Praise for W. M. Spackman's Fiction

"W. M. Spackman, Princetonian, essayist, Rhodes Scholar, and above all, novelist, in *An Armful of Warm Girl, A Presence with Secrets, Heyday,* and *A Difference of Design* invents a startling, askew new syntax, warming while uncovering the oldtime cockles of oldtimers' hearts, offering by the grace of glamor the sly, splendid, and libidinous conceit that we are in the game." —citation from the American Academy and Institute of Arts and Letters' 1984 Harold D. Vursell Memorial Award

Heyday

"If Max Bodenheim, Scott Fitzgerald, and Ezra Pound had at one time pooled their forces (shocking thought) to write a definitive Depression Novel, the chances are it would have turned out something like this parodiable amalgam of classical allusions, large social observations, and explicit sexual vignettes. As a one-man tour de force, *Heyday* is remarkable." —James Kelly, *Saturday Review*

"A lush and emotional story . . ." —William Pfaff, *Commonweal*

An Armful of Warm Girl

"A delightful novel [in which] everything happens: romance, wit, intelligence, geniality, culture without the politics that spoiled it after 1959, sex without tears, a genuinely lovable character . . . [Spackman] reminds us that once upon a time there was a civilization." —John Leonard, *New York Times*

"It's about baffled love, young love, older love, an evasive golden girl, and it tells itself in a worked-up rhythm of fairy tale and coaxing that amounts to a rediscovery of style. Imagine Nabokov and Fitzgerald with a soupçon of Anita Loos." —Herbert Gold, *Los Angeles Times*

"Spackman is a very Fabergé among novelists, and this novel is not fluffy. but mannered, elegant, enameled. . . . Only a barbarous Boeotian could fail to be tickled by the amorous intricacies of this delightful book. It is Watteau's *Embarkation for Cythera* rendered as a fugue by Cole Porter: an incomparably civilized trip." —Frances Taliaferro, *Harper's*

"Wonderful! Absolutely delicious, a total delight. It's so much fun to read that you forget how much skill has to go into such control, such perfect pitch." —Alice Adams

"This elegant light novel is the lace on the Valentine, the *marron* on the parfait. . . . It is perfectly executed, flawlessly performed. The dialogue is a delight. . . . *An Armful of Warm Girl* offers nostalgia with a shining quality, high comedy, true wit. I loved it, every word, and so will you." — Eugenia Thornton, *Cleveland Plain Dealer*

"A triumph in miniature. It is 130 pages of absolute entertainment." —
Larry Swindell, *Philadelphia Inquirer*

"What makes his book entertaining is not merely the mosquito hum of
erotic tension but the way that Love damnable Love keeps butting its pes-
tering head through the door and portal. . . . Love is everywhere, crisp and
inescapable." —James Wolcott, *Harper's*

"Talk about stylists! W. M. Spackman . . . has turned up with as snappy
and original a novel as you'll read in a lifetime." —William Cole, *Saturday Review*

A Presence with Secrets

"Imagine a modern Don Juan playing the lead in *Women in Love*, directed by Nabokov with lyrics by Cole Porter, and you'll have a rough—if
somewhat overblown estimate of *A Presence with Secrets*. . . . A sense of
humor about sex is a rare thing in contemporary writing, and Spackman
drenches these dalliances in laughter and light. . . . On finishing *A Presence with Secrets*, I turned right back to page 1 to read it again." —Jean
Strouse, *Newsweek*

"It is the most stylish, vital, and worldly book to emerge—well, since his
last book. . . . His art is the very distillation of enchantment." —Edmund
White, *Village Voice*

"Spackman's highly elegant and original style turns sentences inside out
and makes a leaping torrent of stream-of-consciousness." —*Chicago Tri-
bune*

"[An] intricate, knowing, precious style that Henry James might have
risen to if he possessed sexuality and a sense of humor." —J. D. O'Hara,
New England Review

"Spackman is a virtuoso with words, using them as a painter does to convey color and texture. This novel is a tour de force sure to please literate
readers." —*Publishers Weekly*

"Each woman is different, a surprise, and splendidly evoked. . . . Each has
her own singular voice; Mr. Spackman is as accomplished at dialogue as
he is at erotic descriptions." —John Leonard, *New York Times*

"For readers of Spackman's fiction it is no wonder that Spackman should
be ranked along with Nabokov: he is a major writer whose worlds of
naughty angels and diamond voices are no less original, whose style is no
less distinctive." —Keith Fleming, *Chicago Literary Review*

"A marvelous novel by an extraordinarily gifted writer." —*Virginia Quarterly Review*

"Reading *A Presence with Secrets* is like taking a warm bath in a luxurious prose style. . . . The considerable charm of the book lies in the ironic, off-hand elegance of Spackman's style. This is confectionery fiction bound to delight anyone with a taste for sophisticated whimsy." —*Boston Globe*

"W. M. Spackman is one of our great writers. Like Henry Green and Laurence Sterne, he is a storyteller, a comic, an enchanter, but first and foremost a master stylist; the magic of his books arises from the eccentric elegance of his sentences. . . . A masterpiece." —*Soho News*

A Difference of Design

"Swift, elegant, unconventional, Spackman's latest arch novel is Jamesian in plot and theme, Colette-like in its deep sensuality. . . . This is a soufflé sort of novel: rich and filling while, ironically, seemingly spun from thin air." —*Booklist*

"An exceedingly elegant . . . novel by a writer whose reputation lately has been burgeoning in certain sectors of the literary intelligentsia. Quite deservedly so." —Stephen Koch, *Washington Post Book World*

"Fine cerebral fun." —*Los Angeles Times Book Review*

"A gem of a novel." —*Los Angeles Herald-Examiner*

"This thin, rich book is a divertissement designed both to compliment James and to make fun of the plodding old moralist-esthete." —*Fort Worth Star-Telegram*

"Spackman wittily reveals misconceptions and petty self-deceptions and transforms a Gallic near-farce into bittersweet musings on contemporary love." —*Library Journal*

"Spackman writes of women in [a] style that is rarely encountered in male authors. At times I found myself astounded that so delicate a book could be written by a man." —*Best Sellers*

"A novel of manners and high style which can claim as its ancestors the novels of Henry Green, Ronald Firbank, and even Thomas Love Peacock. . . . It is not an overstatement to say that Mr. Spackman's novels are as much of the fabric of memorable American literature on their scale as the works of Melville, Gaddis, and Pynchon are on theirs." —Maurice B. Cloud, *Colorado Monthly Magazine*

"In a certain sense, Spackman reveals himself as a committed Jamesian. His meringue glacé prose, his reactionary devotion to feminine wiles, his seeming belief that all truth and pleasure reside in gamesmanship—these constitute the code of a sophisticate, however self-mocking, who aspires to be one upon whom 'nothing is lost.' . . . This man demands a high price: that we master a literary classic, not to mention the French language which he in part expresses himself, before we can even begin to appreciate his effort. Will you? Your answer will reveal your entire attitude toward art, life and continental cuisine." —Edna Stumpf, *Philadelphia Inquirer*

A Little Decorum, for Once

"The tone is light but intelligent, careful but colloquial, and the overall effect is one of witty disregard, making A *Little Decorum, for Once* the type of work one can easily imagine people describing as a *jeu d'esprit.*" — Wendy Lesser, *New York Times Book Review*

"Spackman is a literary stylist of dizzying refinement." —Carolyn See, *Los Angeles Times*

"A whirly, madcap battle of the sexes. . . . The marvelous Spackman dialogue, with its ironic asides, stream of consciousness nonsense, and brackets of affection should be patented." —Christopher Schemering, *Washington Post Book World*

"His books are dream books, pure idealism, full of somehow unfattening scrumptious dessert and champagne and lovers who manage to be faithful *and* unfaithful and happy in the face of everything." —Malcolm Jones, *St. Petersburg Times*

THE

COMPLETE FICTION OF

W. M. SPACKMAN

THE
COMPLETE FICTION OF
W. M. SPACKMAN

Edited and with an afterword by Steven Moore

WITHDRAWN

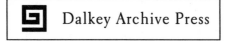 Dalkey Archive Press

First Edition, 1997

Spackman, W. M. (William Mode), 1905-
[Selections. 1997]
Complete fiction of W.M. Spackman / W.M. Spackman ; with an
afterword by Steven Moore. — 1st ed.
p.   cm.
ISBN 1-56478-157-7 (cloth) — ISBN 1-56478-137-2 (paper)
I. Title.
PS3569.P3A15   1997   813'.54—dc21   96-51798

This publication is partially supported by grants from the Lannan
Foundation, the National Endowment for the Arts, a federal agency,
and the Illinois Arts Council, a state agency.

Dalkey Archive Press
Illinois State University
Campus Box 4241
Normal, IL 61790-4241

*Printed on permanent/durable acid-free paper and bound in the
United States of America.*

CONTENTS

HEYDAY

To Mary Ann Matthews
past and present

Mike Fletcher met Kitty Locke for the first time at an all-night New York drinking party in Jill and Davy Starr's apartment in East 11th Street in the spring of 1931, an affair catalogued for history as the Third-and-a-Half Annual Gin Social. The First Gin Social had been a stag affair at Oxford, three springs before, to celebrate Davy's birthday: invitations had in principle been limited to members of the Class of 1927 then in residence at Oxford and Cambridge; real gin had been served. The Second Annual, in New York, had been expanded to include everybody's girl, and had just missed resulting in one man's being cuckolded in a roomy hall-closet; he *had* been, by the time of the Third Annual, though by a different man and not I imagine in a closet, and everyone was invited as a matter of course.

The Third-and-a-Half was in full roar when Mike stepped down into the Starrs' areaway and rang their bell. It was an areaway that already, perhaps, had become as familiar to him as home: he was very fond of Jill and Davy; he and Davy had been in the same Club at Princeton and he had been Davy's best man at the wedding two years before; he saw them at least once a week and usually oftener. A big sleek blond man he'd never seen flung open the door instantly, cried "By god, come *in*, *wonnn*derful see you again!" and struck him on the shoulder with a plump well-manicured hand; and then the polyphonic din of the party was like walking into a wall of sound. He worked his way gradually through the jam towards the bedroom to leave his coat and hat and got tangled up with a man and a girl blocking the doorway: she was on the verge of tears and was saying, "But I tell you he *did* see us Friday, he *did,*" and as Mike shoved past the man's butt he heard him murmur some reply. The bedroom also was milling with people. Our classmate Steve Cannon and a handsome dark girl were lying full-length on the bed, he with his hands clasped behind his head and she with her curls in the hollow of his shoulder and her cheek against his (listening to the Class Trotskyist). A huge pile of hats and coats had been shoved from the bed onto the floor. Mike chucked his on top of them and shouldered his way back into the livingroom again looking for Jill.

She was in a knot of shouting people near a table which, by the big glass jugs on it, was the bar. She had a new upswept hairdo that made the slim nape of her neck utterly delicious; he went up and kissed it. She turned gently around in his arms; she looked flushed and glittering all over and a little tight, and terribly pretty.

"Oh my sweet old Malachi," she sang with soft affection, wriggling an arm around his neck and spilling some of her drink down his sleeve. "Why, I haven't seen you for a whole long day. No, please, you mustn't stroke my bottom, Davy has just made a rule about it."

"I was patting it."

"Davy doesn't allow it anymore; patting either. Nobody but him. It's a Davy preserve."

"He's a selfish hog."

"Oh Malachi he isn't. *You* know—how he says everyone is either a bottoms or a bosoms, and he's been years deciding which he is but now he's decided he's a bottoms. So now all our friends have to give my bottom up."

"Even in that lovely dress? You look wonderful."

"Do I? Only do you really like it, Mike? Oh well, I do too, I guess. I've nearly got used to it, anyhow."

"It's perfectly wonderful, pet."

"You don't think it makes me look sort of— Oh well anyway it's new. Davy bought it for me just this afternoon. So there wouldn't have been time to take it back and exchange it. He bought it to give me more sex appeal, he said. Wasn't that sweet?"

"You look good enough to eat."

"That's what Davy used to say to me in Paris. When he was seducing me. Oh, Mike, this is the third dress he's brought home for me this year so I'll have sex appeal. You know that crimson dress—not an evening dress, that one wasn't—that almost showed all my little bosoms?"

"I've evidently got to see it!"

"Oh but poor lovely Mike you *can't!* It made me feel— It didn't really fit at all well so I gave it to the maid. I expect she needed sex appeal too, poor dismal thing."

"You gave it to Anna? How'd anything that—"

"Oh, not Anna. We've got a new one. Greta or something. She can't cook and she's old and Davy says I have to fire her."

"Couldn't Anna cook?"

"Anna was *rude!* And she hardly ever washed dishes clean and she left the beds all rumpled. And she stole Davy's liquor. So I fired her."

"No wonder."

"She was just so awful, Mike, too. She kept making passes at Davy. He'd go into the kitchen to make cocktails before dinner and she'd make passes at him and delay him, and I'd not have seen him the whole day long and he'd be a long time. And one night I heard him say to her, you know the things he says, I heard him ask her why not a drink on her day off, then, was there some socio-economic principle involved? and she *sniggered* at him, Mike. She sniggered at him and I fired her. Why, look, you haven't got a drink."

"Nobody led me to the bar."

"*I'll* lead you to the bar, poor empty Malachi. Come along with your very own loving Jill. Oh, I *am* loving, Mike; I am I *am!* Kiss me and see. Kiss me hard. . . . Does that excite you, Mike? This way, too? . . . Does it? Does it?"

"Of course it does!"

"Oh dear, now I've embarrassed you. Come hide your sweet pink amorous old face in a drink. Only, Mike, if I'd ever slept with anybody but Davy, do you suppose the boy would have told me how I pleased him, told me over and over and over and over, so then now I'd know?"

"*I'd* tell you!"

"Oh, Mike, I really do please Davy. *I do.* Shall I tell you what he— Oh dear, I don't suppose I can. Oh, well. You just push all these sluggish piggish people away and get yourself a drink, it's straight alcohol Steve brought down from some lab or somewhere at the Yale gradschool. You mix something called lime squash with it. Steve says it's what you have to do, it's worse than anything he ever drank."

Around one or two in the morning, at most parties of that era, the milling company would begin to dwindle, and take on a kind of planetary movement, like an orrery, endlessly tangential and revolving. Constellations of guests would widen or contract, sidereal outlines swaying and loosening and re-forming under the hurtling impact of accretions flung loose from other revolving or decomposing worlds and seeking new orbits to join; a whole galaxy would explode in a sudden surge for drinks all round, to scatter carrying with them to other spheres, in a rain of fiery intellectual matter, the jokes, the topics, the disputes, the ideas, which the parent-star had generated to a white and whirling heat. Or one couple, a man and a girl, would flame suddenly forth across the system's undulating peripheries in the flash of an unexpected and worldless understanding—a flash that would vanish almost instantly into a void of discretion: the pounding heart, the quick sidelong glances of tardy precaution; and then the eyes again for a flicker of time opening to each other wide, engulfing, and possessed; and lips barely shaping the word, the breathed *Tomorrow*. . . .

And Malachi?

At what late point, for example, in that unmemorable evening did he exchange, Kitty, his first now undecipherable words with *you?* At what particular moment of time did he cross your slender progression from group to group, noting the straight and charming back, the high-held head with its loose-swinging bell of curls, the lovely carriage of your shoulders, the slim ingratiating thighs? At what point did he salute you with a casual smile? Perhaps he was standing at the bar; it may be that he was pouring some colorless liquid into a glass. Perhaps you moved out of some disintegrating planet of humanity and flowed toward him across some exact and measurable parallelogram of room; while he noted for unlikely historical purposes that you were the handsome dark girl he had seen earlier on a bed with Steve Cannon listening to intellectual exposition. Or he noted only that you were laughing, and calling to him?

Or Steve himself may have been with you then also; and perhaps, Kitty, he stood close beside you as you confronted Mike, his friendly abstracted face by your cheek, his arm about your waist, his fingers lightly and inattentively tapping your side, his eyes darting restlessly about the room as you talked to Mike, plunging their tense glances into a passing face with some fierce inner vehemence, only to find nothing there and shift their baffled and desolate urgency to another. It may be that, as so often, Steve's abrupt barking laugh burst into your sentences, though why, it was sometimes hard to say; or that his glance beat for a moment emptily and questingly upon your profile before turning once again its bleak and endless search upon the room—though with what purposes I would be put to it to explain.

Or tell me: what did you say?

"This is *a* most hideous drink, Mr. Cannon, *if* I may be so candid," perhaps you said. "Should we let this unoffending man here disable himself with more?"

Steve sounded his laugh; at any rate he had heard his name; his cheek rubbed yours absentmindedly, and his straining gaze shot into some other face unseen beyond Mike's shoulder before he laughed again and looked at you.

"You know this Fletcher fellow here, Kit?" he demanded briskly. "This is a terrible fellow! You want to keep away from him and all people like him."

Perhaps you patted Steve's cheek and Mike was surprised, for what did you see in him? but surely, when you answered, Mike must have heard the lilt, the eager hurrying quality your voice had, as if what you had in mind to say next was so amusing, so delicious, that your lips could hardly wait to say it. Mike was presented to you, certainly; but what then? I do not know.

And Steve? Did he stand there by you, inattentively drumming on your side, his eyes sliding over the flanks of a red-haired girl who had come to pour herself a drink, sliding up again to her profile and then down over her breasts, which he analyzed intently for some moments before flicking his eyes for a second at you and then on past your cheek again to some unreplying face you did not see? Did Mike speak to you there alone?

Or was is it only during the closing hours of that party that, for the first time in his life, Mike Fletcher spoke to Kitty Locke alone? The conversation was without dignity or symbolic interest, and I record it, as Kitty recorded it later for me, only as a *terminus a quo*. Mike seems to have got unnecessarily drunk. He was not yet in that agonizing stage when the eyeball-bruising rectangles of walls and floors, and the loud buzzing lights, and the cubic faces seen through broken glass and in cracked mirrors and with mouths clapping open and shut in their foreheads, all go swinging and slithering by and around in vast thrumming arcs at varying speeds and in different, tilting planes. But he had perhaps an intuition that this stage might not be far away; for at any rate he seems to have gone through the Starrs' kitchen and out into the little bricked areaway behind, from which four or five steps led up to the level of the garden. A late three-quarters moon was flooding the blank backs of the houses with a luminous silence. There was a great inky cube of shadow at the far end of the garden by the wall, and slivery leaf-patterned shadows under the stunted plane-trees along the sides; the sparse new lawn immediately in front of him was brimming and naked with moonlight.

He climbed the steps and sat unsteadily down; and then he noticed a girl standing with her forehead pressed against a crossbar of the areaway trellis, both hands clutching one of its wooden pillars. It looked like Kitty. *Was* Kitty. Going to be sick, he thought. "Feeling sick," he said.

"Yes. Thank you prettily for asking and kindly go away."

"Very ru'." He felt around in a pocket for something; probably a match. "Talk y' in'mate friends that way all right. Don't feel know me *well* enough."

"You're drunk!"

"Well-known philological state. Status."

She said with a sudden vicious flash of temper, "Can't you see I want to be *alone?*"

"Help you."

"Oh go *away!*"

"Help you many methods. Incaluble. Furnish large any number ref'ences."

She had vanished into the house. "Abrupt," he said weightily. Presently he got himself over into the shadow of the nearest plane-tree, with his back against the wall, and as I reconstruct it went to sleep. Looking back now on this brief exchange of whatever you can say it was they were exchanging, I observe that in some discreditable way, in terms of what happened to the two of them later, the scene does perhaps have a certain symbolic interest after all.

That spring and summer following this indecipherable introduction, Mike seems to have taken Kitty around more and more often, almost as frequently perhaps as her affair with Steve left her the unoccupied and convenient time for. (Steve after all was mostly in New Haven.) But whether Mike was then in love with her is probably unestablishable: even Kitty herself, she told me later, was far from sure:

"He was just *after* me in an attractive way; you know?"

"Why, the heel!"

"Webb my dear you all *do*."

"I suppose so."

"Of course he did try to undress me in a routine way from time to time. Only not, may I say? convincingly. *Bumpingly!* You know?"

"No real concentration," I suggested.

"Oh most hideously *un*concentrated, you have *no* idea!"

"No."

"In love with me then, *dear* me surely not!"

The topic was boring me, so I killed it off with an epigram I was employing at the time: "Men have only one idea," I said. "Women, on the contrary, have only one idea too," and we went on to something else.

Actually I suppose Mike's trouble was the universal one, the Depression, which by 1931 was deepening and spreading about us like an arctic twilight everywhere. Mike's firm had begun losing accounts as early as June of 1929; by June of '30 it had been mortally hit and Mike was unemployed, and by the summer of 1931 it was down to the original partners and one stenographer. And how clearly I can see those ex-editors of the *Prince* in my memory—the handsome familiar faces strained now and taut, the tension in the smile, a tic perhaps in the muscles around the eyes; the dread every day clearer and clearer under the charm. They were still, spiritually, editors of the *Prince*; that was the reward, the natural reward, of having played it right and worked the formula (perhaps hadn't quite been chairman of the *Prince* board, but *he* was a dull bastard, God knew; and anyhow look at all these poor dopeless guys that sucked round and never even made the *Prince* at all!). They were still editors of the *Prince* even when their wives had found jobs in dress-shops on Madison Avenue (even on Lexington) and the kids had been sent (where else was there?) to some grandfather's farm in Indiana: the *Prince* being a monopoly couldn't possibly get in a jam; or if it had, the College always stood there gothic and protective; and had anybody ever heard in any economics course anything to the contrary? Was there in short anything other than an editor of the *Prince* for a man to BE?

And now from that warmth, that youth, that careless confidence, to be plunged (and how soon) into this long frost of the human spirit! Abruptly, and for reasons there certainly was no professor to explain, everything we had been bred to and trained for, everything the College had polished us to attain—the easy good manners, the charm, the intelligence, the stations in life hereditary to the ruling caste whose blossoming generation we had been told we were—all this vanished under a mountainous rubble of avalanching quotations from a thousand chattering stocktickers; and suddenly nothing remained to us at all—our training and competence nothing, our prerogatives nothing, our intelligence with nothing to be applied to, our lives with nothing they could return to or think of as their own.

We were not at all, I suppose, equally close to desperation. There may even have been warmth and hope for a few; though a very few. Certainly everyone I myself knew seemed to think that his fellow was better off than he: I found out years later, for instance, that Mike had imagined *I* had a perfectly solid job on one of the *Sun's* Tammany beats, though he had somewhat bitterly decided that I must have had a drag of some kind in the city room or higher up to hold it; he even thought, God help me, that I looked happy and prosperous! Davy Starr of course *was* doing well. He had been writing copy for his agency's big account, a tobacco account grossing around three million; and when the agency vice-president who'd been handling it pulled out to form his own company and of course took the account with him, he took Davy along as assistant copy-chief. Davy and Jill celebrated Christmas and January in the Bahamas in consequence, and Mike lived in their apartment while they were away—the $2.75 a week he thus saved in room-rent, during those six weeks, was a serious item.

But Davy was an exception. Steve was on some sort of sociology-research fellowship at Yale in such poverty that Kitty bought him cigarettes and train-fare to town out of her weekly $27.50 as a fact-checker on *Time*. Mike himself lived at one period on the proceeds of gags unearthed during mornings at the Public Library, pillaging eighteenth-century jokebooks, doggedly modernizing his findings, and peddling them to reluctant editors at $2 a throw. If he hadn't also sold an occasional free-lance radio script to UBS or to Davy's agency, he would quite literally have been on the breadlines. The only really lucky man I myself heard of was an old Hearst reporter who'd packed flour, sugar, salt, and a hunting rifle into the wilds of the Olympia Peninsula and ridden out the Depression there from 1930 to early 1935, living in abundance and in liberty, on a total five-year outlay of about $80. For those are the terms in which we think of that era: the factor-analysis mathematics of happiness, the occupational statistics of hope and of desire; and by what long catastrophe of the human heart do I still see as economic units, see even today, the handclasps, the welcoming doorways, the laughs warm with greeting; or the lifting of an eyelid, the tender glow in the iris, and the answering smile? For worst perhaps of all was the loneliness of man. Through the echoing corridors of how many stately buildings, in what squalid bars, had Mike not heard the voices of his classmates break with their subtle accent of terror and humiliation, to glide with a faltering modulation beyond his ear? *We've cut personnel to the bone and past, Mike; and even now. I may as well tell you, Mike, put it frankly in fact, two weeks from tomorrow. They're closing us down, fella, no kidding they're just plain closing us down.* Him also they had closed down; and sometimes in the spring afternoons he would pace the sunlit rectangles of the streets, a tall man with a touch of crimson on the clean-shaven cheekbones, glancing emptily at the numbers over doorways (Might he some day live here? The basement apartment would include a garden; the front door would be painted a deep and handsome green, with a knocker and doorknob of brass; he would add Venetian blinds to those windows, perhaps lime-green. Or might it instead be *there* he would live?), noting down the address, perhaps, in a small black notebook, or sketching out a plan for the garden in idle hypothetical design. It may even be that you yourself stopped him to ask some trivial question: the whereabouts of the nearest public telephone, the location of Van Ness Place; you two may have spoken together for a moment, and he told you his name was Thatcher (or was it Fisher he said?) before you passed onward in your tilting orbit, leaving him to follow you with an irresolute stare.

From these brinks of loneliness, of dislocation, Kitty was I suppose an escape for Mike, at this era, as much as she was anything. For how else can one explain why for example it was specifically Kitty that his spiritual insomnia drove him to phone, one day in the summer of that year, with a project in mind which almost certainly he himself did not fully understand.

As Kitty recounted it to me later, he had woken one morning with an irrational but overwhelming longing to visit again (though his sleep-drenched mind seems to have phrased it *to return to*) the farm where he had been born, where his father and grandfather had lived, and their fathers and grandfathers before them; *where I sprang from* is how at one point he expressed it to Kitty, though obviously that is a very odd locution indeed in an urban vocabulary; anyhow, where his people had been for so many generations, in quiet and in security, in those green and peaceful woodslope hundreds from which our traditions came. What is significant, possibly, is that it was Kitty whom he phoned, as a companion into the reassurances of the imagined past.

He rang her up at *Time*. "This is Mike."

"Yes Mike?"

Her voice sounded lovely—lilting and young, with a haunting note of his own nostalgia; and he told her how lovely it sounded.

"How *very* kind of you, Malachi. Thank you prettily."

"Look, Kit. I've an idea."

"Yes Mike?"

"Isn't tomorrow *Time's* day off?"

"Yes, why?"

"Could I talk you into going down into Pennsylvania tomorrow?"

"*Go* with you, Mike? I do hope of a Monday morning you don't mean in quite a dishonorable way?"

"That would of course be the ideal," he said; and they discussed this hypothesis; as usual, without result.

"You mean you've just had some sort of pleasant irrational whim?"

"I thought I might borrow Davy's car."

"Mike it is a *wonderful* idea! When must I be ready?"

"You, uh, mind sort of earlyish?"

"What a hideous idea! I completely *hate* it!"

"Don't you want to see the sun come up all rosy over the New Jersey countryside as we drive along?"

"Oh dear God *no!*"

But in the morning she almost immediately curled up in the seat beside him and didn't wake until they had nearly crossed New Jersey and the green rolling valley of the middle Delaware was in sight.

And was hungry.

"Malachi, do you think we should perhaps eat another breakfast moderately soon?"

"How about Downingtown? We're nearly there."

"I seem somehow to eat breakfast with you a *great* deal, Malachi. I can't think the implications look quite maidenly."

"Live in sin with me," he suggested, "and we can make statistical observations."

[...]*

---

*Bracketed ellipses indicate places in the manuscript where the author intended to insert new material; see the afterword, p. 213.

". . . Even with Steve, did you know?" she said, coolly. "I am *very* fond of him and yet I am inhuman to him in the morning."

It was one of those oblique references to her affair with Steve which she apparently couldn't help making from time to time, and I suppose Mike felt the customary irrational pang: even if one is not suffocatingly in love with a young woman it is irritating to have her remind one that she can wake up in bed with someone else. And Kitty's public behavior could be exasperating in the extreme to any man emotionally involved in her—at parties, for instance, there she would be, *hanging* on the bastard! And all the while at her very side Steve's lonely search beating desolately upon the room, glancing into Kitty's face perhaps only for a brief and abstracted instant, as if asking how she ever came to be there, before it plunged bleakly onward in its solitary quest. And then, with an equally infuriating metamorphosis, in a matter of hours one might once more see Kitty untouched and cool, the charming head held delicately and fastidiously high, the blue eyes at once gentle and amused; and why in the mornings (she would ask you) had she to be so *inevitably* vile!

But Mike I suppose rode out the pang; and he said why not just get sandwiches made up now and take them along.

"That would be remarkably fine, Malachi."

"Then we could roam around Coatesville and eat whenever we felt like it. Be free."

"You know, Mike? I somehow always thought you were from Baltimore."

"I grew up there. But I was born in Coatesville."

He gave her the case history in detail as they drove on, while she listened peacefully—his grandfather's farm at first, and his parents' deaths; and then Baltimore and a great-aunt's rich house of hand-made brick, with its brass knocker gleaming from two centuries of polish, and the holystoned steps; and how strange those half-Southern accents had sounded; and his white-cotton gloves at dancing school and the well-bred starched little girls and his great-aunt's glistening cut-under calling for him at childhood dances, with Ebert and his yellow gloves and the smart angle he held the whip, and the crop-tailed converted hunter Selim stepping high and fast toward home.

But Chester Valley was where he had lived before his parents died; and now he and Kitty were nearly there, the names sounding in his ears their loved and honorable history: Downingtown, Ercildoune, Neave's Mills, Doe Run, the Brandywine, Chadds

Ford; and soon they had covered the remaining miles and he was among them again, as he had not been among them since childhood—Fallowfield Meeting House, and the Neave headstones, the names of his mother's people; Neave's Mills and the mill-race and his grandfather's paper-mills, and the memory of a letterhead he still had somewhere, with a steel engraving of the mills about 1862 and W. & A. Neave, East Fallowfield Township, Chester County, Pa., the paper as white and fine as the day it issued from the rollers; and though his grandfather's and great-uncle's stately houses were hardly more than slums now, he could still see behind them the fragrant barn where he had tried to undress a little girl-cousin when they both were three (an early failure), and the gable where runaway slaves had passed so many a night on the underground railway, or woken to find his grandfather's shining blue eyes above them in the gathering dusk and hear his tranquil voice say, A handbill is out for thee; I think it is perhaps high time thee was on thy way.

At any rate his heart was warm and peaceful; and presently they drove back through Coatesville toward his grandfather Fletcher's farm on the wooded hills north of the town. Soon they were in the country again, the road leading through the thicketed woods of second-growth hickory and black walnut, the warm shadows of early afternoon spattering the undergrowth of fern and laurel. He drove slowly, almost drowsily; his eyes drinking it in; completely at peace. What was there about the very name of shag-bark hickory that filled him with this still and wordless contentment? A woods-road joined them from the left; at its corner a narrow low building of stone, covered with stained and scaling plaster, its shutters closed, its shingles curled and silvered with the rains of unrecorded years. An open carriage-shed stood behind it in the woods. He stopped the car.

"What's this, Malachi?"

Almost dreamily he said, "I think it's Caln."

"Caln?"

"Caln Meeting House. It stood on a corner of Grandfather's farm. His grandfather gave the land."

"Do we inspect it?"

"I want to see the burying-ground."

"Isn't that somewhat morbid of us, Malachi?"

"Who has a better right to be morbid?"

"You don't look morbid, did you know? You look happy."

He smiled at her in silence. They got out and crossed the road.

There was a stone hitching-block in front of the meetinghouse; he stopped beside it and stood there gazing, thinking he hardly knew what, thinking perhaps only how many years must have gone by.

"What *are* you doing, Malachi dear!"

He went toward her laughing. "As a matter of fact," he said, "I guess I was helping a pretty girl named Eliza Branson into a buggy."

"What?"

"She was my grandmother." He took Kit's warm fingers, and they paced slowly along the low stone façade. "See the two front doors," he said. "There must have been two meetings, built in one piece like that, end to end, with the dividing wall in common. One side Hicksite, the other Orthodox."

"Why did they separate?"

"I don't think I ever really knew."

"Which were you?"

"Hicksite. Am, pretty Miss Locke."

"At any rate, 'am' for today."

"Yes. At any rate today."

The burying-ground by the meetinghouse was green and overgrown knee-deep with a wilderness of brambles and trumpet-vine. He could find no names he knew. The headstones had sunk and settled, and the shallow lettering was dim with lichen. Then some voice in his memory spoke an echo of phrases: *The soil was too sandy here; after reflection he offered them a new plot of land; it was across the road, where the ground was firmer; after discussion, they accepted it.* The two of them strolled across. The new burying-ground had been tended with care: the turf was green and springy, the low wall newly whitewashed. And the names, he must have thought, the names are *mine!* Amanda Fletcher, 1821-1849. Alexander Branson, 1802-1820. Isaac Fletcher, 1814-1885.

"That was my grandfather," he said to Kitty. She slid an arm through his and rested her cheek against his shoulder.

"All this somehow makes you very happy, Mike dear."

"Yes."

"I've never felt you so happy, did you know?"

"There's another," he said. "Look. That one. 'Malachi Fletcher 1775-1812.' "

"Practically you!"

"Yes."

"Do you know who he was, Mike?"

"No."

"Have you always been here?"

"Nearly always."

"These are your people."

"Yes."

Some collateral cousins lived at the old Fletcher farm. Even in the Depression, they had money: the place was in handsome repair. The house rose in stone among elms on a green-turfed knoll, massive and severe, with a stone springhouse below it and a stone smokehouse off to one side; behind, the huge square bastions of the barn shone with the annual whitewash of a century's incrustation. Under the eaves of the farmhouse, picked out in handmade brick, was the inscription

"Isaac Fletcher," he said. "My great-grandfather."

"If," said Kitty suddenly, with a soft inflection he didn't understand.

"What?" he said. "How do you mean?"

She didn't answer, and he turned and stared at her in surprise; but his mind was too full of the dreaming history all around him to wonder very long, and his gaze went back to the house and the farm buildings and the fields and sun-filled woods beyond. ("I just felt all melted about him," Kit told me long afterwards. "He looked so young and all this made him so alive. You know? You know?")

They knocked; but no one was at home, and presently they sauntered down the gleaming meadow along the rill of water from the springhouse and into the fringe of woods below, and munched the last of their sandwiches in a glade of ferns. They caught a big stag-beetle and pestered him idly; they lay on their bellies and plucked blades of grass and chewed the sweet shoots lazily.

"You don't look so lonely now, Mike."

"No."

"Or did you know you were lonely?"

"Maybe I didn't."

"Would you like to know something, Mike dear? Neither did I."

He rolled her gently over and stroked her temples, his fingertips sliding peacefully through the warm thick curls.

"Mike?"

"Mmmmm?"

"I feel—I think you should know how *tender* I feel that it was me you asked to come along. Why?"

"Why I asked you you mean?"

"Mmmmm."

"When I phoned you I guess I hardly knew myself."

"But you do now."

"Yes."

"Why did you, then?"

"I guess you must be my people."

She said laughing softly, "Should I perhaps warn you? I'm a Presbyterian."

"Presbyterians sometimes get fond of Quakers."

"Ah, Mike. Ah, Mike, sometimes very fond." Her arm slid around his neck and pulled him down. Her mouth was not so expert as he had expected but it was delicious and utterly obedient, and for the first time in many, many months he felt alive. The hand around his neck strayed upward, quietly stroking his hair. He slid the cardigan aside and ran his lips slowly along her sleek shoulder; he heard a sharp indrawn breath, and then the tip of her tongue curled with its light message of caress in the hollow of his ear and he felt the fingers of her other hand close shivering upon his side.

He said against her throat, "I want you. Badly."

"Oh, sweet, had you better?"

"Yes."

"Ah, Mike."

"Yes. Yes."

"Oh, Mike, Mike, I'm afraid I want you very much too."

"Ahhh you lovely!"

"Only Mike *no!*"

"Yes!"

"No *no!* Oh what makes me so bitchy to you?"

"You're not, you're—!"

"Yes I am, oh sweet we *can't!*"

"We can!"

"*No!*" She rolled away from him. He reached after her. "Oh no, Mike!" She sat up and gazed at him dolefully. "I *am* such a hideous bitch about things!"

"My lovely Kit, why on earth can't we just—"

"Oh Malachi. Dear me." She laughed ruefully. "What can one say? My physiology and I are most regretful!"

"*Hell.*"

"Yes! Oh don't I know!" She lay down again, looking at him under her lids, her eyes sulky and desirous. I suppose he merely (and why not!) looked glum.

But then, for a not oversensitive young man, an odd and somehow comforting idea came to him:

"Kit?"

"Yes Mike?"

"Will you tell me something?"

"Ah, sweet, the way I feel about you now I'll tell you everything and anything."

"Was this what, well, what you meant up by the house?"

"By the house?"

"I mean when you said 'If'?"

"Aaaaaaaahhhhh Mike!" All the tenseness went out of her in a soft crying rush of breath, and in an instant she was cradling in his arms as smooth and melting as if she had lain there all her life. "Oh, Malachi, I am going to cry. Of all the things to— Oh Malachi Fletcher why do you *do* these things to a sentimental girl!"

I doubt if in all those years Mike ever felt such contentment as during the hours they drove back to New York in, saying hardly a word, with her head on his shoulder and her hand deep in his coat-pocket; and when he left her at her door and she said, "Ah, Mike, you *are* such a charming guy," it could hardly have been a surprising peroration to either of them.

Was Mike in love with her then? I do not know.

I do not know, but love (let me put it) is not unsolitude nor is it economics, and the Depression was not compounded of such enchanting misunderstandings of Pennsylvania landscape, such breathless non sequiturs in the life we lived and the longings that stirred the reluctant muscles of our tongues; and if ever again Mike read that brick inscription under the eaves of his great-grand-father's farmhouse, it might not without special scrutiny have appeared a monosyllable. Kitty was a girl of nebulous moods; very soon after their trip her affair with Steve went into one of those periodic tensions that seemed to her to demand her full emotional attention; and at any rate nothing came of their charming day.

Or rather, there was no neatly satisfying logical sequence. For there was always Steve; the asymmetry of Steve. And so Mike's and

Kitty's meetings, between his insecurity and hers, as often as not ended in bickerings, to be partly forgotten of course before they met the next time, yet subconsciously never quite forgotten; a wearing down, a wearying, of whatever it was at this era they might just conceivably have been.

"What is it you think you *get* from the guy anyway?" he said pettishly one evening, toward the end of a long wrangling tête-à-tête at some party or other.

"Oh Malachi."

"You mean you haven't even my god analyzed it? After all these months or however the hell long it is?"

"Would you expect me to *analyze* that day with you?"

He was instantly furious. "That was a special sort of day, damn it!"

"Are you so sure?"

"Of course I'm sure!!"

"Now you *are* being un-grown-up."

"Just because you're trying to tell me there's no difference be-tween—"

"You and Steve?" she said coolly.

"No!! Trying to tell me my great-grandfather's fa—"

"I'm not trying to tell you anything, am I? Am I? Oh *really* all how utterly juvenile! Aren't you merely insisting on telling *me*?"

"Kit—"

"Oh Mike *let's* not go on with it; *if* you would for once be so kind? And I would also feel most happy at a new drink?"

He took the glass from her hand in hurt and sullen rage, got her goddam drink, and stepped furiously back across the room into (so to speak) the Depression.

Back into the Depression was where all of us stepped, it seems to me, from every transitory moment of hope or anticipation we tried to linger in, from every ruined sanctuary of innocence our training had persuaded us to retain. The low point statistically, I understand, is now set somewhere in 1932. But for the Class of 1927 it fell in the preceding winter, for it is then that we sustained (if that is the verb) no less than four of our suicides, and within a space of twenty days. I had known them all fairly well. One rolled gently down the side of a railroad embankment and under a train. Another, an only child, leaning with his pretty mother on the rail of a vacation-liner bound for Bermuda, remarked to her tenderly, "If you fell over *this* part of the stern, you'd be swept straight into the propellers, wouldn't I, darling?" and vaulted overboard. Another was found floating in the reeds off Staten Island; the crabs had been at his face and hands. The fourth hanged himself with two pairs of woman's garters in an actors' hotel. Officially, the Class could not notice the incidents as such: they were in principle not what a Wasp education formed one for; psychiatrically no possible connection with the Class could have been established anyhow; and from the standpoint of prose style even the amateur necrologer of the *Alumni Weekly* could feel that *particularly shocking end* was not only inarticulate but (when you remembered so clearly the echoing voice, the welcoming doorway, the answering smile) a bleak travesty and in fact a plain goddam shame.

Mind you, the Class are not instruments of censorship or circumlocution. It is merely that in some strange way we have at times the cell-for-cell identity of four years together and then a lifetime; and when one of our Twenty-Year Book notices reads (say) *Frank retired from his prosperous business connection in 1930 and since that date has been occupied in the main with personal matters,* who but a member of the Class glimpses the crazed and flapping features in the "disturbed" wing of a private sanitarium, or who but a member of the Class can tell you that we do not describe it or allude to it because we could describe it too accurately and too well?

But of course the parties went on.

It was at one of these latter that—quite unexpectedly and accidentally; as a matter of fact even unknowingly—I found myself involved with Kitty Locke. The party was down in Barrow Street, in one of those severe but attractive old brick houses that were built all over that part of New York in the decades around 1800; the ceilings were very low, the drawingrooms stately but small, and in no time the party was uproariously overflowing into the first floor of bedrooms above and cascading with a charming din into the back-basement diningroom. I had two or three drinks and it was a wonderful party, casual acquaintances beating me affectionately on the back in the milling tumult or a light hand sliding under my arm and pretty eyes making half-ungovernable love to me as I turned. But then I had four drinks or five, and it was all beginning to change—I was beginning to feel alone, utterly and desolately alone in the very middle of that warm shouting human hubbub—when over the lifting rim of my drink Kitty materialized

before me. (Was it my bleak countenance, some wounded inter-
cepted glance, perhaps, which her soft heart had glimpsed for an
instant as in a window unexpectedly thrown open through the
chattering, laughing crowd? Had my lonely gaze, thinking itself
forever unobserved, brought her to my side?)

"Look *up!*" she was laughing.

I looked up, and my forehead grazed the dangling crimson
ribbons of a sprig of mistletoe. I bent my head and kissed her, a
long consoling kiss; I said in the idiom of the time, "That's a lovely
mouth you have there, Miss Locke."

"Why thank you *most* kindly, Webb dear! We do strive so
undroopingly to please!"

I kissed her again. A couple hurtling jovially past us caromed
into us with a fusillade of apologies and broke it up, so I kissed her
a third time; until finally she turned her head down and away.

She murmured, "Of course it is something a wiser Miss Locke
would never allow herself to say, but I feel suddenly quite warm
and *tender*, Webb, about you, perhaps you know?"

"..."

But luckily for decorum, at this point we were abruptly swept up
in a group that was headed for Saetti's or some such speakeasy and
by some nearly forgotten prearrangement was taking Kitty along;
so I went too; and in a wildly swaying foliation of wraps we burst
out into the snowy night. An icy wind drove the flakes thick and
headlong in stinging tarantellas; I grew soberer rapidly. So, very
soon, did the others, helped along by bowls of scalding min-
estrone, and I remember a hilarious but perfectly coherent
account, in which half the table seemed to be telling the story to
the other half, of a fabulous adventure of our recent hostess's
which she had been broadcasting at the party we had just left.
The week before she had suddenly found herself short a man for
a moderately formal dinner, and in desperation had at last rung
up something called the N. Y. Guide & Escort Service, a recent
Depression-born organization which for $10 an evening supplied
you with a guaranteed-engaging practically-Ivy-League young unattached male—dinnerjacket, white tie, or even daytime brooks-
brothers—to fill out your dinnerparty and accompany you anywhere through any reasonable evening. ("Stud fees are extra!"
shouted somebody down the table.) Our hostess had naturally
considered the whole expedient wildly funny, and told all her
dinner-guests in advance ("—of course *no* idea what the creature
will be like but he's certain to be the most-slumming-possible

fun!"); the female guests had without exception begged to be assigned to go in to dinner with him, all giving highly indecent reasons. And then, at the appointed hour, in had walked the most aristocratically handsome, the best-bred and most beautifully mannered, the stuffiest Princeton junior any of them had ever seen. His last name was old-Dutch almost beyond belief; he had two given names which were old-Dutch also and two more the most Morgan-partner of Morgan-partner; he not only at once presented his stunned hostess with a magnificent orchid corsage but casually bought her three or four fresh ones at regular intervals during the evening; and as for his fee—well, it turned out that he too was slumming. "Know the fluh runs this escort place," he'd confided to her later in the evening. "Just happened to be by seeing him, huh? when you rang up. Said *Barrow* Street? cod, people actually *live* down that place? He said yes, go see myself why not, broadens! So here I am, huh; *cod!*" He had tired rapidly after three o'clock and had to be sent home, but he refused his host's proffered fee to the last: "After all, old man, when I got there and found you were people I might very easily meet *socially!*—" Saetti's shook from wall to wall with our delighted bellowing; and presently, full-fed, everyone decided to go dancing, and with happy cries we rushed out again hunting for taxis through the sailing snow.

I had simply intended leaving them: I should not have afforded even Saetti's excellent dinner, and the 52nd Street dive they were now headed for (named with some elegance The Men's Room) was completely beyond my economic competence. Then to my astonishment Kitty had argued me, very sweetly and gently, into her paying for our going dancing *à deux* at a modest Greenwich Village speakeasy instead. I was touched.

"What *is* this?" I said gruffly. "You holding my hand?"

"In an affectionately sisterly way I do hope, dear me!"

So we picked up a bag of mine at the West Side Y and drove up to her apartment to dress; but when we were dressed we decided we both looked far too *soignés* to be wasted on the Village so we changed our plans to the Iridium Room; and naturally by this time we were hungry again so when we got there we immediately had supper. The singer was a magnificent Gullah with a most diversified repertory; she began with a standard

> Lovey lovey lovey
> Keep yo back feep drah

then came back in a nakeder dress under a dimmer baby-spot to sing in a raped and tragic contralto

> I have forgotten you; and yet
> Why does my heart still cry "Forget"?

and closed with a parody: "Be Still, My Heart, Aintcha Never Seen a Man Before?" Then she vanished; and we could dance.

Turning and turning in the indolent orchestral topographies we found that we were discussing love. Kitty said, "Being a girl is just a little too difficult for the average girl, don't you suppose probably?"

"Nonsense," I said laughing.

"Oh Webb my dear *yes!* You *have* no idea!"

"Not for you, how could it be, not possibly."

"Because dear me, how you all do come *at* us."

"I guess at that we do."

"Panting and heaving; oh too humiliating!"

I thought this was as good an opening as any for an epigram of mine I'd used widely since college. "It takes all kinds of people to make a woman," I said smoothly.

She paid no attention: she was pursuing some lacerating private memory of her own. "And yet it can all be *so* perfectly sweet at first," she was saying in a haunted voice, her head drooping and her curls brushing my shoulder. "Such lovely *fun*. You know? Even oaf as he is?"

"As who is?" Though of course the second I had said it I realized she was just talking about Steve again, so I added, "You just talking about the generalized male again?"

". . . I suppose I am, how dejecting."

"What's this how-dejecting, what's the matter with us?"

Her head came up laughing. "You're all *perfectly* lovely, may I be understood as saying? There *there!* At Vassar my throbbing little heart would turn to pink glucose."

"The dear dead days."

"The dear dead days—now *do*-let-us-thank-God beyond recall!"

"Then what are you complaining about?" I said.

Her head drooped down and away from me again until I could hardly see even her profile; she said in a shamed voice, "Oh Webb I *am* so dismally incompetent about men."

"What?" I said in astonishment.

"*And* so helplessly inefficient and dispirited and confused."

"Look, Kit—"

"Oh Webb, how can anyone tell really, how can anyone know, how anyone ever anywhere!"

"What in god's—!"

"Sometimes I am all so terrified, so *lost.*"

"There *there!*" I said. "We generalized males can't be as staggering a thing as all that."

She flashed up at me in instantaneous fury, "Oh can't you *just* though! The notion has only to enter some matted male brow that Miss Locke is the solution to his temporary problem!"

"I suppose so."

"Yes! And then there one is, sitting listening, because poor dear Mummy said always dear be ladylike, to the creature's description of how appetizing it would be for *him* if one just slunk meekly into bed with him!"

"Hey now—"

"When dear god all a girl sometimes wants on earth," she cried, "is to forget that one was ever born with one's hormones at all!"

"Easy *easy*," I said, "what is this anyhow?"

Her forehead drooped to my shoulder. "I'm sorry," she said in a muffled, savage voice.

"Sit down and get to work on our drinking?" I suggested mildly.

"I *said* I was sorry!"

We danced a few steps in silence. "What's wrong?" I said.

"Nothing!"

"Then what are you shivering for?"

No answer. If you hate men then naturally you hate yourself for having a yen for them, I thought, but why pick on me? and I said soothingly, "It's all right, Kit."

"It's just that I do grow so *worn.* You know?"

"I know."

"And then it *is* so unnerving and *agaçant*," she flared up at me again, "this dull male conviction that agreeable Miss Locke is not at all exhausted even at the end of her most utterly slain day!"

"Must be."

"And with that hideous lying awake night after night wondering whether one can go on just *living* through this nightmare Depression and headaches all next day and *then* we are understood to be utterly melting with nubility!! *Oh really* how irrelevant!!"

Providentially the music stopped here and we went back to our table, and ordering the ice and soda made a change. I said look, it was probably not really men but the Depression; sex in itself was hardly devised to give mankind a nervous breakdown;

not seriously surely; it must be, rather, sex *plus* the Depression that was bothering her; in other words it was basically (wasn't it?) the Depression itself and not sex at all? How could anyone with her charm, her sweetness, all that lovely (what else could I call it?) femaleness possibly feel 'incompetent' my god about handling her men??!! And then look at what the Depression had done to us, consider what we had been like only a few years ago in college: what hopes, what smiling anticipations, what innocence. And ahead what incarnate dooms! I described them. We danced again and I described the Class's suicides as well (such a damn shame; when you reflected that every single one of them had once been— had once hoped for—somehow had once—well, damn it, it was somehow such a plain goddam *shame*), while she chimed sadly in about her boardingschool prefect, adored at thirteen and now dead following an abortion, or her Vassar roommate's sister (the pretty one) and the overdose of Veronal. We went back to our table and drank while the Gullah appeared and sang again, and discussed how unexpectedly it probably always was—a man would put on his hat and coat and go out in the most ordinary way for a stroll, say, looking back from the corner with a smile and an easy, a friendly wave of the hand; and then quite simply no one would ever see him again alive. (The Class book perhaps still reading, "He is an Episcopalian and a Republican.") Maybe she knew, I said, those grim lines, I couldn't somehow remember whose, that went

> with a casual smile
> Saunter round corners to their doom

Damn thing made the hair rise cold and stiff along my spine with its unstated menace, didn't she feel it too? ("Webb sweet, you are plying me with drink, surely a girl shouldn't just let ply?") We danced again and she clung to me; how long it had been, I thought, how long, since I had held in my arms anyone so sweet and so alive, and I said hey it was nearly three o'clock and maybe I'd better take her home.

In the taxi she clung to me again, kissing me shivering and with abandon; but long before we reached her apartment she had disentangled herself and was saying things like,

"Ah Webb, we have to stop."

"Don't understand you."

"Because otherwise it's too complicated."

" 'Complicated'!"

"I mean nearly home, and all stirred up like this, oh sweet!"

"Implying 'bout in your apartment, my bag, huh."

"Yes and your having to come up anyhow and get it, you *do* see?"

"No complication," I said firmly.

"Yes!"

"Ah Kit, but been so lovely tonight don't want leave ever."

"*You see?*"

"Even behaving myself then?" I argued.

"No!"

"Certainly ought stay at least my god tuck you *in*. Any real gent, only polite course open!"

"'Tuck me in,' oh *dear* me!"

"*Swear* that's all."

We wrangled all the way up the elevator, with growing tenseness and antagonism. But once inside her door, faced with the habitual room, the loneliness so soon ahead, she changed without warning, in the unsteady intake of a breath; and in the very act of kissing me good night, abruptly she was asking me with chattering teeth not to go.

"I suppose perfectly all right!" I said amazed.

"Only *not* sex, Webb, would you mind too hideously?"

"Why, not at all!"

"Because I *do* so—I can't *stand* having love made to me, *at me*, not tonight!"

"Why, sure."

"It's just that I'm— Not the dark exactly, but I just—"

"Fair enough, perfectly!"

"Oh when I am such a bitch to you?" she cried haggardly. "Only it can close down so black and suffocating, Webb!"

"What? Certainly can."

"*And so solitary!* You know? You know?"

The scarcely muffled shrillness of nerves I had noted earlier in the evening, so near the surface, so taut, once again was in her hurrying and desperate voice; and suddenly as it were all around us, under the orderly bucolic antiphonies of drunken argument, I could hear swelling wild, swift, and ominous the pibroch of hysteria. She clung to me sobbing and sobbing, her fingers digging into my biceps, her forehead gouging my shoulder, her body helpless in long gales of shuddering, while I patted and stroked her and intoned meaninglessly on and on and on the dim, assuasive, lullaby vocabulary of solace. Gradually of course the hurricane began to blow itself out; from the midst of the strangling tears she began to gasp things like "Oh why *must* I inflict this on you"; I got her to sit down; then to lie down; the dreadful sobs diminished to hiccups; I mixed her a drink and persuaded her to gulp at it intermittently; the gulps dwindled to a sniffle and she mopped at her eyes and blew her nose and tremulously lit a cigarette; and at long last, teeth still chattering, she achieved a white-lipped and humiliated smile.

There is no doubt what was called for medically speaking: three grains of sodium amytal rectally and throw her into bed, my god. But does one ring up a medical man, even a classmate, at 5:30 of a bleak and icy winter when the cause is—arguably—nothing more serious than a routine Puritan ambivalence about going to bed with a member of the Class of 1927? Sodium amytal may well have been indicated; but what historically she was given was a huge breakfast of *œufs sur le plat* with beautifully grilled tomatoes and sausages, *café au lait* in proper quantity, and Webb Fletcher yawning at her in an amiably full-fed way at the end of it. I am an excellent cook, and when I am fifty I will probably prefer the breakfast to the girl anyhow.

But as, later, I lugged my bag out into the first frost-grey early light and walked through the snowy streets to the nearest bus stop, I reached a workable conclusion: When in future young women proposed holding my hand and making me less lonely in the gay Christmas season, I decided it would be sounder sense to make sure in advance that they had defined with reasonable accuracy what exactly it was they had in mind.

What formal symbolism that winter has for me I do not know; but I do know that when I try to see clearly the events, the passions, the meetings, of that era, I find everything dimmed by the black and hanging night of the Depression, each of us glimpsed obscurely and afar, like solitary travelers in the bleak winter twilight of the horizon against a lowering and frozen sky. And how different too from those winters at Princeton a few short years before—the air then no doubt as raw and snow-filled, the elms' icy branches clashing in the gale, the driven sleet cutting the face as one stumbled back from an early lecture, but always in those vanished and confident days *a place to return to*, an arched stone entry dim yet homelike through the whirling snow, the welcoming doorway, the logs ablaze and the room warm with greeting; and always too that sense of century-long security, of custom, of tradition; of a loved and comfortable history; of return.

Or winter in those rich and spendthrift days might be long weekends in New York, the deb parties and the speakeasies; or a girl down to meet you from Northampton or Poughkeepsie and a taxi through Central Park, perhaps, at the evening's end, the dark air thick with hurrying snow, her body eager under the furs, her lips wary yet clinging, and sometimes her eyes opening to you wide and gleaming in the snowy luminousness of the streetlamps whirling past.

And always too the unalterable certainty of spring; of spring incommutably to follow; the sun-warm flooding of new green by day and the damp fragrant flowering of the nights of spring; and how often in dim starlight the glimmer of a girl's dress through a darker archway, on weekends or at house parties, and light laughter drifting back over the campus in the echoing night.

But in the burgeoning springtide of 1932 there was no sense of annual promise: all we could see was that spreading and immedicable blight. For the crumbling of inherited structures had been if not unforeseeable at any rate unforeseen; and why question even in 1932 (or how?) the credo trained into us of economic propraetorships inevitably to come, the steady steak-fed beating of the Big Board heart, and naturally at the last the opulent, the eupatrid retirement?

For to many of us in the Depression (now, it is clear) all that did remain of the customary abilities of man was the search for love. I think of a scene for example which, once again, I heard of only years later (Mike had told Stephanie, and she me); at the Waldorf or the Marguery, or perhaps it was a midtown speakeasy; and Mike and Jill are finishing a long and intimate lunch, dawdling over their coffee into the early afternoon, and her wistful lost-child's voice saying,

"You must not pay the bill, sweet affectionate Malachi, I will pay for our lunch and you must not."

"Take your dirty little hand off that check."

"I will not."

"Come on, pet."

"Oh, why are you so wicked and mean to me, Malachi? And today of all days when I am so specially rich."

"How, specially?"

"I didn't tell you. Because of a new rule of Davy's, rich."

"What now?"

"It will make me feel shy to tell you."

"Better not, huh."

"It's a new rule about the way we—about Davy's other girls. Or shouldn't I tell you. What do you think?"

"Maybe not, I guess."

"Though maybe it would amuse you, Malachi. Do you think it will? Oh dear, I guess it will, I can see the look in your inquisitive pink old face."

"Matter of fact, pet, maybe we ought to be getting along? Shall I get the—"

"Davy thought up the rule months ago. It's terribly sordid, Malachi."

"Have to be!"

"Of course not *really* his girls, Malachi."

"Course not."

"No. Because I do please Davy, I *do*. But just ones he thinks are pretty, I meant."

"I see."

"Or ones that are exciting to him, I guess, too. So he takes them to lunch. Or to dinner even, sometimes, Malachi, and a show."

"Show, huh."

"Yes; and so then to be fair, the new rule is, when he takes them out he gives me a check."

"*What??*"

"Ten dollars. Or usually ten, anyhow. To make up for my being deserted and alone. So I can buy something I want, Davy says. And not feel sad."

" . . . "

"That makes it all fair. So he can feel free. Do men always want so many of us so often, sweetest Malachi? Are you all like that?"

"I guess so."

"I guess so. Or else Davy wouldn't be either."

One hardly blames Mike for not knowing what to say. She went on, "Though sometimes it has to be more than ten dollars, Davy says. Because if he stays out with her longer I deserve a larger compensation. Or if he—if he has more fun with her."

"Look, Jill—"

"Two nights ago he— Oh, Mike, it was a check for *fifty dollars!*"

Obviously there was nothing to say at all.

"Of course he tells me all about them, Malachi, so it is all right really."

"So now you're rolling in money," said Mike desperately, "and buying me lunches. A fine thing!"

"Why does he like it so, Malachi?"

"How do I know, my god!"

"You *do*. You're a man and you do know and you have to tell me."

"I can't!"

"Oh *please* tell me, Mike. How can I ever be a— be the way Davy wants me to be if you won't tell me?"

"If *I* don't tell you!"

"Would you ever be, well, be that way yourself? Say what's true."

"Not particularly."

"Cross your heart?"

"I guess so."

"I know so! Why, there was a perfectly *sweet* boy who took me to a prom once at New Haven and— Oh, my poor Malachi, I *can't* tell you!"

"No."

"*No!* Not *this!* I tell you everything, everything you ever ask me, because I love you with all my wild fond love, but I can't tell you *this!* Oh please please please don't make me tell you!"

"Good *god* Jill—!"

"Oh, Malachi, I need a drink. I do, I do need a drink. Oh please I know we've only just finished lunch but is it really too early to go back to the apartment and have a drink?"

It was five or six drinks before he left her at the very handsome new apartment in Sutton Place, with its magnificent white-leather sofa that had taken a prize for modern design; but how he got away at last, God knows.

✧

That summer, however, Mike got an extraordinary break, and ended with a job at UBS.

He had conceived an idea for a sustaining program late in the winter and had spent a good many spare hours working out the details; and in the summer he played safe with the usual common-law copyright and took it up to the boys at the net. You have probably heard the show. It was one of the first ballad-singer programs on the air. The idea was to have some grade-A out-of-work guitar-beater spend each week in a different town, visit around intensively with the home-folks, pick up any feasible local ballads, and put them on the air the following Sunday for the after-church audience, with a half-hour script distilling the usable corn from indigenous legendry and two or three standard old-English folk-ballads per show to give the mess backbone. Test it ten weeks as a summer sustainer, he said to them, and you'll have something you can peddle to any pancake-flour sponsor in the country. Because look! You've got audience-participation with write-in votes for Amurrica's Best-Loved Ballad and a big 16-page ballad-booklet-for-the-home-piano printed in seven beautiful natural colors with quarter-life-size cut-out art-views of historic balladry suitable for framing in every package. You've got retailer-and-distributor tie-ins in every hick town from Bangor to Diego. You've got this guitar-jockey parading these towns the whole goddam week building toward your broadcast with a concert in the local opry-house *and* movie personal appearances Saturday nights to wrap in the exhibitor publicity. You've got program-inclusion of local talent building to a Julliard scholarship or Salzburg for all I care by big-name judging of a nation-wide audience vote. You've even got the good-old-Amurrican-way angle in every conjugating commercial to help blast out any wild men this Temporary Recession may try to bring into Washington. Do I have to go on in words of as near one syllable as your cultured audiences can understand or is it a natural? If you can't make a client presentation with *that* material, what are you doing in radio? Why, God help us, the thing's even art!

I doubt if Mike knocked himself to advertisingman's whey over the art argument; but the show clicked. By late August it had even passed a two-hour aesthetics conference of nail-biting and ulcered network vice-presidents; by September it had been sold to a food-chain, and the guitar-hackie and Mike were on the road. In some ways, it appears, the balladist wasn't a bad guy; Duke University theology graduate, I believe; name of Luther something; aside from an uncontrollable oestrus he turned out to have for neighbor-hood-grocers' wives, and one or two low incidents in consequence, Mike had no trouble with him whatever, and at one time even grew mildly fond of the tiresome son-of-a-bitch. I still recall some of the parodies of his own stuff which Mike reported he produced in their evening drinking sessions. One of them went

> Ah'm a-goen whirr they's kleenex fir mah no-ose,
> Ah'm a-goen whirr they's kleenex fir mah nose,
> So's Ah kin wop mah fingiz when Ah blows,
>   Ah ain gaw
>   Nubby tree did
>   Naw such a way.
> Ah'm a-goen whirr the ants got trouziz too-oo.
> Ah'm a-goen whirr the ants got trouziz too,
> Got vulna-rabble pants lak I an you,
>   Ah ain gaw
>   Nubby tree did
>   Naw such a way.

Or he'd say, "Now hyeh boy is a rillil ole art saong," and out would pour a long tragic history that began

> Take yo po'celain teef outta mah beee-eefsteck,
> Take yo dribbelen face outta mah gin

though all Mike could remember of the rest of it was the melancholy chorus, full of heartache and minor chords ("sings alaong mahtie smooths an hummy-lak, hey boy?")

> Fill yo mush wid de good green spinach,
> Fill yo mush wid de good green spinach,
> Fill yo mush wid de good green spinach
>   An leave mah sowbelly be.

Mike himself seems to have specialized on these occasions in parodies of citified songs, *A pretty girl is like a malady* and so on; and he developed a talent for conversing with rustics that left him dropping g's from his present participles (*and* gerunds) even after he got back to New York.

But when the *lauriers* are *coupés* they are *coupés* and let us have no more of them; and by the spring of 1933 he had seen enough of his brachycephalous crossroads fellow-citizens to last him a reasonable lifetime. His nostalgia for New York was reaching psychopathic proportions. He had lived in second-class hotels and out of suitcases autumn, winter, and now spring: like the poet he could with feeling say *we have known the seasons and to hell with them.* With the onset of spring, also, Luther had begun to lower his sights below the age of consent, and while it is theoretically arguable that fifteen-year-old pregnancies have their homespun-Amurrican aspect, Mike said later he preferred to have someone else take over that sheet of the presentation to the sponsor. He finally hopped a train from some broadbottomed citadel of the American Way in south-central Illinois, and in two fast-talking and high-pressure hours at UBS had traded himself off the road into a script-and-trouble-shooter job back at the net. With expense-money out, this meant a stiff working cut in his income. But the only man at UBS who thought he was crazy was the pink-cheeked *petite oie blanche* who was sent happily out to take his place with Luther's Coke-swilling scatological aphorisms and the pancakes.

Mike celebrated his repatriation with a full-scale party. The Starrs lent him their apartment for it. They also filled him in on who was in the old group; and it was thus, Stephanie my love, that for the first time in his unexamined life he met that cool, chic, fragrant, delicious, tantalizing, scandalous parkavenue girl, who was You. His welcoming smile was without portents, comets, or attendant monsters; your answering smile wanted the customary punctuation of thunderclaps from an unclouded if premonitory sky. If he said it was wonderful you had come to his party, we may assess the declaration as conventional-to-gallant; while if you replied "Davy's told me so much about you," we may assume from motives of tact that you were inattentive when he did, for you imagined, my love, that Mike was somebody from Illinois. No doubt if you had known that he was at UBS and hence an entrée to that potential market for your imagination, your knowledge of him would have fattened on immediate and accurate supplements, nor need he have waited (unaware that he was waiting) for the light and lovely accolade of your accent on his office phone. But I am concerned with statable fact; and as far as you or I or anybody can remember, you didn't exchange with Mike twenty words more.

In any case, his mind was incandescent with the dazzling illusion that he had returned less to New York as such than to Kitty Locke. Often I do not see how the human intelligence can accept its own judgments and remain sane; but apparently he had forgotten every squabble, every frustration, and simply thought oftener and oftener of that lovely day in Coatesville, during the weeks before he finally decided to abandon Luther to his dreams of statutory rape. It was some dreary hotel in eastern Arkansas, and Mike remembered lying on his bed in the steaming spring night and trying to concentrate on just what it was he had felt ("Felt about *me* I do hope," Kitty said brightly, "rather than some rural center of population in Pennsylvania!") against an obbligato of shrill giggles and unconvincing falsetto protests from Luther's room next door. (I do not know whether the language here is Kitty's or Mike's own.) The amorous squeals of an adolescent girl have no doubt their place but Mike was not interested in determining it; and his distaste at Luther's Southern lunge for the handiest delinquent child was by this time acute. The retarded brat also punctuated the evening with outbursts of sobbing at hourly intervals. Mike took a Nembutal and still he could not sleep; and unconsciously his decision to wangle his way back to civilization must have been made that night. Anyhow, back he came, a headlong engine of sentimental enthusiasm, with Coatesville and Kitty and New York unanalyzably mixed in his carburetor; and he couldn't even wait till his repatriation party to see her.

He could hardly have chosen (though naturally he had no way of knowing it) a period of more unpromising auspices. In the months he had been away, all of us in New York had changed. The somber invisible night of the Depression, its wintry dusk spreading and deepening about us on and on, had worn us down, as if by an endless insomnia, out of all proportion to the passage of chronological time. The parties of course went on; the gay meetings were enacted, reenacted; the rituals observed. Yet more and more nakedly one saw the rictus of nerves under the smile, the sleek urban integument tight and thin as lacquer upon the skull. The happy froth and bubble was gone; we drank much more and much oftener; we would abruptly quarrel. One member of the Class remarked that we even made love "damn near the way you step into a hamburger joint on a freezing night—at least get for god's sake *warm* before starting home to bed." And of course we communicated our tension to our girls. It seems clear enough, for instance, that Kitty's bitter and somehow degrading affair with Steve might have exhausted the gay part of her less—might even have made her completely happy in some neurotic fashion—if there had been no Depression to tear endlessly and viciously at their nerves. As it was, they merely wore each other out. I remember witnessing an ugly scene of theirs, and I think it was at about this period, the period of Mike's return. I'd been unable to avoid overhearing it, or part of it: been penned in the kitchen at some party or other by Kitty and Steve quarreling in the doorway, paying not the least attention to my presence.

"What're you talking about anyhow, my god?" Steve was saying. "I haven't done a goddam thing to you all evening!"

Kitty was flaming. "Oh, haven't you though!!"

"I tell you I—"

"If you could keep your hands off her *at* least in public!"

"What're you— Now who?"

"Oh you utter child, Steve! 'Now who'!"

"Davy's kid cousin? You mean to tell me you—"

"You're so completely low!"

He laughed abruptly and angrily. "Low, huh! You know goddam good and well what you can always do about *that!*"

"Do I?"

"Want me to tell you, baby?"

"Perhaps it's exactly what I *will* do!" she cried.

"Go right ahead!"

"*I will!!*"

"Yeah? You really think he can make the grade?"

She slapped him; stinging and hard; a real roundhouse swing that knocked him into the doorjamb; and vanished with some inarticulate cry into the room beyond; I thought for a moment that Steve was going to leap after. Then he saw me standing there, and his face changed; and then of course the whole thing became embarrassing.

(She said to me later: "—and so the whole history of what I had done with Steve, how can I put it? just wasted! You know? Just hideous and sordid? *Dear* me what a state! Deserted. I suppose I should have felt, I'm free. Only how dismal, I wasn't! Nothing so simple. Just deserted!")

That was how things stood when Mike sentimentally and unknowingly returned to New York, so full of his feeling for Kitty that he couldn't even wait until his party to see her.

She met him for lunch at the Meadowbrook the first day after he got back to town. He was eager and early. He left his hat at the vestiaire in the little octagonal room downstairs and went up to the tiny round bar in the baywindowed front room above to wait for her. The bartender said he was happy to see him back so soon, where was it again he'd been? and they discussed economic conditions in the Middle West while he mixed Mike a beautiful Martini. Mike let it sit on the bar, watching the lovely clear white-gold frost over, thinking with pleasure that here was an honest-to-god Martini that he could start drinking right from the wood.

"They can't make 'em like this in the West," he said.

"How was that, Mr. Fisher?"

"I said I haven't had a decent Martini in months."

"Don't mix 'em like that out West, I hear; no sir, that's a fact."

Then Mike heard from the stairs her soft-chiming "Malachi, *Malachi!*" and she was kissing him in a flurry of curls and spring furs and delighted eyes and gloved hands patting his shoulders;

and in an instantaneous blaze of illusion he *knew* why he had come back to New York. It was so self-evident a thing to him that, as they sat at the bar sipping their cocktails and smiling contentedly at each other, it seemed to him that she too must have guessed it and felt it. Guessed it and agreed: for he saw something new in her manner to him as well.

"Ah, Malachi, it *is* so splendid seeing you again, were you aware?"

"I could eat you."

"How did we live without you all these unbelievably ghastly months away? And how did you?"

"I don't think I did."

"*May* I tell you how frightful it has all been? Everyone concluded you had vanished forever."

"*You* knew better, Kit."

"I thought of you most often and tenderly, Malachi."

"I thought of you so often I finally came back to you."

"Now Malachi. Come come."

"I did! For no other reason!"

She smiled at him, eyes and all; but it was a little wan, and she said, "Malachi, I am touched. But should we perhaps maintain a sternly reasoned attitude, don't you find it generally wise?"

He blurted, "'Reasoned'! Suppose I'm in love with you!"

"Oh Malachi."

"Anything strange? It's not new, my god! You've always known, well, why I for instance asked you to go to Coatesville with me that day, as an example!"

"It was such a lovely day, wasn't it."

"I felt it then."

"You were most kind that day, Malachi."

"Only you weren't ever, call it 'free,' before."

She looked up at him like a flash, "'Free,' Malachi?"

"Hardly know how else to say it."

"Am I 'free' now, you think?"

"I think so, somehow."

"Somehow. Mike, the expressions you sometimes *use*."

"Well, aren't you?"

"I *look* that way to you, Malachi? I look publicly an unbespoken Miss Locke?"

"I don't know exactly why I felt it," he said defensively.

Her eyes flashed at him and her chin went up. "Only fancy!" she said in a voice of ice. Then suddenly she drooped; her eyes slid down; she was hunting for a cigarette in her handbag. "Though perhaps after all I *am*, Malachi, did you know? *Quite* free really, one might almost say; and how odd."

He gave her a cigarette; as he held a match for her he felt her eyes on his face again, and he glanced up from the match into a long, tense look he mistakenly thought he was reading.

"Don't you know we're very fond of each other, Kit?"

"Oh undeniably fond."

"I want you badly. I always have."

"I know I know."

"And you want me."

Her eyes left him abruptly; she said in a very weary tone, "But then I want so many so much so often."

"But always me."

She said shrilly, "Oh dear heaven what *good* does it do to *add up* words like fond and want, what *good* is it!"

"That isn't what I mean."

"Oh isn't it just!"

"Fond and want are just— Kit, they're only a kind of logical framework for—"

"Oh dear god, Mike, are you setting out with solemn missionary zeal to convince—God help me what a word!—to *convince* people about such things?"

"I wasn't arguing at you. I was only—"

"Oh *no*, Mike!"

"Damn it, Kit, when you were in my arms you didn't—"

"Oh Mike what a *really* undergraduate remark!"

That was a difficult observation to back away from; and in fact I have had some difficulty in imagining how, after it, they managed to get through that lunch at all.

Naturally that little speech of Kitty's ought to have been of great therapeutic value to Mike. It should have told him, once for all, it seems to me, that this was not what he was seeking. (Was *this* high-held head ever likely to send him, across no matter how welcoming a room, the dazed and lovely look that might have been his salvation? and obviously the answer is, No.) But it was only his vanity that seems to have been touched among all possible phases of his sensibility; and when they parted at the end of that difficult meal he handed her into her taxi merely with an expression of outraged dignity. It is not an expression that suggests the refinements of intelligence. He had learned nothing. He was merely fed up with her and her goddam moods, that was all; and a fine return to civilization *this* was!

That lunch did end, it is true, one long phase of their relations; the sentimental phase, call it; and after it they saw very little of each other for a long time. But it was not, as it could have been, the real end; and only partly because meantime Stephanie came between.

And in any case Kitty and Steve made up their quarrel as usual; their affair went on. It always did.

It had been earlier in that same spring, before Mike came back to town, that someone—Jack Geddie, I believe—had proposed the idea of our maintenance farm. I understand that such a term does in fact exist. At any rate, the proposal was that a number of us band together, under partnership terms to be worked out presently, buy a farm in Virginia or southern Maryland, or anyhow where it would be warm, and ride out the Depression from there, working the land just enough to supply us with our food and a small cash-crop over. The work-it-just-enough clause was, naturally, inserted to leave us plenty of leisure for things we really wanted to do. Mike was of course included on his return.

There was a great deal of theory attached to the project, some of it relatively simple. The investment part of the theory, for example, was this: insurance-company and bank portfolios were so choked with practically non-negotiable farm mortgages that we could very nearly name our own price; even if there occurred some hardly conceivable further decline, land was still a sound long-run equity; if the Depression ever did end, we stood to gain substantially on the swing; and meanwhile our rent-free life would represent a real rate of return far higher than our capital could get elsewhere. The basic economic theory was even simpler: no known industrial index was predicting anything worth looking at, the Depression might for all the experts could tell last a decade, and in short our basic economic theory was simply the hell with it. I cannot quite believe my ears as I repeat all this incantation to myself today; but at the time it affected us as if it had been a new religion.

"Yes but what happens to *us*?" Jane Meineke demanded at one of the parties somebody gave for discussion and organization of the project. She was a young cousin of Davy's from Denver, a tall blonde constructed for the most satisfactory possible lay, who threw herself directly and unreservedly, as these Western girls do, at an idea or a man. "You going to communize us too?"

"The women?" said Jack Geddie, grinning. "Certainly *are!*"

"Jack *darling!* You mean I have to let myself be dragged off naked and shrieking to whosever bed—"

"Shrieking, dear?" said Kitty.

"Well of course," said Jane with hardly a look at her, "I can't speak for anyone but myself. But who wouldn't shriek if you never had the slightest idea whose babies— Or wouldn't you care?"

"*Dear* god," breathed Kitty, "do you plan to go around farrowing right and left?"

Steve laughed abruptly.

"I didn't imagine I'd have to explain it to you," said Jane. "Have you always been lucky or something?"

Steve laughed again. Kitty flicked a cool glance at him and addressed the company: "Let me make it *entirely* clear, if you will all be so kind, that Miss Locke does not propose to spend the rest of the Depression wiping tiny noses in some nursery school for other women's by-blows. *Nor* her own, may I add!!"

Jack began peaceably, "Matter of plain fact—"

"On the nights when Jane has to have sex with Steve," said Davy with his meatiest infliction, "does that count as her share of the chores for the day?"

Steve ejected his laugh, and Jane screamed "*Davy!*" delightedly. "What if she liked it?" Steve said, and laughed again, throatily.

Jack was grinning. "We might set up a scientifically graduated scale of satisfaction for the women—"

"*You* set up the scale!" cried Jane.

And so on and so on. I can't say that I understood much of this: I'd met Jane only a few times, and though Jack Geddie was a charter member of the Gin Social group as well as a member of the Class, I knew little about him. He was tall and pale, with a long thin head and a handsomely pointed face; he had been very rich in college, but his family's holdings had been in bank stocks and Chicago real estate, and he was now working as an article editor on, I think, *Collier's*. What he was doing in an adventure like this farm project I had no notion whatever (except what were *any* of us doing in it?); his place in the triangle Kitty–Steve–Jane, if it *was* a triangle and if he was in it, was totally obscure.

But *in* the farm project he indisputably was; he was in fact its chief theoretician; and it was he and I, with Kitty as distaff critic, who drove south late that spring to scout the territory and tentatively decide on the farm itself.

We spent the first night at Harper's Ferry; and it was near there, as it turned out, that we found the only likely-looking place of the whole trip, the very next afternoon, on the wooded bluffs along the Shenandoah. What I remember chiefly, however, was the drive south, through the lovely hazy sunlight and bloom of spring. It affected me strangely. To my surprise (or was it really to my surprise?) I found myself thinking back with a curious and almost caressing insistence to the countryside our route to Harper's Ferry had led us through—the towns we passed into and out of in the green, rolling, peaceful, back-Maryland afternoon, drowsy and still in the early stirrings of spring; the glistening green blades of the reeds in the marshes, the names we had seen on bridges over streams: Leg Creek, Bynum Run; names I supposed of some unknown but loved and honorable history. There had been a bare wooden sign that had in some irrational way moved me deeply, at the edge of an alder thicket by the highway, weather-whitened against the clustering emerald newness of the leaves:

> GIVE GOD YOUR HEART

I had felt, I realized, some tender but unrecognizable emotion when I saw it first; and I felt it later too, running the phrase over in my mind, seeing it again in my memory, faded red letters on a bleached sign. At more than one maple-shaded graveyard with its low white wall and springy turf, I had almost suggested to the others that we stop for a moment and wander among the headstones: I would have liked, I do not know why, to scrutinize the perhaps familiar names; I had even the unexpected fancy that I might come upon my own. And there had been inscriptions under the eaves of farmhouses, letters hardly more than glimpsed as we drove along; some time, surely, I would travel that route again and stop, for I was curious to know what they said, and why.

The farm near Harper's Ferry I had not felt at all so warmly drawn toward, though it did have certain possibilities. It was some two hundred acres, partly woodland and abandoned apple orchards, the land along the tops of the bluffs worn out and desolate, but with some fifty acres of rich ground in the river-bottom below. There had been a mule's carcass in the fringe of trees along the bluff; a pair of turkey buzzards were at it as we walked by. There was an ancient stone farmhouse with walls nearly two feet thick, and though it stank now of a century of frying sowbelly it had fine proportions and spacious rooms; a wall up the center had converted it into a two-family slum but that could be knocked out again easily. There was a wonderful springhouse of stone: the water welled up cold and pure from a spring beneath and rilled in a wide, shallow, stone-paved channel around the walls inside, with basins of milk cooling in it and the cream rising, and half a cheese on a floating plank; the overflow outside was into a mossy cattle-trough with the sign REPUBLICANS above it! A family of tenant-farmers lived there now, trying to build up the land for the insurance company that owned the mortgage. I'd not been strongly attracted to the place, but the price mentioned was amazingly low; and the agent had told us there were two Newtown pippins in the orchard that still bore; and after all (I added sardonically) the farm as a whole did seem to have everything we needed except toilets and running hot water, and of course a shower.

The remaining two days of the trip were completely unfruitful. We went deep into southern Tennessee and found nothing but eroded crimson earth and people that made me feel foreign. Though perhaps the farm group could stand it. Anyhow, Kitty said, now they could all rush down to Harper's Ferry and look for themselves and decide.

(Of course, we never did decide. Even the partnership terms would have been impossible to draw up: the diverse capital investments and salary sacrifices, obviously, from the start irreconcilable. We might just as profitably have spent the time and energy listening to the well-known Mr. Eliot going on about his fear in a handful of dust—a bit muddy with all those infusions of holy water, no doubt, but calculated, surely, to dispel a passing economic dismay. And, anyhow, Stephanie my love, what would *you* have done on a maintenance farm?)

Jack and Kitty dropped me off at Wilmington on the way home: I was being an usher at a wedding there. And I might as well say at once that even the trip through the Maryland countryside does not come back to me so strongly as that evening at the trip's end which I spent—it is a curious thing, I know—walking the deserted streets of Wilmington in the darkness. I was not born in Wilmington, but I had grown up there; and it is the landscape of one's childhood that is one's true *patrie*.

I had not been there for some time. I was being an usher, as it happened, at the wedding of the brother of the first girl I had ever kissed—she and I were both pushing five at the time—at Miss Sellers' private kindergarten on Pennsylvania Avenue between

Franklin and Broome; in a flurry of wild giggles and waving wraps in the coatroom; I think I remember her tasting delicious, but I never kissed her again and she had died in childbirth in 1930. It was a big lavish wedding, full of faces I had grown up with and gone to Friends' School with in the years before my parents had died, but now a shade alien and not seen since the last big wedding in Wilmington. Somehow (though I don't think I phrased it so myself) there should have been comfort in all those faces once so reassuringly near and familiar—the Baronne niece next door who had looked like a Sèvres shepherdess since she was two, and still did (charming!); the Baronne nephew I'd nearly made TNT with once in the chem lab at school (I supplied the toluol, he what he swore was the Company process); the Baronne daughter from the other end of the block, absolutely gorgeous from the age of nine; but then all the Baronne daughters were absolutely gorgeous. For the reception, some Baronne vice-presidential cellar or other had cascaded out endless cases of Heidsieck; and I had one moment of warm remembrance when I turned to a passing trayful of glasses to find that the footman serving it was William, who had been our butler-coachman two decades before—he grinned at me and I had a sudden vision of him sitting high and stiff in the gig, holding the whip smartly aslant, grinning down at me that same indulgent grin as I sat close against him away from the spinning yellow-spoked flash of the wheels, a pink-cheeked little boy on the way to the exciting curb-market on a bright November morning; and now I grinned back and shouted how glad by god I was to see him and what was he doing *here*, and I slapped him on the back till he nearly upset his brimming tray. Everywhere gay and welcoming people pumped my hand and pounded me too on the shoulders; or I would turn at the sound of a half-familiar voice in the happy din around me to find some member of the Class beaming at me with his warm and welcoming smile:

"Old Webb *Fletcher!* Jesus, fella, I haven't seen you since college, how *are* ya by god! Didn't even know you were back in Wilmington!"

"Didn't know you were settling here, by god!"

"You say you're *settling* here? Now by god that *is* wonderful news—why, man, we'll be seeing each other practically every day! My wife and I— Now where the hell she got to? I swear she was right here a minute ago."

So I began to feel lonely early; and presently I had one of the chauffeurs drive me back into town. Anyhow, as far as 8th Street Park. I had to tell him where it was.

"You all right, sir?" he asked as I got out.

"What d'you mean?"

"Well, sir, excuse me, but *this* place. The station's—"

"*I* know where the station is."

"Yes, sir, I just thought—"

"Good night."

"Good night, sir."

I watched his taillight disappear down Broome Street and over the slope at 9th, and then stood gazing emptily across the pool of streetlight into the dusky park beyond. Why was I standing here, what was I seeking, on this northwest corner of 8th and Broome, I asked myself dully, and what is it that I expect to find? Here I had stood (how often!) on this well-remembered pavement, its worn parquet-laid bricks heaved into gentle undulations by the swelling roots of the maples, its edges mossy and lost in the fine grass at the sides; here I had stood how many times, a small boy of two, perhaps, or three, leaning eagerly from the curb at the farthest stretch of my mother's hand, peering expectantly and impatiently down 8th for the trolley that would bring my father from the office home; or in the park opposite I would patter about the fountain as it splashed into its wide shallow basin in elegant lines, chattering orders to my boat of leaves; until the trolley stopped and my father stepped down and caught me and whirled me high into the air till I was way up level with his smiling brown eyes; and the three of us walked the two blocks home, the safe-sounding murmur of their voices in the evening air above my head, and I with a hand clinging to each of them skipping and stumbling over the root-enacted brick waves of the pavement. Why am I standing here, when I can turn and saunter down Broome Street under the maples in the deepening dusk the way I have gone so often? naming to you the houses and who lived in them nearly a quarter-century before; past the granite wall and to 9th; past the broad, spaced-out, comfortable, architecturally incredible houses to 10th; which was home. Yet why can I say I am standing even here, under our wide sassafras tree? a tall man in a morning coat and ascot tie, a light overcoat hanging from his arm, gazing emptily up at the dark porch and the lights in the windows, seeing in his mind the interior, room by room; or turning the corner to pace along 10th toward Rodney past the long garden, a small intent figure squatting among the lettuce-rows, watching the absorbing progress of my father's firm fingers through the loam, or lifting for approval a snapped-off weed-leaf to the answering smile.

At the corner I paused; I turned down Rodney; I paced slowly (for where after all had I to go?), slowly past smaller houses with the look of landmarks though lacking in symbolism; past Pennsylvania Avenue and into a region of shade-trees and lawns in the dark; past Delaware Avenue, past Gilpin and Shallcross, names known later but with affection; the towering masses of Brandywine Park's trees looming like dusty bastions ahead of me, the undulating uneven root-warped parquet of the bricks beneath my feet. Why here? Or here? Why am I pacing here? In what expectations historically impossible; from what wearisome and unattainable whim? Or was this longing only the lack of some companion to formulate questions, to note my answers, to gaze upon landmarks with understanding, to hear the complicated resonances of names?

I must have walked thus for many hours. I tried experiments of singular geographical vanity. Until at last and hopelessly I visited the old brick meetinghouse at 4th and West. Its beautiful 1812 Quaker severity was unaltered, the fine spare lines the same, the block-square turf of its graveyard in the dark under the maples unchanged; but I had forgotten the tall iron fence that encircles it, and of course I could not get in. Yet what, anyhow, would I have found? I could guess at a scattering of the names upon the headstones: Peirce, Comly, Pennock, Fordingbridge, Neave. But none of them would have been my own; and presently I walked wearily down 4th Street hill to French and down French to the station, and caught a late train back to New York. Whatever it was I was after, whatever landscape, whatever childhood *patrie*, I had neither known nor found.

Mike had been at UBS a month or so—the chronology here is less certain than one would have expected—when one midmorning his office phone rang; and at last he heard directed at him those cool, lazy, drawling, delicious accents which were to bring so much confusion into the story I am telling.

"Mi-i-ike?"

"Yes?"

"Or do you like to be called Ma-la-chi?"

"In *that* lovely tone, anything!"

A chiming little laugh, with a touch of malicious amusement in it. "Do you al-ways say such pretty things when you don't even know who it i-i-is?"

"I don't know?"

"You know perfectly well you have no-o-o idea. So don't argue. But shall we not play little games about it? Because they don't re-al-ly amuse me, do they you? This is Stephanie Lowndesden. You don't remember, but I—"

"I certainly do remember!"

"I have no idea how you can, you paid not the sli-i-ightest attention to me all that evening."

"Nonsense. I was the guy that kept your glass full."

"You mean I was drunk and revolting, Ma-la-chi?"

"Nothing of the sort! I—"

"I don't see how you kno-o-ow. You never once even glanced in my direction."

"Ahh, Stephanie—"

The lovely malicious laugh again. "You didn't you *didn't!* So don't ar-gue. Whereas I looked at you pra-a-actically without interruption all evening long and I want you to come to my party. Jack's giving me one for my birthday, it's *ver*-ry sweet of him, and I am particularly inviting you. A week from Thursday."

"Why, I'd love to come."

"It's ver-ry tiresome but you will have to dress. *White* tie. Which is perfectly silly but we are going to the ballet, of course I've seen it twice already, and Jack is stuffy about tails and the old regime and it is so-o-o much easier just not to ar-gue."

Mike's subconscious mind can hardly have remembered what she looked like, but at a male name it made him say, "You going to wear something lovely and naked?"

Suddenly her laugh was down in her throat. "Do you have to have your girls already naked, Ma-la-chi? Don't you know how to undress us?"

"It's this damn modern cloth. Just doesn't come away in the teeth the way it used to."

A shriek of musical delight. "I don't think I had better come see you after all!"

"What?"

"I was coming to your office, Ma-la-chi, some day soon."

"Well, *do.* Don't let a few scampering half-naked—"

"In fact I suppose that was partly why I am phoning you, now I think of it. I par-tic-u-lar-ly want you to tell me who I ought to see about a script."

"A script? Whose script?"

"Why, mine. Naturally."

"What's it about?"

She told him and they discussed it (it was an idea for a series rather than a one-shot) and he told her the man to see.

"Then you'll be sweet and make an appointment for me, Ma-la-chi? Or isn't he important enough?"

"He's always free."

"But it would be a little better if he knew who I am?"

"I don't know. It might be."

"So you *will* make an appointment for me?"

"Glad to."

"And then take me in and introduce him?"

"Why, sure."

"And explain who I am? Because he might ju-u-st as well know I'm not just an-y-bo-dy. Or walking in cold. Don't you think that's better?"

"Why not have lunch with me," he said suddenly, "and we can lay out a whole campaign." The smooth mixture of warm and cool in her voice, and the mingling overtones of calculating career girl and calculating deb, had begun to fascinate his imagination; and anyhow he hadn't had lunch with a girl in ten days and why not?

And so therefore; and in most natural consequence.

She was late; as she was always late. But presently they were perched together at the little circular bar in the baywindowed room at the Meadowbrook, lifting between them in uncomprehended ritual those first of how long and how unforeseen a series of his Martinis and her whiskey sours—the angel-grey eyes smiling at him their cool and tantalizing appraisal between the wink of the lifted glass and the smart black angle of the hatbrim; the gloved wrist at the cheek, the sleek arm rising to it from her elbow on the bar; the straw-gold hair drawn smooth and tight above the ear; the slim body indolent and delicious through the tailored severity, with a creamy froth of ruffles at her throat; the sweet red curving kiss at the cocktail's rim—and all that for the first and fatal time poised and discharged *exprès* at *him*; and ranged in on him and on him only, with lazy and expert calculation, that point-blank battery of teasing, sensual, so-I-please-you charm, that struck straight into his eyes and half took his breath away with the directness of its impact, half made him uneasy by the very insolence of its execution. *I may never need to acquire you* (it said) *in fact why should I ever? but just in case* . . . and the serenely smiling eyes would drop for an instant to his mouth, with a little half-checked lowering and flutter of the lids, the mere soft flicker of a glance that suddenly lingered there a breathless second too long, as if she had intended only to note and file away his individual savor against some hardly probable future moment of cool exploration, yet had found it—her eyes said for an erotic instant as they came up again to his—unexpectedly and floodingly delicious to anticipate, and she half wished it were worth while tasting it now. It was a look that blinded him with its mingling of wantonness and lazy postponement; and between it and the Martinis he was soon exactly as enchanted as she had intended him to be, namely enough to be very useful but not so much as to be a nuisance; and she was investigating his case history in detail.

"Ma-la-chi, why did Jack never tell me you are at UBS?"

"Doesn't get around, I guess."

"You know what I mean. Here you are practically running the place and I wasn't even properly told."

"I've only been there a few months."

"Don't be sil-ly, you know you're *ver*-ry important."

"Yes but they can't make me chairman of the board under a year, they told me. There's some kind of rule."

"Be serious. I want to know what you do-o-o. Aren't you ever serious?"

"Yes."

"When? No, never mind! I don't think I want to hear, I can tell perfectly by the carnal look on your face." The cool, mocking laugh. "Do try to remember I'm just having lu-u-unch with you, Ma-la-chi. I have no-o-o intention of getting into bed with you the minute you've had your coffee!"

"I can't explain the advantages of that?"

"You may explain *what you do* at UBS and you may also order another drink for me."

So he dutifully explained: he'd just recently got his office job at the net by persuading an intellectual virgin to go out and script for Luther; he described Luther and the show, which Stephanie had not heard.

"Was this Luther whoever-he-is any good?" she asked, bending down to sip her new drink from the wood, while he looked at the angelic curve of her body with sheer stupefaction. "Why have I never heard of him? What's his last na-a-ame?"

"I've never been able to remember it."

"But my dear man you were with him for months!"

"All I seem to remember is his women. And his parodies."

"Did you fancy any of his women, Ma-la-chi?"

"Good god no!"

"I suppose Luther's parodies were on the same level?"

"Some of them. Some of them were a bit more complicated."

"Ho-o-ow?"

"You want a complicated specimen, you mean?"

"But of course."

So he sang obediently,

> "I had a little nut-sy,
>   Nothing did she wear
> But a golden G-string
>   And a baby stare;
> The vice-president-in-charge of-sales-and-
>   customer-relations' daughter
> Made a play for me,
> But just to get a crack at
>   My little nut-sy."

She shrieked with delight, so he sang her a couple more. They had another cocktail apiece and carried their thirds or fourths into the restaurant and he began to tell her what he had done to Luther's time-sheets.

"Hadn't you better or-der, Ma-la-chi? You've spent so much time getting me drunk enough to seduce that it's now *ver*-ry late."

"Huh? Nonsense!"

"And I am hungry. So order my lunch."

"What do you want?"

"*I* am not ordering. *You* are."

"Well, but—"

"Don't be lazy, Ma-la-chi. You're taking me to lunch, so order."

"Do you like, well, sweetbreads? They do them here with some kind of black sauce."

"I told you. Or-der!"

So he ordered; and went on about Luther. UBS had sent them a thick sheath of mimeographed time-forms to fill in: one for each day, 8½ x 11 sheets, dull pink, three-hole punchings at the left, blank spaces at the top for name, office phone, date, position held, program, and check-here-if-sustaining, and all the rest of the sheet marked out into little boxes dividing the twenty-four hours into fifteen-minute stints. A management firm had presumably sold some particularly retarded UBS vice-president a bill of goods on personnel efficiencies; and so Mike and Luther were instructed to fill in every fifteen-minute box with a scrupulous itemizing of their activities during that specific quarter-hour. Mike's own forms had been easy: he simply typed up five carbons at a time of *planned program* in the first box, *researched program* in the next two, and *wrote* (or ditto marks) in all the rest; occasionally he varied the entries with a *walked reflectively to water-cooler* or a *perpended*. But he'd told Luther *he* could hardly write his name, much less contribute to the efficiency of a great industrial bureaucracy, so he (Mike) would fill in his forms for him. Except for one day devoted entirely to *swilled Cokes* and *scratched armpits and buttocks while meditating about program*, he gave Luther a romantically full life. Luther was made to read fanmail asking if he was a Baptist and saying they thought about his voice after their husbands were through with them at night; he interviewed a police lieutenant in Tallahassee over a complaint brought by the superintendent of a consolidated junior-high school in Utah; he washed his undershirt and handkerchief every Tuesday 10:15-10:30 A.M. except for the week he unaccountably missed in Wichita; he consulted lawyers an average of three fifteen-minute periods a week about parentage suits brought by people named Lutie and Truleah and Rayliene Ann—oh, well, anyway it had all seemed mildly funny at the time, Mike told Stephanie; and anyhow this was enough about what *he* did and what did *she* do and what was her idea about the scripts?

"Jack hasn't told you about me, Ma-la-chi? I'm at Trotter & LeBon."

"The publicity shop?"

"But of course. Though I am *ver*-ry bored with my accounts. Except one. That's why I'm thinking of trying radio."

" 'Except one'?"

The sweetly derisive flash of her eyes. "Yes. But I don't think I will tell you, Ma-la-chi. It might make you jea— It might upset you."

"Does it make Jack jea— Upset him?"

A giggle. "Only you're not Jack, Ma-la-chi, are you?"

"How do you know," he said. He ran the backs of his fingers very lightly up the line of the lovely sleek pale-gold hair and touched the lobe of her ear. She moved her head half an inch away with practiced composure, and tranquilly returned his hand to the table.

"I don't think I want you to be tiresome and I dislike being tickled."

"How do you know I'm not like Jack?" he said.

She looked at him coolly, but her eyes were smiling. "Do you want to hear about this one account? Or don't you?"

"You think I can control myself?"

"Don't you'd think you'd better, Ma-la-chi?"

"Subjectively think? Or objectively?"

"It's a minor Hollywood account; an agent," she said composedly. "Not that the *agent's* minor—he's *ver*-ry important—but of course it's not like a big industrial account." Her eyelids slid down. "Though I'm afraid he is really rather ex-ci-ting."

"The Hollywood lunge, huh."

"Oh, no. He always tries to be *ver*-ry correct and eastern with me. He's my account so of course I have to be nice to him and take him around when he comes to New York, and he wants to be terribly hard to resist *in a New York way*, he told me. Can you imagine?"

" 'd charm anybody."

"And of course he's so ut-ter-ly crude through and through," she said with her eyes deep in Mike's again, "that I keep thinking what a fascinating ex-per-i-ment he might be. You'll never guess what he said to me!"

"Quoted Shakespeare?"

"No. It was the next-to-last time he was in town. We were talking about jobs in Hollywood and of course he can do *any*-thing out there. And naturally I'm always feeling tempted by a job there, and what do you suppose he said!"

"What?"

"He said, 'Look, baby, *you* want a job in Hollywood and *I* want to lay you, so whadda ya gonna do about it?' Did you ev-er hear—!"

"A direct bastard!"

"Isn't he! And then he flew out east only ten days ago *just* to see me, and he sent me a perfect ham-per of flowers every day for a week before that—'little floral build-up,' he called it—and brought me a bracelet I haven't even dared let Jack *see*. He says he 'goes for me,' isn't he unbelievable?"

"Is he?"

She looked at him under her eyelids, and her eyes were gleaming. "I'm afraid he is *ver*-ry attractive, I never met anyone quite so vulgar and stallion-y. What do you think I ought to do about him, Ma-la-chi?"

"Well, you're still here in New York, aren't you!"

"Well, *dar* ling! What a question! Do you expect me to have se-e-ex with a man just because of a plane trip and a *ba-a-angle?*"

Looking back now at that long and trivial lunch, Stephanie my love, at the strict and leisurely procession of the hors d'oeuvres, the sweetbreads, the *zabbaioni*, the coffees, the brandies you two sat dallying over until nearly a quarter to four, seeing it through a haze of much alcohol and much history, I can discern no scientifically admissible portents trailing their fiery and authenticated tails across the mind of Malachi Fletcher in this junior period. One incident only may have induced a later moment of more lingering speculation in the mind of Malachi Fletcher, Lt. Comdr. USNR, gazing out idly perhaps over a flight deck at unnumbered fathoms of advertisement-blue water; thinking perhaps of Noumea now many days astern, there a few points to starboard, past the sunlight-flattened fantail of an attendant destroyer; or of Pearl and the islands, the lion-colored sand, and Diego farther homeward still; or thinking even, for an unwinking instant, of nothing other than you—to wit, the sharp little indrawn breath you took when at 1542 hours he finally rose from your table, and you caught your delectable underlip in your teeth, and

"Dar ling," you said, "when you stand up like that I had no idea you were so beautifully *ta-a-all....*"

Between that anatomical predication and the day of her birthday party, Mike seems to have seen Stephanie twice. The first time was when she came to UBS for an interview that left her script still up in the air—due to her interviewer's befuddled belief, she told me later laughing, that she was representing some publicity outfit or other trying to grab free time. The second occasion was when, two days after that, Mike took her to dinner and a show and was sweetly and deftly said good night to at her door. Very likely nothing would have occurred the night of her party either if Jack Geddie had not had the singularly silly idea of driving them to the Met in his old Bentley instead of taking a taxi like a man of sound mind. Though admittedly one could understand more or less how he felt about the Bentley: they'd had to sell the Daimlers in 1930.

Anyhow. To begin with, the cocktails were catastrophic. They were something called a Depth Bomb: half cognac half calvados in theory, but in fact half Jersey applejack and half Maryland brandy. Within half an hour everybody was tight; and they all got tighter rapidly. They seem to have wolfed a big buffet of food but Stephanie remembers none of it whatever; they must simply have choked it down in chunks; and by the time they got to the ballet, which was two-thirds over, they were all lunging rather than walking, and shouting-drunk. None of them gave the ballet more than a glance. They merely regrouped the box chairs more conveniently for tête-à-têtes and went right on with their conversations. Stephanie was nearly as drunk as Mike was, and all conventions were off: their eyes were twined in one long, suffocating, ragingly impatient and libidinous embrace.

Going back after the show, he had no trouble maneuvering Stephanie and himself into the rumble seat of the Bentley. There was a drizzle of rain, but they were quite simply too drunk and too ravenous for each other to care. He threw his coat over them like a leaky tent; and in the same avid instant that he turned to her, she turned to him.

How to describe that unique and lovely mouth I do not know. It is a matter of textures, Stephanie my love; and masculine English cannot describe textures; not *your* texture. Those cool, delicious, tantalizing lips must have seemed to Mike hardly to graze his (though the verb we need is evidently something lighter than graze or even *effleurer*); no matter how hungrily he thrust back your head, their angelic and unharvestable freshness remained beyond him. How often, day after day, how many hours at a time, must he have drunk at that mouth yet never drained it, never touched the welling springs of its inaccessibility. And that first time, it drove him wholly wild, and still you lay there in his arms frustrating and aloof. Until you said,

"Stop it. You *must*, I tell you! We're nearly *there!*"

"Hell with where we are!"

"I know exactly how you feel, oh heaven I never felt so in bed with a man in my life."

"Bed! You're fully dressed damn it!"

"Well not *quite*, dar ling! The way you go af-ter what you— *No*, you utter animal!"

"Stephanie, why can't we just get rid of these people."

"*I'm soaking!* My hair must— Mike it's simply *pour-ing!* Rid of what people? *Now?*"

"After we get back to your apartment."

"Don't be *sil*-ly!"

"How's it silly? I could leave early and come back again after they all—"

"*Don't be childish!*"

"It's not!"

"It most certainly is and in any case I do not propose to wake up with you tomorrow morning and nurse your tiresome hangover."

"I won't have one."

"You most certainly *will! No!!* Here we *are!*"

"Can I see you tomorrow?"

Her eyes gleamed. "You know perfectly well you can."

"Lunch?"

"Na-tur-al-ly."

"Phone you?"

"Well *not* before eleven. Because I simply won't answer if you do, oh heaven how hung I'll be."

"The afternoon too? *All* afternoon?"

Drunk as she was, the smiling eyes were as deridingly and as coolly appraising as ever. "Do you think you can make pla-a-ans about me, Malachi? Please remember I am *not* going to lunch with you in a be-e-edroom."

Nor did she. She had such a hangover that when he phoned her she simply hung up on him, and he had such a hangover that he was very glad she did. It was not, in fact, till half a dozen lunches and nearly a month later, and after the most detached and teasing coquetry, that they went back to her apartment after their coffees and brandies, and his hungry vehemence was at long last answered with a cool, drawling, "Oh, well, I suppose I do have to humor you so-o-ome time," though her eyes were smiling at him wide and possessing; and so (if I may use the phrase) they made their formal entrance upon love. Though oddly enough Mike's chief memory of that afternoon seems to have been of her standing serenely by her bed, with a cool expectancy in her eyes and nothing but the most perfect composure in her voice, and, saying, with that faintly malicious intonation,

"Surely you don't expect me to undress myself, Ma-la-chi? *You're* the one who wants to make love to me. Aren't you? Or aren't you?"

"Ahh, you lovely sleek—"

"Yes, dar ling, but aren't you going to take off my clothes?"

"You think I'm not going to?"

"But you're not exactly doing it, Ma-la-chi, are you. I told you. Undress me! Don't you know ho-o-ow?"

✦

[. . .]

Kitty was having a savage row with Steve about that period, and why for once shouldn't the beneficiary be me?

I know when I first felt so. Kitty, Jill, Davy, and I had planned an evening *à quatre*; but the Starrs were late coming down from their shore-cottage in Connecticut and Kitty and I, in their Sutton Place apartment, had to wait. I had gone out to the kitchen and got the maid to produce some liquor and poked around making us drinks to wait with; and it was then that I heard Kitty at the piano, playing something straight out of the jazz age, every sinful and lonesome-sounding syncope in place. Some wild quality in the performance made me leave the drinks half-made and go to the livingroom door.

"And what's *that?*" I called across above the pounding chords.

She said without looking up, "'Penthouse Romance.'"

"What!"

"By a Mr. Rube Bloom."

"Never heard of him."

"Steve says it always sounds to him like a kept woman's serenade to her soul."

I went across and took her sleek shoulders in my fingers. She put both her hands up over one of mine and tilted her cheek down against them; and presently she said, "Steve and I are having *a* particularly degrading blow-up just now, of course you know?" and abruptly got up and flung herself into my arms, kissing me with a kind of bitter abandon; and I don't think even the goddam maid, forty feet away in the pantry, would have stopped us if Jill and Davy hadn't almost immediately arrived. We separated quickly as their heels clattered on the landing; but even as Jill burst in, trilling apologies, my lips were saying in Kitty's ear, in a last flare of lawless and cold-hearted desire, "*This* one we are going to *have.*"

And certainly the beleaguerment progressed with satisfying speed: it was at some party only a few nights later that Kitty came up to me in the deserted kitchen, kissed me with a wild, reckless, and unprecedented drunkenness, and told me to take her home. It was merely momentarily regrettable that she should pass out in the entry of her apartment and have to be put to bed, under a quilt, in the irritating chastity of full party attire. But what really matters is that a few days later, as Kitty and I rode up the Connecticut shore in the rumble seat of Davy's car for an impromptu party at the Starrs' cottage on the coast, *our* personal plans for that night had already been fully agreed upon. Not with contentment, no doubt;

and not without moments of strained and pettish argument. But agreed upon.

As Jill remarked of that brief house party late the next morning, with a sting of epigram that eased the tension for nobody, "This is the *farm!*" And in fact spiritually it was, though Mike among others happened to be missing from our muster, and though also the farm project had been tacitly abandoned many months before. Mike's not coming along, Mike's being allowed to plead work or Stephanie or whatever it was, that was the error. With Mike there, an equilibrium might have been achieved, whether by simple mathematics or by aesthetic formula. But he was not there; and so, with Davy and Jill paired off for or against, we were Kitty, Jane, Steve, Jack, and I, two females and three males, and the whole thing was so badly thought out that it was at least eleven that night, with the drinking in full career, before I noticed in Davy's eyes the glinting speculation, Which of you three guys is planning to sleep alone? And at that early hour I would have had no difficulty whatever in informing him.

And why not? I had of course only a working acquaintance with the special geometry of Jane, Jack, and Steve, and no knowledge at all of its theory of axioms. But here was Steve getting drunk with a casualness, not to say a cheery and happy-go-lucky exuberance, that made it all look Euclideanly straightforward. So help me, I said to myself, he's *relaxed* my god: a guy I've never seen relaxed when there was a woman under forty-five within half a mile. Kitty must have been leading him one hell of a life if his final manumission's taking him like this!

The corollary *Then what about me?* didn't bother me a minute: I knew what I was after and that I would have all of it, and I had guessed to the fraction of a pulse-beat how much it would affect me and what it would cost me. My only real concern with Steve was that he didn't seem to me to be getting drunk fast enough: if only the tedious bastard would get on with it and pass decently out, the process of lugging him off to bed would serve as a sort of tacit curfew, the party would expire, and Kitty and I would be alone.

She was standing across the room telling Jack some anecdote, her eyes shining and her curls swinging in their charming bell and her fingers pirouetting in the air to illustrate what she was saying. My glance shifted with sudden expectation to Steve—he was at an open window, announcing that the goddam room was revolving in an unpleasantly spiraling arc and he, personally, needed air. I noticed that he'd left his glass on a chair-arm and handed it to him with a friendly exhortation: there was no rational purpose to be served by prolonging things. But no: the goddam air actually sobered him; and I was so infuriated that I snatched the glass back from his unnoticing hand, took it to the kitchen, and flung its contents down the sink.

Jill was in the doorway when I turned. "Why my poor lonesome deserted Webb," she said anxiously, "are you being a poor sick man all by your solitary self?"

"What?" I said irritably.

"Or are you just off here feeling cross and mean?"

"Do I look cross?"

"You look all so blue-faced and furious it makes my heart sad."

"What makes you sad, my angel love?" said Davy tenderly, coming up behind her and stooping his cheek to hers. "Is this man here putting sad thoughts into your little bosoms?"

"Oh, Davy, how can we cheer Webb up?"

"There are ways I can think of, my love."

"Oh, what ways, Davy. We must do them for poor Webb."

"Shall we tell him our new private game?"

"*Oh no.*"

Davy laughed softly, his eyes brooding at me under his half-closed eyelids with some heavy faunlike speculation. "Tell him, pet. How can your tender heart refuse? Tell him."

"Oh, Davy, it's such a silly game."

"But you said you liked it, my heartless angel."

"Webb will think it's sordid, I *know* he—"

It was then that a voice from the livingroom cried sharply and alarmingly, "But where could she have *gone!*"

Steve lunged abruptly into the doorway. "Kitty not with you?" he demanded unsteadily.

"What's the matter?"

"She's—*disappeared!*"

"Nonsense."

"Nonsense hell! I tell you something's damn *wrong!*"

Jane appeared behind Steve, her eyes bright with excitement. "She's not in the john. Or anywhere around the house."

"You *sure?*"

"We just looked. Do you suppose something *has* happened?"

"What could happen?"

"Anything could happen."

"Nothing could happen, she must just be somewhere being sick or something."

"She didn't look sick to me." Jane's voice was lovely with interest. "I saw her face when she went out of the livingroom and she didn't look sick at all."

"How did she look, then?" Steve cried.

"Her eyes were funny."

"*What?*"

"I don't know how to say it. Like somebody else's eyes looking out of Kitty's head. But not *sick*."

For an uneasy instant we were all silent. Then Steve muttered half inaudibly, "Oh jesus, not *again!*" and in a sudden nameless dread we poured out of the house and scattered calling through the empty night. There had been a moon, but now the sky was heavy with clouds: everything was impenetrably black. The Starrs' cottage lay on a stretch of coast entirely deserted in those days, in a depression rolling back from the dunes, with sandy brush-fringed cliffs rising to right and left and a scrubby wood above us to landward; there were no lights, no neighboring houses; and though Jack (I believe it was) had snatched up a flashlight from his car as we scattered, I could see it only as a dim beam jigging about far off to my right among the thickets, and then it too vanished. I could hear Steve stumbling and thrashing through a fringe of trees somewhere to my right; once I heard a heavy grunt, as he ran into something head-on in the blackness. I remember thinking with acute irritation that all this violent exercise in the fresh air would almost certainly sober him up still farther and God knew *when* the party would close down. I myself was skirting the wood: I had started out into its edge but I'd run into a low-hanging limb, and I had therefore veered to my left out of the trees and along the edge of a field of some kind. I intended to find Kitty; certainly; but why beat myself up doing it?

Then I heard a low sobbing behind me and spun around toward it; and abruptly she flashed up out of the darkness and flung herself into my arms.

"Oh Webb it is so dark here Webb!" Her face was streaming tears; she kept kissing the lobe of my ear and murmuring softly and brokenheartedly, "I am so glad you came at last, I am all so dark here, never in the lighthearted light always anymore, did you know? ever always till you came." She stopped, and stood shaking and shuddering in my arms, her sobs going on and on. I had no idea whatever what to do except murmur to her and stroke her disheveled curls. I thought of calling to the others; but then I had no notion what a sudden loud sound like a call might not do to her; whether it might not simply set her off again. Gradually, at last, her sobs began to slacken, and then died away entirely; and presently, to my relief, she gave me an affectionate little hug, put up her head and looked me in the eyes, and said in a humiliated voice, "Webb, the *moods* Miss Locke works herself into sometimes! Have you a hankie? *Dear* me!"

I gave her one. She blew her nose and dabbed and patted her eyes. "*Wringing* wet," she said, glancing up at me and laughing shakily. "Now, please, may I be entrusted with a cigarette?"

As I fumbled in my pocket she suddenly stared around us in surprise, "Why Webb look where we are!"

"Not far," I said.

"But how did we—" and then abruptly in a different voice, "Yes here. Yes here. Way out along the cliffs oh quickquickquickquick!" and like a flash of light she was away from me and racing toward the edge.

I still don't quite see how I caught her in time. Perhaps unconsciously I was keyed up for anything she might do next. But anyhow she hadn't got twenty feet before I brought her down with a tackle that flung both of us headlong and rolling. I pinned her arms almost before we hit the earth, but for an instant she fought my grip like an animal. Then abruptly she was lying there quietly on her back under me and looking up at me with tender, honest eyes.

"I wasn't going to, Webb."

"What's the *matter* with you for god's sake!"

"*Really* I wasn't going to."

"You have a hell of a funny way of not doing things!" She giggled. I said, "You've also got the start of a pretty bruise up here on your temple."

"I expect so, Webb dear. I could rub it if you weren't crushing my arms in this earnest masculine way."

"Anything else you might do if I weren't crushing you?"

"No, Webb."

I looked into her meek eyes for a long time. "Maybe," I said. Suddenly, to my complete surprise, I was feeling just terribly fond of her; all of her; fond and *tender* my god!

"Webb sweet, *honestly* I'm all right now."

LISTEN *to the patient* is what the doctors all tell you. I let her up. She slid her hand through my arm and gave my biceps a hard, affectionate squeeze, and we walked side by side back toward the cottage, shouting to the others that everything was OK. We had a story worked out before we got there, and passed it on to Steve, who met us just beyond the circle of the cottage's lights.

I have no clear memory of the next couple of hours. I know we all had fresh drinks. I also have the impression that Jane, Steve, and Jack transferred their base of operations outside and sat sipping their drinks on the terrace, discussing something intensely; I seem to recall that it was politics and/or the labor movement. At one point Davy must have joined them, for I remember that Kitty and Jill and I were alone inside when Jill said Kitty was looking terribly white and didn't she want to go to bed? and Kitty said would we all feel it was terribly rude if she did. But when she got up she nearly keeled over and Jill and I half-carried her upstairs, and she fainted for good at the bedroom door. I went down and sent Jane up to help Jill get her to bed; and then I stayed on the terrace hardly listening to Jack and Steve and Davy arguing about some revolution or other, I forget in what country and whether it had already taken place or was with dialectical certainty just about to take place; my mind full and brimming with my unexpected deep tenderness for Kit. Who was obviously a *darling*. And all I'd been planning was—I blushed: *nothing* was going to happen between me and Kit tonight or *any* time until she was well and happy again, and I was glad it wasn't. Because I felt so tender and fond of her. And because when she'd recovered it would be another private tenderness of ours that nothing had happened or *needed* to, by god. She was a noble girl and I was a splendid young man and we were both highly sensitive people and you could have cut the magnanimity with a knife.

Presently Jill and Jane came down and said Kitty was asleep now; and soon after that I finished my drink and went up to bed alone. My room was next to Kitty's; I went to sleep in a touching admixture of proximity, alcohol, idealism, and deep content.

What was it that awoke me? A heavy step, perhaps, in the stillness? The muffled clump of a closing door, the creak of a plank, the blind fumbling of outstretched palms along a corridor wall? I had no idea. But there I was suddenly tense awake in the dark and silent house, holding my breath to listen for the sound my sleeping ear had warned me I might hear again. Was it in my room? Had it been *there*, just beyond the foot of my bed? Or there, over by the window, whose rectangle the deep black of the unmoving night outside made almost invisible? Did I hear the echo of it still? I listened unbreathing. Or would I hear its muffled repetition at all?

Then I did hear it again. The soft hollow scuffle of an empty shoe being deposited on bare wood; the thump of an anonymous shoe dropped stealthily by an anonymous hand. On a floor beside a chair. *And in the room next to mine.*

The senses already tense and quickened in my ear shot their outrageous message through me so instantaneously that I think I must have flung myself from bed and been already upright on my feet, every inch of me a soundless yell of fury, before my conscious mind had articulated or interpreted a syllable. Looking back on it now, I believe my body must have acted for itself, for a few seconds anyhow, in a sort of atavistic delirium. For when I came consciously to myself, standing there on the floor, with my modernized brain uttering the incredible intelligence that the deposited shoe was not anonymous but Steve Cannon's, my body was already far along in the kind of epileptic cataclysm of primeval jealousy and primeval rage that must have wrenched and shaken in their bulky sockets the bones of primitive man. (I swear I think the fine hairs down my neck bristled from their roots and rose up into a stiff vestigial mane.) But the pathetic difference—I will even settle for the adjective *dérisoire*—between me and *Homo javensis* was that *he* could bellow out his raging and unendurable frustration, while I, strangled by centuries of inherited meiosis, could only stand there incredulous as I heard (or did I as much hear as *feel?*) the soft slip of Steve's discarded clothing to the floor, the pad of his feet toward her bed, the covers rustle back, the noiseless weight of the descending knee and the meaty roll of the body following it; and then, my jaw hanging in an unroared roar of disbelief and fury, the sweet drowsy question only half surprised, the penitent rumble of Steve's answer, the low tender murmur of infinite reply, and the hush of their kiss.

And I stood there, I have thought since, like one of those stuffy cartoons labeled Plight of Modern Man on the second page of Section IV of the Sunday *New York Times*—naked, straddled, crouching, my chest barreled out, my fists like great clubs, my eyes murderous and glaring, my jaw swung out and downward for its bite at the spurting jugular—there I stood primitive to the final infuriated raw tag-end of ganglion, complete in everything but the bellow; and moreover with all of *modern* man's delicate sensibilities to tell me, with a more exquisitely torturing accuracy than ever troubled my lunk of an ancestor, *exactly* every shade of outrageous pleasure that could be inflicted on My Property in the next room, and *exactly* how, and how badly, it was hurting me and would continue to hurt. Yet mind you, all this magnificent instrument of headlong murder stopped in its tracks by that one airy thread of cerebral tissue, Euclidean intelligence! *I shake*, wrote Ovid once in similar circumstance, *I shake at what you may do for I have done it all myself, and I am wrung with the expert terror of my own example.* Yet Ovid, twenty centuries nearer the dawn of history than I, had still to check *Homo javensis* with a polished couplet; two thousand years his junior, I stayed my clubbed hand too—though I went and lay down on my solitary bed without the advantages of literary composition.

I have no real notion of how long I lay there, shaking in every fiber and yet utterly rigid and unmoving, in a kind of thrumming paralysis of fury and hate. It seemed to me that my infuriated hands were jerking and gesticulating to a phantom audience around my bed, summoning them and heaven to witness this apocalypse of enormity. I swear I did not hear I FELT her first pierced indrawn sibilance of delight, as my fingers vibrated with the slaughter they were *not* entrail-deep in, and my lips simultaneously mouthed their appeals to impossible legalities. It was the most exhausting tantrum I ever indulged in; and when the window grew pale with the first dewy early light and my body fell into a sudden eclipsing slumber, I was so burnt out and consumed that I could not have summoned the strength for a casual wave of the hand.

So burnt out and totally consumed, in fact, that I woke an hour later with no emotion left of any kind except a raging desire for an immediate and especially delicious breakfast. A thick golden fleece of buttered eggs! Three eggs at least, I thought to myself in wild excitement as I pulled on my clothes; or make it *four!* a rich slug of cream beaten into them just before they go on the fire! *Boy!* Cooked gently and slowly and stirred constantly and ending up just *baveux!* and toast scorching hot and magnificent black-charred brown with slabs of butter melting their swimming gold into the rich black; and coffee *properly made* my god with *plenty* of hot milk!! It was so rapturous to be alive with all that ecstatic food in my mind that I practically galloped down the corridor, almost forgetting (though not quite) to open Kitty's door en route. I stared coldly at the two of them in their unbreakfasting slumber, Steve curled into a semifetal position with his forehead on Kitty's breast (how the hell could the guy breathe in that position?), thought contemptuously that all they'd eat when they did come down was canned orange juice and weak coffee made still weaker with *cream* my god; and ran briskly and happily downstairs.

It was as beautiful a breakfast as I ever served up to myself. I took my *café au lait* out onto the terrace and had five cups and three delicious cigarettes in the lovely gold-shadowed early-morning stillness; and when Kitty and Steve finally came down for their dishwater orange-juice-and-coffee I looked into their sleep-sodden and unappetizing faces with the smug pity of the decently fed.

It is true, my detachment could not be complete. There is a way a woman behaves the next day, to the body that has given her delight, which is wonderfully gratifying if the body was yours but perfectly sickening if it was not. Her eyes follow him about with a drugged and adoring constancy, her hands reach out to him of their own loving accord as he passes carelessly by; she trots humbly after him as he moves between kitchen and terrace, her senses so drenched with him that she even forgets the fatuous joy of taking cups and saucers from his hands and carrying them, as an enraptured service, in his stead; she leans her whole remembering body on his doltish and preoccupied back as he boils his coffee at the stove. *And insipid coffee at that!!* The most voluptuous and groveling worship oozes from her; and I could have wrung this one's damned neck at the revolting display.

It was at this point that Jill remarked to the assembled company, *"This* is the *farm!"* The epigram amused but did not really disturb me. I had just thought of a so much funnier one myself.

As Mike got to know his way around UBS in more accurate and sardonic detail, he set out on the advertisingman's habitual campaign of lining himself up for somebody else's job; and with an eye that had never lost the cunning of its earlier agency days, he settled on a producer named Crawford, an almost unique combination of good salary, easy job, and stomach ulcers in an already advanced stage. What Crawford produced was incidental: it merely happened to be that internationally familiar news-commentator voice called Fothergill Martin, a household word so useful to UBS in explaining its public-service side to the American people (and intermittently to the FCC) that he had been a net-sustainer show for years in spite of fabulous bids from every industrial titan in the country. Gill himself was a charming ex-newspaper rummy who had been flung out of half the city rooms in the Middle Atlantic States. The nearest he ever got to the news now, outside an occasional bookie-sheet, was the beautifully turned out 1200 words that

Crawford handed him every day just before Gill squared off at the mike. He worshipped Crawford; I never saw such happy devotion anywhere. But his awe of Crawford's knowledge and brains made him too shy to show what he felt, and he had to take out his love in barraging Crawford's kids with every expensive new toy that came into Schwarz's, and Crawford's wife with everything from a half-gross of roses on her birthday to a dozen Maine lobsters flown down by special plane for a supper party or for no reason at all. Everyone in radio below the level of vice-president knew the story of his coming out of the studio one day with tears pouring down his face.

"Did you catch that show?" he asked in a strangling voice. "Did you *hear* the script that lovely big-hearted unselfish son-of-a-bitch put together for me, just for *me*? All that berazzle about China or whatever it was? Where's he *find* all that wonderful goddam stuff? How's he know so goddam much about *everything*? You think honest to god there's going to be some sort of war over there like I said?"

He was right on one thing, anyhow: Crawford did do an A-1 script. What's more, written in the *tone*, if I can put it that way, the exact reconstruction in vowel sounds of Gill's magnificent, stirring, authoritative baritone. And Crawford was a hell of a nice guy as well, Mike said: if his ulcers had to get him anyway, his job might just as well go to somebody like Mike who thought highly of him and understood his merit.

Mike seems to have started out with a suggestion about the 1934 election campaign. I'd happened to ask him once the inevitable questions about free political time; and after we'd dropped around together to City Hall and Tammany and I'd helped him in a little amicable trading, we worked out a deal. Crawford was to get all reasonable special information from National Headquarters he asked for, and in return would see to it that Gill's copy stayed un-slanted. It went off very nicely. The vice-presidents who thought Gill wrote his own copy were afraid to ask questions of so valuable a UBS property, and the vice-presidents who knew where the copy came from knew also of Gill's wild devotion to every word that issued from the beloved carriage of Crawford's typewriter; so they let it ride. It wasn't a presidential year anyhow; only 1934. Besides, genuine apoplexy was still rare. So it all helped Mike along.

The day he went in with his ultimate proposal, Crawford must have been especially worn down. He was standing slouched at the window of his office, staring down into Madison Avenue; looking as tired and thin as Mike had ever seen him. The room was in its usual pre-script mess, newspapers strewn on the big couch and on the floor, and a couple of ragged stacks of reference books on the typewriter desk.

"Craw, why the hell don't you see a doctor?"

Crawford didn't turn. "Why?" he asked. "They pretty?"

"Get him to prescribe, well, something like Nassau."

Crawford turned and looked at him for a long minute, and finally grinned slowly. "You aren't trying to promote yourself something, Mike?"

"I am, sure. But for you too, Craw. As you damn well know."

He inspected Mike again; then smiled rather shyly. "You know, fella, I guess at that you are. For me too. And this is radio. But I guess maybe you really are."

"You know you need *somebody*," Mike said.

"Do I?"

"Assistant producer in fact, anyhow. The hell with the title; call it understudy. Don't even call it anything. But this straight-across-the-board thing's beating the final whey out of you, way it is now."

"Maybe."

"Maybe hell, Craw! It's just that you're goddamned if you're going to step out and let some fat-headed young bastard from downstairs walk into what you've built up."

"And so?"

"So I'm suggesting you line up a non-bastard and take an honest-to-god rest."

"The non-bastard, Mike, being you?"

"Me."

"You sure about non-bastard? You're a Quaker. Isn't there something kind of funny about these Quaker weddings?"

So Mike moved his office and his salary up, and it was almost like being on the *Prince* again; and he gave a party for Stephanie and everybody else in celebration. He gave it at the Starrs' apartment, because his own room-and-a-half was of course too small, and except for its final scene it was like any other party of the era. He introduced Fish House Punch, buying a particularly huge stoneware crock somewhere on Second Avenue for the occasion and finding the essential pippins after many hours' search. It was a new drink to the crowd: in spite of the stinging fumes of evaporating alcohol that sprang from the crock whenever the lid was lifted, everyone insisted on pouring it down as if it had been a fruit punch of some kind, and the party turned into a madhouse with encouraging speed. Somebody started a game called Oh Mister Farley, or Post Office for Grown-Ups: a man sat blindfolded in a chair, successive girls kissed him, and he was expected to identify each kiss and rate it for inherent ecstasy. It is embarrassing to record that this game was wildly successful, though it did cause one bitter marital quarrel and eight new cases of trench mouth (these latter due, according to an epigram of Jack Geddie's, to "Jane's habit of keeping a civil tongue in all her friends' mouths"). In fact the whole party was such a success that, except for a few casualties like some unknown Yaleman's falling down a flight of stairs and breaking half a dozen ribs, everyone stayed on till nearly three.

While the last happy bellows of departure were still echoing up the stairwell, Mike left Jill leaning over the banisters, smiling and calling to the groups still struggling out through the foyer below, and went back to the livingroom to start collecting the battalions of dirty glasses. Davy was seeing one of the unattached girls home and might not be back for a while; Mike wasn't going to leave Jill to face that battered and disheveled room singlehanded. He found a tray in the kitchen and moved about filling it with debris, listening to her gay voice calling the final farewells into the emptying house below. He carted the load to the kitchen and came back for another. She had unslatted the Venetian blinds at one of the front windows and stood with her forehead pressed against the window frame watching the last guests scatter in the inevitable search for a night-owl taxi or two. When he came back for his final trayful she was still there; and he must have been rinsing glasses and stacking them on the drainboard for several minutes before he heard her walk slowly through the livingroom and diningroom, and stand in the kitchen door. She didn't speak; and rather to his surprise she didn't come over to the sink and help. He turned his head and started a smile over his shoulder and then saw she wasn't looking at him: she was folding and unfolding a paper napkin in her hand, and then folding it again, staring down at it composedly with an expression he couldn't see. He turned back to his rinsing; and they stood thus for a long, long time, he at the sink in the faint busy splashing of the faucet, she in the doorway in silent and unstirring meditation; until at last,

"What time is it, Malachi?"

He bent his arm and looked at his watch. "Seven past three."

"It's late."

"Moderately."

"Was it a nice party, Malachi? Do you think we all had fun?"

"Didn't you think so?"

Again they were silent. Was something wrong? he wondered vaguely, his thoughts as much on the sticky glasses as on her, and on the monotonous splash of the running water, lulling his already somnolent mind; had something happened at the party he hadn't seen?

"When did he leave, Malachi?"

"Hunh? Leave?"

"When did Davy leave. What time."

"Davy? I don't think I noticed."

"You didn't see him leave?"

"Don't remember it."

"Or notice what time it was, Malachi?"

"No. Why?" She didn't answer; and suddenly his brain shook itself awake and snapped a warning at him.

"Though matter of fact *yes*," he said. "I remember now I did see him. Almost at the last there, it must have been. Shoving his arms into his overcoat sleeves."

"What time was it then, Malachi?"

"Time? Well, some time around the last. Or a little before. He was taking a couple of girls home, I think. Why?"

"At the last?"

"Maybe a little before."

"No, Malachi."

"You, uh, probably in the livingroom or somewhere."

"Oh Malachi *why* do you protect him so?"

"Why do I do *what*?"

"Why do men always hang together? So heartlessly so heartlessly; always; always."

"What on earth are you—"

"Oh, Malachi, you know so well. He's been gone a long, long time. Suppose I don't even know when he left. Or didn't see him go. Do you know where he went?"

"No."

"Yes, Malachi. You do. Only why do I always have to know too? Why does he always make me know?"

What was there to say? He rinsed another glass; and then another. She came up slowly behind him; she rested her forehead against the back of his shoulder and her hands slid around his biceps and gently pressed his arms to his sides. He stopped rinsing obediently. The faucet ran quietly and monotonously on and on, the water splashed softly into the sink and flowed with a soundless eddy down the drain: and he stood there motionless with a half-rinsed glass in one hand and the other on the corner of the drainboard, and she motionless with her head tilted slightly forward against the angle of his shoulder.

"Malachi."

"What."

"What time is it?"

"About a quarter past three."

"Yes; but exactly."

He turned his wrist and glanced down. "Three-eighteen."

"How much time would the taxi take?"

"*What?*"

"You know, Malachi. She lives down in the Village; in Barrow Street. Would it take twenty minutes?"

"I guess so."

"Don't you think I ought to allow half an hour, though? Because it's late and he might have trouble finding a taxi."

"Maybe longer."

"I'll give him forty minutes each way, Malachi. Don't you think that's fair?"

"Yes."

"Forty and forty is eighty: an hour and twenty minutes."

Of course there was nothing he could say.

"And then another twenty minutes, sweet Malachi, to say good night and see whether he can get into bed with her. No, half an hour, because he can be very insistent and hard to manage."

"I guess he can."

"Even for her to manage. That makes an hour and fifty minutes but I have to make it two hours to be fair. Even though that's too long."

"Jill, pet, look here: this—"

"He took her home at ten minutes to two, so at ten minutes to four—"

"*What?*"

"Oh poor helpful Malachi, did you think I didn't really see them go?"

" . . . I see."

"Or haven't learned in all these months to notice the time?"

(Yet ten to one all Mike's mind could think of was, But why do you have to tell *me* about it? why always *me?*)

"So at ten minutes to four, Malachi, you—you have to do something for me."

"No I don't!"

"Yes."

"*No*, Jill!!"

"Yes, Malachi, you do. Because you were our best man. And there was an old Roman custom about the best man, Davy told me all about it; that was why there *was* a best man. to have her first. Even though this isn't quite the same. But you *have* to, Malachi, you have to do it for me."

He knocked her fingers from his arms and spun around and started to shake her, and then he knew he couldn't do that but what could he do? and he stood there shaking her lightly and stupidly, hardly a shake at all. Her eyes stared back at him unblinking and expressionless; her words began to vibrate, though not with the ridiculous shaking but as if chattering with cold: "You have to Malachi you must, oh please for me, you all hang even in that so heartless together always, but not this once always oh please no." She broke loose and flung her arms around him, talking with her lips softly against his throat, "Oh I will be so wonderful and *please* you so, Malachi, I *am* exciting oh I am oh I am oh sweetest Malachi please please I am—" though God help me how can anyone remember everything the poor crazy baby said in that desolate icy voice with never a pause except that once she thrust him wildly away and seized his wrist and looked at his watch; and then clung to him and began again; and while I suppose it was only a few minutes until they heard Davy come in that apartment door, it must have seemed to Mike that it was already dawn.

She sprang away from him like an animal and vanished into the livingroom. There was a brief silence; then Mike heard a staccato spray of syllables and a sharp, quick conflict of voices; then a door slammed viciously (the bedroom door?); then again there was silence. He turned back to the sink and finished rinsing the sticky glasses; and presently walked slowly into the livingroom. Jill was sitting on the couch. She asked him whether there was any punch left and he went back to the kitchen and got a glass for each of them; and they sat and had another drink, talking about radio programs; and finally he kissed her good night and left. To this day Davy no doubt thinks they made love there on the couch; but the plain fact is, Davy, they simply sat there discussing radio programs.

✦

[. . .]

It was in a moment otherwise unmemorable in the extreme, between the clauses of a two-stick story, perhaps, on an Upper East Side love nest, that my phone rang at my elbow in the *Sun* city room, and I heard the light and lovely accolade of a soon-to-be-familiar accent; and presently I was waiting (for she was always late) at the little round bar in the baywindowed room in the Meadowbrook, for the first point-blank impact of that teasing, indolent, smiling, so-I-please-you charm. Stephanie was editing a department then on *Chic*; and she had called me to see about placing a publicity story—she saying *release* and I saying *handout* and she delicately repeating *release*; and as I never had time for a civilized lunch, I took her to dinner at the Meadowbrook to work out the angles.

She opened with her standard I-charm-you-so-promise-me—the angel-grey eyes seducing me right then and there, and all the rest of it. But I responded with a deadpan exposition of why *she* should help *me* sell her editor an article series; so our eyes smiled a friendly quits over the second cocktail, and we never drew a foil on each other again; the next time she phoned me, in fact, it was to give *me* a tip she'd picked up, a political story that was about to break. I liked her through and through. She was such a lovely decorative piece to take around the night spots; she was also a very smart journalist. But above everything, damn it, she was *fun!* She was also, I discovered bit by bit, one of the most extraordinarily honest girls I ever met, and in time one of our private games was predicated on just that difference of hers from the average—she would spend as much as half an hour erecting some structure of delicate lies in a wonderful parody of the best feminine tradition, baroque in every line, and then, when neither of us could keep sober a minute longer, she would dissolve the whole airy farce in a throatful of laughter. I suspect that we knew from that first evening, both of us, where we were heading, and that there would be no coquetries to delay us when we arrived.

We arrived one Sunday morning early in the winter. She had roughed out a *Chic* story she wanted me to help her on: it was spiced-up advice to the ambitious prom-trotter on how to behave and what to expect when a Princeton boy had you down for a prom weekend, and Stephanie wanted me to dub in the masculine point of view. It was a bright frosty Sunday morning. I picked up some scrapple and a jar of Cooper's Oxford marmalade at a delicatessen on the way to her apartment. I had to ring twice before I heard her sleepy voice beyond the door.

"We-e-ebb?"

"Let me in, I'm starved!"

"Can you count ten dar ling? Before you come in?"

"*I*'m awake, my god!"

"Don't sound virtuous and su-per-i-or. Just because you're sil-ly enough to be out of bed for hours."

"It's nearly eleven."

"I don't care what it is. I'm not *up* yet."

"Hell, you're not."

"Not officially, dar ling."

"Let me *in*."

"Well, count *ten*. And then you can come in. Because I am far too sleepy to be looked at, I haven't even bathed. The door's off the latch now. *Count!*"

I got breakfast while she splashed in the tub; I had it nearly ready when I heard her back in the bedroom again, humming something off-key. "Webb?"

"Hurry up. Breakfast's practically ready."

A wail. "But I haven't done my ha-a-air!"

"Sweep it up in a topknot and come on."

"I will look *fri-i-ightful!*"

"You'll look delicious."

"How do *you* know, dar ling? You've never woken up with me."

She came out in a shining-white copy of a Chinese scholar's gown, with gold dragons embroidered down the front and the long skirt slit at the sides, her face fresh-washed and waked-up-looking, and her straw-gold hair piled high on her head like a little girl's in a bath. I'd set the table over by the deep windowseat that ran across the front of the livingroom, with the sun pouring in in glowing parallelograms. It was a fine breakfast: scrapple cakes and shirred eggs *au beurre noir*, unbuttered toast with the bitter Seville-orange marmalade, and *un café au lait sérieux*.

"What's scrapple, Webb, I never had it before."

"You're just a dern city girl."

"And how glad you are. What's it made of?"

"It's ground-up Pennsylvania Dutch *Heimweh*."

"Fletcher's not Pennsylvania Dutch."

"The family wouldn't let us play with the Dutch."

"Is 'play' the Quaker word for it?"

"Well," I said, "it's got four letters."

"Do you make love in dialect too dar ling? I don't think it

sounds at a-a-all attractive."

We dawdled over breakfast in the luxurious leisure and wonderful idle feeling of Sunday, and didn't get down to work till early afternoon. We argued about who was to clear the table; she won, and then sprang up and cleared it herself and brought in her typewriter. Her rough draft was a good job, and in an hour or so we'd discussed and added the male angle and I was typing up the finished story. She was kneeling behind me on the windowseat, half-leaning on my shoulder, reading copy as I typed and making an occasional final suggestion or emendation.

I tapped out the last two-fingered line and stretched back lazily. My head pressed against her breast; we left it there, and I turned the axis of my arm and slid it around her.

"I wish you'd come around *this* side of me," I said.

"*I* know you do."

"Then why don't you?"

"I'm not the least convinced you've been wishing it long enough to be really flattering."

"I've been thinking about it for months."

A giggle. "But you never fed me scrapple before, dar ling. Is it an aphrodisiac?"

"Haven't, huh."

"No you haven't, dar ling. You've been concentrating on that tiresome article among other things."

"You were concentrating on it too," I said.

"How do *you* know what I've been concentrating on?"

I pulled her gently around across my knees; and she lay there smiling and calm in the hollow of my arm. After a while she said, "Do you think you ought to undress me like this, dar ling, right here in the win-dow?"

It was a lovely mauling. I remember the one last half-questioning flash of a glance from the pillow, the final half-rational how-is-it-going-to-be look they give; and then the wildness engulfed us and we drowned.

I came out of that blind dive to find her kneeling beside me panting and laughing, her eyes shining, her hands trying to hold aside the disheveled pale-gold sweep of her hair as she inspected a shoulder.

"Will you look what you've done to me? You animal, I won't be able to wear an evening dress for weeks!"

"Good."

"'*Good*'!"

"If you can't wear an evening dress you'll have to stay home in bed with me."

"And be black-and-blued all over again, dar ling? I most certainly will not!"

We examined the shoulder solicitously. Her hair cascaded tickling along my cheek, and I turned my head; and suddenly we were gazing at each other with a long, happy, full-fed, confiding smile.

"*Repu*, dar ling?" she said softly.

"Never."

"Hardly ever."

"*Never*, the way I feel now."

"The way you're supposed to feel now is all *repu* and sleepy. Didn't your father tell you the facts?"

"Stay in bed with you forever!"

"Yes, dar ling, I know; only you'd very soon just start thinking about food."

I lay back and looked at her. "I can't describe you."

"Would it flatter me if you did?"

"Ought to!"

"And anyway you can't. Hemingway keeps trying to describe, well, that *sort* of thing and all that happens is paragraphs about owls in the twilight."

"Just because Hemingway can't I can't?"

"Of course not. You just write about Tammany and he's our greatest-living sex-writer."

"How's it happen he doesn't write about sex?"

A wicked little laugh. "Don't be ca-a-at, dar ling. I thought you were going to describe me."

I smiled at her. "Well, now, if I were a sentimentalist I'd say you had a little heart-shaped face."

This was somehow terribly funny, and she plunged down on me with a shriek of delight and we lay there entangled and giggling. Eventually she said,

"Dar ling. Will you admit something?"

"Why not?"

"I never asked this of any other man."

"Then better not be a fool and ask me."

"Oh, I know the answer already." She rolled up onto her elbows, chin in hands, her face very near mine, and inspected me closely. "I just want to watch your expression when you tell the truth."

"It's something to see."

"Tell the *truth*, Webb?"

"What d'you want to know?"

"Haven't you finally met your match?"

It was true in the form she'd expressed it in. "Yes," I said.

She collapsed gently onto me and slid her nose under my ear. "Dar ling, I think you do really mean it." She nuzzled my neck. "Oh heaven I can feel you all through me. Even when I'm so battered that all I can feel is one endless throb. Dar ling, is your arm comfy this way?"

"Yes."

"Sure?"

"Yes."

"It won't go all pins and needles?"

"No."

"Then stop talking, please, dar ling. Because I'm going to sleep." And she did, like descending night.

So it began; and by morning we might have known each other all our lives. I woke early (it was strange being in bed not alone) and put on her dressing gown and went and stood framed dimly in the window against the dark of dawn, watching the thick winter-morning twilight glow gradually into hazy light and the frost on the roofs wink and sparkle in the pale sun's first rays. It was still dusky in the room. I went over to the bed again and gazed down at her as she slept, her eyelids smooth and her mouth relaxed and tender; looking about twelve. I would bring her breakfast in bed, she deserved such affectionate attentions (if they had ever oc-curred to *Mike*, then I understood less why he loved Stephanie than I imagined). So presently I turned on the oven in the kitchen-ette for *œufs au plat*, and made coffee and heated milk; I even drew a bath for her when things were nearly ready and carried her, murmuring in sleepy protest, into the bathroom.

Yet afterwards I lay back lazily on the bed in her dressing gown and watched her doing her hair: a nude poised you would have said by Renoir (though so slender!) on the pouffe before the pier glass, the delicious rounded angles of the lifted arms, the deft and delicate ballet of the fingers, the stylized undulations of the slim back, the naiad thighs; and above (and so amusing!) the rapt and solemn intentness of her eyes.

"You always do your face before you even put panties on?"

"But of course." She nipped her underlip in her teeth with con-centration; her eyes never shifting for a moment from their earnest running analysis of the image in the glass.

"Why 'of course'?"

"Stop dis-*tract*-ing me!"

"I want to kiss the nape of your neck."

"Well, dar ling, you may. If you won't muss me."

"Well, come here so I can."

"I most certainly will not. *You're* the one who wants to kiss my neck. So come over here."

"Why, you cold-hearted—"

"Besides, if I come over, you'd muss me."

"You haven't got anything on to muss."

"You'd muss my hair. Now stop talk-ing to me, I have to do my mouth."

"But before you do?"

Her eyes smiled at me from the mirror. "No."

"Please."

"I know exactly what you think you want and you're not being in the least subtle about it."

"You don't know."

"Don't be sil-ly. And anyhow it's qui-i-ite impossible, dar ling, because I have to be at my office at nine and I'm late already."

"Don't you even want to hear what I'd like to—"

"No! You'd get me all excited again."

"I like you excited."

"*I* know you do."

"You're so l—"

"If I came over for just a second would you promise not to do anything but kiss the back of my neck?"

"We couldn't compromise on both back and front?"

"The front isn't my neck, it's my throat."

"And tastes even lovelier."

"Then I won't come over to you. Oh Webb it's not *fair* when I've already— Oh damn *damn*, now I'll think about making love all morning and not get a thing done!"

"Will you leave work early?"

"You know I will! Can *you* get away?"

"Four o'clock. You promise?"

"Oh, dar ling, I'll try! Oh heaven if I keep on feeling about you like *this* I won't be any use at the office anyway."

I got back to her apartment that afternoon before she did, and the pretty Negro girl who cleaned for her let me in. All Stephanie can have said to her on the phone was something like, "Let Mr. Fletcher in when he comes—the other Mr. Fletcher," naturally without a shade of inflection in her voice. There could have been nothing more. Yet the special smile of greeting the girl gave me, as she opened the apartment door to my ring, expressed with the most polished and delicate courtesy, the most finished urbanity, her private and approving welcome to the new master of the house.

✧

[. . .] It happened one evening when Mike had taken Stephanie home from a nightclub evening a little tight; if she had been a little less tight it might not have happened then; but she was not so tight that it wouldn't be fun to make love, you decided, and you had just argued her out of her dress on the pouffe when the phone rang, and she reached for it in a flash before you could discourage her unanswering.

"Hel-lo?"

" . . . "

"You! But I *told* you—"

" . . . "

"You can't."

" . . . "

"Certainly not!"

" . . . "

"You ought to know why."

" . . . "

"Ob-vi-ous-ly I can't tell you!"

" . . . "

"But of course!"

" . . . "

"You *can't* guess!"

" . . . "

"Na-tur-al-ly."

" . . . "

A giggle. "Most certainly *not!*"

" . . . "

"Don't be sil-ly. At this hour? How could I pos—"

" . . . "

Her eyes smiled suddenly into yours; but they were not smiling at you, they had merely just remembered to watch you. "I never heard any-thing so ridiculous," she was saying. "I've had a *per-fect-ly* ghastly day and I'm dead and I'm going to sl—"

"   "
    . . .

"I won't tell you."

"   "
    . . .

"No! Oh god you most certainly *must not!!*"

"   "
    . . .

"No *no*, oh be *sensible!* If you—"

"   "
    . .

A little laughing wail. "But how can I? You ask such—"

"   "
    . . .

"Oh *that's enough!!* It is *per*-fectly out of the question and you know it (her eyes were on you again) and you're simply keeping me awake, I am exhausted and good *night!*"

She hung up. "Really!" she cried indignantly. "The things Davy does and says now Jill's safely out of the way up at Neurological! Did you *hear* what he wanted to do?"—but smoothly as she covered, somehow you knew it wasn't Davy.

Nor could dignity be saved by pretending you didn't know. If the bastard had rung her up three minutes sooner, she'd still have had her dress on, and you could have passed the whole thing off with perfect urbanity, kissed her good night, and left. But *no*, he had to wait till she was half naked, curling there on the bedspread lovely and laughing as she told you about *Davy*, with hardly a shadow of nervousness in her eyes—had to wait till you had *committed* yourself to lovemaking! You heard yourself say in a frozen voice, "I find I'm leaving, good night," and you left her in the middle of her delicious confections, picked up your hat in the hall, heard her call a question you didn't even understand, much less answer, and tore down the stairs stone-blind to everything except the dazzling and anguished vision of what at every moment you could imagine happening in her room. She would of course have rung the bastard back the moment she heard the door slam; lying there in bra and panties on her belly on the bed, sleek and wriggling, propped on her elbows, her chin cupped in a hand, one sweet knee bent and the stockinged toe waving its slender ballet in the air; the red lips curving in their lovely mocking smile, the voice breaking with laughter ("and dar ling, his fa-a-ace when he left the room . . ."). Or perhaps she had composedly finished undressing, coolly lighting a cigarette even as you were pounding down her stairs; deliciously marshaling the phrases in her mind before she lay back stretched in luxurious indolence and dialed the number, and the tantalizing accents were *at this very moment* saying, "But how can I tell you over the pho-o-one, when it needs gestures? Do I have to ex-cite you, dar ling, into coming to see me?" [...]

I can imagine all too well your mingled gloom and uneasiness when you would dial her number, only to sit and hear her distant phone ring on and on; on and on; on and on; on and on; unanswered in her empty room. Or you visualize it as an empty room, the long curtains drawn before the windows, motionless in the silent air; the dusky stillness somehow listening and alive, as if a voice had been suddenly hushed, instantly been checked; as if someone held his breath, someone just beyond the range of your ear, and listened poised and unstirring, unbreathing, for your departure; as if in the silence your straining senses could almost catch the last soft impact of a word's vibration across the dim and motionless air; as if to your desperate question there were almost the ghost, the echo, of the taunting answer *She was here*. The double ring of the phone would take up that phrase: *she was here* it would seem to say, on and on; on and on; *she was here*; and you would see in your mind the hushed and twilight still-life of the familiar room, a pair of grey gloves tossed emptily on the smooth bed, a gold compact lying open on the dressing table, its mirror a dull gleam on the dusky rectangle; an open letter, perhaps, beside it, the page now curling upward with mute and imperceptible slowness in the quiet air. What message had it brought, of urgency or of appointment? What amusing but irrecoverable secret had it conveyed? To what rendezvous forever undisclosed may it not have summoned her, her lips fresh-reddened with eager swiftness, her eyes cool and expert in their last appraising glance at her image in the pier glass but then suddenly bright with expectancy as she snatched up her purse (had she forgotten her gloves?) and hurried to what breathless meeting beyond her door? *She was here*, the phone would ring, *she was here*; until at last you would drop the receiver despondently back on its stand again and the room would vanish with the endlessly reiterated phrase; and sometimes you would sit for a quarter of an hour, staring emptily at nothing, wondering glumly and pointlessly where it might have been that she had gone.

Evidently I learned more about Mike from Stephanie, in the long, happy months of her affair with me, than I ever learned in all the years that had gone before. For had what all of Mike's and my encounters been, if you didn't mind simplifying a little, but a casual greeting, an easy and unreflecting wave of the hand? from that first meeting (if it was the first) on the sun-filled Princeton campus in the spring of our sophomore year, down to the last time I ever saw him, in a Naval tailor's near Grand Central, in 1940: he apparently had a list of gear in a small black notebook which he kept consulting during our desultory conversation as we were being fitted; we addressed each other as lieutenant, I remember, as we said good-bye.

But through Stephanie I saw Mike with precision because she had had to deal with him with precision, manipulate his moods; and of course she had made love with him with a more finely toleranced precision still.

"He was ex-cit-ing, dar ling; that's why. He used to—" and we had a couple of paragraphs demurely unprintable, her body shifting lightly with delicious reminiscence as it lay half on mine. "He was ver-ry ex— Webb. What are you do ing?"

"Something else."

"I know you are."

"Then why ask?"

"Because I don't think you— Webb!"

"Don't go away."

"Then stop being tire-some."

"Not being."

"No? What are you being?"

"Just properly cordial. Amicable."

"'Amicable'!"

"Please come back."

"I am back."

"No. The way you were."

"What a spoiled voluptuary. Like this?"

"Wonderfully comfortable, thank 'ee."

"Well, I should think so!"

"But why did you go on with Mike?"

"You see? You aren't thinking about me at all."

"I am."

"You aren't and I don't think it's in the least flattering."

"Why did you keep on with him?"

There was so long a silence that I thought she wasn't going to answer. I could feel her breath gently against my throat. Finally she said, "I hadn't really planned to tell you."

"Why not?"

"I thought you wouldn't ask. I thought you'd guessed."

"I haven't."

"And also it is just a little shy-making, dar ling, to have to say."

"Then never mind."

"No. I might as well tell you. Only you mustn't tease me about it."

"*Tease* you!"

"Because it will sound—it will give away—"

"Oh nonsense."

"Yes it will, dar ling. I'm an utter fool to tell you."

"Angel, you don't have—"

"Mike wanted me to marry him."

"What's shy-making about that?"

"No, that part isn't."

"But you didn't want to?"

"Certainly *not*! Why on earth should I marry him when what I wanted was— Well, after all I was only twenty-three, dar ling, and marriage is so sort of governmental and settled-down. Then I— I met you and I—I— Oh, well, you *know* it perfectly well, I met you and I wanted you. Only you—" [. . .]

My fondness for Kitty had grown; and whenever we met, even if we had not seen each other for as much as a month, the warm fingers of affection would enlace out of the real or imagined past: we would smile at each other at a party, past a score of intervening and irrelevant heads, as one of us entered to find the other already there; and this gave us an hallucination of continuity. Not that we could have said, had you asked us, what on earth it was we were continuing. A baseness turned inside out and become a bond? A wordless apology to the other from each? Or she may have had some peculiarly female feeling that part of me still was and always would be hers: perhaps merely *I owe him this tender if slightly embarrassing duty; and in any case surely much of him is mine.* At times, when I saw her answering smile across a milling room, I had almost the sensation I so often had with Stephanie, as if past all these inconsequential heads our bodies were remembering their enlacements, and shoulder were smiling at unforgetting shoulder, the globed breast suddenly warm under the envisioned cheek, a whole tender wordless murmuring dialogue of limbs across a vanished room:

—*The hollow of your arm felt thus to my lips, and thus.*
—*Your lips felt thus (and thus) as they brushed the hollow of my arm.*
—*Your breast was cupped thus in my hand; do you remember?*
—*I remember, delicious hand; I do remember.*

Or again, in some group newer than Kitty's and mine, formed perhaps years after *our* first meeting, some group that had no share in our knowledge of what we had been in the days before they had known us, we would find ourselves by some unconscious process of maneuver *à deux* in a crowded and clamoring party, and with a laugh of pleasure would realize how we had got there.

"You are looking *very* charming, Webb, may I say?"

"Fancy seeing you here."

"Fancy."

"And looking so good to eat."

"You do sometimes have a knife-and-fork way of thinking about me, Webb, have you been told?"

"Look, Kit, haven't you had nearly enough of this party?"

"I can't think our hostess would be terribly pleased at the way you put these things!"

"Let's give it a miss and have a drink."

"Webb you mean a drink in a private way?"

"I haven't seen you in private for days."

"It's rather late though, do you think?"

"Only a little after one."

"You mean merely a little before two?"

"Look, Kit, I have my car."

"And I am certainly far too worn for a taxi!"

"Then do let us go?"

"Then *do* let us go at once!"

Sometimes, in my apartment, I would want her, in a sudden gust of sheer exasperation at any one of a number of lost and irrecoverable occasions when we might so easily have made love with complete satisfaction to (I would tell myself) everybody concerned. But mostly I wanted little more than to loll, say, with my head in her lap and hear her chiming voice, while her fingers made affectionate ringlets in my hair or fed me my cigarette. By this time she was, or so I thought, engaged to Steve anyhow, and she certainly suspected my affair with Stephanie; but I believe our half-conscious feeling must have been—though it certainly is a hell of an odd way to put it—that our making love just wasn't really worth while. We perhaps owned part of each other; we had the illusion of that possession; but did we honest to god want to assume the complicated responsibilities of owning very much more? and the answer was No. Except that—as every now and then the sudden savagery of a caress would inform us—we had never quite plumbed the final curiosity of each other, many of our evenings were as peaceful as exhausted lovers slumbering side by side.

"My head too heavy?"

"Objectively or subjectively, Webb?"

"Whose standpoint?"

"What charming hair. This is an *entirely* fetching curl you have here."

"Where?"

"Here."

"This one?"

"Yes." [. . .]

"Oh Webb darling, I just feel so completely tender I don't know where you stop and I begin."

That much, of course, I had regrettably been able to tell her for several years; but naturally the immediate practical problem was not the geography of mysticism but, rather, to formulate, in the appropriate mood, the decently romantic tactics of gentlemanly flight. (Had I for nothing got a first group in the Dean's French 402 Le Romantisme Français?)

And yet, after what years of soul-searching and agonized indecisions; after how tedious a series of dramas and debates and hesitations, now finally, and in what a culmination of irrelevance, *voilà qu'elle me tombe sur le râble!*

"You sweet sweet Kit. I never had a lovelier proposition."

"Ah, don't call it that. I do so mean it with all of me."

I kissed her gently. "No one could ever have said it but you. No one I know on earth." The tone sounded right: its mode beautifully minor, the cadence of its phrasing incomparably renunciatory. "But what would it do to *me*, Kit. I might just fall in love with you all over again instead of what you mean."

I described in detail how it might be; every trope in the catalogue; I was even moved by the passage myself. And so bit by bit our normal equilibrium returned; and presently I could take her home.

Yet as I drove down 96th and turned down Park, some of the special charm she had cast over that evening remained. My arm was around her; and whenever we stopped for traffic lights, she would reach out and shift into neutral while I pressed the clutch pedal, then shift again, from low to second to high, as the lights turned green and we drove on. I thought at the time (and I still think even today) what extraordinary sweetness her imagination managed to find, and by how simple a gesture, in that essence of all mechanisms. Her light hand on the gear-lever said *I love you* (illusion as it was) as no intonation of her voice had ever succeeded in saying it. I damn near went into her apartment with her after all.

✧

It was from Stephanie, perhaps I should have said earlier, that I had first learned of Mike's joining the Naval Reserve. We were in one of those amiable weekends we had made a practice of, when I simply moved into her apartment Saturday afternoon with an armful of fancy foods and didn't leave till Monday morning; when we let the phone ring unanswered and time passed without even the most casual regard for the formal divisions of night and day; when we ate the minute we were hungry and made love the minute it seemed interesting again, sleeping and waking as the mood took us, and the hell with Greenwich astronomy and the time of day.

"Did I tell you about Mi-i-ke, dar ling?"

"Hhmmm?"

"Will you stop beating that tiresome *béchamel* and pay at-tention? Mike's learning to *fly!*"

"What for, my god?"

"In the Naval Reserve. He goes to Connecticut every weekend and learns. He's solo'd already."

"You mean he's *joined* the Reserve?"

"But of course."

"I'll be damned."

"Though you'll never guess why."

"And you can hardly wait to tell me?"

The delicious smooth-little-girl laugh. "You mean I'm a hateful ca-a-at, dar ling?"

"Well, why has he?"

"Three reasons, at least. He wants to have something *to do* on weekends, that's the first reason and I'm sure it's *ver*-ry good for him. And then there's an old girl of his married to somebody in New London."

"Tsk."

"Last year he had lunch with her at least twice. When she was down shopping in town. He told me she wasn't at *all* happy with her husband. What are you looking for?"

"Got a fine sieve?" I asked.

"Certainly not."

"What a kitchen," I said. "What's the third reason?"

"I oughtn't to tell you, dar ling."

"Discreditable, huh."

"Not in the least. It's just that— Oh, well, he's always *worry*-ing so about his figure, I have no idea why, he has a lovely shape and the most beautiful shoulders. He doesn't have to worry in the least. But he does, Webb. So I'm per-fect-ly sure he thinks all those set-ting-up exercises they have to do— Dar ling, are you ever going to start worrying about your figure too?"

Again, it was from Stephanie (though later) that I learned of that final explosion between Kitty and Steve from whose wreckage arose, after the customary acts of demolition, the baroque pergola of the affair between Kitty and Mike; and then their marriage; and if I had been seeing Stephanie still later, she would have told me about that too.

Or again, the sudden glimpses I sometimes had, through Stephanie's eyes, down some dimly lit and unsuspected corridor of Mike's mind. I remember for instance the night I returned, early in 1936, from nearly a month's idiotic exile in the West. Some fatuous apoplectic, upstairs at the *Sun*, had decided that we needed a town-by-town series showing how Republicanism every-where was about to sweep those madmen out of Washington; and so (in the year of As Maine Goes So Goes Vermont) for twenty-eight consecutive days I was filing my stories from a different solid-Democratic stronghold of Republicanism every night and getting hungrier for Stephanie with every date-line. I raced straight from the train to her apartment, and we nearly tore the place apart.

"My god," I said in one breathless between-rounds, "you must have been *faithful* to me all these weeks!"

"I *was*, you undeserving animal!"

"So was I, Steph."

She had never smiled at me in quite that way before. "Oh sweet, *were* you? Oh Webb."

"You wanted me to be."

"Yes. But I never said so. How did you know?"

"How did you know I wanted *you* to be?"

"Oh Webb come *here!*"

It was hours before we really got around to conversation.

"Weren't you even tempted, dar ling?"

"No."

"Not even to sleep with somebody's secretary?"

"No."

"*I* was tempted."

"By anyone I know?"

"But of course."

"Who?"

A giggle. "Just your namesake, dar ling."

"*Mike?*"

"Naturally."

"Why, the adulterous hound!"

"But I was feeling sorry for him, he was really terribly upset, and feeling sorry is such a silly reason for having sex with anybody."

"Upset?" I asked.

"About Jill. Oh, but you were away and don't *know!*"

"What's the matter with Jill now?"

"She killed herself."

"Good *god*, Stephanie!"

The whole thing had been ghastly, she said. Jill had been allowed to go home from Neurological: she was practically well and anyhow she had a nurse with her. Stephanie herself had met them shopping; Jill had been happy and glowing and told her she and Davy were off to Nassau in a couple of weeks; everything was *wonderful* again, and Davy his old sweet self and sending her flowers every day. And then. Two days later Jill had taken a fresh box of flowers into the pantry to arrange, after showing them off to the nurse and their both explaining how lovely they were, and the nurse had helped her choose a vase; and the next thing the nurse heard was a wild sob and a splintering crash, and she spun around and dove for the pantry, but Jill had slashed a wrist and her throat with the flower shears and was already nearly dead when the nurse reached her.

"Oh god," I said numbly.

"And no one knows why, Webb. Though Mike thinks he does."

Mike had been utterly haggard at the funeral, she said; at one point had broken down completely; and afterwards she had brought him back to her apartment and sat with him and let him talk until four in the morning. ("That was when he wanted to sleep with me. He didn't say so; but I knew.") He seemed to feel he should have been able to *do* something, to save Jill; he had been their best man, there *must* have been something he could have done, he kept insisting, if only he could have thought of it; if only he could have discovered what it was. He had gone over with Stephanie scene after scene he had had with Jill in the past, despondently examining them in endless detail, wearily asking her what she thought, where he might have done differently or said something differently, postponed a climax, found a solicitous and saving plan, lightened a strain before it became intolerable, relieved some unendurable uncertainty. One scene he had come back to again and again had occurred only the summer before. Jill was at the Starrs' cottage up in Connecticut, and Mike had moved in with Davy while his own apartment was being repainted. Early one evening Jill had unexpectedly appeared, and they had had an amicable drink or two together waiting for Davy (though Mike had been a little uneasy that Jill might cross-question him about where Davy was, for he happened to know). But Davy hadn't arrived; and when by two in the morning he still hadn't arrived, Mike had finally persuaded Jill to go to bed and had wearily turned in himself on the couch in the livingroom.

He didn't know when Davy got home, or what had then happened. But he had been violently awoken by the crashing slam of their bedroom door; and then Jill was all over him, sobbing and giggling and shaking and tearing at him and gabbling stuff that made the hair stand up along his spine.

What should he have *done*, Mike had demanded with the tears rolling down his cheeks, how could he have *helped* the poor distracted darling? Couldn't Stephanie suggest anything, to check that desperate spiral down and down and down? What did she think? Where had he failed?

"There was nothing, Stephanie," I said sadly.

"Except that she needed him."

"It was too late for that."

"No, Webb. Not if he had seen it."

"*The poor guy.* You didn't tell him there was anything?"

"No."

"Because there just wasn't anything at all."

"I know."

Abruptly she looked away; and I lay there gazing at that lovely profile, so warm with life yet now suddenly caught up in a marble stillness, both of us in a wordless and fearful pause that hung upon the air like the heavy folds of a curtain descending and descending. Stephanie, for that evening at least we were haunted; and when, after I thought you had been long asleep, you turned suddenly in my arms in the dark and clutched me and whispered, "*Hold me. I wasn't lonely while you were away. Oh, Webb, I was too frightened,*" I needed no answering mortal shiver in my spine to tell me what it was that you wished to say.

Beyond any doubt, that evening, so wildly and splendidly erotic when it began, and at its end grazed so close by the fluttering draperies of terror, left Stephanie and me embraced more tightly and more inextricably than either of us had ever imagined would be possible. Of the early Mr. Eliot's famous three-piece eternity, birth copulation and death, we had shared the only two that man experiences consciously for himself, and in a span of time no longer than it would take you to saunter around a corner with a backward wave of your hand; and even as I held her close in my arms, my mind felt in the rushing dark the naked wind of that winged metaphysical chariot of mortality, and *le silence éternel de ces espaces infinis.* What the over-educated and remembering brain of Western man echoes in his solitary hours before the dawn has no doubt a spurious validity: those epigraphs chiseled in eternal Roman capitals on the granite midnight may turn out to be graffiti in the morning. But still the desolation has been experienced, the *tenet et nox longa tenebit* recorded, the sleek and perilous body has been clutched against one's own. I do not know, nor does she remember, how Stephanie and I went to sleep that night; but the next morning we looked at each other for the first time in our lives a little unsteadily; and when I got up to find that *she* had already made our breakfasts, and asked her teasingly what on earth had come over her, the sudden depthless look she gave me had none of her usual composure in it at all.

And how else, perhaps, should I explain the night, a fortnight later, when she got so helplessly drunk—something she had never done with me before—that I had practically to carry her from the taxi to her room? I undressed her and put her to bed, and was just going out the bedroom door when her voice stopped me where I stood:

"I am ver ry drunk dar ling but I have to say this." She was speaking slowly and carefully, with only a slight slurring. "I love you but what can I do. If I were not so drunk I would be too shy. But I can say it now and I have to. For I will never be able to tell you this again. You think because we are so gay in bed that I am never serious. And now you think that I am just drunk. And don't know what I am saying. But I do Webb. Only I have to be drunk or I can't look at you and say it. I love you and now you know. But I can't say it ever again. Now good night dar ling please go away."

And finally: In those last months before the war, it is certain that Stephanie was gradually and deliberately weaning me. It was not that she saw me much less often, or that there seemed to be the least change in our meetings, our habits together, our conversations, our lovemaking. How she accomplished it I do not really understand. But there was an indefinable feeling of valediction about some of our nights together in the winter of 1937-38; and when one afternoon she told me, over cocktails at the Gladstone, that she was going to marry Jack Geddie, I had unconsciously been so well prepared that I found I was hardly surprised.

"He wants me to marry him, dar ling." The angel-grey eyes teased at me under the smart black angle of the hatbrim as they always did, but there was a gleam of new excitement in their depths. "Shall I? Or shall I?"

"Well, you want to get married, don't you?"

"I'm nearly twenty-six."

"Is he good enough for you?"

"He's— I'm afraid you won't like this, dar ling, but he's ver-ry like you," and suddenly a throatful of delighted laughter.

"So you've been cocu-ing me!"

"Well, dar ling!"

"Is he good?"

"The questions you a-a-ask."

"Just a courteous interest, try to show always."

"Do you really think I'll tell you such things? About my future hus-band? I told you you wouldn't like it."

"You know you're dying to tell me."

"I most certainly am not, why should I?"

"I don't know. Only somehow you— Stephanie, you somehow want me to approve of what you're doing."

She didn't answer for a moment. "Not 'somehow,' Webb."

"All I meant was—"

"You know why I want you to. Though sometimes I wish you didn't."

I sat looking into her eyes for so long a time that when my answer came it sounded almost oblique, but I had to realize (now finally) what it was that I was at long last about to say: "There'll never be anybody like you for me either, Stephanie."

"You oughtn't to say it, Webb. Unless you mean it."

"I do mean it."

"Never anyone?"

"Never anyone."

"You never said it before," she said quietly. "*Did* you, dar ling? In all that time, not even to be specially sweet to me once, you never could quite bring yourself to say it before."

✦

I feel a similar sense of valediction as I see Mike's figure too move out and away from me in that unrehearsed pas de deux we had been so long involved in. I will however add one inconsequential theme more—the charming redhead he had met again, one weekend when he was flying, at a Naval party in New London. Years before he'd had her to a prom when he was in Princeton and she in a Bryn Mawr finishing school; she had since married some kind of Wall Street lieutenant commander; she disliked her husband and she liked Mike; she often ran down to New York for a day's shopping; and a few weeks after Mike stomped down Stephanie's stairs, she ran down to New York for a mutually liberating afternoon in bed, Malachi, with you. It was the first affair she had ever had and she was disastrously nervous—if the elevator stopped at Mike's floor she went frigid with fright—but her taut nerves made her recklessly erotic and she fed on love as if she had been starving. It must have been a wonderfully satiating afternoon; and no doubt when he saw her to her train that evening he felt as if he had got Stephanie out of his blood forever.

They had several afternoons as fine as the first; and then one day she came to his apartment retching and white and he hadn't even closed the door before she said, "Oh god Mike I'm going to have a baby." She didn't know whether it was his or her husband's; she lay on his couch weeping the whole afternoon; when he tried to talk her calm enough to decide what she wanted to do about it, her wild sobbing doubled; and when he merely touched her hand she went into high-decibel hysterics. She literally shrieked her refusal to let him see her to the train; and after she stepped into the elevator he never saw her again.

Perhaps I should not have labeled this incident inconsequential: it involves, after all, Mike's only posterity, even if the bend of the little thing's coat of arms and the color of its hair are momentarily surprising. (And even though, in a psychiatric sense, we may hope that it has inherited the temperament of its begetting rather than the atmosphere of its annunciation.) But I must call it inconsequential because Mike himself thought of it as inconsequential; if indeed he thought of it much afterwards at all. For when our paths crossed during that winter of 1937-38, what I remember in him is a kind of carelessness of the course of his life, an irrational apathy toward all existence, a look of spiritual desolation, that seemed to indicate a draining of the emotions too deep and too enervating to allow him to think even of his own.

Yet there must have been times when he too expressed the thing to himself with a certain gloomy rhetoric. He may, for all I know, have been sitting in a bar; the Biltmore; the Waldorf; over on Second Avenue; it could have been (say) Thanksgiving night of 1937, and he was watching the pale-gold frost gather right to the brim of his second Martini; thinking how delicious it would taste in a moment when he bent for the first sip; and then suddenly thinking, What is this alien and night-enshrouded era in which I find myself? What am I doing here? Or here? Along what echoing avenues, past what weed-grown and deserted lots, what empty corners, have I made my unaccompanied way? And he would think with melancholy humor, Why, half the girls I know seem to be dead or else in bed with somebody else. Or pregnant, for all I know, with a redheaded firstborn of mine whom I shall almost certainly never see. What bleak landscape (he could have phrased it), what setting was this of hope or of desire? What was this frame from which his face looked out for the inspection of his fellows, the eyes black and sparkling, a handsome touch of crimson on the cheekbones? looked out with a judicious mingling of opulence and tired concern, the expression at once sardonic and urbane.

Though for all we can tell he found, as he finished his Martini and decided against a third, that he was not even sure such a fanfare of queries had much interest; and what the hell kind of frame was apathy anyhow?

It must then have been in some such sterility of the spirit that his affair with Kitty began. I have few details; Stephanie had few to supply; and of what happened after the affair ended in marriage, in the summer of 1939, I knew nothing at all. But I gather that one evening in December of 1937 Mike was feeling bleak and fed-up, and finally flipped a coin between going inexpensively to bed and doing a pub-crawl; and when the pub-crawl won he phoned Jane and when Jane's phone didn't answer he phoned Kitty; and Kitty happened to be free. But naturally pubs are all the same and they grew finicky early, and eventually went back to his rooms for a nightcap with enough liquor in it at least to taste.

Kitty was tired. She stretched out on his couch, and he sat on the floor beside her and fed her her drink at requested intervals; and quite accidentally, as far as Stephanie could tell, presently he began sliding his fingers softly through Kitty's warm curls. They'd not been talking much, and now they stopped entirely; and the silence spread and muffled them in its quiet folds, she lying there gazing at him peacefully and a little wearily, and he slowly stroking the soft thick locks back and back from her temples and feeling their dark rings slip smoothly and satisfyingly through his fingertips; the room wordless and unstirring around them, the lamp's twilight hanging as if suspended upon the air. Until finally she took his hand and held it gently to her cheek.

"You are such a charming guy, Malachi, did you know?"

"Why, thank 'ee."

"Tell me something?"

"What?"

"What was it you were after that day?"

"What day?"

"In Coatesville."

"You remember it too."

"Ah, Mike my dear, quite fondly."

"I don't think I really know."

"What you were after, you mean?"

"Yes. Or know, Kit, even now."

"At one point, if I may make so bold, I should have said you were principally after *me!*"

They smiled at each other; and I suppose he thought, Of course I cannot live backward in time or revisit that day or that trance or feel again as I felt then; and neither can she; and no one but a fool would try to; but is there a law against at least going through the motions? and who's to say the motions are not the thing itself? And even if they aren't (and they aren't) they're better than this nothing; or can I persuade myself they're better; since after all what objective proof am I likely to be provided with that I will ever feel more than I do now anyhow? So he said,

"You warned me off. Remember?"

". . . I remember. Oh quite well. And other things also."

"You said Presbyterians were sometimes fond of Quakers."

"Yes, Malachi. Miscegenative, it must have sounded!"

He said, "Quakers are very affectionate people too."

". . . Are you so sure, Malachi?"

"Sure."

"And I am sure too, would you say?"

"Why not?"

"So many words. All so persuasive." She looked at him spiritlessly. "And all, oh dear me, how weary and worn."

They were silent. He kissed her experimentally; her lips were soft and obedient but there was no real response, and presently she said,

"Does this all feel very— in some way very strange to you, Malachi dear?"

"Strange? No."

"I mean— Wasn't Coatesville all somehow very long ago?"

"This hasn't really changed, Kit."

"Ah Mike, Mike my dear, that may be just what's so—"

"We're the same."

"Are we, Malachi? Are we? Am I?"

"Except that now we know better."

"There isn't really much else to think, did you know? Or much else to try, Mike dear? Or anyhow, for me."

Perhaps for a moment he thought of saying *But even if there were*; or perhaps even half-thought *The hell with all of it*; but there was nothing rational to say so instead he kissed her, a long kiss; and slowly her arms tightened about his shoulders and drew him down; and after a suitable time he turned off the light.

After all (he could argue) it worked. They were married in the summer; he gave her three of the nakedest nightgowns he could buy as an engagement present. They were certainly extremely fond of each other, and with what preposterous and misplaced idealism will anyone undertake to demonstrate that that isn't as good as anything?

AN ARMFUL OF WARM GIRL

DIS MÂNIBVS
ALFREDI YOUNG FISHER
COMMILITONIS

He was born pretty damn' irked, with a Caldwell's spoon in his mouth, to a family of short-tempered Philadelphia-Quaker private bankers, on a stifling country-summer morning in 1909. Or a Bailey Banks & Biddle spoon, what difference does it make, father could've bought and sold 'em both twice over. Weighed twelve pounds; they all did then; grew up big too. And in due course graduated from Princeton in the Class of 1931, though who didn't.

Though as it happens only just graduated, having got himself under sentence of rustication, spring of his junior year, for half breaking a classmate's back after a lush June wedding at Trinity. In a stripped and bare-handed midnight duel, of all things!—dim starlight down by the Lake, grass skiddy with blood and dew, some pre-med classmate standing by and a couple of Virginia classmates for seconds, this fellow-usher having had the incredible damn' taste to describe the bride, mind you the guy's own roommate's girl! as "built like a brick Gertrude Stein." But the common bastard turned out not to be paralyzed, so they dropped the rustication.

Additionally, come to think of it, got his nose broken in the Place du Théâtre in Dijon during his formal grand tour in the summer of '31. Served him right: made some mannerless generalization ("Faut-il quand même qu'on y foute du lait maternel?") on the indiscriminate riches of Burgundian cookery.

Otherwise a life like anybody's—married a delicious Main Line deb; usual children usual love affairs; succeeded as a chairman, at their Bank, his bellowing father. But who wants to bother with this background claptrap? or for that matter like Homer invoke a Muse on the subject matter of mere size and bad temper, when the point about a protagonist is that here he is here-and-now, this big-boned striding irascible man with his bloodshot and arrogant blue eyes— what's *he* care for his boyhood and the rest of it? Let Freud fuss with all that. Or for variety Aristarchus.

So then this is 1959, and down to business.

On *this* country-summer morning, then (here and now), a summer morning already hot and still, every drowsing green ride of landscape toppling with light, this Nicholas Romney, a Philadelphia private banker aged fifty years or as good as, a Chester County squire now stiff-faced with rage and deep affront, left his inherited groves, his woodland chases, his messuage and out-farms, and in particular his wife, and banged off in his ancient Bentley down his great-grandfather's furlong of carriage-drive toward the outrage of exile in New York.

Having no more than reached a time of life when all he or any man in his senses wanted was to settle down with some agreeable woman or other, at the very least a wife he was used to and fond of—"and the irresponsible bitch *leaves* me!!" he yelled.

So away, alone.

In his meadows, in the flash and dazzle of the morning, his fat black cattle grazed through the jingleweed, his white guineas ran huddling. In his parks of oak and hickory the woods' high crowns discharged their splintered emeralds of light, the dogwoods shook out in flower, pink or cream, their weightless sprays. In his grove his great-grandfather's beeches, nave on nave, shone in their argent elegance, his glossy peacocks straggled, his grandfather's marble folly reared its Palladian ruins, studded with busts of ottocento celebrities, now seriously begrimed. In his box maze glittered the fantailed Cytherean tumbling of his doves.

And all this, by one pretty woman's perversity, now done with, unreal; as lost to him as if by disseizin; plundered; *gone!*

For not twelve hours ago she'd stood cool and tall before him and said in her stylish drawl he didn't expect her to account to him did he? not any longer now surely; or for that matter explain; or in any case expect her to mock ordinary good manners by asking him would he mind? when why pretend he'd in the least mind "beyond the temporary vexation to yourself, Nicholas"—this, if you'll credit such a thing, from a woman he'd thought he'd known every sweet inch of, and for years!

Many years; many happy years, to reckon the plain fact! A whole warm and smiling chronicle, a sentient lifetime. And now here what was she but become this stranger.

Thus then he'd packed and gone.

What with her preposterous "not another day"—fancy making use of such an expression! had she no more sense of prose style than that after a quarter-century of his company?

So like any man in his right mind he ground out between his teeth a discountenanced "Wife wants to go let her by heaven *go,* up to *her* infatuated levity not mine!"

Adding, stunned, "Tired of *me,* can you imagine!" though the emerging fact was, now he'd got around to noticing it—and here was the final disobliging and unnatural affront—as to this requested divorce she never in so many words had told him why!

So this baffled man drove through West Chester and on toward Chester and the ferry dispirited and glaring dismally, his mind as good as vacant apart from the customary interior rodomontade.

For what had he done to be deserted like this, loved her hadn't he? And if not exclusively, still by heaven these many many years! And as much as he or any man had it in him to, hadn't he, all things considered? Well, then!

Or if he'd bored her why not say so!

Though what real likelihood, she hadn't bored *him* had she? Or not much. Or not more than was normal and understood. Or anyhow not bored often, and damned if he'd had the bad breeding to show it in any case. In any case he hadn't held it against her had he? And so at last, muttering complaints by this time at her irresponsible damn' technique of merely handling a husband, this endless confronting him instead of maneuvering round him nuzzling and femalizing at him like a European woman ("like a *woman* dammit!") he drove onto the ferry.

Where, as it happened, in the car next his there was a delicious-looking girl to stare at.

Who finally smiled at him; so presently drove into New York, where he'd not passed a night in many years, feeling rather less embittered than had promised. And at Veale's Hotel, though now changed from the Thirties almost past his disconcerted recognition, he had a very decent squab, à la Marigny or some such, with a bottle of Hermitage, and half a dozen pretty women in good view—two of whom, a normal enough percentage, ogled him charmingly through drooping lashes.

In fact he felt much better.

So after a nap, fourish or so, he rang up his New York daughter. "Melissa?"

"Hello?"

"Mélisse how *are* you my sweet baby, regret I've got to inform you at once an infuriating thing's occurred. Matter of fact an outrage, I've been badly ups—"

"I'm terribly sorry but who is this?" she said in her fashionable young voice. "I can hardly—"

"How's that? This is your father!"

"Hello? Hello?"

He blared into the phone, "Now see here Melissa dammit I'm resigned to a few symbolic communication-difficulties of a routine order by heaven—"

"Why *Daddy!*" her pleased voice cried, "why how perfectly, why darling where are you then!"

"What?"

"I mean how blissful hearing you out of the seamless blue like this, where are you phoning *from?*"

"What? I'm at Veale's. Naturally. Where else?"

"Could you speak just a little louder d'you think?"

He shouted "*Can you hear this?*" at her.

"Yes *much* better, where are you?"

"An old-fashioned private hotel called—"

"You're in New York, why Daddy what's this!"

"Look, my precious child, if you'll just—"

"Mummy too?"

"No!"

"Oh Mummy *not* with you, where's she?"

"How do I know dammit!"

"What, darling?"

He violently announced, "Your unhinged mother's taken it into her head to divorce me, is what!"

"Oh Daddy not so loud, I can't hear anything but a sort of bellow."

So he translated down, and into a tone nearer the Horatian irony called for, "Your mother has I regret to say taken it into her pretty head to propose that she divorce me."

"..............*divorce!!*" cried their daughter in accents of shock and universal scandal.

"Yes by god!"

"Oh Daddy, oh poor loves!"

"A sheer outrage!" he told her in a despondent roar.

"Yes but Daddy but *Mummy!*"

"Deliberate affront of a pretty damn' unrefined—"

"But *who* on earth?"

"What?"

"Yes; who in love with; oh hideous!"

"Now what in God's name has love got to do with it!"

"Oh darling don't yell so, getting her divorce *for* I mean. I mean to marry him or whoever."

He snarled, "Your mother has not it appears seen fit to provide me with the customary rival, if you want to know. No doubt flattered herself I'd fling the swine in the pond."

"Pond, Daddy?"

"Well, the tenants' pond, what difference does it— Now look here Melissa the point doesn't arise. I've just said. Your mother's not in love with somebody else. Or with anybody, merely doesn't appear to want to live any longer with *me*."

"There couldn't be some, well, *terribly* stealthy—"

"Now listen to me Melissa—"

"Only pet but nobody at *all?*" wailed the former Miss Romney dismayed.

"The structures of female romanticism aside," her father pronounced testily, "why should there be somebody? Or is the question one one's daughters reply to?"

"What, Daddy?"

"What d'ye mean 'what' dammit, anyhow the point's perfectly clear and undebatable: wretched woman doesn't want any longer to be married to anybody. Or so in the absence of any responsible explanation from her I'm forced to conclude. Doesn't anyhow want to live with *me*—can you conceive of such behavior?"

"Now *pet* she must have said!"

"What?"

"Darling *said*."

"Said what? Said you two girls were both married now (she 'supposed' happily), both married and your brothers at least *in* college, as if that had anything to do with it! When how's anyone know? herself included, for all I— Do you realize that now for weeks on end I'll have to commute down to that root-canal man in West Philadelphia?"

"But darling couldn't you persuade her that a—"

" 'Persuade her'! You out of your pretty senses? If she was done she was done, *I* wasn't going to beseech her to change her mind. Out of *her* senses! As I told her!"

"Oh Daddy you yelled at her?"

"Naturally I yelled at her!"

"Oh blessing," she mourned, "oh what a thing, oh poor loves; oh just when we *all*."

"Isn't it though? Isn't it?"

"And all your darling little marottes."

"My what?"

"Like the peacocks. And great-grandfather's stone poets you were going to have scoured, ah how sad."

"*Well*," he agreed, in unhappy tones.

"Will Mummy see to them?"

He cried, "How do I know!"

"And when it's all yours!"

"Now see here my lovely baby, I couldn't in reason throw your da— your poor mother out! Of hearth and home? Limits, I have to assume, even to *my* late-Edwardian attitudes."

"But I mean it was grandfather's, dearest, *your* father's not Mummy's. And great-grandfather's and so forth; why, back and back forever, you're always telling."

"Now imagine your being concerned!"

"Well but Daddy *yes!*"

"Well it is a lovely old place in practice by god isn't it."

"Why, it's my whole lost sweet growing-up girlhood," she laughed, lightly delivering this line at him, as from footlights.

"The groves, the high woods, the light," he lamented tenderly, "the eighteenth-century solitudes, why Melissa I was a boy, a tiny child, there."

"Such dreaming summers; ah, what sweets."

"Not that you're ever even near the place now particularly," he said with sudden deep gloom.

"What? why I *am!*"

"Or really stay."

"When I was there only this Easter?"

"In what seems long long years."

She was wildly astonished.

He concluded loudly, "*Miss* you in fact, darling child!"

"Well *dearest* then!"

So he mumbled something.

"I mean but *darling* Daddy!" she cried. "Why of *all* the!"

"See something more of you now anyhow, huh. Going to open the little Barrow Street house, all things considered: it's been—"

"But then you can't mean you're settling here then, I mean Daddy the 'dower house' and all?"

"Well, for the next few months I—"

"But what can your plans be? why sweetie all your friends are around I thought Philadelphia."

"Now Mélisse," he said, amused, "no more friends than that, good god?"

"But New York! when you haven't *been* in twenty years."

"Seventeen."

"Well, seventeen."

"Must know dozens of people here still. All my old New York girls, for a start."

"Oh Daddy seventeen *years*, and married to other people now anyhow, aren't they."

"Married to other people *then*," he snickered.

"Daddy!"

"Ah, well, though," he resumed, in tones of threnody. "You do of course have a point. Seventeen years," he pronounced heavily. "Not even I suppose excluded that some of them may be even dead, poor sweet creatures. Happened to a classmate of mine only day before yesterday."

"What, Daddy?"

"Being buried today. Be there for the service too, you know, except for your confounded mother."

"Oh darling someone you knew?"

"Well, no, actually; or anyhow hardly; just another damn' Philadelphia banker. But a member of the Class!" he cried in acute self-pity.

She crooned, "Ah, dearest," rather moved.

"Saw him not forty-eight hours before he died, too, poor guy. Pink and vigorous; absolutely glowing with health."

"Ah Daddy."

"Poor guy. Must have had his plans too. Like all of us. Then next day, or the next, quite simply we miss him from the accustomed hill. Ah well. Such a shame, somehow, Melissa."

"Ah but old *sweet*," she grieved.

"Though as it happens," her father said in a different tone altogether, "a complete stuffed shirt actually, if you want the fact of it, bored the blessings out of anybody but his fellow Republicans. Class is full of these well-behaved people, what's Princeton do to 'em? Frightful thing: no real standards, just *behave* well, poor decent amiable dying mugs. Where's the short-tempered Achilles that we knew? Well though here dammit, mustn't keep you with this dismal sort of stuff, when can I see you? By the way how's your husband?" he demanded suddenly. "Marrying these wretched Yale success-boys," he tailed off grumbling.

"Now Daddy ssssshh, he's lovely."

"Well when can *I* see you!" he cried.

"Why, any time! why *sweetie!*"

"Lunch tomorrow then? Or's dinner better?"

"Well I'm afraid *tomorrow—*"

"Day after, then, huh."

"When if I'd only known you were coming!"

"Weekend then? or that impossible too!"

"Oh Daddy I *am* so sorry but the thing is we've got this endlessly long-standing weekend up in Connecticut with—"

"Well then *Monday!*"

"Only don't you see the frightful fact *is* we hadn't actually meant to get back till very possibly— Now look *darling* could you ring up then? when I mean we can keep it open? and find out what you intend *doing*, I mean *here* and so forth! because then we can have you all properly up in full fig and all!"

So he said rather testily he'd give her a ring then, why certainly, be delighted to; and hung up.

Presently he rang first one Princeton son, then the other. Neither of these miserable boys was in, and not one of their clods of roommates either; and his other daughter being that fortnight with her proconsular young husband in Istanbul of all places, he had nothing to do but shave and shower.

Under the razor his face had never glowed with a pinker health. ". . . poor guy," he muttered elegiacally, slupping the lather around his firm jaw; after a while adding, "Heu, modo tantus, ubi es?" thanks to a decent Classical education.

So evening came on; and after seventeen years (or even conceding in this case it was twenty) in agreeable expectation he rang up Angelina Hume.

Having first debated aloud with himself, in the clouting torrents of the shower, what pictures of her his memory's eye was actually on, what pageants glimpsed down what flowery perspectives; since otherwise he might just be remembering What's-his-name's gainsboroughization of her in the National Gallery instead. So now in a knotted towel, combed and cologned, he rang her up, in his hand a frayed rectangle of paper he'd kept all these years happily ever after, which once upon a time the two of them had passed back and forth and back and forth, at whatever stuffed bankers' banquet it had been twenty years ago, with her damn' husband (her first one) at the speakers' table and she and Nicholas feeding side by side below the salt an urbane eight inches apart, while scribbling on *this very paper*, here now in his eager hand, their antiphonal enchantment:

    — 8 inches much too *far* [his pen had written]
    — *Yes!* [had answered her scrawling backhand]
    — Don't be monosyllabic, think of synonyms
    — *All right—I'll think and what I think is you're adorable—3 syllables—Want more?*
    —I want any and *all*
    —*I'd like to go make love—All monosyllables—and you* dont *like them?*
    — [a crease, his reply illegible; paper rubbed and worn]
    — *Come on that wasn't an answer—Write something like I write—Such as you have sweet curls on your head*

('Curls'?) But now anyhow in her 73rd Street palazzo her phone rang and was answered, and he said with smiling anticipation, "Like to speak to Mrs. Hume please; Mr. Romney, tell her."
    " . . ."
"Well, be in shortly I presume? ask her if she'll—"
    " . . ."
"What? why g— Why that's *extremely disappointing* dammit, where can I reach her then?"
    " . . ."
"Can't 'give out' her out-of-town address, what d'ye mean 'out,' dammy I've known your mistress twenty years!"
    " . . ."
"Now see here then, where *is* Mrs. Hume?"
    " . . ."
" '*In Europe*'!" he exploded.
Wildly staring.
And dressed stunned and speechless.
"Yes *speechless!*" he trumpeted, thrashing his way into a shirt. "Is every unaccountable damn' woman I want to see up to something else by god? A display of insensibility that I— of inconsider— Have they *no* responsi— And where in the name of God are my black socks!" he snarled, flinging the trunk-till onto the bed.
And rooted in vain: wife gone, heartless daughter off weeks on end in some Connecticut commuters' slum with her huge child of a husband, and now for a third, and past any system of probabilities known to man, his own Angelina not even in the same

hemisphere! and in a word, "*Deserted* by god!" he shouted at his image in the glass, flailing a fistful of sober ties.

Pulled on his socks muttering, "Been too kind to the finicky bitches, is what," pretty dismally.

For spend your whole self-sacrificing lifetime on 'em, in single-minded devotion mind you! and now here for reward where was he but some hog's-own hotel changed out of all semblance of memory!

The bed not merely too soft but too short!

Yes! and with the plumbing roaring and racketing day and ever-lasting night!

Yes! and no sooner settle down for a night's decent rest in due course than in all likelihood from some next-door room there'd come a rushing and trampling, a delighted nubile screeching, and the hoarse male grunts of Edwardian desire. . . .

So by *god* he stomped out of his room and down into the bar pretty damn' near speechless again.

And waiting for the first glass of his evening champagne he sat in a corner glaring: one cloyed flitting self-indulgent unreachable female after another, the whole performance beyond belief; and if now like a reasonable man he rang up his angel Victoria Barclay next, what unforeseeable dither of universal disorder mightn't he find there too!

And to cap everything he had to call the gerent over, or what-ever the man was, to complain glowering about this champagne, was it ullaged or what? and as the fellow scuttled off for a fresh bottle, snapped after him "Not even your bar's the same!"—this once familiar room changed now as those redecorated hearts; all he'd known vanishing; so that what was there that once had been and still was.

The second glass was better. So he stumped over to the bar glass in hand and lectured the bartender on négociants, vignobles, and the like, with testy brevity.

Or at first brevity; for soon, while having his third glass to exem-plify, in warmer detail.

Till ultimately, from the vapors of the fourth or fifth along the now crowded and affronting bar, he strolled forth from their damned din and took the air in an archaizing trance—forth alone, into the murmuring early-summer evening, to pace up-town for a block or two through the tender diamonds of Park Avenue twilight; eye bright enough though the fact was without anybody much now to ogle; and so, rather soon, ah well, back toward Veale's again, under his breath humming "Passacaglia with Floy-Floy" in amiablest nostalgia; and so to dinner, alone.

Eating which, he recalled other tunes now foundered in time. For example what was that great flabby Gullah's name in the Thirties that sang at supper in the Iridium Room? woman had practically no teeth, sang with her great lavender gums somehow, anyway he finished his fruits de mer (they appeared to be done with burnt pernod) humming her famous

> Settin' around in mah underclo'es
> Gettin' a piece o' yo' mind.

Probably extremely talented singer actually technically, wherever now lost or gone.

And over his tournedos recalled a nachtmusik that once upon a time had been composed explicitly for *him,* had it somewhere or other still, must have, mind's eye saw the score with absolute clarity: this hand-inked score. For that sweet creature temporarily his, what had she done but set some verses she found pleased him, as a pavan, some seventeenth-century-sounding thing, "Stay Lovely Peasant What Wild Flights Are These" — only then the mad angel had inscribed his copy "To Nicholas from his un-fled non-peasant" (a fine piece of embroilment for a wife to find, God help everybody involved!), and what if afterward she had had a final fiery tantrum at him and raged off never to return, had that love been any the less delicious an échange de deux fantaisies?

So he went on, next, to remember (it having come next) — remembered sighing one brief and tender affair with ah, how different an ending, and her last letter he still knew every sad syllable of by heart: *Darling*— *One of the conditions of maturity is that no one is free to perform heroic rescues. Adieu.*

Thus by dessert why not concede the well-fed melancholy Renaissance point then? *They flee from me that sometyme did me seke* and what man of sense (and with other resources anyhow) would call it unforeseen no matter what the lovely skittish things did or didn't adopt as behavior? including past all reason an adieu.

"When who knows what they may fancy they've set their heat-simple little pink hearts on next goddammit," he complained in mellow affection; and having sent the man for a marc concluded, "Whereas when have *I* by heaven *not* been in love with some agreeable creature or other?" and so, finally, began to laugh.

He'd ring Victoria. First thing in the morning.

And swayed off with dignity to bed.

✧

Next forenoon at a reasonable hour, then, having done the chores (bought black socks in the Grand Central area and then, being thereabouts, dropped in on a banker classmate at the Guaranty and increased his account there substantially, refusing a not only extremely civil but even warmly pressing invitation to lunch while arranging to be put up for a couple of clubs they agreed were suitable, and then dropped in on another classmate at Chase to discuss his Bank's account there and having to plead and smilingly defend a previous lunch engagement in the face of all kinds of friendly importunity, only to find himself proposed for a third club before he got away, and in short was decently treated everywhere and why not), on his way back to Veale's through the sun-flooded haze of late morning stepped into a florist's and had Melissa sent a great swaying tangled armful of city-spring flowers; and so at last, heart brimming with vernal nostalgia, even with libertine hope, rang up Mrs. Barclay after these seventeen years.

"Victoria?"

"Yes?"

"Victoria!"

"Yes who is this please?"

"This is Nicholas; Nicholas Romney."

A charming little diamond of a cry: "Oh Nicholas not you *really* not actually oh *no!*"

At that happy voice, that cascade of light and jewelled syllables, like no other woman's ever, what could the man's remembering tongue do? but utter once again, after seventeen years, as of its own seraphic volition, the opening phrases of that incantation known to the two of them alone, exordium once (ah me) to how many an undiscovered dialogue; so he breathed, "Mi vuoi sempre bene?"

And sure enough, heard the sweet antiphonal reproach (as how often, ahimè how long ago), "Nicola, Nicola. . . ."

Had any man in history ever heard a lovelier voice? He stammered, shaken with delight, "Well then *say*, dammit: mi vuoi bene?"

"Ma se te ne vogl— Oh no but really Nicholas *fancy* hearing you over a phone again, how unimaginable! I mean how unimaginably *pleasant!*" she finished rapidly, in châtelaine tones.

"Se sapessi quanto io—"

"Now Nicholas. After all *this* time after all! We should say 'Lei' anyhow, we—"

"It's timeless!"

"—shouldn't even be talking Italian, now you must tell me where you merely *are*," she ordered brightly, "why where can you be staying then, oh really what a thing!"

"You pretend you don't even remember how it goes on from there?" he accused her.

"What, Nicholas? From where? How *what* goes?"

"Angel Victoria, our 'dialogue.'"

"Oh, that. Oh."

"What comes after 'ma se te ne voglio.'"

"Nicholas, I—"

"After you've said 'se te ne voglio!' with that lovely, love-stricken music of reproach in it, remember? What I used to say next?"

"*Really Nicholas!*"

"So you do remember!" he exulted, with delighted laughter.

"Nicholas I will simply hang up!"

"You do remember, by heaven how could either of us forget!"

"Very easily indeed!" she said in a tremulous voice, "when after all one hasn't thought of any of it, even, practically, for years."

"Haven't you?"

"Now Nicholas why on earth should I!"

"But haven't you anyhow?"

"Certainly not!"

"You're a sweet married liar," he said amiably. "*I* have."

"Now Nicholas."

"By god I have!"

"Yes but never quite enough to make you ever come to see me even, *did* you Nicholas dear!"

He shouted into the phone, "Good god Victoria do you seriously pretend to think with one lovely melting melted atom of you that a single atom of me will ever forget anything about you till the day the last breath sighs out of my body?"

She said, in moved tones, "Such a rhetorical liar, oh Nicholas."

"Calling me 'Lei'! As if every nerve in my—"

"Ah Nicholas."

"You even planning to pretend you've forgotten Alassio?"

" . . . Ah Nicholas."

"And that hotel in Pisa?"

"Were we ever so frozen anywhere, oh *darling* how cold!"

"Then your damn' husband wired!" he denounced her.

" . . . I know."

"Meet him in Geneva or some such place; perfect outrage; you came running up to me across the Piazza dei Cavalieri waving the blackguard's wire—"

She murmured, stricken, "You even remember the piazza's name."

"Didn't you?"

"Oh Nicholas *yes!* But I never thought you would."

"What? Infallible geographic memory, drive you round Rome blindfold, even now."

"Like a homing pigeon, cocchiere mio," she fondly sighed, "only who was it drove us out to lunch at Frascati the noon we ended *up* at Castel Gondolfo?"

"Everything, you remember everything!" he cried out in jubilation.

"Oh Nicholas isn't it suddenly frightening, *I do!*"

So they pronounced each other's names three or four times over in accents of happy lamentation. He then groaned, "When *can* I see you my utter angel?"

"Oh *yes!*"

"No, I said 'when.'"

"What, darling?" she breathed, lost in dream.

"I said, 'I said "wh—" ' *god* Victoria when this absolute minute—"

"Ah I know!"

"Where will you meet me then my angel!"

"So sweet."

"I mean for lunch; today; now."

". . . '*Now*'!" she cried out, as abruptly awoken.

"Dinner tonight then if I have to wait till then!"

At this she uttered a little musical scream of sheer common sense.

"Now you can't inform me you're tied up!"

"Oh Nicholas *of course* we're tied up, we're having a—"

"Well then tomorrow!"

"Oh when I so long to see you it's *dementing*, why I've been tied up tomorrow for utter months!" she wailed in star-crossed despair.

"But I—"

"Why, this whole coming weekend for months!"

"Now Victoria how can you!" he expostulated in tones of the most picturesque unhappiness.

"But we're due in Concord then! You don't even know that I have a huge great fifth-former son?"

"Your *son!*" he shouted in affront.

On which she demanded with spirit whether in sixteen years, or in point of fact longer than sixteen years, a heartless expanse of time and she forbore to reckon it, he had even bothered his faithless head to inquire!

So they wrangled gently.

For she told him now she was looking in her book he could see for himself she hadn't two free minutes end to end this whole frenetic coming *week* because of his treatment of her! when what could he merely have expected? when self-evidently she was helpless if he dropped out of any casual cloud! by which time he'd just be back in that dismal Philadelphia long ago again anyhow wouldn't he?

He had therefore to explain to her in outline this vagary of his irresponsible wife's, this divorce, Mrs. Barclay uttering little arpeggios of innocence and concern in comment.

So by god she could see he had no intention whatever of returning to Philadelphia *or* his West Chester place until their lawyers had got every last parochial inequivocation signed and sealed with their interminable crimson wax. Take months. Take a year; so he had to see her at once, surely she saw?

Hadn't he even listened? she'd been telling him till she was hoarse (she cried in a voice of music) that every exhausting minute of her time was already pledged twice over for ten absolute days, when he hadn't even told her where he was putting up, where she could reach him if, because where *was* he? when she was just enmeshed!

He said at Veale's, natur—

His *impossible* self-centered unpractical demands, 'dinner tomorrow' indeed!

He instantly said teatime.

Was she to fling to the winds her every appointment? every ordered plan she'd made in her book, was he some mere savage?

Absolute Boeotian, he conceded in an ingratiating whine.

Utterly putting out everyone else for a wretched twenty minutes her soft misguided heart might just conceivably—

He gave an enraptured pealing cry.

Well she was *concerned* about him then! she cried out at him, when here he was sounding upset and lonely and she was *fond* of him, did he expect her to deny that? for *old times'* sake she was fond, also his immediately ringing her up about this mad decision of his wife's, well, she was touched, well who wouldn't be touched then! and she felt *sorry* for him so there! she more or less snapped at him in conclusion.

He said she was the uttermost of archangels.

Unless by some chance (she said in a different tone altogether) *he* were the one getting this divorce. He rather than his wife. Something she of course couldn't say, not knowing.

He said certainly not, it—

Or however it was in fact occurring, whatever had taken place, she meant; or possibly was still taking place; he not having yet given her a specific account; or details.

He said what? occur? what'd she mean?

Yes, she meant what had. The particulars.

He said but what was there to 'occur'? woman'd simply walked out on him, not literally of course because she was still there in his house packing, but—

Where was she going then?

How was he to know!

He was just letting her stay on? as she pleased?

But when he growled now what difference did it make to him or anybody how long she dilatorily dallied, *he* had her out of his hair hadn't he? Mrs. Barclay lightly made known her sheer incuriosity, he could tell her everything tomorrow if he insisted, when for fifteen minutes she would have one rushed cocktail with him at Veale's, oh what did he merely *look* like again? for she could hardly wait to see!

And so, lingeringly, and (merely think!) till so soon, till almost in fact subito, she softly said their rivedersi; and hung up.

He sat beaming at the phone.

One moderately responsible woman left to him anyhow!

And went on beaming even when, having presently rung up Melissa for no real reason, he heard her phone sound on and on in an empty room and no one answered.

Under the dazzling country-summer morning, on a hilltop bowling green set about thick with yews, Melissa's hostess and Melissa lolled by the plinth of a stone sundial and dried their hair, brushing brushing brushing, stylized little bodies ivory and gold in the immense light; brushing like young madwomen as they idly animadverted upon love.

"—adultery. Though who cares? Only Sam argues so!" the hostess was at that point complaining, of her husband, whose shorts, inside out, she was kneeling naked up in.

"Well she's insane, or d'you mean," yawned Melissa, naked too except for her own husband's, seam-out also.

"Well *admittedly* Liss, when she came right out of the grove with this boy!"

"Mm."

"In front of everybody!"

"Though even if nothing, you mean."

"Yes, after all *that* time!"

Melissa murmured "ouch, ow" to her brush, in languor. Her hostess fussed on, "Every tousled inch of her of course *looking* it."

"Mm."

"Why, it's just mindless of her."

"Yes, when *any* husband would—"

"Lissa *love*, as if she cared!"

"But dear, even not; I mean one can just hear one's mothers on how irresponsible."

"Oh but that's Sam's interminable point, oh how stuffy Melissa you are!" wailed her best friend in muffled tones, head bowed in her silky tent, brush wildly fluffing and flying.

Melissa however, her short curls dry, had risen; she was posturing absently and languishingly, as in dance. "Why of course, poor love, oh darling mmm," she agreed, humming something.

"Oh where isn't it *dry* Liss, can you see?"

"What, dearest?" she vaguely sang, this young woman having been her roommate, at one time.

"Where not *dry*."

"*Not* dry?"

"Here?"

"Where?"

"Here!"

Melissa crooned, "Where, *here?*" approaching to touch deftly the cascading gold.

"And all in under."

"Well, no, not."

"Oh Lissa *hell!*"

"*Still* wants brushed," pronounced her guest in their private bogus Pennsylvania Dutch.

"Because husbands, what a creature they are," the hostess chafed, brushing in mad anguish once more. "Because I mean everybody always calls everybody else irresponsible when who knows what it is, responsibility I mean, well goodness!"

"Mmm."

"So unfair!"

"Oh darling men," Melissa sang, "darling darling men," turning in idle dance about the dial, sleek arms tenderly flailing.

"No but such *agony*, because Liss what would he do if *I*, I mean for pure hypothesis for example, what would Sam I mean, if I went to bed with somebody just melting and I couldn't help it, oh it's all so risky and unpredictable!" she whimpered.

"Dear, mm."

"No but they're so *arbitrary*, when you think!"

Now gravely resolving in gavotte, Melissa intoned a dreamy "so anulnerous" in adenoidal.

"Oh of course who wouldn't be endlessly faithful to the great thing like a swooning thing," Sam's young wife fretted, brushing and brushing, "even married two everlasting years to him! Or anyhow nearly two; forever. Though Lissa?"

That one, however, wordlessly singing, turned and turned in the blissful day.

"Assuming merely. *Lissa!*"

"Mm?"

"Now admittedly *she* was mindless, if only fancy having herself caught like that, why as we said she *is* mad! but Liss if one were just this once on the whole *utterly* fetched, I mean by someone so— I mean what else is there but love one ever really thinks of!"

"So fond, so sad."

"Like Patrick for an example or someone madly sweetie like that, I mean d'you think? I mean for an *opinion* Lissa."

"Oh though look at them!" Melissa commanded, pirouetting to peer through the wall of yews down the green country slope at their two huge young husbands toiling in the streambed far below, in a thousand-fold flashing tessellation of aspens.

"No but *Lissa!*" her dearest friend agonized.

"How can they, oh how infantile!"

"Well they're delirious then," the hostess agreed in sheer distraction, coming up still brushing to peer too.

"How do men survive."

"Yes, when did *we* last build dams!"

"Will you merely *look!*"

"*Paddling in water!*"

They uttered little melodious screams.

"Wading!"

"When we were seven perhaps?"

"One's sweet little muddy panties sopping!"

So, swaying, hilarious, white and gold, these glossy little beauties clutched each other in helplessness, hooting at indecorous memories.

"Having in mere desperation to play half the summer with any little monster available!"

"Or Mummy inviting those perfect little *rapists* from that great moldering place beyond, so irresponsible!"

They drifted away. "Ah but Lissa think," her friend besought sadly, crouched drooping by the sundial once more, hair swaying down and aside as she brushed lovingly, indolently, on, "as to 'faithful' Liss I mean."

Melissa twisted her pretty torso in the blaze of noon, to see whether both little rocking breasts would cast their shadows, murmuring in agreement, "Hm? oh, *mm.*"

"No but *listen,*" the hostess said in her most careless tone, "because in her case it's admitted the boy wasn't married and all maddeningly involved already, but suppose he is, *both* sides of an affair I mean, assuming one were in love with some man who is. Was."

"Mm."

"Patrick as you suggested, for an example."

"What, love, who?" Melissa dreamed, a dying swan.

"If you'd only listen!" her roommate shrieked.

"Dearest, Patrick's married."

"Yes! and so what would that horrible little wife of his *do,* I mean, leave him for example or what? or might he even leave her or d'you think," she mused dreamily on, sweet head leaned aside.

"Well about *Daddy* I certainly never thought!" Melissa cried out, standing still in shock.

"No but Liss, Patrick told me once that he—"

"Or about Mummy leaving him! Well, I was beside myself, just *beside* myself!" she declaimed.

"Oh my arm is *dead!*" her hostess at once moaned, piteously writhing.

"I mean fancy Mummy having so much spirit!"

"Dearest *could* you brush? if only till my arm—"

"Why *dearest!*" soothed her guest, "why *here!* But leaving Daddy, of all possible men to want to leave! No bend *more,*" she commanded the swaying gold, beginning to brush in gently sweeping parabolas.

"Yes you said."

"Because he isn't just anyone!"

"Oh terribly sweetie, why I adore him," the roommate absently agreed, twisting her little head half off to see down her pretty back.

"*Hold still!*" shrieked Melissa.

"No but I mean Liss—"

"Dearest you do have it long, you're mad."

"But when they want it long, because what can one do with them really, one *is* helpless Lissa."

"Ptah, not compared."

"Oh how can you, when I mean here we are responsible for men when it isn't even as if we were *responsible* for them!"

"Bend *over.*"

"Thhhhfffff," fuffed the friend, little scarlet mouth now full of gold.

"Of course Mummy has no idea how to handle him."

"But when one can never quite be sure what they may do! Though what can one do in any case, Liss, ah, just drenched and drunk with a man the way one gets."

"There. Dry."

"Even when you *know* how they can be!"

"Mm."

"*So* irresponsible about us!"

"Ah, well," Melissa mourned, gazing down the slope once more at their pond-building husbands, gleaming among the aspens far below.

"Ah, they're *stones*, Liss," the hostess agreed.

As by the dark yews they clung together, slackly, in woe.

"Mad."

"This pool."

"This hysterical pool *exactly* and banking banking banking banking and who is it thinks up all the perversions."

So down they gazed in the enormous light, limply clinging, gazed and gazed, white and gold against the somber yews; swaying; spent.

" . . . but they're *huge*," the glinting little hostess whispered presently, as in nameless dread.

They gaped at their great earth-moving animals, aghast.

Or dazed, in dream.

"This light," one murmured, in ultimate languor at last, breaking listlessly away.

"Dry now."

"Dry."

"Even long, dry."

"Even long, ah why does he," Melissa's hostess grieved, of whatever he, and drifted now finally across the clipped green and on, in, toward the vast cool glass livingroom beyond.

But Melissa, glittering indolently after her in the towering light, uttered only an indecipherable cry.

✧

Mrs. Barclay being as it turned out late and Nicholas early, or as early anyway as a man in his right mind waiting for a pretty woman, he'd sat damn' near twenty minutes in Veale's unrecognizable bar, bolt-upright and presently glaring, before with a ripple of high heels in fluttered his angel in this breathless rush at last, blissfully gasping "Oh Nicholas oh simply now imagine!" as he lunged up from the banquette with a happy bellow to grab her—though this act she parried, after one radiant flash of blue eyes, by seizing and tenderly pressing his hands while uttering little winded cries of salutation and reminiscence; and having let him merely peck at one heavenly cheek eeled out of his arms to the seat, onto which she at once sank, blown.

"Now by heaven I was half-certain you weren't coming!" he cried out scrambling after her.

"............!" she panted wordlessly, batting those great eyes at him under a propitiatory hatbrim.

"When my god Victoria what an unearthly stylish lovely thing you are!"

"You're looking so *well*, Nicholas!" she replied to this.

"You've even got the sort of hat on by heaven you know makes me light-headed at the mere sight of you!"

"—and so beautifully turned out, really when can anyone have seen you looking so handsome," she ran on, flinging a spring fur neatly between them and scattering gloves and handbag about her in practiced piles.

He rumbled, "Now, an unbolted old wreck actually," much pleased.

"So tall, so imperial, *fancy* forgetting, oh why simply look at you, now you must tell me instantly how you've been Nicholas, how *are* you, oh I could lose my heart to you all over again from sheer good manners!" she cried lightly. Immediately adding, "Actually of course I bought it weeks ago," of the hat.

Adrift at this, he said, "Did, huh," signaling the waiter.

"*Long* before you rang up!"

"Unh? first person I called!"

"So you see quite plainly, even if it did, or does, happen to be your sort!"

"Now my lovely Victoria what's this now?" he demanded competently, eye on a waiter charging headlong.

"Well Nicholas *who* in her right mind! when you know as well as I do we hadn't thought of each other for d— for years," the lovely untrustworthy thing assured him, tilting down her hatbrim momentarily as a shield against the only polite answer anybody could make to this, viz., that it was a damn' lie.

The waiter here plunged up trundling a champagne-cooler asplash with frost. A heavy captain followed, and now with his thick thumbs grasped the cork, breathing through his mouth fussily. So while the fellow lengthily poured, Nicholas groaned, "Drinks with you again my utter blessed woman my god imagine it!" in the stricken accents of idolatry.

They drank. She murmured in tones of happiest misgiving, blue eyes for one melting instant deep in his, that he knew she had in twelve minutes quite literally to fly.

"Now my sweet Victoria you can't intend to go *on* like this dammit!" he burst out, "in the manner of that icy salutation? Giving me a *cheek* to kiss my god."

At this she had the sensibility to cast her eyes down, sipping.

"Ah that lovely mouth, color of pink dogwood," he droned along, as in most moving elegy, "and then to treat me in that absol—"

"After seventeen years?" she cried at him. "*Oh* how unfair!"

"'Unfair'!"

"And *upsetting* then to be meeting you again Nicholas! If you'd even thought about me enough to *see* how I must feel!"

"But my sweetest angel—"

"Am I then to dash forgivingly here there and everywhere falling into the arms of strangers in any bar they happen to name?"

"'*Strangers*'!" he bayed.

"And now you yell at me!" she breathed, absolutely shutting her pretty eyes.

So it seemed time for him to say, beginning to laugh, "Not yell, why how can I converse then?"

She pouted, sipping.

"Well, can I?"

"Oh you *wound* me so, Nicholas!" she announced through the rim of her glass, which she now drained. And as he refilled it, "When seeing you is such a— When merely meeting you again like this is—is so—"

"I just want to point out my restraint, my decorum!" he cried.

"And you *know* we have to be!"

"My blessed Victoria—"

"We do we *do!*" she wailed.

Here the captain loomed over them again, heavy jaw civilly ajar, to turn the bottle in its floes.

The moment however the fellow got around to taking himself off, Nicholas declared she *knew* he'd for days done nothing but think about her in the most heart-shaking terms; with the most eager, the most affecting anticipation; 'd hardly slept, anticipating; and now here she took it into her heavenly head to drive him distracted with expressions like 'decorum'! and in a word what sin was she pleased to assign him in the room of adoring her? he ended in his most bravura Restoration manner, draining off his glass with a smack of his lips and picking up her furs from between them to deposit the damn' things out of the way. But by this time that mouth-breather stood over them again pouring; now, sucking his thick tongue, he uttered judgments concerning this blanc de blancs, which he described as 'Heidsieck.' So they had to sit while for some time this went on.

Mrs. Barclay then at once lightly veered and began prying delicately into his divorce: how did he feel about it then, so tedious for him, she told him in well-groomed tones and gave him little shuttered glances, so distressing and putting-out of his wife, how could she!

He pronounced it in his view an insult of a not very refined sort.

"*She's in love?*"

"Now what's this," he growled.

"Well but she must be you mean naturally," Mrs. Barclay urged, fixing him with great watchful eyes.

"*My* wife?"

"Or in love with somebody you don't know?"

"Why should she be dammit, no!"

"But nobody at *all?*" the charming thing cried as if distracted.

"Ah, well, possibly some insulting second marriage soon enough, I make no doubt!" he snarled, conceding. "Ought to wring her pretty neck now, for all I know; save her from some subsequent god's-own folly. How's anyone to say what'll take your babbling undiscriminating bewildered hearts next!" he ended in exasperation, and poured again, drizzling.

"But Nicholas my dear didn't she say?"

"Say what? My point is—"

"But Nicholas she—"

"Point I'm trying to make dammit," he insisted, "is, here she was for years, a most delicious sweet creature actually, I suppose; for *years*, Victoria! Yet now this happens, and abruptly I find I have to ask myself after all was she," he said in dejection, draining off his glass.

Mrs. Barclay let fall into hers, "in love, how sad," sipping.

"*Well* then," he rumbled, deeply cast down.

"But *you* now, poor darling," she said in instant encouragement, "what have you in mind then, your *plans* Nicholas I mean," she urged him, sipping several little mouthfuls more, of which she absently sighed, " . . . delicious."

And as he said nothing, "No but your coming *here* I meant," she gently probed, and pushed her glass for him to refill yet again.

He appeared to think, pouring. "Urban type, why not," he offered, morosely.

"Because don't you remember your own epigram about New York all that time ago, is why," she explained and drank. "Ah Nicholas *so* delicious again!" she admitted, of whatever, smiling over the glass's rim into his eyes. "Spilling it, oh darling shaming," she mumbled happily, having slopped.

"Epigram, huh."

"What, darling?"

"This epigram about New York you claim I made."

"Yes you said New York was a terrible place but other places were *terrible* places."

"By god now did I?" he said, delighted.

"You found it terribly funny," she murmured, little nose dreamily in her glass once more.

"And you remembered it, my angel!"

"Well you kept using it for weeks; so sweet, oh Nicholas."

"But anyhow naturally I came here, d'you maintain you've had for one seraphic second to wrack your brain wondering why?"

"Ah Nicholas."

"My sweetest Victoria as if you didn't—"

"I *never* think about you!" she cried out tearfully.

"Now you're not pretending you hadn't even thought about me coming here to meet me!"

"Oh what mad egotism! while I was *shopping?*"

"Well so then you did though!"

"Well how childish, well of course why wouldn't I or anybody?" she told him crossly.

"And made this unnerving decision to maneuver me into merely kissing your cheek by heaven!"

" 'Decide,' " she quoted with heat, " 'decide,' as if one 'decided' on the only natural normal— Nicholas!" she hissed in sudden outrage, for the waiter had swooped in rolling a second wine-cooler to set beside the first, the captain following with his catarrh to twist out the cork and meatily pour.

At this piece of foresight, the moment they withdrew Mrs. Barclay organized a scene. "Your preparations!" she blazed.

"Of course now the fellow's an imbecile dammit! All I—"

"*Two bottles!* as if I were—"

"Now Victoria it simply struck me, 'd strike anybody, one bottle's a mere couple of glasses."

"Oh what an utter staring lie, a sheer dozen!"

"Two glasses apiece at the outs—"

"A *dozen!*" she as good as screamed at him. "Call back that smirking waiter and see then!" she commanded smoldering, "oh how can you be so carelessly unfeeling to me!"

"'Careless'!" he cried, in tones of one reeling.

"So impervious to how you upset me, *ask* him how many glasses in a bottle, ask that snuffing ox of a captain, oh how selfish you are!" she rebuked him, draining off her glass.

So he had to summon the man back.

"Now Mr. Romney's agreed you shall settle a bet for us," she cooed at him, explaining what—the fellow wheezing, "ah, precise, madam, aha," and the like.

"Simply how many glasses in a bottle d'you figure on normally then," Nicholas demanded.

"Is a metter call for nize judgment, sair."

"I mean by and large dammit."

"A tremendous number, I'm persuaded," Mrs. Barclay serenely proclaimed.

"Allows a mostly seven, madam."

"You see?" she crowed happily at Nicholas.

"I said there weren't anything like a doz—"

"You said four, *four*, whereas this man who has to pour cases and cases every day in mere line of duty said seven as you heard as a minimum," she explained to him in tones of charm.

"If you call a three-ounce restaurant glass—"

"I suppose you'll pretend to me you'd think nothing of draining off four three-ounce glasses of Martinis then!"

He shouted "Now by god you know I won't have a Martini in the house! As seventeen years ago you were perfectly well aware!"

"You not only yell at me," she at once charged in a low quivering voice, "and are as unkind and purposely intransigent as you know how but you pretend I've forgotten your stuffy prejudiced habits too!"

On this he instantly pounced. "And so you *have* forgotten, and boast of it!" he happily proclaimed.

Mrs. Barclay, not having quite seen this coming, sat with her lovely mouth ajar.

"Heartlessly and unfeelingly forgotten!" he ran on, eyes alight, "whereas not one single thing you ever did with me has left my mind for a day, not one sweet word you ever said, Victoria, not a day or night I swear to you in all this endless gloom of time!"

She glared in miserable silence.

"Why, you've even forgotten what you swore that last night at— *Have* you forgotten?"

"I won't tell you," she sniffled, nose in her glass.

"When I'd waited half that afternoon in the Via del Babuino—"

"I didn't mean to make you wait!" she cried in remorse.

"You came racing toward me through the traffic, every man in sight staring his heart out at the mere lovely glimpse of you!"

"You were teaching me to drink those horrible Roman drinks. And now you bring me here and abuse me about champagne," she accused him in melting tones, sadly draining her glass.

"My lovely Victoria, as if you didn't know I'm as wild over you this minute, no matter what damn' wrangle, as I was the last instant I had you in my arms."

(Which phrase simultaneously and at once recalled to them that this had occurred, to specify, in a huge Roman cinquecento bedroom, early in a summer dawn, in a bed littered with the fragrant though by then ruined petals of three or four dozen gardenias.)

". . . so spoiled, such an actual child," she said dolefully.

" 'Spoiled'! when your very kiss of greeting—"

"When I indulge you so, ah when I do everything you want and I shouldn't; why here I am *meeting* you!"

"And you never meet anybody for a drink? you lovely transparent— Just meeting me for a simple drink you feel adulterous, do you, you heavenly thing!" he told her, in rapture, pouring once more.

"*Nicholas!*"

"Then by god what did that angel's remark mean?"

"I won't tell you!"

"You sweet guilty—"

"Oh how *irresponsible* you are!" she screamed at him, pink with exasperation.

And so on and so on. As they went on down into the second cool delicious bottle.

The conversation becoming still less worth setting even ceremonially down.

So next morning she had to ring him up in bland complaisance to have him know it had been so agreeable to see him that could he imagine what she'd forgotten to tell him? the one thing she'd meant to say to him, too! it had just skidded out of her mind utterly, she urbanely informed him, and it had been almost her main reason for meeting him as she had, only fancy!

Viz., why couldn't she lend him a man for his little Barrow Street house if that was where he was going to be for a time—look after him, or till he'd hired one for himself, this man happening she said to serve as chef on her chef's days out though bred for a valet, so it took care of everything. For why for one unlikely moment think that he (Nicholas) could put up with staying at Veale's when as he well knew hotels just upset him, they had ways of doing things he wasn't used to and he had tantrums, even at Veale's, so she wanted to lend him this *excellent* man. So then he could move in practically at once then, did he see? into his charming small empty house in Barrow Street as soon as he pleased, with its little oval Adam stair and she remembered *tiny* elegant low-ceilinged rooms, fancy a Philadelphia family's having these eighteenth-century properties in New York, how unexpected.

(There being however nothing remarkable about this—a great-grandmother of Nicholas's had simply been this New York heiress et voilà—what Mrs. Barclay presumably meant instead was that she forbade all mention of a folly she now so wholly repented of that she did not even remember it, namely how she'd made love with him in nearly every room in the place at one time and another, even, as he well knew also, on the elegant stair.)

So, he could shortly move in; and did.

To find nothing changed, moreover everything in good condition, though by some madness of apparently Melissa's (who'd lived there the first year she was married) the Copley ancestor over the fireplace in the front drawing-room had been lugged off to the garret and in its place there hung, of all possible portraits, that damn' painter's *Early Prospect of Mrs. Hume* or whatever title he'd assigned it. So this had to be carried up to the garret and the Copley fetched down again and hung.

And he himself unpacked (while Victoria's man was unpacking him) a manila folder of assorted private relics, which he stowed one by one in the upstairs scrutoire—an engraved *William and Priscilla Neave desire thy presence at the wedding of* a girl who in due course became his mother; an old New Year's card written out in a college roommate's easy scrawl "with every warmest platitude of the season"

> Well, Nick boy? Both of us alive,
> Another year receipted.
> Here's luck—in 1955,
> Almighty God, we'll need it!

—kept not for luck, God knows, the poor devil having been shot dead in Walnut Street hardly a month after writing the thing, by some crazed Camden shipwright who mistook him for somebody he thought was keeping his daughter, never really cleared up who; an enlarged snapshot of two baby boys and two sub-adolescent girls (Melissa mugging) with a dog named Dirdy Giotto, now dead; and then suddenly here was his tall charming young wife years ago, her eyes looking lovingly straight at him, faintly smiling. So he stared at this for some time.

Still, when presently he went down to where in the back drawing-room that gave on the garden the man had the evening champagne iced and ready and an evening tabloid in (headlined SEX SHILL CZAR PROBE FIX HIT) and sat sipping till dinner, musing on Victoria he felt better, in fact went down to dinner murmuring be damned if for all he could tell he'd been relieved of the endearing fatigues of one of the sweet creatures only to have the vaporings of another imposed.

For the place was how agreeably haunted again! and after dinner he rang her up to move her by telling her so, meaning also to report that the guinea-with-gin she'd had her man serve him (now imagine her remembering of all his dishes that one!) had been admirably cooked, he'd had a Clos de Vougeot with it, and then the fellow's poires dorées, cool and fragrant and all the more so from *her* having ordered it all for him, she was as womanly sweet as she was sexually delicious did she know that? so he'd taken his coffee and marc out into the little brick-walled garden in this early-June night so full of her *and* her dinner that he could hardly wait to hear her angelic accents over the wire.

Except when some confounded domestic answered by god she wasn't even in!

Nor what's more had left word when she might be!

So will you credit it? he had to put in the evening planning his house-warming himself, lists lists lists, endless goddam roster of his friends, names and faces and matching them up and with not even secretarial womanly help sorting out memory.

So, he borrowed a couple of Victoria's maids too and asked enough people after these twenty years to pack his little house to the walls, couldn't have been more agreeably nostalgic, might have been the Thirties all over again, rooms jammed and milling, uproar deafening, guests in no time overflowing in clamoring waves out over the flagstones and turf of the garden and down into the little dining-room, sitting gabbling on the stairs, even racketing up into the bedroom and the writing-room behind it—bankers brokers New York classmates amiably baying at him across the din in welcoming and heart-warming quantity, wives offering a cheek to his kiss, a few even putting up a smiling mouth in undeceived reminiscence, even the usual number of people he damn' well disliked; also his lawyer up from Philadelphia with his bulging briefcase, the sheer tax-maneuvering his wife's behavior had now got him into! his own cursing yeoman forebears hadn't been amerced with a blacker set of reliefs and merchets, church-scot and plough-alms and smoke-farthings and hearthpenny on Holy Thursday, and nowadays who could he tallage in return? and of course Melissa.

Who fled in darting glances of piercing young appraisal at everything as she proclaimed, "Sweetie, champaginny and all, well how *coo*," absently presenting her angel cheek.

Which he kissed, grumbling happily, "Now what's this, afraid I'll muss you dammit?"

"Well *Daddy*."

"Tirée à quatre épingles like that," he beamed.

But she cried, "Why, you've changed everything, now who's *that?*" of the Copley ancestor; though what difference who? she hadn't had a notion who Angelina's portrait had been of either.

Also several New York nieces and nephews he had recalled he had and a young cousin or two. And to keep that generation at least amused he'd told Melissa ask some of her friends if she liked, why not (husband too of course if the fellow could forget his bank long enough); also Victoria had her stepson, son of her husband by a first marriage, name of Toby or something of the sort, who it appeared might well bring a girl he was in a daze at (a little actress, rather sweet and mad, Victoria said). So in a word he'd asked pretty much everybody, even children. Though not his sons, they having final exams.

Everybody crying out with indulgent urbanity how wonderful again, how well he looked and what a jewel-box of a little house lost way down here, how had they ever forgotten how it enchanted them, this small elegant eighteenth-century house he had, these tiny charming rooms, this heavenly stair, bawling at him across the commemorating pandemonium how particularly fine *now* when everyone was pulling down everything everywhere, demolishing demolishing, the Brevoort rubble the Meadowbrook a scavo, why was there nothing anyone could do? though they demanded what could anyone *do!* when if wishes were horses (had he heard this one?) if wishes were horses we'd have a population of centaurs.

Also what were his plans, as a corollary would he perhaps now live way down here? this part of the Village having after all, since the Thirties, changed.

So it took time before he got in two words edgewise with his Victoria by backing her for a happy moment into the curve of the piano, on which some drunken couple he'd never seen in his life were accompanying themselves in what sounded like

Se amor non è, che dunque è quel ch'io sento

—this-can't-be-love but probably turn out to be Petrarch he roared in her ear and he *loved* her, would she for once get it through her stylish head how he adored her? because *god* what a lovely thing she was and why in His bellowing name had he ever invited these crashing intruding people that kept her from walking into his arms that instant, for had she any notion how frightful it was? because how could she!

She however as if conducting this at some undisingenuous pace had already begun to tell him she'd been thinking about what he'd not really said, had he; of their conversation the other day, she meant; she meant at Veale's.

He said said what.

Couldn't he pay even passing attention? said *why*. This divorce she wanted; why she wanted it; his wife. After all these years why of all moments this one!

Did he have to keep saying and then saying again? she had not said! Which was one reason that final infamous interview—

But surely no matter what he might evasively or even guiltily say in denial he must nevertheless know! She must have had some reason, possibly some very *good* reason, oh what had he contrived to spill on his waistcoat now? she cried in pique, scrubbing at it, or was the hideous truth (which he dared not admit to her) simply that he'd made love to one other woman more than his wife's nerves could finally stand! she finished in a passion.

But as he was about to reply in amazed innocence the drunks from the piano bench joined them. So then they all had to converse in halting Italian for some minutes, the man of this couple turning out to the universal surprise to be a classmate who'd roomed in the same entry of '79 Hall.

Until some courtly ox joined them proclaiming (in English) what a hell of a fine little house this was, had he lived here all these years by god? made him think of what's-his-name's over in East 10th, astonishing how similar, what *was* the poor devil's name, knew it as well as he knew his own, everybody knew him, knew about him anyhow, used to rent a handsome baby to wheel round Washington Square as a conversation-starter, they remember? used to say he was its uncle! Or its grandfather, depended on how he assessed the temperament of whatever pretty little piece he was engaged in picking up; *dead* now, of a thundering heart attack not six months before, poor charming lecherous old devil, 'change and decay on ev'ry hand descry,' however it went whatever it was; who'd expect the law of averages applied to the upper classes!

After this threnody he and the drunken Petrarchians rambled off. Nicholas instantly resumed, demanding of Mrs. Barclay with amazed innocence other women other women must she like a pervicacious angel think that because he loved her with every beat of his heart, loved and had loved, as she herself well remembered and in this house should remember best of all—

Mrs. Barclay regretted seeing that he still had the discreditable habit of avoiding a review of his conduct by reminding her of flaws in her own! because she had simply been *very young* then, then when she'd loved him, young and as he was well aware infatuated, what did one know of one's emotional responsibilities at that age? what *could* one know!

He said but—

And what arguments could *he* marshal of innocence and youth, then or now, what pretext of a heart's sweet first love, in the sheer rake's progress of his protestations! she cried at him through the hubbub around them, driving his wife too she had no doubt at long-suffering last to such despair!

But as he was replying with tenderest raillery now what ever gave woman the notion that she was monogamous, here came a ponderous old dandy to kiss Mrs. Barclay's hand, describing to her what a happy assault on his peace of mind the mere sight of her was! thank God the convulsing of man's equanimity still constituted female comportment, and then in turn describing to Nicholas how damn' heartening to see a man in his own establishment for once, would he conceive the Club nowadays couldn't even set out a routine breakfast? porridge thin and they pretended they'd never heard of Demarara sugar, the buttered eggs weren't buttered but *scrambled* in God's name! a catalogue of barbarism he'd not offend Mrs. Barclay's lovely ear by reciting further. Would they tell him what had become of the ordinary decencies? with nothing left but a new outrage daily to add to the series of indignant bellows with which thank God he still greeted reality!

So Nicholas had to say yes by god take an ordinary interest in what food one ate and what resulted? his own children denominated him a pig! and Victoria said snappishly there at *last* was her never-on-time young mountain of a stepson, had he never met Nicholas's Melissa? because she must see he did instantly! and was off.

So the old boy demanded of Nicholas who were all these children? by god they baffled him, this generation, they appeared to think sex was a branch of psychotherapy. Now his and Nicholas's generation—well, take a leathery cousin of his own who when divorced had set up this showgirl in a little flat, perfectly normal showgirl, tendency to go to bed with outfielders; but all the same—

Here however a huge handsome white-haired classmate flung himself jovially upon them, one great ape's arm round each, to beg in a whooping and waggish stage whisper don't stop him *now* goddammit, his ear had just this moment picked up across the din a sound it had been delightedly attuned to catching lo these many years, the hunting cry of a pretty woman who'd suddenly realized how *much* her damn' husband bored her—the angel promise of which music he for one could hear over the braying of a party mob four times the size of this one and would they in God's happy name not delay him till some low lecher got to her first? so off he caromed in that direction. And Nicholas at once in another, it being high time he worked his way down to the kitchen to see to supplies.

So that was where he was, leaning against a counter and having this peripatetic extra glass of champagne to himself in momentary peace for once (nothing *against* his friends and contemporaries of course but they poured champagne down as if they took it for gin, by heaven)—the kitchen was where he was, pouring himself still another glass in fact, when speaking of the younger generation the door swung gently open and closed again, and in had stepped this beautiful child.

Who came softly up to him and stood smiling into his eyes as if she not just worshipped him but meekly owned him, and said in a voice like a lovely bell, "Ah, I knew I'd meet you again, some day somehow Nicholas, if I only waited and oh, so hoped."

And there he was, dazzled.

Mind utterly ajar.

"You don't even *remember* me!" she cried, instantly pink.

He managed to get out what on earth'd she mean? not remember, why good god!

"You don't remember my name even!" she upbraided him, a great topaz tear trembling in either eye. "Whereas I remember every time I was even in miles of West Chester!"

From some desperate mineshaft of recollection he came up with a what nonsense her name was Morgan, *Morgan*, and she'd permit him to add as pretty as a—

"Well when after all Nicholas I was at your house that whole weekend at your own daughter's house party, I mean who could be so stupid," she demanded as if reasonably. "Though of course she says it's Melissa you pay all the attention to."

So thus he was able to assure her in heartiest tones why certainly! why, she'd been at some acting school or other over on the Main Line then hadn't she; or wait, she'd been about to play Ophelia in some off-Broadway art loft at the time, anyhow Juliet perhaps or some equally star-crossed but unhelpless ingénue, he beamed.

"Well there was also something else that weekend you might be nice enough to me to remember too Nicholas if you weren't so puritanical and formal," she complained serenely, casting down her eyes. "Except I bet you don't even think I should call you by your first name even, do you! when what would you *expect* me to call you? when of course I always call you Nicholas to myself, how else could I even think about you!"

He started to remark, well, he imagined that if that obsolete noun punctilio were to be observed—

But she was murmuring with a sweet look at him, "I don't suppose it ever crosses your mind that I think about you even more than I think about myself, oh people are such *mysteries* to each other, Nicholas," she confided, while with his courtliest air he made to fill her glass. "No one ever suspects what I really think inside! Except once in one's life one can meet this one person one wants to know one's whole secret mystery—and I don't see why you won't just *admit* when it is you, my dearest!" she finished in a sudden little fury.

He gaped out a what?! now what on earth was she—

"Well, we women are simply *helpless* then sometimes in our dealings with you, why can't you see!" she fumed as if explaining, stamping her little foot. "Oh but I forgive you anyhow though Nicholas," she went on happily, "because after all that weekend, well of course I was just too young and inexperienced to work on you wasn't I, oh if I'd known then what I know now oh think what I could have made you do! It was a whole year ago, well I was simply young and *infatuated* if you insist on knowing."

He said, looking at her pretty warily, now now now now, she wasn't forgetting the way her whole charming sex tended to operate, was she? and when all a man might be doing was his poor reeling best!

And before she could decipher this, he a bit too rapidly cantered on: why, just try persuading some heavenly creature you adored her, would she consent to listen accurately to the honest pounding of your heart? on the contrary she flounced and turned her back on you and pouted that you didn't *really* love her (mind you, the poor stricken devil expiring of love right there under her elegant little nose!) didn't really *love* her, you didn't you didn't you only wanted to get into bed with her and why was she ever born! yes, and before you could summon the wits to combat this heartless libel the lovely thing would moan, 'Because you *do* want to go to bed with me don't you?' and when you stammered out good-god-*yes*, what did she do but shriek *'You see?'* and burst into tears!

So she looked at him with shining eyes.

So then he more or less unavoidably had to pat her shoulder assuasively, smiling down.

After what may have been a long moment therefore the child drooped her lashes at him, softly saying, "Well you ought to be able to *see*, Nicholas, that you're so darling to me so much of the time that when you're mean to me what could I be but furious."

He said now now.

But she went on, lower still, "Ah, couldn't you be kind enough to me just this once to admit you remember what you know did happen that weekend, any of it?" And now not looking at him, in fact sinking against him sighing, she whispered as if, ah, undone, "Even that one lovely kiss, my dearest?"

So what was the great gruff man to do?

—Except that almost before he could utter some croaked reply this sudden little suppliant of his was out of his arms again and standing there before him in instantaneous composure. As the door opened; and not unnaturally at all, there was Mrs. Barclay.

Who at once, or nearly at once, exclaimed in a wholesome voice, "So *here's* where you are, my dear d'you know your young man's been hunting high and low for you this good half-hour? This child has bewitched my stepson, or can you wonder!" she cried at Nicholas. "Now Morgan dear you know how he gets to *be*, he goes along quite capably but then suddenly it comes to him he's hungry! so hadn't you better cope? The huge thing, he's a j.g. already, Nicholas, fancy! or did you even realize his mother was that sister of Angelina Hume's?—somebody I'm sorry to say Mr. Romney imagined he was particularly fetched by at one time," she explained in tones of womanly forbearance, to Morgan, smiling at these bygone foibles, for how immature.

So Morgan smoothly chatted, yes *poor* Toby, taking her to dinner when she'd told him what could she do but feed and imperatively *fly?* with studio rehearsals at the hour they were! even just when he had his first leave in so long. Whereupon in he lumbered beaming and bore his little actress away.

Mrs. Barclay at once said in a different tone altogether now please might she ask to have a drop more champagne in a glass he seemed unaware had been empty she had no notion how long, his attention having been elsewhere? in fact what exactly *had* he conceived he was doing all this time! Or did he even know? she demanded in disdain.

He said, stunned, 'doing'? she mean here? canvassing supplies in his own kitchen?

Oh how convenient it must be not to recognize criticism when he heard it! A man of his age! And when this hardly stable girl— Why, even if no other impediment, even if no early misconduct of his, marriage with Toby would make her Angelina's niece!

He stammered what? completely at sea.

She said violently what did he *mean* 'what'!!

Why, he begged her, was she suggesting— What *was* she suggesting?

He had the effrontery to pretend he didn't *know*?

But what possible implication of consanguinity— Even if it were possible it would be an *impossible* thing! when there hadn't been a shadow of— And in any case, why, dammit, the girl had no more than just come into the kitchen! the plain inhospitable fact being moreover that he hadn't known the little thing from Eve!

Then why was he kissing her in a kitchen!

He cried by god he'd done no such thing! this much being the simple truth anyhow.

Was he then saying in addition to every other slur that she lacked the most elementary powers of observation? Though what had she ever had from him but one mistruth after another! Or had he forgotten his ignoble epigram: 'A man lies to women because they won't know what to believe if he doesn't'! she quoted, pale with rage, and for all she knew he did have that affair with the unhappy boy's mother too!

He implored her—

In fact the *real* question was not whether Toby might be his own huge innocent son but whether she, Victoria, ought ever to speak to him again at all! she raved.

And fled the very sight of him.

—This, mind you, when he hadn't done one damn' thing! Had merely stood there! In ordinary civilized good manners! And the boy didn't in the least look like him anyway.

Past all expectation, then, after the party, his rooms empty now and echoing, servants gone, he stalked through his deserted house pretty down in the mouth, pretty *glum* if you want a word! baring his teeth at that boiled mutton of a Copley, a goddam bleached Puritan and no conceivable ancestor for a man who liked pretty women.

Or stood, too, for a time, at one of the tall front windows staring in irresolution out into the luminous city night (how charged with memory); or again, drifted back once more, to touch the empty curve of the piano with his remembering hand.

And in this dim hallway too she had so often stood! this scrolled and gilded glass had held her image in its blackening depths; why, it was here she had fought him laughing that day he bought her the Hindu nose-jewel and pinioned her struggling and gently slipped it on (which with little salvoes of apologetic kisses she had at once slipped off, and never worn again); at this stair-foot too she had once stood weeping in his arms. And up the interlacing ovals of the stair, the half-landing with its clasped and happy ghosts (they'd all but rolled down), and so on up, in emptiness, in desolation, until here was the very room, the rosewood field-bed with its vased turnings, sheet laid smoothly back in its waiting triangle — *here*, where once he'd woken and found her, lapped in the first early warm-ivory light, hand held high in the dawn-rose shadows at the end of that Botticelli arm, staring as if unseeing at the dull gold of her husband's ring. So he stood at that room's windows too; looking out in *rebuke*, by heaven! growling despondently his Ovidian tag (hic fuit, hic cubuit, however the thing went); and so, out, finally, sighing, alone, into the unobliterating night.

For there too, as he wandered east along 10th Street, in which house had it been, between Sixth Avenue and Fifth? behind the French windows with their fine ironwork filigree, that he and a girl in a fluttery jonquil-colored summer dress, in the amiable din of an all-night party, or anyhow in the moonless garden behind — But what had even been her name? and perhaps hadn't it happened over east of Fifth Avenue anyhow? at that advertising classmate's with a dyke of a wife?

—But in God's name *where was the Brevoort?* A hoarding screened the site; wreckers' hooded and implacable engines lay moored at the nighted curb.

Pulling it down! *Gone!*

In the violet air the gutted brick cellars gaped, the roofless walls reeled and fell ("Pompeii!" he cried hollowly aloud) amid a litter of stucco-duro medallions and tumbled capstones, the sprawling plinths of rubble in an ordered Palatine desolation. "And to make room for *what* supererogatory forty-story glass slum," he said at last, turning heavily (and now, forever) away: terrasse dark, sidewalk tables gone, an outrage, an ultimate outrage, not just to him but to a whole geography of human recollection, memories by the tens of thousands, of honorable established people who wanted a gleaming properly laid table and good food well served and some delicious creature or other to have dinner with on a fine early-summer evening as the lights came on in the baldachin of dusk and the nightfall murmur of traffic died slowly away uptown along the Avenue and down into Washington Square, this very Brevoort moreover where he and his Victoria had met for lunch that first fatal and enchanted rendezvous, the mere second time they'd ever laid eyes on each other, ah God what a prelude to what an afternoon and a lifetime! her poise the glossiest finishing-school cloisonné as he paid off her taxi but her eyes overflowing with light at him before she'd even sipped her vermouth cassis, full of happy terror by the entree and ah, by dessert hardly able to look at him, the lovely undefended undefendable angel! and God knows he himself hardly able to breathe! in the sunlit delirium of youth both of them, shaken and dizzy at the sheer miracle of each other—until at last over their brandy her eyes opening to him radiant and amorous, and as if she would never look away from him again.

And now that tender ghost vanished; lost; the toppling wreckage untenanted and menacing before him; and here ahead (in the most piteous possible phrasing) stretched out empty the long night-reaches of the soul.

So he stumped home to bed.

Homesick for his woods too by heaven, in this impalpable night; his ancient beeches, or in his parks of oak the wild azalea now, the dogwood, still in flower; and up the darkening lawns of that irrecoverable past his silly charming children scampering shrieking; lost they too; done with him; gone. So he poured himself a marc in lieu of nightcap and the hell with what it did to his liver, and went moodily to bed.

Where he then lay tossing in the dark, snarling.

For what could anybody maintain he'd done to this unaccountable wife of his? when he'd done nothing! *Literally* nothing and what fault might be lay at her door not his!

Or if change his character, what change? Moreover what change could she or anybody expect of a man of fifty? Or as good as.

How did a lifetime of decent-minded experience prepare a man for being flat deserted? And why *now?* for what was he the day she'd coldly said good-bye to him that he hadn't been every day for decades, what had he done? Or not done? Or had a man's behavior toward woman anything at all to do, finally, with whether she fluttered into his astounded arms or, conversely, out of them.

So he flumped, sleepless.

All these years and then suddenly a woman not there anymore! Years of the most conspicuous and patient Responsibility, too, if that was the argument! And admittedly a man who liked women had to put up with being responsible about them in some degree. Though responsible responsible, in what sense responsible goddammit? aside from treating them with a cushiony consideration.

"And how's anybody know!" he burst out at last, snapping on the bedside light, glaring, "with mankind for all I can tell not responsible just involved—hopeless from start to finish," he railed, and flung on his dressing gown. "What if there's no fault then, tell me that, none on either side, hers or mine, poor creature, poor sweet creature, what then? with for all I know all love a flow, a flux, a phase, an end," he droned dispiritedly and rhetorically on, shuffling out and to the stair.

And muttering "—talking to myself like a goddam great-aunt" padded down for another marc.

Which might have put him to sleep except that at two in the morning his senior son rang him up.

He roared in utter affront, "Now God *damn* it Nickie you aware what *hour* this is?!"

" . . ."

"You *what?*"

" . . ."

"What's that hellish racket, where the deafening hell are you anyway!"

" . . ."

"Some fetid dive in short!"

" . . ."

"*Damn* what the swine play, foul dive like any other!"

" . . ."

"In any case I was given to understand you were off at Poughkeepsie, what the devil are you rutting around after some mincing girl for when as I understood it by god haven't you got exams?"

" . . ."

"*Told* me you were in Poughkeepsie."

" . . . "

"One of that stampeding horde you room with, how do I know which?"

" . . . "

"Oh but *she* had an exam! now how damn' insensible of her! in a word though you had to *go* all the way to Poughkeepsie to discover they give exams at this time of the year too?"

" . . . "

"Yes but if you don't have her with you why in God's nightlong name aren't you down at Princeton studying yourself?"

" . . . "

"*Who* instead?"

" . . . "

"How do I know their names, describe her. Is this that stylish little Goucher—"

" . . . "

"Had an exam *too*, yes I do see! So with the most fertile masculine resourcefulness you've conjured up still a third young woman to share this pandemonium you're phoning from."

" . . . "

"Well, 'fourth' then; a fourth."

" . . . "

"But in the medieval monastic phrase how many of these little angels do you conceive you're balancing on the point of a needle simultaneously?"

" . . . "

"I said, how many damn' girls are you responsible for at the moment, what d'ye think I said!"

" . . . "

"Well, *ir*responsible for then. Involved with."

" . . . "

"No but I mean it's all very well to collect young women in this flattering quantity, even in variety Nickie, couldn't *be* a more fashionable pastime I know and I do sympathize, if not a rake why else born? undergraduate myself once let me remind you! And heaven defend us from a mere parochial taste in women anyhow. Nevertheless, Nickie, has it, uh, never struck you—"

" . . . "

"Well *obviously* my dear boy they're there to be made love to within selected limits but you can't have the Boeotian insensibility to imagine that that's all!"

"
. . . "

"A limit I naturally mean to the extent a man feels free to be-
muse what may in fact be a, huh, be a very tender and uncertain
little heart dammit!"

"
. . . "

"Now don't talk like a *child* Nickie!"

"
. . . "

"Look here dammit just *correct* this attitude of yours a little in
the direction of reason and good manners will you! I don't propose
to be rung up at three in the morning to be instructed in the defects of my judgment, fondness for you or no fondness!"

And hung *up*, by god! And sat fuming.

Presently, yawning, he went down to the kitchen in the back
basement and rummaged in sheer parental exasperation in the ice-
box and sliced a few slivers from a ham. With four eggs in a little
parsley omelette he made to go with it. Also a bowl of porridge the
man had quite properly made overnight in advance. Sampled a
couple of jars of jam, too, on some leftover croissants; and a peach
and a slice of melon, the melon not very good so he got rid of the
taste with two more peaches. Last him anyhow till breakfast.

The day after this, Melissa and Melissa's dearest friend met up-
town at their charity, doing thankless Lists.

Hours long, a soft gabble, musing, as in Arcadia, choral turn
and turn.

Melissa chanting, "—this simple black Moygashell-linen
sheath with horizontal tucking at the yoke with I think a box jacket
though she had it over her arm so who could tell? with that Aztec-
ish embroidery, and the *hat* one of those little cones of straw and
lattice veiling, so how would you decide?" of Mrs. Barclay.

"Except as you said she did seem to know your father terribly
well."

"An old family friend? when why not, well goodness!"

"So what d'you think then, in practice," the friend said, yawning in her little white swan throat.

"Dear love generation-wise I just *said*, she's Toby's father's second wife or whatever."

"Lissa *love*, what I meant was—"

"No but what I *meant* was, she said to me the thing was his immediate practical plans, where otherwise was he merely to stay

poor old spoiled darling until he was even half-settled? so she'd sent her man who's this very good cook."

"But dearest turning over her whole butler or whoever to him like this?"

"Because she said it *upset* her to think of his trying to exist in hotels when their sheer service if nothing else would just start him yelling, as I must know."

"So then she knew him then obviously as I said!"

"Hm?"

"Will you *listen?*" her friend shrilled.

"What, dear?"

"Oh this years-ago affair they *must* have had, oh Lissa why can't you ever listen! when what other possible expl—"

"With *Daddy?*" Melissa hooted. "Dear you *are* mad!"

"No but—"

"Why, there was *just nothing* in her manner!"

"Well sweet ninny of course not in *hers!*"

"Now dear tell me what else Daddy's *ordinary* social manner is normally! I mean he goes on as if any woman he met were some lovely portrait to beam at or whatever."

"Oh their entire generation's simply too goa— too gallant for words, well admittedly," the friend babbled absently, squinting her lovely eyes to read her watch, at which she then muttered in anxiety, "—must *go.*"

"Anyway she's not even near his age," Melissa announced.

"But everybody can't invariably have said no even in those days! in principle one's parents can have had these just dozens of affairs Lissa. Or do you think. Of course with their *contemporaries.*"

"Twenty years ago?"

"So hard you mean to tell about customs then, well, mm."

"Why, she can't be even forty; dear I was amazed."

"So then he'll marry again anyhow you think."

"*My father?!*"

"Ptah Liss they all do."

" 'Always do,' why how can you know possibly, oh hideous!" she chattered, wild.

"Usually some sheerest bitch too," her worldliest friend told her.

"Why how can he!"

"Well Liss he *is* very good-looking. I mean in a distinguished way."

"Ah but then so darling, so just charming," that one mourned, bereft. "And when he does adore home so, poor wandering old love," she cried, as if wretched, "his precious box maze and his endless spreading green gloom of a beechwood and the old smokehouse we even *use*, dear can you imagine!"

"Though what will he do, I mean Liss in your view his plans. Because possibly you'd thought of taking a hand or d'you think."

"You can't mean *run* him!"

"Not 'run,' heaven! but this Mrs. —"

"Run *Daddy?*" Melissa shrieked, in loving derision. "Or even hang over him like some groaning Greek chorus, chanting and admonishing, dearest you're unhinged!"

"Well, yes, *parents.*"

"Though with Mummy deserting him admittedly I am involved; responsible even, if one has to use the word."

"Sam does, oh I could scream," his young wife whimpered, peering at her watch.

"Because I have to suggest things he can fill up his time with. Or just now anyway. For example I suggested why didn't he write his memoirs. Then I've been thinking of having him take Morgan out or whatever."

"*Your father?*"

"Sweetie she came to me frantic! you know how she is, so beset, if she goes out with the same boy three times in a row she *has* to break the sequence with a date with somebody else or it's terribly anti-magic for her, yet she isn't allowed to *refuse* the three-times one if he asks for a fourth date first. So she's defenseless."

"Yes why can't she have sensible magics like anybody? oh she's unstrung."

"Dearest she's *oral*-level, she says there has to be this genuine other date so she can *genuinely* refuse the three-times boy, so in consequence she's always frenziedly plotting after the second date with anyone because on the third they think the fourth's just automatic. So when she came to me half out of her mind with Toby absolutely *looming* and begged me to make Daddy ask her out even for cocktails—well, after all, my own sister's roommate, dear! and when obviously it would also fill out an evening for him, or d'you think?"

"Mm."

"He *loves* ordering meals and being exigent."

"Well dear I think you're heroic."

"Well admittedly he does have these rather serious debit sides, poor old at-loose-ends darling, he *yells* so and then every woman in sight leering hopingly at him since I was an infant in arms, just disgusting!"

"Oh, their manners, Liss."

"While uninterruptedly lecturing us on ours!"

"And *going on* so about sex and all right in front of one for years, so boasty!"

"So unfeeling!"

"Of course what else *is* there to think of really. But still, so irresponsible! and when one couldn't compete! Or wasn't supposed to, oh I despaired."

"Only what can Mummy think she'll even find, compared I mean!" the indignant daughter burst out.

"Well Liss at that age."

"Why, Daddy was so *amusing* merely! Simply his epigrams, for example now *wait*, I learned it by heart, his most-polished-ever he called it: 'I have spent my life making epigrams that apply to women and I have never yet found a woman they apply to' and he was *only twenty* when he thought it up!"

"Ah what must simply go on in their heads about us, practically," the friend let helplessly fall. "Why just *unsettling!*" she moaned.

"Why, twenty's what my mere baby brother is!"

"Nickie's twenty?"

"Dear *not* Nickie; my *baby* brother; I just *said*. Oh he's in this phase, he has these perfectly manic 'engagements,' dear I told you."

"Mm."

"He comes home all obsessed and ranting with these tales of how he's just proposed to some child in college and she's said yes! *sheerest* id-fantasy of course and naturally it turns out *she* not only wouldn't dream of marrying him but didn't even know he thought he was asking her to!"

" 'Engaged,' well just juvenile!"

"It's a *visitation!* Mummy's driven beside herself by him!"

"Yes you said, mm."

"Though of course as to Daddy, it isn't as if Mummy'd ever known even to begin with how to handle *Daddy*," Melissa said in contented disparagement.

But the friend grieved, "Ah though Lissa, as to handling them, how can one ever know, so unwarned, even what they'll think of to do."

"Impenetrable, mm."

"Ah *so* precarious, how know what they're ever like, when one's
so lost in them; so helpless and all at bay."

"What, dear?"

"Oh Liss we *are* powerless, or d'you think."

"So then you mean how does one ever know one's 'handling'
them at all, well dear *yes.*"

"So therefore why won't they look after us more then, ah, the
way we are," the lovely confidante mourned; adding sadly and
softly to herself, "if they love us; *really* love . . . " eyes now dreaming, unseeing, on what appeared to be her watch.

"So exhausting, so endless," Melissa started on.

But here her best adviser suddenly shrieked *look* at the time it
was, she was lost, she must utterly *vanish*, springing up scattering
tiresome lists like autumn leaves, Vallombrosa or anywhere for
that matter, for as she bleated she was *utterly* late!! and scuttled.

Though when Melissa lightly called "Say buon giorno to him
for me" into the hallway after her she yelped "Why who ever *said!*"
stopped in her tracks, stricken, eyes suddenly huge; or stopped for
one foundering moment anyway—before screaming back in airi-
est disparagement, "Oh, Liss, men, *coo* how oestrous!" this being
beyond cavil universally established, even God's plan, que sais-je?
and raced charmingly off.

Next day then Nicholas's dear daughter interrupted him in mid-
feed by ringing him up if you please with some nonsensical
hortatory supervising about his evenings.

Because she was *worried* about his just staying home in them
merely because the food was better.

Because she was ringing him up even though she was on the
point of rushing out to be lunched, which one's husband *didn't*,
her father of course hadn't met this particular new man in their
set but he'd roomed with Sam at Yale but then abroad for years
but now back but terribly *interesting*, all involved at practically
policy-level in that hushy échelon liaison with SHAPE and State
and whoever they were at Fontainebleau when they were *there*
(or at Bonn too for months at one period about which she was not
free even to breathe) and in Fontainebleau her father would *approve* for he no less than drove a gig! well, being French, it was
un wiski actually she supposed, with this smart little Tourangelle
mare he'd won from the General on a bet he snickeringly refused

to tell her what over, anyway her father would approve because here was a Yale man who *did* know how to order a meal properly, even magisterially, so she had in fact to fly out her door on mad wings that instant and *couldn't* be later already or more dithery, but she felt in his evenings he should overcome his feelings about this disgusting divorce and go *out.*

Why, he said, how sweet of her to be concerned! but he said was nightclub cuisine a form of stoicism he was prepared to dedicate even one evening to?

Not nightclubs but something like the St. Regis and what she'd thought was, with all his own contemporaries married and unavailable, obviously he should simply take out somebody young and hence not attached yet, it was only logical, Morgan for instance whom he knew fairly well already, also she danced beautifully which he loved—and he needn't sound stuffy and amazed like that, what could possibly be leveler-headed!

He said pretty doubtfully, why, he supposed he could have her in if she liked, but the trouble was—

But not *in!* because why couldn't he be his courtly old-sweetie self and just very angelically take her for once *out?* and *not* abuse the food. Because what did he think she meant was good for *him* if not out? what could he imagine? when for a woman this was an emphasis, it was like jewels; besides meaning in practice one could dress up, to be dazzling to him.

He said what about St. Regis food though, place be full of Texans wouldn't it? he'd heard the waiters yapped to one another audibly, and the maître d'hotel— Where in New York could a man who knew about food eat anyway no matter what he paid out? ah well though, mustn't bore her with all that again, merely his customary strictures on the Creator's arrangements, shouldn't upset her—nor Him either, as far as he could see.

At which she quoted her great-grandmother at him: "I doubt whether thee upsets thy Creator as much as thee thinks thee does," this being a family jest; now she must *fly,* and hung up.

So when he got back to his lunch it was cold.

Thus he had to ring up Morgan disgruntled by this too, having (after a review of all tactical risks involved) settled with resignation on the Iridium Room after all: at least see it again, be nostalgically *in* the place—that much gloomy satisfaction anyhow amid this endless suicidal impermanence and demolishment, with nothing left to him as it had once been, or was.

So, wincing, he rang Morgan up. Said in his best courtly man-

ner, would she take dinner with him? he meant tonight even; felt
they might dance too if that worked in, she care to? and she said
she would love to in tones of such simple happiness that when
he'd hung up by god he found he'd not actually noticed before
what a lovely young voice she had, what sapphire enchantments in
it, what tender, what haunted promisings; as in fact he supposed
however any bewitching little actress why not.

So anyhow.

So anyhow he called for her all charm mobilized, what's more
in a fiacre from the Plaza, which he decided would be full romantic fig for her years—actually, too, have been a simple pity not to,
through the warm murmurous urban evening, the streetlamps
hanging nodding like the blooms of great peonies in the gathering
dusk, through this jewel-box twilight, and she by heaven a dazzle
beside him half-naked in her summer black, with her eyes like
stars for him, down Fifth Avenue to the Iridium Room—in the
impossible anachronism of which he briskly got vermouths cassis
ordered and, grabbing her little hand, shouldered their way into
the packed and solid wall of dancing couples and took her in his
arms.

In these she instantly leaned back to announce with shining
eyes, "Oh Nicholas to *start* this evening of all evenings with a thing
I never heard of, oh what angel luck!"

He answered with a kindly interrogative grunt, having spotted
through the mob a distant pretty back.

Morgan said, "I bet you didn't even guess it was a First for me,
what you ordered for us I mean."

"What, why, decent enough drink I suppose," he agreed, still
absent. "New to you, huh; *well* now."

"And so sweet it's with you it's this First," she told him happily,
clinging to him, as through the music's reiterated formal archways
they began to turn and turn.

He explained, now paying attention, "Can't have you starting a
hard evening's dalliance on champagne."

But she dreamed at him, saying "My omen," in radiant awe.

"Vermouth cassis? perfectly normal summer aperitif."

"Well I know it seems child— I mean it's not important to you
and I know it Nicholas, just ordering a drink I've never had before
or heard of, but you might try to see why for *me* it's a special happiness."

"Now what's this," he demanded uneasily.

She said in the lowest tone that would reach his ear, "Because for a woman every smallest thing from her lover has such new meanings," and put her face down on his shoulder. But when he instantly stiffened, just as swiftly she was lilting up at him in her gayest mode, "Well of course you're not technically my lover or any other way, are you, no matter how shamelessly I wish you were, so you needn't defend yourself glaring like a bull, Nicholas! Anyway Nicholas all I *meant*," she went meekly on, "was now it will be one sweet secret thing more to remember whenever I order a vermouth cassis, which now will be always, I don't see why you should mind. Much less glower like that, ah *please* don't, if I'm a woman and can't help behaving the way we have to with you! As you of all people know," she finished, with a soft look at him.

"Now what random informal feminine instruction's all this!" he exclaimed in general alarm.

"Well if you don't play Firsts you won't understand why, but you must *see* that in threes they're omens! I mean if they work for you," she said soberly. "Well, so the very first thing you ordered for me the first time you ever took me dancing is my first taste of it! so it's an omen."

"Well dammy now," he rumbled.

"Which means I can stop *working* at you in such agonies for what I hope it's an omen about. Because now all I want will just happen of itself, oh Nicholas imagine! Without my having to drive myself frantic dragooning you!"

"Why, fine!" he said, not understanding any of this.

She said in a voice as soft as a breath "oh my dearest" and settled her cheek in sighing repossession of his collarbone.

So the band went into some Bantu business or other with the title of "Greasy-Toe Stomp." "Though I bet even now you haven't spotted the *main* three Firsts, Nicholas," she went on then.

"Not, huh."

"It even interlocks with the set I just told you about. Which makes it stronger and more binding still, oh my darling you're surrounded!" she sang in tender exultation, eyes aglow.

"Now what unbelted b.j. species of—"

"Well obviously, first, it's our first rendezvous isn't it! I know that isn't the word but it's the *thing* Nicholas; and next, the first thing you did on this First was dance with me, for the first time. That makes two. And *this* second First I'm in your arms, don't interrupt, I *am!* and even this formally it still counts, I bet you do anyhow believe in symbols, Nicholas, just as frantically as I do."

So beginning to laugh he asked then what was her third.

"Well it's something you haven't noticed. Or I don't think you have."

"Pretty extrasensory type though," he said amiably, patting her.

"But if I tell you, I don't know what you'll do, can't you see?" she cried tensely. "Only if I *don't* maybe then it spoils the omen!"

"So you see you do have to tell me then," he summed up, as the band slid along toppling melancholy walls of sound into "Yo Sho Pick a Hot Tahm to Cool Off."

"But it's about how you are *toward* me, Nicholas, and if I tell you you'll change, oh how can I, I can't!" she wept in a swoon of misery deep there in his arms, as through the unassembled shards of the music, its bare ruined choirs, they suitably turned and turned.

"Now *now*," he consoled her, for whatever it was. (Beyond *him!*)

She gazed at him with great misty eyes, gulping.

So he prompted, "So now then what."

"Well if I have to tell you," she said in a choking voice, "it's that this is the first time, in all these months I've loved you so blindingly, that you've ever once *really* treated me as if I were even nice enough to more than politely glance at," and buried her face in his shoulder, clinging.

"But my dear little thing but good *god!*" he cried, stunned, "why what possibly, now you can't mean I've been some damn' brute!"

She flashed one range-finding look at him and hid again, moaning something too stricken to be articulate.

"Now my sweet child!" he implored her.

To this she replied, still muffled, by pronouncing his name as if it were music.

"Now dammit Morgan—"

She wailed, "Oh you've wounded me so! Because you really *hadn't* noticed, had you," she accused him, flinging up her head and staring at him with great wet eyes, "but tonight you've been so sweet and wonderful, only now you've made me tell you you'll change, it's all spoiled, you'll be *conscious* of it, you'll probably even start hating me for not leaving it unsaid," she ended in piteous tones.

"I swear I—"

"Oh Nicholas I so didn't want to upset you tonight, on this first night of all nights, I didn't even intend to harass you by telling you I love you."

" 'Harass'!" he echoed, taken aback still again.

"Well, I had it planned to be just docile and *happy* with you, if you must know. Anyhow not like the— that morning," she amended, dropping her eyes. "Oh Nicholas I know I've fought you and dragooned you and driven you, and I've thrown myself at you, but now I'm not going to again, ever. I am just going to be yours. And *obey* you Nicholas. Anyhow now I have my lovely omen," she cooed contentedly.

"'Surrounded,' huh!" he said in amusement.

"Well it can't upset you, because you don't believe in it! So you can't object to my using it, so there!"

"Necromancy by god!"

"Then I can *have* my omen? even if it snares you for me?" she laughed in a voice all jewels.

"Why, snared already I expect, why not, only gentlemanly course open," he conceded, "though now how about drinking the thing for once," and took her back to their table.

So they sat; and next, lifting her glass to his she said shyly, "Well it *is* the first time and you don't really mind after all," then sipping she cried out, "Why, it's delicious!" in surprise.

He mildly teased her, " 'Mind,' why should I 'mind,' pretty guilty little conscience to think so!"

"Well then it slipped out," she muttered, faintly pink; but at once adding, "Well you know as well as I do, Nicholas, it's just that I *am* so yours that I can't hide anything I ought to. I have no pride with you. Which is why I have so much trouble controlling you, damn it!" she burst out.

Nicholas snagged a waiter who was catapulting past and told him bring two more vermouths cassis, and the confounded menu while he was at it.

"Because men doing what I want them's no problem, heavens. But you, Nicholas, are just infuriating," she said in tones of adoration. "But if I do tell you all my humiliating secrets, and I *do*, Nicholas," she pleaded, practically as if this were so, "can't you see it's because I am trying to display *every* side of what I am like for your approval, hoping there'll be something somewhere to please you?"

"You ought to, huh, study my old namesake's portraits of ladies," he threw in distractedly, as couples inched bumping past them from the dance-floor, for the music had now stopped.

She buried her little nose in her drink and stared at him over the rim in bafflement and dudgeon.

"Not from Wiltshire, that Romney," this Romney said, "but I mean to say he picked some damn' delicious women to sit to him. As every brush-stroke makes plain he knew, too!"

In a flash she'd set down her glass and cried in rapture, "Oh my dearest then it *wasn't* spoiled!"

He gaped.

"I mean you do like me, you really do!"

"*Well* now!" he growled.

"Well you think I'm pretty!" And before he could open his mouth in reply, "Oh think, I'm *good* for you!" she crooned in happy wonder, stretching her young arms to him over the gleaming white and silver of their table.

He groaned, "Well you're a mad sex," taking in his fingers one elegant little wrist, which he pawed tenderly.

"But Nicholas you don't know about *me* yet, really," she eagerly went on.

"Different, huh."

She snatched her wrist away crying, "You don't have to gloat at me, I *know* you think all women are alike, Melissa warned me, oh I think it's horrifying!"

"'Melissa'!"

"Well, she told the way you make these cold-hearted epigrams about us, oh I know they're witty but when I love you like this they make my heart *sink*, my darling!"

He blandly quoted himself: "Women, like tragedy, should inspire pity and terror."

"*You see?*" she bleated.

"Made 'em in French too at one time, she tell you? La faiblesse des femmes n'est pas qu'elles se laissent persuader mais qu'elles se persuadent elles-mêmes for example; quite true too."

Into her eyes there sprang great clear tears.

"*Now* what've I said, oh what an impossible damn' sex," he bayed. "Look dammit I made the thing up *in college*, you weren't even born when I m—"

"It isn't the *things* you say that wound me," she said very low, blinking bravely, "oh my dearest what hurts so is that how I feel isn't even enough on your mind to make you see how they'll wound me when you say them."

"Now you know quite well," he was beginning at her when the band threw up a sudden wild fountain of sound, any practical lighting went out, and in the embellished gloom a big luscious bangled girl sprang onto the dance-floor under a dizzying spotlight and began singing "Got No Budder onto It," in niggra.

When this din was over Nicholas clobbered a waiter and got the goddam menu. But the young woman at once came demurely back onto the floor and to what sounded like Haydn with grave charm sang

> What laurels, ah, what sauntering thighs are these,
> What sweets profundive to dismay

or whatever the actual words were. Everybody with any culture applauded this in riot; so for an encore this babe flaunted her handsome way through

> Caint git started wid de fuss-class tidings,
> Caint git goin' wid de glow-ry news

waving a bustle that gently broke a man's heart.

"She's *pretty!*" Morgan raged in a whisper. "I bet you think so, too!" she cried, eyes on the woman like knives.

"Hardly be simple-minded enough to say so, huh."

"So you do so then!" she gasped, stricken. "You think she's *desirable!*"

"What's this? now dammy I hardly as much as—"

She drooped, lamenting. "No but Nicholas I do have to find out what you really like, can't you see?"

"Some *singer?*" he demanded incredulously.

"Oh Nicholas please you aren't just lying to me again?"

"'Lying'!"

"Well I never have any security with you, you know it! Oh but tonight I wasn't going to reproach you! Oh Nicholas I'm truly *not* reproaching you! Even for playing safe by bringing me here. Instead of some small elegant restaurant where I could be alone with you. The way I'd pl— dreamed it."

"Why see here," he instantly said (having prepared this much anyhow), "I brought you here especially, to dance with you."

"Oh Nicholas, did you really, oh darling! Oh but how can I be sure you did! Because *did* you?"

"Dance for instance right now," he suggested smoothly, as the band's brass blew a preluding fanfare.

"Even if you didn't, you said it to make me happy," she whispered.

"So then come on," he boomed, standing up. The band plunged into some moody nostalgia out of the early Thirties:

> O honey
> Honeyhoney
> Lil ca'iage-trade honey

What de good word
Fum
Heah
On
Down

They danced. She murmured from the blest bower of his arms, "So you do like me. Enough to be willing to be kind to me. To *recognize* that I do love you. So see? I'm saying the so-see to myself," she purred up at him, and stretching radiantly up kissed a corner of his jaw with her soft little mouth. And then back again against his collarbone.

Though immediately turning up this perfectly teasing face to misexplain to him, "Just trying to palliate the harshness of your circumstances, my darling!"

—So in a word he didn't get home and into bed till God knows what hour.

He was hardly up, midmorning next day, when round his Victoria came as if she'd never addressed an unadoring syllable to him "—to see for one split second how you simply are, Nicholas!" she announced in brightest tones and not looking at him at all, eluding his embrace by neatly popping into it an armful of small parcels.

And on lightly past him into the back drawing-room. Here she struck an amorous chord on the piano and cried, "Make sure for *myself* you're being well taken care of, poor unhinged darling!" before fluttering back and across to the chimney-piece in the front drawing-room, where she straightened the Copley ancestor, who was already straight.

Nicholas dumped the damn' parcels into a chair and took her by the shoulders and pulled her around (while she indulgently reminded him her car *couldn't* wait, blocking everything) and for a moment got his enchanting maddening creature in his arms; but these, after one brilliant look at him, she placatingly squirmed out of and ran out into the little garden, crying out tenderly he must have the piano *tuned*, and, next, that the flowers, as he must have seen for himself, what there was of them, were past their glorious prime. To which he naturally replied that she had made him so wretched he hadn't slept a wink for these *two nights* after the way she'd left the party, if she wanted the truth!

At this she conceded in happy tones, "Now I've merely run by to see how you're getting on," and tripped into the house again, where this time when he caught her he held her. So for some minutes they stood there while she gently murmured from against his heart the roll-call of her immediate engagements, and he described his agonies.

Until eventually she did have to go, *really* must, she assured him, so many things merely to do before even lunch; and drew lingeringly away and out of his arms, to the piano bench, whither he at once followed. So there she butted her forehead against his shoulder while they disputed dreamily on.

For how could he consider constantly embroiling her, could he think of nothing but selfishly complicating her life? and when at this he groaned well where then by heaven had she gone after the party, leaving him desolate! she thrust herself away exclaiming did he for one peremptory moment mean she was to have developed no life of her own in these seventeen years he'd deserted her in? had she no duty no responsibility to herself? to her sweet fifth-former son? or did he dare hope she would now be light-minded because *then* she had been!

And when he begged her to explain why she kept repeating this 'deserted' when she knew the real reason as well as he? she instantly cried, shushing him, if he was going to be odious to her, did he want her never to be able to come visit him again!

Though now she was here, she said perhaps he would try to explain to her what he had been up to in the kitchen with that unstable little thing of her stepson's, poor boy.

He said if she cared for a candid answer the question struck him as being not what he but what the girl'd been up to.

But what had this still undefined activity been? which was what she'd asked.

Hiding she meant in the kitchen? to rouse that hulk of a boy to chasing her, he supposed she meant. Or did she mean the girl was a shade tight? Or even, as she'd suggested, unstable. Or upset or—

Mrs. Barclay said in a glossy tone the girl upset? on the contrary it had seemed to her that he, rather, had been rattled-sounding. So unlike him, she went on in affectionate concern. Because how could he at his age be upset by this ingénue, this child!

He said, beginning to laugh, he'd always hoped in his modest way he was attractive, now'd she claim he was even a menace to schoolgirls?

She said whether 'schoolgirl' as he put it was a relevant category was a datum she did not possess; but what was not clear (she continued, meekly buttoning her top blouse-button which he had just undone), not clear to her anyway, nothing in the whole odd little episode was clear— Now merely where had he met this child before? since perhaps he had better fall back on some simpler presentation, for example chronological order which after all she said had its advocates.

So he affectionately unbuttoned the button again and said wasn't it plain? the girl was some school friend of his younger daughter's apparently. Been in this weekend party at West Chester, it seemed. Flunked out of Radcliffe freshman year, he now recalled being told. What possible aesthetic or sociological end was served by her buttoning it again? Though why they'd taken this particular girl in the first place heaven knew: mad-women!

This she said disengaging herself slightly might be part of a dean's history of Radcliffe, assuming such a book was printable, but did he think it fully explained what he pretended to be explaining? Buttoning it moreover was not a sociological question but a matter of his immaturity and childishness, which were incurable.

He cried out that to shut so heavenly a bosom from the sight of a man who adored both it and her was the act of a pig; furthermore if she held that the desire of male for female was proper only to the years before puberty how did she propose to explain the reproduction of the species? So she permitted him to kiss her lightly, smiling; and got him narrating again.

Except what was there to tell? The narrative was no narrative at all, simply this house-party afternoon, a cold dull-crimson afterglare from a November sunset and this house party of kids had come straggling up from the stables through the autumn dusk in their mired riding-clothes and clumped stiffly into the library for tea (*late*, he need hardly inform her!), Morgan he recalled hand-in-hand with some gangling boy or other; she'd had on a dead-black turtleneck sweater and her boots and breeches and face mud-splashed, and as far as he could remember not even lipstick.

Mrs. Barclay said in an unexpected tone she was pleased to see that after eighteen years he had at last, if abruptly, learned to observe what a woman was wearing.

Huh? a visual memory he'd had all his life? why, he could— But anyhow! This girl— Well, when introduced she'd given him one of those long sultry looks that experience had taught him wasn't sultry but just nearsighted, and then turned her little back on him and loitered over to where her young man was slouched on the padded fender and sat down close beside him with her hand in his pocket. Well, it was an indecent unreticent generation by heaven! and he thanked God his own children didn't behave like some of their friends! Would she have the simple womanly decency to keep her pretty hands *off* a button he'd just arranged to his satisfaction? Anyhow this girl'd sat there with her temple lolled against the boy's bony young shoulder and as far as he could recall not a word out of her. So that was it. Hardly seen her again. Boy he presumed had monopolized her all the weekend. Or she him, depending on which sex it was sank its delighted fangs in the other.

Mrs. Barclay wished he had somehow learned to distinguish between a woman and an entree.

He said an entree has no buttons. So he'd never seen the girl again.

What did he mean by his 'never'?

Oh, well, yes, come to think of it, yes, he'd taken her with some of the others on a little tour of the valley farm and let her drive tractor for the tree-planter for a few furrows when she'd asked to. So then that was the whole story. Now why didn't she like the angel she was stay have lunch with him.

'*Lunch*'!

Yes, he'd ordered a particularly pleasant—

Lunch *today*?! when he'd already utterly thrown out her schedule with his evasions? her car waiting hours! And she herself waiting too, for him to finish this curious little story of his!

He said 'finish,' how'd she mean.

Its point. How it had gone on.

But pointless was just what the story was, he'd told her that to begin with!

Because all one had to do was glance at his great dissembling face, she answered him smiling, to see that there had been something more.

Point? there'd been no— Unless you could say, he supposed, that there had been one *time* more that he'd seen the girl that weekend, if that was the point, strictly speaking, that is, come to think of it, if that was what she meant; the girl having, uh, kissed him good-bye Monday morning she mean that? for what kind of a nugatory point was that!

Mrs. Barclay said 'nugatory' was hardly the adjective she would have expected him to choose when it was obvious there were others.

What? why it was a routine thing! He'd just settled himself at the wheel, there in the porte-cochère, to drive to the Bank as usual, why, this was something he did every morning! And she'd merely appeared beside the car. And bent down and in, without a word. And, well, huh, for the space of two bewildering heartbeats laid her mouth on his. There in the sleek hanging tent of her hair. And was gone!

And *before* she framed a comment let him point out to her, how routine! A mere bread-and-butter kiss! Or, all right, 'impetuous' then! He'd concede that; concede even that the girl had behaved a bit like a, well, like a Celt perhaps, for he supposed any jeune fille bien élevée would hardly have had the—

Mrs. Barclay at this gave a pretty little musical cry.

Now what? what did that mean! he besought her, taken aback. Oh had he to be told?

She'd *laughed?*

Well, she was amused. He amused her.

'Amused' her!

She was amused by his fussy distinctions.

'Fussy'!

Could he do nothing but repeat her words back at her in this gaping way? His scruples, then! It would amuse any woman!

His scruples! when to the contrary it was the *girl's* want of modesty that—

Mrs. Barclay cooed at him he didn't really have the least notion, had he, how a woman's mind worked.

—So it was sheer luck that he could counter, leaning tenderly toward her, was she really bothered then, heavenly thing that she was? and was she at long last ready to ravish his senses by admitting it? Though if she meant had he at his age bewitched the child, well, why shouldn't he have? he asked her agreeably, weren't the textbooks full of such cases? Or did she like everyone else, at the first genuine sign of our most normal of passions, propose to summon in psychiatry and sociology! And turn *those* appalling fellows loose on our rituals of reproduction as well? with Nicholas Romney lectured by some whinnying percentage-monger on the statistical norms of love!

And she knew they'd just maintain (and here he finally began to smile) that every girl who'd ever loved him had done so because she was maladjusted, in fact that he was merely one of the charming thing's symptoms! And if this was alleged universally (as it was) had she reflected that its significance was therefore zero? and laughing contentedly into her now faintly smiling face he begged her to instruct him what medical excuse she herself felt able to proffer, what specific psychopathology, for the loveliest moments a woman's sweetness had ever conferred upon a man, those days and nights she had loved him, as never anyone before or he hoped since; nor would she, she must know as well as he, until she consented to love him once again.

And so on and so on until like an angel she stayed for lunch.

✧

Moreover next day she dropped in for the briefest moment more, between a hair-dresser and a fitting, to have tea with him.

Or rather, since he hadn't intended going to the trouble of making tea, it being the man's afternoon out (Oh was it? so it was! she cried in pretty surprise), did she see any real grounds for not starting in on the evening champagne a shade earlier than usual? so presently she followed him tractably down to the kitchen to ice it.

Because she said she really could not (surely he saw for himself!) go on with this silliness of kissing him minutes at a time on every occasion she merely ran by to see him for fifteen seconds: she was fond of him, she was even indulgent, but couldn't he be serious? for she was so fond of him she hated to see him without plans.

No plans? he laughed, grabbing her again, when just the sight of her—

She pulled away crying he put her out of all patience! frivolous and intemperate as he was, when she was kind to him to his heart's content! had he come down to ice champagne or hadn't he?

So he had to clatter down to the wine-cellar and fetch a bottle and set to chopping ice.

Because she said smiling again didn't he think so too? which was another reason she'd had for coming back again to see him again so soon; or did he intend to spend his life philandering in kitchens, so irresponsible.

He said would she in her heaven-sent way fetch him the wine-cooler from the dining-room? from the sideboard. He supposed she was talking about that girl again, what was her name. *In* the sideboard, then. Whom he'd hardly more than met!

Neither on the sideboard nor in it but in the chimney-cup-board, she informed him, and brought it forgivingly; what she meant was he must not think he could have everything both ways.

He snorted now now, what was the use of being born into the privileged classes if one couldn't have it both ways? Had Mrs. Barclay herself at a party never agreeably trifled with her host's sensibility if only from good manners? and forgot the whole thing in a quarter-hour! Probably a high percentage of our national passes were made in kitchens anyhow, had to be made some-where! Though this girl hadn't done anything of the kind!

'Done,' Mrs. Barclay mimicked him, what had 'done' to do with it, she quoted unfeelingly; as if what an experienced little actress decided she wanted to implant in his head were to be given the status of evidence!

He said dammit no man with fifty years' astonished acquain-tance with female conduct was going to wear down his imagina-tion guessing why a young woman leaned wordlessly against him in a kitchen to inform him she found him temporarily fetching! Girls had no judgment; they had a political talent, but common sense, no; moreover they looked only at that part of the future, even at that part of the next five minutes, that suited their dreamy fancy. It was cool enough to sip now, should they take it up to the drawing-room?

So they went up, she inquiring in a special tone what did he mean by 'wordlessly'? and he arguing that girls of twenty of course spoke but what did they ever say in so many words.

For he said had Mrs. Barclay herself at that age in similar cir-cumstances for example— Suppose she'd temporarily set her pant-ing heart on a wary man of fifty, why, if she opened her little red mouth she'd just find herself out-argued. Now here: the wine was beautifully cool. Whereas the ambiguities of a throbbing silence, how unanswerable! Nor was it something she need snort about, did she really think?

She had *anything* but snorted!

And did she have to fuss at him like this over something that hadn't even *happened* good god? just when the champagne was cool? when how was *he* responsible for some pretty child's moods!

Mrs. Barclay asked in a hardly temperate tone whether he actu-ally wished her to believe him such a dolt as to think himself help-less—at his age! and with what she blushed at having to refer to as his experience!—helpless against any random misconduct of any common little thing that flung herself at his irresponsible head?

'Flung'? when she must know the whole roster of alternate motivations as well as he did:—The girl'd been temporarily separated from what's-his-name, Toby, and wanted to touch something male. Or it was just the end of a long day and she felt down. Or she felt dramatic. Or it had been a mere *game* then, dammit! enfin tout le bazar! Or with a young actress doubtless the phrase was toute la comédie. Or a mere bet with herself! Or even simply she wanted to make him admit she was femalely *there*, why not! And Mrs. Barclay needn't make that pretty pouting face, had she forgotten the time she herself, in this very kitchen—

Would she drink her drink and stop this flouncing? for even on the preposterous hypothesis that the girl had for fifteen seconds conceived a passion for him, did that alter the fundamental fact that it was *she*, Mrs. Barclay, that he single-heartedly adored? *Well*, then!

For ah, these memoirs she'd suggested he write, what would they be (assuming he wrote them) but a record of her? And need she look at him with such sadness? was it 'sad' that there was no woman on earth he had loved like this? For to revise the metaphor what was his memory but a gallery of portraits of her!

And refilled their glasses, sighing.

So in order to sip this round comfortably they sat on the piano bench.

His whole mind a gallery, Victoria after Victoria framed side by side, this radiant girl (he droned in tenderest persuasiveness), eyes looking their happy questions out at him from whatever irrelevant chiaroscuro of a background it was, the wedding they'd first met at, the Brevoort terrasse; the same breathtaking girl on and on à perte de vue in new frames and new poses and other costumes and often no costume on by god at all thank God! he ended in a meatier tone, seizing her free hand.

Which barely fussing she seemed to decide to let him have.

For how constantly his memory saw her as if coming to meet him, emerging for *him* out of whatever landscape his mind painted, along this or that elegant Palladian perspective—

At which tender and time-confounding point the goddam phone rang and it was his tomcat of a son!

"You're *what!*" this father bellowed.

" . . . "

"But what the devil are you doing in Northampton of all pos—"

" . . . "

"Met *which* young woman of yours, doesn't it by god occur to you I may have quite enough trouble keeping track of my own?"

" . . . "

"Still more recent even than *that* one, I see!"

" . . . "

"Um."

" . . . "

"She *what?*"

" . . . "

"'Platonism'!"

" . . . "

"But good heavens Nickie—"

" . . . "

"Well but is the child in love with this goddam associate professor of philosophy or with *you?*"

" . . . "

"No, but what earthly—"

" . . . "

"Nothing special about your particular generation, it'd make no sense in *any* era!"

" . . . "

"Then what *is* the nature of this unfathomable understanding or whatever the hell it is you succeed in not explaining!"

" . . . "

"But look here Nickie, any girl that falls in love with men old enough to be her father—"

" . . . "

"Now Nickie my dear boy if I may for one moment interpose a—"

" . . . "

"No but I wonder whether you'll mind my making a sug— my asking a question of a most benevolent kind. A most *concerned* kind, Nickie, if I may put it in an old-fashioned way; I mean this is none of my business at all. But my point is: now, you're going to Italy this summer. Now, as you know—"

" . . . "

"Well *exactly* Nickie, only I meant a *nice* Italian girl."

" . . . "

"What the devil does that tone mean!"

" . . . "

"Well for one thing they're female by god!"

" . . . "

"*I* know American girls are female!"

"   . . ."

"Well, European girls don't go around behaving as if the fact unnerved them so!"

"   . . ."

"This one doesn't, uh."

"   . . ."

"Oh, she is? I see."

"   . . ."

"Is, huh; *well!*"

"   . . ."

"I know, I know, but a really nice Ital—"

"   . . ."

"For one thing they were civilized when our own Sassenach ancestors were still rutting around in caves!"

"   . . ."

"Ah well, as civilized as girls are ever likely to be; my point is—"

"   . . ."

"*Need* variety, goddammit!"

"   . . ."

"The hell with progressive education!"

And so on, declaring to this idiot boy that if God, or Iddio rather, ever put an inclination for him into some lovely little Roman head he'd assure him he'd never say a disrespectful thing about Him again, perfect old *angel* by god was what he'd call Him! and so on and so on. So by the time the damn' boy had rung off, Victoria had of course literally to fly to her fitting.

Accordingly he was boring the hell out of himself that evening over some piece of current arrière-avantgarde fiction or other (who'd guess there had ever been a time when the subject of fiction was simply Achilles? before all these interior decorators turned author! or before we had all these standard Southern masterpieces, all disembowelings and relatives with two heads), when the door-pull sounded in his empty house and there on his doorstep in the deep June night was his obed[t] little serv[t] Morgan.

Who at once with a tender air of appeasement stepped in and stood in his arms lifting her mouth with meek assurance to be kissed.

". . . so see darling?" she murmured in time then, taking that sweet young mouth gently away from him at last; and when he rumbled some sort of reply, unlocked his embrace by submissive degrees, lingering still; but ultimately on into the drawing-room, he following, while she sighed to him, "I suppose you'll want some *explanation* Nicholas, when all I'm really doing is stop by for five minutes, well who'd explain that?" and in the pier glass between the front windows smiled placatingly into his reflected eyes.

"Though couldn't the whole reason," she softly cried, turning to him, "just be the sheer luxury of not being held off at a distance at last any longer? — being able to come to you in this heavenly peace? Or was that actually what you meant, my dearest?"

Whatever he replied to this was still too far on the gruff side to be made out.

"I mean what you said when you took me dancing, about a serious talk," she explained things to him.

At this, starting to laugh, he told her if she recalled her Dante, quel giorno più there'd been precious little serious talk!

"Well I don't know what you're talking about but it was just too sweet an evening to be serious," she said in happy accents, sinking into his chair. "So now I came by in case you still wanted to be," she expounded further, picking up and sampling a sip from his half-empty glass, which she made a face at and set down.

So he offered, get her a drink?

"No because I'm not going to *stay*, Nicholas. Though as you might guess this 'serious talk' was a reason I stopped by."

He said *what* serious talk!

"Or partly was. Or Nicholas if you still really want one. Oh if you knew how sweet it is to be able to tell you anything and everything! Because I also came, partly, if you insist on knowing, because my psychiatrist advised against it."

He mildly resounded.

"Well *of course* I'm seeing a psychiatrist about you! For months and months! After what you did to me that morning — why, you Rejected me!" she reproached him, in indignant technicality. "Well actually she's a woman psychiatrist and you can sneer but she understands me Nicholas! Oh will *you* some day? Though she did do just what you predicted she would!" she cooed in sudden derision.

He asked her, rather staggered, how could he have foreseen the behavior of this woman when he'd not even foreseen the prerequisite likelihood of her existence?

"Well I remember *everything* you've said!" she cried at him in loving surprise, "and you said *this* that weekend at West Chester the day we had lunch champêtre deep in that wonderful grove of beeches stretching on and on and on, by that half-ruined Doric folly with its frusts and columns."

He said actually, he believed, it was Corinthian if anything. Also perhaps she meant the pieducci.

"Well *anyway* Nicholas you were yelling at Melissa and her husband, and at Nickie too partly, about psychiatrists, and you said that if for instance a girl was no-matter-how bored with her husband and in love with somebody else, still the average psychiatrist didn't 'pay the most rudimentary attention to these *facts*' (was how you said it), he just shooed her back to her husband, because no matter what they *say*, you said what they *do* is prescribe as if the ideal course is for everybody to be exactly and endlessly like everybody else and only do what everybody else thinks should be done, 'adjusted,' and you were outraged."

He said who wouldn't be? unless she cared to except Immanuel Kant!

"So sure enough *she* tried to shoo me back toward Toby and I just *hooted!*"

Nicholas civilly snorted too, and lugged his glass back to the cellaret.

"So she went *very* stiff, could I have just one vermouth cassis then?" she begged, coming to stand obediently beside him. "So I can have my third on my first peaceful loving visit to you," she explained, resting her cheek shyly against his big arm. "Still she does sympathize, Nicholas."

He said *fine*; and in addition, that he was delighted to hear it.

"Though Nicholas she did make this hilariously un-psychiatrist remark! It was once when I was weeping my heart out over you in her office, and she said, 'My dear, I too have loved and lost,' *imagine!*"

He said the woman should transfer her God-given inabilities to some less taxing sphere.

"Well of course she lost! I mean she dresses beautifully but Nicholas she looks just like a sweet little pouter pigeon!" she exulted, and in one swift whirl curvetting away from him to the pier glass gazed with love at the smiling beauty poised in the shadowy depths there. "Oh but will you *truthfully* answer me something?" she cried.

Why, he'd never lied to a pretty girl in his life!

"Well, 'pretty,' Nicholas you've already granted that much you know, and anyway I *am*; but what I want you to admit," she instructed him, eyes still wide with delight at that glowing young image, "is, don't you secretly *like* having somebody this pretty in love with you like this?"

So in common decency what else could he by god say?

She whispered trembling, "Ah you do you *do*, oh Nicholas dance with me!" stepping in luxury into his arms, and (the lack of any music being evident enough to both of them) stood there as in happy swoon.

But he quickly said, patting her—and might he for one moment switch back a little in all this? to something she'd said just before? —he said of course the woman appeared to have a chiefly statistical and textbook knowledge of the human heart, and certainly very little talent for expressing what information she did possess: no one would agree more than he on her lack of competence. But on the other hand Morgan must not over-simplify either! and in short what about this undiscussed question of what-was-his-name? her young man.

This, she glided effortlessly past at once: "Oh but *now* Nicholas? when it might take hours, when after all I'm just here for these two minutes luxuriating in your not being all solemn and formidable with me Nicholas darling. And when anyhow the real reason I dropped by is something I thought of that I bet you never in the world would guess but I hope will please you."

He nevertheless, he said, saw no reason—

But she ran on in tones of adoration, "Oh Nicholas I've been so wanting to think of something I could do for you that no other woman's ever done, something you'd *accept* my doing I mean, and this afternoon I thought of it!"

And while his mind tried to deal with this, prattled on, "Well, I know it may not seem like much to you, but little things are *important* things to a woman, Nicholas, if only you knew enough about us to understand; and this is just that nose-jewel."

He said blankly now when on earth had he told her about *that* early piece of amatory fol-de-rol!

"Why Nicholas how can you possibly need reminding?" she cried in disbelief, "why, it was coming back from the tree-planting thing, you *can't* forget walking me back all that way with my arm through yours! when naturally I'd let the others get ahead. So you were grumbling about food in Princeton at first, at your Reunions, but then you began about the girls the seniors had flocking round at commencement or whenever it was, fiancées and sisters too you supposed, and your first impression had been my *god* what hundreds of pretty young girls but then you'd seen that it was just that they were young. So my heart sank; except I knew I *was* pretty; and also I knew I could somehow make you notice it eventually, as a matter of fact I thought you possibly had already but were too stiff to admit it to yourself, I mean here you were walking with me weren't you? so by this time you were saying you'd got used to looking at your sons' classmates and seeing they looked exactly like your own classmates decades ago, but it was a *shock* when you found yourself doing the same thing with girls, looking at this shining little head or that melting slope of shoulder (you said) and realizing that what you were seeing was not this girl here in 1958 but someone who'd looked just like her only it'd been 1931! of course with a different hairdo, you admitted. 'I mean to say boys, who gives a damn about boys,' you said, 'but when I start seeing *girls* in this how-like-your-breathtaking-mother-you-are sort of way . . . !' —so you see I decided they did please you, then, so I was in heaven, for I thought oh then *I*'d please you even more, I mean being prettier, and oh I clung so softly and with such hope to your arm—the first time ever, oh Nicholas I'd never been so close to you before! Only then you began grumbling about their tenue, these girls', Bermuda shorts and so on, you said where had all the baroque charm gone? and you said for example you wanted a sweet dessert to be really and elaborately *sweet*, no nonsense about de-cloying it, and in the same way a pretty girl ought to—but then you broke off and began to laugh and said here you'd spent a lifetime trying to persuade one·pretty woman after another to even just occasionally wear those nose-jewels that made Hindu women look so delicious, you'd actually had one made up years ago, a tiny clustering rose of diamonds that clipped gently on with a little spring-clip like an earring's, but not one woman would wear it for you, not even to give you two minutes' delight looking at her beauty with it on. Only then there we were at the house and everybody out front waiting for us so I had to let go your arm before we'd crossed even that threshold together, oh how *easy* it is to tell you all this or anything, my dearest, now that you're almost ready to love me a little at last!" she said happily, smiling into his eyes.

He at once replied that while he couldn't say he recalled all this in, uh, quite such unerring detail, still, if a lifetime's delight in the mere look, the mere tournure, of women, in the posed and lovely portraits they always somehow made him half-think they were—

"Oh Nicholas *please*, I'm not 'women,' I'm—"

He told her now wait, he'd been about to recite and translate for her a verse of Ovid's, that went

saepe tepent alii iuvenes, ego semper amavi

which he'd render 'Can't answer for my tepid competitors, but I've always been in love with some agreeable woman or other,' he assured her; and perhaps, he said he meant, it was just this that she must not be tempted to misinterpret.

To this piece of delicacy she paid no attention (except for five seconds to gaze into her drink instead of at him), meekly saying, "So then you must still have it then, your lovely jewel I mean."

Well he supposed naturally he did somewhere or other.

"I mean here *with* you Nicholas, in this house?"

He asked her sighing now how could he be sure about the answer to a question of that sort without prolonged and thoroughgoing search? what with these masses of baggage and boxes and what-all this miserable domestic crisis of his had forced upon him.

"You couldn't have just this one *quick* look in a place you'd *probably* have put it, Nicholas, like a jewel-box?"

So he said with a snort of laughter she certainly did want to try the bauble on didn't she! and when he fetched his stud-box there of course it was in plain sight right on top among cuff-links and studs, this small white blazing rose.

Which he picked out and dropped in her palm, and she took with a little soft sound of wonder and delight and flew to the pier glass. And slipped it on, submissively muttering "ow."

Now she saw what he meant? he cried in self-approbation, justified: see how delicious she looked in the thing, what it did for a charming nostril!

Tilting her enchanted head in this pose and that, she pored in a passion over this new image the glass held poised there, saying "oh Nicholas oh think" meanwhile in no particular tone.

Well was she convinced?

"Well it's the most uncomfortable thing I ever wore in my life if you must know darling," she told him lovingly. "But you see I wear it for you, no *other* woman ever did! Only I do everything I do merely to please you, can't you tell that by now?"

And running to him begged, "Oh shall I wear it for you, my dearest? Oh Nicholas shall I?"

So he said, laughing, settle for that would she, huh! battle if not the war?

But laughing, glittering, back, "Why you're not even *pretending* to fuss!" she cried in angel complicity; and shortly thereupon wore the bauble home.

✧

Melissa said at lunch at Il Baloccone, scooping from her melon rose-pink cusps, to her dearest friend (who was eating a sfogliata) that all things considered she had now decided, poor old sweet, to pack her father off almost at once to Europe, or in practice she supposed Paris, this being the classic "return" for his generation, they'd never set foot in Italy.

"Because I had this perfectly penetrating feeling he wants to be *alone*," she theorized. "I mean who at his age doesn't, do they, so he must. No responsibilities and just *enjoy* himself, so when he rang me up and said he'd decided to go abroad, even fairly soon, well I said I *agreed*. So possibly he's going."

"To be out of the way for her divorce you mean too, oh I see," the friend said, in antistrophe.

"Yes, when now he has just nobody."

"Also when your mother marries whoever."

"Dearest *your* hypothesis not mine! because as I told you Daddy quite definitely said—"

"Oh Liss of course there *is*, he's just too vain to admit."

"Well but—"

"Well love if *I* were going to be unfaithful it'd be *with* somebody!"

They both screamed musically with laughter.

"Of course once he's *there*," the friend went on, waving her little bangled wrist for their coffee, "who knows who he'll pick up, your own baby sister told me he has this affetto if not worse for Italian girls."

"*Daddy?*"

"Because Nickie told her your father discusses them in detail with him, pare che sopratutto gli piacciono *Roman* girls, dear, so now you know."

Here, smirking courteously, the maggiordomo bowed low over them pouring their coffee; so for a choice of languages Melissa said more or less in English, "Oh well dear love what Nickie says, ptah."

"No but he might know!"

"No but you know the perfectly possessed things he says! last time I saw him he was 'cultivating un petit air faisandé,' leering; dear he's an adversity!"

"Well Liss he *is* very good-looking. Or in that great gangling way."

"Oh at least he doesn't maunder like my *baby* brother, goodness! *He* did I tell you has just announced to us he's engaged again, 'really' this time, to some child at Radcliffe, poor Daddy's having to go up there merely to see! Because of course he isn't, only of course each time one has to make sure in case he is!"

"Yes infantile, no but going *back* Lissa, about your father I mean, dearest your own sister said Nickie said—"

"Well she's mad, Nickie knows *just nothing* about Daddy! Some clutching little Italian thing? When he's *fifty?*"

"Now Liss you know how they are."

"But Daddy simply wouldn't *notice* outside his own generation! what on earth can my sister— Why for example she knows he didn't even notice Morgan when Morgan was *publicly* mooning at him at her own house party last year! when I mean it was so dismal even Daddy's good manners couldn't have coped if he'd so much as looked at her and seen! So when nothing happened what could happen?"

"But then what *happened?*" her friend implored.

"Oh what d'you think? she languished at him in this quivering schoolchild way the way they do, just pathetic."

"Repulsive, yes."

"*Exactly,* and making these immature excuses all weekend to be near him, following him about to Be Alone with him, well it was sheer girlish *dream* dear, of course I was only there these two nights, because I was sorting out my part of the attic because Mummy'd taken *on* so, though what does one do with wedding presents forever? I mean what does she expect, goodness! and that second night Morgan was as good as out of her mind in my room till *dawn* with these drooping lovelorn details in her despair!"

"Love, how sad."

"Love-how-sad and who doesn't sympathize! only anybody would have thought she was *authentically* in love with Daddy, just disgusting!"

"Then this was before she'd got Toby, then."

"Toby, oh ptah."

"Well Toby's huge and rather sweetie *I* thought," her best friend said, yawning delicately.

"Oh in that great helpless *way* sweetie if you like," Melissa conceded, "but then what man isn't? and he was a mere child in officer school. I mean he just hangs open at Morgan mouthwise, who'd give him a second thought."

"Yes I suppose."

"I don't mean that I didn't still feel this most complete pity-and-terror for her, sleepy as I was. Because adolescence, well goodness. Though this Mrs. Barclay that Daddy knows, you know how that generation can be, just seemed terribly *amused* when I told her."

"No now but where was all this."

"Because she said I must realize (love, imagine my *not!*) I must realize that Daddy was a perfect old angel, our whole sex was endlessly fetched by him (I ran into her at my fitting, is where) so why not children like Morgan too she said? in any case she said it was practically a family trait in Morgan's family, Morgan's own mother —you know, the composer—was aswoon at him for a year."

"*Morgan's mother!*"

"Well so it seems! and she dedicated a concerto to him, I mean love what one finds out! Though she said of course it wasn't likely Morgan knew about all that, did I happen to know whether she did? this passion her mother had for Daddy having been just before Morgan was born."

The friend uttered a scream.

"What, dear?"

"You mean she meant that was a *reason* for not knowing?"

"Not knowing what, dear."

"Why, not *knowing!* because Lissa you don't almost certainly think she must have been rather clearly hinting to you Morgan might be *his own daughter?*"

"*Daddy's?* love you're deranged, how could she, *all* she said was it seemed to her the sort of thing Morgan might not have been told, didn't I think?—one's mother's hopeless passions, after all! There being no one to tell her, would there be."

"So then you're going to tell Morgan."

"What, dear?"

"Well because why else d'you think Mrs. Barclay told you all this if not to pass it on, goodness!"

"Well but how could I possibly 'tell' Morgan whatever it is when I don't see what there could be to tell, anyhow it might remind Morgan how she tried to hang herself round his stately old neck in her adolescence when he didn't even notice she was *there*, dear! Rather cruel."

"No, but Mrs. Barclay must have—"

"Particularly when he just recently sacrificed this whole evening taking her to the Maisonnette *merely* as she knows because I argued him into it to have a little peace and qui— They saw *you*, dear, by the way! well *dearest* how skulking!" she suddenly purred.

That one uttered a shrill cry.

At which instantly the huntress swooped: "What my darling? when love I'd never guessed you had this dog for him!" she sang, bright and innocent of eye.

"Why what can you mean!" cried her frantic prey.

"'Mean,' why dearest what could I, why nothing!"

"No but—"

"Simply who'd ever thought Patrick fetched you so!"

"'Fetched'!" she yelped.

"And no one knows? or not *Sam*, I mean how terribly stealthy you must merely have been!"

"Oh Liss oh what *possibly?*" babbled the quarry. "Why, for anyone to have noticed, oh *what*, to make you for one second *dream?*"

"'Notice,' why what can you be remembering," exulted Melissa, now smoothly casting down her eyes.

"But for example at some party can you mean?"

"Dearest nothing, why *nowhere!*"

"Or anywhere, oh Lissa *tell me!*" the lovely stricken thing gibbered on. "You *can't* have thought we ever even looked as if we— Ahhhh but Lissa Lissa it's been so hard *such an agony* to hide," she wailed in self-pity at last; and so on into the long murmuring sweet confessional afternoon: the roster of meetings, of partings, the separations, at routs and balls, in the guilt of clandestine and unaccustomed bars, in milling companies with one's husband sometimes a mere eight inches away in the welcoming din; the anguishes and inconveniences of adultery (as well as of course its sheer heaven)—this emotion described by among others Sophocles with unusual turbidity of sequence as "unwithstandable; love that in a girl's cheek lies nightlong masked aglow; nor can the immortals flee it, land or sea, or man brief as a day"; for ah Love,

> he that has thee has gone mad.

This, mind you, in sober stilted Attic tragedy!—one place, it might have been confidently supposed, where by convention a woman would sometimes (for short periods; and, it is conceded, artificially) think of other than of love.

✧

All Nicholas Romney was doing was enjoying one hour of peace and quiet himself, the innocent next morning, at the piano, fiddling with a setting for

> What amorous pearl, where Lycid lies,
> Pouts her adornment to his eyes

when of all people his son took it into his carnal young head to ring up for permission to bolt off to Europe not end-of-June as planned but (in ravening pursuit of some sleek child Nicholas had never even heard of) tomorrow!

"Now goddammit Nickie," this responsible father had to roar, "now which one is this!"

"   "
. . .

"*What* madman's daughter!"

"   "
. . .

"How should I remember what I call 'em, all somebody's daughters, mad or not, aren't they?"

"   "
. . .

"Oh."

"   "
. . .

"I said, 'oh,' what d'ye want me to say!"

"   "
. . .

" 'Tone,' what tone, can't say I used any tone I'm aware of."

"   "
. . .

"Remember her perfectly; damned unlikely to forget in fact!"

"   "
. . .

"My dear boy *no*, all I meant was—"

"   "
. . .

"A *vivid* child I suppose I meant if I meant anything, even rather a high-strung little thing perhaps; 'high-mettled' one might even say; but I assure you—"

"   "
. . .

"Now my dear Nickie I'm sure she is!"

. "   "
. . .

"Why of course she is, temperament's the most natur—"

"   "
. . .

"Now see here you mustn't think for one moment that I'd consider a lovely sultry young dancer wasn't perfectly—"

"   "
. . .

"What the devil's your mother's remark got to do with it!"

"   "

"Well among other things you did spring her on us pretty abruptly you'll admit! and now here she is just as abruptly back again."

"   "

"I see."

"   "

"Yes but dammit all, months gone by and not a breath out of you about her since."

"   "

"Yes but what about that delicious little Goucher one you've—"

"   "

"Oh *she's* not going over till *July*; I see!"

"   "

"One in Paris one in Geneva, mm."

"   "

"Oh, three hundred, three hundred twenty-five miles, I suppose you could call it a shuttle if you liked, why not."

"   "

"Except that Nickie my *dearest* boy don't you think two of these highly charged lovely mechanisms at the same time dammit is—"

"   "

"Affairs with two girls simultaneously, you must be out of your senses!"

"   "

"All right all right 'in love with' two simultaneously then: at your age it's a damn' quibble!"

"   "

"All right a quibble at any age!"

"   "

"Now I'm really not prepared to tolerate this irresponsibility of yours d'ye hear? getting into bed with 'em isn't the whole story!"

"   "

"Responsible to her, yes, only by heaven you do seem to feel that about several of the charming little things in a row, don't you!"

"   "

"I mean they want to be *looked after* dammit; what else?"

"   "

"How do I know why they do? simply do."

"   "

"Because if you want to grow up into a 'man who understands

women' as you put it, responsible happens to be the absolute first thing you have got to be by god!"

"   ."

"Upset, of course they're upset!"

"   ."

"Well they haven't *got* anything but undergraduates, if that isn't enough to upset a girl what is?"

So in a word all he was doing, after abusing his dear son, was putter in blameless peace and quiet over a musical setting for

> What amorous pearl, where Lycid lies,
> Pouts her adornment to his eyes,

when his Victoria rang up and intemperately demanded what wickedness was he up to! because this for-years friend, one of her four or five *closest* friends, had seen him of all things irresponsibly dancing at the St. Regis with some sweet little minx or other, what *was* he doing!

He cried out, "Now what's this!" taken aback.

"She *saw* you there!" Mrs. Barclay denounced him. "And in that brummagem Maisonnette or whatever it is!"

"In the what? why dammit I was in the Iridium Room."

"*Where?*"

"Why my angel I was simply off on this new policy of Melissa's," he reasonably besought her. "Now you can't be calling it irresponsible!"

"You took Melissa *dancing?*"

"*God* no, Victoria, merely she suggested the entire—bullied me into it actually, if you care for the blunt fact."

"Nicholas what are you talking about, *what* policy!"

"This policy of Melissa's? why what about it? simply my evenings! said go out on the town now and then as a policy, why not."

"Yes I mean who then was it."

"Now see here my angel, she said the thing was, and I thought after all how sensible, she said why not take out someone unattached I already knew, meaning no involvement d'ye see? Because I mean she *suggested* all this, Victoria! Even more or less, uh, picked the young woman for me as a matter of fact."

"Do you insist I am actually to believe this dementing tale?" she cried in a voice of rage.

"But it's the truth!" he bayed guiltily.

"'*Truth*'!"

"Now surely Victoria you can't seriously—"

"Nicholas are you going to admit the name of this surreptitious girl you had with you or aren't you!"

So he croaked, "Well the fact is it was I suppose Morgan."

Mrs. Barclay appeared to be speechless.

"My utter angel," he began—

"Not that deranged child! you can't mean you've been seeing her!"

"But Melissa sug—"

"*Encouraging* her, Nicholas you must be out of your senses!"

"'Encourage'! but what frivolous interpretation's this? when you yourself said she and your stepson—"

Mrs. Barclay uttered a little jeweled scream.

"But dammit Victoria fundamentally the child's for all we know merely unoccupied now the young oaf's back at sea again, what more natural."

"'Child,' 'unoccupied,' oh *really* Nicholas your expressions!"

"But what perverse—"

"And now you'll of course try to conceal the whole guilty performance, oh how unprincipled and graceless you are!" she cried at him.

"Why what is there to conceal, now by god what's suddenly depraved in taking some young woman feeding and dancing?"

"*Dancing*, I've not the slightest doubt the little thing complacently pointed out to you that there she was all evening in your arms!"

Nicholas uttered a cry.

"*And* saw to it that you kissed her the most lingering and murmurous good night! Or was there even occasion to say good night, did you instead simply— Do you *dare* admit it? Oh where can that dolt that *lout* of a Toby ever have picked up this scheming abandoned knife-wielding little—"

"Victoria will you *listen* to me!" he bellowed.

"*No!*" she screamed at him, and hung up.

She then instantly rang him back. "Nicholas what can your daughter have been even *thinking* of!" she demanded in a passion.

"My angel Vict—"

"Do you have the face to deny it?"

"I was merely—"

"Because Nicholas how can you *treat* me so!" she raved.

"A girl young enough to be my daughter? now what else beyond a little dancing could I pos—"

"*What* else!"

"I tell you I—"

"How often have you seen her again then!"

"Seen Morgan again? what on earth makes you think—"

"Do you realize," Mrs. Barclay told him in tones of menace, "that this is almost *literally* the despicable lying sort of phrase you used to me years ago on another odious occasion? In one of the most wounding scenes your indefensible conduct ever forced me to go through!"

"My angelic creature what is all this even about?" he implored as if unhinged.

"You don't *remember* how you lied?!"

"I—"

"About that horrible little Angelina Hume!" she yelled.

He gaped, stunned.

"I don't suppose I know even yet how often you may or may not have lied to me! And at the very time when we—when I was so—"

"My blessed Victoria—"

"I was *so* in love with you, and I simply went off to Nassau for *ten days* and you took up with her again!"

"'Took up'!" he gobbled.

"*Slept with* the over-dressed simpering little tart again then, in plain English, oh how could you!" she sniveled, weeping with rage; and *crash!!* went her phone.

Nor this time did she ring him back.

Though he waited long past any reasonable time, gloomily banging the piano (a divertimento called Percussion Sonata for a Pretty Bottom), women being what they alas were.

For how could she! Here were the rooms they'd made love in, the hallways of what greetings, what partings, the oval stair's half-landing too where once— Had she no memory of their love's landscapes? or saw him as he, ah how constantly, saw her, coming toward him along some unforgotten perspective, some Roman street that year, a via, a viale, racing toward him waving perhaps, eyes shining. Or in sunlight on some stone stair, as down from Santa Trinità de' Monti that day, "at the first landing of the elegant stair owly Thomas pray for us," he quoted himself as of some eighteen years earlier, apostrophizing his generation's bard.

Had she no memory? Did she forget their Alpine meadow, deep in spring? and how in those brilliant mornings he waited in the forests' rim above, in the gloom of the hemlocks, waiting when how could a man wait! for her to come climbing the long mountain-meadow from her hotel far below in the blaze of day, up and up and up and up, swaying on her high heels, panting, happy eyes searching the dark thickets for him as she clambered near at last (ah come se ne ricordave!) and then the final gasping laughing rush into his eager arms, and the brown pine-needled forest floor.

Did she now propose to deny all that?

Because by god if she chose to forget there were thank God other women who'd be delighted to remember! — Arabella Hobbes for one! and stamping to the scrutoire he rummaged for the latest of those sporadic letters this sweet Celt from his past still tossed at him now and then from Lyon or Paris or Geneva or wherever any current husband happened to be:

Insufferable Sassenach why do you never arrive where *I* have a milieu? I love you. I love you and I miss you permanently. Sweet pig are you going to let the locks close with me in one continent and you in another? Je t'embrasse fort *fort*.

A.

For then why *not* go abroad at once? . . .

They might meet somewhere like (say) the Closerie des Lilas, a visit of piety, purely classical in feeling, to that monument of so many humane generations, including even Henry James. And, meeting *there*, Arabella and he might well feel once more the happy weight of the hours, the sheer total days, they must in all have spent on the breathless scheduling of when they'd manage to see each other next, be in each other's arms, what with that insufferable French husband's comings and goings! the very Closerie where (ah me) that madcap Celt of his had once murmured, dreamily sucking a fingertip, "If we had it all to live over again *darling* Nicholas d'you suppose we'd really go to all this *trouble?*" and collapsed upon him in helpless laughter, in Arcadian un-innocence and joy.

So why not!

✦

So he'd go. Clear up this Radcliffe-child chore of his stupefying son's, and *go*.

He had therefore just bellowed down into the basement to his man to pack him a couple of bags would he? for a night in Boston and have the car brought around right after lunch, when his front door was flung open and there on his threshold was Morgan, little scarlet lip quivering, eyes enormous with outrage and humiliation

—who cut the air past him and into the front drawing-room like the swish of a kriss, crashing into a fine light French-walnut chair knocking it sens dessus dessous and caroming off with some fuming little sound, to end up at the long front windows absolutely without a look at him, glaring nearsightedly out at her unpaid taxi or whatever she wanted him to think she *was* glaring at, possibly nothing.

Nicholas collected his wits enough to follow, with a re-assembled smile, informing her shivering little back, in a voice of well-brought-up un-astonishment, that this visit was an agreeable surprise.

She simply sank her head lower, clapped her slim palms over her ears to shut out his loathsome libertine accents, and responded, if response was what it was, with a mewling cry.

He being naturally unable to make anything out of any of this, was fool enough to say so.

At which she spun round upon him, eyes as good as blind with tears, and blazed at him she wondered his unfeeling black heart as much as bothered, why did he even let her cross his doorsill at all!!

Nicholas's jaw opened and hung, a permanency.

"If *that*'s all you think of me I mean!" she cried at him chokingly. And when he gaped on, rushed at him stamping, splashing him and everything around with great topaz tears, "Or do you just *hate* me then, why don't you admit it, you don't even think I'm pretty, you wish I'd never been born don't you!" and baring her little white teeth at him, "*Italian girls!*" she screeched, and fled wildly into the back drawing-room, where she flung herself onto the piano bench and set about shattering the air with volley after volley of horrible treble chords.

Nicholas followed, wincing.

"*And don't touch me!*" she instantly bleated, and sprang up and scuttled round into the stair-hall, "I will *not* be soothed and got around and patted patted patted patted, I loathe the very touch of you," she babbled, rushing through the hall and around into the front drawing-room again, "how would you feel if I only pretended you attracted me, oh how stupid how gullible you'd be, oh how I despise you! Oh how can you *bear* to just stand there and disgust me so!" she squalled, and fled into the hall again and up the stairs and into his bedroom, where she plunged face-down into his great bed, howling.

What could he do but follow? and stand there glaring down at her, speechless, as she wallowed and hiccupped!

So she at once demanded in a muffled shriek *must* he stand
there staring at her agony, gloating over how he had made her
weep till she looked hideous? so he'd have an excuse for never
looking at her disfigured as she was again!

He essayed a tentative there there, in a resigned fashion. To
which she responded with moans of hatred and misery.

Presently, in a gingerly way, he risked sitting down by her, a
position on which she immediately turned her delightful little
back, punching and biting into his pillows and showering him
with still more fragments of sob-mangled rodomontade, "Because
you never liked me, not once in all that time, every sweet thing
you ever said to me was a heartless lie, even letting me think I
interested you and *pleased* you" and so forth; anybody can reconstruct the sort of thing. But when he thereupon proceeded to
the routine next stage of mildly patting her shoulder, up she
jumped and ran round the bed ranting, and round the room and
into the bathroom and out, and did he for one instant fancy in his
great smug oaf of a heart that she hadn't lied to him too? for what
else could she do when he treated her so! how could anyone treat
anyone so! "even if you loathed everything I ever did to try to
please you how *could* you treat— Oh Nicholas Nicholas Nicholas
I am so lost so slain!" she ended, casting herself contentedly weeping into his completely apprehensive arms.

So this went on.

It took in fact no less than half an hour of what was left of the
whole outrageous morning by god just to draw enough cold water
to wash her tear-blackened little face!

Then, she felt so faint there was a question whether she didn't
need a brandy instantly, so he was sent shambling off for that while
she lay weak and lovely in a slipper chair, but when he got back
with the stuff she felt enough better *not* to need it, he was sweet
to fetch it but she reminded him he might perfectly well have
remembered she *dis*liked brandy, detailing to him two occasions
at his own baby daughter's house party when, in his very presence, she had refused it. Or else he had noticed but simply didn't
care.

After that he was sent off so she could do her face.

But if he had nothing else to do while she *did* her face, he might
for example fetch a fresh pillowcase before the maid (or whoever)
came and found *this* lipstick-smeared rag, which (she sweetly
cooed at him) looked as if she'd gnawed it in the most heavenly
transports while he was having his beastly will with her.

So he went to the linen closet looking. But she also immediately called that she'd left her bag with lipstick and compact in it *naturally* downstairs it would be right under his nose, how could anybody miss it? so he went down and rummaged about and brought it. Also got her two more clean towels, and a box of Kleenex. And a box of that fluffed cotton. And went down and paid off her taxi.

No sooner back in the house though, and sunk in a chair in the drawing-room to wait, than sure enough he heard her crying again. So he heaved himself to his feet and trundled up for the whateverth time. But now all she broken-heartedly wanted was for him to forgive her. For how could she have subjected him to all that? and so on—the whole smothered rhetoric of contrition, nose buried in his lapel and her arms quivering round as much of his big torso as she felt she might humbly move in on, lifting at last a wet but peaceful face, which inevitably he kissed; and so on round to cold-water compresses again.

Though would he please *stay* this time because there was something she would almost certainly want to say to him before she did her face.

This turned out to be an appeasing complaint: "I *know* I said things I shouldn't 've, Nicholas, but there is one thing I bet you didn't notice as much as you would have if I'd ever got you to behaving the way I want to me."

"Is, huh!" the man more or less snarled.

"See? you didn't notice at all!"

He smoldered at her, speechless.

"Or I suppose it's perfectly pointless to ask," she said in now meek tones, "whether you ever think about any of the things you might guess I do because of you, *for* you. When you didn't even notice."

"Notice *what!*"

"Why should I even tell you! All you do is humiliate me!"

" '*All* I do'!"

"You said to that red-faced man with the dirty stock— Oh how can I admit everything to you! Oh well damn damn, you know it anyway, I have no pride with you! So I do have to hate you sometimes, so there! so I heard you say to him in the paddock why aren't American women woman enough to admit the necessity of high heels and my heart utterly foundered and that night I crept out and threw two pairs of shoes that hadn't absolutely *spike* heels under the first culvert down the carriage-drive. Because my legs *are* nice," she finished, thrusting them out from the bed in sleek display.

Delicious, he gruffly admitted.

She turned them on their high heels in gentle gourmandise, saying, "From any angle, too."

"Well, damn' pretty legs evidently!" he exclaimed, nervous.

But she mourned, "Oh I always have to prompt you so!"

"Now my sweet child, look, a man of my age can't just—"

She leaped to her feet and shrieked at him *stop* saying such things, age age age age age *age*, he maddened her with it, he said it *only* to madden her, to shatter her with frustration! and she ran round the room chattering like a little demon what had his *age* to do with it, hadn't she wanted him the minute she'd laid eyes on him? was it age that kept him from simply stretching out his hand and taking her, sick with love as he *perfectly well* knew she was? or was it his hideous archaic standards of conduct instead! his hateful victorianism or whenever he'd been born, leaving her in this fever of longing and submission and shame, "or are you going to pretend you didn't want me too at least that one morning as much as I wanted you?" she gasped in pain.

Nicholas gaped at this roommate of his own baby daughter's drop-jawed and speechless again.

"Ah but it was so sweet so *sweet*," she wept, crumpling in self-pity into the nearest chair. "My one pitiful threadbare memory of you," she sniffled, forlorn; and collapsed still further, this time to the floor, where she sank effortlessly into the lines of ultimate classic despair. "I crept into your room," she said in a voice so low that no first-row balcony could have caught a word of it, "oh it was barely dawn; so dewy, so cool; so hushed; there was no one in the world but you and me, and there you lay huge and sprawled, and oh Nicholas—"

He bellowed, "By god you know as well as I do I thought you were some confounded daughter come to pester me awake!"

"You patted my shoulder, and then your hand—"

"Different hairdo, damn' unexpected shock if you care to know it!" he cried at her.

"Then you opened your eyes and looked at me in that lovely pallid light and I sat there and oh no woman ever in your bed was more tenderly and strickenly yours my dearest, ah I could see everything you were thinking, your eyes were so near, all sorts of shining floating expressions, and I in this utter sweet terror and determination; and then suddenly you asked me in that *therapeu-*

tic tone if I was all right, and I was so—I was so— Well what *could* I say damn you!" she shrieked, on her feet again, stamping at him, "when all the *matter* was I wanted to get into your bed only you looked as if you'd fling me straight out the window, wouldn't you 've, bully and brute that you are, you *would* have too!" she sobbed. And hurled herself into the bathroom and violently locked the door, and started splashing cold water all over again.

So he went downstairs.

And sat, shaken.

Because all very well to say learned his lesson, but *what* lesson! When why *not* 'stretch out his hand and take'? Was he after all these years changing his goddam spots?

Got to his feet and paced from front drawing-room to back drawing-room, and glared at his watch; then front again and glared at the Copley, and if he was changing then why squat here in a paleolithic stew merely because this wild little beauty of his lacked a certain reserve?

When what was it anyhow but a pure matter of female style: merely she hadn't the usual billowy decorum!

So then a touch of tolerance dammit! At his age he could afford to! Or when forced to, anyhow!

This little Cartesian review, in fact, presented the state of affairs not only without the scrabbling about and the discomfort but with many of the stately appas of pure reason thrown in; so by the time his young lady finally came tripping down, all sweet and self-possessed once more, he could ungruffly remark time had sort of got *on* what with this and that hadn't it! and urge her why not stay take lunch with him wouldn't she? in the sunny brilliance of the garden and all? short notice of course but considering the hour? actually a minor meal, just a cold soup, a crème de concombre he thought it was, then a suprême de volaille, and a salad to glisten in the noon light. He'd also had the man add a little crêpe farcie to help keep body and soul together, glazed crêpes actually and very pretty with their glossy little crests of sliced and lozenged truffles; and though for dessert he couldn't offer her fraises des bois he was afraid, still there was this bavarois with kirsch-soaked strawberries piled round in crimson dunes; and the man had a Montrachet flashing green and gold in its ice.

She said with a sweet look at him that she'd love to.

"Because dammit," he hurried on, "this outlandish whatever-it-is, relationship, hardly know what, between you and me—total absence of any term from the language if you want my opinion!

And I include Freudian technicalities!" he ended with violence.

"Now dammit can't I get you a sherry?" he in part shouted, springing up again.

This, eyes cast down, she meekly accepted.

"The thing is, to take these things *calmly*, in the name of heaven!" he made her see.

She murmured the most docile assent, and sipped.

"In a word, my lovely little thing, you and I do really have to get our, huh, our mutual history into some sort of handle-able order my god!"

"But then Nicholas this was exactly my plan."

". . . uh?"

"Oh but surely this morning you can't—"

"I mean once for all, hope you *see* that!"

"Well of course, only *not* now, when I do think my dearest you might spare me that now of all moments."

"How's that?" he cried hollowly.

"Why, when you've just put me through such hell over you, I mean all morning long!"

"When *I've* just—!"

"Well when anyway you won't dare say I haven't been *through* it! Because how in any case could I possibly suffer like this if it weren't for you, my darling? Or are you going to wound me still more by some cruel unfeeling pretence that you don't believe I do suffer?"

"*Dammit* Morgan—"

"In fact I don't see how you could ever have brought yourself to suggest it," she reproached him in a voice full of pain. "And Nicholas we do have all the time in the world really. I mean for explanations. So, my dearest, I forgive you after all."

He started to say, "Now Morgan I want you to realize I don't even—"

But "Now do we have to just suffocate in here with that lovely sunny glowing little walled garden to wait for lunch in instead?" she sang to him, springing lightly up and stepping with a click of high heels toward the garden doorway, where she paused waiting, great eyes wide and softly upon him until (for what else could he do?) he'd got up and tagged along and come up with her, whereupon she took one step and stood against his heart, lifting her mouth to say now couldn't she just once be kissed? without fussing? just, very sweetly, once?

So therefore.

Then they went out, and shortly had lunch. To which he had the man add a goat-cheese.

✧

He was therefore later than planned leaving for Boston after lunch, in fact a quarter to five.

And with no especial moral to point, either, as he wove northward through the glowing green and gold of early-summer-evening countryside; none that is that a man of brains need bother about. What was this business of homilies anyhow but mankind's fatuous and age-old yearning for the Book of Answers! There never had been answers; never would be; merely a linguistic mistake of Greek philosophy's we'd taken over, that if the word existed the thing it denoted existed too. Why, the only serious desiderata for a normal Indo-European are a pretty girl within grabbing range, a dazing drink, and somebody to knock down. Hymns of self-praise or self-pity on these topics are standard too, being in fact our literature. But answers, no. So he sang

> What call ye this? — my fausse, my fair,
> My gilded honey says me nay

most of the way to the Connecticut line.

Answers he would admit would be very cosy: if everybody could for example find out how everybody else felt, by running one of these beef-witted opinion surveys on it, then everybody might temporarily be less uneasy about how they felt themselves.

Or again, answers filled up space very decoratively if one had nothing urgent to say about what was actually going on: he'd instance what's-his-name from his own generation, Eliot, that Pindar of the prie-dieu, *wonderfully* lyric and readable on there's-nothing-to-be-done-about-anything. Well, there never had been, but was that a reason for inventing answers saying there had?

This warm and lovely little Morgan and her psychiatrist merely for one example: ah, what irresponsibility. Or else what haunting ignorance. And what a conception of Man! for fancy 'happiness' as a goal for a being whose immemorial ambience is catastrophe! Here we'd been, since the dawn of history, stumbling onward and upward, as if that were the right direction, dodging the endless thunderbolts (le bon Dieu, si archaïsant) and now here came psychiatry to 'adjust' us to being knocked sprawling! Did they seriously conceive of Achilles or for variety Michelangelo being 'happy'? Why, in this badly lighted world we take one pratfall after another over whatever it is props up the scenery, complaining of our contusions and abrasions and denouncing the inconveniences, and this is normal and understood; and moreover (as just said) is all literature.

> Ahi, nel dolore nasce
> L'Italo canto

and who'll say what mightn't have become of the unobliterated spirit of man if they'd been able to rid Michelangelo of his 'conflicts' by god, or applied group therapy to the tantrums of Achilles!

The immediate problem wasn't Morgan however or for that matter mankind, but he *did* have to compose a little note to be sent round by messenger to this daughter-in-law, if that was what for once it'd turn out to be, at Radcliffe.

✦

Who presented herself in polite wonder at his Cambridge hotel midmorning next day, a sleek little golden thing in Bermuda shorts and a boy's shirt, feet moreover in sneakers, and as feared not only didn't consider herself in the least engaged to his huge infant of a younger son but visibly didn't even really remember what boy this might be.

This gaping hole in the amenities they both rushed, shaken, to fill, in something of an excess of hasty good manners—he expressing the profuse hope that she'd take dinner with him that very evening, bestow *that* pleasure on him anyhow if only as salvage from this, huh, this rather misled little encounter, and she simultaneously producing the most melting look to beg him come with *her* to this lecture she had to go to this next hour on book 30 of the *Paradiso*, because there was *just* time for them to make it if they went at once and this professor was brilliant, he was *brilliant*, and if Mr. Romney was a Princeton man he'd probably never in his life been to an intellectual Harvard lecture had he, how sad how deprived-sounding, so it would be an Experience. Thus seemliness was retrieved, he saying that this suggestion of hers delighted him, and she, of his dinner, that she would adore it.

The lecture, reversing accepted academic methodology, illumined Dante by special insights into Kierkegaard, the suovetaurilia, Fermi, Braque, Keynes, Peter the Great, and the geography of Dublin.

His dolce dottore then very civilly walked him back to his hotel. Where, as the first thing to catch his eye was Mrs. Barclay's Daimler glittering at the curb, he made his adieus outside.

Mrs. Barclay however was in his sitting-room. Why, *here* he was (she said in tones of pardon) where on earth had he been? because she was on her way to Concord to see the headmaster over something she needn't go into, a very minor contretemps and in any case what did they expect? fifth-formers being what they were, and she just happened to have rung up his house in a chance and idle moment before she left New York, chiefly to say perhaps she should not have rung off so brusquely as to have deprived him of the chance to express the regrets he might well have been suffering from ever since (she now saw) for his conduct toward her. So that was how by pure accident she'd found out where he'd run off to. So *that* was how she'd decided, since she was making this trip to Concord in any case, to break it at Cambridge and show her willingness to forgive him by letting him feed her lunch. So that he could explain.

After this they went amiably down to the dining-room, where, once he'd ordered, he began describing his dilemma, for as she knew he obeyed her lightest word of command, yet in what terms could a Platonic evening be 'explained' to her? other than as Platonic.

"Now really Nicholas," she said reasonably, "will you maintain that a word like 'Platonic' is even in character?"

"But when I keep swearing to you—"

"Now for example what tone do you use with this girl of my poor stepson's, what do you talk about."

"Talk about, how can *I* remember!"

"You mean you don't propose to tell me?"

"Dammit Victoria you know as well as I do I can't remember conversations; never did!"

"You can't recall one single thing she's said to you?" Mrs. Barclay charged.

"Now as it happens I can! Why, it was an outrageous thing, too!"

"Something *she* said to you was?"

"Yes; now this place was packed d'ye see, no agreeable sense of space the way it was in the Thirties, Victoria, dammy if I'm sure it's even the same room, *done* something to it somehow, and in this swaying mob Morgan suddenly spotted of all people Melissa's college roommate."

"Who?"

"Don't remember her married name, but if you'll credit this there she quite openly was with some young whelp she's by heaven having an affair with, Morgan informed me! She *told* me this!" he fulminated, and fell dismally silent.

So she had to urge him, "Yes, so in what sense then?"

"Ahn?"

"I mean so then what."

"*That* doesn't strike you as enough?"

"No I mean the *point* of this story Nicholas."

"I said it wasn't young Sam with her! Wasn't the wretched girl's husband, it's some disconcerting damn' affair!"

"Well but Nicholas young people *do.*"

He said glumly, "But dammit Victoria *Melissa's* roommate!"

"Now you can't forget *I* was married when I fell in love with you!" she cried.

"No but can't you see it's startling, Victoria," he argued, pouring the wine, which he then tasted with sceptical grimaces, "to find the extent of what I hadn't even suspected about my own daughter?"

Mrs. Barclay said in an augmented tone, "But it's not your precious Melissa who's having this miserable affair!"

"Victoria be sensible, what I mean is here's this standard little u·ban amour not merely ventilated with the maddest romanticism in my baby daughter's circle mind you, but by heaven it's her best friend!"

"Nicholas of *all* tiresome misplaced—"

"My own sweet daughter by god and I'm at a loss to understand even the elements of her comportment!"

Mrs. Barclay emptied her glass in irritation and told him he knew *perfectly* well!

"All the same it makes me damned uneasy if you want to know," he mumbled.

"So then what did this bewitching child say to you next about this," she prompted him.

"Uh? what child's this?"

"This chattering little Morgan whatever's-her-name, you know perfectly *well* who I mean!" she cried piercingly. "And how can you bear to be so transparent, well go on go on why won't you go *on!*" she accused him, though all he was doing was attentively refill her glass.

"Well, about this generation? or how d'you mean."

"Your irresponsible conduct with this devious child, what else could I possibly mean!"

So in sheer defense he rambled into an analysis: "Now my lovely Victoria what's this everlasting 'irresponsible'? merest routine good manners to let a woman feel she's a woman surely, what other course's conceivable! I grant a woman adores this sometimes to the point of thinking she adores the man too; but if this happens to convince the giddy thing she has to acquire him as well, poor devil how's that *his* fault? Then when he declines to break his accommodating neck undertaking this responsibility, in other words to acquire *her* by god permanently, she shrieks at him how irresponsible he is!"

"So then this is what this clandestine little thing's been giving you to understand!"

"Uh?"

"That she adores you, what else!" Mrs. Barclay denounced him in a glittering voice.

"Now my reasonable angel you can't be maintaining—"

"It's *disgustingly* clear!"

"But Victoria—"

"And what am *I* to do about you? when you behave like this with one maladjusted clinging child after another!" she fumed.

So he was driven to telling her in manly declamation, "You might *trust* me then for once by almighty heaven!" open and honest as daylight—for where were there a woman and man on earth with a remembered history like theirs? and hadn't he told her and told her?—how happily, how constantly, his memory saw her coming to meet him, toward him, *to* him, out of that unfading past, through the warm noons of Roman streets, the splash of fountains, or she was in sunlight on some broad marble stair, arms full of flowers, descending, coming to him, *his*—and now she spoke as if none of this had ever been, he said heavily.

And refilled their glasses, sighing.

While she sat with lovely eyes cast down.

For what he asked did she conceive love to be if not this continuum, the present what it was because of what was before? why otherwise should he remind her of what lay in memory between them? for didn't she, as he, remember their Alpine meadow deep in spring—

"I should never have had anything to do with you, ah Nicholas," she lamented tenderly.

"You're shaking inside this minute as you did then, admit you are!"

This, eyes deep in his, she mistily pronounced simply untrue.

"Shaking like a sheer girl!" he exulted, making a happy grab for her hand.

"Ah Nicholas what wild conceit."

"But you are, you lovely unforgetting—"

"I am not, oh darling, no," she breathed.

"*I'm* shaking, just at seeing you for this mere—"

But she said, "You'd just had your hair cut," as in dream.

"I'd *what?*"

"Hair cut, oh Nicholas think," she mourned.

"Now when was this, why what an endlessly sweet thing to have remembered somehow!"

"Well you *had*. When naturally I remember how you looked."

"All I meant—"

"And when the way you looked was that you *had* just had your hair cut why should I remember you as having it long? When it was short."

"Why, I suppose so!" he cried, amazed.

"Oh cuore mio *remember?*"

So they gazed at each other through a haze of angels. She murmured, "Must go, caro," in virgin revery, "darling literally fly," not stirring.

"Now how could I ever let you go!"

"Or want to, ah sweet," she sighed, eyes drifting to their entwined contented hands.

But as he was triumphantly announcing, "Then angel stay!" the maître d'hotel bowed over them, madam's chauffeur having sent in word, as madam had instructed, to remind madam that madam had wished to set out at two.

They stared at each other dashed, beset.

In anguish or in outrage, "My angel then will you dammit come to dinner tomorrow, you never come visit me!" he charged.

"Ah Nicholas I know I've been neglecting you," she lied to him in tenderest penitence.

"So then come on then!"

"For example I haven't even come by to make sure you're comfortably settled, have I."

"How's that?" he cried out.

"Really looked after and *cared* for you Nicholas darling, I should keep seeing to it!"

"Then will you come to dinner?"

"*Tomorrow?*"

"Or day after then?"

"Oh *how* miserable, when dinners, oh Nicholas you might very well guess how impos—"

"*Lunch* then day after tomorrow, dammit my lovely Victoria now say you will!"

"Well possibly lunch the day after *that* was what I actually had in mind," she confessed in a voice now as smooth as cream, neither of them needing (at their age) to be so insensible as even to remember that this would be the man's day off.

So that evening he could light-heartedly feed the Radcliffe child (who, it turned out at considerable length at dinner, had thought of doing her junior paper on Bramante's early Milanese period but the subject was *so* broad) and deliver her punctually at this 8:30 seminar she had on Kepler; thus he was back in his sitting-room in the hotel, yawning pleasurably and on the point of bed in good time for once, in fact only waiting for the radio to finish off one of Bach's everlasting ethereal variations on the Sailor's Hornpipe, when of all possible things the door opened and there was Morgan.

Looking this time like a somber and sulky little thundercloud and muttering, "Well I am just desperate Nicholas so there!" before she'd even lifted her haunted face to be kissed.

Indeed hardly kissed him at all before she was fretting, "I know it's all very convenient and comfortable for *you* Nicholas, but you might realize *I* had to cut a rehearsal to come here after you. And I'd never see you if I didn't!" she concluded peevishly, rebuking him still further by not only not kissing him again but in fact taking herself ungraciously right out of his arms.

And in a pet flicked the radio from Bach to some young woman who sang in a voice of sugary delinquency "wunna be bad rill baaad" before Nicholas could leap snarling and snap the thing off.

Morgan immediately said, "Well Nicholas I know I shouldn't be furious with you but it *is* your fault that I'm so worried now about Toby that I'm in this unending sleepless anguish over it! So *of course* I had to come discuss it with you!"

'*His* fault'!

"Well my dearest it *is*, why, you brought it all up, you *reproved* me for not thinking about Toby when I'm engaged to him and now I *keep* thinking about it, oh how could you!" she chattered, eyes filling with tears.

He started to say he was blest if he saw offhand what pos—

"So naturally I had to follow you then!" she cried in indignation. "Because when I'm so complex who else understands me, my darling? Not that you do—*oh* you can be so blind! But I mean you do at least partly know how utterly—oh Nicholas how *enslavedly* I seem to love you! because truly don't you?" she pleaded, coming to him.

He patted her, and declared with a belated lightness of tone that he wasn't so insensible as to deny she'd had the flattering good manners to make it plain she felt so.

"Oh well when I couldn't help myself as you know perfectly well; but I mean what would Toby *do* is what I want you to explain, is why I came. I mean would he get special leave d'you think or something equally desperate?"

Nothing desperate about a leave! what if he did?

" 'Nothing desperate'!" she echoed, almost in a shriek. "When only yesterday Melissa for example told me her own best friend asked her whether she thought Sam might even kill her if he found out about Patrick? and Melissa says she *just doesn't know!*" she whispered in horror.

He said now what staring nonsense was this! did her generation take its coups de théâtre from the tabloids?

But she said, "Yes only what will Toby *do?* oh Nicholas how does any woman ever find out what goes on in your heads, the way you plunge wildly past and all."

He said these Yale boys, ptuh, needn't worry her pretty head about 'em, nothing against Toby personally of course but Yale boys like the Victorians always thought up was *up*.

"Well Nicholas what difference does it make where you went to college, but you *have* to warn me what he may do, can't you see?" she implored him. "Because you are responsible for me, Nicholas!"

Now look, he said humanely, now couldn't she realize? her enchanting sex had been saying *Look at me, dance with me* and the like to him ever since he could remember, and that was the whole damn' trouble.

"Oh I know I'm not a new experience to you, you don't have to remind me!" she said with a gasp, drooping, delivering herself instantly from his arms. "I know you're a libertine, my psychiatrist says so, anyway I know you won't ever love me, love *deeply* Nicholas, the way I love you, it's just not in your nature I guess," she said in a low tone, blinking rapidly. "Which you know *is* why she keeps saying there's no happy future for me in loving you. Oh as if I cared! Or as if living without you could seem a 'future' to me, my darling, even if it stretched out till I'm a hundred. Oh but Nicholas she does have my good at heart though," she fretted all woe-begone, "even saying you're bad for me."

He said with some natural heat the woman was a fool, *he* 'bad for her'!

"Yes but the *worst* is, she tries to make me think I'm bad for you too, I can't bear it!"

Not good for him? what, when here she was caressing his advancing years with this sweetest blandishment, this most touching of all flatteries, her young beauty's devotion?

"Oh oh please not about *age* my dearest!" she mourned. "Oh you understand women so little—*so little!*—when you talk about age like that!" she half-wept in exasperation and despondency. "I'd love you when you were eighty—*will* love you when!" she wailed, starting up, confronting him.

Long before *that* unaccommodating milestone, he said soberly, he hoped some honest old friend would have the common humanity to put him down.

"Oh but Nicholas this *isn't* just that I'm young and in love, *terribly* in love, for the first time, can't you see that? Have I ever said I wasn't young and inexperienced? Or can't you admit that even though I am, you still could be the one love of my life? Because you are! and why couldn't my first love be my real one!"

He said, well, in principle—

"So I can't even *make* my mind think about Toby, oh I just don't love him at all," she moaned in loveliest distraction. "Because oh even you must see I have a duty to myself, women just *do* I don't care what you say, am I to be irresponsible and deny my love for you? only when I write and tell Toby I'm your mistress he may *kill* himself, my dearest, and then I'll be haunted, oh Nicholas what shall I even do?" she babbled, clinging to him.

He got enough of his thunderstruck voice back to expostulate now now now now, why she must be out of her sweet little female bedlamite mind!! did she suppose at *his* age he'd be so insensible, or her own word 'irresponsible' dammit, as to disseize a perfectly decent boy, no matter how hulking, of a girl he—

"Oh how can you misunderstand me so, *hurt* me so!" she choked, through a tide of tears. "As if I'd ever more than glanced— As if what I feel for you could be compared— Well what if I did for one mere moment consider marrying Toby and say I would, was it for anything but to be connected with you? once I'd found out his stepmother is this old family friend so you couldn't just have over-looked me anymore the way you'd like to," she ran wretchedly on, tears now showering, "when besides I'd at least have been *seeing* you, Nicholas, not often perhaps but still often, so your image would always have been there under my eyelids, every day fresh and renewed and new, how can you not understand!"

Would she let him finish a sentence? because he was *perfectly* willing to concede her psychiatrist's shooing her back toward Toby was not merely misplaced but a piece of damned imbecility, fancy telling a girl who was in love with one man that she ought to fall in love with another man instead! Nevertheless—

"I never even suspected what love was till I loved you!"

Nevertheless dammit—

"This half-unbearable joy, oh this certainty that I'd found the one being I was created for," she recited softly, as if a quotation, "after my whole lifetime of just ordinary boys and men, my dearest!"

So he sat down, sighing; and started out to suggest that perhaps she hadn't entirely—

"As if till now I'd always lived in some deep hopeless night but now suddenly there is this lovely light of day over everything every-where, ah can't you see how I must feel at last?"

He said well, yes; because he supposed poetry for example was something anybody wrote till age twenty-five and then gave up (or of course in some cases went on writing, with more studied enigma to it but no less dull) and he wondered whether just as poetry was a kind of first-love of language, so this feeling of hers—

"Well but you *are* the only man I've ever loved, Nicholas," she told him, coming to kneel in front of him before he could scramble up from where he was sitting (which unfortunately was a mock-Empire sofa as big as a bed made for love) and leaning toward him so that he had at all hazards to gaze straight into the child's eyes if only to keep from looking down her dress.

He said well she was a sweet temptress, by god she was; and damn' well she knew it, too, he added, patting her; but now couldn't she all the same recognize the sort of situation—because wasn't it?—that she and he and everybody they knew had been raised *not* to—

"Oh but Nicholas that was only before I'd given *up* Toby, can't you see? when now there's nobody!"

He let out some vacuous unhappy sound as if he no longer had any really workable notion of what this might even mean.

"Because all I have to do is sit down and write to him right now to tell him, and prove to you; and then even you will have to admit, oh my dearest then I *will* be yours!"

He pronounced her name a couple of times over, as if it were in some sheer foreign language.

She said in a choking whisper, "And so then *not* have to wait oh please please after all these endless months any longer my darling?" and stretched blissfully up to be kissed and taken, saying his name as silkily as if she were already swooning enravished in his bed.

Poor devil he besought her now *look* in heaven's reasonable name! wouldn't she like the lovely thing she was merely *listen* to him for ten consecutive seconds for once? for even assuming as the last hypothesis conceivable, the *purest* of absolute assumptions, suppose he did for one putative bewildering minute happen to want her as much as she wanted him—

She said in her throat, "*You do.*"

By god he gobbled if he was going to kiss her be damned if it'd be in *this* preposterous squat, would she stand *up?* scrambling to his feet and hauling her up with him; but then instead of kissing the lovely pleading child like a man in his right mind, he took her determinedly by the shoulders as if possibly to shake her and launched into a homily on (of all topics) maturity.

So naturally she broke in: "But can't you see with your own eyes how loving you has turned me into a woman at last, my dearest?"

Now he *assured* her—

"You think I'm *not!*" she cried, going white.

He said he simply—

"Only then I'm *not!*" she choked, springing away from him. "Oh how can you taunt me so cruelly!" and fled to the sofa, on which she dropped, gasping.

But when he more or less flabbergasted came after her with the ready assuasive rhetoric of solace (or whatever *was* needed) she sprang up in his face squalling "Well then I'm a *virgin* if you must make me tell you damn you!" in mortification and rage, and catapulted past him into the dark bedroom, and banged and bolted the door.

Nicholas slumped back onto the sofa, looking his glummest. And, presently, yawning.

Then, as the silence went on, he stood for a time staring in vacancy and depression out the window onto the nighted street.

And went back and sat down again; and almost dozed.

For a long time there was silence. But at last he heard her unbolt and open the door, and then her hand came around the doorjamb and found the switch and turned out the lights. But when in the dimness he went solicitously toward her she slipped past him and stood in the deeper dusk by the doorway to the hall.

Where then she mumbled something in a tone so low that he had to go right up to her to make out what it was.

She whispered with her little back to him that he must not look at her, she was hideous with tears, she knew she was hideous, she'd cried so long and so hopelessly, in her misery, in (for why should she not say it?) her final despair.

He said gently *not* despair, now what sort of Regency performance was this? when here she was with every prospect, with every bright hope.

But she said how could he call it a 'performance' when it was just that she loved him, it *was* love, this was what love was, and she murmured an alexandrine which it struck him must be Racine; she loved him and she did not see how he could expect her to just stop. But if it would please him she would try to stop throwing herself humiliatingly at him, if that would make him feel less harassed, for would it? for then she would try, she finished softly, and opened the door.

And as she stepped through said in a sad little voice, "Because Nicholas this *shows* I am grown up. I can Renounce you." And with gentle dignity went down the hall away.

So he had to drive back to New York next morning talking to himself in bafflement and inhibition.

For responsible responsible, who knew what it meant anyhow? flung in his face morning noon and night like this!

As if a man's soul were there to be yelled at!

The soul is a private affair, even the religious bureaucrats were beginning to admit it without all these threats of documented hellfire; le bon Dieu had had better sense all along, and he remembered once in his boyhood his father leaping from the stanhope in a towering passion—they'd been on the road to Peirce's Mills, up a branch of the Black Brandywine, getting a hunter used to driving harness—his father had leaped down and ripped off a pious posted sign

SIN AND YOU'LL FIND OUT

which he'd beaten to flinders on a stump, roaring *he*'d keep their impertinent yatter out of Chester County for 'em by god! and his father had been *right* by god, no birthright Philadelphia Quaker ever bothered his head over their slave-class preoccupation with the safety of their unappetizing souls, what was this anyhow, the whingeing hagiolatrous tenth century all over again?

—Except of course it was not, admittedly, an answer to much of anything about this sweet little Morgan of his.

Why did this generation suffer so drearily? Where was the styled and handsome anguish of tradition? the whole ravishing diapason, from Edwardian vapors to those wonderful screeching bosom-beating Mediterranean tantrums, how decorative, how in keeping!

Whereas in this present desolate ambience— Why, for instance, for sheer contrast that phrase of Paris's to Helen, in the *Iliad*, when he can hardly wait for her to get her clothes off, *glukus hímeros hairei*, he pronounced in his mind, *"sweet* desire," could one imagine any intellectually fashionable novelist these days, of any of the four contemporary sexes, calling desire sweet? by heaven they talked as if the only similitude for love were the terminal agonies of cancer!

So in the end he drove into New York lustily singing

> Almighty Sir, of Whose my soul
> An ancient indecision is,

an undergraduate pastiche the prosody of which, and the syntax, still pleased him.

What he'd first thought of feeding his Victoria was an early-summer lunch out of Paul Reboux: a cool gazpacho, then a little glazed crème de cervelle (which, as he wouldn't inform her was cervelle, she'd love), followed by a fine pink-fleshed lake trout garnished in two shades of green, viz., artichoke hearts and green mayonnaise, and end with a vanilla ice gleaming with slivers of almond and slivers of truffles. But then he remembered she made a tiresome fuss at truffles, which she held were not merely over-rated but rubbery, so after trying in vain to find fraises des bois he had just this cherry tart with a crème aux marrons piped onto it in rococo swags.

That then was what she arrived looking lovely to eat.

He'd laid the table out under the lace-shadowed locust tree in his little walled garden, and almost at once as they ate (she'd barely finished her crème de cervelle—what *was* this delicious thing, a mousse de viande? he said yes) almost at once she said she was concerned over how he proposed to occupy his time once he was in Europe, would he merely like all bankers go to Geneva? because he'd spoken of writing his memoirs or had he really meant a novel, which was what everybody seemed to write instead, and in either case she'd have expected him to go to Paris where he'd always said August and September were his favorite months, with that heavenly golden haze over the Seine in the mornings and enough of everybody away en vacances to make the lovely city seem nearly deserted, for example that time he and she had had the whole Place St. Sulpice to themselves, such a blessing, did he remember? so if he was going to write something, or even set his songs, was Paris possibly where he planned to go and perhaps stay?

So he replied, taking their empty ramekins down and in, to the little back-basement kitchen, and bringing out the glistening trout, on seeing which she cried out how magnificently handsome (as it was), he replied hardly memoirs but now would she notice this Montrachet particularly? because this was a Tastevin bottling which he'd never found before outside of France, he'd come on it only last week uptown, a sheer trouvaille.

Oh *wasn't* it, she exclaimed, sipping, and then with a little sound of delight sipping again, how *really* delectable, he must not just tell her where he'd got it but remind her later too, but did he then mean he remembered that Place St. Sulpice day, what they'd done?

He said with a snort he was aware of this female dogma that men have no memory, even of love, but she didn't seriously expect him to forget the priest her conduct had upset? the suggestion was mere coquetry. No memoirs, no; who'd read a banker's memoirs; and what could he call it if he did, A *Short Wait for the Butcher* or what? holding up his glass to gaze at the green gold of the wine against the brilliance of early afternoon.

Well then she said he meant he'd be in Paris in for example August?

All August probably; why not.

Because she said she'd asked because she herself might very easily be in Paris too in August for a day or so, anyhow she was not going to follow her husband to Geneva, so this was why she'd

wondered about Paris and accordingly asked him; namely because
of this possibility she was describing; of being there herself; she
meant in August.

To this he naturally if prematurely replied, dropping knife and
fork in delight, thank God was she really about to make up her
mind about him then, angel that she was?

She cried out in petulance what an utterly wicked lying thing
even to say!

So he served her again to trout, dashed.

Which she forgave his indiscretion enough to eat. And
launched next into a reporting, or anyhow a selective report,
which she contrived to make sound very much like an accounting
to him alone, of her life for the period he'd deserted her in, that
space of seventeen years which he'd spent she had no way of ever
knowing how, or sunk in what wallowing self-indulgences.

He protested that on the contrary these years had been crowded
with hardly supportable acts of God, some of them of an almost
medieval savagery.

A space she repeated of seventeen years which he could as guiltily compute as she but which she was not asking him to justify to
her, now or ever, neither was she really rebuking him, she said
with a gentle glance, since she was *fond* of him, and also she was
forgiving and besides it had after all not been really his fault that
their affair had ended as it had, she admitted, drooping her pretty
eyelids, but she did wish him to know that though in those seventeen years she'd been tempted by other men often, and twice *agonizingly* (she had never told anyone about either of these and
never would tell anyone but him, but early in the war this utterly
charming Free French attaché had fallen terribly movingly in love
with her, the most stormy and haunting siege, and ah such tenderness of desire, he of course desiring but she on her part too, oh
she'd *never* been quite so wrung he was so handsome and bereft,
and this affair she chronicled for him scene by scene, but he'd
been caught on a secret mission to Toulon in 1944 and stood
against a wall and shot and she hadn't even the consolation of
having made love with him even once and made him happy, she
said in grief, taking out a little jewel-studded Louis XVI pillbox, a
small capsule from which she washed down with Montrachet, and
then later this other, the second husband of one of her three best
friends, a *heart*-breakingly attractive Carolinian who'd pursued
her with the most intoxicating gaiety for nearly two years, and she
described in detail the tender, frustrate, and harrowing course of

this adulterous passion too) but in spite of these, in spite of others too at times almost as blissfully devastating as they, as close as they to the ideal exemplar and paradigm of the delicately panting female heart, yet she had nevertheless stayed *faithful* to him, did he realize that? she cried almost angrily, foolishly faithful *thanklessly* faithful, she'd not ever had another affair, so there! or she supposed ever even fallen in love again really, she told him softly, in fact probably he'd spoiled her life for her and he was a pig, she charged, smiling contentedly into his eyes.

During all this he had taken away the trout, which they'd nearly consumed, and carried the plates to the kitchen and brought out dessert plates and the cherry tart with its creamy swags and gadroons, and they had eaten a good part of it and he had additionally eaten a couple of peaches and some green almonds, and then he had brought the coffee out to the table so as not to interrupt her, and they'd drunk that and she had had a Cointreau and he a kirsch, and she had helped him clear the table and rinse-and-stack in the little kitchen as of old; so it turned out that at the moment she called him a pig she happened to be standing so near him as to be as good as in his arms.

Taking the sweet stylish creature into them therefore he begged if he now might know whether all this could by some divine benevolence mean (what he hardly dared hope) that she still did love him (who God knew had never ceased adoring *her*); and when she murmured in happy acquiescence how could he possibly suppose this, so unlikely, so utterly out of the question, resting her forehead on his collarbone where it had rested so many thousands of times, he kissed the elegantly sculptured shaft of her neck where its curve was at its most heavenly and where he remembered it moved her most.

Whereupon clinging to him she whimpered she must go. He said would she be quiet? when he'd been on the point of reciting for her (and translating) that couplet of Ovid's that went

> ego semper amavi
> et si quid faciam nunc quoque quaeris, amo

which he'd render impromptu for her

> Always in love till now, till now's been true.
> And now? Why, dammy, I'm in love now too.

For like Ovid, he (Nicholas) being a man of sensibility was a damn' sight more devotedly faithful than the reputation which in mere feminine maneuvering she kept gracelessly trying to give him: she'd plundered his senses twenty years ago once for all and every beat of her own responding heart must tell her so!—a claim which she informed him dreamily he must know was false from end to end.

So then they kissed for some time.

Until tenderly taking her mouth away from him she half-said, ". . . mustn't," and opening her eyes to him at last, ". . . so untrustworthy," she breathed, her look all soft radiance, lost, lifting her mouth again for a kiss which this time went on for some while too.

Thus they stood shaken and clinging, in this mild daze; hardly even practical, vacuous in fact and abandoned; mindlessly sighing as in time past so many thousands of times; she saying at last ". . . and you've been so long ah Nicholas," in comment on which he like a fool mumbled the first thing that came into his head, an amiable "—these damn' people you marry."

At which to his flat astonishment she burst into tears and fled from him into the basement hall!

"*Now* what in God's name can I have said now!" he groaned out, chasing after and grabbing her at the foot of the stair, where while she wept in his arms she absolutely would not look at him or speak.

"But Victoria!" he implored her, distracted, "Now my *sweetest* of women!"

Still she wept.

"My darling creature you can't mean to tell me," he havered on (as she had told him nothing), "that some mere fortuitous reference like that to your damn' husb—"

"How *could* you!" she raged, stopping her tears instantly.

"But I merely—"

"Just at the most tender— *Just* when I was so—"

"But in God's thunderstruck name—"

"—heartless taunting rake!" she choked, snatching his handkerchief from his breast-pocket and dabbing in fury.

"But I—"

She shrieked, "Oh when you can't even realize what your selfish grabbing insensitive nature *involves* me in even!" thrusting him off and flying up the stair, and (when he scrambled after her) flinging his handkerchief back down at his disconcerted face. "Have I no life of my own then?" she raved from the top step, whirling upon him panting.

"Now my utterly blessed woman what earthly elaborate disorder *is* this?" he begged, jarring to a halt a step below her, quailing.

"And when you don't even know what you ask!"

"'Not know'!"

"*Oh you put me off so!*"

"But I *love* you goddammit!" he shouted.

" 'Love me,' when you've not even the most doltish retarded notion— How *could* you misunderstand me for seventeen whole years!"

He moaned, "My darling will you merely once listen to me at all?" stretching out his hands in what seemed entreaty, though where they came to rest was her sleek waist.

"When everything I ever felt about you—"

"But that's exactly the point I've—"

"Why, you can't even see what thinking you love me as you used to will merely do to me!" she upbraided him, great blue eyes filling with tears of sheer reproof.

"Are you in some mad contriving feminine imposture going to pretend that from the moment I first laid eyes on you, there at your baby sister's wedding," he cried in the most moving unhappiness, "without the intervention of a single day—Victoria my one darling among women I don't need to swear it, you *know* it, every lovely inch of you knows it!" he declaimed.

So she gazed at him more reasonably.

And in fact next said, "But my darling it isn't that I doubt you, or anyhow not really, though of course you heartlessly lie to me constantly," she gently regretted, taking one of his hands from her waist to hold it against her cheek, "but when I had to organize some sort of life for myself when you left me, you must *see!*"

"But my love I 'left' you only because you—"

This tactless topic she condoningly hushed by instantly putting her fingers over his lips, while conceding, "Yes, and this autumn who'd merely *believe* now he'll be a huge sixth-former," before continuing, "but Nicholas you do have to see what loving you all over again will do to my responsibilities if I were for one minute to let you have your selfish way."

"My angel—"

"And simply upset everything I've lived with, oh Nicholas my whole ordered life all these years and my delightful son and my husb— my house," she ran sadly on, stroking his temple apologetically with a fingertip, "why, simply all these peaceful family emotions I'm used to, my poor old darling. Only now you want to bully me into letting you sweep everything away and how *can* I, how could I stand it if I let everything I felt for you— And I *never* felt about anyone what I did for you, oh caro look your hair's getting grey," she sniffed in misery.

"But just by god had it cut again too!" he snickered, remembering; and with a snort of laughter took her back in his arms—where after a moment she had the complaisance to giggle.

"Ahhhh think of it all though!" he exulted tenderly. "There you were at your sister's wedding in that damn' receiving line, I couldn't even touch your hand!"

"Well, you did, you brought me that first glass of champagne; *so* noticing, Nicholas."

"Looked thirsty," he smirked, reasonably.

"So sweet."

"More than your damn' husband did for you!"

"Oh the way you *looked* at me when you came up with my champagne, oh darling I never felt so undefendable and I didn't even know who you were."

"My god Victoria how d'you think *I* felt!"

"We fell in love with each other right there, in front of everybody on earth, you never realized that?" she told him soberly.

"Your face gave everything away."

". . . I know."

"You knew *then!*"

"Well you were *lovely*-looking!" she cried in happy extenuation; and suddenly in immemorial flight slipping from his hands and (when neighing her name he lunged after her) seized his hands and kissed the heel of the thumb of one of them with little silly kisses, while he declaimed (rather more in the manner of, say, the Earl of Rochester than in his own) that he wished the whole round world were as entirely hers as he was, now or ever, for then she would have no reason to complain of anything!

But "oh Nicholas, oh we mustn't, I can't," she mumbled amorously, giving him a great kiss; and then pulling herself away fluttered along the hall and into the front drawing-room.

Here however when he caught her she utterly handed herself over, every charming inch, for the whole heaven-sent eternity of a dozen heartbeats.

So when she then again began to struggle, how could he help ranting (in words as straight from the heart as under Charles II or any other king by god) that she was the most afflicting fair creature in the world! for whence came this peevish prudence that hourly advised her concerning him how 'dangerous' it was to be kind to the one man on earth who loved her best?

"Ah never!" she cried in sheer laughing happiness, and fled him.

What, was he to be permitted to gaze upon the miracle she was, yet forever have the miracle she might do him forbidden him? he chased her proclaiming, with a shout of laughter; for could she not pick her deserving serv^t, himself, and place her kindness *there?* — an act so lofty as would show the greatness of her spirit, and distinguish her in love, as she was in all things else, from womankind. And still laughing caught her and kissed her, a long long kiss.

Until she again took that heavenly mouth away from him sighing and quivering, mournfully whispering, ". . . is awful," eyes one unending confiding smile; and then with one more flurry of quick pouted kisses (nyim-nyim-nyim-nyim) escaped him again, in little laughing sighing rushes from room to room, he now delightedly crying could she reproach to him that he had no ways, save words, to express that love to her, yet uncivilly still refuse him all means, save words, to acquaint her with it? for was he to have thought her more of an angel than he now found her a woman? and ran her down in the back drawing-room against the curve of the piano at last, whereupon she nuzzled and cooed and femalized at him in general.

And let him lead her to the foot of the stairs, where she gave him a long kiss. "Oh how I want you when I mustn't even *consider* you!" she lamented, kissing him again, blue eyes melted. "And when it is so impossible oh darling," kissing him once more, in a gale of sighs.

And in a perfect haze of love let him take her up his stairs.

So, then, in a kind of wild calm at last, breathless with rushing and with laughter, both of them, on in, to his elegant rosewood bed—both of them having after all, for hours, known exactly what they were doing.

He was working his contented way through his mail next day between tender attempts to phone his Victoria (who kept being out: "Corinna's gone with all her brokers maying," he muttered, a line he'd after all written to her and no other, however many years ago it now was), working his way through a grotesque mail in fact, a snapshot of loquat trees and a dirty impluvium, endorsed "Here is nothing of great interest old boy but at least everyone keeps his meals down, how good God is," and a Class of 1931 Reunion announcement captioned in blackletter "A Clean Old Man Never Decays," not to mention other letters equally disfigured by signs of widespread and various world disorder, including a manuscript-size communication from his wife's lawyers which he merely bundled off to his own (who were the same men anyhow), when Melissa rang up.

"Now Daddy what *is* this, what unpredictable thing have you done to Morgan!"

Taken flat aback, he uttered a resounding cry.

"Well Daddy it's *Melissa*: I said 'to Morgan'; I mean darling is the connection bad or something? because what have you been doing to her?"

"*I* done!"

"So you did perfectly well understand all the time!"

"How's that?" he bayed.

"Well Daddy I do think it's not only irresponsible but just *provoking* of you, I mean forgive me and all, sweetie, but after all here she just *is!*"

"But dammit what if she is!"

"But she's *hysterical* from you!"

"She's *what?*"

"Oh dearest don't yell; hysterical."

"Who says this?"

"I'm just *telling* you, goodness! she's been here in my hands this whole half-morning crying her heart out over your treatment of her and I do think it's utterly pathetic!"

He roared, "May I interrupt this flood of womanly pity long enough to make out—"

"Daddy *please!*"

"Yes but what am I accused of dammit!"

"Dearest I *wasn't* accusing you; why, what a thing to say; it was Morgan."

"Then what's Morgan accus—"

"Well goodness how do *I* know, I called you to *ask!* Daddy she's just too upset to say, except you were terribly unfeeling and unkind and as good as—"

" 'Unfeeling'!"

"Well she's so incoherent and sobbing, what *did* you do to her?"

" 'Do,' by god Melissa on your own insistence I took her to the Iridium Room and what's more I additionally gave a damn' good lunch if you want to know to the squalling little she-brat!"

This produced a shocked silence. Finally she said, "Well but *Daddy*." And then, "Well sweetie all I can say is, that isn't exactly *her* story!"

"I don't by god doubt *that* in the least!"

"But *something* upset her, you will admit?"

On this, he choked.

"What, dearest? because if I am trying to merely make some sense of all this it's on *your* account Daddy after all!"

He said in an attempt at a lighter tone, "Now Melissa the plain apodeictic fact is nobody is very sensible," but she paid no attention to this truth, on the contrary went on:

"When I suppose with Toby off at sea again and *no* letters, I know you're just a man and don't know about things Daddy but girls get perfectly *panicky*, anyhow if in frantic loneliness or whatever she went around to see you *of course* it's your fault! why, you took her dancing and then you fed her this very good lunch as you just admitted yourself!"

"My dear Melissa the child hardly—"

"Because at any rate she admittedly did go round to see you for whatever reason, you won't deny!"

"By god didn't she!"

"So sweetie I do think you might see your responsibilities a little more promptly don't you? And go soothingly around to see her and apologize! Because I'm taking her back to her apartment, I can't just go *on* having her weeping here, goodness! Because is it really too outlandishly difficult for you just to step into a taxi when you haven't anything actually to do anyhow? and go make it up with the poor bruised bereft thing! And like a sweet *not* yell? but just go appease her. Instead of brutalize and terrify, Daddy!"

So if the man was not to yell at his precious daughter, what could he do.

—Even though goddammit how was *his* conduct toward that unhelpless little seductress of his 'irresponsible' but not hers toward him! a question he'd by heaven like to propound to people who think answers answer! Such for example as that Edwardian lawyer of his with his comfortable fifteen-stone felicitousnesses ("After all, no one, surely now, Nick old man, more aware than yourself? Of the pitfalls? Furor ille revisit and so forth, how's it go. Girls being, after all, flighty veering little things at best! And these first virginal fancies, Nick, after all!") and Time the Healer and so forth till doomsday—when the plain fact was that the only course for a decent man was both to take her and not to take her!

Whom in a word loved or unloved he must equally destroy, if one cared to use these stately terms!

"—and let him who is without luck among ye cast the first die!" he snarled; and sent the man for a taxi.

—On the whole better not take her flowers: might well just become dried keepsakes; keep memories needlessly alive.

But then, *no* by heaven, for had le bon Dieu created the touching, the charming memory of woman only for psychiatry to prevent its filling itself with the sweet woe it cherished most? so first thing he did was lay his flowers on his young love's bed, though her room was in such sad darkness he barely made out where she lay.

And sending her dithering maid away and pulling up a chair to her bedside he said now poor little sweet what *was* this.

From a shadowy tent of silence her hand slid out and sought his, which it weakly clung to; but she said nothing.

So he solicitously prodded but *what* then, for wouldn't she say? Because he went on to assure her here he was, d'she see? as she'd asked that he be; if she'd take her pretty nose out of those suffocating pillows and look at him she'd see for herself he was not only here but here from the tenderest *concern* for her.

But what at last from the muffling depths of her bed she miserably whispered was that she loved him.

He said but—

Loved him, and a woman's only life was love; and then her voice died piteously away.

He said he knew. He *knew*. Nevertheless—

Concern was the word he'd used but what he'd meant was pity. So she was going away, to spare him. Even possibly to a sanitarium. But not burden him again. She was going to be what he wanted her to, responsible. All she could do was say adieu. With her lips; for with her heart, never.

Why, he said, she had her whole young life before her, what kind of talk was this! with in fact only one thing not in her power, viz., to reward any man in the world with half so much sweetness as she had thrown away on his worthless and irrelevant self.

She wanted to die. She was so worn. But she would not. Truly not. If only because then he might blame himself. When it was not his fault that she loved him so. She could never blame him. She could only love him.

He tried saying now what was so damn' charming about *him*? even if some sweet creature had the indulgence to let a man see she thought so, still the plain truth was— Would she bear for a moment with a Classical analogy? for take the *Iliad*: the *Iliad* it often appeared was like a ballet, matched heroes dancing forward at each other in opposing pairs to fling their antiphonal taunts and spears, then dancing back, and then after a choral movement of the ordinary infantry another pair coming on, another pas de deux; and this he said was how it often seemed to be with love, the shafts of woman's transfixing beauty ran him through, their sighs answering his antiphonally in turn, and if it was ever-changing and new still was it each time any the less utterly a death? and so there it was.

She replied, but now so low he could barely hear her, that a woman never forgot the man who first made her feel she was a woman, there was nobody like him for her ever, but her love for him was more than merely this, he *was* the love of her life, that was all, even now she had renounced him; and if he was shallow and she loved him more deeply than he had ever loved her, or loved any woman, or could love, that was her fate; her doom; he could love one woman, as he said, and then in time another, and love the second as much as he had the first, but *her* heart she had given him for life, and she had only one to give. And how was she merely to get through the fifty years more, the half-century, that he kept telling her she had every reason to look forward to, with no more of him than this? she ended brokenly, beginning as in sheer weakness to cry.

Well poor devil what could he or any man say.

But presently she stopped; and then she said, sniffling, here was her diary, and from somewhere under her in the tumbled linen she pushed a warm grubby little volume toward him. Because he was to take it. It was the chronicle of her love. He was to take it as a last act of ritual kindness since he would not take her. For it broke off on the day— Well, he would see, because the last entry she had made would tell him *how* she loved him, no longer the girl she had been that now lost November afternoon when she'd come into his library from the stables to tea and seen him and known her destiny but like the *woman* her loving him had made her. For this much honor at least he could do her, to read what she had set down. He must promise to. This was all she any longer sought.

He stammered out that the warmth, the sweetness, of her imagination—why, what could be more understandable? and this honest attachment— And yet no woman could be more aware of the pitfalls, surely, than herself? Ah but dammit he'd not have the insensibility to moralize at her when certainly none of this could be forgotten by *him* by heaven, not ever, her beauty, her lovely impulsive—

But she gasped, now crying bitterly, oh kiss her and go.

So he went, gulping; her diary clenched still warm from her in his hand. And walked heavily to Park Avenue and then downtown, on and on through the early-summer brilliance of afternoon, sighing and cast down, the whole sad dilemma an insoluble damn' shame. And all because of *his* decision, that poor little sweet a mere turning point! and so, helplessly, at last (muttering he by god *must* be suffering an elemental change if he walked out of a pretty girl's bedroom for her own good!) hailed a cab to take him home. Where he finally read her diary's last entry:

Charme de l'amour, oh this enchanted certainty that I have found the one being I was created for; this sudden light of day over everything—and what was mystery, so clear! this unsuspected worth in the merest nothings; these swift hours whose details by their very sweetness elude my memory yet leave this long furrow of happiness through my heart; such bliss in your presence, and even when you are away, such hope—

But hadn't he read something like this somewhere or other before?

✧

Soon he would sail.

But meanwhile his Victoria now had the complaisance to find time for him often in her book, he having as she said to be looked after, *seen* to.

Thus for example "............," this angel wordlessly murmured one happy dusk; drowsy, entangled; in a word all his again, they being in the great dim rosewood bed at the time. And he, in agreeable stupor, sprawled all anyhow, in time groaned out amiably into her shoulder what might have been an answering "..........mm."

This conversation then died in contentment away.

Until at length in a torpid voice he got out, ". . . at *this* age, ah Victoria, to say 'I love you.' "

She made some fond and languid sound.

"Knowing now what it means," he yawned.

Her knees slid, slackly hugging him. These lovers then shifted position a bit, deprecatingly; then once again lay there, now comfortable, this dialogue too stalled. Or as if there were no language in the world.

But at long last he sighed, and, eyes now open, appeared even to think. In due course rolled up onto his big elbow, to where she no longer blurred on him, and delivered himself of droning reminiscence: by what towers, what ancient streets, down what narrowing marble geometries, ah by what fountains, had not her image turned to him, smiling and silent; then he lounged down to where, for this, she let him have her sleepy mouth as he pleased again.

He mumbled, "Of all our memories, which."

In their private twilight she opened her eyes to him, gazing, wordless and grave.

"Then which, Victoria."

But as at some softer question, in pause, she mused, bending this long sweet fathomless look on him still.

"All these years, snared like this in the tender net of you."

Her eyes closed.

"Until now we're here by god," he concluded vaguely, and patting his angel he yawned.

"Here, and after all that," he drowsily expanded. "After all that shared and inextricable history. Yet now it still goes on!" So she drifted closer against him, settling.

"Which I suppose by god then," he went on in a different tone, "is why your sweet fussing sex is everlastingly engaged in making us feel 'responsible' for you, isn't it! Hand yourselves over batting those great reproachful eyes, and if this all-of-you isn't important enough for a— Now will you not flounce away pouting dammit?" he commanded, rolling after her. "I said, if the insensate hog does nothing but add you to his inventory— Turn *over* here!" he cried, grabbing and uncoiling her.

So she let herself be re-arranged to suit him.

"Ahhh what's all your mad flittery maneuvering for anyway," he laughed in pure affection, "if not that you want us to *accept* the fact of what you are, is that it? the whole wild vertigo of you, why dammy for all I know you'll decide your feelings are hurt if I haven't demanded *you* get a divorce from your damn'— Thought of *that* before you thought I had by heaven didn't I?" he snorted, for in the gloom she had opened her eyes to him again, and she was faintly smiling.

"So I put *up* with your moods, d'you see? if only so you'll feel spoiled to your heart's content," he explained. "And if I didn't occasionally yell at you how'd you be sure I took you seriously, isn't that how you want it, my slumbering Macchiavellian angel? Are you listening to me at all?"

For her eyes had closed once more, and in the dusky air, as from down some footfall passageway, came no more than the breathed echo of a reply.

He stroked her, grumbling tenderly, "If we're not willing to be that much accountable, I suppose you don't feel like a woman do you. Lacking the final proof. That one unstatable attestation to what you were born to be. Is that why you love me then?" he demanded of her shadowy face. "Because I do by god accept putting up with you, you delectable thing?" and hauled her into his arms.

Where, though for all anybody could tell she was already a good two-thirds asleep, she lovingly let him do with her as he pleased.

✧

In a country-summer sunset now a mere nightfall dim gold, all gilding gone, Melissa and once more Melissa's hostess sat murmuring, wayworn, on the plinth of the sundial in its darkening lawn, ivory in their evening silks; as if spent, night upon them; the sweet friend fretting " — so love I am driven *mad*, then," quivering.

"Mm."

"Ah who wouldn't be left maddened? when how can I even wait till I meet him in Italy yet here is this utter quandary *where!*"

"Poor love."

"Because if I go with him to this lovely stealthy out-of-the-way little place he wants it won't sound like turismo even to Sam! Who I'll have to phone every night to make sure merely! Yet we *have* to keep away from places we'd run into people we know in and then anyway who wants to see tiresome Sights? when what will I even be able to think of but him, I mean Liss where *are* we to go!" she lamented, drooping.

"Dear I do see!"

"Mi fa impazzire!"

"Ma dove che sia—"

"No but I'm just *impaired* by it all! and all Patrick does is laugh, he says why not simply some huge cool dim cinquecento bedroom then in for example Siena and *stay* in bed! when he ought to know he'd very soon just start thinking about food!"

Melissa cried lightly, "Well pity on *him!*" in what may have been their college-era dialect.

"No but when all I want to know is what he'd *truly* like, why can't he see?"

"Sweetie I thought your great angel of a husband—"

"Ptah he'll say he's tied up in Geneva all August. Or half. Oh Lissa how can I even begin to wait!"

Melissa yawned "Thee must just possess thy soul in patience," quoting her great-grandmother at her.

"But how can I, oh how dismal you are, when for this whole month or almost I can authentically live with Patrick and look *after* him and not just play house in these sheer agonies of having to part in a few sad vanishing hours, so rushing and gone."

"Yes you said."

"And I *never* felt responsible for anybody like this before," she wailed to the gathering night. "Oh one's parents were so lucky, just affairs affairs and never bother their heads, when Lissa what is there merely to think about seriously but this!"

"Mm."

"And Patrick *admits!* Or anyhow as applying to women he says he admits. That what else is there to think of ever but love, I mean. Except I think he feels every agonizing bit the way I do, dearest he *must*, or d'you think? for example only two times ago he said had I any notion how hellish it was? because he said how could I!"

"So bliss then."

"So *bliss* then, well exactly! If he does mean it, that is. But he *does* Lissa! Or don't you think," she whimpered.

"Dear love *mmm.*"

But the friend cried in hopelessness, "Oh though how can I look after him Liss when it isn't even as if I could look *after* him, when what else were we made to do but be with them, oh I endlessly despair!"

"Love, how sad."

"Ah and he's so darling, so amusing," that one mourned, bereft. "Simply the things he'll say, I mean he's just constantly tossing these wildly unexpected sardonic epigrams *off* Lissa, he just impromptu made up that phrase 'as un-American as *good* apple pie.'"

"Mm."

"And the last time we were at the St. Regis they served him what he said was this *perfectly* cynical incompetent duck-and-olives, he says if they don't give up catering to Texans *he's* going to stop going there, and he called the maître d'hôtel over and said to him, 'Your chef missed his calling, whatever it was,' well just *demolishing!* Oh I love him I *love* him he's teaching me to drink those horrible Italian aperitifs or did I tell you," she ended, gazing into the night, in happy dream.

But Melissa airily stretched her young arms high, saying yawning, absently, after all what could one expect? when how could anyone after all know!

Then the floodlights came abruptly on over the rich terrace and it was what her father would have called their damn' husbands. Who yelled out across were they coming to get a drink for God's sake or weren't they.

✦

One hot midafternoon at last anybody who was still in town came down to Nicholas's ship to say bon voyage.

And it might have been the Thirties all over again, his cabin jammed, flowers everywhere and the most agreeable urban din, Victoria's man eeling his way through the hubbub with the champagne and the usual horde of well-wishing contemporaries in full cry, classmates admen whatnot, even his lawyer from Philadelphia again with dockets of last-minute-be-on-the-safe-side stifling stuff to be signed; and then too (and pleased and touched him) a random three or four of his New York nieces and nephews and whoever they'd severally had lunch with that day, the girls sleek as colts in their summery dresses and a couple of them calling him *sir* Southern-style while drooping their unmaidenly eyelids at him; and presently Melissa too, racing in out of breath, with some smooth well-mannered young giant he'd never set eyes on in his life who *sir*'d him with that tiresome Yale deference while Melissa conveyed the most dutiful best wishes of her husband, who hadn't been able to get away from his bank, absolutely greatest regret of his life; and finally Victoria, looking not in the least as if she were due in Paris herself in a fortnight and would ring him the moment she got in. So he grumbled in affection now he *wished* she'd have the sensibility to reconsider and let him motor down and meet her properly and comfortably at Cherbourg, they'd drive for lunch for instance to Caen, where he'd once had the best coq au vin of his life, then up to Paris in easy stages, spending the night in that beech forest around Lyons why not? for what if it wasn't the direct route, was she going to deny him the pleasure of the first night he'd ever spent in the Forêt de Lyons with the woman he loved?

But she said ssshhh, now who was that with Melissa.

"How would I know a thing like that, missed his name, generation of mumblers in *my* view," he complained.

"Then he came with her? so good-looking, Nicholas!"

"Of course I'm persuaded she must be out of her silly mind!" he burst out in great unhappiness.

And when Mrs. Barclay opened her eyes wide at this, muttered in raging explanation, "Abruptly been stricken, if you must know, with this infuriating conviction I'm being presented with a new damn' son-in-law!"

"Oh Nicholas no!"

"An *outrage!*" he fumed, as she turned to see for herself and murmuring ". . . not Melissa surely" took in Melissa and her young man in one instantaneous assize.

"Even wrong side of the blanket, how do *I* know," Nicholas told her in dejection.

"Now my old darling he obviously does adore her!"

"By god he'd better!"

"*She* I must say looks entirely self-possessed."

He made some hollow maundering sound.

"She is a sweet, Nicholas."

"Well, evidently, yes, what man could help himself I suppose," he conceded, sunk.

"Why a perfect darling!" she sang in encouragement. "And in point of fact of course he's terribly attractive-looking."

"Whatever that's got to do with it!"

"Oh Nicholas what utter—"

He snarled, "Ah well, young and healthy enough I suppose, yes!"

"Though hardly more than a child actually is she," Mrs. Barclay at once acknowledged.

"Well exactly by god!"

"Your oldest or is she Nicholas too."

"My own daughter!" he cried morosely, staring.

"Your first actually?"

He grunted in gloom, draining his glass. "Though what difference?" he declaimed in valediction. "Walk out on you don't they? Of age or not? One after another! Leaving me knee-deep among these unpredicted ruins!"

But smiling into his eyes she gently teased, "Now old darling don't be an old stupid."

"See how it is?" he snorted, making some sort of bogus face, "show a natural affection for a pretty daughter and every woman in earshot begins denigrating my intelligence."

"Nicholas haven't you ever thought what my own sweet apoplectic father would have said, and *done* to you darling! if he'd once had the faintest notion—"

"Well, then, why, you're a terrible damn' sex, aren't you?" he decided to agree, beginning to smile back. "Ah well," he went on, more cheerfully, "it's what comes of letting one's daughters marry any young man that happens to take their silly fancy," he ended, even beginning to laugh.

Here however his lawyer worked his weighty way through the uproar and started holding these dockets up against the cabin wall for him to sign one after another, affably bawling his full-phrased enucleation of each in turn into his ear, for example the sheer *extra* papers because what had his Bank's treasurer done but slump to the pavement in Chestnut Street not forty-eight hours before and die before they'd even got a doctor to him, *shockingly* sudden thing, poor stuffy devil, member of all his own clubs, man he'd yelled at five days a week for twenty-odd years, man in a word from his own well-fed well-brought-up decent dying generation, to whom by god there was still a residual meaning in Domesday Book's ancient cadastral *quantum silvae quantum prati* (but now co-parceners of what moss-hung and abandoned avenues, what crumbling porticoes) and it made his heart heavy to think he'd had to yell at him as he had; so they discussed a proper successor. Then they began working their way through the second briefcase and he signed and signed.

Except that, through the river of well-read legal prose, he kept hearing some discountenancing young whelp or other just within earshot in the gay pandemonium behind him muttering (to some girl, he presumed) first something about "the little cloud of angels surrounding you," a nice enough phrase, but next thing he knew followed in a guarded carnal undertone by "even these damned eight inches away from your arms!" to which (and at his very shoulder if you please!) came her teasing little music-box laugh of delighted reply.

The unseen damn' boy panted, "Oh my *loveliest* angel!"

"Oh sweetie be careful!"

"Tomorrow afternoon too? Please *please?*"

"So hongish, ssshh," she tantalized him, in adenoidal, sounding amorous.

The wretched children then began mumbling unintelligibly. Until the boy's voice rose in outrage to the hoarse whisper " —your husband, when I want you!"

"Sweet."

"All of you! All the time!"

"Or do you sweetie, because I can't always think you do."

"*What,* when hardly an hour ago we were—"

"So anulnerous," she cooed, "so wingèd!"

At this they both snickered extravagantly. "So termly san," she giggled; and they were off again. Until from deep in some private joke he said, "Who wants to get on first base anyhow?"

"So *lonely!*" —and they snickered wildly this time for a good half-minute.

While all about them the unheeding company bayed in its brightest party tone.

But when Nicholas turned round at last from signing, the couple, whoever, were already lost among those salvoes of oblivious sound.

Anyway half the company was rustily talking French by this time, it having been found that the girl of one of his nephews was not Southern at all but from Paris. Also, by this time nobody was any longer tasting his drink, just drinking it. Melissa moreover buttonholed him and conveyed the most dutiful wishes, the very sincerest best regards possible, if only he could know, of her husband, did he know he hadn't been able even to get *away!* Then the all-ashore gong began sounding and all the girls except the girl from Paris (who however had turned out to be Swiss) kissed him languishing good-byes and off everybody went, chattering in English again.

And last, at the very gangway, his sweet Victoria kissed him, mistily; and for just that instant clung to him, wordless; and was gone.

Presently everybody else had gone too, for long before dusk they had to be at sea.

And when at dinner he stared agreeably about for some engaging creature to pick up next day (*eat* with her anyhow), there seemed to be no one. Though in any case, he at once virtuously remembered, he had now changed his spots, hadn't he! Worn down as he was after everything to the man he was here and now.

Why, even the thought of Arabella Hobbes hardly crossed his mind!

And so eventually out then under the ocean night with its soft wind from home, to lean in dim starlight on the sports-deck rail, his full-fed gaze toward France; away; alone. "Or alone for this hour anyhow," he said aloud to those dark leagues of sea ahead, to Europe in fact, in declamatory apostrophe.

So not even Arabella; no. If only because Neuilly and the Place Vendôme weren't far enough apart geographically to keep separate two pretty women who'd run into each other in the rue du Faubourg St. Honoré in any case. And fancy at his age organizing a shuttle anyhow! Even apart from such sighing tangential questions as whether memories were ever what one is after.

And besides, as said, hadn't he changed?

For if there are no answers (if virtue is for example not an acquired characteristic; or conversely if when leopards change their spots it is not their spots they change), if there are no answers there are still perorations, and "Have I then mended my ways for *you* Victoria goddammit?" he cried aloud, and began to laugh; and waving a tamed hand westward to her through the dark seaward rush of the ocean night, proclaimed in final self-approbation, "So then onward and upward by god!"

And turning aft went below.

To where, in the companionway to which he was affably descending, life comfortably settled, all virtue scheduled at last, there stood waiting (here and now), her little scarlet lip quivering, her eyes enormous with terror and determination, his sweet besieger, his suppliant, his captive, his very loving stowaway, his Morgan.

A PRESENCE WITH SECRETS

To Laurice
Present and Future

I. A PRESENCE WITH SECRETS

1

". . . and, well, *shy*, then!" she said in her haughtiest clear young voice and not looking even near him in the rosy fire-flowered darkness, speaking in fact less to this lover just acquired than to the bed's dusky canopies, or to the soaring Renaissance night of the ceiling where now the hearth's reflected images breathed their tumbled and disintegrating crimsons—a Miss Rosemary Decazalet by name, abed as it happened in Firenze, on a night of tumult and deep spring, a properly brought up girl for any reasonable purpose including this one, and in any case, and already, as good as twenty years old.

So in the hooded Giotto bed, ". . . feeling shy," she mumbled, lolling her pretty head down into the deepest pillows away from him, folding her legs chidingly aside and aloof on their tender hinge, in fact half turning her charming young back on him, wanting suddenly very much, as it seemed, to hide.

So in a kindly way he was amused.

But having been so humbly kissed there by that soft young mouth, who could think of smiling at the child? so although she was not looking at him, still he made his face show a gentlemanly concern.

Also he was a good deal embarrassed at what he had let happen.

For they had not taken refuge in this elegant room to make love good god! but in a hairsbreadth run for it out of the path of that headlong mob suddenly from nowhere on their very heels— though then it had hurtled past and on, toward the questura it may have been, the narrow quattrocento street such a tossing flood of packed and racing bodies the powdery old walls you felt shook with the weight catapulting along past them and on, so at the last moment he'd as good as flung her out from under its impact, aside, into the courtyard of this pensione or whatever it was, gasping. And *shaken*, by god! Then he'd seen she was white with terror, even going faint, so he'd banged on the door. And had the padrona give them a room for her for a bit, and had brandy sent up.

Casa d'appuntamenti though he very shortly saw (and now, with irony) the place must be.

But *this* to have happened!—and when this angel beside him he'd known little more than to say buon giorno to: a conversazione evening or two at the Fonteviots', a tea at the British circolo. Even this time merely happened on her, she was window-shopping in the Vicolo del Forno and it was absolute chance, he'd no more than been taking that way back from the Lungarno. Then, and there had been no warning to them whatever, a distant shout or two but in Italy what was that, they were standing chatting, she was asking deferential questions about his portrait of Mrs. Fonteviot, when suddenly up at the far end of the vicolo that wild scattering of people running, slipping on the smooth old cobbles and one man had gone down, and next instant this massive rolling wall of mob swept round the corner with the speed of a tide-bore right over the fellow and down upon *them*.

So no wonder the brandy, when that sleek padrona brought it, the girl had near spilled with trembling. Eyes enormous; and her teeth had chattered so against the shivering glass he'd had to take it from her cold fingers and hold it for her, steady, and get sips into her between shuddering sobs.

Because *nothing* like this had she conceived could happen before her eyes *ever* or she be so terrified, she told him chokingly— for what was *happening*, could it even be did he think the end of not the world perhaps but the whole government? for oh this *was* how revolutions began, with awful murderous mobs like that, how could he say they didn't? And that poor man who'd stumbled and fallen had been *trampled to death* hadn't he? Before their *eyes!*

So he had been a good long time lulling her.

Till, then, finally, well, the end of the world was what finally she'd behaved as if she thought it was, and no tomorrow.

And now was overcome at herself.

—He saw therefore he had to be wary for a while about how he put things.

For about this child he knew nothing. It was unpredictable. They can go he knew flutteringly shy at being seen in a bath yet be in tears if you misguidedly didn't; and there, it is only about vanity. Here it could be about anything. So he was silent. He did not see what a man of sense could risk unless she said more.

But she was now it seemed too humbled to say anything, indeed in that warm fire-hung darkness her body's tender arabesques he thought drew farther, if anything, away from him and apart, in upon themselves, so that he saw the slender buckling curve of waist and back he could paint with a delight as deep as only just now had plundered his senses. But he also thought that if for the moment he should touch her it was unpredictable.

So for the moment he let it go

In any case, staying on, as now arranged, by morning he might have decently seen to it she was left unhumiliated. For otherwise it was too heartless.

Also, as he'd said to that padrona when he'd gone down to say they'd stay, why risk making it back to his own quarter of the city on a night of carnage like this?—running battles in the streets if nothing deadlier, non finivano mai, questi baccani!

Ma come, "baccani"! Was a *nothing* (she humored him, Etruscan eyes dark with innuendo)—un pochino di baruffa municipale, the signore needn't—

Call it a little fuss or what she liked, he said, the young lady'd been *badly* upset by it. Still was, in fact.

Ma se conviene al signore—

Thank 'ee yes, he'd said blandly, suit him it would; so they'd stay on. And he'd want a little dinner sent up to them shortly, too; something light if she'd have the kindness to manage it?

Though as to any dinner—that had turned out not to be what he'd gone back up for, the complicities of a kindly Iddio being what sometimes they were. He lay and looked at this unexpected blessing of his, and in the luxury of it, almost yawned.

But suddenly in the night outside, and from so nearby somewhere that right under their windows it sounded, this shocking cry, half a scream, and in an instant the child had uncoiled up out of her pillows like a spring, eyes enormous again into his, wordlessly imploring, and just then along the house wall below feet went racketing past, frantic, and with a little stricken sound she sat bolt upright, the hearth's now faltering and shadowy crimsons staining every madonna slope of throat and breast, or as if she were strewn deep in those dying roses, spray upon spray, so that before she'd clutched the coverlet childishly up he thought once more what a lovely bribe to have Iddio (or Whoever) simply hand him like this, which however anybody can of course be indulged with now and then who knows why, but what sheer blazing luck from Heaven it is, what a blessing, when they do.

Still, to reassure her, he groped to the window; though when he slung the heavy satins of the curtain aside he made out whoever it had been was gone.

All beyond was in deep darkness, under he saw thick mist above, night-glow from the luminous city around them thrown up saffron against filmy overcast, to be drawn in there, under great lifting curtains and pale coils of cloud, so that light was shed back down too faint anywhere, he hardly made out what this window gave on, below, muffled in black geometries of shadow; a small private square it seemed. And even elegant, a seicento façade over across, arcaded and ornate, the galleria a run of rounded arches all along it, also what must be the shape of a fountain, some spouting nymph he supposed, or riding marble waves a boy and dolphin, anyhow he heard the cold splash of water on stone. Silence again too everywhere, only damp breaths of night-sound rising like exhalations from dark streets and squares, where at last it smelt of spring.

So ecco, he said over his shoulder, in reassurance, and let the long folds of the curtain swing down straight again—there was nothing; had been nothing; late-night passanti scuffling. In any case not that rabble they'd run into, or anything like. But this without looking round at her, for he thought fright, yes, but also the delicate point now was, more likely, how with kindness to get her over what she was so stricken had happened, this helpless shock at herself he supposed: trouble with innocence was historical perspective, it had still to learn what was praxis. So, first, then, deal also with this woebegone nudity. Engaging or not.

There should be the usual toweling vestaglie warming on pipes in the bathroom. Where when he went to look there of course were. So he draped himself in one and brought her the other, saying amiably, here, put this round her pretty shoulders, she couldn't spend her life under these comic European eiderdowns could she? while he saw to the fire.

On whose incandescent hummocks of ember he took his time shaking from the scuttle dribblings of fresh coal. Culm, it appeared: soft dusts kindled instantly, showering sparks, then soon the whole hearth glowed again, strewing its roses deep into the room's vaults of shadow, so that when he turned round at last and found great innocent eyes dolefully upon him, those crimsons fluttering in her cheek anyone would have taken for hopeless blushing, so deep among the bed's canopies of night had the hearth distributed its insubstantial emblems.

And blushing she may have been—helplessly not even he supposed being sure merely what next, or expected to know, for in the fire-fringed shadows she dropped her eyes from his to her cold hands. It seemed she could not speak for misery. Or gêne, for he saw it might be she had no idea what in this situation a girl found—desperately, or even at all—to say. A topic, even. Or, generally, what was, well, *expected!*

This unforeseen . . . could he label it "threshold-ritual"? anthropologically speaking it had been gone through like an angel, but on from there is not so near second nature. Including light drawing-room conversation if called for.

So, humanely, and still from across the room, imagine, he said to her (as if in complaint), getting caught in another of these pointless Mediterranean revolutions, what a damn' nuisance. Assuming revolution was actually what it was, for he said genially he hardly thought Italy, Firenze anyhow, was a place any practical-minded Marxist would pick to start one. With *their* millennial history of total political cynicism? *And* all the black-marketable antiquities!

But she said in a shamed voice, "I thought we were going to die."

Yes, well, after a moment he conceded, he supposed it was mostly that ominous lowering sound of a mob coming, like a typhoon. It *was* daunting; daunted anybody. So in pure primitive reflex people turned and ran.

Whereas she'd seen for herself all they'd really needed to do, she and he, was step into the nearest doorway, or a courtyard, or anywhere out of the way. He was appalled he'd frightened her by not doing that on the spot. Instead of haring off first like a fool—luxurious as this pensione (or whatever it was) had in the event turned out to be.

But still it seemed she could not look at him, it was such a hopelessness, only murmuring something downcast about ". . . una condotta di collegio . . ." as if she did not see how, in English, she could possibly ever bring herself to face such a thing.

"Boarding-school behavior" he thought was one libel it was not!—when was this woebegone angel going to divagate back into sense?

But he asked her, coaxing, trying though not to sound kindly—asked her what on earth made anyone as lovely as she was think she had to take refuge (or whatever) in Italian? And from what!

Stunned still, he thought, looking at her, by that mob. The sheer sundering momentum of it is what stuns—the huge rolling weight of this one like an immense wave flung in along the seawall of some narrow shod of a bay, to burst in its thunders on the drowned stones of the quay; the earth's foundation seems to shake; and so no wonder if even now perhaps she was in dread, these walls ready in her mind to reel and fall.

So dammit he said was she perversely trying to make *him* wretched with regret, compunction rather, over what had happened?—when there wasn't an atom of his body not in a kind of wonder at what her sweetness had blessed him with!

This rather overworldly rhetoric at least got her eyes back to him, though still she seemed too uncertain what to say next to speak.

To give her time, then, he went to the wine-bucket for what might be left. And a good half bottle was; he was surprised. So he poured and brought her her glass and at any rate she took it.

He therefore risked settling on a chaste corner of the bed with his own glass. And brought the bottle along.

For he said look, he knew she sounded as if she wanted him to explain her to herself but did he really need to? As wouldn't she consent to see? He meant she didn't need *him* to tell her how lovely she was, did she? And meantime the wine in that glass in her hand was there to be drunk: beautifully cold, and as moelleux a white Hermitage as he ever remembered tasting outside France, a pleasure to happen on.

So at least she meekly raised the glass to her lips and sipped a little, great rueful eyes now to plead.

Having still, though, no real idea what to say, he was continuing more or less rhetorically, had she no sense of what between one heartbeat and the next sometimes—when she decided to explain.

Viz., "But this—this— What I— Well, *this!*" in a little wail of woe.

In fact as good as reproaching him.

"And when don't you see I'd never so much as called you by your first *name* even before I simply— Oh *how could I!*" she mourned. "And it wasn't even partly your fault!" she accused him, choking.

The answer to this hardly being that he'd never happened to call her anything but Miss Decazalet either, and a mere couple of times at that, he had for the moment no idea what form of reassurance he could fall back on to comfort her with.

But she said in a sad little voice, "Because when you're so famous how was I to think of you except that way," as if making sense.

He said, amused, "But how did—"

"Well but aren't you?" she cried. "You're a terribly famous painter—you *are*, there was a part of a whole *lecture* in our art department moderns course on you! And even here you're 'il Tatnall'! So when you came into Mrs. Fonteviot's salotto that first time—I mean how could I possibly think I'd ever be like *this* with you," she entreated him. "Even Mrs. Fonteviot did laugh and say goodness should she risk introducing a girl her godmother had put her in charge to a painter who—who made even a still life look as if—"

Yes, yes, he said, and laughed, that was Alex's standard epigram about him—an elegant creature, Mrs. Fonteviot, but she couldn't it seemed tell him from Courbet! And the English upper classes did go in for low language, earls' daughters and other ladyships it sometimes seemed in particular.

"Well, but," the child said in a diffident voice, "that wonderful whoever-she-was of yours in the National Gallery sort of does look . . ."

Camilla?—good god he said what a nonsense, he'd posed her in the exact posture of Michelangelo's Erythrean Sibyl! why, what on earth, he said agreeably, did she think the picture was about ?

So, not knowing, she was silent.

Or anyhow for a moment, before gently conceding, "Well of course then I found you were charming *too*, I mean I saw you at evening parties, and that time at the circolo, and you were terribly nice to me, anyhow I thought you were. But that could have been I knew because of Mrs. Fonteviot and good manners. Anyway I'm not—I just don't have the mondanità for *this*," she said humbly, "because anyway all I thought was what it would be like to know you well. And what you might feel about me if I did, being famous. But now even after *this* I don't know!" she cried at him in a sudden little fume. "I might no more than have just met you! And then to *go to bed* with you!"

And before he could answer a word mumbled, "When I haven't said your first name even *yet* . . ." in a voice of tears.

—All of which anyone could see was leading nowhere.

In mere humanity therefore he moved up toward her, set the Hermitage and his glass too on the table de chevet, sat down again on the edge of the shadowy bed a respectful six inches from the nearest part of this mournful child, and said oh now now now.

This maneuver however only made her look at him a little wildly, eyes wide with new misgivings.

So he slid a hand, palm up and harmless, under hers that lay on the coverlet there between them; and when after a quivering moment she seemed to nerve herself to look down at this piece of unseduction (though what more innocent could any man do?) he let his fingertips slip their blameless way an inch or so farther, to where the pulse beat in her soft wrist, which they caressed as if in affection or simple cajolery, there in the smooth folds of her sleeve; though otherwise for a space the two of them were as motionless there as amanti in some sepulchral marble, among tombs.

Till finally she swallowed and murmured, ". . . Well, *Hugh*, then" in a sheepish voice, and looked at him, placating. Though she drew her hand away.

And, also, complained gently, "Except Hugh you do see how I did have to feel, I mean how am I to think you really feel anything about me, don't you see? When the way I've behaved— And I know you think being upset is just silly! And anyway it *is*, isn't it! And after all the girls who must've made—who've been in love with you!"

Now now, she needn't make him sound, he said, like some damn' pasha!—and a pasha at the end of a long and well-supplied life, at that.

Or was she just saying (as near as good manners would let her) that he was too old for her, he asked amiably.

"Why, you're not old!" she cried, astonished at him. "But you can't be! I mean, how old are you?"

Thirty-seven he told her next birthday.

"But Hugh, that isn't *old!*"

Old enough to 've conducted himself with more regard for the ordinary amenities than he had, he said he thought was pretty obvious. To have upset an angel like her like this? A certain disinvoltura was all very well and expected, but not as unthinkingly as this! Here, give him her glass, at least he could see to that properly.

So as if bemused by this, in wonder, she watched him pour. And pour into his own glass and set the bottle down, in silence. Till at last she said in a meek voice, "Yes only Hugh because I was so frightened and silly doesn't mean I still didn't feel about you as if—"

Frightened and silly if she liked, yes, he said, but was he at his age to be innocent of eventualities?—what could happen he meant too often did.

". . . But I let it," she said, looking down at her glass.

So after a moment therefore he slid his hand under hers again. And said as if conversationally yes but the *point* was, and she must have been aware of it, from that first time in Alex's salotto he'd thought what a lovely thing she was—hardly meant for him he meant, but what painter in his senses wouldn't have? But dammit making love was not something to be done "all'improvvisto"! and what reason had he had to imagine she'd even had occasion to think about him? Much more do anything like make up her mind about him if she had, in short what he was saying was that he was dismayed at himself.

"Oh, *thought* about you, yes! I don't see how you could expect any girl— Why, but you're llllllovely!" she laughed, exulting. "It was just, well, *how* it happened, Hugh, I mean 'improvvisto' sounds so horrid!"

But wasn't when it wasn't, he said amiably, and picking up her hand turned it palm up and put his lips to the inside of her sweet young wrist.

"Oh Hugh. Oh *dear* this is all so hard on my objectivity! Only don't let's talk Italian. I know I was, but I felt shy. No but d'you know what's surprising?"

Nothing so surprising he said about feeling shy.

"But surprising about making *love*, silly! It's how sort of devoted to you it seems to make me feel about you afterwards, is surprising."

What flattery, he said, smiling.

"Am I? I mean aren't you supposed to deserve it?" she asked, smiling too. "It's just that it isn't what you hear makes you expect you'll feel, somehow, is all."

But he said didn't even *her* rather offhand generation occasionally—

"Oh well at *school*," she said, coolly pitying this, for how immature. "At school of course everybody says it seems to be a sheer toss-up what it's like, it's with just boys. Anyway," she murmured, "not like *this*, Hugh—oh my!"

So then she didn't really need, did she (he asked, and in fact what could have been more reasonable), *didn't* need to be upset anymore about it surely at all? What was there to gaze at him with those great doubtful eyes about?

"Yes except *then*, Hugh, I hadn't— I mean it was because I was so beside myself."

But good god what had that to do with it? he protested, as if this were true, setting his glass on the table de chevet (and hers out of the way there too, come to think of it) for he *swore* to her—

"But if I made love with you now," she said in an uncertain voice, "I mean *again*, how could I ever, well, explain it to myself later? I don't mean it isn't that I don't feel—that you're not terribly— Oh well oh *dear!*" she ended dolefully, for he had taken both her hands.

And saying couldn't she see for herself that six inches was a senseless distance now between them anyhow? kissed her submissive mouth at last; and though she whispered as if in gentle despair, aux abois, lost, "Are you my love? . . ." in the warm hearthlit shadows of their bed she collapsed obediently into his arms.

—It might therefore have been hardly an hour, but however long, for in that fire-soft darkness they lay half-entangled still, that as if dozingly at last she murmured, "Only Hugh does she— Have other women felt devoted to you like this too? . . ." having now in any case, all things considered, beyond doubt some sort of right to ask.

So, finally, he had to look at things as they coldly were. And were, whether Alexandra was still alive somewhere in a looted and burning city or not.

2

Eighteen, nineteen hours now she was gone. Though back well past that, faint dawn again it must have been, the second day's rioting had woken him. And he thought worse than the first, huge mobs scattering out before police. And it had gone on, half the city in wild disorder now, out of control it seemed altogether. And in that mindless tumult Alexandra these long hours vanished no notion where.

And she'd quit him without so much as a kiss—turned on her elegant heels with that final "You *can* be a tiresome pet at times my sweet can't you!" cool English voice taut with displeasure, out his door and down to her car in his courtyard and off into the soft Tuscan morning, unwarned, to meet her husband's plane.

Then, perhaps an hour it had been, the great pleasant trusting chap's voice on the phone: "Hugh? Aubrey here. At the airport. Any clue where Alex might have got to? Was to 've met me, she tell you? Nothing could have held her up, surely? Not to worry of

course, nothing I hope like that. But she was to have *met* me! . . ."
And then, toward noon, the questura had reported her burnt-out
car.

—Yet here now was he, Hugh Tatnall, a year her lover, no more
concerned you'd have thought in this agreeable bed than if she'd
(say) merely gone out of town and nothing beyond an offhand infidelity were the point, a mere role in the usual masque, instead of
that subtle body he knew by heart lying it might be battered and
unidentified in some nighted emergency ward, or in a lightless
alley or down an embankment even, still to be found. If indeed
alive at all.

Except why on earth anything of the sort!—Alex, if anyone ever,
serenely looked after herself. As to her car, for whatever reason
why, simply she'd abandoned it.

Reason moreover might very well be, if some part of the rioting
it was had stopped her, she'd amused herself by joining in—the
English upper classes had been having fun in worthy demonstra-
tions ever since Spain in '36.

Why in short should anything melodramatic have happened to
her at all? That being the *off* chance.

And why assume she hadn't already turned up safe and sound
hours ago anyhow!

—A letter from his London agent it had been began it: did he
still now and then rent a friend that other half of his piano nobile?
Because a friend of *his*, chap named Fonteviot, many years' friend
in fact, known him since Oxford, been up at Merton with him, 'd
rowed for the College, *charming* great man, and now it happened
he wanted a pied-à-terre in Florence—was just it appeared adding
factories near Prato and also at Empoli to the main complex of
plants he owned in the Piedmont. Wife elegant Anglo-Irish; in fact
very nearly a great beauty. Likelihood was they'd want the apartment for a good year minimum. "Ce sont de braves gens, Hugh—
and the lovely Alexandra's an absolute Gainsborough for you." Or,
he'd said to himself, a Van Dyck: sounded a bit that *Countess of
Clanbrassil* sort of thing in the Frick. Though anyhow why not? So
in due course she'd come from London to have a look.

And his connoisseur of an agent had been right: a beauty by god
she was, Gainsborough or not. He'd been grinding pigment when
she came; he was a mess; it amused them both. He showed her
through "l'attraverso"; they strolled slowly, even dawdled, as she
looked at everything, room by room, with little courteous cries and
murmurs of pleasure—what a heaven of a palazzo he had, what a

blessing it all was, what pictures what tapestries, what a great angel he was to be willing to rent it to her: the whole bland polished extravaganza of British upper-class rhetoric. They'd pleased each other at sight.

Later, Fonteviot too had seen and liked it. In due course they'd moved in. He had given a couple of dinners for them (though they knew people already). They saw a good deal of one another; he did a Gainsborough of her after all; Fonteviot gave him a Degas sketch of Mary Cassatt.

Then, one day, and this had been a day of sudden wild spring cloudbursts which, shopping, she'd got caught in—great splattering gouts of rain bursting on those stone streets, the gutters a rushing flood, whirlpools racing ankle-deep over the drowned cobbles, and he had spotted her poised in stylish dismay in her jeweler's doorway, trapped aghast in the utter crash and din of it. He had skidded his car in to the curb and flung open the door shouting to her, and she'd leaped from the doorway and with happy little yelps of laughter skittered in beside him. *What* a godsend he was, in pure relief her lilting English voice told him, these *damned* brutes of taxis that wouldn't stop for one! shaking raindrops over him from her hat, from her gloved fingers; and half the way home, as he wove through the deafening wet hiss of the traffic, she fumed at it all, for what nameless Florentine pigs they were, what a canagliaccia!

Though then in the courtyard of the palazzo they had to sit on in the car, waiting for the deluge to slacken, the rain now coming down in great ropes, beating on the flooded cobbles, so fierce it leaped up again knee-high almost, drumming on the car roof till they barely heard each other.

So, waiting, they'd agreeably gossiped; and presently he had told her how he'd just got a fresh-caught Loire salmon flown in, from Nantes, he was going to have it cold with that green mayonnaise of his Lucrezia's, so why wouldn't she and Aubrey come take lunch tomorrow? it being Sunday.

But *how* wonderfully kind of him, she'd cried formally, that lovely food that absolute jewel of his did for him; but she said—

With that same wine (he put in) which, last time they'd had dinner with him—

But now he was making her *totally* despairing, she wailed as in sheer good manners, that heavenly hock of his, but didn't he remember she'd said Aubrey was off tomorrow for Zurich again, early?—those squalid bankers of his adored the place, *oh* how it all put one out! and just when he was offering her this lovely lure of his, his Loire salmon.

Out of nowhere, no more than the word 'lure' even it may have been, or the lingering caress of her lips shaping it—who knows why, ever?—suddenly he was so breathless with the sense of her, and so shaken at what he found he was about to say, that he did not see how he could say it without faltering. But she, though, surely (he managed to get out, holding his breath, for what if she knew as well as he that this was not what he was asking), at least *she'd* come, wouldn't she, Aubrey or not?

But he *knew* she never stayed when Aubrey took off, it was detestable and she was bored, she took off herself (she told him, great eyes all gentian-blue light suddenly deep in his), she simply got into her car—"Me ne vo e basta!" didn't they say? she'd seen *immense* parts of Italy. Though this time she'd go she thought see her brother, he'd just bought a villa on the Corniche beyond Cannes, she adored him, it was all arranged.

So he had taken a deep breath and said but couldn't she be at least tempted into leaving *after* lunch? Or good god he said (since what he was asking was not what he was asking) even next day?

So for a long moment she looked at him and anyone might have thought she was only thinking how surprising.

All however she then said was a faintly mocking "Si figuri!" and the rain having at last abruptly stopped they went in. At her door she said, "Aubrey's plane's at eleven," and he answered, "Come at three then?" and she slid her heavy key into the slotted brass of the escutcheon, let her eyes rest on him for one long cozening moment, and then, wordless, was gone.

He let himself in his own door as breathless again suddenly as some dazzled boy, for such beauty for oneself who can ever quite believe it? for as anybody could see, it had been decided.

Next day though it might have seemed an ambiguity of caprice they blandly lingered on in, over the splendors of his salmon, the cool cheeses, the crimson dunes of wild strawberries on their paillasses of bright leaves, the torrone molle they left untouched at the end, spinning out instead the slow enchantment of unspoken enticements and acquiescences on and on into the long murmuring afternoon, the approach of night as if hardly yet in their pulses, only this comedy of unavowal still to be played out to the last unneeded word—time itself in fact one unsurfeitable luxury the more to them, that final feast of each other who cared when it was to come. So they were long; it was delight.

Or as he had thought once, many hours gone — deep night then it was, though still for neither of them the night at an end or for discoveries near it even, his senses so drenched with her by then they hardly recorded what elegance of line the draftmanship of his tracing fingers told him her body was — making love with such goddess-given luck (he'd said to himself) making love being with luck like this a pleasure not a conquest it can seem never to be over, never, even when one is in it it is not to be believed how it is, for what savoring of herself as of him she indulged him with, even the mockery of her "So unbridled, goodness!" a wantonness to lure him on.

Very late, too, and if they had parted his tall curtains and looked this might almost have been the first cool pallors of dawn, she had said, lightly adrift up over him, sated at last and amused, "Though how frightful, having to seduce one's men! M'ma always gave one to understand it was the other way about."

He was too dazed with her still to think of anything, even mindless, to say.

"Or did you fancy you were luring me to the lovely wickednesses of your bed with a *fish*? — goodness what middle-class guile!"

He made an effort against his stupor: she had upper-class reasons instead?

"Well may you uninnocently ask!" she murmured, and in their eclipsing darkness slithered like a lovely dolphin back down into his arms.

—And it was *this* enchantment, he now had to say to himself, *this* angel he might conceivably never see again, for who can ever even expect them until in pure wonder there they are. And now, it was possible, there no longer.

For a bad morning he and Fonteviot had had of it. She'd have gone, for they thought surely how else, out the Via della Scala, then by the Via delle Porte Nuove and so on straight to the airport. So each had worked from his own end, Fonteviot in toward the city, he outward to meet him, phoning hospitals and the questura first. No word of her at any of them; and soon Fonteviot phoned, frightened now: he'd drawn a blank too — taxi'd been stopped by a damned police block at his end of the Via della Scala, flat refused to let him through. So he'd turned back and covered the Via delle Porte Nuove and the Via Toselli and so forth back to the airport again. Not a sign of her car. Nor in the airport park either.

So they'd had to look along the Via della Scala on foot, each from his own end. But at the Via Santa Caterina intersection he himself had come near being turned back—police vans and a jeep stood end to end across and he was having no luck at all talking his way through when there was this muffled sudden uproar from the direction of the station off to the right, shouting, and all at once thick black smoke came up over those buildings in great rolling spirals, then they heard bursts of tear gas and the police started piling into their vans and shot away, sirens howling.

So in the confusion he'd bolted, and got through. He had made it nearly to the intersection of the Viale Rosselli before he saw Fonteviot lumbering along toward him, and no trace of her.

So then to search the cross-streets (for who knew?) they separated.

For also she might they saw have taken the Via Palazzuolo route instead, or, again, around Santa Maria Novella and past the station. So Fonteviot turned off toward the Arno along the Via Rucellai and he himself up the Via degli Orti.

At once though he saw he'd get nowhere. Around the station it was chaos. The mob had it seemed run but the whole piazza was choky with tear gas, and police were beating up a handful of stragglers trapped against a wrecked shop-front and dragging them off to the vans. Just in front of the station four bodies lay sprawled by an overturned kiosk; they looked trampled. In front of a hotel opposite, great licks of flame and black smoke were rolling up out of a burning tanker-trailer; the hotel's façade was scorched; glass had shattered from its windows, in the heat, and muntins were catching fire.

It was the questura reported her burnt-out car: been driven they said up onto a sidewalk in the Via degli Avelli. So she must have tried to bypass some block or other and gone round behind Santa Maria Novella toward the station. So during a silent lunch they took turns phoning hospitals.

Presently, though, the questura rang up again: now they had found the signora's handbag. Tossed aside, it appeared, against a wall of the church. The signora's driver's license was in it, yes, but if there had been valuables, these they regretted were gone. So Fonteviot had taken off for the hospitals: no unidentified admissions now meant nothing, emergency wards everywhere were traboccanti they said with casualties and more constantly being brought in, *many* more, as the rioting spread. Nothing therefore to do but make the rounds, hour after hour, until, somewhere, she might be brought in.

He himself hadn't even that to kill time with.

In a doomed way, then, presently, in the studio he took out his portfolio of sketches he'd done of her. That whole year's worth, and he went through them slowly, thinking as he looked at each drawing, and remembered the act of drawing it, of the day he'd done it, the circumstances of her pose, the light, what else too they'd done that day in particular; the stage of happy desire for each other their knowledge of each other by then had brought them to; almost he thought now and then as he looked at these images what *was she* then? on the day of this sketch or that, what had she felt as he worked? for now it had begun to occur to him that possibly he had never actually known. He came on a charcoal they'd had a row over. A sheer petulance: she'd been doing her face at her glass and he was sketching her with amusement and she had got very cross, he no longer remembered why, only the unpleasantness. Which had lasted a week nearly. He put the portfolio back in its drawer.

An elderly jest came into his mind of his rich old libertine of an uncle's, whose palazzo this once had been: "Popes have those endless sequences of lady saints. Humble laymen like you and me, my dear boy, must make do with an occasional pagan goddess." In his uncle's day the studio had been a ballroom.

It had its baroque balcony still. He stepped out, aimless, thinking of ways he had seen the light fall on the planes of her face. Over across, the French windows of the Fonteviots' balcony stood open too. Somewhere on inside a maid was singing as she cleaned, *Ahi che mi hai fatto, Amore*, and in abrupt desolation he saw in his memory that summer evening Alex and he had lain here, here on his old uncle's great rococo divan, stilled suddenly as lovers turned to marble, unbreathing, listening to Fonteviot come in across and wander nearer calling her name through those other rooms and out at last onto that balcony across, murmuring by then in bafflement and deep disquiet a no more than whispered *Alex? . . . Alex?* . . . for where could she conceivably be? —and this was what, for all he could tell, he himself had now lost too.

Early June that had been, afternoon he remembered faded already into the edges of night, and next day it was she and Fonteviot were to be off, at daybreak, for England; trunks long since packed and gone, maids sent on ahead; be away from him poor libidinous sweet till grouse season, she'd cooed at him; even beyond, even; goodness how often he'd have trompée'd her she'd expected by then! and kissed him *sweetly* laughing good-bye.

But for one last farewell sight of her still he'd gone across the landing later again anyhow, and in. The place was stripped, sheeted away for summer, furniture shrouded white, dim now already with coming night, the tall formal rooms a silence of unstirring air, hooded pictures lost in shadows—life could have been gone, nightfall and abbandono everywhere. She had heard his key clatter in the door, and come quickly from somewhere deep in the house; he had got no farther than the piccolo salotto. Though how could she have known the key was his?—for perhaps instead it was his footfall she had heard as he came looking for her through those rooms that were nighted now and echoing, floors shining dark-polished in the summer dusk. She was in white, or white in that now deep obscurity it seemed to him: hair twirled up into a high Italian knot, and she had stuck a peacock's feather through it; and what on earth did he want now? for she was writing letters.

So he had said, deprecative and half in jest, resigned, for in any case it was all too far past hope to risk asking for in English, in English in fact the phrase was so childish-sounding that for months it had been a minor ritual joke they made now and then about making love—he'd said in his best mock-sospirante voice Nemmeno he supposed *una* ultima volta di più? . . . and what had the angel done but laugh and it was like a miracle, indulge him with the ritual's mocking reply, "*You* ever just *one* last time more? Ho!"—it was unbelievable what luck it was, and back across to his studio they'd sprinted (or by god as good as!) without another word.

But then soon they had heard Fonteviot. From the salotto it sounded he called her first, just come in, calling with bland assurance, where was she? though then coming nearer through those great hooded empty rooms in the now fading light, calling now in a sort of soft surprise, "Alex? Where've you got to? . . . Alex!" But then soon with less confidence, indeed there was now an edge of panic in that pleasant voice, "Alex aren't you here? What's happened dammit? *Alex!*"—the big man hurrying now, tiptoe as if swift with dread, calling nearer and nearer her unanswering name, till there out on that balcony across finally he stood, emptily staring, knowing now she was not there, not anywhere, it was pointless, yet still whispering, in a mere rustle of breath, his baffled *Alex? . . . Alex? . . .* into the gathering night.

In an instant, at that first far-off sound of her name, she was up out of their embrace, breath caught, fiercely listening, at bay—

pitched up half over him still on one Botticelli arm, hair tumbling, and in its dim tent what he could see of her eyes might have been a gaze of marble, unseeing, down into his own. They lay transfixed, wild. And as shapes he thought can in the dark silver of mirrors at night loom out of some menacing perspective of shadows and suddenly it seems they are upon you, so these lovers could each have been watching, in fearful vigilance, for that image the other's mirroring pupils might at any moment hold, the great bulky pleasant unsuspecting man blundering through those darkening rooms toward what they both knew would be his heart's dismay, handsome face even now chapfallen, the bafflement beyond human explanation. And, as he came, calling.

Till there on the balcony across then he'd stood, twenty foot away if that, the sound of her name no more than that dumfounded whisper.

Then that too died away on the nighted air; and suddenly with a soft fluttering throaty sound he'd never heard her make before— ferine, erotic, seigneurial, derisive, God knows what—down her head came in a lovely arc seeking his mouth, and her body slid back down onto his.

—Never *had* found out what explanation she'd offered Fonteviot afterwards. A scribbled note thrust next morning under his door said merely

Va bene here my sweet, have a pig of an Italian summer. But then *I* shall be back, remember!—trilling 'Ere I calm wiz a rose in my teece, anch'io!

signed with a lipstick kiss.

3

All of which now, in the shadowy fire-soft landscape of this bed, this lovely child might for all he knew have decided she had earned a supplanter's pitiless right to explore, even intrude upon, though this for the moment he could not tell, the hearth's ruined and dying crimsons now barely breathed into that dusk it was so deep, also she lay close, he could not see her eyes to tell; for in any case, as if in this new wild flooding of her senses beginning never to want not, or shyly learning, her soft young mouth had just kissed his throat now he seemed so lovely to her.

He thought damn all women, the things they are capable of saying! for when this one asked impossible questions what possible answer did she in heaven's name think he could make to her?

Ah, but then, he said to himself, but then they all do, wherever, this off-chance ritrovo or a civilized bedroom and long love, not seeing he supposed that we can only lie and they what but be made frightened we do. And it is from pure egotism, less to please than to make sure they please more; so go even as far as there *has* been what they seek to know and the truth (or whatever) is more heartless still.

Even bringing their hopeless questions up they suffer, he as good as said aloud: they know beforehand they will suffer and that if we love them we must lie.

And as this one, either, didn't see it should never have been asked, or that it is always impossible, indecent even, then the child was in for more sconcertamento than a first roll in the hay ought to involve any girl in as much an angel as this one. So he hoped she'd drift asleep, and then forget. And with luck why not? for he felt her soft breath in the hollow of his shoulder, soft as dreams.

But from her nightfall lawns of silence now she settled closer against him and this he supposed she did to seem to confide or the like rather than what he called explore, for as if meek she now said, "Or I guess you don't really though think I ought to ask, do you."

This being neither a question to put nor the way to have put it even if it were, it was perhaps apology, though in the rose-depths of darkness they now lay in she seemed to have opened her dreaming eyes and be looking at him, as for some reply, for he felt her long lashes brush his ear.

(Though however he might reply he did not see how she or any woman could believe him. Women they would not be if they did, and this was why what a folly such questions were, so he said nothing.)

Anyhow she went on, as if explaining, "Except Hugh I have you know seen you and Mrs. Fonteviot, well, *look* at each other. At parties I mean. I mean when I sort of thought you didn't think anyone was noticing. Twice," she said.

So damn all their intuitions too, he said to himself, they are fabulous, they are trained to see love everywhere so those eyes that it seems to us are like great jewels miss nothing anywhere, an unknown girl's eyelids cannot flutter a wordless *Soon* to her lover across some milling company to drive him wild with fatuous lust but they see it; or if he is near her it is not even the secret smile in the iris and for him alone that is secret from them—why, paint itself he thought cannot show what they see! and he said, "What worldly nonsense."

For a submissive moment therefore she was silent again.

—And his old libertine of an uncle's goddesses too, he thought, those elegant idle worldly girls, though to the small boy he had been they seemed old as his uncle (but who was then of course in fact as young as they)—his uncle had lived a lifetime being put through it like this, girl after girl at him as so to speak her turn for it came and often they must have wept with rage, he'd once himself in wide-eyed six-year-old bewilderment heard a molten young Roman beauty as good as raving at the man, screeching even. Absolutely primitive-wild, and he had thought, stunned, "Le donne have tantrums too? . . ."

Sheer opera; and now here was this one of his own.

—Who however appeared to have turned dreamy again for the moment instead. Even adoring, though it might have been this also was apology, for moving murmuring closer still she said softly it was so strange, she'd never imagined one would feel sort of "well, Italian-second-person-singular about you," she mumbled, mouth against his neck. "Mi *piaci!*—what a lovely thing to be able to say, *oh* it sounds so nice! Mi piaci piaci piaci piaci—and ti voglio bene too, don't I! oh it's so *convincing* in Italian!"

"Also safer," he said, and smiled.

But this she seemed not to understand, in fact only nuzzled his collarbone and was silent so long, warm there against him in the fire-fluttered shadows, that he half-dozed.

Except then, and this too might have been an apology, this child went back to explaining: "But Hugh even before she introduced us I'd wondered *whether.* You don't have to remember I know but she'd taken me to that party at the contessa's, I'd only just arrived in Florence, I mean I didn't know anybody and of course not you then either, I didn't even know you lived here, goodness how surprised I was! Except naturally I knew who you were, after all I'd *studied* you hadn't I? I'd even wanted to do my course term-paper on you, only this professor was insane about the Chadds Ford school so he wouldn't let me, anyway you came in terribly late, even for Italy late, I was talking to that Curzio Saetti near the door, because I was thinking Mrs. Fonteviot looked very bored and was nearly ready to leave anyhow, and there you came in right *past* me! Though of course you didn't know I was, well, *me* yet, anyway I thought you were looking for your hostess, Mrs. Fonteviot had told me everyone here is terribly formal, even Americans. But then

I thought *were* you looking, because you didn't seem even to glance round for the contessa, you went straight to Mrs. Fonteviot. Though I mean all I thought *then* was heavens that's *Hugh Tatnall the painter* and I was breathless, I thought but then she knows him! *my* Mrs. Fonteviot knows him! and I was just amazed—why, I'd only presented my godmother's letter to her the week before and now here you were! But then almost at once she came over to me and said did I mind if she ran me back to my pensione now? it was almost time for the party to begin breaking up anyway it was so late, so we left. But at the pensione when I turned round at the door to wave good night to her in the car, why, she'd turned on the dome-light and was doing her mouth in the rearview mirror! So I was astonished, I thought is she going *back* to the party? Or *some*-where, anyway not home! only then why hadn't she said so? and I thought how strange. Though there wasn't of course any reason for her to tell me what she was perhaps going to do. Because really there wasn't. But then I remembered all of a sudden that you'd just come in and said something to her, it took no time at all, and al-most right off she'd come and said it was time to leave. So don't you see, Hugh? later I wondered, was all. But about Mrs. Fonteviot please I wasn't trying to pry, Hugh. But just to sort of tell you you didn't have to explain it," she finished.

Though then after a brooding moment, as he said nothing, she added in a gentle voice, "Then there was that one other time," as if she did not see how he could possibly need reminding.

When this one other time might have been, however, she did not go on to say, instead seemed to explain again:—

"All Hugh I meant was, I did wonder. Because you weren't you know *just* terribly nice to me once I'd met you, you paid attention to me as if really you were thinking about me—me as *me*. So natu-rally I did begin to think about you. I don't mean like, well, like *this*, really Hugh I didn't. Except I guess anybody always does a little don't they, even if only as hypothesis sort of, but I thought there you *were*, the way you are, famous and pratico del mondo and charming, goodness *any* woman would wonder who you—I mean *everybody* here it seems to be understood *all* the men have mistresses, don't they? Of course I'd read about cavalieri serventi during the Romantic Period, Lord Byron for instance and that Contessa Guiccioli. But that was *then*, centuries ago. Or two cen-turies nearly, anyway, and then there were all those bel mondo women Stendhal's autobiography tells about his affairs with when he was consul at Civitavecchia, though I didn't think it always sounded as if he'd actually *slept* with them very much. So Hugh I wondered. Because you certainly didn't seem to pay any special attention to any of Mrs. Fonteviot's Italian friends. Or any Italian women. Or do you think I shouldn't have noticed that either," she said humbly.

He was amused, and thought for a moment of telling her, and almost did, no no, bel mondo seduction-Italian it took an expatriate to be good at. Like an old uncle of his own, his mother's brother: been as good as irresistible to the wives of the local nobility. Delinquent English ladyships too, off and on: made for variety. But in principle'd lived off the country, what old campaigner didn't.

—But he could not upset this rueful child further still! she was lost as it was in sad uncertainties, one unintended seducer was bad enough good god without the debaucheries of an irrelevant uncle to be overcome about too!

But soberly, and in particular, was he heartless?—he could not let her go *on* seeking comparisons like this, what was there in mere innocence of the world, in simply being young, for her to upset herself over!

Also he was a little upset about it again himself.

So he lolled her gently up out of the curve of his shoulder and slid her to where in those dying shadows he could make out her fire-lit eyes, which now he thought looked at him so uncertain she might once more not be feeling sure of anything about him, even whether he wanted her to smile.

In mere kindness therefore he said look, wasn't it time she began to see that this was—for want of a sensible word—normal? this being how it did happen. Foreseen or not was he told her hardly the point: making love was always it seemed somehow new and unexpected, and who you made love with always this stranger, always new, this lovely phoenix. Which was why making love he said, stroking her, was an exploration he did not see how he or any man could ever come to an end of or want to—here was this Being in your bed, this secret presence, and what could you feel you'd ever want more on earth than to discover who she was, this charming stranger.

And added, to make it sound less ponderous, off-chance it could even be Aphrodite herself, he said amiably, thinking of his uncle, for why not? *had* been for Anchises!

So she looked at him with solemn eyes. Believing. Even it appeared memorizing. As how beautiful. As (in hopes anyway) the Mystery itself.

At any rate she came up gently onto an elbow over him, to gaze down at him now it almost seemed with the sweetness of trust, this grave brooding gaze. "Then really do people then?" she asked presently. "Because I never I guess thought of anybody's thinking about love that lovely way. But Hugh *men* don't though, do they, surely?"

Ah, well, no, he said, the information was most didn't, shifting his arm that had lain under her, up agreeably over and around, fingers tracing the elegances of that docile young back, downwards too, thumb modeling the plunge of waist into slender thigh. "No real notion what they're even doing," he told her in mild derision, in self-gratulation too in fact it sounded (though under the circumstances why not?). "Here's this lovely labyrinth of you to explore, good as *waiting* to be explored, mind you! and they don't even suspect it! Past belief," he told her great soft eyes. So the breathtaking (you'd have thought) question *who* this angel is, right there in their arms to be asked, they never he said think of asking—though for all they know about her she could be some total apparition, not three-dimensional reality by god at all. "Whereas the fact is, only *you* know it non è vero? and no more than part of the time at that," he ended, laughing at her, and taking her charming waist in both hands he woggled her tenderly.

This she paid no attention to, but gazed down at him there as if wildly absorbed, as at practically a revelation, eyes poring over his face.

So ecco, there was the reason, he concluded it, why the average man wasn't much competition—a truth however of so little conceivable interest to any girl, in bed with him or not, and here, with this one, so irrelevant, she did not even bother to hear it.

Saying instead, in a musing voice, "But then Hugh how does anybody get over feeling shy if it's always still strange? Because partly, maybe, I feel shy because Hugh I just don't know enough about making love to *guess* what you think about me! I—feel so— I don't even know how to *say* it! I almost feel like the girl I roomed with sophomore year, she'd been frantically trying to decide to go to bed with some boy, because you may not know it but virginity can be very difficult *socially* at college if nothing else, but she couldn't make up her mind for months because Hugh it *is* everybody says so much a toss-up with just boys. But finally late one night she came back to the room looking sort of totally astounded and said, 'Well, I've finally *done* it!' in this bewildered voice, but then what she said about how it had been didn't make it sound as if she was at all certain she felt as impressed, for instance, as she thought she ought to, only she didn't even know whether this *was* how you felt. I don't mean she thought was this *all*, disappointed I mean or whatever, because she said it *was* really fantastic in a way, but she just seemed terribly baffled by not having any way of deciding whether what she felt was *standard*, sort of, was this what one *does* look for, aside from all the bliss-propaganda. It had seemed so unspecial she sounded practically *alarmed* Hugh about it! And the boy had been no help. Even whether anything had gone on in his head about her she couldn't imagine, he looked so stupid. *Nothing* might have happened between them! In a way she said she supposed it was in principle special, being this First Time, but about *him* she didn't seem to feel anything special at all, even trying to. Or trying to feel 'tender.' Or seventh-heavenish and swoony. She just didn't! Also what was silliest of all, she said, she didn't even begin to know whether she was, well, *you* know, 'any good'—or whether this boy was either, how *was* she to know! So she was practically out of her mind with exasperation at how little about making love she'd even found out—emotionally she didn't seem to have learned anything more about it afterwards than she'd known before. Which meant she therefore actually knew less! And she's the only girl I've ever talked to *really* about making love, Hugh. In depth that is. But now here about *you* nothing she said seems to make any sense at all, it just doesn't *apply*—or the way you described it either, so how can I help being confused? Especially when the way I seem to feel about you—well, I just *feel!*" she cried as if helpless. "I don't even think what other girls say makes much difference, I wouldn't have known what to expect any more than I did. Because I'd never have expected *this*," she said, collapsing tenderly on him again. "Are you just sort of specially charming, or what?"

So he said a mildly deprecating "Hoh!" to her; but he thought, at least she sounds deflected from Alex.

And decided to encourage the diversion. Other girls, he therefore said he agreed, probably were little help. Women, anyhow, he suspected, didn't discuss lovers with other women, except to boast, or to disparage—or find fault, like that roommate of hers. Or of course to swap hilarious indecencies of detail now and then. But a love affair that deeply pleased them was it seemed a secret sweetness, there was no delight so deep, why shouldn't they hug it to themselves? And afterwards often its memory too. It was lovers women were pleased with they "talked" to, not other women, if to anybody. Was she for instance going to tell her roommate about *this* night?

"When I've been *silly?*" she cried, shocked, whirling up over him on her elbow again, curls tumbling wild.

He said oh nonsense, she didn't actually any longer think she'd been 'silly' dammit, why pretend, anyhow she knew quite well she could offhand dream up twenty plausible explanations for her roommate of *how* it had happened, what was woman's angelic imagination for?—it wasn't the circumstances, no, it was the lovemaking she and he had so entranced each other with.

"But Hugh I did everything in such a—in oh this schoolgirl helpless way!" she mourned.

He said was she past belief too? trying to tell herself she hadn't *felt* every lovely atom of her was in it as headlong as he!—how could she have more?

"Oh I know how I feel, I don't mean I've been too busy being dazed with you not to know that," she said soberly. "But I can't very well know, can I, whether this *is* the way anybody who's had all these very affectionate attentions of yours should feel, don't you see that? Or *do* girls ask about other girls?"

He supposed not particularly, he said, more or less lying.

"About how they—what happens."

She meant *she* wasn't asking?

"No but for instance Hugh I know this will sound silly but how does an Italian girl start calling a man she likes 'tu' instead of 'Lei' without sort of giving her feelings away to him, how does she keep it from being terribly abrupt-sounding? Because it doesn't often happen like, well, *this*, does it?" she mumbled, abashed. "But in English, with 'you' for everybody, it's simply not a problem that ever even occurred to me existed."

Why, Italian girls he didn't much know about, he told her (and this was a sensible lie). But the 'problem' would, he expected, be more likely not language nuances but the cultural differences people grew up with. The bred-in assumptions wouldn't match, for instance the signals one learned about the other sex's Yes and No. Because anybody's behavior was helpless routine like the rest of the damn' populace's. Except of course painters', he added, and patted her, smiling.

These generalities she appeared however to see no point in. "Well, but what I meant," she said, going back, "was for instance the first time a girl sleeps with a man? Stays I mean the night, so there is this next day, and it *is* all strange, Hugh part of *me* isn't even sure it's still me, what happens to one's ordinary reflexes about even trivialities seems to be just wild! So what sort of thing does the girl for instance *say* when they wake up?"

—This nonsense *really* he said to himself it could not go on! at what point do they stop being apprentices and learn the full luster of their beauty?

But he managed to say, teasing, good god had her professors got her to believing there was such a thing as answers? if a girl woke up in her lover's arms what *could* she say but whatever happened to come into her sleepy head? One flippant coquette he remembered had for example said to him just *Miss me?*

But the child did not seem to follow this either.

In fact, after a silence, "But about other girls," she said in an uncertain voice, "what sort of thing—I mean a *man* telling a girl about other girls?"

He was tired of it. Still, he conceded, had she been a blessing or hadn't she? so he said, gently or as good as, look, it was not a *question* of other girls, what were other girls? let her have the confidence her beauty should give her!

So for a long moment she gazed down at him, eyes dreaming and grave, as if pondering this; persuaded almost, spellbound.

"But Hugh aren't there ways?" she asked presently, stroking his temple with a fingertip. "I mean things I could do," she said apologetically, "except you're too darling to me about it to say."

He said " 'Things'?" idly, fingers spanning that slim young waist again. "What things?"

"But which I don't *know,* Hugh!"

Ah but look, he said in pure indulgence, what on earth was there to 'learn' or whatever verb it was she was fussing about? And anyhow basta with all these endearing *buts* of hers, wouldn't she in God's besought name *trust* him for once when what he told her was absolute truth? which was that she couldn't have *been* more Woman-a-paradigm-of-herself?—rolling her down beside him again where she was more convenient.

"You mean you're tired of all my amateur questions!"

"Outraged," he said, and pulling the child to him he kissed her enchanted eyes.

At which, mumbling "Oh Hugh . . ." she slid her arms as if in obedience around his libertine neck.

So, like any man of sense who'd had something as delicious as this practically god-given him, he saw, resigned, that clearly it would be considered a nonsense, after this gentlemanly interval, not to begin to think about having it again.

4

Room cooling, it might have been, woke him.

Stuporous, in unknown black whelm of night no notion where; foundering; lost. And, next instant, mind a maelstrom: for this *who* was — —?

Then remembered. Who and where both.

And so gently it seemed she slept as if fondled there still, all blood-warm sweet against him, face tenderly smothering in his neck, softest breath riffling his hair.

Warm because warm he'd kept her.

Except at once this woke him further, for, to recapitulate, simply had that whole fire gone out?

So saw he had to ease an arm out from under, gingerly, to tilt half up, to see.

—Sunk to *ash.* . . .

Stared at it in affront, blank, propped on an elbow in total darkness, mind saying *blast.*

—Though, then, blast or not what was there for it but see to it? so, warily, had to try inching his legs from among hers, such pitch-black night it all was he could not even see how. But it did not appear she stirred. So with extreme caution, touch-and-go still, he did work finally around to rolling slowly clear. But that eiderdown to cover her in his place, he could no more find feeling about in that blackness for than see.

Or find a dressing gown they'd let fall either—till it was when he had slid stealthily out of the bed at last and fumbled his way along its swags and hangings he tripped into the things in a heap on the floor at the foot.

So he groped round to the other side with the eiderdown and spread it over his sleeping blessing, or as well over as in that blind dark he could guess at. Then back and picked up a vestaglia. Which he wrapped himself in, shivering.

But when he knelt and blew on the fire it was too far gone.

—Well, but surely a ritrovo as elegant as this one he decided would be run for all departments of benessere in general wouldn't it? this being Italy. For had no other secret lovers woken in this room to dying embers, or so sad a symbolism not been foreseen, to be provided against? and sure enough, when he felt about in the great brass hearth-box there was charcoal and those little drum-shaped bundles of neatly split faggots, even a sheaf of paper spills.

So, shortly, fire at least kindling again, he sat back on his heels staring into it, yawning.

It was slow. Charcoal was slow, catching.

So he dropped another handful of faggots on, loose. And this worked: the stuff caught in a burst—blazed up in so white a sudden dazzle the room's great cube of darkness was as if struck back, simply it fell apart into shards toppling every which way, it could have been huge shadows leaping frantic into corners. So, soon enough then, he could begin putting coals on, this first lump or two.

Sat watching it begin to glow, mind a pleasant blank.

Was warm again. No ambitions; just was warm. With those coals now slowly aglow. And himself warm. And three-dimensional: sensibility coming agreeably operative. *Himself* again.

—And aware that he could not, then, any longer, not phone.

If even for nothing more than find out whether.

To, at least, perhaps know. . . .

—Nor could he lightly go on telling himself, either, hour after unexamined hour, that there would in any case be no one there to answer if phone he did, Fonteviot out plodding on and on through black streets and echoing squares, frantic by now, haggard, if by now he had not found her, or else at her bedside if he had, in a hospital somewhere or emergency ward, phoning pointless either way.

For now it had to be faced. Whatever, faced. He got to his feet and turned uneasily to the room.

Whose vaults of darkness were now filling he saw with the hearth's reanimated crimsons again, corners emerging, murmurous with soft dusk; and as if from aisles of twilight the bed loomed out now before him palely luminous, night gone from its tall canopies, through which the coals' fluttering images were cast so faint in under that where the girl lay he could not make out for sure, thickets of shadow were so dense, only the folds of the bed's hangings fell fire-dyed, damasks and wavering vermilions, and in the brocade of its swags glints of dull gold.

For a moment he was at a loss where they could have put the phone.

Though then her table de chevet he saw was where, and he thought *blast*, for suppose she woke.

But keeping his voice down why should she? Since anyhow phone he had to: could no longer not. So across he went, careful tiptoe.

Phone had call-buttons. He had to bend down, close over, to make out the etichette. *Direzione Maggiordomo Staffiere Cameriera Bar*: all Italy leaping to serve, to caress. He buzzed the staffiere and waited, staring at nothing.

"Pronto, signore!"

He said to the man, low, muffling the phone, ring this number he was giving him, would he kindly.

And, waiting, seeing in his mind that other table de chevet where now by her bed he heard her phone ring and ring, unanswered, he also became aware that what he was dully staring at, blank-blind before his face, was the Hermitage. He lifted it up near his eyes, squinting at it. A quarter full it looked still.

But barely cool. Moving with care, he stretched slowly off with it to the wine-bucket, phone-cord snaking after, and soundlessly eased the bottle back in. Out of anyhow the way.

Ice left or not.

"Non risponde, signore."

He muttered well dammit to keep trying.

Though turning now to look he decided the girl would not perhaps wake after all. For in those clustering shadows she lay it seemed almost as he had left her, unstirring, lapped in sleep, under the eiderdown he had spread over her (askew, he now saw), sweet young head half-smothering still in the pillow where he had lain, lashes as if dreamless on her cheek, though the hearth's burgeoning roses were too faint through those heavy hangings for him to be sure. And waiting there he stood gazing, simpleminded, savoring how it had been, the remembered pleasure of her—and this in a kind of wonder, even, for always how is it one has never, beforehand, quite seen the beauty, the amazement, of detail they can be; and suddenly *Alex* he heard his mind say to him, so that for a moment he was dazed with the uncertainty, totally lost, it could have been either of them lying asleep there, it seemed he had no way of telling which, the sweetness drowning his senses an enigma of memory forever; and he thought, with accusation, *I am unteachable.*

"Sempre nessuno, signore. Ma se ci vuol che—"

No he said never mind: non importava, and turned away. Though then good god he thought what was this heartless *non importa* when the night had still to go on! *on* and on and with nothing even to do. Or keep still, even, poking empty-minded at the fire.

He went to the window, and looked out, aimless, into the dark cortile.

Night outside was he saw no longer that immense cumber of shadows. For a moment, surprised, he thought faint glow it must be from some burning quarter of the city beyond was being shed down, reflected, from lowering cloud-mass. But it came and went, intermittent gulps of oily light, from it seemed off to his left. He leaned close to the panes to see, and it was an abandoned car, burnt out it looked but still burning sluggishly, gouts of dirty flame now and then; and in that light he saw what he had taken in the blackness earlier for some sort of small private square, or perhaps courtyard, now opened he saw at that far end onto a tangle of narrow streets, and these led off God knew where, into fathoms of darkness beyond.

A thin rain had been falling. The smoldering car as he looked flared up as if in a puff of wind, thousands of points of gold light burst up and fled scattering out over the wet black cobbles below him, so that for an instant he made out the whole piazzetta plain, end to end. Arcaded façade ran he saw the whole length over across, the arches rounded and their soffits picked out with eccentric abbellimenti of some sort in the stone, ball-flowers perhaps or crockets; and the severe march of long Roman bricks was broken, between the formal courses of the windows, by fylfots and enameled medallions alternating. Under the central cornice a baroque cramp-iron carried what looked like a date, or a scrolled initial. Architecturally it could be anything.

And a bare twenty foot out, below, was the fountain whose overflow splashing he had heard. Now he saw it was a Roman patera sort of thing: simply, water welled up through this low stem into the flat circle of its cup, to spill, thin slopping sheets of it, out over and down into the round stone basin its foot stood in. At its imagined corners some later taste had set four battered coehorns on the cobbles, linked by chains.

Then that abrupt flare of smoky light guttered and went out, snuffed. It was black again.

And silent; or if sound came from the rumorous city beyond, of somewhere mobs still, it would have been like surf far off among dunes in darkness, or like when in a cove at night long seas roll in to burst thundering and thudding under the rotting timbers of a jetty long years disused, and if the tide is making it is a sound he thought as of an omen among ruins.

He let the long folds of the curtain swing closed.

— But turning away, to the fire-soft dusk of the room again, now he could not think what there might be merely to do, night it seemed was without end everywhere. He was mindless with disquiet. For ring Fonteviot so soon again he could not, in reason: no time had gone by. Or not enough, though in the deeper shadows there by the window he found he could not make out the face of his watch, to see.

But going toward the fire for light, he thought, with a kind of sardonic dismay, was he God help him merely *bored?* . . . For eccolo, here he was at a ritrovo with as sweet, as acquiescent, a delizia as the Bona Dea and Iddio combined had ever indulged him with, and in *this* situation he felt at a loose end good god?—grumbling and put upon? . . .

—But all the same, night in fact lay before him for long hours still. And whatever the time was (presently he saw), was he to sit on and on in the dark doing undistractedly nothing whatever?—since going back to bed was he supposed not possible, the child would be woken, and if then sadly shamed again it would have been unkind.

So in his mind he tossed, fuming.

Having been exasperated further by discovering he could not make out the hands of his watch at the hearth either, the coals glowed too dim.

—Which on top of by heaven boredom was too *much!* if he had hours of it still to face he'd at least find out how many!—though then round the hooded bed he still stepped softly, wary eye on that sleeping pleasure of his this time too.

Though, then, waiting phone in hand, he thought sardonically again what matter—was he any the less clear about this probably misguided episode than if she were awake and prattling? For what operators they are, he said to himself, even novices they are capable of every disingenuousness. This one, and after the happiest complicity, mind you—*three* complicities—Iddio Himself could not keep this one from arraigning him for 'seduction' if she decided to, lovely eyes wells of betrayal and tears. When all he had done was humanely save her, perhaps, from a fate as dejecting as her preposterous roommate's—deflowered by an undergraduate, dear god what a thing for any girl to have nerved herself up to! Whereas *he* had helped her bypass disillusionment altogether, an absolute beneficenza d'Iddio. Or of the Bona Dea's, it being of course unknown Which happened to have the duty that evening.

Except that it was alas not he supposed clear to him what he thought about this or perhaps any love. If only because what girl is

it one sees as she is, or even to herself is? so alike they can seem.
Alex too, even, he said to himself in depression: each charming
body as if beckoning up from the infidelities of memory those
ghosts of others'—so that again *unteachable* he found himself
saying in his mind, uselessly, or it may be he muttered it half
aloud, to whatever drifting presences glared in rage at him from
the shadows, torva tuentes like Vergil's Dido; though in gloomy
fact, he thought, it is all out of our hands and is also hopeless, we
lie to them out of decency, as said. And often, likely as not, they lie
to us from that strange tenderness in return.

"Pronto, signore!"

He said, low, "Che ora è?"

"Signore? Quasi le tre, signore. Si fa tardi!"

—Fellow being *insolent?*

But no: no insolence in the tone. Not trained properly, was all,
place being what it was. "Grazie," he said, and set the phone back
on its stand.

—Two in the morning *then* it had been, not three, Alex had left
him, merciless with anger.

And this, after a special lussuria of love long into the small
hours—past surfeit they had even spun it on, for with Fonteviot
returning who knew when such freedom could be counted on
again: it was ritual. But then, and this she had never done on such
an occasion before, she had taken him aback saying she must
go—had he forgot she was to meet Aubrey's plane? And *early?*
goodness! so go she must, too desolating, poor great lecherous
sweet, but surely he could see? So they had gently wrangled.

Except that then, and from mere carelessness he said to himself
it can happen in love—one wheedling word too many; the deft-
ness of a caress misconstrued—abruptly it had turned out they
were quarreling. For most *certainly* she would not stay! Had he no
more sensibilità than a, than some lout of a, what was the word for
a stableboy?—che uno stalliere, then! She did *not* propose to set
out from *his* bed to meet Aubrey—in fact what an *utterly* squalid
idea! And LET GO of her!

To which, in his folly, and he might have been some petulant
mere boy, he'd very nearly replied what sudden onset of wifeliness
made her fuss about which bed she started being faithful again
from?—but, said or not, she had read it in his face; and though at
the last he had appeased her enough to say she'd come have breakfast with him before she set out for the airport, she had left cold
with displeasure still.

And gloomily now he had to say to himself God help him why not?—he'd as good as made a year's easy ambiguities explicit, insisting. Which bed, simply it mattered—if only for maskings and unmaskings of cool images in her pier glass, for unhurried complacencies, between sets of feelings and customs, and these for all he knew of her a bal travesti too. For what could he say she had ever been to his senses but a beckoning masque from some *Assemblée dans un Parc*, smiling and heartless, some sweet Watteau marauder?—it having begun to be clear to him that he had not asked himself who, enchantment aside, this charming being had perhaps become.

Even that cold tantrum of Alex's it must be he had not known enough of her to understand. For it had hardly crossed his mind that she might not, by breakfast, be over it.

—In the curtained night of the bed the child mumbled something, and stirred, whimpering. He stopped dead, numb.

For, abruptly, so little about her he felt he knew either, that if now by bad luck he had woken her, bolt upright out of her pillows she could spring in the intake of a breath, eyes flying open at him wild, lips parted to shriek, at what deep terror he could never know; and then, as swiftly, all coming back to her—in a rush, everything—she might for all he knew feel oh what must he think of such frightenedness, and bunch down into the bed they had tumbled again, sheepish, overcome.

And if then in reassurance he went over to her she would humbly make room for him to sit on the edge there, slim body diffidently reassembling its symmetries of light and line, as if in apology drawing aside and away.

—But then, ah, well, his memory said, they can come awake mood anything.

They are an unknown, he said to himself, resigned; unknowns, the lot of them; and what was he to make of this new one either?—for whether he was to regard himself as having (carelessly or not) acquired her, he did not see how it was possible to decide.

But for the moment it turned out she did not wake; so presently it was safe to step softly away, to the fire.

Which as he saw could do with more coal, he knelt and one by one took more lumps from the scuttle and put them on.

—The third morning this would soon be the chaos in the streets had gone on. Gunfire, that first one, he had thought it was woke him, and this had been very early—no more, it might have been, than first light, which fell, a pale bar, through some slot in the heavy folds of his bedroom curtains, this ingot of cool white gold. Or perhaps it had been tear-gas bursts, for when he heard it a second time it had those flat slaps of sound.

Though what matter which. He had dozed.

But then, sluggish, barely drifted up into waking again, with a pang he had begun to remember that ah, no farther off than tomorrow, now, Fonteviot was due; would be back, coming between, reclaiming, dispossessing; would *be* there, and his lovely Alexandra—though how he thought of her, sensual with sleep as he still was, was of the savors of that sleekness nightlong elegant and entwined, and at these splendors of remembered lust he had groaned longingly aloud.

Upon which, instantly, in his mind another English voice breathed to him, lazy with making love, though this had been in a bed in London, years gone, hardly the war over, *Tell me about your sweet lovely American girls, do they do all sorts of wicked wonderful things for you? . . .* light fingers stroking his belly, dream-crossed greedy body tangled with him still—except that then the sheer libertine faithlessness of all this had so amused him that he opened his eyes snickering.

So he yawned, happily, stretching.

And lay thinking about schedulings ahead, for tonight yes, but then Fonteviot back. Though he saw what was to happen was not clear. So then he had lain there, idly drowsing.

But at length had got up out of his bed and was shrugging into the sleeves of his dressing gown, yawning still, when from what sounded some distance he heard shouting, from over across the Giardini it seemed to come, so he slung back the curtains from the French window and stepped through, to see, onto the little oriel of a balcony.

Up into the pale cool ivory of dawn—and it was beyond the gardens, on past the Strologaio corner too, where cold mist still coiled, or clung in wisps to walls, muffling them soft in wreaths of drifting white—up into the still air black smoke stood straight as a pillar just at the vicolo, and now he heard it had not been shouts, or articulate even, but a sort of toneless baying of sound, it could have been the sad bellowing of deaf-mutes.

And then this sudden flap of orange flame cut part of the mist through and he saw a camion afire, it was overturned across the vicolo, half-blocking the way into it; and just then this huge scattering mob, hundreds, had come pouring wildly out and around the other corner and in behind the Strologaio, and with a heavy clattering roar a police helicopter shot down past from nowhere over his head and scudded off low over the gardens as if in pursuit.

And police, he now made out too, had caught up with some of the last clusters of the running mob at the far edge over across, and were clubbing them.

He had said, "Well, be damned," a good deal surprised. But by then he was chilled.

Had gone back in and run a bath.

And when, presently, dressed, he had stepped out to look again, it had all seemed over. The camion, burnt out, they had pushed up out of the way onto a traffic divider. The uproar of the early Vespas was on.

Ominous who'd possibly have thought it! Riots are a European routine. They are politics; since votes are not.

He had even joked about it to Lucrezia as she served him break-fast: what had been that porco of a row that woke him—her Rivoluzione this time at long last?

She'd dismissed it with Marxist jeers: "Da dilettanti, signore! Da studenti!"

And "Tanto più fa paura!" he had tossed it off with, and gone on with orders for the day. He was lunching out. Expected no one for drinks. The signora inglese was coming to dinner. Start with an insalata alla Nizza, or some such, then he thought a rabbit, with that pine-nut and raisin marinade; and see if that fruttaiolo of hers had any wild strawberries yet. . . . *Now*, the light-mindedness of it left him stunned.

—And what that morning had she said and whirled on her stylish heels and gone out his door without a backward glance?— the cool displeasure he could remember, but the words she had flung at him, no. Yet why? When from deep tunnels of the past voices drift up like echoings in dreams, as if from those ancient catacombs and lost corridors of the self the waking self has never groped its way down to, they are so unknown. Yet so clear are they, almost it can seem those girls live on there, not memories but beings, and they speak.

—He could not stand it. He crossed to the phone and buzzed the staffiere one time more.

And as that far-off ringing began again, unanswered still, again he saw in his mind the tall cool room that for this whole year now the faint scent of her presence had made her own, and the scrolled and gilded pier glass that a thousand times must have held her image in its blackening depths; and from *it*, he thought despondently, her eyes would have looked out at her open and undissembling, as at no lover ever, but unguarded, primeval, solitary, all-knowing, and serene. But as for who the being is that looks out at us from the eyes even of our longest love or oldest friend, he said to himself it was as if there were the shimmer of a summer veil between.

—Then against all hope, so that believe it almost he could not, he heard, answering, Fonteviot's voice, ragged and fretful with it seemed fatigue: "Yes? Pronto—cosa c'è—chi parla?" but then, when he had said who, in a sort of headlong cry, "Hugh, *Hugh* where've you been! not still out *looking*, man, surely? Why in heaven's name haven't you rung in now and then—*hours* ago I ran Alex down! They've turned that old hospice into emergency and there the blessed woman was, fuming—couldn't make even the damn' sisters get word to me: language absolutely livid, *wonderful* spirits! She's a *bit* knocked about, Hugh, broken collarbone and rather a nasty scrape all down that side—got tumbled down one of those flights of stone stairs by the river, running from the police. But in *miracle* form, spitting fury at nobody's phoning me where she was. Sent you her *love*. Where *are* you, by the way?"

He let the phone crackle on: now it made no difference. Not only perfectly safe, Fonteviot was saying, but they'd bring her home in the morning straight off. Was sleeping now, poor sweet creature: he'd taken pills with him, in case, and given her one. But Christ what a tamasha! Couldn't either of them remember for the life of them when she'd had a tetanus booster last. Thank God it was over. He felt *drained*. As, he feared, must Hugh poor old chap too—he *was* most frightfully sorry for the sheer bloody-mindedness they'd repaid all his kindnesses to them by involving him in— these *Neapolitan* unbridled Tuscans! But tomorrow, though, he *would* look in on her wouldn't he? She'd want to thank him—been so quite marvelously devoted and kind! So then see him tomorrow then? Then good night, *must* try and get what there was left of a night's sleep, he finished it, in a voice of now total exhaustion, and rang off.

—Though it was of course tomorrow now.

In fact today; "quasi le tre" long past. In mere hours he would see her.

As his mind did now—sitting up smiling he hoped at him from her heaped pillows, eyes his again, a light hand out happily toward him across the sun-moted morning of her room for him to lift to his lips, scattering her stylized English extravagances of blandishment and apology into the glowing gold of the air about him as he came, little courteous murmurs mingled it might be in, of penitence for what an *endless* night of his it must, poor sweet, have been. . . . He would even be thanked, the sudden sardonic gaiety of his relief said to him, for his nightlong devotion, and no way to forestall the equivoco. He set the phone gently back on its stand and turned toward the bed.

Where it would be tomorrow-today sooner. And nothing for that either but wait.

—Except ah, he was tired of it. Wake, sooner or later, she had to. So hardly mattered by now if she did: be deep dawn before long in any case. He sat down on the corner of the bed where he'd sat before, and settled back against the tester-post, among the dark folds of the hangings, yawning.

In his mind, drowsily, he saw the first scene, how it might go. She lay mid-bed there; turned away; he would not see her eyes open. Drift perhaps then closed again, back into the last moments of oblivion: hardly conscious of seeing, of having taken in, the pillow her dreaming head lay lost in still. But then, again she would wake. She would make a little sniffling sound or two; would swallow a yawn; and then in faint surprise she would find herself looking at the unexplained curtains of this unknown bed, and her gaze would stray up, astonished now, to the tester-rails above. Then she would remember, and turn and see him; and, he hoped, would smile.

He would deal with it as it came.

With whatever matter-of-fact decencies of affection it turned out for the moment were called for.

—But for the tomorrows beyond? The structure of another scene to come rose in his mind like a tiny model of a set for a play, and this could well be no farther off than the real tomorrow. Alex would be abed still, recovering. But recovered enough for a levee. Friends would have been dropping in. With flowers, with fruit, with the jeweled rhetoric of bel mondo commiseration, with circolo scandal.

And in the particular scene his mind now saw, Rosemary would have brought flowers, and a book perhaps; and Alexandra would have patted the bed at her side and made her sit there; they would be amiably gossiping. He would have crossed the piccolo salotto, and the gilt and ivory of the anticamera, and have halted in the white panel of the doorway, with a phrase of greeting. And as for that instant of pause he stood there, beginning to smile, those lustrous heads would turn to him as one, rosy tongues stopped in midsentence; and for a moment of absolute stillness, side by side, their eyes in wide unguarded welcome would be in his. . . .

—But first, as said, there was today. And this one.

He settled his head against the post's vased turnings and closed his eyes. He wondered, when she woke, what she would say.

II. Pays de Connaissance

I remember I thought, kneeling there in the blaze of that summer morning, how hot and still, how heavenly, it all might have seemed to me instead, the towering château walls and the neglected gardens in the enormous light, and the low-lying green headland shimmering off à perte de vue to the immense shining circle of the sea beyond, the whole world a brilliance of enamel, turquoise and azure and gold, oh everywhere the high summer I love and the sun like warm slow bombs, and Hugh lounging there long-limbed and easy on the stone stair, and looking at me; but of course by then none of all that was how I could any longer see it, too much awful had happened, I remember wondering how long it had been since either of us had spoken even a word, and when at last he did, looking straight at me with almost no expression at all, he just said, "Why did you come with me?" like that.

I thought oh heaven as if I *knew*, and I said, "But Hugh darling I love you, even after all this time I love you, I never stopped," with my soft look at him under my eyelids to make sure he believed me.

I did I remember wonder a little what that look of his was, did he think I was heartless? as if that mattered!—though mostly I was wondering whether now all this would perhaps have spoiled things, making love: he might decide he saw it all in my eyes like a tiny scene carved in a cameo, minute but terribly clear—that empty Breton headland sloping up through its meadows to the glitter of the ruined gardens and the sun hot on the cobbles of the courtyard, the château walls over me splintering light, and even under the great beeches in the parc around, sun splattering down through the foliage here and there like beads and coins of gold.

And when all this was just total mistake and tiresome! — and not the domaine Hugh had come to look over at all. But then, one winding fern-fringed ancient Basse Bretagne lane like every other till finally we were lost, and we saw this long avenue of huge old tilleuls leading back in from the voie to it seemed a wooded parc behind one of those rough-stone walls they all have, with wrought-iron gates standing open for once and an elegant little Renaissance lodge just inside, and, beyond, the avenue disappeared into the green gloom of the beechwood and I said to Hugh why on earth not drive in and simply *ask* directions. Of course he said, ". . . Just blandly intrude?" in his not-approving voice, so I had to say, "What a stuffy-Philadelphia darling you can be, goodness!" to get him to, only then there was no concierge at the lodge to ask.

So he said all right *all right* goddammit, though he sounded amused, and we drove on in, till after a minute I began to see glints of sunlight on masonry ahead through the green aisles of the wood, and suddenly out we came into the dazzle of a forecourt, under this great sun-flooded façade of rose-gray stone, up and up, balconies and balustrades and finialed cornices and an armorial escutcheon, prancing heraldic beasts and all, carved in the stone over the entablature of the portal, goodness what a place, and we rolled across the cobbles and pulled up beside four men in gunning jackets who'd just got out of a big black Citroën and turned to watch us drive up to them, and I remember saying to Hugh hunting in *summer?* except by the time I saw it was mitraillettes not shotguns in their hands they'd surrounded our car and it was too late.

One of them called out, "Va chercher le patron!" to a man in a blue houseman's apron who had just come round the far corner of the château, and then they just stood there looking at us empty-eyed — totally silent, and even when Hugh said, "What the devil d'you think you're doing!" they just went on bleakly staring, and not a word.

I was thinking but Hugh speaks perfectly good French, why's he behaving as if he doesn't? when this tall man in riding breeches came hurrying out of the château with the blue-apron man, and the minute he saw the men around us he called out, "Mais non non non *non!*" and ran across the balustraded terrasse and down the half-dozen broad stairs down to the cobbles and over to where we all were, and I thought heavens what a beautiful man, bel homme doesn't begin to say it, he's breathtaking, but I supposed he was the "patron," anyway now he'd call these idiots thank God off, so we could go, how was *I* to know he couldn't.

But there at first he was so perfectly charming—and in English english, in the wilds of Outer Brittany of all places!—so perfectly distressed-sounding too about "this desolating overreaction of his friends' " that really I don't see how I could have suspected, I don't think Hugh did either, then. Because we knew there *had* been this second or third attentat on General de Gaulle, and *Le Figaro* said it was believed the gunmen hid out in Brittany somewhere this time afterwards too, so when he stood there tall and elegant by the car, the sun on his fair hair and so exactly noonish overhead it threw the shadows of his eyelashes on his cheeks as he looked at me, goodness how blue his eyes were, I mean why *shouldn't* we have believed this wasn't a part of the general battue he said it was, "manhunt" didn't we call it in English? on battait la campagne all over the département, this back-country sous-préfecture in particular, and his friends had simply been overzealous, but now *would* we have the gentillesse to let him try he hoped to make up for this lamentable malentendu by staying to luncheon with him? delayed as they had hélas by now made us, miles he feared from anywhere we could eat decently in any case? . . . so before Hugh could say no I started the process of saying yes we would by saying it was sweet of him but of course we couldn't. So of course he charmingly insisted—and if Hugh looked sardonic I didn't *care*. So in due course we introduced ourselves, he said he was Alain de Moëtland and Hugh said our name was Tatnall before I could stop him, and we went in; and it wasn't really till after lunch that we began to discover they wouldn't have let us leave anyway.

And then, not two days later, and oh so *sudden*, to have such savagery to remember. . . .

—So I was still sort of in shock, kneeling there that lovely morning, though why I told Hugh I'd come with him was true enough if you felt romantic, because in a *way* I'd certainly wanted him practically from—Was it the winter I was nine? yes because Georgiana was nearly sixteen, he was taking her to a Penn Charter dance and Mummy'd asked him for the weekend, he was our cousin anyway. Of course I'd *seen* him before. Lots of times, I expect, but never the way *that* time he was, goodness!—he was like some fierce corsair the way he was after Georgie, he looked as if he could lunge at her right there in the drawing room and carry her off, and *she* I could see was absolutely in pieces about him inside—well, *ridiculous*, but it was an epiphany, my first-ever sense of Man after Woman, and *understanding* it! Of course part of me was sexy-wild, out of my mind over what was going to happen, but also I felt cold and brilliant all over, for now I *knew*, I can even remember the exact words I thought it in: *So this is how men are, wonderful and dangerous*, and I wanted to own him though I wasn't certain what for exactly, technically. Ho, but that night I found that half out too, I'd woken and gone to the loo and was just about to patter back along the dark third-floor hall when I saw him, he was tiptoeing, and I was *very* astonished, but just as I was about to ask him what he was doing he opened the door to Georgie's room, I remember particularly he didn't even stealthily knock, and he went *in!* Well, my heart was in ruins, I stood there simply out of my mind I've no idea how long, *oh* how I hated her, I seethed with it. I rushed back to my room and tried to listen to them through the wall, jabbering *D'you suppose he's kissing her?* to myself in rage and misery, and *Suppose she's* LETTING *him!* I plotted horrible revenges half the rest of the night, and at breakfast I sat glaring across the table at them till she got so upset and wild she tried to make Mummy send me away from the table. And later I stole a letter of hers to him, from the hall table, I loathed her so. But then I found all it said was "Each night I imagine our meeting. Shall it be where our lovely First was? Already I know what I'll wear, and how the sky will look, and you." So I didn't even bother to tear it up, goodness.

—Then on the passenger list there his name was. And I thought of all those times and times again I had seen him since, at dances and horse shows and family tennis and at weddings, he was an usher at both of mine, and how each time I would find myself being taken with him all over again, and I thought maybe this is the time nothing will stand in the way? and I sent the cabin steward round with a note to him. And in hardly any time at all there he stood in my doorway laughing and calling out, "Good god, angel, *you!*" and he was as lovely-dangerous-looking as ever and I said, "Don't you ever knock?" wondering how I was going to keep my fingers off him long enough for ordinary good manners. But of course I did: it wasn't till the next day, he saw me back to my cabin after lunch and I couldn't resist saying, "Are you being charming, or just seducing me?" and it was lovely even the first time.

And that whole way across to Cherbourg, just lovely—I *never* thought I could spend so much that-sort-of time with a man, partly I suppose wild helpless girlish béguin I was working off years of, heavens some of my behavior! but oh a man sort of your whole body can feel knows what it is you do and how you feel inside doing it—by the night before we landed alarm bells were going off all through me, head and everywhere, je m'en passais la fantaisie, yes, but what if I wasn't going to *recover* from this just anyhow! but then at dinner he said look, whether I'd been describing us to myself as an affectionate experiment in symbiosis or just an extended roll in the hay he was too out of his mind over me to care, but for *him* there hadn't been anywhere near enough, there might never be, the way he felt, he *adored* me and why didn't I come help him try to find some for-sale manoir he'd told me he was thinking of looking for, in Brittany, to buy for summers, wasn't my French more than good enough to make American fusses at the stingy inconveniences of their fruits-de-mer vacation hotels? and I thought of a phrase I'd read somewhere that took care of the first part of his question too, and I said, "Ça me ferait l'air de quoi, que de pester contre l'amour?" and at Cherbourg his car was the third up out of the hold, an *omen* he said, so we'd have lunch at L'Avaugour at Dinan.

But we ran into the assassination alert even before we'd got out of Normandy, on the straightaway after Avranches there must have been half a mile of cars backed up at the bridge before Pontaubault being one by one *searched* of all things! you pulled up under the mitraillettes of four or five young soldiers in that baggy battle dress, hardly any of them more than boys, looking bored and manly, and a very good-looking officer Hugh said was a para came to the car and saluted and politely asked us to step out and might he see our pièces d'identité, and while he did two more of his men went through the car; and just on the far side of Pontaubault we found the same sort of patrol was stopping traffic joining us from a road on our left, from Alençon Hugh said, but we didn't find out what was going on till in Dinan Hugh bought a paper, though outside Dol we did see this huge DE GAULLE À L'ASILE — VIEUX CINGLÉ daubed in red paint across the wall of an abandoned stone barn.

I said to Hugh but to want to *assassinate* the poor man? but he said why not? — they'd come within hours of pulling off a military coup last year, and they'd have stood him up in front of a firing squad if they had; been absolute touch-and-go as it was. Because roughly speaking he said de Gaulle was the French equivalent of the kind of English landed gentry that went to Sandhurst and held the Empire together in the Guards, so, now, to the French army and navy and the landed families their officers came from, the General was simply a traitor to his country *and* his class; and when I said but over just Algeria or whatever? he said if you need pretexts you invent them — wasn't one of the slogans "Algérie Française"?

One of the coup generals had even gone round proclaiming, "Ma passion pour mon sol natal me rend enragé!" foaming at the mouth to prove it, god what people.

—But for us to have got caught in anything so utterly unlikely— and so *French*-unlikely, heavens!—who would expect any of it? And from a man as old-régime-elegant as our beau Breton of a host above all!

Though from almost the first moment of that first day, even before lunch, I remember I thought there was a constraint about him one didn't somehow expect in such an ambience: why didn't he I wondered really properly introduce those men for instance, instead of just a wave of the hand and an easy phrase about his "local friends and colleagues." Of course the French can be very odd about mentioning names sometimes. But these men were so obviously out of place to pass for country neighbors or social equals, Hugh told me later they were so hard-eyed he'd taken them at first for off-duty police. And then, well, the *lunch* was so ordinary to give friends, just ray with black butter and then escalopes, wouldn't he I thought at least have a hunt board of some sort even if it wasn't that sort of a battue? so it was strange, bel homme or not.

We had lunch in a great wainscoted room he said had been the corps-de-garde originally, with one of those enormous Renaissance fireplaces, the coat-of-arms over it had its prancing beasts gilded, and the quarterings in the field were enameled, azure and I guess it had been gules, but the wainscoting he said some eighteenth-century ancestor had added—even in summer the bare ashlar walls must have been bleak, so this aïeul had turned it into still another salon. But then it had been his own father who'd made a dining room of it, they'd no longer been using most of the château anyway, what could one do with nearly seventy rooms!— lambris dorés or not, one simply no longer found servants enough, so it was closed off, some of the attics he thought from Second Empire times. But the furniture surprised me—a beautiful dark-gleaming Hepplewhite dining table and shield-back chairs and a *pair* of serpentine-front sideboards with those banded inlays, and as we sat down I said to him how light and charming they made the room, what a pleasure to come on such English elegance in France, and he said he'd had an elegant Irish great-grandmother, these had been a part of her dowry.

And he was telling me more about her, he did make conversation beautifully, but those unexplained "friends" of his were just sitting humped over their plates at the other end of the table not even talking among themselves, from their faces not understanding even, and I thought *really* what people, not that I cared what they did or whether he was just having them eat with us because of the battue, but were we going through a whole meal like this? because goodness how awful, also how uncomfortable and silly, so I said to him, "Hugh and I, you know, do speak French, so why don't we, so much easier perhaps d'you think for your friends," so we did. But then they didn't take part in the conversation in French either, just sat feeding like lumps, staring sullenly down into their plates. Except of course now and then I could feel them sliding looks at me out of the corner of their unpleasant eyes the way that sort of men do, but who'd care.

Anyway, in French, naturally we were soon making conversation about the attempt to assassinate General de Gaulle, Hugh told about the "perquisitions" at Pontaubault, and I asked but why did everybody seem to expect these attentat people to hide out here in Brittany, when wasn't it Algeria they were in such a rage with the General about? One of the men at the end of the table muttered something, but Monsieur de Moëtland looked amused and said but madame where could any happy assassin of a French politician possibly be safer?—Bretons were *Celts* bon Dieu not Franks or Burgundians or Provençaux! Brittany wasn't even part of France for any true Breton—it was *occupied*, ces gredins de rois français had "annexed" it, by marrying Breton duchesses when they were helpless orphans: "Vous ne saviez vraiment pas, madame, que notre petite Duchesse Anne—" and on about Louis XII and François I and the young Duchesse Claude in 1514, tout le bazar, smiling into my eyes.

But I was hardly listening really, I was thinking *Mon Dieu qu'il est beau*, he's unbelievable, the skin of his neck is so white I feel as if I could taste it, and I wondered what he did for love. Because surely not I thought just some pretty peasant girl he'd have couche-toi-là, it had to be someone of his own class for such beauty, there's their endless talk about honor of course, but still. Because that head on your pillow, heavens! And I thought, if he were an American, by now I'd have begun to call him Alain, and even looking in his eyes what could I be but conscious of the rest of him, even his hands, so deft, gesturing, and I wondered how they would feel, touching me. But then Hugh must have said something, anyway I began listening again, and of all things they were discussing their *traditions*. . . .

Or at least Alain was explaining about the Breton old nobility, the only careers they could with honor follow were what they'd followed from Agincourt or before even, they became generals or admirals et voilà, what else was possible, and when Hugh said but not the Church too? he said laughing what battle-honors did a monseigneur or an abbé de cour get, and Hugh looked amused and said *his* family didn't go in for religion thank God either, just bibelot-collecting in a distinguished way and Main Line polo, and I thought goodness do I even know how I feel about either of them.

But also during all this I'd been noticing the surly-looking man across the table at the end more and more fidgeting, and looking hard at Alain, and now suddenly he scraped back his chair and stood up, and sort of blurted out, "Je m'excuse, monsieur le vicomte, mais vous savez . . . enfin . . . vu le boulot?" and the other three scrambled to their feet looking awkward too, and I wondered why he'd use a word like "job" for their battue; but all Alain said was, "Mais allez-y donc, sauvez-vous," hardly more than glancing down the table at them; so they mumbled *sieur-dame* the way they do, and slid their eyes at me a last time and went out, and the maid with them.

And then for a moment, it was no more than a wordless breath of time, the three of us sat there in one of those strange soft silences, like a transition between two worlds—as if from the tone one talks in when there are people there who aren't like us, to how we talk when there aren't. I mean we are brought up to say things in ways such people will understand, it saves time. And, really, their feelings I expect too. Because with them we *say* instead of just half-say with implications and references taken for granted that would make them see they were left out, anyhow now here was this sudden little silence, and I said to myself we are all three en pays de connaissance and thinking the same things about these men but won't say so, and this is what the silence is about.

But then Hugh broke it with a remark that showed it was something else too—though really he might have known Alain for years, the way he looked at him and said it—"I'm afraid our presence has put you in more of a difficulty than your good manners are letting show," and I thought, why, he's speaking English again, but what an odd thing to say, and looked at Alain and then I saw something *was* the matter.

For a minute, though, he had such a strange uncertain expression that all I thought was he must think it's odd too; but then he sort of took a long breath, and turned to me looking unhappy and humble, and said, "The difficulty is, I have to tell you something, madame, and it distresses me to," and then he turned to Hugh again and said, "It's not quite the battue I've been giving you to understand," and I suppose I might have foreseen it all, right then.

Because the fact was, he said, simply these men were "separatists." Bretons had suffered under French rule for centuries, he was as good as a partisan of autonomy himself, he said, looking at me in a kind of apology, for really madame how not? — what Breton hadn't ancestors killed fighting them, c'était dans le sang to detest them! Did I know they still even refused to let Breton be used in Breton schools? — that outrageous piece of petty tyranny alone had turned Bretons by the thousands into fiery autonomists, and a few practically into maquisards! So, now, with these attempts on the General's life turning the police loose, anybody in any movement they could label "dissident" was being harassed, and these men in particular were understandably wary — two of them had been picked up already by the police after the earlier attentat, and roughly handled; so in short he had had he felt to assure them no possible word of their presence here would get out. *He* of course realized it wouldn't, from us, but — ah well, we saw the sort they were. And since now they did need a few hours to get safely off to another cachette, he found himself in the desolating necessity of asking us whether —

"Is what you're saying we *can't* leave?" Hugh said, and I thought but it's almost as if he'd been expecting it! and I was almost too surprised to think.

Simply it was a matter of the few remaining hours it would take, Alain said, to make arrangements, and get these men safely hors de portée somewhere else. Right or wrong, they felt *this* cachette had been rendered useless. What he was asking us was to have the indulgence, the vraie gentillesse, he said almost pleadingly, to give him the pleasure of having us under his roof meantime.

Then nobody said anything.

But I thought *really* what an unbelievable conversation! — this drawing-room punctilio and politesse when are we or *aren't* we in something rather unpleasant? *And* odd!

So I said but heavens — well *somebody* had to say something! — I said but weren't his sympathies known? he being "pays" after all, wasn't he? because his lovely château I meant I'd have thought would have been one of the first places a police "rafle" closed in on. But he said ah but madame a "sweep" through a paysage touffu like this they knew would be hopeless, in Basse Bretagne every second field disappeared into woods or hedgerows, Dieu might have made the landscape exprès to hide in: no, the police would spot-check, and more or less at random. Hugh said mildly by "random" he supposed he meant "with luck"? but he said why not?—with the château's seventy-odd rooms *and* attics and cellars a handful of men no more than these could vanish at a minute's warning, there were even three or four—wasn't "priests' holes" the English for it? in the thicknesses of chimney walls, from Chouan times.

Hugh sort of looked at him, and even I thought 'warning'? with the lodge gates wide open and no concierge? . . . But then Hugh decided to say it anyway: what if, that morning, it had happened to be a police scout car l'intrus, not us? and of course what was there to say.

So Alain just made this sort of rueful face and said ah well, his friends hadn't, he admitted, "pris leurs dispositions" very efficiently, in fact they'd been offhand to the point of folly, he threw up his hands at them; but what was inexcusable—and past all apology, he said humbly, looking at me—was the vexation, the contrariété impardonnable, to madame above all, of what had occurred; and I remember thinking but can he actually be helpless or something about these men? and I looked at Hugh.

But he might have been no more than amused!—he said to Alain, "You mean these nervous friends of yours shouldn't have let us find them with their mitraillettes showing?" as if it were a joke. But Alain looked so nonplussed for a moment, by the irony or whatever, that Hugh must have decided to make it plain, anyway he added, "In other words all this is just our bad luck?"

I thought, what is going to happen. Because now Hugh was looking at him with no expression at all, and I said to myself but a fiery animal like *Hugh*? . . . But then after a moment he said in a perfectly amiable tone, "You damn' well wouldn't put up with this yourself, why under the sun d'you think I will?"—really it might merely have been some bantering argument they were having! And Alain answered in practically the identical easy tone, "Mais si à ma place c'était vous le responsable?" But he'd I thought flushed just a little saying it, and why had he gone back to French? and Hugh looked as if he were thinking oh nonsense too, and said, "You can't seriously think these people are in *danger* dammit?" and suddenly Alain did flush, and said in a sort of haughty voice, "Il ne s'agit pas, monsieur, de ce que j'en pense—j'ai donné parole!"

Hugh said to me later, "I damn' near asked him flat how in God's papist name he'd ever let himself get trapped in anything as simple as high-mindedness—*god* I was exasperated!" but all he looked was sort of politely sardonic, and he said, "L'avantageux de la vérité est qu'elle a un cachet," and the maid brought in the coffee, and at least it was a transition, for all of us.

Anyhow if Hugh wasn't disturbed why should I be? Also if this was an outrage, Alain was the one to be upset about it, not Hugh or I, but *this* was not the moment to discuss it! so quite simply I said to Alain what lovely old gardens it looked as if he had, the meadows beyond all golden with gorse in flower, and the ferny fronds of—was it bracken? and the green headland above the sea; so presently we walked there. And he began to apologize all over again after a little, he was totally *dejected*, he said, not just at the inconvenance but what must we think of a loyalty to a cause we'd never heard of, loyalty it *was* but then what it was subjecting us to! could we forgive it *or* him for that?—forgive even (he begged me) to the point of considering coming back some day soon under happier circumstances? So I said but where really had we intended to go in particular anyway? so why not; also he couldn't have made us feel more en pays de connaissance if we'd known him already, I'd almost begun wondering what I should call him, I said, and I suppose my eyes did caress him a little—well, he was beautiful, heavens!—though I said of course first names between us ah *this* soon would be so unheard-of un-French I thought we shouldn't try to cross that particular cultural frontier quite yet, even if we weren't perhaps entirely thinking of each other as monsieur and madame. And I thought if Hugh weren't here what would he do? and I said to myself shall I charm him and see?—at least the theory of it? I have to pass the time *somehow* and amuse myself don't I? so all the long lazy afternoon I sort of did, and we had tea by the carp pool and fed crumbs to the huge old carp, and by the time we went in I could almost have laughed, he was so uneasy about me already.

Because all this talk about honor, heavens! when I thought what if really I have only to stretch out my hand for him, wife of his guest or not? oh mon pauvre Alain how mean I could so easily be to you, I could be absolutely pétrie de méchanceté, goodness what lovely fun, shall I, or shall I? Especially since Hugh had spotted how things were too.

And what arrogance, was just *amused!* We'd come up to our room to change for dinner, I was at the pier glass tiffing my hair, and he came up behind me and took my waist in his fingers and said, "What are your angel plans for this helpless viscount?" brushing his lips softly down my neck and along into the hollow of my shoulder. I said, "What ever made you think you were supposed to have noticed?" and wriggled, but he snorted that scoffing way he does and said, "You and your blue-eyed apostasies!" and held me. So naturally I said, "You don't really think *this* is an ambience I'd have picked, do you?—for an affair with you either!" Because 'apostasy' anyway! From *him!* I said, "You're mussing me," and he said, "But to my taste," snickering, and he let me go and we went down to dinner. And thank goodness those men—the surly one in particular: Hugh said later he thought he was a Belgian, an unreconstructed Rexist even, from wartime—anyway thank goodness none of them were there. And Alain didn't bother to explain why. Also it was a *good* dinner—beautiful pink heaps of cold langoustines with mayonnaise, then tournedos with a lovely glaze with rounds of marrow and artichoke hearts, and for dessert a montblanc aux marrons, and the wines astonishing, I suppose they always are when one first gets back to France again, but these *were*, and we must have dawdled over the cheese and the fruit and the coffee and the calvados till well on toward eleven, and in such a lovely haze I had to be careful how I let Alain look at me, I didn't even want to go out for a minute in the moonlight before bed I was so sleepy and delicious.

And then it was so amusing, there was no electricity except downstairs—how long had it been, I said to Hugh, since he or I had gone up to bed by candlelight!—so charming, too, when we'd lit the two oil chimney-lamps the maid had left for us on the coiffeuse, the bedroom all shadows and soft dusk and the tall curtains drawn against the night and the bed properly turned down, even a brass bidon à goulot of hot water by the washstand—a century mightn't have passed, Hugh said, it was so tranquil, so unchanged, did I feel like my pantalooned great-grandmother? I said then hadn't he better test the bed? He said for softness or for feed? and bounced. I asked, "Rather hard?" and he said, "Hair mattress," and made a face. But that wasn't what our minds were on, and presently he came over behind me as I was finishing my face for the night at the coiffeuse, and our eyes met in the glass and he said, "What a thing."

I hadn't decided whether or not I'd begun to feel a little cross, or about what, so I said, "Why on earth did it have to occur to you to say I was your *wife*."

He said, "Whose damn' business if you're not?"

"But so stuffy don't you think, Hugh darling!"

He smirked at me in the glass and slid his hand affectionately down into my nightgown and said, "Turning out perfectly agreeable this way isn't it?"

As of course it was; so l wrinkled my nose at him and said, "You mean here I anyway am, sharing that rather hard bed with a wicked cousin instead of not?"

He said, "I do what thank God I'm wickedly tempted to"— and there in the glass we were, faintly smiling conspirators, the long lovely night waiting to close us round still one time more.

—Except later it was, much later I guess it could have been by then, I'd thought he was asleep, and I nearly was, lying there all drowsy-warm and close, hardly thinking of anything but the feel of him all through me still, all the lingering luxury, heaven what a thing it can be when they are like this, and the memory of how, and half-dozing I wondered d'you suppose he was like this with Georgie? though then of course I thought but how could he have been, so young. And only with *her* anyhow! Though I wonder what he would say if I asked him—except hoh! would he even remember! So then I thought why not have a conversation-in-my-mind with him, I could for instance use an amused coaxing voice and just say darling what was Georgie, you know, *like?* so then he might yawn and say what's anybody like, and I'd say I don't mean just in bed, I mean her—her— But how would I say it to him? her 'taste in men'? because imagine, after *him*, marrying a man she could call "Petchie"! oh the poor silly, and then that first time she was unfaithful to him bleating, "But I thought I'd feel *weird!*" to me afterwards. . . . Or no; I'd say Hugh darling why don't you ever tell me about your women, I tell you about my men, what *they* do, I'd say, kissing his throat, do you make us over to your specifications while you have us? or do different ones of us just have different impressions of you, and maybe feelings about you too, because our effects on you differ? and I was wondering how much perhaps did we when suddenly he sort of lazily stretched all along against me and shifted the arm that was under me, and said yawning, "You believe this honnête-homme account of his?"— wide *awake!* I thought how absolutely so soon *can* they forget how we must still feel, heavens! but I said, ". . . What account, darling," trying to think.

He said, "This host of ours's, what d'ye suppose? About these 'separatists.' You believe it?"

I thought why shouldn't I have? but I said, "Oughtn't I to?"

"You took those mitraillettes for costume drama or something? With for God's sake the safeties off?"

I said goodness, were they? but how strange, I supposed I hadn't thought (and I guess really of course I hadn't)—just I said I'd wondered, at lunch, why if these men were the vicomte's friends they didn't more seem to be. Or at ease even.

He snorted, and said good *god*—hard-eyed Paris underworld thugs like these in the back-nowhere of *Brittany* and I hadn't wondered? Or wondered what this seigneurial host of ours was giving them asylum for? Hiding political dissidents, d'accord; because the police were picking up anybody and everybody, parfait. But a national manhunt for assassins was hardly a danger for mere *dissidents*. If the police picked them up they'd be knocked about a little, and held a day or so, and turned loose. "But suppose, my angel," he said, "suppose part of the gang *is* what they are—had you thought of *that* explanation? With this helplessly honorable viscount now in it over his head entirely?"

I thought *Alain?* . . . . I was appalled, and I said, "Oh Hugh *no!*"

"Hasn't he as good as told us where he stands?" he said. "Simply loyalty to what his race and his upright heritage tell him to do! Only, unluckily, the danger of honor is, it puts you at the mercy of extremists. So here he is, involved with *these* people!"

And what could I do but see it. I said, "Oh Hugh how awful."

"And some of the kind of men behind them very likely old fellow-officers of his into the bargain," he said, sort of grimly, "or cadets with him at Saint-Cyr," and when I said, "But Hugh you sound *upset* for him?" he said, "Well, dammit, I am!"

So we lay there.

But then I said, "But you looked as if you *believed* what he told us about it."

Why not? he said—there was no danger. It was a damn' quick-witted and plausible scenario: why should they think a stray couple of touring American innocents didn't believe what they were entertainingly told? It was seeming *not* to would have been the danger. And what would I suggest he shoot our way out with then?

So why *not* give this entirely presentable viscount the pleasure of our company he asked for?—had the impoverished old nobility so often, on sight, begged me to stay the weekend that I hadn't even a civilized curiosity about their amenities? Bed hard or not, he added, and stroked me.

But then, ah well, he went on, everybody was stupid, yes, only did the privileged classes have to be stupid so often too?—people who simply didn't seem to realize they were still going on being their ancestors? It wasn't dammit that he didn't sympathize (what after all did *he* do!) but good god could there be unlikelier unlikenesses? *Us*, for instance, and that oaf of an ancestor who'd landed in Philadelphia in the 1680s—what genetic fraction of *my* elegant ninth-generation body and man-beguiling soul was Wiltshire yeoman? Why, I wouldn't so much as know what to make light conversation with the old guy about if I met him. And de Moëtland went back *five* and a half centuries, to Agincourt! There wouldn't be even a drawing-room pronunciation in common! Yet now *that* one-nth ancestral genetic fraction was exactly the folly that had him on the absolute blind brink of catastrophe. . . .

I said, "Such a rhetorical darling, aren't you," but as I went to sleep I wondered whether I *should* perhaps be a little upset about Alain.

But in the morning we went swimming—sunbathing, anyway: the water was *cold*; and then at lunch Alain asked whether it would perhaps amuse us to see some of the long-disused part of the château?—there was a ballroom for instance that had considerable period charm, originally it had been the great hall and still had one of those huge baronial fireplaces at each end, with stone sockets for flambeaux, but in Louis XV's time it had been made into a ballroom in the best Louis XV taste, would it at all help divert us if he showed us through? and naturally I said how lovely, but Hugh said two of the château's exterior façades had rather taken his eye, some of the architectural detail was remarkable, in fact it was the sort of thing that brought out the Piranesi in him, so would we forgive him, he said, looking blandly at me, if he wandered about outside and sketched instead?—and I almost laughed aloud, he knew exactly what I'd think of doing, and what other man would have had the arrogance to turn me loose to do it! ("Arrogance my eye," he said that night. "Just scientific curiosity." But it *was*.)

So after lunch out he sauntered with his sketching pad, and Alain and I began our tour. The ballroom first, and he was right: even dusky and long-disused it was enchanting, a long tall room all white-and-gold rococo lambrissage, and when the myriads of candles in the great lustres were lit it must have been as gay as it was magnificent, though alas Alain said they hadn't been lit in many years, not since the wedding of a young cousine of his, long before the war, it was the first ball he'd ever seen, he was a small boy, he'd been absolutely ébahi, *stunned* practically, by the white brilliance of the dresses of waltzing girls and the glitter of their partners' uniforms—and the lovely child, he now remembered, had died in childbirth before the year had gone.

Beyond, there was a graceful oval antechamber, with white-and-gold paneling too, but then the reception rooms that opened off it on the other three sides had waxed wainscoting instead, beautiful dark boiseries with fielded panels in the English style, and bead-and-ovolo moldings instead of rococo, the beading delicately gilded, and glints of gilding in the cornices too and in the course of guilloches under them—*lovely*, and in these rooms the furniture was very good Louis XV or XVI though it needn't have come from Paris. But there *was* mostly provincial furniture in the salons in the wing Alain took me to next, the wing he lived in, some of it even that awful Renaissance stuff, and here the lambrissage was much simpler, even severe—plain bolection moldings, applied, or that tiresome linenfold paneling, with battens or astragals, and in the large salon simply tapestries instead, faded really the color of mildewed porridge, huge ghastly classical scenes that must have begun fading in Bourbon times.

But then, as we wandered on, and up this stairway or that to other floors, all was stone. And a *feeling* of the silence, as if it were something hooded and softly waiting, at the end of a curving passageway, or in some dusty cul-de-sac a voice had perhaps not echoed in for a hundred years, lost to everything but the scuffling of a squirrel across the floors of deserted rooms. Or at the end of some dim corridor we would come on a turret stair winding up around the worn stone of its newel, and climb to a tower chamber where the slow dusts had settled so feathery fine our shoes left prints where we crossed to peer from a window down, if only to see what side of the endless maze we had come out on, and once I found I was looking down into a little interior courtyard I never did work out the position of, oh it was a kind of utterly charming dust-and-desolation everywhere I told Alain, but goodness what a place to look after! and he said yes even the bare *detail*—did I know there had had to be one man who did nothing except lug wood twelve hours a day for the fires ? . . .

Sometimes in the long enchanted afternoon a room would have a history he'd tell me, he'd been no more than five or six when his grandfather had begun making him learn the château's history by heart, practically room by room, then when he'd grown he'd of course found out about amusing scandals as well, two of his eighteenth-century ancestresses seemed to have been particularly light-minded—one of them had even had a *Huguenot* lover as an added flippancy! perhaps the ancestor she was married to had been a bit stuffier a dévot than the average run. Or she'd just been plantée là in deepest Brittany a little longer than a pretty woman's vanity would put up with, who could say; and then there was the impassioned Vicomtesse Aurélie, whose husband unluckily ran her lover through the heart and killed him—that very day she'd got the fallen man's sword from his second, knotted her scarf around the hilt, plunged it to the cross-guard into the mattress of her husband's bed, ordered up her calèche and her groom, and vanished. Myth if one liked, he said happily; myth possibly also that she'd vanished a second time, and for good, into Russia, in the coach of Catherine the Great's ambassador. But not to believe in selected myth of one's heritage would hardly be good manners, didn't I believe in mine? and of course I said heavens yes: I couldn't after all very well say they *were* rather less simpleminded.

And from some of the rooms, bare and deep in dust or not, what views there were out over the sunlit sea, we stood at one and I said could it always did he suppose have seemed as lovely and by itself as this? such long centuries on this shining headland, with the depths of the beechwood behind like a green wall against the intrusions of the world—the landscape might have lain here dreaming and unchanged for a thousand years, from didn't they call it "the long peace of Henry I"? people going on pilgrimages slowly everywhere, and perhaps abbeys too were founded in those remote valleys to rediscover the wonder of being alone. . . .

He said in an uncertain voice but "the wonder"?—was he to believe that *I* could wish to be alone? and I looked into his blue eyes and thought, As if either of us were made to be anything ever but à deux! but I said, softly, but ah hadn't he, too, moments to be alone to himself in?—to withdraw out of time, the time that goes hour by hour by hour, into one's own space and frame of time, where one saw things one had done not as one felt about them as one did them but as if they were history, seeing it all, I meant, in the real time of memory; but I thought, heavens I'll confuse him, so I said maybe this was why his ancestors had stayed here those centuries, to be alone, and I turned to the window again and added, gently, maybe that was why he did too.

And, waiting, I thought how still it was in those ancient rooms, the sunlight fell through the dusty panes like a pattern of pale tiles across the bare brown oak of the floor, or hung like a haze of gold, sifting motes slowly revolving, as if in that unstirring air of years even our silence, our caught breath, were a motion somehow. I was turned gazing off and away over the flowering headland and the blue sea far out as if forever, and Alain was so close now at my shoulder I felt the warmth of his breath flutter the hair over my ear, and in the middle of a phrase his voice had stopped. I thought, Now? . . . and certainly the air about us was charged with that lovely electricity, I could almost feel him trembling, and I waited. Except then I began to think is his arrogance as different from Hugh's as this? so I turned, so near now I heard the thudding of his heart, and I let my eyes say *Here then I am?* . . .

So of course how could he stand it, he was like a steel spring as it was, wild, I thought but really can no woman ever have done quite *this* to him? goodness how agreeable—and he did do his honnête-homme best not to, he stammered something desperately light about ". . . your eyes' soft threat," I remember wondering what the French for it would be, ah but his face was absolutely agonized, he was lost, so all I had to say was, "But you must see I cannot mon cher listen to such things, how can I honorably, I mustn't, to such disturbing sweetness," in oh how soft a voice and he gave up— "J'en suis comme transpercé!" he said in his throat, and something choky about de part en part le corps, and simply, well, *grabbed* me, and bent my head back kissing me, and when I twisted my face away kissed my throat, just as violently, and my neck and the curve of my shoulder, and my earring fell off.

I thought goodness d'you suppose this is the sort of mauling makes French women swoon? what verb would they I wonder use, se rendre?—or no, céder's better: that's it, on cède. Except I thought but *I* don't, mon petit vicomte, tu es beau comme le jour, but making love is not a biological confrontation, how can you know so little, oh have been *taught* so little, you are probably the most beautiful bel homme I shall ever lay eyes on *and* a charmer but I am not here to be manhandled for your instruction.

Still, by this time it was beginning to come to him that I wasn't swooning or doing in fact anything but wait to be let go, so after a little more I gently took myself out of his arms. But I touched his cheek with the tips of my fingers for an instant, and murmured, "You are unsettlingly sweet, ah how you are! but mon ami I—I—" and left it unfinished so as not to seem heartless or unmoved. Or have him feel just rejected. Though with nobody to see, what matter, heavens. So of course then he took me in his arms again, trembling, this time, and I put my forehead down against his shoulder and for a little while let him. As Hugh says, if love is a duel it ought to enjoy at least the courtesies of eighteenth-century rules.

But then at last I had to say, "But mon très doux Alain I do you know happen to be the wife of a man who's your guest," and I lifted my head and kissed his cheek, *really* what I do and what I'm doing it's *wild* how different! and then I said, "Now please will you let me go," and he did, looking so shaken I half-repented. Oh but what incantations I've recited to myself sometimes afterwards, as reason or excuse, or as mere good manners. Or just as emotional décor. Hugh said once I was a matter of style. And I am.

But then of course there was the rest of the day and the evening to be got through as if nothing had happened, and the proprieties reactivated, and I was glad when at dinner Hugh said he couldn't remember when *he*'d had two pleasanter days, circumstances or no circumstances, but now he really thought we'd given Alain's friends head start enough wouldn't he agree? — tomorrow morning would make it forty-eight hours he'd not noticed any of the men around any longer except that Belgian or whatever he was, so after breakfast we'd say what he hoped Alain too would feel might be only au revoir, and be on our way — "and with proper directions this time!" and Alain said steadily, without looking at me, that alas he supposed he'd no right to keep us, much as he'd like to; and so next morning after breakfast we packed, and Hugh and the man took our bags down, and in a little I followed.

The brilliance of summer morning was over everything, such a dazzle of light it half-blinded me as I came out of the château into it with the maid and my dressing case — sun hot on the gardens and the headland, and the sea like blue haze off and off beyond, and I was just crossing the terrasse to the broad stair down to the court-yard, thinking what loveliness, what country peacefulness, almost I wish we were staying on, when I heard this sort of snarling shout, "Eh, halte-là, le copain! Laissez!" and I came to the balustrade and there at the foot of the stair Hugh was standing, hatless in the tow-ering light, by the open trunk of his car, our suitcases lined up on the cobbles beside him, and sprinting across toward him from the corner of the château was that surly brute of a Belgian with his mitraillette pointed straight at him. Hugh must have been bend-ing over into the trunk shifting things to make room for our suit-cases, and had just straightened up and turned, anyway he had a tire iron in his hand, or maybe it was the jack handle, and he sort of balanced it, and the man stopped fifteen feet away and snapped, "Essayez pas de coup, hein?" and at my shoulder I heard the maid gasp something very scared, I suppose in Breton, and then for a long moment Hugh and the man just stood there in the sun, the breadth of the stair-foot between them, rigid, each by the stone newel his side, poised as motionless as if time had stopped; and then suddenly I saw Hugh just very gently heft the tire iron, and I said, "Hugh, don't!"

His head jerked around up toward me, startled, and he looked at me as if I were a child who'd said something absolutely mannerless; but then his face relaxed, and he said almost banteringly, "You want to bet on it?" and I said to the maid, "Allez vite *vite* chercher Monsieur," and she scuttered back into the château wailing, and I saw Hugh turn toward the man again and oh god I thought how can I stop him, stop either of them, is this insane thing going to just go ahead and *happen?* and all I could seem to do was think *oh please please* so hard I almost wasn't sure I wasn't saying it aloud.

But then next moment here *did* come Alain out of the château at a dead run, he must have been on his way to see us off and nearly there already anyhow, and he sprinted across the terrasse to where I stood at the top of the stair and burst into such an absolute fury of rapid French down at the man that really I didn't understand a word.

The man didn't even look up at him, just sort of drawled out, "And *my* neck if they take off, mon beau commandant? . . ." as if he were talking to a child.

Alain said, in a voice of steel, "Je vous le repète—monsieur m'en a donné sa parole!"

The man said contemptuously, "Et puis après?" not taking his eyes from Hugh.

Alain went as white as if he'd been struck. He cried, "Vous vous *rangerez*, nom de Dieu!" and plunged down the stair two steps at a time straight at him, and out of the corner of my eye suddenly I saw Hugh starting toward him too and I thought *and I am here helpless.* The man had sprung back two or three steps away from the newel and spun round facing Alain, flinging up his mitraillette and shouting, "Halte-là—*halte!*" terrified, and as Alain reached the foot of the stair he—I *heard* that awful sort of multiple thudding!—he fired this *full burst* from his gun point-blank into Alain's poor breast, it knocked him straight over backwards onto the bottom steps of the stair as if he'd been picked up and slammed there, and just that instant too late Hugh smashed his tire iron or whatever it was into the man's crazed shouting-open face and sent him catapulting back headfirst over one of the mounting-blocks and down on the other side, the mitraillette clattering out of his hands onto the cobbles, and as I ran horrified down the stair to where Alain's body had begun to slump and roll I saw Hugh spring up onto the block and look down with his arm up to strike again, though then I saw his shoulder relax, and then I was on my knees by Alain.

He'd nearly rolled off the bottom step, he was face down and blood was absolutely welling out from under him, little scarlet rivulets of it running into the cracks of the cobbles and turning dark and thick in the dust between, and I thought but if I turn him over and find that beautiful head *too* has been . . . ? And I supposed I ought to try to turn him over but I felt too half-sick to, and anyway I heard Hugh coming back across to me and then he was looming over me saying, "He's *dead?*" in a shocked voice, and I said, "Yes. Yes, he is," like conversation in a dream, and I looked up at him, the sun blazing down on his uncovered head so white-hot gold his face almost seemed deep in shadow, his hand was sort of clenching and unclenching the tire iron as if he couldn't make up his mind what to do with it, and he said with distaste, "I may have hit the other one too hard," and then for a long moment there in the sunblaze around us the world was as summer-morning still as if there had never been sound.

I said, rather wildly I expect, "Will you put that thing *down?*" but he'd turned and was calling up to the maid, she was leaning weakly against one of the urn'd newels at the top of the stair balustrade, she was making gagging noises and when Hugh snapped at her, "Mais filez donc!—téléphonez à la police, nom de Dieu!" I thought she was going into hysterics. But then Hugh saw, and softened his tone—*soyez une brave fille* and *du courage, hein?* and so forth, and she was to get the doctor here at *once*, would she?—and after just a little, softly weeping, she ran obediently back into the château, and Hugh went across to the mounting-block and looked down over. But right away he turned back toward me, making a face, and looked round for the mitraillette, and I must have said, "Fingerprints" or something, because I remember he said, "Not that a doctor'll matter much either," but he dropped the tire iron by the gun; and then what did he do but come back across and kneel down by me and pick up my hand and turn it gently over and put his lips to my palm. For just that moment. The sun on his hair. Then he looked up at me and said, ". . . if you know why the hell I am doing this," and I thought *against the awfulness, really,* but I said, "One has to do something," except suddenly I was seeing him so differently, how had he done what he had done, the sheer bursting violence of him, and the speed of it, yet now *this* look, and he was saying, "Are you all right?" and it was all such horrifying confusion and shock, and I heard myself saying, "Oughtn't we to turn him over?" and him saying, "You've got blood on your skirt" as if that were an answer.

But I said, "His poor face is in the *dust*, Hugh!" and he said, "Get back a little, then," and I did. But of course, because of the bottom step, he had to turn him right into the wet pool of his blood and for a moment I thought I couldn't look. But then of course I did, and I suppose moving him made more blood gulp out soaking still, the stain seemed to spread out farther over his poor bullet-slashed shirt before our eyes, it was horrible, I thought shall I ever again remember *anything* in such savage detail? but his face was unscathed.

And his blue eyes through those long dark-gold lashes were half open, he might almost I thought if I moved into the line of their vision be looking at me still, even if only the way people do in delirium, glazed over sort of; but to look and *not* see? not to *be* there to see?—though what explanation is death I thought either, and I said to Hugh, "Shouldn't we close his eyes?" Though then when I reached out over to, I felt the sun strike hot on the back of my hand and I wondered would his eyelids be—well, still warm? but then I thought how silly; and stretched out my hand and saw its shadow fall across his face and then down over that empty gaze, and when my palm touched his forehead of course it was sun-warm too; and I said to myself I am closing a dead lover's eyes.

I don't quite remember what happened for a little after that. I knelt there. Then there was a clatter I remember of wooden clogs across the terrasse, and the houseman appeared at the top of the stair looking out of his mind and clutching a shotgun and Hugh was a time calming him down; but then he came and looked at Alain from a little distance and crossed himself, and his lips moved, praying. But then Hugh sent him off at a run to the lodge to see the gates were open for the police, and sat down at the top of the stairs and said, "You just going to sit there?" and I said, "Kneel," and he said, mildly, "Kneel there, then?" and I thought oh Hugh darling let us alone, all three of us, Hugh, until I can decide whether I knew him much either.

Because listen, I said to him in my mind: as in girlhood I knew the wild weeds, but by their sprays in the summer dusk, Hugh, not their names, so, now, whom must I think I know except as they seem to me? even a lover is an ally against loneliness who still hasn't claim enough to encroach upon my solitude for me to 'know.' Is there some *rule* one has to, about men?—except for perhaps convenience, I wanted to say to him, sitting there so long-familiar and easy against the lichened scrollings of the balustrade, the sun in those cocksure libertine eyes, gazing down at me but perhaps a little through me too, though at what, I am not sure I shall ever be quite certain again.

Ah though, really, I thought, I might almost not be a part of any of this, and not horrified or in this strange grief for whatever it is, as if all this were somehow no more than a tiny scene painted on crystal and I were here merely to tell you how brittle and quick to shatter it is, this scene how can anyone civilized ever explain—the château on its low headland above the sea, the blaze of morning over the gardens, and I kneeling here on the cobbles, waiting, an edge of the bartizan's shadow just touching the fingers of my hand; and ah how peaceful, how wordless-still my lovers, in the long murmur of this day, Hugh who since this is France is mon amant, and Alain who—ah, well, might have gone gallantly back to being some other woman's I suppose really, poor French darling, and I *me* between them; and I remember I had just noticed that the slow, still-mortal spreading of the red stain through his shirt had stopped, when Hugh said, "Why did you come with me?" and I had to think of something to reply.

III. A Few Final Data During the Funeral

Searching the cave gallery of your face
My torch meets fresco after fresco
— EMPSON

1

A proper upbringing being what it is, I can't say I had expected to set out for a memorial service to my oldest friend—even now a long month dead—after a night in the arms of his eighth-or-ninth-from-the-last ex-girl, but then beautiful Camilla had always been a woman of sentiment.

Drowsily murmuring now, in our contented night, "Sweet Simon were you surprised? . . ." though obviously it was by then many hours too late to be.

". . . and abashed?"—unquestions ending in a bland "But think if we'd known *then!* . . ." the flutter of soft breath in my ear just not quite a giggle.

A dreamy pause.

As of an angel musing.

On what, however, turned out to be the indecorums of feminine reminiscence: "Sweetie you'd never *guess* what he'd do sometimes . . ."—mildly scatological particulars; little splutters of ladylike ribaldry at the comedy she made of it—". . . like some *navvy*, Simon—imagine !"

A pause.

"Though goodness what a time to tell such things!"

Pause.

"Though *sweet* Simon how unbosoming we do seem to 've become, goodness!" a knee sliding its silky flattery between mine; and so, in tranquil posthumous infidelity, off to sleep.

I too, shortly.

After having decently wondered, for a moment, as one marauding male about another, whether Hugh's ghost mightn't, just conceivably, in the circumstances, be walking.

Here and now. In the felicities of *this* nth-from-the-last ex-bed-room.

But Hugh a bystander?—ghost or not? It would be wildly out of character. Theologically speaking, anyhow, why should he leave those flowery retinues of girls about him in Elysium? Girls in love were an appanage of his immortality his libertine's eye hardly even dissembled when he painted them. Why, this sleek and sleeping armful here of mine you can gaze at, any day, on her wall in the Corcoran, and observe (and be right) that though she's painted in the pose of Michelangelo's Erythrean Sibyl, a hallowed sibyl is hardly what you'd conclude the painter knew her as, nor is the way the paint's put on a bystander's.

So, just in case, I muttered an avaunt: Ghost of my lifelong friend, old unbystanding Hugh, have the Philadelphia decency to be gone! Take to your spectral heart those opening eloquences of the *Corriere della Sera*'s Non starà più a contemplarci obituary: "The great distinguished head is to look upon us no more." Un-haunt us, Hugh—bless us like a gent, and back to the hypotheses of Eternity.

Mind you, canvases or girls—and deplored or not—Hugh Tat-nall's is a renown he was entitled to. Even if for nothing else, that arrogant rake's persona of his stood for something through an era when the intellectual ambience in fashion had been a wincing and haggard self-pity at the eliot prospects of the soul. Not for Hugh: *his* subject was the landscapes and still lifes of Man's and his own individuated rut. Very reassuring, too—being after all how we had all behaved (and approved of behaving) before the psychagonists and the education-mongers explained it all away. For Hugh still did behave that way: as a high-church critic who detested him put it, "Even Tatnall's madonnas, if the appalling fellow had ever painted any, would look as if they'd just got out of bed with him!"

(A baffling observation. Not only did he paint madonnas—in the years he amused himself being artist-sometimes-in-residence at Smith he did a series of them. They were, I admit, from the light-minded side of him. Parody amused him: Manet's *Olympia*, he used to say, was a quotation of Titian's *Venus of Urbino*, so why shouldn't he "quote" Raphael's madonnas? They were jeux d'esprit, to be given to his friends rather than exhibited. I own two of them myself, including his enchanting Nadezhda [*The Virgin as Bona Dea*], and many of the rest of them are at Smith too. All the models were, after all, Smith girls. And if they all look as if they have just been in bed with him, why not? They all had.)

Now this famous old charmer of a rake was gone.

And famous now not least, a Sophoclean chorus would have chanted at you, for the manner of his death. For Hugh had been shot down point-blank by an overwrought young Pisana in the most newsworthy sexual circumstances.

European newspapers had been fond of him for years, Italian especially. He spent nearly half his time in Italy; he was known there widely; his work was known. He even made news for them — the academic uproar he'd caused, for instance, the time he made Dante the subject of an hilarious fresco he painted on the ceiling of La Buonabolgia, the nightclub of a local friend of his: there were outraged cries of everything from enormità to bambineria. ("What the devil are they fussing about?" he complained. "Composition's impeccable — it's Rubens's sketch for his *Apotheosis of the Duke of Buckingham* practically to the square inch. . . .") Even his airport interviews sold papers: if nothing else, he was always good for an off-the-cuff analysis of la ragazza americana, that year's illustrative specimen on his arm for the photographers. And now, alas, it was almost as journalistically natural as it was sadly final: there he lay dead in Italy under Paris *Herald* headlines.

I read them, at breakfast, in Grenoble, at a United Nations conference on the Humanities. I had been agreeably laying siege (in French: a bit cramping) to a dreamy-eyed young instructress in semasiology from Bucharest. With a heavy heart I raised the siege, packed my bag, hopped a plane across the Alps, and was in Florence even before our cultural attaché got in from Rome.

Hugh had inherited, from an expatriate uncle, a late-baroque palazzo, off the Vicolo Saltimbeni. He had been letting half the piano nobile, most recently to an aging marchesa, a years-past gallantry it seems of his uncle's; the rest he kept as a pied-à-terre. And, of course, studio: nothing like Tuscan light, he said, to mold the contours of a pretty bottom or crotch. I found the quarter an anthill of reporters: news must have been phenomenally short. Even the *Economist* and *Le Monde* stringers showed up. When they discovered that I was Hugh's executor, they went into happy mass-production: for days, headlines were black and exclamatory with every scabrous invention the quarter could come up with. In Italy, tutto si sa — it is the inviolably clandestine, your midnight secrets known only to God, that are on your every neighbor's tongue.

(I might as well have stayed on in Grenoble a day or so. The Dacian accent in French is delicious. So had been the tactics: surely un si beau classiciste should remember that Dacia had held out against the Roman Empire itself for three whole centuries—"et vous voulez qu'on cède à un simple colon au bout d'autant de jours? . . .")

—Hugh had spent late winter and the cold Tuscan spring in Florence. The Smith girl with him this time was an Art-and-Architecture major conveniently doing her departmental junior-year-abroad; her name was Persis Dove. She was very serious-minded. But also she was satiny and sweetly shaped, a slender pale-gold blonde with great green eyes and an enchanting voice, a voice that absolutely caressed you, and to complete her amenities Hugh had been teaching her to cook.

But by grotesquely bad luck Persis had met a rinnovatrice at the Uffizi, a girl in her late twenties named Francesca. She was a talented but also a moody painter, who hardly ever sold a canvas: in effect she was working as a restorer full time. She was a tall, tawny-haired, rather smoldering Pisan, with one of those stylized angular bodies, and a kind of fiery chic. And she wanted to improve her English. And didn't Persis need—ma sul serio, need!—a great deal more practice in Italian? So the two of them had been instructively exchanging language lessons as spring came on.

But ahimè, language is not parts of speech alone. *Miri la bocca,* Ariosto's sonnet exhorts you, that mouth

> Which sweet the smile hath as sweet word it speaketh.

As spring came on, enchantment came on too.

"Because oh *dear,*" Persis mourned to me (in that soft voice that made every word she spoke sound as if she were about to breathe *oh my darling love* at you), "one day Francesca began, well, courting me! And naturally I— Well, we were 'a tu per tu,' isn't that what they say? though that doesn't *mean* that, does it?—except, well, it was an aspect of my sexuality I hadn't known, I mean she made me aware, Professor Shipley! I don't mean I wasn't Hugh's all the time, but she began to court me and after a while, well, Hugh *saw.* And he refused to have her in, even! Except when we had her stupid husband too, for drinks, or there'd be this meal Hugh felt like showing off his cooking with, he used to say Toulouse-Lautrec was a chef too, wasn't he? so it was all just horrid and mixing-up—and *dreadful* at first, Francesca was so furiously angry, once she realized, oh just *blazing!* She rushed up to me in the pinacoteca and began screaming the most— She called me a— She c-called me—" and began to weep.

(Called her what? I ran through my La Scala vocabulary. Empia? Infame? Sfrontata? Sciagurata? TRA-DI-TRI-CE?)

"Then I didn't see her for oh *days!*" she choked. "Oh I was in such dread such fear for her, and that minchione of a husband kept coming round moaning and bleating hadn't we heard from her? because she'd just *vanished*, Professor Shipley, and not even a word to me, as if she and I had never—I mean by that last morning I— Well actually I was in the kitchen peeling garlic, I was making an agliata and Hugh was in the salotto writing up his journal the way he'd started doing, *rearranging* what happened, half the time, and suddenly I heard this—suddenly Francesca— Oh, it happened!" she softly wailed; and her tears, this time, were for Hugh.

Francesca had it seems burst into the salotto absolutely raging —a cold foaming fountain of barely articulated Tuscan. Hugh must have got to his feet in courtliest astonishment, and the crazy girl pulled a little black pistol from her bag and shot him five times point-blank, the first three straight into his breast: he toppled back onto the writing table, gone already. Persis rushed in, wild with foreboding and disbelief, just in time to see his body slither like a heavy snake to the floor and hit flailing, and the sightless head thud and roll; and then it all eased, and lay still.

She pitched to her knees beside him, clutching at him, crying out, "But I love you *I love you!*" (the mindless, the beseeching magic of that incantation!)—and in helpless dismay found her fingers crimson with his blood. The plump little twin maids from across the landing raced in and at once began screeching. This brought their marchesa, who after one shocked glance cried, "But in the name of Our Lady of Heaven can't you run for a doctor?" at the now white and dully staring Francesca. Meekly beginning to weep, Francesca went. The old lady whipped an apron from a maid to staunch the weakening hiccups of blood; the maids fell to their knees crossing themselves and gabbled terrified prayers at Eternity. These various apotropaic measures were, of course, far too late.

All of which made a most rewarding news feature, the *Corriere della Sera* stringer having arrived with the doctor and the police.

—And eventually I brought Hugh's body home. But the sepulchral and the fiscal bureaucracies that can embalm the Mediterranean dead, the winding-sheets of red tape, would, as they say in

Rome, make Iddio's hair stand on end if He were bald. And Hugh was not just a corpse: he was a rather illustrious corpse. It was even maintained that, morally speaking, he was a cultural possession — classified, unexportable, in fact an Italian monument. So the patenti, the ricevute, the stylized and ritual disputes in this, that, and the other ministero or esattoria were as good as endless.

Not to mention the question of his — Il signore ci scuserà, ma Signore Tatnall's . . . to say "houseguest"? (Ahhh what a man of taste, l'illustre defunto! — what year after year after *year* always new beautifuls!) But exactly what, Signore Scippli, was this one's condizione civile? A man of the world like il signore testamentary executor had hardly to be reminded that in these cases one gravely risks — if il signore knew the term? — *mal-ver-sa-zi-o-ne*: "Sir, they *make off* with things!" By the time I got Hugh landed dockside in Boston I was in a state of exasperation that stopped just short of scrawling *Corpse — no value* on the customs declaration.

—And now (I thought drowsily) in how few hours more, the heavy dust I had had my lifelong friend reduced to was to be put into the earth at last, a few formal sad final words spoken over it as epicedium, and then — ah, Hugh, good-bye.

Except that here — history being we are told a series of logical consequences — here I now found myself with *this* particular benison of girl, and never mind the ghosts.

And dozed unregretfully off.

—Though somewhere in the night she woke me, to murmur, ". . . you're still *there?* sweetie what fidelity," tucking her bottom affectionately into my midriff.

Adding, all sleepy softnesses again, ". . . like two spoons." And back to dream.

2

The charm of such phrases ought not, I need hardly say, to have lingered on, indulging my memory with their blandishments, as we sat side by side in the pious hush of the meetinghouse late the next morning.

I was, after all, brought up a Quaker. Loosely and nonobservantly, yes. But at least taught the ordinary godless decencies of Hicksite good manners.

Even reminded, *if* now and then my parents thought of it, that Meeting is a time when thy mind is to be engaged with Befitting

Things—including whatever happens to be thy notion of God, even if peculiar.

At any event *not* anything as theologically out of place as thinking about the pleasure of Camilla with pleasure.

For, simply, she happened to be beside me there, eyes cast down as in angel meditation, gloved hands clasping what looked like an Episcopal prayerbook, at a memorial service for a years-past lover. And I was merely the escort who had, as is proper, fetched her.

Just as I had fetched Persis too, here on my blameless other side, a very sleek young widow indeed, in black even to the faceted glitter of jet at the lobe of that charming ear, the pale gold of her hair drawn flashingly back and up into a classic knot.

Nevertheless, it was Hugh's mortal part that was to be commemorated here, not his fine taste in young women. I had fetched them both for sober Quaker purposes. Nothing more.

(And besides: If I were to glance at Camilla, and she by simultaneous chance at me, it might well turn out not to be Hugh our eyes would say to each other we were remembering.)

So we sat, the place now rapidly filling.

—My Arts-faculty colleagues were turning up en masse. Not that they approved of Hugh: many of them even thought him an outrage. But he had been artist-in-residence at Smith, off and on, for the better part of two decades—at any rate often there at least part of a semester, and the college had in principle the cachet of his presence even when he was somewhere else. Scandalized or not, our colleagues were having the piety, or at least the good manners, to acknowledge it.

A Quaker meetinghouse, if it is as old as it should be, has a vestigial partition down its center, each half with its own wide old entrance door from the street. A century and a half ago, one side was for women, one for men, and no glancing across: thee can just possess thy soul in patience till after Meeting. This meetinghouse had had its partition removed generations ago, but the ranks of long rail-backed deal benches stood where they had always stood, and marked the immemorial line. The tall old galleried room was dim in spite of the brilliance of early-summer noon outside, and full now of a kind of intense hush: silent and unstirring, eyes cast soberly down, the still host of Hugh's colleagues and mourners were settling into the sculptured attitudes of contemplation.

What I myself was contemplating, as the tedious minutes began to drone along, was not man's dutiful expectation of Eternity, as was solemn and approved, nor even Hugh's random prospects of it, or my own. Simply I began to think how long I had known him. How long and, I suppose, how well. And not just the fiery drive and arrogance of his painting, or his happy rampage after this or that fluttering girl—not even whether the painter and the libertine were two aspects or components of a creative unity—but merely the warm social animal he was with me instead, seen now through the haze of time.

For Hugh Tatnall had been my friend and second self from prep school and Princeton on. Arcades ambo, though the benchmarks of our spiritual topographies were altogether unlike. I come of well-to-do Chester County Quaker mill-owners; but Hugh was so impeccably upper-class Philadelphia that only the accident of an exotic upbringing can have saved him from being that and not much else. For until he was twelve he was raised, his parents having died young, by a rich expatriate uncle, an amiable rake who had a palazzo in Rome as well as the one in Florence, a castelletto in Portofino, an eighteenth-century view of life, and in particular a succession of titled mistresses, English and Italian, who fussed indulgently over little Hugh in flattery of his uncle, and in effect formed his young mind. As Hugh once said to me, "By god I was *ten* before it occurred to me that he might ever have gone to bed with a girl who wasn't at least a viscountess. . . ."

The consequence of this elegant misinformation was not however the snobbery one might expect. Rather, the company of his uncle's poppets made him precociously humane. Their beauty and bel canto blandishments, their stylized good manners, the idle affections of the whole ambience, combined to give him a kind of Renaissance page's enlightenment. He grew up in the caress of transience. For these were love affairs, they were fleeting, no matter what passion or what fantasy had been their occasion, and Hugh's uncle was always therefore still enchantedly paying court, the girl always still indulged to her exulting heart's content—"the air was full of angels," Hugh put it once, and on every side was the half-incredulous delight one has in a new love. Even if, sometimes, when a sweet creature left, there were tears, this too was a lesson in the humane. And finally (and very practically) Hugh had as a model a man who believed that a woman in love is the luxury of luxuries, and behaved so, and was therefore rewarded in kind.

The sense of social maneuver that this developed in Hugh was of course too suave for the scruffy Philadelphia prep-school life his uncle eventually shipped him back to. But it paid off even there: at one time Hugh had a string of dazzled Main Line little girls each of whom tenderly fed him fudge on her weekly afternoon. ("Weekends," he used to say in a voice of kindly amusement, "they have off.")

It was Italy, also, that turned him into a painter. The furniture of his uncle's palazzi included art in Italian profusion, and Hugh's first canvas was a try at copying a lush Roman copy of "an anonymous Tiepolo." At prep school he drew Palladian ruins, a form of homesickness that did wonders for his draftsmanship. By our last year at Penn Charter, though, he was drawing "girls as architecture" as well as Renaissance landscape: he did that virtuoso *Still Life with Cousin Georgiana's Bosom* (now at Cooper Union—discreetly retitled) the spring we graduated, to commemorate a rather breathless family seduction.

He had begun to be a virtuoso at that too by then—and mind you, in those days the spiritual logistics of talking even a very dazzled girl into bed with you could be daunting. I can't think of anyone of Hugh's level of competence then, in fact, except Buck (Decimus) St. Ledger, a Virginian classmate of ours that autumn at Princeton, and Buck was merely Apollonianly good-looking besides. "A lazy bastard who just happens to be catnip," Hugh used to complain. "Goddammit Shipley here are you and I manfully screwing our way up out of adolescence, doing our Darwinian damnedest, and all this indolent snake St. Ledger ever has to do— Doesn't he my god take any pleasure in the *craftsmanship* of the thing? What kind of mannerless behavior to a girl's finer feelings is that?"

This talent of Hugh's, however, by our junior year was developing into an assurance, not to say a heartlessness, that I now and then found disturbed me. I come from a quieter persuasion of Quakers than Hugh's sometimes wordly Philadelphians. I was of course brought up, like any "birthright Friend," without any nonsense about not doing pretty much as I pleased. My parents had the sophistications of what would now be called an existentialist tradition, my mother's father having even been "read out of Meeting" for marrying a girl he'd decided to without bothering about the Meeting's permission first. (They soon took him back, and my new grandmother with him—after all, he owned the bank as well as the paper mills.) But existential or not, I was still given fairly clear notions of "what thee does and does not do" from the time I'd been taught to pay attention to what was said to me, and the criterion, if not the canon, usually turned out to be less what was or wasn't 'moral' than simply what was kind or unkind. These are hardly college-age adjectives. But Hugh's marauding had I thought become something that girls of that decently behaved era had nothing even near the tactical apprenticeship to cope with. Dionysiac charm is all very well, and the flower-crowned rites of spring are our cultural heritage; but Hugh's persuasions to delinquency struck me as offhand to the point of self-complacency, and in fact his campus reputation (undergraduate scuttlebutt being what it is) took on the imperishable vitality of myth—as late as our thirtieth reunion I found myself still having to tell a classmate that that famous seduction of the daughters of a professor of animal psychology was *Casanova's*, dammit, not Hugh's.

Still, I have to say, in extenuation, that there were girls even then, possibly plenty of them, who were now and then up to him. I remember, spring of junior year, overhearing a set of his preliminaries with one of them, a velvety Southern-belle type named Lucinda. It was the last club party before finals, and I had gone outside for a drink. The club kept its weekend applejack in the ivy outside a dining-room window, and I was just reaching for the jug when Hugh's voice came through the open window above me, murmuring something I couldn't distinguish, and then a girl's voice, tense.

"But where will you—would you be?"

"Edge of the golf course back of the Inn."

"What if I can't get away from him?"

"You *helpless?*"

Silence. I could almost feel the electricity. And mind you, he'd hardly met the girl till before dinner! He said something else too low to make out, and she said, "But when he's jealous *already?*"

Again I couldn't hear what he answered—probably something disingenuous: what had they done to be jealous *about*, for God's sake. But then I heard her voice, secret and soft, taunting, "If *I* can almost taste you, silly, don't you suppose he's noticed? . . ." and as I disentangled the jug from the ivy they drifted out of hearing.

And so help me, it wasn't two hours till he picked her up behind the Inn and drove her off for the rest of the weekend to a stud farm of his grandfather's across the Delaware in Bucks County.

I was stunned when he told me. I said, "But for God's sweet sake, Tatnall, *no chaperone?*"

". . . Farm manager's wife was there."

"In the house with you?"

"Wouldn't bed-check if she had been."

"But didn't she do the rooms?"

"What if she did?"

"What's this what-if-she-did? dammit, the sheets—"

"For God's sake who *sleeps* together?"

That part of the carnal logistics hadn't occurred to me. My innocence abashed me; I switched to an aspect I knew about. "But what in hell'd you and this Lucinda *do* all day between nights?"

"Sat around."

"Charming each other, huh."

"Charmed *me!*"

"Just sitting around, for God's sake?"

"Rode some too."

"Where'd she get a habit?"

"Trunk in the tack room."

"Ride well?"

"Hunts at home."

"Just rode and sat around, huh."

"Huh."

"Didn't get her to pose for you or anything?"

". . . Sort of."

"Sort of what? Shirt off? Pretty bosom and all?"

". . . Made a fuss."

"You're losing your grip," I said, "and a good thing for American womanhood," but who knows what did happen? My guess has always been that Lucinda is the (shirtless) girl in that lighthearted Picasso parody in Boston, *Lady Looking Minotaur Straight in the Eye*, though the face is too Picasso'd to be sure about.

(Except which of several ways a girl can look you straight in the eye is she looking you straight in the eye?)

—She may of course have had explanations at home, and they may not have been convincing. Hugh I remember received a postcard with nothing but !!!!!!! on it, went haring off to Richmond to find out what she meant by it, was ordered violently out of the house by her father, in an atmosphere crackling with metaphorical horse-whips, and I'm not sure ever saw her again. Certainly he spent an unruffled summer painting Mediterranean light at his uncle's castelletto in Portofino.

—Well, as Auden said about something else, Come, peregrine nymphs, delight your shepherds. But by our senior year, luckily, they'd begun to humanize (and re-educate) Hugh as well. This can be disconcerting: I've always suspected Hugh wasn't far from thunderstruck the early-winter weekend when, of all people, the serene young second wife of his departmental adviser decided she would acquire him.

When honest to god all he'd done was go round to pay a *duty* call on the guy!

Merely *happened* he was at a conference in Utah!

Or one of those places. So he'd stayed for tea anyhow. She was a lot younger than her husband. Also it developed she did avant-garde reviews for the *Dial.* So he'd stayed for dinner too.

Then after dinner they'd sat by the fire and, well, she'd read Marianne Moore and stuff to him.

So, in brief, goddammit, and as good as straight out of Dante, *Marianna fu il libro e chi lo scrisse,* hard as that is to credit—

I said but for God's—

Was I going to tell him a mere Princeton senior was expected to argue with a *Dial* critic in *bed?* And dammit what was I laughing at?—she was *wonderful!* And also, for all he knew he might have got her in a hell of a jam: it had *snowed* in the night (of all possible acts of God to have occurred!), and there in the new snow were his footprints only coming *out*—with every faculty neighbor in Broadmead sure as hell to know exactly when the stuff had started falling *and* when it had stopped!

—Drawing-room farce, yes. And it didn't have a long run: second term her husband disobligingly took her off with him on a sabbatical. But it was Hugh's first affair with a girl just enough sensual and civilizing years older to put an end to his adolescence; and the face with a look of hers that turned up in Hugh's canvases for several years afterwards is less I think a symbol or a memory than payment of a debt.

Senior year, too, he had his first one-man show. It was only local, at the Brick Row Book Shop, and in the main just Mediterranean landscape and Italian hill towns—what a petulant critic later described as "Mr. Tatnall's revolting cold-color lotissements." But two of these same early canvases brought solid prices three years ago at Sotheby's, and even Princeton undergraduates got a sense of what an astonishing young painter he was: in our senior balloting he was even voted *both* "Most brilliant" and "Thinks he is," the second as solid a mark of status as the first.

—So in due course we graduated. More or less cum laude, even doing very little work. Though why work if one has natural prerogatives? Who in Art-and-Architecture could even begin to draw like Hugh? Nor did I think anybody in Classics could, say, turn out neater Latin elegiacs than I did. I was especially fond

of an Ovidian farewell to a two months' Vassar love of mine. I can
still remember how it began:

> Tamquam nocte brevi longum ponamus amorem:
> Voce unâ partam perdat et una fidem—

which I translated for her

> Put off our long, like a brief evening's, love:
> The bond one word began, let one word end.

So cum laude and a credit to our various departments we graduated, and went our several ways.

—And between that lighthearted airy morning long ago and
this one now (I thought, contemplating the hushed and reverent
assemblage of Hugh's colleagues on every side about me, row on
unstirring row)—between then and now think what rectitudes
his life and conduct, by contrast, had comfortingly allowed them
to display. What fastidiously intellectual deprecations he had
been the occasion of, what campus headshakings, what disparage-
ments, how many high-minded and improving senses of outrage,
what universal chiding! All moreover how justified and unanswerable: for paint, yes, certainly—but why not lead a respectable life
too? . . .

The meetinghouse door creaked open and closed again one
last time, the old flat latch clacked, a final late-come friend
bustled breathily to some bench behind us and settled with depre-
catory scuffles. Silence took over. By some unspoken consensus it
came to be understood that the formal hour had begun. The door
held its peace, the latch was mute, the last apologetic rustlings
died away, and in grave and quiet meditation Meeting began.

3

Quaker funerals have no prescriptive ritual. The *Book of Disci-
pline* says merely, "We commend the simplicity of our usual form
of worship" and lets it go at that. But our usual form of worship
happens to be formless: one just sits, in a meetinghouse, in silence, for one hour. Thee may of course get to thy feet and speak if
thee is moved to. And, in principle, on any topic. Even if peculiar.

But, in Hugh's case, what to say? Recite the standard graveside
pieties one could not, Hugh being Hugh: *this* undeceived forgathering knew better. And whatever went on here ought in any case, it

had seemed to me, to be for *his* ghostly entertainment, not the Smith faculty's—their taste in iusta funebria was irrelevant.

Also, who was to say whatever was to be said? Plausible numberers of the usual nonsense wouldn't do. Nor would any speaker who didn't know exactly what he was getting into. I had finally drafted a man who was pretty much a fellow-marauder of Hugh's, an engaging Carolinian named (to give him his full Rebel quarterings) Taige Pulteney Massingberd Heald, a years-long friend, colleague, and campus libertine whose charm was as breathless a student legend as Hugh's own.

I did have some trouble talking him into it (why pick on *him* for my spiritual requirements?). But I'd said now now, think how a fellow-campaigner's words of appreciation would please Hugh's ghost as it passed upward to higher preoccupations. And with a consoling reassurance that it was leaving the student body in such good hands still. So there at any rate he now sat, "facing the Meeting" as it's called, looking put-upon and wary.

The slow, sobering, pointless minutes began to drowse their lengths along. A throat was self-effacingly cleared; somebody sighed deeply. Camilla lifted a black-gloved thumb and finger and delicately adjusted an earring. Persis humbly swallowed a tiny yawn. Up at the front, Taige recrossed his well-tailored knees and settled on the other buttock; his disinclinations began to show. And on every side, in stony tedium, row on row, aligned like sepulchral statues along an ancient Roman way, the silent synod of Hugh's assizers and assoilers began resolutely sitting out the hour.

—But what could any such alliterated establishment ever have made of Hugh, I said to myself, bisected or not into those indispensable academic entities (a) the Man and (b) the Œuvre. His canvases with their maelstroms of fractured and reconstituted light are in museums and millionaires' collections everywhere. Yet here, three rows ahead of me in this intellectual assemblage, sat our famous old physiologist who at a campus show of Hugh's had been overheard remarking, with mild asperity, "Why, bless me, the human genitalia don't look like that!" ("Have I painted a girl then or a goddam dahlia?" Hugh snorted.) But Hugh's renown in the college had never been quite clear: as in other disciplines too, the Work was always being somehow confused with the Man. One sarcastic and slighting colleague had even declared, "The fellow's major work's his endless damn' girls anyhow!" And a Lesbian wit had nicknamed one of his portraits "Tatnall's lunch."

College girls' falling in love with faculty, as any reasonably masculine professor knows, was a rite of academic anthropology many long years before anything as simpleminded as sexual freedom was thought up. The explanation of those days was of course Freudian, a happy search for someone like Father in age and authority—and what's a professor if not an authority? and, well, *sort* of old! And, well, with a professor, voilà, it isn't incest.

(Though think how much Hegelized nonsense Freud might have left unwritten if he'd just been what we used to call *around* a little. Or had even come across that urbane sentence of Steele's: "She naturally thinks, if she is tall enough, she is wise enough for anything for which her education makes her think she is designed.")

The quantification of such an agreeable perquisite did at one time make private-college administrations jumpy. "Though Simon goddammy," Hugh would complain, "am I to tell some trusting child she *doesn't* love me? Frustrating her temporary view of what she's here on earth for? If a campusful of girls feel they have to fall in love, what business have our trustees behaving as if they thought this decorous young ladies' seminary was an upper-class house of call?"

But, generally no doubt, why or how Hugh painted was beyond his average colleague's grasp. Whereas often I knew even the trivial detail. That madonna series, for instance: if future art scholars bother with it, they will naturally spot the parody of the Raphael series in which the Virgin holds the bambino in the curve of one arm, and, in the other hand, some symbol of the crucifixion to come. But how are they to guess that Hugh's series began as a private joke?

One of his first girls at Smith was, it happened, a very pretty but also a very proper Mormon. Her name was Susannah; and though she seems to have had only sporadic religious crises about making love with Hugh, once she got used to it, he never could get the child to pose for him. She was terribly sweet and humble about this, but she absolutely would not. A chaste head and shoulders, yes, but oh please please nothing more.

"And was *I* to put up with that kind of disingenuous farce?" he demanded of me. "So I *painted* her as a virgin by god! That book in her hand's the Book of Mormon to prove it. The bambino's chubby little hand that's just pulled her shirt off's a work of the imagination too."

But when he let his model see it, her shock of dismay at the composition was shattering. She gave a little cry of woe and stared at it speechless, and when at last she turned to Hugh her face was sheer hopeless misery.

Now now *now*, he'd said, why, what on earth was this?—had she forgot her art history altogether? Did he need to remind as good a student as she was that, say, Fouquet had painted Agnès Sorel as the Virgin? *And* with that charming left bosom of hers as bare as in her secular portraits? Was she a fine-arts major or wasn't she?

She looked at him with great wet eyes, wordlessly betrayed.

"So, like a perfect gent," he said to me in his humanest tone, "I simply handed the child a palette knife and said all right, all right, it's yours anyway, my angel, slash the wicked thing to ribbons."

I said but naturally she hadn't?

"When *I'd* painted her portrait?" he cried, affronted.

Or again, what historian can guess the cockeyed history of the 'Bona Dea Motif' of later canvases in the series, that veiled female figure one faintly makes out lurking half-hidden in the edge of a shadowy Tuscan-hillside wood in so many of the backgrounds.

The Bona Dea is an obscure Latin vegetation spirit who became, as times grew less primitive, an anthropomorphic goddess of love; but for some reason Hugh had taken her as his tutela. I'm not sure he didn't half-believe it *was* She Who gave him (or sometimes, for Her own amusement, denied him) whatever girl he had at the moment an eye on. This nonsense had derived from a casual affair at Nîmes, years before. A ship's stewardess, a pretty Nîmoise, had obligingly sewn a button on a shirt for him, and while she sewed they had talked; and later talked several times more; and a few weeks later, en route from Nice to Biarritz, he seems to have thought why not stop off and see.

His train had pulled into Nîmes during a violent thunderstorm. At the very moment he stepped off, there was a frightful rending crash, the platform shook, women travelers shrieked and swooned, and simultaneously (he presently discovered) the Maison Carrée was struck by lightning. This, in a landscape of ancient pagan gods like Provence, was a clear Omen.

And of what, he soon found out. The girl not only sighed into his arms without a moment's demurring, she spent the rest of her vacation there, except when she was posing for him, or cooking for him, or washing his clothes.

This struck him as a demonstration of Who was In Charge of him (and with thunderbolts at Her disposal!); and when presently he wandered through the public gardens looking for the Maison Carrée but somehow failed to find it, that was part of the monstrum too: the Bona Dea had caused it to vanish, to remind him. "Elle exagère, ta déesse," said the girl.

(Whom he immortalized as befits such an epiphany. She is that glowing *Girl with Two Shirts* in the art museum at Princeton, perched on the windowsill of her kitchen in the flooding pagan brilliance of Mediterranean noon, legs dangling bare; she has just sewn a button on a yellow shirt and is biting off the thread; the other shirt, unbuttoned, is what she more or less has on. Picked out in black tiles on the red-tiled floor, as if an ancient Roman had put his admonitory CAVE CANEM there, you can just make out a DÉESSE MÉCHANTE.)

—On the far side of the meetinghouse a towering old man I had never seen before in my life abruptly stood up, and in a strong gobbling voice ejected a couple of stanzas of what I took to be, from their tone of meek piety and general theological smarm, some Quaker poet or other. He then sat down as suddenly as he had got up, and the silence of empty-headed meditation engulfed us once more.

Persis looked at me with great startled lovely eyes. Camilla made a faintly mocking face, lips shaping a soundless *Who?*

I soundlessly mouthed back *Gonnd.*

4

And we'll get more of it from the same exhortatory Source, I said to myself, delight in the repetition of claptrap being what it is, if Taige doesn't get *on* with whatever his prepared damn' remarks about Hugh turn out to be.

—Though what was I to conclude Hugh 'was,' here at the melancholy end of it? What had the guesses of history ever made of, say, Benvenuto Cellini? How explain any of these sporadic fusions of creative genius and incurable libertine that decorate the record of our cultural heritage? What made that wild meteor of the Restoration, Lord Rochester, go in for so much sheer outrage—how explain Liszt, or Byron? Half the girls in their endless baggage-trains seem to have as good as mistaken them for reincarnations of the primordial Dionysus, and themselves as initiates in their thiasoi.

> If history points a moral (and we *say* it does)
>   Don Juans are immortal—that wild spirit
> That makes the female heart behave the way it does
>   The moment a marauding male comes near it.

("And often to its fluttering own dismay it does," one can add, cooings of palumbiform goddesses or not.)

But certainly, in Hugh's case, the expatriate uncle's example, if not his influence, had somehow to have molded him. I remember his telling me of a long-ago morning when, as a very small boy, he was pattering about the terraced gardens of his uncle's castelletto in Portofino, and first saw, dazzled, what was probably the loveliest, and certainly the most scandalous, of his uncle's beltà, Lady Mary Castinge: that instant could have formed the pattern.

Lady Mary (this generation has to be told) was one of *the* international beauties of her day. The *Tatlers* and *Spectators* and *Sketches* of the twenties are one long photographers' tribute to her angelic English loveliness, and to the Almanach de Gotha of her misbehaviors. She was born (see Debrett) Lady Mary Sare; but by the customary processes of British upper-class marriage, adultery, divorce, remarriage, and nomenclature, she successively became Lady Mary Savenake-Hope, Lady Mary de Wennerent, Lady Charles Penhér, and finally, married to Capt. the Hon. Philip Castinge, became Lady Mary again. That time at Portofino, if I have the chronology right, she was being divorced to become Lady Charles. Or was Penhér the fellow who was divorcing her? Not that it matters, or mattered then. She used to come floating devotedly back to Hugh's uncle between husbands anyhow. "*Much* her favorite co-respondent," Hugh said.

But to five-year-old Hugh, trotting busily about the climbing gardens that innocent morning, when he looked up and saw her coming languidly up the flights of broad stone steps on his uncle's arm, white and gold in that clarity of Ligurian light, she was divinity. He had had a mildly mythological bringing-up: we were all read to at bedtime then from a genteel scarlet-bound expurgation of cultural anthropology called *The Children's Hour*, so he knew what gods and goddesses were. But the draftsmanship of *The Children's Hour* illustrations was on the muddy side: what goddesses, in particular, looked like was hard to make out. Now he *saw*: they looked like This Lady.

She was saying in one of those cool rippling English voices "—but you can't think Robert what a doting wife I should have made you darling, who else do I indulge with this spouse-like and wedded constancy, you will admit? Eccomi, after every marriage! Or should one rebuke your vanity and say 'before'?" (Or this is what Hugh thought she said. To a small boy it was meaningless. Also, the fluting English of her accent made him uncertain whether she was speaking a language he knew.) "*Ohhh* how you look at me, you look as if all you can think of when you see me is the wicked things you persuade me to do with you, goodness isn't it heaven! But now Robert who's *this*, you're not to tell me he's some son of yours darling, I suppose his mother's some sweet farrowing little Italian piece you've had somewhere?"

Hugh's uncle said firmly no, no: nephew, nephew. Right side of the blanket too, far as *he* knew; and Hugh come here be presented.

But she was saying, "Now Robert *how* implausible, he's the most melting image of you!"

(So he *was* understanding what she said—this remark he had heard before. That girl who'd spent part of the spring with them, and left in a fiery tantrum of tears only a few days before, had once in his hearing told his uncle the same thing: "Ma fa paura, carino, quanto ha il tuo aspetto. . . .")

His uncle said oh nonsense, resemblance didn't make the boy a by-blow—*he* didn't indulge in the coarse practices of the peerage and landed gentry! and she said yes he *was* always maintaining he was a landed peasant instead, wasn't he, what a staring snob he was! and laughing affectionately in each other's faces they went lazily on up into the castelletto beyond.

All little Hugh could do was gaze and gaze, his senses drowning in her radiance. He gave up breathing entirely. He was not merely transfigured with awe, he was stunned with love. "In fact," he once told me, "I forgot that adorable contessa of Uncle Robert's on the spot—a girl who'd been tenderly mothering me for weeks, girl who'd leave my uncle and race to my room at two in the morning if I had a nightmare, and snatch me up in her warm young arms and croon comforting Italian to me and carry me back to her own bed with her. I even remember my uncle standing there once at the foot of her bed, in a pool of moonlight, laughing 'Dunque!—sono cornuto anch'io!' There I'd been, five years old in bed by god with my first girl—and I forgot her *instantly*, for that cool and heavenly being on Uncle Robert's arm. What perfidy! What benefits forgot!"

—Though, again, how much of Hugh's behavior at Smith was due, rather, to the delectable environment, that always changing campus population of girls he had lived among off and on for so long? There they were—self-willed, flighty, ungovernably amorous, dithery, lawless, innocent, ruthlessly designing, demure, sly. Ma ahimè, incantevoli too; and how they threw themselves in his way! Having an affair with Hugh Tatnall, I've heard it sardonically argued, had become practically a status symbol. "Who sees goat-ishness as goatishness at nineteen?" Hugh used to argue. "Why, dammy, they still think it may be the Great God Pan."

(The fact, more likely, is that they used him and knew they did, and also more or less knew why. Whether he was an advanced lab course or the higher theory of the thing no doubt depended on a girl's previous disillusionments. But there he was, an undeniable paradigm of what a lover was supposed to be; and if in due course he too disillusioned them, it was disillusion as good as certified on a higher level entirely.)

Faculty wives were sometimes affected too. He had hardly settled in, I remember, his first year at Smith, before the young wife of an instructor in French (a Structuralist, come to think of it—compounding the nonsense!) took to 'confiding' in him. Did he think, she would ask him mournfully, that everybody worked as *tirelessly* at their dissertations as her husband? Did they all spend so much *time* at the college—evenings too? Did he think some horrid sneaky girl— She wept, flowerlike and enravishing, against Hugh's breast pocket; had to be comforted, brow kissed and so forth; soon, too, those great tear-filled and doleful eyes. Lovely grieving curve of her neck too, below her little jeweled ear. And so, ah well, around, at last, to lips still wet and tremulous with her tears. This is all so childish that I am embarrassed to re-member it of a friend.

Yet all Hugh had to say was what was I snorting at! Had I forgot Benjamin Constant's pointed phrase about "le despotisme de leur douleur"? Was it *his* fault if some over-articulate sod in Modern Languages hadn't structured his wife's reading in the Romantics? And anyhow, dammit,

> Elles nous font autant
> De pluies que de beaux temps

for our own good, don't they? To keep our sensibilities in working order, at no matter what cost to their own? Was he *not* to assuage such high-minded tears? Was I a stone ? . . .

—Well, as Lord Byron wrote to Lady Melbourne, of Lady Frances Webster's oaf of a husband, "If a man is not contented with a pretty woman, he must not be surprised if others admire that which he knows not how to value." Anthropologists tell us that stealing women is only exogamy anyhow.

5

A soft sound from Camilla: Taige had got to his feet and was stepping gravely down into the broad aisle across the front of the meetinghouse.

Where he now stood for a silent moment contemplating us—bland, courtly, archaic-looking, and easy, as if this were a graduate seminar and his subject Aristotle's Ethics rather than Hugh's. But in fact it was in lay-sermon tones that he began:

"We are a people, I suggest to you, of the here and now."

A practiced Ciceronian pause. He'd decided to bore us high-minded? And talk *around* the factual Hugh; very ingenious.

He went on: "The theme of death as a long rest is as alien to us as it is Asiatic—the hopelessness of the slave mines of antiquity, Platonized into a contempt for life, and then, by lesser Platos, into a distaste for it."

I was amused. Not four hours earlier the disingenuous bastard had interrupted my breakfast at Camilla's to fuss about what under the sun he could say—he was doing my spiritual dirty work for me wasn't he? so then how about a few paragraphs of classical throwaways dammit from *me!*

—I had woken alone.

. . . Heartlessly deserted?

But no: off in the studio her grand piano was showering the summer morning with baroque cadenzas. Not deserted—sweetly let sleep. The glittering notes fled in like handfuls of spilled jewels. Rehearsing for her next concert. So no "eyelids lifting upon a matutinal Pygmalion." Just Mozart.

And breakfast fed me by her willowy au pair sophomore, leering as if sophisticated. I was still feeding when in sauntered Taige.

"Not having found you at home," he explained in courteous unsurprise. He pulled a chair to the table and stared round at the food. So I'd taken to acquiring musical culture too, had I?—though would I *listen* to what that unfeeling girl was playing? And on the very day of her once-cherished Hugh's funeral!

I said come come. And to have some coffee.

"Ah but Simon *this* sonata!" he cried. "Have you any notion how it brings back my own charming little—bless my soul what was her name? Had a silly affair with Hugh before I got her."

He meant Emma?

"That's it—*Emma*. Dear heaven Simon what a fantasia of a girl! Past poor Hugh's ability to appreciate I suspect altogether. D'you know, she'd say, 'Oh my darling when you weep for me what do you weep for me *to*?' What's a man to say?—so at random I told her to *this* adagio: good as anything else. It became our 'theme.' Bless your heart, I *must* have told you."

I said he had, yes.

"But does it I wonder still move me now, though," he said, as if judicially, listening. "What if I found myself fearing it no longer does, Simon. Have I a heart of granite, would you say? Or less sensibility than I hope my sensibilities deserve? Ah, well. Yes. Emma. She'd say, '*Oh* how I love you temporarily!' Isn't that charming? Isn't that witty? All what long years now past and gone. Why do any of us. Yes. Well. Happiness, how sad. And now we've got to put dear old fornicating Hugh's dust in the grave too. We shall miss the turmoil of his depredations."

Though now what about this oration he'd had the madness to say he'd undertake for me. Would I tell him what he could possibly say with a straight face? "Hugh's undeviating interest in the individual student." Ho ho ho. "The enviable campus reputation of the Tatnall seminar." *Ho* ho ho. As they sat there tutting their moral tuts. Had I forgotten what faculty meetings were like?

—A sunburst of crashing final chords from the studio, then silence; and then in a moment there in the doorway had been Camilla, eyes as if veiled in the sonata's concluding intensities— barely even taking us in, lost still in the Mozart, in purest technician's trance. She drifted across to the table, a musing angel in work shirt and torero breeches, black curls pulled up into her concert chignon all anyhow, absently holding up a polite cheek to each of us in turn to be kissed—murmuring a still abstracted "Mmmmm *pet*" to Taige from her reverie, and a dreamy "*Mmmmm* sweetie" to me.

Then so to speak she saw me. And came mockingly awake. "You got *up?*—goodness!" she said, sat sweetly down in my chair, and rang for a fresh verseuse of coffee.

(O lovely dish from heaven that you are, I said to myself, by what dazing Mediterranean inadvertence of Hugh's goddess was last night appointed and conferred on *me?* . . .)

She was saying to Taige, "But goodness what a great glum fussing face, what *can* be wrong?" so the cynical anguishes of his dilemma were still being re-explained when I finished my breakfast and left to fetch Persis.

Camilla saw me off.

I said, "Kiss for the road?"

"Why?"

"I got *up!*"

"Such enterprise!"

I drove off laughing. But then I found myself thinking about her with such happy violence that I pulled into the next filling station and rang her up.

"Why, it's you," she said. "Where are you?"

"In a phone booth."

"A phone booth where?"

"It doesn't say."

"But what's wrong?"

"Nothing's wrong."

"I thought you were fetching the little widow."

"I am. I'm en route."

"Then *what*, sweetie?"

"You mean I don't make sense?"

A silence. Then, "Are you going to *say* why you're calling?"

"What I wasn't given a chance to, this morning."

Another silence, shorter. Then she said sweetly, "Was good for your morale, last night?"

"What a question!"

"Well I should think so!"

"Was good for yours?"

"What vanity!"

We hung up, snickering, and I drove off.

It had been late, the night before. We had just finished shutting up her house for the night, I the polite guest lending a hand; we were just leaving the studio. All evening we had discussed Hugh. Or perhaps I should put it, thematically we were discussing Hugh, and what ostensibly we were discussing was our relationships to him, but in simple fact what we were doing was exploring our relationship with each other now Hugh was gone. Memories we shared of him were also memories of our own unstated hankering earlier, and not stating it now was beside the point: every phrase of reminiscence had become a kind of subliminal serenade, hour after hour.

We left the studio; she flicked off the light at a switch by the door into the hall. And at that moment she turned to me in the darkened doorway and said, as if summing up the evening about Hugh and his girls, "And that was always the trouble, sweetie, he didn't always *like* us as we are."

So all I had to say was, "But you've decided maybe I do? . . ."

and she said, "Well, you *do*," with suave approval, and stepped into my arms.

—What an angel what an angel. I pulled into another filling station like an infatuated boy and rang her number.

". . . You *again?*"

"I thought perhaps by this time Taige—"

"He hasn't."

"You mean he's *still* discuss—?"

"Sweetie are you calling for information or do you just love me?"

(What kind of lopsided disjunction was that? I was simple-mindedly out of my mind about her!)

I said, "The first time I ever saw you—"

"But you were just an old friend of his that he'd bored me going on about half the summer, at Portofino."

"Whereas *I*, with a certain adulterous gallantry—"

"Sweet Simon did I *stay* bored?"

Silence again; it was all elliptical anyhow. Our minds went wordlessly on. Until I said, "Are you smiling?"

"Yes."

"At bogus discussions?"

"You mean I discussed him with you and see what happened?"

"Angel *angel*," I said, "why did you get up?"

". . . That wasn't in your plans?"

" 'Plans'?—when I hadn't seen you for months?"

". . . Well what did you think then, before?"

"What seeing you again would be like."

"See, you did plan!"

"What did *you* think, before?"

"Oh . . . I wondered what you'd be like again, too. After all these months. Nearly a year. And I thought, well, here we'd *be*. In my empty house, all alone. Just the private two of us, in my dark empty house. Listening to the beating of our hearts. . . . Oh, just the customary maidenly thoughts, sweetie! And wondering whether— well, what *were* you like. . . ."

6

I surfaced, sighing.

And found Taige in full gnomic cry: ". . . so that for the average man among us, hardly will even the syllables of his name outlive the fading recollections of those who knew him. In the ancient Attic idiom, élathe biôn—'he escaped notice living,' and this is the common lot. But for illustrious men, as Pericles said of the Athenian dead, a whole earth is a memorial, extinction in part suspended. . . ."

—And this was the panourgos who'd come badgering me for classical throwaways!

What's more, with a theme like extinction, it struck me Taige was running risks. Those flesh-hacking battlefields of 431 B.C. are on record and, now and then, remembered; but the lumbering hoplites cut down on them are not—Pericles's grandiose "a whole earth" is not an identifying stele. Yet who, out of Hugh's lifetime roster of infatuated girls, could Taige or anyone be sure had so much as bothered to read the news of his death? Or been saddened if they had. Or had come here this summer morning if only for a wordless moment of farewell. (Or for that matter, Camilla my angel, been one night faithful to a ghost before its nunc dimittis into oblivion.)

This, mind you, when girl after girl had imagined she was making over her life for him; and I thought of Caroline, an absolutely classic case of a love affair with a thoroughly nice girl.

Caroline was the fifth young wife (or perhaps the sixth: one lost count) of a majestic professor of English Lit named Coplestone Colville, a much-sought-after performing poet cum visiting lecturer, both here and abroad, who had made a practice of marrying his students. Caroline was almost thirty years younger than he and hadn't I believe gone to bed with him her senior year, but otherwise she was very much like her predecessors—demure, sensual, innocent, determined, and, as far as the Bona Dea sees fit, idealistic.

At the wedding, Hugh had been more sardonic about Cope than usual. "Are his damn' girls coming in primary colors now?" he grumbled to me. "*Look* at the Velásquez red of that delicious mouth. And the misty radiance of her eyes—Corot-blue by god if there ever was!"

I said why not borrow the girl?—he could do a *Virgin on the Dean's List* from her.

"Dean's List *was* she then?" he cried, delighted. "*That's* what Cope thinks the List's for? . . ." And I doubt if he gave her another thought.

But that next summer, on Cape Cod, he'd rented a cottage in a part of Chatham known as Skunks Neck (he was working on the

second version of his *Sea-Light Triptych*) and Caroline happened
to be on the Cape too. And temporarily alone: Cope had gone
magisterially off on a cultural tour of the Balkans for the State
Department—*not* her sort of project, he'd explained to her: living
conditions were primitive, the schedule was exhausting, he'd have
to be what was called available-to-students fifteen hours a day, and
there was no food worth eating east of Vienna anyway; so he had
deposited her in a house somebody had lent him in Wellfleet. As a
summer project, she was reading Virginia Woolf entire. This, in a
young wife as beautiful as Caroline, is an inscrutable omen.

And Hugh, at a loose end somewhat too, found himself seeing to
her social life. He sailed with her; he amiably lugged her hamper at
picnics; he squired her to parties. He even got hold of a small racing
sloop and had her as crew. She fed him lunch a couple of times a
week in return. They discussed Virginia Woolf, the erotic sociology
of the Eastern college girl, marine navigation, the father–daughter
relationship, and (often) each other. Probably for ten days they were
as blameless as Homer's blameless Ethiopians.

But then one night a Harwich Port millionaire with intellectual leanings gave a party for a Cambridge don who was on a pil-
grimage to Edmund Wilson. Wilson himself didn't come but
socially it was a great success: everyone drank to the point of
oratory. I myself, I find I remember, no longer conversed—I declaimed. My classicist's bred-in dismissal of English Lit was
available to anybody who'd shut up and listen. I even remember
charging out into the warm summer starlight, glass in hand, as
Hugh was taking Caroline home, crying out where was *he* going,
in God's name, with a girl who'd affronted our cultural heritage by
marrying into *English?*—'d he mistaken *their* departmental taste
for sexual selection God help us all? Caroline had had to kiss me
half a dozen laughing good nights before I'd let them take off.

It was one of those black and brilliant early-summer nights, a
dusky splendor of starlight over everything, the earth in inky
shadow. And very late, the moon long set; the sleeping villages
they drove through were dark and silent, the roads deserted, the
distant beaches invisible, only now and then the ivory lines of surf
glimmering faint and far off as they thrust their fans of foam up the
unseen sand. But for a car's headlights once far away among the
dunes, the towering night was like a great dim ballroom in which
they found themselves alone. A more elegant setting for a seduction a girl couldn't reasonably have asked for. Or the Bona Dea
provided.

At Caroline's gate, when he handed her out of his car, for a wordless moment she faced him, poised in the dark radiance of starlight like starlight herself in her floating summer dress— *She's like jewels* he told me he remembered thinking. Her beauty astonished him as if he were seeing it for the first time—and the dreaming gaze, the eyes lifted to him as Corot-blue no doubt he thought as ever but in the darkness what was their expression? a soft wonder, like the night about them? . . . Never mind what; he reached out and took her in his arms.

And was instantly incredulous. Like a telegraph of doom, his libertine synapses flashed it to him almost before their delight: this delicious girl was not just in his arms but, beyond any ambiguity, was *his!*—even this lovely mouth had never kissed anyone with *this* abandon. He was scandalized. And from the periphery what corroborating data were flooding in—the warm weight of her, clinging, melting, handed over, title and tenure as good as conferred in fee simple forever.

And how past dissembling it was clear she knew it too when at last she fought loose, gasping and wild, hair tumbling, eyes dazed, lost—for, simply, everything had been said. They faced each other, and you could have said what they faced, like a starlight presence between them, was Cope. Then she broke free, with a choking little cry of dismay, and fled into the house.

He was more or less dumfounded. The light went on in her hall; then the light on the stair; then the light in the hall went out and in her bedroom a light went on. But at once went off again, and when it came on the curtains had been drawn. If he had not been so upset for her he would have laughed aloud. He got back into his car and drove back to Chatham, shaking his head at himself.

Though God *damn* Cope! This unguarded *angel* of a girl!— who now couldn't pretend even to herself that the difference between Cope and him wasn't open, explicit, calamitous, irreversible, and apparently heaven.

With every immemorial station and sequence of love now how inevitable!—meetings; tears; transports; protestations and accusations; flights. . . .

And he himself, routine or not, he too might easily by god find himself declaring—even believing: for how often had he not!— that this delectable state of things, this tender woe, a girl *in love* like this, might never if he did not take her come his way again. He pulled in at his cottage groaning with simplemindedness.

His telephone was ringing. He charged through the door.

It had stopped. He was *outraged*.

Though what could he have said, if he'd got to it in time, that any longer needed saying anyhow?

She of course in no time rang again. "Hugh?"

"Are you all right?" he cried.

Silence. Then she said, "I wanted—I just— You did get home all right? I just thought—"

The connection broke.

She immediately rang back. "Oh my darling I didn't mean to hang up!"

"Huh?"

"You— We didn't say good night."

Neither did she say it now. Or hang up. But said softly, "Will I see you tomorrow? When will I see you?"

"It's already tomorrow."

"Today then? This morning? *Soon?*"

"I was going to Boston."

"I know. You said. *Are* you going?"

"After *tonight?*" he said, in shocked gallantry.

She cried, "Well how could I be sure!" as if furious.

Silence again. He said, "*Are* you all right, Caro?"

"Will you *stop* asking me that *stupid* question!"

"I was only—"

"When you went away and *left* me like that!—when for all I knew I might never see you again, you could have been killed in an accident! And just when we'd— My darling, you *left* me! I thought of that Henry James girl who said 'If I knew how I felt I should die,' and I could have shrieked it aloud, so there!"

And hung up.

Hugh sat there. Dutifully feeling, I imagine, that he should feel stricken. The very phone in his hand denounced him: what had he done? Perhaps at that very moment she had begun to weep. *That* was what he had done!

Though what was civilization good god coming to?—modern girls *upset* at being upset about a man!

And look what he'd got anyway from meditating seduction in the English department: quotations from Henry James. . . .

So he went snickering amiably to bed.

—Tossed for a good while, though. For what, humanely, was he to make of her being overcome at herself to this degree? Or make of such a vaudeville of contradictions, both horns of the dilemma showing simultaneously. . . . It was the first pallors of summer dawn before he slept.

—A little cry of rage was what woke him. He opened his eyes; and there she stood, poised in his bedroom doorway, smoldering.

"You could *sleep?*" she cried at him, in a passion.

He was too stunned at how beautiful she was to know what she was talking about.

"*Asleep!*—what we've done doesn't mean anything more to you than that?" she upbraided him, tears of sheer affront in her eyes. "My darling love don't you even understand what's *happened?*"

He sat up, saying, "Caro—"

"And now you don't even care enough about my feelings to put a dressing gown on!" she choked, and vanished from the doorway.

Well but dear god he at least had pajama trousers on!—so he sprang out of bed and plunged after her. She was just running out of the cottage. He yelled "But goddammit I *adore* you!" at her, and she stopped in her tracks and leaned against the doorjamb, weak and lovely, looking at him in wet-eyed misery, lips quivering.

Was she out of her *senses?* he cried. Did she think that any man, ever, had been blessed with a more—

"But we can't!" she wept (answering some other question). "Oh Hugh we *can't!*" in sheer woe dissolving into his arms. "Because *do* you love me—last night I thought you did, but do you?"—nonsense which he naturally answered by kissing her mournful mouth.

But she thrust him away. "Don't you understand what *has* happened, my darling?" she lamented. "This absolute heaven, of being in love like this, only then *not* free for it?"

He said what had a word like "free" have to do with the way a coup de foudre—

"Then oh *kiss me!*" she said violently; and this time, everything had been admitted in advance.

But as the logical sequence to what she was doing was what with anguish she had just assured him she could not do, presently she fell back against the doorjamb, disheveled and radiant, blissful, blue eyes dazed with deliverance. "*Ohhhh* the way you kiss me! oh if you ever got me into a bedroom and kissed me like that— Oh you *please* me so!" she babbled, mindless with happiness. The folly was complete: if he'd had any sense he'd have taken her then and there.

—The delirium of a new love is, normally, a kind of slow fever. But to Caroline it had happened instantaneously, in a thunderclap of shattered innocence, and she took off into the trecento like a cuor gentil born. She lost eight pounds in the first three days. She couldn't eat. She would wake at four in the morning and lie staring at the ceiling deep into the summer dawn. She began to have frightening dreams, often of an appalling clarity.

"You and I were standing in that arbor Cope has," she for example told Hugh, "but we didn't know each other somehow, not names or anything; my darling love we were just two figures in an arbor. I began telling you about a girl I knew who'd got amnesia. It was terribly sad, I said, because it had happened while she and her husband were making love, so of course there she was with *no idea* who this huge heaving man even was! It was *ignoble!* So you said to me, 'If that turned out to be you, you must or mustn't say so,' and I said, 'I ought never to know who you are again,' and I woke up *sobbing!*"

By the end of three days, between guilt and wild longing, she was half out of her mind in a kind of seething depression. She would say, in misery, "If I had any honor I wouldn't even listen to the lovely things you say to me, and if you had any honor you wouldn't make them sound so lovely—you wouldn't *mean* them, my darling!" The first bliss and wonder no longer sustained her. She wept for the frustration she was causing him, and for herself for causing it. She must somehow kill this unlucky love, Hugh must help her kill it, he must stop seeing her, she must simply leave the Cape, run *away*, if he didn't stop. He found himself patiently saying but if he helped her kill it she'd only weep the more, didn't she see that? and she wept in grateful agreement. The sheer confusion of her scruples began to make all her other relationships seem insubstantial to her compared to Hugh, even impossible to feel as once she had felt them. Love in particular was becoming so completely Hugh that it was being Cope's wife she found strange—"I don't really *remember* anymore how I felt about him when we were married," she lamented. She lost two pounds more.

Her wretchedness was so endearing that Hugh found himself flattered into being amiably upset too. There were times, in the unconscious campaign of counter-seduction her tears were confronting him with, when he disentangled himself and left her plus étonné de son propre cœur, as Stendhal put it, que de tout ce qui lui arrivait.

Then finally, one lamenting afternoon, he asked her how long did she expect either of them to go on putting up with all this.

". . . I know," she said meekly. "I know we can't."

"And known it for days," he said, getting to his feet. "So come on," as if what they were talking about were something very brisk and kind, and pulled her up too.

She said, ". . . your bed then not mine," in a doleful and docile voice, and let him lead her to his car; and they drove to his cottage without another word.

But, as they drove, he could almost feel her begin to quake. A sort of dread settled over them; the air between them filled with a sense of hovering doom. (He could have shot himself: why in God's name had he ever let this quivering angel of his maneuver him into any such mood-ruining démarche? There were other beds in her damn' cottage; there was a splendid roomy sofa; there was that hearthrug, even! . . .) But sure enough, when they pulled up at his door she put her face in her hands and whispered miserably, "Hugh I can't."

For a moment what came into his head was a grandmother's firm-minded "It isn't what thee wants, it's what's good for thee." But no. Poor angel, he put an arm around her and petted her and said there there, and when it was no, no was what it had to be said it was; and now how about his taking her out to lunch and putting off seducing her till tomorrow.

—But then it was late that same afternoon that he heard her car drive up again as he was cleaning his brushes in the kitchen, and she walked into his arms without a word.

—First times tend to be too much of an Event. Also, crossing an unknown frontier one proceeds warily, for what are the natives like? This time, too, as a mild nuisance, Hugh found himself thinking critically of Cope's grounding. Still, when late that night she rang him up from her own bed to say good night again, she was mumurous with happiness, all miseries of indecision melted and gone.

—But next morning it was the happiness that was gone. Her voice on the phone was cold with accusation.

"I've betrayed Cope and I've betrayed myself. I can't even understand myself! Or *you*, Hugh! I'm not the *sort* of wife that has affairs! I've never even—"

What'd she mean, 'affairs'—he *loved* her!

"Does saying 'I love you' to me make it *not* an affair? Everything I thought about myself's gone! Oh I think it's horrifying to have upset my life so—my darling love how can you treat me like this!" she cried at him, as if making sense.

And when he interrupted this tirade to say he'd be in Wellfleet in ten minutes, she answered drearily, "I don't want to see you. Hugh I can't even look at you, I don't want to see you at *all*, can't you understand?" and hung up.

He of course set out instantly for Wellfleet anyhow.

She met him at the door, barring his way. "Hugh if he finds out I love you, if he even *suspects*, I'll tell him!"

"You out of your head?"

"But *of course* I'd tell him! If he suspects he'll suffer—could I bear to let him do that? It would be letting him down! And with *you*, my darling!"

He thought what did she call going to bed with him? but he managed to say only that he didn't altogether follow the consistencies in all this.

"Are you stupid? If he doesn't suspect that we've—that I love you so, how can he suffer? *I* have to suffer. But I have to. For being furtive and clandestine and— Can't you understand how *horrified* I am at being an adulteress? I can't even explain myself to myself! You don't even try to understand me!" she cried at him, in a perfect tantrum of woe, and flung into the house.

Sed enim tener ecce Cupido: this is what a love affair with a thoroughly nice girl can be like. So he took a deep breath and followed her in, and, as it turned out, didn't go home again for two days.

—But back, soon enough, came Cope from the edified Balkans; and at the party Caroline gave for his return she was so meek and husbandward that Hugh she seemed barely to look at. This infuriated and alarmed him. ("I wasn't 'jealous' goddammit," he told me, later. "Who's jealous of husbands? What I was, was *outraged*. . . .") He left early, grim. And drove back to Chatham snarling an Ovidian

> "Why should this uninvited swine
> Enjoy you, blast him, now you're mine!"

in no more worthwhile a state of mind than if he'd been sixteen.

But there on his pillow (how under the sun had the angel managed to put it there?) he found a letter:

Please, my darling, don't worry about me, and I will try not to worry about you. We will both have our horrifying and miserable moments—but is that new to us by now. Somehow this time *will* be gotten through. I love you, I am bursting with it, and it is lovely and terrible—you have made me more warm and alive and my human self than any other woman can ever feel. I need you because I love you. And that's what "I love you" means today.

He was stricken. Could any man on earth have foreseen such a tenderness of consolation? He charged out his cottage door and shot away in his car back to the party, almost laughing aloud.

—But now they had the tedium of being circumspect—and sometimes they were not. At one evening party, discussing a next day's picnic with Caroline and their hostess, he suddenly heard his voice *telling* Caroline what to bring, in a tone of proprietorship for anybody to hear; and in an instant saw the woman's eyes widen at him, then glance swiftly at Caroline's face, and then, with a new light in them, back into his. All she said, presently, was a bland, "You know, you two are perfectly beautiful together." But that was merely luck.

It was not until college opened again that they felt free. What Hugh then did with his time, an occasional seminar aside, nobody could verify. Caroline and he could spend long hours together, at this or that rendezvous, without its ever occurring to anybody that they were missing, much less missing at the same time—parting (to his amusement) with the lovers' precautionary phrase she had borrowed for them from *The Golden Bowl*, "What shall you say . . . that you've been doing?"

They could plan. They could meet at parties unfrustrated and hence at ease: life was always an enchanted *soon*. . . . They even managed a night now and then in Boston. Her ordinary daily life was what now seemed to her, she told him, a secondary kind of reality, like scenery on a darkened stage in a deserted theatre, where she found herself walking through a part she could still just remember she had once played.

And as the college year went on they evolved rituals. She asked him what she should wear to parties. She betrayed her dearest friends' most compromising secrets to him ("I promised her I wouldn't tell anybody ever. Will you *promise* never to tell?"). They discussed money. She refused to make love on the maid's day out. He balanced her checkbook for her.

But the scheduling of adultery in a college town is not an exercise for laymen. The circumspection itself unnerved her. "My darling love I'm afraid of all sort of things I'm afraid I haven't even *thought* of! And I have to *act!*—even if we've just been making love and I'm in that haze about you I have to act! When what I want is for everything I do to show I love you. And *you* are so careful and cool when you look at me at parties that my heart *sinks!* You don't even look as if you loved me! And how can I be sure you still do?"

She developed wild superstitions. Their meetings had omens. If a day of planned rendezvous began well, this was the Bona Dea reassuring her; if something happened to prevent a meeting, that too was the Bona Dea, watching over them—the rendezvous (for reasons they of course couldn't know) would have been terribly, even fatally, dangerous. "We're being indulged, whether you think so or not," she would tell him, with a convert's serenity. "For all we know, my darling, we've been saved again and again. . . ."

So at last, perhaps inevitably in the course of things, one night late in the spring she asked Cope for a divorce.

She and Hugh had spent the night before in Boston. She had driven back in dreamy reminiscences of everything they had done and said, her whole body a remembrance; and when, that evening, there was Cope amiably saying come to bed, "suddenly I just couldn't," she told Hugh on the phone.

"I didn't know myself I was going to say it!—divorce I mean. But when he said come to bed, I— How *could* I let him? So I just—I said I hoped he'd forgive me but I didn't love him anymore, I knew it was awful but I'd fallen in love and please would he divorce me. So he said *who with?* in a terrible voice, so I said nobody he knew, a man I'd met last summer. So he said in a snarly sort of way then I'd been having an affair, *that* was why I went to Boston? and I said no I *had not!* oh my love what else was there to say? when it was you! So then he—oh Hugh it went on and on and on and finally he said all right *all right* he'd divorce me, by this time he ought to be used to his parade of fluttering capricious love-simple temporary wives! and I went into the guest room and slept there. So I'm still all yours. And I'll stay that way, are you glad?"

He said he'd be with her in five minutes, and took off.

She was picking out her books from Cope's shelves. Three or four stacks already stood on the long library table. She dropped a handful of volumes and ran to him, crying, "I locked my door!" and clung to him.

But when he approvingly kissed her she pulled away. "Oh Hugh we can't, not *now.* I mean now he knows. I feel too odd to, can't you see that anyway? I almost don't know who I am all over again. My darling I woke up so early, it was hardly sunrise even, and I lay there saying to myself, out loud, over and over, I could hardly believe it, 'I'm not Cope's wife anymore, I'm not Coplestone Colville's *wife!* I'm Hugh Tatnall's faithful mistress, is who I am!'

I felt terribly light and free, I felt like dancing! I got up and dressed and crept out of the house and walked and walked in that cool early-dawn light, just feeling *new*. Then I began to feel shy—my darling love, almost as if I'd just met you! so I came home and made break— No you must not kiss me, please Hugh not in his house, not *now*, I don't care if you do think I'm superstitious, you have to go, don't you see you must? until I'm not *here!*"

She went to a classmate's in Amherst for the night; and next afternoon Cope, with the grim gallantry of experience, drove her to her sister's in Cambridge.

So at last she was Hugh's.

But at a damn' inconvenient distance; and this at once led to nonsensical telephone dialogue.

"What are you doing, are you working? My darling I know I shouldn't interrupt you. But I long for you so! And all evening I've been imagining I'm jealous, do you think that's silly?"

He said even damn' silly.

"Are you stupid? All your students are in love with you, do you dare deny it? Some slinky little thing could *this next minute* come languishing in with her drawings!"

He said but—

"As if any of you ever say No! Have you ever said it? *Have you?*"

So after a couple of weeks of this sort of thing he said to her dammit look, the term was practically speaking over, why shouldn't he cut his last seminars short and take off with her for Portofino right away, she like to?—next week why not!

She was silent.

Mildly surprised, he said but surely it couldn't take her more than a week to pack, for God's sake, could it? Portofino—

She said, ". . . *live* with you?" in an uncertain voice.

She afraid it might lead to seduction or something?

Silence.

He said, taken aback, but what *was* this ?

". . . Everybody would know!"

But good god, he said, nobody did, right out practically in plain view, day after day on the Cape!

"Oh Hugh *of course* they'd know! People drop *in!* And all your Italian friends would— Hugh, Italy's *Italy!* And then it would all get back here!"

Was she making this hair-raising fuss, he demanded, totally baffled, about nothing more than a little *gossip?*

"... and what would come of it," she said, in a voice of tears.

And go she absolutely would not! Nor did Hugh it seems ever get a lucid reason out of her. Long afterward, once, he told me he'd had to conclude it was probably nothing but a cockeyed sense of decorum. Or of responsibility. "Or some idiotic other kind of behavior about her damn' husband's feelings—people saying 'What, his still undivorced wife living openly with a *colleague?*' and the like. Who ever knows anyhow?"

—Enchantment will for a time go on. But suppose one has happened to ask oneself toward what? . . . Often in the dusk of that summer's evenings, perhaps, Caroline would lean on the balustrade of her sister's balcony and watch the last gulls winging dully seaward down the Charles as night came on, and all her life would seem to her planless and bereft. And Hugh, like Cope, was a quarter-century older than she was.

So who can suppose he was surprised, home that winter from a leisurely visit to his London and Paris agents, at her telling him that she was, well, she was thinking of— Oh how could she make him see that really it was the best thing for them both!—she was thinking of marrying a very nice, a very *kind* Harvard ecologist, and would he perhaps, oh please, still love her enough to understand? . . .

"And by god Simon d'you know she wouldn't even spend one last consoling night of adieu with me?—*wept* when I reasoned with her!" Hugh was still complaining, months later. "Can you account for such peremptory heartlessness? As if I'd been just any goddam passing affair!"

God help us, I thought, has it never been borne in on him, with some girl or other, that these taperings-off are just a masculine ("but oh sweet not really a *sensible* . . .") romanticism. But all I said was, ah well, he'd gone to the wedding like a gent.

"What's a wedding? Tribal ceremony like any other—you drink what looks like champagne, and in decent families tastes like it too, but you're just drinking potlatch. *Yes* I went! Even behaved well, dammit—even when I kissed *my* angel in the receiving line, and found all I was given to kiss was a cheek!"

7

A resonance as of peroration in Taige's voice brought my mind back to the meetinghouse.

And sure enough,' at long oratorical last he had generalized himself to an eloquent final throwaway:

> ". . . For a little our deathbound
> delight grows high, in a little falls to the dust,
> toppled by a Heed I quail at.
>   What are we, or are not?—a shadow's phasm
> is Man,"

he intoned nobly, turned, stepped gravely back to his place on the facing benches, and sat down.

—Pindar. That Homer of the ho-hum. I glanced at Camilla: been dozing. Very practical. And at Persis—and was gratified to see she'd responded to Taige's sonorities with tears. Like a good girl: that was what I'd fetched her for, high Pindaric nonsense or not.

—Except, finally, what *is* one to say of the dead? Listing a man's qualities reduces the throbbing human animal, the everyday sociable sardonic friend, to anonymity: *tolerant generous loyal* are not the predicates of a unique being but of that universal bore Everyman. And *wise* is no better: all it signifies is having sat and amiably listened while assorted fools made up their minds aloud at you in detail.

Why defame a dead friend with the truth about him in any case! What business of Hugh's gossiping mourners, for instance, were things like that cache of libertine mementos I had come across in the palazzo in Florence?—in a locked drawer of his uncle's red-and-gold Venetian baroque secretary, a great wadded-in mass of old letters, photographs, bloc-notes, journals, a sketch or two—a midden of nameless litter that bulged up out of the drawer the moment I pulled it open, and sent the top sheets of it sailing and slithering in handfuls across the waxed red tiles of the salotto floor. In what innocence I picked the first sheaf up!

And was stunned. Could the entire drawer be this giggling record of a quarter-century of campus assignations? Amorous little notes that had been sneaked, breathless, under doors; slipped tenderly under pillows; stuffed wildly down the fronts of pajama trousers, shrieking and giddy with laughter; tucked into pockets of lovingly laundered shirts in chests of drawers. Notes signed ("à *Toi*") with what flattering sighs, with what submissive redesignings of a persona ("Schmutzling—and I found out what it means, so there!"). Signatures too of total unmaidenliness—a Pill scotch-taped on, a chastely beribboned little lock of unambiguous curls, a magenta-lipsticked *Scroomie?* squirming with archness. I love you I loff you I loave you I louve you I L*O*V*E you.

Or, for a plus-ça-change, that sentence on the letterhead of Northampton's extremely stern-minded young lady psychiatrist: "Don't be beastly to Blossom—Blossom doesn't like it beastly."

Why under heaven had of all people *Hugh* stored this hilarious gabble away? Against what conceivable ruins? What had it even to do with the fact of Hugh, as in the unmasked and lawless privacy of his mind he himself must have known himself? . . .

The drawer did, here and there, I found, hold random bits of respectable sanity. There was for example, near the top, a light-hearted postcard of Restoration adieu:

> Once on a time a nightingale
> To changes prone,
> Unconstant, fickle, whimsicall,
> (A female one) . . .
> Addio, amoreggiato!

Or again, such touches of civilized tradition as a colorphoto of a sweetly laughing Nadezhda in a sun-flooded noonday angle of the torricella terrace at Portofino, mixing a glittering salad in a blue faenze bowl, at the long table down whose top twin black-and-gold scagliola dragons coiled languidly toward the far end laid for lunch for two, the turquoise sea foaming and adazzle behind her far below, through the dark thickets of cypress and olive—che bella che indimenticabile ragazza! black hair piled high on her stylish head gleaming and glossy in the sun, cameo profile turned half toward him; sweetly laughing; sweetly indulging him with her beauty.

As Taige had said: all what long years now past and gone. . . .

—Yes; but what note of elegy could one hear in the choral echoes of that drawer as a whole? Hardly half an inch down, for instance, I came on Hugh's wriggling affectionate Rachel.

Whom I remembered with unusual disapprobation. She had a long swishing mane of blue-black hair and wore a different set of bangles each time one saw her. The moment she'd spotted Hugh she'd loved him. She had, it's true, just got herself engaged to some helpless instructor at Yale. But she loved him *too*, she explained to Hugh: he was her betrothed *husband* —would Hugh have her marry without love? She spent so much of that term in

Hugh's bed that she nearly lost her place on the Dean's List. But she didn't *actually* lose it, did she? *Well* then!

I concede that many a Smith girl might have thought this conduct on the exotic side. Or, depending on temperament, on the idealistic. But would any of them have indulged their daydreams with the sequel?—for what did Rachel do but come dancing back from her honeymoon to spend the second term as lovingly in Hugh's bed, and as assiduously, as she had spent the first.

Even Hugh was staggered. He did, for a time, try like a gent to rally his good manners and explain to her (her naked young arms round his neck) that after all one can't just— One doesn't perhaps quite so *soon* simply— He was never allowed to finish. Tears. Great mournful eyes. Heartbreak. What in God's thundering name, Hugh bayed at me, was a lifetime's devoted attention to womanly démarches, if he now found them baffling his declining years like *this!*

(I must have laughed at him for a month. *Poor* old bastard, what a shock! Why, nobody who hadn't taught at the best women's colleges would ever have *conceived* such things could happen!)

—Yet I must often myself have known some of this drawer's seraphic little simpletons and never once dreamed what visions of the burgeoning feminine soul were being denied me! My simple doting faith in women as women, I supposed, their hair-raising mélange of sense and sensibility—how my simplemindedness had sheltered me! I gave the drawer up, daunted. The angelic babble was unreadable.

The journals too I soon gave up—stupri vetus consuetudo, Sallust would have said, a resounding phrase meaning "a long practice of seduction" or "many years' habituation to delinquency," depending on your frame of mind when you translate it. There were, of course, here too, amusing exceptions. I particularly remember a note on Persis, apparently the first time she'd come to see him, about admission to his seminar:

Great wide innocent green eyes (gold & virid?) as full of wonder as if she'd just been making love while having what she was doing gently explained to her as she did it. Winterhalter's young *Princesse de Morny* at Compiègne! I see Winterhalter's point! Said to me, "Oh people are such mysteries, Mr. Tatnall, why a girl can look at the boy she's been seeing [Christ what a verb!] and just turn *cold* with not knowing what he's really like, oh how lonely and despairing it can be!"

What business had biography with any of this? For think what variations of unreality this preposterous drawer showed even me, a lifelong friend, I had mistaken for familiar fact. What scholarly nonsense, accordingly, art historians of the future could be expected to make of the contents. For aren't data data? Isn't Hugh Tatnall himself the unimpeachable final factual word on Hugh Tatnall? *Poor* Hugh!—guggenheim'd and transmuted, the minutiae of his misconduct sorted and reassembled to make sense, the whole random picaresco of his loves scrupulously fitted into whatever the psychaesthetics in fashion held his canvases to mean, Hugh would rise from the dead a learned Project, rational, exhaustive, fact-packed, and unrecognizable. And undefended.

I burned the lot, except for the picture of Nadezhda.

—But if my bonfire had saved Hugh from the indignities of future speculation, still how account for his keeping such stuff in the first place? Notes and reminders for Casanovan memoirs struck me as out of character. Incidental detail for a formal autobiography was likelier, to be worked up perhaps as ironic running commentary on the follies he had seen and lived through and put up with: a kind of memento sapere. Or was it nothing but his casualness?—and the stuff had simply so little importance for him that he'd never so much as got around to deciding what to do with it. That was in character, certainly. But then also in character, it occurred to me, would have been a memento sapere sardonically addressed to himself ("a little common *sense* next time for once goddammit! . . .")—for the offhand follies he let himself in for were sometimes as plain to him as they were to me.

His affair, for example, with that mocking young daimon Maura Mac a'Bhoghainn: almost anybody would have known better on sight. Young women writers can be pure hazard; and to make it worse, this one was as talented as she was dangerous. The college thought her perhaps an even more gifted undergraduate poet than Plath had been. And she was more precocious: not only had her first volume of poems come out when she was still a sophomore, but the Eastern literary establishment had reviewed it with respectful discursiveness. It was a collection of some forty flaunting and tumescent lyrics entitled *Triskelion*, a Celtic symbol with a Greek name but no language needed to make the point, the three legs being self-translating. Several individual poems had titles on the same principle, and if "Trismyriakis" isn't in *Liddell and Scott* its meaning "30,000 times" is clear enough, times what not having to be stated. I doubt if Hugh ever read any of them.

Yet what could he have been in ignorance of?—the book had been a newspaper scandal as well. A Boston reviewer had been so outraged by a short set of lyrics with the wicked title "Noctuary for an Impotent Lover" that she denounced not only them and their title, but the volume, its concept, its message, and (gifted or not) its shameless author as well; and when the academic community weighed in with intellectual defense, even the explications de texte turned into publicity. Was this young woman to be seen as Lib, anti-Lib, or just a merciless young free-lance sexist deriding our national calamity? Further, which of the six contemporary sexes was this text addressed to? (Or, perhaps, aimed at? . . .) And how should we assess the style: was it high anti-mandarin, or just vulgar?

Not Hugh's type.

Also, unluckily, he happened on her at a dangerous moment. One spring night he had gone into a late-open snack bar for a bite. It was toward midnight; the place was empty except for a fry-cook behind the counter and, at a table, the girl, a suitcase on the floor beside her. Hugh sat down and made campus conversation: what was she doing with that bag?—off weekending in the middle of the week?

Oh, weekends (she'd said, in a soft Irish-sounding drawl), who bothered about weekends, did he? Nah, she was leaving. Leaving college. Till she felt like coming back. If she did.

Classes boring her that much?

She'd answered, letting her tawny eyes rest on him as if his civilities amused her, oh, it wasn't classes, what were classes. She was just running off, was all. Did he mind?

So he'd asked what from?

Had it got to be 'from' something? she said, as if contemptuously; and then, in a voice so indolently erotic it startled him, "I'm going adrift," she said, eyes in his. "Anywhere I please, Mr. Traditional Tatnall. And any *how* . . ."

The derisiveness, not to say the easy arrogance, of any such provocation as that should have turned any man wary. The best one can say for Hugh, probably, is that he was so used to invitation that he could no longer tell when it was challenge. So in his folly he said well then if she was off come have one for the road with him, wouldn't she?—"and by god Simon the coldhearted young trollop was in my bed before her glass was more than sipped from!"

She wasn't beautiful: her face he said was "like a sleepy cat's." But never *never* had he had such a— Well, in two days he was *hooked*, and she'd stayed with him four. . . .

Then he had woken, in the first early paleness of dawn, alone.

In an instant he knew the status, the depths, of his outrage. He leaped from his forsworn bed and ran through his rooms half-deranged. She was not there; she was gone; her suitcase was gone; she was *gone*. He threw on his clothes and charged savagely out into the dawn silence of the streets groaning aloud with the affront of it. It was still barely light; as he raced in rage toward the bus station the first cool streaks of sunrise were no more than a chiaroscuro in the sky.

He was in time. The early bus had not even rolled in: the dusky slab of the loading-lot stretched out blank and deserted in the greying light, and he made out her solitary figure at the shadowy end of the ticket shed.

She was sitting on her suitcase, head leaned indolently back against the shed wall, the smoke of her cigarette curling slowly up into the still dawn air—watching him come, her long gaze coolly expecting him. He jolted to a halt before her, shaken and panting, too winded to speak; and there she sat, looking up into his face with a kind of indulgent mockery, waiting—unconcernedly waiting—for whatever his fury or his anguish would decide to say.

But at last, "Why, look at you," she drawled, in amusement, "up and all sexy so bright and early . . . ," and with an easy sweep of her body she was up and smoothly against him, palm stroking his cheek, voice of honey murmuring, "And you *missed* me? . . ." softly laughing into his distorted face. "Did he wake up alone by his great self and miss me then? oh but what a pet he was to miss her!" she crooned, all teasing caress. "And when all he wanted was so easy, so *easy*. . . ."

But stay she would not.

"I like you, *pet* pet," she murmured that night, very late, sprawled on him all anyhow in the tumbled bed, rosy tongue delicately tasting him, lips grazing and smoothing, "I like you I like you, all so yummy and pretty. And ooooooh how I love screwing. But I told you. I am *Me*. And I'm going adrift. Because I want to, see? Don't you listen? And I am not to be chased after! What d'you expect me to do, pet—*love* you or something?"

But, shortly, he had talked her into going abroad with him. He had shown her Italy. She wanted to see Tangiers. He got her an abortion in Denmark. She recuperated in Ireland. He did no painting at all.

I was appalled at him. "Didn't even paint her?" I said.

"Refused to sit."

" '*Refused*'!"

"Said she was an artist herself, not a damn' model! Wrote me a nasty poem called 'Lay-Figure' to prove it."

"But holy god," I said, "how long did this preposterous— Her family think she was here still?"

How'd *he* know what story the unfeeling young slut had told them? Father was some grim Gogmagog of a Catholic-ward police captain in Boston. Used to beat her with a strap, she said. Maybe the black-avised old aurochs had a point!

I said ah well we can't all expect to limit our Boston infatuations to Brahmins. Not that tampering with the iron chastity of Celtic womanhood was an alternative I'd have thought *he*'d have hit on. But then what, after Europe? Back to Boston?

What else? He'd got her an apartment.

He'd *set up* a poetess?!—like a showgirl for God's sake?

Did *I* classify what I took to bed sociologically? And anyhow, he'd snarled, trollop or not, for months she's certainly been *his* kind of bedfellow, and he hers. Even when, presently, she'd now and then put a visit off, weekends, her excuses had been reasonable enough: even at a last minute, reasonable. That soft voice over the phone was an illusion of reality. And if he didn't paint her, what of it?

All this I'd known about, and thought pretty poorly of, for half the semester. But curae est sua cuique voluptas—you *see* to what you fancy, and what did I know about poetesses anyway. Maybe in bed they're not so scary. Possibly he even knew what he was doing. Or, with this one, was in luck. God behaving as He sees fit to, anything is possible.

But unluckily luck runs out. It happened an autumn evening a cool young houri of a sophomore in my Ancient Greek Religions course had asked to come consult me about her term paper. But she had been drooping her unmaidenly eyelids at me for a month, so I concluded that her demure "Would it be all right if I came round *after* dinner, Professor Shipley?" was a ladylike fair warning, and I was to make up my mind. But we had no more than finished the ritual discussion of her paper ("Orphism at Eion-on-Strymon"—not that anyone knows anything much about Orphism anywhere else either), and I was admiringly watching her work her way along the transitional sequences, when there came a buffet of a knock on my door and in stomped Hugh, almost before my young huntress could stifle a shriek and spring away.

Hugh lifted his eyebrows at us, murmured something about

consultations at *this* hour, what next what next, was my brandy still in the kitchen? and stalked pointedly past.

So the girl had to go. Though at the door she turned for a sultry moment, poised hand on knob, eyes saying what she thought of my incompetent hospitality, then with a deadly flash toward the kitchen and an "It's-been-awfully-helpful-Professor-Shipley-you-were-terribly-kind!" she was gone.

Hugh came strolling back in, asking where in fact *was* my good brandy kept goddammit anyway!

I said it had never been in the kitchen in the first place; was in the tantalus; always was always had been; and whose tottering virtue had he thought he was preserving, hers or mine?

Then I saw he was seething.

And what a story: He and his Mac a'Bhoghainn had had a weekend feast planned. He'd got a couple of twenty-ounce Maine lobsters, for an homard Delmonico. She was to have port and cream in, and a Meursault. All arranged. As often before. Except that, this time, she and her flouting subconscious had miscalculated the day.

His key therefore had opened her door onto a disarray, a locker-room squalor, beyond civilized sanity. The apartment looked west, and now, through the living-room windows he faced, the last sunset light fell in great fading bars of ocher and cadmium red across a coffee table slopped with the leavings of a lovers' breakfast. Detail by detail his eye took the sleazy still life in, his minutely concentrated painter's eye—the smeared grey-whites of the plates, the highlights in the dull-umber dregs of a coffee cup, the glint of a gutted sardine tin, a yellow sludge of lipsticked butter on a gob of toast. A bath towel, still damp, hung limp down the back of a chair; another lay in a wad on the floor by the sofa.

The slattern anarchy of the kitchen was worse: what looked like half a week's unwashed dishes stood in the motionless scum of the sink. He was stupefied.

Sack of lobsters dangling from his fingers, he went into the bedroom. "And *there* by god," he burst out at me, "I saw the psychopathic disorder of her for what it is!"—the disheveled bed, stained pillows all anyhow, a torn slip in a silky heap at the bed's foot with a pair of dirty socks, half a dozen empty beer cans and a rosary under the table de chevet—"Simon goddammit I was looking into cold chaos on every side, a total attestation to *what* all these months I'd thought I was living on. . . ." He was paralyzed with apperception.

Then he gave a great laugh of rage, hurled the lobsters head-long onto that wallowed-in and unspeakable bed, and came savagely away.

—I can still hardly believe I heard such stuff. Or that it was Hugh Tatnall I was listening to, whose charged and luminous canvases of girls (he'd once blandly said) made Matisse's odalisques look as if they were "right out of a plush maison de passe in the Bourse quarter." And the problem not even a problem!—simply that a libertine had come up against a female libertine and, naturally, she'd out-libertined him. And why leave her two perfectly good lobsters?

But one cannot confront a lifelong friend with the unkindness of the self-evident. Humane diversion was what was called for, not the horrors of common sense.

—Still, I thought, whether he had come to me for disabused advice or just as a handy audience for the rhetoric of moral resentment, he was in fact suffering from what Ovid once urbanely called indignae regna puellae, "the reign of an unworthy girl," and among Ovid's detailed recipes for getting oneself out of subjection I remembered one that was as good as written for Hugh's case. "Have two girls," says Ovid. With two infatuations you're unlikely to be more than half-infatuated with either, et voilà.

So I said to Hugh (in sympathy) outrage by god I agreed it was. And unprecedented. They go sweetly to bed with us or they don't; we call the gods down to witness their perfidies or we don't have to; but *this* one he'd got hold of was both kinds at once—what was the world coming to!

All the same, what had got into *him*? Did he expect the complaisancies of an offhand carnality to last longer in a young poetess than in one of those fifty-five kilos of young finishing-school experimenters his seminar was usually full of? And, this term, was as full of as ever? Was I to believe he hadn't even looked at them? Had he gone lazy on us? What were seminars *for*? . . .

He snorted at me. I meant another girl for God's sake, and as *therapy*? What sort of heartless inattention to a girl's feelings would *that* be?—what kind of insensibility was I crediting him with? And he didn't want another girl anyhow, blast it—he wanted *this* one!

I said he dejected me. Had he got so used to just taking what was handy that he'd got so he couldn't deal with what wasn't? And the plain fact was, he wasn't going to be able to stand this cool-headed young tramp of his much longer in any case:

Entre de si beaux bras de *tels* emmerdements?

I said he was too damn' spoiled to! Women had been enchantedly building up his amour propre for him from his uncle's pets on, and it wasn't going to put up now with anything else. *Or* stick around.

So would he give over? And run over his seminar class list with —if not therapy—at least agréments in mind?

—It took less time than I expected; quite soon in fact I got him off into the night, if not convinced about the seminar, at least committed to a campus survey. From the door I called encouragingly after him not to forget Ovid's advice on lovers' diets too ("Don't eat onions or cabbage. Nibble at a bunch of rue now and then."). I went back into my rooms laughing, much pleased with myself. And with Ovid.

Well, yes. But just at that self-satisfied moment there came a light tap at my door; and never mind Ovid on the subject, there was my term-paper angel again.

Who smiled blandly into my eyes, murmuring, "I don't *like* people to interrupt me, do you either?" and stepped sweetly in.

"And anyhow I made up a French alexandrine about you while I was waiting," she went on, as if conversationally, pulling off her mittens and unbuttoning her coat. "It's sort of cute and surrealist. Do you understand French, Professor Shipley? I mean, spoken French? Anyhow, it goes

Que j'ajoute a ton Un les zéros de mon cœur—

d'you like it? I thought I could have it say toi to you in poetry, they all do," she explained smoothly, dropping her coat in sheerest ballet onto a chair. "Except oh, though, do you really mind?" she asked, suddenly all eyes at me. "Because I hope really you don't— don't maybe *you?* . . . ," and came serenely across the room toward whatever I was going to do about it.

So naturally I said, "I even understand unspoken English," and that was how, on a night of damage to a friend's enchantment, I acquired Hildegarde.

—Or Hildegarde me, depending on one's Darwinian assumptions. Though, either way, I hardly know whether to call it a blessing or a luxury—a light-headed and airily self-willed young luxury, I admit, but what an impiety toward the Bona Dea or Whoever to find fault, the coquetting body poised on its slender elbows over me, the voice delightedly teasing, "Do you love me? But do you *love* me? . . ." eyes alight with amusement at the sheer wanton inconsequence of the parody.

Though why she fancied me? Discussion was not for Hildegarde. Her eyes would turn mocking and demure, her body wriggle and flounce: no answers. Or in pure frivolous ambiguity, "Oh but think if I *loved* you!"—and that was that.

"And anyway oh ptah," she would say patronizingly. "Most of the girls don't even *start* deciding to seduce a professor till they're juniors or seniors—*so silly!* And time-wasting! You aren't pleased I'm practical?"

Among her amenities, she kept me documented in campus scandal, in particular the fatuities she amused herself by tantalizing this or that gulping colleague of mine into. Her favorite at one time was our yearning Sociology chairman. She would report, sweetly smirking, "Harry the Pad discussed frigidity this morning in lecture. Looking right *at* me. Oh how sad!"

Harry was known as "The Pad" to distinguish the area of his quantified concerns from that of a departmental colleague called Harry "d'Urgence." Not that d'Urgence was around the campus often enough to make a distinction essential: he spent much of his time rushing up and down the Eastern seaboard testifying fervently before legislative committees, or vaticinating on learned panels, in anguished support of downtrodden causes. The Pad was our *relaxed* sociologist. Or had been, until his besotment with Hildegarde.

Who would mockingly report to me, trailing light fingertips along my spine, "I'm a college-girl love-object, did you know that? Harry the Pad said so. See why you adore me?"

I said 'said so'?

"Well, he did! After class. And patted my bottom."

"Nonsense."

"Well, he wanted to!"

"Interpersonally, this was?"

"Oh you're always so old-sneery about sociology!"

"You have to be told why?—in bed with a humanist?"

"You're just kind of old-fashioned, I guess, aren't you," she said, sliding a flowerlike hand under my belly. "*Sunch a pinny!* How am I to explain you to my roommate?"

"No cachet?"

But "Why won't you turn *over?*" she complained, collapsing tenderly onto me, tongue-tip in my ear. "Because why not explicitize some parameters of interpersonal *humanist* structuring, then—don't you *want* to? Aren't you ever going to Be Lovely again?"

Hugh had once caught her eye at a faculty–student tea. "Ooooh how beautiful! And I had him talking to me a *long* time. He wanted me to model for him!" Should she add him to her Circe's stable? Maybe she ought to explore him, she said in her love-making voice, what did I think?

"Let him sink his great yellowing dentures in you?"

"Well, you're all of you always telling us we should broaden our horizons, aren't you?"

"So you're going to cuckold me with a damn' painter!"

"Going to *what?*"

"Cuckold."

"What's that?"

I said, "God help me, Hildegarde, have you survived the batterings of reality all the way into sophomore year at Smith without acquiring the basic vocabulary of your lifework? Go look it up in the Concise Oxford!"

"Way off in the study? Why should I!"

"You're at Smith College to learn!"

"What *you*'ve been teaching me? Hoh!"

"Get going, you illiterate siren."

"I don't know how you spell your stupid word anyway!"

"Get out of my bed, dammit, and look it up!"

"You're so *spoiled*," she grumbled.

She came back saying, ". . . oh," slanting her eyes at me.

"Horizon broadened?"

"Well, I knew it in French, or practically, so there!"

"Spoken French?"

She pounced down on me, spluttering laughter. And romped.

—With what cool efficiency, too, she moved in on me. I hadn't *really* decided, had I, on my summer plans? Because she herself (she explained, fingers delicately rearranging my hair—"All this greying charm: so *sexy!*") she herself was going to be on the Normandy coast. Because Mummy was renting this manoir of a cousin of hers's. Not actually *on* the coast, sort of back in the country a few kilometers: *undisturbed*. Deauville was nearish, but nobody had to socialize. Mummy said the place wasn't what it was anyway.

"And you've thought of some villa nearby for me."

"Mm."

"Where you can keep a ladylike eye on me."

"Mm."

"Some jeune fille à tout faire go with this place?"

"Well naturally I told Mummy one of my most presentable professors was looking for a summer research assistant."

"Who wouldn't mind working late?"

"But silly, a *live-in* one!"

I was brought up to be taken aback by this sort of thing. I found myself saying but had her mother—

"Well *naturally* I told her how sort of terribly stuffy and correct you were, she could have you to lunch and see for herself. Why, you were just *traditional*, I said."

One is reduced to the clichés of parental guidance.

"But what do you want me to do all summer then, Simon darling?" she asked, all innocence. "Sleep with some *boy?*"

—Years, since then. Other entrancements too; other échanges de deux fantaisies. Other illusions. Yet Hildegarde still seems to me, the distortions of time and tenderness aside, an irreproachable demonstration of what the Bona Dea presumably has in view; and if there is always folly to offset, I should argue we offset it with attachment. Nor do the pruderies of Freudian explanation explain. Freud has his theological uses; but the straightforwardnesses of love were not his specialty, and his experience was with those who had not found love humane.

By Hildegarde's senior year, at any rate, that lighthearted Norman summer had little by little become a ménage, and on the glowing final June morning of her graduation our eyes silently said so to each other across the formal distance that lay between us, I in the robed and solemn ranks of the faculty on the rostrum, she in her alphabetical place among her classmates out below. Afterwards, too, I walked back to my rooms thinking how empty now, how silent, I might for a good time feel they had become. I even found myself remembering a mulatto lament that Malraux had been moved by in the Caribbean—

> Doudou à moi elle est partie
> Hélas hélas c'est pour toujours.

For how primitive my desolation!—and for how many hundreds of irrecoverable dawns by then! the last sleepy lovemaking before she'd leave so long-familiar, so wedded, a ritual by now that even on this final morning we had hardly behaved as if, this time, it was farewell.

Nor was it quite. I heard a car roll up to my curb, and she sprang out and was up my walk and in, cool and elegant in a summer-linen suit I'd never seen, lightly announcing, "Well I have to just *race*, Daddy's out there fuming as it is!"

I managed to say but I thought we'd decided—

"*Yes I know*—only is that any reason I can't come say good-bye to you with clothes on for once?"

But at that flippant pretext, her gaze—helplessly—flickered for an instant past me to the open bedroom door, and through it to the bed, a pillow still dented where she'd left it in the cool quiet of dawn so few hours before, and when her eyes came back to mine they were stricken.

I could think of nothing to say. What was there to meet that look of wordless woe that wouldn't sound like the valediction it had to be? I started an assuaging—

"I *know!*" she said fiercely. "I saw you looking at me. At Commencement. I looked at you too, oh I never took my eyes off you. Oh Simon suppose there isn't ever going to be anybody, in all my life ever again, like you. . . ."

Too much to hope for perhaps I should have answered; something light and false like that; something faithless-hearted for us both. Something practical, even—simple et sensé comme au grand jour. But after three years like those we had lived, how?

She said shakily, "Are you going to be sad?"

"Both of us are."

"You're not helping."

"Helping doesn't help."

In a soft wail she said, "I never thought it was going to feel like this. My darling I'm *in mourning* for you! And oh Simon I don't even dare kiss you, I'll have to make conversation with Daddy all the way home, and if I—if you—"

She choked. But then she lifted her hand, kissed the tips of her fingers, and touched them miserably to my lips. "So there, anyhow!" she whispered. Then one last blinding, endless look, and she'd whirled on her heels, gasping, and was gone.

—It was not till the end of summer that I found, in the drawer of the table de chevet, a ring I had given her three years before. It lay on a scribbled note:

Ne peints pas sur ton cœur nos images d'adieu.

Very stylized: ended with an alexandrine, as begun.

8

A stir at my side. Camilla was looking at her watch.

She was right: the hour must be nearly up. The sober overseers on the facing benches would soberly rise, shake hands with each other and with Taige, and soberly end it; and what were any of us likely to say the solemn ritual of our forgathering had done to lift the heaviness of mortality from any heart? Whose heart could I assume was heavy anyhow, except my own? The rhetoric of Taige's euphemisms had its splendors and its uses, but, here, every canting colleague had known what was not being said about what was being said.

Memories I suppose there were. I had had one or two letters about Hugh's death that seemed to be trying to say so. But only a note from Nadezhda, sent from Paris the week he died, had said it as I'd have thought it might decently have been said by many more:

I went to St. Sulpice and lit a candle for him. Not to pull him out of Hell or indulge him into another life, but to smell the burning wick, and see the flicker in the cup.

And to think it had been Nadezhda, of all his girls (he'd told me, months afterward), who had first made him feel *old*.

—I remember I was biking across campus one June morning, the first time I saw her. I had been away, on a sabbatical. I heard myself hailed, and there was Hugh with this marvel of a girl— where on God's bagnio of an earth, I thought as I wheeled across to them, does the undeserving bastard *find* this young-goddess loveliness, these marvels? Her black hair shone in the sun, twirled up into a lustrous topknot à l'italienne, the lacy patterns of sun and leaf-shadow came and went across her face like veils of summer light as we stood there, her bare arm through his, her shoulder lightly against him, her dark eyes indulgently on his face as he talked, or on mine, with all the young wariness of beauty, as I answered. She let Hugh and me talk, learning I suppose how we were with each other, the climate and the shared landscapes of our friendship: she had heard from Hugh what I was like, but what was I *like*? . . . I remember saying to them finally come along have some coffee, thinking tolerantly enough-of-this-lovemaking-let's-get-to-the-table, for in fact they looked as if they hadn't been out of bed a decent quarter-hour.

I can't say I ever really worked out the aesthetics of their affair entirely. Nadezhda was cool, elegant, exotic, and perfectly serene. Her serenity had moreover a kind of foreign poise, her family having been some sort of White Russian exiles. The contrast with Hugh's customary operations was an anomaly I couldn't let pass.

"There been some mutation in your charm while I was away?" I asked him. "Grown-*up* girls go for you now?"

A grunt.

"I mean what are you doing with a girl like this one!"

"This an incivility, or felicitation? Kept her from the usual follies, haven't I?"

"You're not a folly?"

He said sarcastically, "Compared to what?"—though for that matter I hardly thought, then, that she knew why she'd acquired him either. I remember saying to her, "What on earth got into as cool an exotic head as yours anyhow!"

". . . Exotic thoughts, perhaps?"

"You mean a whim?"

"What a word, Shipley dear!"

"Want me to call it just a ladylike horsing-around?"

"Oh *poor* man," she mocked, patting my cheek, "haven't you ever had anything but Anglo-Saxon girls?"

Though the explanation, I concluded as I came to know her better, was her sense of her own mise en scène. "Does one have to be 'in love'?" she said to me. "Why not just charmed, or enchanted? Parts of me do behave as if they ought to feel frightened, and I think 'Where am I going, and why?' But then—someone's impossibly sweet, and I can't resist. It was a summer romance, and I just stepped into the story."

(And gently expunged a brief earlier enchantedness as she did so. This was a visiting poet, the spring before, who had given three lectures on *Paradise Lost*, and charmed her; she had spent the Easter weekend with him at an old farm the college used as a guest house. That autumn, to lay the ghost, she had taken Hugh there, picnicking. No one was there; the place lay deserted in the sun of early afternoon. They walked ritually around the house, peering in at the blank windows; she described the layout, the kitchen, the fireplaces in the bedrooms upstairs. They poked about in the barn; she indulged him and made love with him in the haymow. It was an exorcism: when, later, they walked in the woods behind, she wept a little, standing in his arms. "Once or twice I glimpsed my other self, the one who'd been there at Easter," she wrote to him later. "But she and I had nothing to exchange. I cried, there in the autumn beauty of the woods, because I didn't feel what I thought perhaps I should. But how easy to share the beauty with you!—and return to a room with *you*, not to Milton's prosody and him. . . .")

—That it should have been *this* girl who caused Hugh's first grim disquiet at the prospect of age could be thought a piece of Bona Dea pleasantry.

It had happened one morning early in their affair. She was in his dressing room, in bra and bikini, doing her hair up into its gleaming topknot in the gilded baroque scrolling of his glass. He was still lounging lazily in their bed, in simple pleasure watching the ballet of her through the open door; and suddenly, in the glass, she caught him gazing.

For an inscrutable moment her eyes held his. Then she made a mouth at him, as if in sweet derision at anything so wanting in savoir-vivre as that kind of stare. ("I suppose I did look, dammit, like some yokel gawking from a hedgerow," he admitted, "though by god what was I doing but gaze in pure aesthetic delight—a sort of awe, Simon!—at the whole sleek flaunting beauty of her!") She finished doing her hair; then, with another moue at him, did her mouth; then her eyelids, and put in her earrings; and finally she slipped into her dressing gown and came in by the bed. She stood there for a moment, looking down at him with indulgence. Then, "How nice to be new," she said gently, and twirled off to make their breakfast.

"And I went in to shave," he told me. "And in the glass— Are you going to understand what I mean, Simon?—in that damn' glass I *saw* my old face!"

He was thunderstruck. One's face does not change: one sees it as a continuum. But not *that* morning—that morning he had seen the young face of beauty in a glass where now the face he saw was his own, and the face it mirrored he saw had aged by more than thirty years.

"—the thirty years there were between us, d'you understand what it is I'm trying to express?" he cried at me. "I'd never seen her face in *my* glass—never seen her face *like that*—and then, a moment or so after, this withering one of my own! . . ."

—I felt badly for him over this outburst. No doubt man's private pastime is feeling sorry for himself; but hadn't Hugh been through this sort of experience without a pang often before? He had even been so touched by one girl's mournful "Oh if only you were just *ten* years younger . . ." that its solemn absurdity never struck him. But this time, with Nadezhda—and in bafflement perhaps more than in dismay—he had somehow seen the ghost intervene. This may be what ghosts are for: mortal instruction is traditionally their métier. But here, the looming briefness of mortality, its unfactorable elements compounding the predicament of man, had risen up as if before his eyes, deadly and undeniable, and the consolations of philosophy were wanting.

He of course recovered. But it was not long afterward that he painted the oddly inscrutable self-portrait now in the library collection at Princeton, and on the back of it lettered, with a fine brush, a sardonic epigram:

> Gristle and bone, too leathery now to please,
> Here th' aging painter Tatnall takes his ease—
> While the three Graces, with a teenage blush,
> Sneak out behind him tiptoe, tittering *Hush*. . . .

—And now I thought too of what only that morning, from Persis, I had learned about his last months, in Italy.

I had fetched her to the funeral from her departmental supervisor's, a languid blue-eyed Norwegian sculptress who had a studio in the country beyond Middlefield, an ancient farm now long abandoned and overgrown, where she worked on weekends. She had taken Persis with her, possibly for a report on her research in Italy, possibly (with Hugh in mind) from curiosity.

No one was in sight when I drove in. A woods road, ruts already deep in the soft dust of summer, led in from the highway past a decaying barn to a Bauhaus-rustic pavilion squatting dogmatically in the sun beyond. I went up and banged at the knocker. There was a scuttering of feet inside, the door leaped open, and there, a solemn little golden dream in studious horn-rims and tousled pajamas, and instantly aghast at me, stood Persis.

She uttered a squeak of stricken decorum, whipping off her glasses and desperately smoothing her hair.

"Oh Professor Shipley oh how *awful*, is it already—oh *dear!*" she quavered, in loveliest dismay. "I didn't somehow expect you'd be so—I didn't realize the *time!* and to find me— OH DEAR!" she wailed, scuttling off ahead of me into a wide functionally bleak living room. "I'll be ready in five *minutes*, Professor Shipley, if you'll just— My adviser's not— She went to— *Honestly* only five minutes, Professor!" and fled off into some farther depths of the house.

She then immediately came darting back in.

"Oh while you're waiting would you perhaps like—I mean maybe you knew there was this scholarly article on those sketches Hugh did of all those Roman ruins in Asia Minor, it tried to prove he was parodying Piranesi stylistically?—so I mean while I'm making you *wait* in this awful way," she dithered, scudding across to a trestle table at the far end of the room, where she began scrabbling furiously in the sprawl of papers. "It's called 'Hugh Tatnall: The Rhetoric of Inattention,' I can't imagine why, it's not about literature at all, oh where *is* the thing!" she babbled, loose papers flying. "Anyway this professor who wrote it just doesn't know *anything* about how Hugh worked, Professor Shipley, and why he picked on Piranesi of *all* poss— Oh here it is!" she cried blissfully. "I mean it's not a *real* research project for me, it's just about this one series of Hugh's sketches and I still have to check years of bibliography, he did them way back in 1940, I wasn't even born! But this morning I've been working and I've *proved* how utterly this professor's interpretation— *Would* you like to look at what I've done?" she murmured, eyes like great stars at me. "While I dress? Would you I mean really, because I won't be two minutes if you would"—thrust her discoveries at me with a warm little hand, and was gone again.

The top sheet seemed to be some sort of mistake: it was blank except for a mimeographed

7. "The progression from a realistic to a symbolic mode is recapitulated on a level of consciousness where the mode in which meaning is created becomes itself a special part of the meaning."—Discuss, with reference to any *two* decades since 1900.

Ah, well, English departments go down flags flying. I turned the sheet over, and politely began to read.

The phone rang.

"What are you doing?"

I said, " 'Doing'?"

"Sweetie you haven't rung me up for half an hour!"

"I was supposed to?"

"Well but by *this* time, goodness, shouldn't you have got started back with her?"

"She'll be dressed any minute."

" '*Be* dressed'?"

"She had a learned morning. Did a research paper."

"*Naked?*"

"Or whatever it is girls don't wear when they don't wear it."

"But sweetie the morning of Hugh's *funeral?*"

"Smith girls are serious-minded. We inculcate it. This one's just more inculcated than you're used to."

"What are you talking about?"

"Anyway she's been engaged to a Yale boy all year—serious-mindedness itself."

"Engaged when she was with *Hugh?*"

"Total fidelity. Said to me in Florence, 'Why, Professor Shipley, I write to him every day.'"

The phone was speechless.

So I said, "You don't realize the hair-raising conduct you can confront us with. Not that I understand it either. Merely that with each one of you my ignorance is enriched with additional incomprehensions."

A faintly smiling silence. Then she said, "You tell us you love us and we tell you we love you and really it's a darling metaphor. Or good manners. What one's taught to say. And taught one feels. But *in love* must be a madness."

Silence again. I was still decoding when she went on from whatever it was, "Sweet Simon this *won't* last."

"That make it any the less an enchantment?"

"So you do know that."

"If you'd thought I didn't it wouldn't have happened."

"And you're trying to keep my resistance melted by reminding me that it did?"

"Yes."

"How lucky nothing's so simple as you like to make it sound," she said sweetly, and hung up; and I went back to Persis's research.

The child took more than her two minutes. Or than her earlier five. But the eventual result was a properly seductive production, eyes demure, lips murmuring their penitence, and all aimed at me, so I said how admirably entertained her paper had kept me.

"Oh *do* you like it, Professor Shipley?" she cried, instantly beaming.

I said why on earth not?—if she was as hard-working as this she'd graduate next year with a magna. And obligingly added, nothing against being smart as well as beautiful, so suddenly there she was all dimples at me.

Priorities are however priorities. I said did she want to gather up these papers of hers? because we ought to be starting for the meetinghouse—and, by the way, didn't she still have some sketches of Hugh's too?

A stricken silence.

I said, trying to sound kindly or whatever, I meant that series she'd been the model for.

She looked at me in misery, swallowing.

"Because you do have them, don't you," I said.

"Oh how can I make you understand!" she cried, wretchedly. "I didn't take them to *have*, Professor Shipley, I mean like keepsakes, I only took them to protect his— He was a *wonderful* painter, everything he did had always— But *these* were only some very preliminary sketches for a madonna, I mean just sort of *parts* of me, like my, well, my legs in a lot of different trial poses, and my b-bosom, and the *trouble* was, Professor Shipley, that when I tried to find out why he was planning a *nude* madonna he just laughed at me! Till I was in tears! I felt like, well, you know all those girls of Cellini's in his autobiography?—why, except for that Caterina in Paris, when he was working for François I, Cellini doesn't even mention their names! And they'd *had babies* by him! And then one night we made love twice, and again in the morning, and he started the real composition—and it was the next day that Francesca killed him. And all that was left were *pieces* of me. And then you arrived and I—I— Well, I hid the sketches and everything from you because *all* they would do was mock his reputation," she sniffled. "I don't mean I'm a critic or anything but I couldn't bear to have people see them and *find out* how Hugh— Oh, he was so *valuable*, Professor Shipley, oh *do* you see what I mean about it all?" she choked, and by this time she naturally turned out to be more or less in my arms.

So then she wept there briefly.

But in due course we dried her tears; she scudded off to do her face over; we collected her suitcases; she scribbled a note to her adviser; we proceeded to the car; she raced back for another suitcase; we stowed it with the others in the trunk; she murmured as if in caress "Do you think I'm awful?" I said "Only in principle"; and off we went, into the warm annunciations of noon.

Presently, as we drove, she said dreamily, "Have you always had someone in love with you, Professor Shipley?"

I said hardly a question a man would have the want of punctilio and gratitude to answer No to.

"Oh it is so nice, isn't it!" she cried. "And *necessary*, when you're a girl! Otherwise you feel so discouraged."

Ah, well, I said, there were these vapors, these special declines her sex felt called upon to go into over ours. Whereas if the ordinary male didn't get his young woman after being led some outrageous dallying chase for weeks on end, heavily out of pocket perhaps too, did *he* repine?

"Oh, I *know* about Hugh's girls," she said slightingly, as if this were a reply, and went into a reverie.

After a time she said, in a brooding voice, "Sometimes, *now*, I can't decide whether I was *in* love with Profess—with Hugh, Professor Shipley. Maybe I just sort of wanted to own him. Or d'you think? Of course I had this—I suppose it was romantic, what would it be like, living with him and making love and having him wild about me, and I got him to let me sit in on his senior seminar and then, well, there *I* was in Italy! Oh the things that happen to you are so accidental somehow, aren't they, it doesn't look as if anybody ever planned anything very much at all, does it! I don't know if it was what I'd expected, sort of. I don't mean I was disappointed, I was *living* with him, and he was wonderful, but I was just so surprised sometimes. Maybe because I've never lived like *that* with anybody, or d'you think," she said uneasily. "Because there can be this loneliness in being *with* somebody too. I mean he wanted me *there*, and he got very grim about Francesca, but did he think I was *me*—me, Persis—what I am, I mean? So how am I to know about anything!" she burst out, gazing at me with great softly accusing eyes.

And back into her reverie.

Till in fact we reached Camilla's. Who greeted me with a bland "Why, it's you! You got her clothes back on her again and *got* her here? sweetie how resourceful," and off we drove to the funeral.

9

Sur tant de portes tant de clefs
Le long des couloirs de ton âme

What mistaken conclusions was I to decide to come to here, then, about my lifelong friend and fellowman, before these interminable Quakers called it an hour? What misgaugings or misjudgings or misinterpretations? What simple oversights? What imaginary truths altogether?

A classicist is trained to suspect (and a few of us do) that much of what we know is misinformation, and much of what isn't is

beyond sensible explanation anyhow. If an archaeologist finds
Linear B scribblings on, say, fragments of an Attic black-figure
amphora, what conclusions is he to arrive at? — rewrite the complete chronology of the ancient Ægean still a twentieth time? Suppose Hugh an archaeological scavo, then: how am I to account for
such total unexpectednesses as that drawerful of mementos? No
trained classicist would maintain that I had, as the phrase is, "seen
him without illusions." He had blandly presented me with alternative illusions I could see him under instead, and the historical
'truth' was beyond even hypothesis.

And think of the assorted illusions of the world at large! The man
in the street thought of Hugh's paintings, if he thought of them at
all, as simulacra; the academic establishment saw them, with
equal absurdity, as symbols. And his behavior as metaphor. Hugh
as Hugh had vanished into a haze of myth long since. Painters I
admit are a libertine, arrogant, lawless, and singularly inarticulate
lot; they do exhibit, and without explanation, what Aragon called
"le goût du saccage." But the stereotype is delusory: any "taste for
havoc" that describes, say, Gauguin or van Gogh is obviously neither here nor there about Cézanne or Degas.

Nor did stereotypes explain even the libertine side of Hugh.
The mutual incompetences of our mating habits are immemorial,
and even the expertise of Ovid could be baffled:

Cur mihi *plus aequo* flavi placuêre capilli?

— "Why did that golden head *so immoderately* delight me ? . . ."
But only a sad sociologist would quantify Hugh's fluttering amies
de rechange as Case Studies in Ladylike Nonsense. Perhaps
Hugh's old uncle had unconsciously taught him, but he took a
pleasure in the ballet of coquetry that most men seem never to
suspect is there, the fascination of waiting for this or that sweetly
dallying girl to show you what situation, and what style, she has
imagined for handing herself over in; and whether it was in fact
this or Hugh himself they loved, the covenant had a humaneness it
would never have occurred to a simple libertine was what in fact
made the pleasure a pleasure. Often they found themselves moved
simply by how moved they were; or that nightlong in a lover's arms
they can lie entranced discussing themselves as an Episode, as an
Epiphany, in a dialogue of recited mementos, delighted with
themselves — and hence with him.

— But here now at the end, I said to myself, the secret essence
of him gone, I wish there had been someone with a less disen-

chanted, a kindlier, intelligence than Taige's or mine to have
said what was said, of a friend as much like a brother as one is
ever likely to share the intractable farrago of a lifetime with. As my
fellowman he was a fellow-marauder, but I assessed his performance with I hope a disabused impartiality, noting his methods as
I did any other male's. If, like any other male's, I sometimes found
them surprising, this was perhaps an inevitable vanity. For though
I had known him from our boyhood, one has always to remember
the Dryden—

> Farewell, too nigh me, too familiar grown,
> To think thy nature, as thine image, known.

Nor is the artist ever Man writ large. Make him over to the specifications of humanity and you have upset the ecology of creativity.
So let us unmoralize. The secret essence within is gone.

—At which point, as if I had said it aloud and been heard with
approval, the grave overseers facing the meeting rose and shook
hands with each other and with Taige: the hour was up. We rose,
and began working our several ways along the lines of ancient
benches toward the aisles and the doors.

Except that I heard a whispered "Professor Shipley?" and found
Persis looking up at me starry-eyed.

"Oh Professor Shipley," she breathed, "*would* it d'you think be
all right if I went up and told Professor Heald—I mean what he
said was *so* perfect! Could I just I mean tell him how wonderful I
thought he was? . . ."

Well, she was of age. "My guess is," I said in my kindliest tone,
"he'd be charmed."

"Oh Professor *Shipley*," she sighed to me, and was gone, as
single-mindedly straight for Taige as a bee for nectar.

"But shouldn't you have told her to write her daily letter to her
Yale boy first?" said Camilla.

I said now now, hadn't she at least a spectator's indulgence
watching the logistics of an agreeable future take shape? and
slowly we drifted on toward the doors.

On and out, in our dozens and scores, into the blandishments
of noon. An amiable learned nattering rose around us: we might,
in our groups, have been issuing from the genialities and back-
bitings of a faculty meeting, the agenda of the spirit dealt with,
minds in order, disbursed, and at ease. "And anyway," Camilla
murmured as we sauntered away, "immortality's so reassuring to
hear about—other people's especially."

But it was the low assurances of mortal things that I found my mind was on, and I said, "Are you going to be an angel of angels?"

"... and do what ?"

"Have for instance lunch with me?"

"I make you hungry too? goodness how gratifying!"

"All I thought was—"

"Or did you just mean 'lunch first'?"

"God help me," I said, "what can a man do with a woman he's out of his mind over, but offer her any excuse he can think of for doing what he helplessly hopes she'll do no matter what he says?"

"Oh sweetie are you charming me again?"

"You don't feel you know?"

"Ah Simon who are you and I to suppose it of ourselves that we *examine* what we do with our feelings? ..."

"You couldn't try giving it a try?"

"Sweet Simon," she said, sliding a gloved hand through my arm, "you can't *still* be surprised!"

So, as I recall it, I answered, "Always"—enchantment being (with luck) what it can sometimes turn out to be.

A DIFFERENCE OF DESIGN

To Laurice

. . . My Lord D. has given over variety,
and shuts himself up within my lady's arms.
—SIR GEORGE ETHEREDGE,
in Ratisbon, *19th December, 1687*

1

Was it I wonder when I turned round, there in the car, and found him gazing straight at me.

The sun in his blue eyes. This American five minutes before I had never even seen.

Blandly looking at me.

And had been looking. And in that way. At I suppose my shoulders. At the soft curls at the nape of my neck. At where I am kissed.

And, now, straight into my eyes. The sun hot on his fair hair, the car's top down in the lovely day.

With from either of us not a word. And as if, there between us, suddenly there *was* this not-a-word.

Tranced almost, the blaze of summer morning everywhere.

—Except of course I simply disavowed it, ah mon Dieu *oui*— simple and faithless as bonjour, as who hasn't to be!—anyway the warm wind of our speed was flipping and fluttering the sober stripes of his tie, so simply I murmured, "Chad is blowing us to bits d'you mind" as if that had been all, and let my eyes half smile at him for a moment, then I turned round front again, away.

Not that that helped.

We were hardly out of Versailles. All the way down into Normandy he was going to be there still.

Though heavens what if he was!

All the same I should not have let it happen.

—Though as if it mattered! Because alors bon, I am sometimes careless. And it was the suddenness of it. And the surprise, the unexpectedness. But I do as I please with them don't I always? And no matter what? For I do. I looked at Chad, the sun in his charming eyes too, and I said to myself, amused, on est lamentable.

—Still, it was careless.

I had merely turned round to say I've no idea what to him.

Nothings; the civilities one does. Chad had of course said what this Mr. Sather of his mother's was like, but what was he *like*? So this day at the manoir was to see for myself. We would pick him up in Versailles on the way.

Then I turned round. And he was gazing straight into my eyes. In silence. And as if somehow straight into *me*. I felt—I don't know how I felt! It was so utterly upsetting from what I'd turned round for, that I couldn't think what it had been I was going to say. I felt as if no man, ever in my life, had looked at me like this. And for just that one wordless moment too long I felt myself gazing back at him. As silent as he. And he knew.

—Ah, but knew what.

For in the courtyard of his hotel, five minutes before, when Chad fetched him out and across to me in the car in the haze of summer morning, what had there been to make anyone think there could be, ever, anything to 'know.'

He was a man like any other. Tall élancé easy urbane. For an American, not un-elegant. Comme un autre. Disabused-looking. A little I thought wary-looking too? A *little* greying. Really I felt nothing much about him one way or the other. And now in five minutes am I so uneasy, I said to myself, shocked, that I can't think what I could merely turn round again and say to him?

I felt I was—I could not understand *how* I felt.

It was as if he— It was as if that terribly self-assured gaze had somehow— But was I some helpless savage, tranced by the spinning of a sorcerer's wheel?

—I felt as if suddenly my neck and my shoulders lay naked. I was appalled.

He could reach out I said to myself and touch me and I could do nothing *nothing*.

—I needed *time*!

So I looked at Chad and said, "*Hé!*" mindlessly, and at least he said, "Hé yourself," the way he does. So at random I said, "Mais il est bien, ton homme," and if the man understood French, tant pis.

—I should *never* have let it happen!

We were nearly out of Versailles. I thought should I get in back then? Chad could stop. But then why shouldn't I have straight off, at the hotel?—what had changed? And he would know.

—Except Dieu du Ciel, I thought almost wildly, am I to put helplessly *up* with this? and I turned round smiling, arm along the back of the bucket seat, the leather warm on my arm in the sun, and said *poor* man I was thoughtless, I should have got in back with him at the hotel, he looked *deserted.* Still it *was* hardly an hour's run, did he know Normandy? our part of Normandy? we had this lovely domaine in the Bourgthéroulde area, a forest, wild boar and other gros gibier in quantity still, did he hunt in the States?—thinking how can I *bear* myself and this torrent of inanities on and on, under that bland gaze. . . .

But then there we were at the autoroute, and Chad was gunning his precious Jensen up into the cent-quarantes, we *were* being blown to bits, and I could shrug and smile excuses helplessly and turn front again, and slide down deep into my seat out of the wind, as if into a shield.

—There are no shields. I shut my eyes and thought in a kind of horror what have I let happen to me.

For what has there always been *there,* between me and any man, that so frightens me is not there now?—that *is* there, between a man and a woman, to be oneself behind, and safe! and I thought of Grand'mère's cool voice reminding me of *la barrière des bienséances, ma chérie*—though 'proprieties'? when even thinking about what I was thinking about was 'abandoned'! And a 'barrier'? that after five minutes I can feel is no longer between? I was in total dismay—for was I to think I *wanted* to turn round as it shocked me I was in dread this unknown man was willing me to? *Wanted* to look at him and have him look at me? I could not remember that he had uttered a word. Oh or I given him a chance to! and I *heard* myself babbling! That, dissemble?—I only just stopped myself from whimpering aloud.

Suddenly Chad whooped his "Porsche suisse, taïaut!" and I opened my eyes. We shot past the thing; but the wind of our swerve snatched at my skirt—and voilà, my dress ballooned wildly up before I could hold it. Chad cried, "Hey *hey!*" in his happy voice, like a tally-ho that too, and flicked a laughing look at me, and of course we both thought—it was a phrase of ritual by now; every time, it had been, since that first time on the road to Dreux—we both heard in our private memories the *What de good word, pretty britches?* he'd called out in the delight of our new nearness then, that first time, and I had let my dress balloon as it pleased, to indulge him. And now he always said it when it happened, it was like Swann's cattléyas, only this time we of course just thought it.

Lunch, we'd been going to, that day, at Dreux; and I'd let it balloon for him, and he shot the Jensen off onto the shoulder in a crazy shrieking of brakes and scatterings of gravel and grabbed me, and kissed me and kissed me till I lost my breath being kissed and laughing at him, I thought isn't it enough mon Dieu that I've acquired of all possible savages an American, without the creature's being enthousiasmé into the bargain? Grand'mère would have disowned me!

I looked at him now through my lashes, remembering back before that; and I said to him in my mind, I was behind *you*, mon beau hobereau, the first time I found myself wondering about you. Baudouin and I had hardly known you a—ho, was it a month? yes, because it was after Easter, coming back from Venice we ran into Jock Bingham in Aix and he introduced you. Then back in Paris it was that day Baudouin drove us all out to Raizeux for lunch, and Jock and I sat in the back, and I was behind you. And I began to look at your shoulders. And the nape of your neck filled the collar of your shirt so round and white, the skin such satin my fingertips almost felt themselves touching you, ah felt what it would be like touching you, the fair hair beautifully trimmed and short, just I thought where the bend of my arm would come, wound round, smooth as the smooth hollow of my arm holding you, mind you *all* this time chattering to Jock about n'importe quoi, heavens the things I think of! But I thought them; and a dreamy part of my mind was seeing how it would be, how we would be, you were taller so with my arm there my lips would be where? against your creamy throat, the taste of you on my tongue, and I thought for the first time in so many words Am I d'you suppose going to find myself making love with this man before long? for heavens perhaps I am.

But then *this* I thought is how it happens? As light-mindedly as *this*? Tiens, and as pitilessly! Can the rules one has lived one's life by become, in the flicker of an eyelid, the mask of one's disguise instead? as without a pang one forswears what it was! I looked at Baudouin's handsome head, and without a pang I saw the salon of your flat in the Avenue Bosquet, hazy with the gold of early summer that afternoon he and I first came to tea. Jock was away. Was away, I remembered you said, often; and there in my husband's car, driving to Raizeux, I looked at the handsome column of my husband's neck, not one whit less charming mon bel américain than yours, and with a little shock I found I had begun to plan.

—Months, it had been, since then. A year nearly; and now that was how I felt this silent man was thinking about *me*. I could not understand how I knew. And if I turned round where could I look but into his eyes, and he would know I knew, I could not keep him from knowing. I felt how terribly near he was—*no* barrier, *nothing* between—he had only to stretch out his hand. I knew of course that he would not: they do not, ah *no!* Ah, but if he should?—for this man was I felt closer to me than any man had ever been or I'd thought could be, it was as if in a dream I found myself in a terrifying world which had rules I had not been told and had been forbidden to ask, and I said to myself if he touches me what *can* I do?

Nothing. No matter what, nothing.

—But to sit *still*, being touched? . . .

Yes, but to turn round, admitting it had happened?—there *was* no way to deal with it! And he had not spoken a word. He had not had to. And I said to myself, in horror, this whole day lies before me, in which there will be nothing I can do. . . .

We shot past the exit for Mantes. I shut my eyes.

—I could not go on like this.

Except I thought but am I totally out of my senses? for why should I have to 'do' anything! They enter our tastes, yes; they can enter into our feelings till not a word need they say of what they are thinking, to make us in our folly believe we know, and that it is what we want it to be. But *I*, have I not always more a disposition to appraise, say, than be tender? And is a quarter-hour of folly to have changed me?

D'accord, I was careless. Hoh, but is that a change?—how many another time too haven't I been careless! And why in any case should that be an entrée dans mes goûts, much less dans mes sentiments? I remain Me.

And voilà, all at once I *was* myself. I opened my eyes and looked at Chad, thinking how aimable to be adored, even simple-mindedly; and I said to him—as good as flippantly, I felt suddenly so gay—I said, "Tiens, maybe I like you for reasons I can add up!" laughing, and if he had no idea what I was talking about, poor sweet does he even when I know myself.

But when we leave the autoroute for Louviers, I said in my mind, I will turn round. Without a tremor.

Because this American, after all!

It was only because Chad hadn't said *this* was what he was like.

—Though of course we hadn't discussed him very much. Or very long. Or even why he was here. Just at the very end of that lovely afternoon two days ago, Chad's rooms all soft early-summer nightfall already and I was thinking I must go, I was going to

Maman's for dinner, she'd said *don't* dress ma chérie, you're coming up from the country just come straight here; but from the country I'd have allowed leeway, so I said to Chad, "You're making me late," and sat up. The room was filling with dusk, the tall windows were no more than frames for the fading day beyond, and in the depths of the pier glass I could just make out the gleam of my reflected body, silver against the shadowy room behind, I was leaning on a hand over him, looking down, 'musing' he used to call it, 'ton petit air d'en rêves' (he *is* so sweet, all he will ever need is someone to adore him) ". . . making me late," I said, "and we haven't even discussed what to do with this Sather of yours, what *is* he like?" Because the man had it seems arrived days ago. We weren't in Paris. But now we were, we couldn't *not* meet him. Or put it off.

Of course Chad said what was anybody like? fingers lazily tracing my thigh. Sather was a Wall Street type, how not? A well-turned-out perhaps-fifty. Been he thought widowed; urbane diner-out type anyway. Entirely presentable. Une personne de condition.

I said, ". . . Coureur? Comme toi?"

A chaser at *fifty?*—though of course anybody he supposed why shouldn't he?

I said, "But so *family* an errand," watching his face. "You don't think perhaps he's her lover?"

He snorted *god* no! in amusement—*his* mother with a lover? I was out of my lovely head. Sather *advised* his mother, was all, investing. In and out of the market as well as solid long-term stuff. So he was coming to what the profession called 'look into' him.

I said, "*You* an investment?—hoh!"

Ah, well, his mother was in the habit of 'retaining the services' of anybody and everybody. Meaning she ordered them formidably about. Why doesn't Chadwick come home when I tell him to? Mr. Sather, go find out! Is he gambling? Is he Entangled? "Sather's here, madame l'adorable comtesse, to rescue me from *your* lovely clutches," he finished, snickering, and tried to pull me down by him again.

I thought how silly. I tucked my toes under me and knelt up and away from him, stretching, watching my image in the pier glass arch her slim back and reach her pretty arms high in the dusk too, fluttering her hands at the tips like flowers. We yawned. "Sous mes griffes, how *really* silly," I said. "Are we to— Should we *do* something for the poor misinstructed man, to amuse? . . ."

(Even, I said to myself, pour lui plaire. And control. For why else was I trained to please?—as only, really, I suppose, my light-minded ancestresses and I have ever been trained to please.)

So we'd decided, have the man to luncheon. At the domaine. Feed him, and see.

For I thought ah mes belles aïeules how straightforward being alive must once have been, au grand siècle. Woman or man, the scenario was dans les règles and foreseen. And the rules were like the stage directions for a masque at court. 'Quand l'amour se déclare, une femme vertueuse'—the very style as good as falls into formal verse. When love speaks, a virtuous wife 'lui impose silence.'

Imagine.

And silence imposed not because the declaration has upset her, but because she has made it a principle for herself that it is upsetting. And so (logically) she resists because resist she must. . . .

Ah but the trouble can be, by resisting one can drift without knowing it into the taste for adventure that resisting adventure brings. What charm in the virtuous sentiments she's resisting with! What a high-minded romance they create to play a part in, to adore being the heroine of! And meantime the lover, asking forgiveness for having upset her, upsets her all over again with the passion of his excuses—and how natural the rules make it seem!

And one found oneself excusing his passion—for how deeply sincere it must be to overcome him like this! And how star-crossed and unhappy he sounds—and can it be only rhetoric, that no beauty on earth but one's own has caused it? We fall into a kind of wonder at how noble his sufferings are! And how like our own! And it is our virtue that has caused them!—until suddenly, hoh! we no longer have any, and all that's left us is the virtue of lamenting its loss, oh *really* what a marivaudage!

The green-and-white *Sortie Louviers 1000 M* shot past, and Chad began slowing for the turn-off. I looked at him and almost laughed. For enfin what a consolation in one's ancestresses' day too the sheer good manners of one's undying remorse les règles made possible. Even one's frailty, mon Dieu what a word, all the same they said it!—even one's 'foiblesse' was excused by the virtue of one's sad self-reproaches. In fact, I said to myself as Chad skidded us off into the exit ramp, every advantage of virtue a woman has went to the profit of her misbehavior.

And thank Heaven still does. I sat up and turned round, and let my eyes smile at this dangerous new American of mine, and I said to him, as bland as he, "See what a bad place for you France can be Mr. Sather? Chad's learned to drive like a frenetic Frenchman."

But what I thought am I doing. It is not safe. Especially it is not safe unless one *knows* whether one is throwing down a gauntlet or what Grand'mère used to call 'letting fall a lavender'd glove.'

Not that what *does* one ever do with a man but one or the other! And what help is it knowing which?

And I don't know which anyhow. . . .

—Yes, but until I do?

Should I try simply boring him? If only because mightn't it make him seem safely boring too?

I could prattle us into a polite stupor with, say, a set-piece history of the domaine. Ah but Mr. Sather (I could say) how I do adore the place, the great beech forests, the wooded rides opening on and on and on, it used to be one of the royal maisons de chasse. One of my light-minded ancestresses adored it too (I'd say)—at any rate she was it seems unusually kind to one of the Louis, was it Douze? *totally* kind and I suppose as often as necessary, goodness the things one did, anyway she got it out of his Orléans clutches. And into ours, what heaven. Commodity for commodity. Isn't 'in kind' how you say it? And, well, she *was!* Though she'd have said 'en nature' wouldn't she, how amusing. Or d'you think there's all that difference Mr. Sather. . . . Heavens how common I could make it. But I could set my teeth and do it couldn't I? 'Oh I must show you a portrait of her in the petit salon, Mr. Sather. A *lovely* commodity, one hardly blames the king.'

Aïe.

—Though of course instead of this we were gazing into each other's eyes with every just-met politeness, and disposing of the preliminaries.

A banality was a banality but had he found Paris amusing?

Amusing himself, he said he was sorry he had to say, hadn't been what he'd come for. It was only a brief mission anyway. To oblige a client.

But not, surely, evenings too?

Oh, well, evenings, he said smiling, evenings no. Evenings he'd taken advantage of a very agreeable guide-and-escort service he'd had the good luck to be put in touch with. Astonishing what you found existed, in large cities; but it seemed there were several of these agencies in Paris, with a staff of well-brought-up young French or American women who'd show you round. *Entirely* formalized and proper, need he say, but they looked after you. Where to eat, what there was to see, what to do, what not to—a sort of spiritual chaperoning generally. So, anyhow, this young woman he'd been assigned, a Mrs. Godfrey, had been very kind indeed for his evenings. Gone to the opera once with him. Gone dancing with him too, a couple of times. Couldn't have been kinder.

These people in fact looked after you very well in general. The Paris hotel for instance he'd stopped at first—she'd said how did he expect to put up with these faceless international glass slums? the Empress Eugénie had of course lived there, but that had been a *long* time ago, and, well, was what they'd done to it since to his taste? so she'd immediately moved him to this Versailles place.

And quite right—huge comfortable Edwardian bedrooms, and those enormous tubs in the baths: no comparison! Honorable kitchen too: did a splendid Sunday-lunch buffet among other things. Which he'd noticed a lot of the (by the look of them) local gentry seemed to turn up for.

I said but American young women went I'd been told into liberated rages, didn't they, if men treated them as commodities? So sad, too, somehow—when all we need do is look at you as if you were quite wonderful, murmuring *goodness!* at intervals.

—Banalités de luxe. But did he know enough my mind said to know what they were for. Years, it takes men, even to begin to try to see what we are like. Or as much as begin—so stupid. Still, this man had had time. Chad said he was fifty. Ah, and the kind of man he was anyway! I did not see how he could not be what I felt like this he was.

Or how any woman could not feel he was! And I thought and each of us in her time thinking, la mort dans l'âme, how many others must have felt as we, and against the hovering sweetness of his memories of them the very blandness of his gaze told us we were helpless—even, among so many so like us, were ourselves hardly a difference, so stricken, his power over us itself our dismay. For how strange if that were why I could still feel how frightening that endless stopping of time had been when I turned round. Or was it the panic of *being* frightened? for how strange.

Simply perhaps it is like that epigram of was it Madame de La Fayette's? that if a man has been loved often enough it is hard to imagine his not knowing it when he is loved the next time too.

For this man must.

—Except that it is a longer word than love.

Which Heaven spare me.

For ah it is like one's girlhood midnights again, writing à la chandelle a letter that even then one knows one can never send. *I am awake. Because of You. I know I should not tell you it is because of you. And oh I should not write it. But I am not sleeping. I am feeling. And I want— There is a part of me I want—*a letter perhaps it will be deepest dawn before one shreds it into a thousand tiny squares. But ah, one writes it; and *does* this man I thought know enough to accept it that banalities 'impose silence' as they should? Or does he know they do, but knows also what he is, and will not obey.

And need not, because I know he need not.

—Suddenly I could not stand it.

And I said to myself I *will* not! Let Chad take over the amenities! We're nearly at Elbeuf aren't we?—and in ten kilometers the lodge gates? Un petit quart d'heure? Let Chad take over the entertainment of this monsieur de rencontre!

Have I to go on trapped à deux like this as if there were no one else on earth?

The very look of it a symbol! . . .

C'en était *assez!*—and in the middle of a phrase I simply turned round front again. In the middle of I didn't care what! *Away!*

I felt—I did not know *how* I felt!

—Or even, now, how I seemed to feel about Chad either, and I looked at him in dismay. At his profile, at the delicious corner of his mouth, the sun on his hair, the sun on his throat. His long fingers on the wheel. As if I had expected to find him somehow changed.

For did he look the same? but then of course I saw he did, and I thought oh how absurd anyway, how could I see him as different when how could he be, heavens—he is an era in the private history of *Moi, Fabienne,* is all, even if only an early one, que sais-je. Though if that was all, how at this era I should know it I did not see. But the definition amused me, and I said to him, "Tu as un air plus mérovingien que je ne t'en ai jamais vu!" and he could take it as he liked. But by this time we had got through the market-day noon traffic of Elbeuf and out onto the Pont Audemer road beyond, and I was myself again anyhow.

Then in no time we were there, as so many thousands of times I had been before, the huge old marronniers in flower still all the long avenue in to the lodge gates from the voie, the sun-flecked shade of the allée a tessellation of fallen petals, pink and cream, then the arched grilles of the gateway and Emile's Maryse waddling out of the lodge to kiss my hand and leer at ce beau Monsieur Newman again and swing the tall gates open, then the green shadows of the beeches through the parc, and then suddenly out into the white glare of the courtyard at last, the blaze of noon hot on the cobbles and the sun-drenched ancient stone of the manoir glittering up and up like a bastion for my refuge, and I was out of the car and up the perron and *in*, set free, ah how sweet a house, I was so light-minded and gay again that I thought ah zut why *not* show him her portrait, cette aïeule who so gentiment earned all this for me, and if he thinks I look like her, alors bon, I do. . . .

And ah, moving about now I could look at him, no longer trapped à deux. I could *see* what it was that had happened. Or at least I said to myself I can look at him and look away from him and look back at him again as I please, and either way it will mean nothing at all, *nothing*.

So, then, presently, it was so green and lovely on the garden front I had Emile lay the table for luncheon out at the pavilion, in the little columned Roman atrium some grand-père or other had had built before it, the sun filtering down over us through the new leaves into wavering mosaics and patterns of light on the paving; and as we sat down the brilliance of early afternoon lay on the lawns, and down and away to the pièce d'eau and the water stair and the carp pools at the woods' edge beyond, spilling the glint of the stream into the dark vanishing aisles of the beeches at last, where the forest closes in around again.

And at least mon trouble . . . wasn't it lessening?

For what was there to think I must 'decide,' here between them in this heavenly day? mon beau hobereau d'amant and my— this— Oh *really* how could a man like this one have undertaken any such opéra bouffe of a mission with a straight face! What possible description, even, was he expected to present the situation to me with—'sous vos adorables griffes, madame'?

But then instantly I thought, and it was like a small cold hand closing about my heart, But *is* he perhaps as blandly cynical as that, as *heartless*? Like a gleaming mirror the glass of the tabletop threw its patterns of leaf-shadow like veils of silver light up into his face, into his eyes, he was talking to Chad smiling, winkings of sun in the green gold of his wine reflected up too, and I looked at him and thought is it happening to me all over again, that dismay? For what am I to do, seeing him again—as how am I not to, if I am why he has come. Chad it is of course he was to talk to. But if he should try to see me too? Even if merely to repay this déjeuner. For if then I am alone with him, eyes in his again across a restaurant table? Or there beside him on a banquette, a few mere centimeters away? . . .

He was telling Chad of a visit he'd made to the Normandy battlefields. Filial piety, he said amiably: his father had been wounded there, at a village called Saint-Sauveur-le-Vicomte. Name of the place had so amused his sergeant, theologically, that the fellow hadn't kept his eye on a German patrol. He'd visited Omaha Beach too, a wild day of scudding cloud and onshore gale, the Channel a chaos of toppling combers; spume and spindrift flying. He had left his car by the voie and slogged across, and come out through the dunes into the loneliness of the empty sands. Mile after mile, and no one. And nothing, only the endless thunder of the Atlantic tumbling and bursting on those beaches of desolation, and the bones of German blockhouses like great beasts stranded there, gaping, the beach-grass growing in their doorways. He had been absolutely alone, the salt spray stinging his face and eyes. He had *felt* absolutely alone. What had it been like there, that morning a lifetime ago. Gone differently, he supposed, from *his* war. Which had been he said Korea.

—Does he mean I thought la Corée?—with a shock, for what American war was this? Are there wars one doesn't hear of—or was this just before I was born. For how old must he have been? Though yes, if he was twenty in that war and fifty as Chad said now. Though *twenty?*—for ah what had he been like, young. *Then* would I have— Could a boy of twenty, even he, have so totally— But what if I had, and then he had been killed there. . . .

But the *death* of this man? If it were now? I looked at him through my lashes, and then at Chad, the sun-spattered shadows of summer veiling his blue eyes too; and it was not the difference of age between them but oh I thought how could anything be so not the same.

And I am not claimed.

—Though have I been ever. Or wanted to be.

And from always. Think how I used to sit, those endless dripping afternoons here at the manoir the summer I was twelve, sit at the portes-fenêtres onto the terrasse from the salon, dreaming out in a perfect little fillette fume at the rain coming down in long weightless lines across the mist of the deserted lawns. Or it would clear, and I would trail sulking through the wet green carpets of fern beyond the carp pools in the dusk, and watch the rimless violet of evening darken and fade away over the crown of the forest, *wild* that it was still not time for me to try my eyes on a man and see what would happen.

And so faithful to myself then too, ah mon Dieu what a little savage I was!—so myself already that I even knew I'd never have a passion for whatever lover I'd have fancied without having one too for a rival I'd have picked for him—if for no reason but to find out how it was, two of them! And what it would turn out they were like, to have, differently. And what I should find out about their lovely differences, like that. And oh miracle after miracle after miracle of possible chances!

Yes, and in what sense they would be my *property*. . . .

But Dieu merci never I theirs!

And of course what *amusements*, for instance whether whoever it turned out to be would be like that husband I'd read about in was it de Gramont? who 'wasn't jealous but he always managed to be inconvenient,' and how did it happen if both husband and lover happened to be both.

—Only then, hoh, it turned out to be mon beau Baudouin, who is neither.

And from the first, was neither. Like me. Like all of us. I remember how he and I, at the bal de fiançailles—it *was* a heavenly night, deep country summer everywhere, the manoir like a great jewel-box of light, the whole front and the forecourt lit from high overhead in the dark air by the enormous porte-flambeaux they'd used for balls in Maman's day, and from the salon wing the marquee was like a great glowing ballroom built out into the night, its tenting lined with a deep green toile, that somber First Empire green, swagged and garlanded along the cornices with white, and the white of the fluted pilasters at the piers made whiter still by the soft pallor of the candles in the pier sconces, and down from along the high peaks of the tent the sweep of three great chandeliers, the facetted glitter of their lusters shattering light into thousands of disintegrating particles as it fled endlessly away.

And out on the gardens side of the salon wing the terrasse too was lit by a line of porte-flambeaux, their great guttering torches breathing a kind of luminous dusk down over everything; and we had the buffet there, in the warm night, the music drifting out into it from the marquee, muffled and sweet with distance, and coming through the grand salon between too.

And I remember how Baudouin and I stood with our parents at the salon doorway and thought cars would *never* stop arriving and arriving or we be free from receiving, it must have been two hours nearly we stood like good children there, for his families and mine, cousins and connections and friends, for generations some of them from back forever, those family worlds that had known us from childhood (the same, many of them) and from our pays around us and from Paris and the Midi, from London too, some of them; and my friends and Baudouin's, and a few of Baudouin's from back in his Charterhouse days—oh a company so long known, so kindly, so like us, yes and so timeless that somehow the evening itself might have been a kind of endless pause outside the accident of time, those hours like an island out of all our assembled pasts, an island so enchanted that we should never need to visit it again, and jusqu'à pas d'heure I danced and danced.

Oh, and the first cool pallors of summer dawn were there before it came to an end, the parc slowly filling with silver light, the last coils of mist seeping and sifting back like retreating ghosts into the dusk of the woods behind. The porte-flambeaux in the forecourt were guttering out one by one, high in the greying air, as the last happy babbles of adieux were being chanted, and then the echoes of the last departing cars died one after another in the distance away, and we were alone with the wakening rooks in the enormous stillness.

Over the terrasse the torches had burnt out too, when at last Baudouin and I kissed our parents good night, and went out for a last glass of champagne there. The tiles were glistening with dew, the first white-gold shafts of sunrise were just striking through the crowns of the great beeches behind the pavilion and up across the lawns into our eyes. It must have been almost four. I thought how many hour-after-hour men d'you suppose I've danced with, and Baudouin began humming that waltz from *Faust* and there I was in his arms again, drowsily turning and turning in the dew, alone the two of us turning in the wide world, goodness I was half asleep, my head on his shoulder, his voice in my ear sounding sleepy-happy too, and I thought what a darling, on a bien fait, and he bent his head and kissed under my ear, and down into the hollow of my shoulder and I heard myself murmuring, "Tu vas me séduire?" So of course he snickered, "Serviable!" that joke from our childhood, and I'd have snickered too except I was yawning; but I thought ah but the instant my head touched his pillow I'd be asleep, and I said, "Mais au lit, tu sais . . . ," yawning again, and he began to laugh at me, and then I was laughing too, it was hopeless, it was too sweet to be anything but hopeless, and finally we just took the last champagne in, to the kitchen, and I suppose what we had was breakfast.

—Oui, on a bien fait. And I know as much about him by now as I expect I ever shall. Or as much as one decently should. Or, really, want to—am I for instance to fuss guessing whether he has someone as I have Chad, un amour rangé of his? Or bother whether now and then he even has what Jock Bingham says they called 'bespoke sex' at the university? *what* a thing to waste curiosity on.

Not that I don't I suppose wonder whether Baudouin is ever curious about me—in the sort of loving-onlooker way I am about him sometimes, making love. Because *I* am always alive to *any* change in rituals, in the way we do, there hardly ever are, but where there are my mind is *instantly* busy sorting and explaining them if I can and trying to fit them in. But why shouldn't I expect him to be as good at dissembling his elsewheres as I am mine? One is simply a little careful. Out of respect for each other. And for les bienséances too.

And out of affection, voyons!—un mariage qu'il a su rendre heureux.

—But then I did not want to think about what perhaps I should have to think about next, and there in the brilliance of early afternoon was Chad instead anyway. And his difference from Baudouin a difference I knew. Though how strange, when I thought back over it—had this changed what I saw the three of us as, à la légère, when it began? Because at the very first there I thought the difference was simply the, the, well simply the lovely breathlessness of it. The light-headedness, the freedom, the *delight* somehow—a rendezvous was the way dances were in one's teens, fête pure. And, well, perhaps they were, simplicities and all. Only then, except that Chad was Chad but Baudouin was Baudouin and my husband, was there the difference? Except of course that this time I'd carried myself over the threshold. And except that Baudouin naturally would always be there and I shall always expect him to be—c'était normal, we were brought up that way. Because whether or not one accepts it, one expects to behave as if one did. So if elsewheres are light-hearted, or even if only light-minded or just de gaieté de coeur, they are light-winged and fleeting too; and one returns. Never having, really, been away.

But now ? With the difference of *this* man? . . .

—And I sit here between them I thought in the long murmur of this day (and ah in what ways between them!) as if there were not this curtain about to go up, on a stage set for some lost comedy perhaps of Marivaux's, the set a garden front like this, of a manoir centuries out of time, the pale stone of its walls warm with the seeping gold of summer, the first soft shadows of afternoon already at their slow obliterating climb; and here at a luncheon table center-stage the three of us, each in his stylized part. But then how stylized a trio I suppose Marivaux might have seen us as, la ravissante comédienne Heaven pity her most of all—and not marivaudée but oh, beset! For à quel saint se vouer? And am I to know which way to turn either, better than she?

—And my sweet Baudouin, *now?*

What has happened to me what has happened to me.

—Ah mon Dieu mon Dieu I could not bear it! The sunlight was stifling me with gold, je me sentais *mal*—they must go, *oh* they must go!

And why care how? I stood up. And if Chad looked at me astonished, let him! They could think what they pleased! I would say good-bye at the terrasse. Up the drowsing summer of the lawn I could feel Chad's concern, and I didn't care, dear God I had no strength to, *any moment* I said to myself I may feel that awful trembling start again. And what if, at good-bye, my eyes say a helpless *Do you know what you have done to me?* to this man, and every moment I did not see how I could stand it until I could face what it was, alone.

—Except then, well, at the end he merely said something gallant and smiling about 'enchantment,' and I smiled back into his eyes as if there were nothing but bienséances in the world, and said, "Or do you just mean that women are habit-forming."

Silence imposed.

✦

It was dawn when I woke. The cool early light was drifting in through the hangings of the bed, and I lay and watched it slowly fill the dusk of the canopy above me with white shadows. The lovely stillness of country-summer morning was everywhere. I must hardly have slept an hour.

—Though then how could I have slept at all.

For did I ah even believe in what, finally, I had decided? when it was a longer word than love? . . .

Qu'importe, it was decided. Or at least the démarche decided on. Even, of a kind, a schedule. I looked at my watch; it was not even *five?* Hours still, hours, before I could reasonably try to phone. And begin.

Except even then.

—Well, but at least, soon, Emile's boy would have been for my baguette for breakfast. Alors bon, I would dress for town before.

And then not *wait*. I could phone on the way. The poste in Elbeuf is right on the voie. Or at Louviers, just off. Or I could leave the autoroute. At Mantes, even.

And I could phone the Embassy before I left here, to have Jock asked to expect me.

—Was it going to be hot ? I went to the window. The first white blaze of sunrise was just beginning to glint and dazzle through the tops of the beeches, but the whole wide sweep of the lawns up to the terrasse below me was silver still with mist. A heron stood motionless at the far edge of the pièce d'eau. I watched the pure crystal light grow and unfurl and deepen in hue, and suddenly, on the sundial, the first glowing shaft of sunrise burst through the treetops and struck the tip of the gnomon with golden fire, and then, ah how lovely, along the whole dawn-shadow rim of the parc, bar after glittering bar the saffron light fell slanting through and up the lawns, and slowly the floating radiance of morning was over everything.

I lay in the bath thinking what to wear. It was going to be hot. The sleeveless white shantung? Or was it in the flat in Passy. Over the bathroom's Venetian window a mourning dove roucoulait on the parapet. How the doves had amused Chad. "But they're *French*-speaking!" he said. In the States they coo it seems differently. He was so funny about their 'language problem'—if one tried to crossbreed them would la jolie petite even understand qu'on lui faisait des avances? Would the squabs be bilingual?— would they feel culturally disoriented and not fatten properly? . . . How long ago that was. Early on, between us. His first visit here. Poor sweet. 'Once upon a time.' Comme dans les contes de fées. . . .

—Yes, but also 'il était une fois' you too, ma belle, I said to myself: once upon a time (remember?) earlier on between us still, you too in idle amusement were wondering, for mightn't it perhaps put one out, making love in English?—the whole au lit vocabulary of your Frenchness translated? *redefined* even, in barbarisms? Aïe, and suppose in American it was different still again!

Heavens, the things one thinks of. And then, hoh, how it turned out instead.

—I had breakfast on the terrasse, the lovely morning already hot and still, the sunflooded stones of the manoir behind me towering up against the blue glaze of the sky. A hawk was wheeling, high over, his pinions scattering sapphires of light. Or was it a falcon. The heron was gone.

—But how was I to wait. I was too upset. I took my coffee into the study, and rang the Embassy.

Could I leave a message for Mr. John Bingham. It was urgent; would the standardiste have the great kindness to *make sure* it was handed to Mr. Bingham himself the moment he came in? Could he be told, please, that the Comtesse de Borde-Cessac wanted, d'urgence, to be able to get in touch with him. She would phone again. Between nine and nine-thirty and would he please wait for her call. It must have been a new standardiste: I had to spell my name.

It was not eight yet when I ran down to the car in the forecourt. The house was still pointing its stately shadows; the cobbles were wet still with dew. Elbeuf and Louviers would be much too soon to phone from: Jock wouldn't nearly be in. I decided to make time and phone from the poste in Mantes—nine-fifteen, nine-thirty. And in my mind as I drove off into the sun-spattered ancient aisles of the beeches I saw him in his immaculate office, the soft Parisian morning floating in through his windows over the Rue Boissy-d'Anglas; and perhaps he would be in his shirt sleeves at his desk, he might when I called be dictating dispatches or memoranda to that creamy secretary of his I'm not sure doesn't sleep with him now and then, well he is tempting, why shouldn't she, and at the standard they would put me through to him and he would pick up his phone.

And there would be his nice voice, perhaps concerned: "Fabienne? Angel what's wrong!" and I would say, " 'Wrong'?" and he would say, "But here's your switchboard message saying it's d'urgence," the girl's dark eyes watching him. But I would just say, "Oh, that," but so he could take me to lunch, heavens. I was coming up to town. And then we'd discuss where.

Or he'd say, "But 'urgent' lunch?—*serious* eating, this is for?" and I'd laugh and say, "Well, and Embassy rumors"—because are 'calculated indiscretions' his special Embassy job or aren't they. And he would give that engaging snort of his and say something like *"That's* not the d'urgence I take women to lunch for!" and the girl would laugh.

—But all the same, d'urgence it was.

Because ah poor Chad. Because I am not heartless, I am *not*. Except how was I even to put it, I thought, mon Dieu how did one *do* it! I drove on and out and onto the voie, and off toward Elbeuf through the lovely fresh green paysage of morning, and for a little all my mind seemed to see was the Avenue Bosquet, those rooms for so many light-minded months at least some sort of a part of me, even the salon hazy with the amber of afternoon that first innocent time Baudouin and I went there to tea, but then room after room to the very last one, which who could have guessed was the very last, or a symbol, that bedroom in the summer dusk only three days before; and I said to myself but am I then really not ever going to step across that secret threshold again?—or, I suppose, tell why.

Or *is* this, merely, the way it happens. And has to.

> La terre écarte de sa face
> Ses longs cheveux indifférents—

who reads Pellerin now but who cares? and I remembered how Chad once said to me *Grâce à toi l'univers s'explique*—so sweet and simple of him. Ah well he is simple. And I may as well admit I've known a long time.

But does one feel one's 'plus jamais' no more than this?—or had I simply no other emotion to spare for Chad, no passions de reste, in this nightmare of dismay?

I who had been so politely astonished, so often, at what other women do! . . .

And what had been the use in saying *I must not decide, I must not look at this man*, when oh Heaven help me just saying it was deciding!

Ah mais regarde-moi—regarde comme je fais.

—But I *need* never see him again.

He will leave. He will go back to where he has a milieu. To his Wall Street; to his Maine coast in the summers. For what meaning has France ever had for him. He came now only as a courtesy to a client. Why should he come back, ever? There is nothing for him to come back for. Even if he knew what has happened to me, there is nothing. For I would not see him. All the more not, if he knew. If I don't dare risk seeing him again now, why would I then. I would not. Let me not, now. Oh let me not need to. Let me not think he is ever likely to return.

Let it not be catastrophe. . . .

—Ah, but wasn't the proper prayer, I said to myself, 'Let it not have begun'? And had I decided not to see him again or hadn't I? With nothing more then to remember of him, had I to dread the days to come—five hours remembered of a summer's day the only meaning of a lifetime? *I* forlorn?—that at least I shall have stopped short of! to have had nothing was at least that much un bien.

And if I find his flowers I thought in the Passy flat when I come in this afternoon, and presently he rings up, as he may, to ask to see me, I have only to say no. And that my husband is coming on a fortnight's leave from his regiment, I didn't know his plans but I rather thought we were going off to—well, wherever came to my mind at the time. And it was partly true. For of course Baudouin *was* coming on leave. And I *didn't* know whether it was to be Portugal.

And he was going to be my excuse for Chad too.

—Jock was waiting for my call. *God* yes he'd feed me lunch, what a question! Where'd I thought of going? because look, sweet, would I mind Barbizon? That Bas Bréau place, say. He had to go on to Fontainebleau at four, was why. Line of duty—had to see a man about a spy, very stealthy stuff. Sure I wouldn't mind Barbizon? I was a pleasure! The Bas Bréau then? Quarter to one?

I came out of the poste into the morning street again thinking an hour and a quarter to Barbizon leaves two hours still to fill somehow. Off toward the Seine, a few streets away, the twin towers of the cathedral glittered above the red-tiled roofs of the town: I could go light a candle. And watch it burn slowly down.

Or I could drive into Paris and have Jacques do my hair. He would work me in.

Or I could go to Passy. But what if Chad phoned while I was in the flat. Every morning he does. And I am not, well, not *prepared* yet. And there would be the flowers from— Ah but what if I had to face finding he *hadn't* sent them.

So finally I just drove in and went to Fauchon and took a *long* time buying all sorts of friandises. To be sent to the flat, for Baudouin's arriving.

And I went to Hédiard too and bought things.

And on my way across Paris to the Porte d'Orléans I stopped to light a candle at St. Germain-des-Prés and left by the Porte d'Italie instead.

I was *not* heartless! I was not a Mme. Récamier and Chad would not be a Benjamin Constant lamenting her in his tear-sodden journal day after *day* till Napoleon came back from Elba and distracted him.

And Constant knowing exactly what she was doing!—'she doesn't want the nuisance of feeling sorry her charms make me suffer so, so to spare herself she thinks they don't.' *Pour s'en délivrer elle n'y croit pas.* What a sentence.

But then what a woman. And how did she put up with the man, even for his political usefulness. Heartless or not.

I could not have been like that even if it had been that sort of affair. Or of ending.

—I was ten minutes early in Barbizon, but sweet Jock was there.

Jock Bingham has always charmed me. Of course he was Baudouin's friend first, from lycée days. And it was Jock's father's sending him to Charterhouse that made Baudouin want to go there too. But now he's—this last year in particular—he's more mine. Even, perhaps, just mine. He was standing waiting for me in the court of the Bas Bréau, elegant as usual, in a white linen gilet croisé this time of all things, with jet buttons, and he came across to the car with that kindly air of his of being put-upon-but-I-was-worth-it, his repertory of worldly divertissements mine to command, and he'd begun amusing me almost before he'd ordered apéritifs.

For would I believe what his high-minded dedication to his country's diplomatic competence had just involved him in? There he'd been—(What did I see I longed for in the menu? He hardly thought that duck aux ananas!) There he had been, after my phone call, blamelessly letting this British legal chap from next door start the daily wasting of his time—and with some memorandum of livery of seizin who on earth cared *who*'d endossed on a deed of enfeoffment, except was it authentic ("What am I, the College of Heralds?") and *only* this godsend prospect of lunch across a table from *me* was getting him through the first horrors of Embassy morning (Look, how would I feel about sharing this filet en feuilleté pour deux with him? And what to start with, then? Argenteuil asparagus? Or was I seriously hungry—when *had* I had breakfast? before I'd called him?) when his phone rang, and it was this Yale professor who was a visiting world authority on American literature, at the Sorbonne, and so help him the poor learned idiot was gobbling with fright!

And there was this kind of wild happy singing going on in the background, and once it had come sort of swooping in on the phone and then off and melodiously away—no wonder the poor sod was practically hysterical, 'd unnerve anybody—anyhow in God's shattering name would somebody COME AT ONCE!! Because this student of his, student also of his it seemed back at Yale but she'd followed him abroad, well actually she'd more or less come abroad *with* him—anyhow half an hour ago she'd suddenly gone completely out of her head, and he didn't know how you— What were the proper French— Because good *god* it had never crossed his mind! Student infatuations of course yes; perfectly routine campus behavior; old story; girls *did*. But then this one had— Well yes recently he'd begun to notice she, she'd taken to sort of humming. In he meant bed. You know?—*not paying attention*. And then, this morning (and right in the middle of!) she'd—well she'd burst into song! . . .

Ah, well, Jock said, he supposed nobody was very sensible sexually. Think of some of Stendhal's behavior. Think of Tolstoi's. For that matter think of some of God's. But he'd loyally trundled round (for what else? she had our passport hadn't she, baying mad or not?) he'd trundled round to this incompetent rake's apartment and sure enough there the child was, swooping about, waving the chap's pajama trousers if you please like a heraldic banneret, in the full luster of her lunacy. Fey, he'd decided, though, perhaps, rather than straitjacket barmy. But what a commentary on the mating habits of the race of man. Was one to call it dejecting, or just hilarious? He'd said to the dithering Yalie, What next what next, didn't he ever check with the college psychiatrist before he got into bed with them? and all the ungrateful lecher'd done was snarl, "None of your philandering damn' business!" and rush off to lecture on (he said) Poetic Strategies in Elizabeth Bishop.

So he'd rung the Assistance Publique. And packed an overnight sort of bag for the child. And fended off a couple of giggling attempts to garrotte him with the pajama trousers. And rung the Embassy to give the boys time to handle the damn' thing. And in short he'd preserved the consular amenities until the Assistance Publique had turned up and lugged her away. Singing of summer in full-throated ease.

What next what next indeed.

So that had been *his* morning. Such as it was. Thank God for *me*. I was a lovely giddy creature to feed lunch to and now what did I want him to tell me about this chap Sather.

—For an instant I thought I was going into shock. *How* could he have known? Or guessed! And when I had been so certain I would be safe that I already thought I was. . . . It was so dreadful that for a moment I didn't see that he wasn't looking at me, he was running his eyes down the wine list, ah *I was safe* and I said the first inanity that came babbling into my head, "Don't I have any surprises for you at all?"—and I even managed to laugh.

And he merely glanced up amused and said what surprises? because look, it was only yesterday I'd met the guy, and fed him

Chad said a very decent Pays de Caux lunch hadn't I? but then, this morning, the Embassy switchboard time-stamp recorded that I'd rung *him* up for God's sake at 7:19. But why on earth, at that hour, call him at the Embassy and not the Avenue Bosquet? So what *had* I wanted to discuss out of Chad's hearing? Simple! Hardly needed to wonder.

So of course I said heavens what was there to wonder about, I'd merely wanted a third opinion. Je lui avais trouvé du charme, à ce Sather. But why would a man as civilized and as sympathique as this take on such a—in 1983!—such a really preposterous mission, heavens! Or was he did he think as cynical as it made him perhaps seem?

But Jock said oh come, what did I want the man to do. You couldn't very well explain even to an Iowa client that she was an anachronism could you?—simple question of manners. Maybe in Iowa she wasn't an anachronism anyhow.

Sather'd he said turned up looking for Chad the morning after he'd arrived in Paris. It was a Sunday; he'd been lazing around in the apartment, and Sather'd stayed a good hour and filled him in. He'd it appeared been looking after the Newman family's investment portfolio for a good many years. Even made them money before this latest consignment of nonentities brought their cracker-barrel economics into Washington. Investments, and then inevitably you found yourself being asked to look into other areas now and then as well. Especially now it was just Mrs. Newman. Would he for instance find her a religious broadcaster to buy for tax purposes (but *not* one of those smarmy or whinnying ones). How *much* money, please, should she expect to have to put up with Chadwick's wasting at Princeton. One became resigned. And actually, Sather had said he felt, there was a sound financial side to it anyhow: high time this young man started thinking about coming home and taking over a few of the dynastic chores. How much longer was he going to put it off? Good god, what was he now—twenty-seven? twenty-eight? . . .

—It was as good an opening as any. It could have been exprès. So I decided; and I said, "But sweet why do you suppose I rang you. For a long time I've been thinking shouldn't he go."

Oh, of course I oughtn't perhaps to have said it quite like that, it did sound blunt, saying it—and he *was* absolutely taken aback. Hoh, I thought, so I do hold surprises for you! All the same, was there any real use in 'explaining'? So meaningless, when what would it be but the classical situation, tiresomenesses and all.

With nothing new either side could possibly have thought up that hasn't been thought of and said from the beginning of time, pointlessly pointlessly. . . . He would say but the poor guy adores you! And I would say I know I do know, and he *is* so simple and sweet, and Jock would keep repeating his baffled irrelevant but *adores* you! and I would try to go on sounding meek and to blame and dans mon tort in general, I've no idea *how* many times I might have heard myself murmuring I do feel badly, I do (because I *did!*), perfectly senseless all of it.

So I simply told him. Tout passe, voilà. In a new love perhaps everyone is innocent; then each couple creates its sequences for itself. "I'm turning classic comédienne for you," I said—but thinking of Chad, remembering how it began, that long-ago afternoon, how breathless he was, half afraid of me, he couldn't believe I was saying yes, even when he kissed me he could hardly believe it; he was shaking so, that first time, I thought was it going to be a fiasco? maybe I should soothe him somehow?—except I was so wild myself I could hardly wait till he touched me, for how would it be? and how afterwards too would it be, adultery, all these years from my girlhood wondering, and now I was to know. . . .

But now here, I said to Jock, tout passe; and wasn't this Mr. Sather here with the answer? Anyway *an* answer? "So I rang you first," I said.

So he took a long breath, and said, "Well, God bless God bless," looking resigned. "I'm to give Sather a hand? On souffre courageusement son bonheur! You are an absolutely adorable woman and I never blame anybody for anything. But thanks to your adorableness I have been for a year now in a totally impossible position. Now at least the situation is to be demoted: I shall be a mere retrospectively uncomfortable. And being tired of Chad I can see. Mais autant que *ça?* . . ."

—That at least thank Heaven I thought is what I want the reason to seem to be. But ah did it make it any less sad to put it in French? and I said, "Oh Jock but in French how does it sound."

"Ah, well, dammit, 'quod vides perisse,' then," he said, "over's over, what's the advantage of having classical tags on the tip of my tongue if I'm going to be astonished at anything as immemorial as woman?—what you've collectively sworn to us the winds and the waters carry away. Ventis rapiuntur et undis. And always have been. Look, angel, I call this a gloomy conversation, let's for once have an overpriced Clos de Bèze and be done with it."

So I could laugh at him. "But men recover," I said. "All you need is someone to indulge you if you're simple-minded. Or over-indulge you if you're not," and he said lightly, "Oh, epigrams," and signaled the sommelier.

But I went on to what came next. Had this Mr. Sather said how long he was staying?—did he I meant expect to take Chad back with him. Because how was he managing, with no French. And only this escort service he'd said he'd engaged; this young woman.

Why, Jock said, these agencies, he knew of two or three of them, they did a very competent job, why not. They were a sort of very superior couriers; they took people about. There was supposed to be nothing they didn't know. Including how to keep their clients from committing the next shattering American bévue. Very busi-nesslike. And charming. Very expensive of course too, but the stockholders foot your bills.

I said but couldn't the situation become, well, ambiguë? Mr. Sather's young woman had for instance he'd said changed his hotel for him. And she had gone dancing with him. Several it sounded times.

He said what was her name? he knew several of them. They turned up at the Embassy with clients. Who was this?

I said a Mrs. Godfrey I thought.

Maria Godfrey? but he knew her quite well!—'d met her at parties as well as around the Embassy. *Very* pretty girl. Even deli-cious. Sather *was* in good hands!

I said stupidly he'd said she was very correct.

And of course he laughed at me—what'd I expect? some sort of what his stately grandm'ma used to refer to as 'a lightskirts'? Look, these were—they *had* to be!—jeunes femmes sérieuses. Divorced, most of them, to prove it!

I said well yes I'd wondered. About I meant this Mrs. Godfrey's husband, if she went dancing with clients every other night. And then, well, I'd wondered what kind of expatriate life a young— of course it *was* I supposed a way for an American girl to make a living in Paris, but didn't this Mrs. Godfrey—

But simply it's good god he said a country you like existing in! Drawbacks of course—our intellectuels with their sub-Heideggery fads and sweeping nonsensical aphorisms. Where but France would you hear a Jean Rostand announce 'L'homme est un miracle sans intérêt'?—all right then what *does* interest the fellow! We sometimes struck him as being out of our over-Cartesian minds. Or again: would *any* other nation put up with the suffocating ronds-de-cuir bureaucracy we French did? Still, that was qua citizens. Qua *French*, everybody but the bourgeoisie let everybody else do anything their anarchic fancies suggested to them. So American girls could be themselves here (or for that matter be anybody else they pleased too) without having to strike liberated attitudes about it. And an American writer, say, could sit over a bock half the day at a café table, writing up his personal improvements on the Book of Revelation, and nobody would think it worth a glance. Or a waiter hover. Whereas at home the poor devil would have to earn his unappetizing living teaching freshman-english.

—How quietly, I said to myself, I sit listening to him. I might be that marquise of Musset's—je commençais à avoir trente ans. But how can he tell me what I can't let him see I want to know. And when I haven't 'decided' anyway.

I thought of Fontenelle: 'Wherever there are men there are follies—and the same follies.' Except Fontenelle didn't dignify us by saying *folies*, he said *sottises*.

And poor sniveling Constant bore him out: 'Les femmes m'ont fait faire tant de sottises.' Tiens, how thoughtless of us to trouble men's peace of mind so! . . .

—Ah, but it helped, that lunch! Jock amused me. And cheered me. If only with other people's sottises. At a nightclub he'd heard one of those fluting English voices at the next table—"one of those lovely delinquent ladyships, and she was complaining to a sleek solid guardsman sort she called Arthur about some chap she called poor Charles. 'I said to him, "Oh darling *could* you find it in your heart to just *go away*, I mean *not* fussing about it my very sweet? because I'm afraid you're beginning to give me what may turn out to be the horrors." He was rather put out. Such vanity—what things you *are*, Arthur!'"

And he told me about a folly an old uncle of his in Fiesole had had built, in his grove—a "heptastyle tempietto, its seven sides expressing Uncle Robert's contempt for astrology and his personal independence of the points of the compass." And for all he knew some anti-Palladian notion of where to make love. It had turned out to be rather uncomfortable: his uncle'd finally had to have central heating put in. "But much superior anyway to one a Main Line cousin had had built," he said. "*That* had a stock-ticker installed."

And there was a young American studying piano at the Conservatoire who was making a *very* good living composing demotic ballads for a dive in the Rue Vavin—

> I don't want no mo sweetie-pies
> Ef all they is is you

and so forth. And something called Bach Rock for variety.

And, oh well, Jock is good for me. And désabusé. And for dessert we had fraises des bois.

And when he put me in my car he said what time is Baudouin getting in, and I said for dinner I hoped, and he said how long'd he have this time, and when I said two weeks he looked at me and said blandly but I *was* going to be busy? And I said I expected so, yes. And he said but only perhaps part of the time in Paris? And I said yes we might go to Baudouin's father's, on the Corniche. Or to Portugal perhaps. We'd talked about both. On verrait.

So he hadn't to ask whether the Avenue Bosquet would be seeing us. Which was the message.

And so he smiled at me, and patted my hand on the wheel, and leaned in and kissed my cheek, and I drove away.

That much taken care of.

But we shall all (I said to myself as I drove back along the autoroute)—we shall all need time.

Day-after-day time, too, to grow used to this—to what has happened. Dear Heaven to its *having* happened! Time simply for me to revive from that in!

And for Baudouin perhaps without knowing it to grow used to how I may be until I do. For how *do* I make love with him now. . . .

I drove back to Paris fast. Baudouin might have wangled an earlier plane. I wanted to rest anyway. There was . . . the night ahead.

And it was just as well I did drive fast: at the flat there it was, waiting, a great floating armful of flowers, and an engraved card saying MR. LEWIS LAMBERT SATHER.

Without another word.

Ms. Godfrey tilted herself up over him on an angel arm, and said in a happy voice, "Let me contemplate you"—for they had seen no real point in getting up, it being Sunday.

So, for hours, from the blaze of morning beyond the slatted shutters, bright motes of sun had chinked and filtered in, myriads, her tall room swam with the glints of their floating patterns, and, now, they were sifting with the brilliance of, outside, practically noon.

But since why should this young woman now some five days his have expected an answer, he only took the wrist of her free hand in his fingers, and lazily kissed it, instead. At which, as having no other amusement at the moment anyhow, they both then smiled.

Till at last she murmured, "No but I keep wondering what you were like, when you were only I mean my age," as in dream. "Are you likely to have been rather a pet?" she added, and bending kissed his chin.

Oh, Sather said, been he supposed like pretty much anybody. Undifferentiated marauding pre-stuffy East Coast near-thirty male then; how not. Something of a bastard now and then too of course, like anybody in his right mind. Why bring his that-stage up?—'d give *any* decent man the horrors, remembering, good god!

"'Remembering'?" she said, and watched his face. "Like what?"

He appeared to think. Ah well, he said, after a moment, unkind-nesses, mostly. Inadvertences. What had he known, young! Why didn't she come down again where she was convenient.

But this she paid it seemed no attention to. Or for that matter moved; but, poised atilt there, over, bent her enchanted head as if musing upon him, cherishing, this long fathomless gaze down.

So they lay there half tranced, faintly smiling still.

Till at last, from those depths of dream, she murmured, ". . . must get *up*," not stirring.

He made a lazy expostulating sound: 'up'? for what for.

"You make love instead of lunch *too?*" she protested, laughing. "Goodness!" and, bending, kissed his eyes.

So, naturally, like a man of sense, he pulled her down beside him again. Where she lay, giggling.

"Floreant Gadara by god anyhow," he said (thanks to a decent Quaker education), and stroked her sleek shoulder.

Or was what she'd been trying to say, he added presently, that he was keeping her from mass.

Suddenly there was silence.

She reproving him? he asked, sounding amused.

She seemed, minutely, to detach herself from him; but she said nothing still.

So he rolled up onto his elbow and looked at her. This some technicality'd escaped him? he asked blandly.

"But Lewis you must know," she gently rebuked him. "One doesn't take communion when one's doing, well, what I'm doing, sweetie *anybody* knows that!"

This was for god's sake *sin?*

She have to confess it even if it was?

". . . But Lewis the priest would think it was if he knew," she said meekly. "And it would be a *discourtesy* not to think of his feelings, can't you see?"

The fellow's hypothetical finer feelings, hypothetically well yes, he saw. But how was a poor heretic to follow the niceties of this sort of thing? Because he said look, they were a wonderfully confusing collectivity and what was one to do? He remembered one otherwise tractable girl who wouldn't even consider making love Sunday mornings, because that, she said, was when you went to mass. This, mind you, wasn't because the lovely thing *went* to mass Sunday morning. No no, simply she wouldn't come make love during the time she'd have been at mass if she'd gone! She conceive of such bedlamite piety?—the one perfect time, too, when her damn' husband wouldn't have suffered uneasiness! Two perfect hours (counting to and from) just thrown away—the sheer *inhumanity* of the waste! So now how'd she expect him to— And don't flounce! he cried, and held her—look dammit he wasn't talking about the girl, he was talking about theology pure and simple, this was lofty speculation, built-in superstition or not, he told her, practically as if he expected her to agree.

So she lolled back against him again, and gazed at him, close beside, lovingly. "Do I have to hear about your horrible other girls?" she murmured, and putting out a fingertip traced the line of his mouth. "And anyhow," she said gently, "it isn't superstition. Le bon Dieu has been very kind indeed to you, my love, and so have I."

But so Old Testament hit-or-miss! he said. He put it into the head of an Iowa Baptistess that her son's virtue must be saved from a life of lobsters and fancy women, then persuaded of all people *him* to undertake the cockeyed mission—but to what end? *Her!* Nothing, he agreed, could have been lovelier—Aphrodite herself couldn't have been more thoughtful! But so roundabout, so *inefficient* somehow! God was good, of course, but He often didn't seem to be all that good at it. Was she going to tell her confessor about this? . . .

"Are you stupid?" she cried. ". . . and anyway it's my religion and *my* decision, and if I decide to passer huit jours avec un monsieur it isn't really the church's business at all! You don't know anything about theology anyway. Did that girl confess about you?"

No idea, he said.

"Didn't you ever ask her?"

Why should he have!

"But you asked me!" she accused him.

. . . Different girl entirely.

"How, 'different'?"

How'd *he* know how? he complained amiably. Simply not this lovely dazzle, call it. Never set off rockets in him this way, if she liked.

"*Not* just my Sunday-morning difference?"

He said good god no! as blamelessly as if this were so.

So she kissed the corner of his mouth. "Are you perhaps sort of lying a little?" she asked tenderly.

But didn't she take that for granted? he teased her, and ran the tips of his fingers up through the slipping shadowy tent of her hair. If she expected anything as far-fetched as truth from him, how would she decide which parts of it she wanted to believe?

"You haven't even learned what I want to hear?" she asked, nuzzling him. "Or do you just think I'm so light-headed about you you don't have to bother?"

'Bother'! he echoed—'bother'?

"Oh well and anyhow," she said, "if I decide to lavish myself on you that's *my* decision, Lewis my pet, you have nothing to do with it. Except, I hope, go out of your mind over the total sensuality of it," she ended, little tongue lightly savoring him.

So they lay there in great comfort, and they might simply have been mindless.

But presently she said, "I do think you're silly, sort of, though, to call her again."

A try, he said. Like any other. Because no telling.

"But sweetie, this lunch," she said. "D'you really have to? You've met Mr. Newman's poppet, and she turned out *not* to be a poppet, she's a perfectly ladylike countess. And rich. And you sent her your thank-you flowers. But then when you rang her up and asked her to have lunch with you she said, politely, no. And isn't that that?"

Put that way, he conceded, yes he supposed very likely.

"Then my silly love what can you expect from ringing up and asking her again."

Ah, well, he supposed he had some vague feeling he ought to apologize somehow. Good god, now he'd met her, he not only didn't disapprove, he was all for Chad! And for all *he* knew, she might want to marry him; divorce what's-his-name and marry him.

"But ces gens-là don't *divorce*, heavens!" she said. "Any more than they emigrate or abjure! They think it impious and vulgar."

He meant apologize for the, the affront of his damn' mission. Not of course in so many words—words would only make things worse. But just sort of—

"You mean *charm* her?" Ms. Godfrey demanded, coming up on an elbow to look at him. "Oh dear have I a rival?"

He said oh nonsense—when she'd said no to lunch with him? God no, he didn't think she'd even particularly liked him. Could have disliked, even. No no, all he'd wanted was to, well, close the whole implausible incident with the routine civilities of regret, what else was he to do? Merely, say, leaving a card struck him as pretty damn' bleak. Or did the French leave cards.

But she was gazing down at him as in total disbelief. "Oh *really*, Lewis my darling," she cried, "how can you have the, the effrontery to be so bogus modest!"

But what was he to think.

"As if privately you thought *any* woman would 'not like' you!"

He made some vague grumbling sound.

So for a moment she appeared to contemplate him. As being possibly beyond interpretation.

Then she began to laugh. "Because know what would serve you right?" she asked sweetly. "Because I'm supposed to *advise* you aren't I? and help you carry out your ridiculous mission efficiently

and everything? Well why don't I advise you the *efficient* way
to put a stop to Mr. Newman's truancy would be simply for you
to supplant him in the lady's arms! And don't look shocked, my
heartless pet!" she cooed at him. "*You* object to another seduction-
campaign more or less?—hoh! And in such a worthy family cause,
too, goodness!"

So, shocked (or perhaps in fact not), the man seemed not to
know how to take this, though who would.

And finally merely remarked (mildly) that any man was, naturally, only on loan so to speak anywhere; but, well, she surprised
him.

"Ah *do* I!"

Or did she mean she'd eventually want him back.

" 'Back'!—if you'd done a thing like *that!*"

All he'd meant was—

"Make love with another woman and come back *expecting* I'd
simply—"

But dammit he'd—

"Oh well never *mind!*" she said in a voice of tears. "Except you
are sort of heartless anyway aren't you? and now you as good as
threaten me with— And don't say 'It's just a lunch'!" she commanded, and took herself out of his arms altogether. In fact sat up.
"You don't know anything *about* women! It was at lunch I started
falling in love with you, don't you know that? Or anyway at dinner,
so there!"

—And now he hadn't even let her eat breakfast, he said,
amused, what behavior! and rolling up after her took her in his
arms again. Where at least she had the complaisance to giggle.

And in due course say, "All right *go* be unfaithful then!—now
are you happy? And why aren't you starving too," she complained,
and kissed him. "So let me go. Where did you throw my— Let me
go!" she reproached him, kissing him again.

And so forth and so on.

Except that, presently, at the bedroom door, for an instant she
turned and looked round at him, smiling. "So I shall want you
back," she said in a happy voice again, and vanished toward her
kitchen.

✦

These two, then, were at least past any stage at which lovers, abed
in gratitude and wonder, recite to each other, in alternating song,

the Arcadian miracle of their ever having met; and it had been a good ten days. Counting anyhow from the first.

When out of the brilliant noon of the Rue de Castiglione she had come into the cool glass depths of his hotel so light and quick she was at the concierge's desk asking for him, spun round in fact and halfway across to where the fellow pointed he was sitting, before it seemed he took it in it was he, Sather, she must be heading for—hardly given him time to scramble himself to his feet before there she was, smiling as if delighted into his eyes, slender gloved hand out to him.

And a beauty.

Though this it could have been thought he had clearly not counted on, for he looked, in a courtly fifty-ish way, for a moment as good as wary.

But she was lightly chiming a well-brought-up "Mr. Sather? oh how d'you do I'm Maria Godfrey, but you've been down waiting for me how *kind*," in a voice of music—for how pleasant to be *meeting* at last, lunch instead of just telexes! so now where did he want her to suggest they might go? Or had he perhaps somewhere he'd heard of in mind? as one did!

For in case *not* (she had run on, wide eyes softly taking him in) she'd thought why not Drouant, they were very good again, also it was only this ten minutes' walk away, did he know the quarter? in the Place Gaillon—they could simply stroll there if he liked (they'd be early anyway) through the noon streets in the lovely day, would he care to? for she had reserved a table, in case.

Unless of course he felt too fagged to?—after she meant his plane.

Though he didn't in the least *look* fagged, she told him, for an instant all eyes at him, in fact he'd go beautifully with Drouant, what a pleasure to have so presentable a client (sliding a hand through his arm as they took off), did he know Paris?

So through the glowing maelstroms of Parisian noon they had sorted out the polite preliminaries.

No he'd somehow never got to Europe. Even in college summers. His father had had a big yawl; they'd cruised off the New England coast, summers. Up into the Maritime Provinces; that sort of thing. Then, his service had been Korea, not Europe.

No she lived in Versailles, not Paris. *Far* more square meters of apartment for so many fewer thousands of francs. And then one could commute in to *either* station, St. Lazare or the Invalides, so handy.

And so forth, along the Rue Danielle-Casanova. (No, not *that* Casanova, that was Giovanni Giacopo. Jean-Jacques. Like Rousseau. Terrible male chauvinists both of them, so *silly*.) Shops yes, did he want to buy presents for friends, before he left? she'd shop with him, she loved it. But *this* wasn't the quarter to, they'd *shop*. And across the Avenue de l'Opéra and there they were, and she was translating the menu to him (in detail) over a glass of champagne.

For was he hungry? For how hungry? Though in any case he should have a Drouant sole; everyone should. She, though, was going to have what they called a 'mignonnette de Pauillac,' it had a heavenly tarragon sauce; he would see. But the carte des vins didn't need translating, would he order. And, please, another sip of champagne.

And so, as the sommelier bowed over her, competently around to business.

For he knew what their agency *did*, that part of their set speech she could skip; but also she was supposed to tell him about herself, they'd found it was only sensible. Just people were curious, and why not.

"So then I've been I explain married," she told him. "Only that turned out to have been stupid, too soon after college like everybody, so l am divorced. And then *I* add," she said sweetly, "I add 'But I don't have a lover. *Nor* am I looking for one.' There, that's the other part of my set speech — not that you really in the least look as if you needed having it said to you, Mr. Sather, I mean do you?"

He had murmured, looking amused, why, he hoped none of his fellow clients ever'd needed it said to them either.

"Ah, well, sometimes, no," she'd said. "No, it can even seem safe sometimes to add 'I love being charmed.' If one of you, that is, looks charming. Still, every now and then it can be a *little* like handling one's father's classmates at reunions. You know? in their various happy stages of dignified rut?"

But good god, he'd said, and he might have been as courteously shocked as he made it sound, good god what were he and her agency's clients like then! — they lunge, and that sort of thing? to have called for *this* kind of cards-on-the-table warning-off to him!

"Oh but heavens," she cried, "I didn't mean to *alarm!* What sad primnesses have I put in your mind, Mr. Sather?" she begged him, laughing. "Oh *dear!*"

Not that he'd blame some poor greying devil, he'd said gallantly, for being — what should he call it? 'over-enchanted'?

Certainly he himself hadn't had the pleasure of taking anyone this lovely to lunch, he hoped he might say, for blest if he could remember how long.

This however she had passed over with a bland *poor man how deprived-sounding*—except 'enchantment' wasn't, was it, what he'd come all this way from New York for, even if his letter hadn't (for whatever reasons) quite seemed to her agency to say what the object of his trip in fact was. They were after all a guide-and-escort service; what was it she was to guide-and-escort him into? Or was it out of.

So, before the sole even, he had got down to it.

Well, no, he'd said amiably, perhaps he hadn't been all that specific, no. But the fact was, to put this particular scenario in black and white on the letterhead of a serious-minded investment counsel— Well perhaps the way to put it was just that he was indulging a rich client. A Mrs. Newman. Very rich in fact—widow of Newman Industries. They made couplings; huge plants in Burlington and Ottumwa. Which she had stepped in and run after Newman's death with a rod of iron. *Extremely* strong-minded woman. And used to giving orders. And she had this truant of a son.

Who had she said spent *quite enough* time dawdling about Europe since college. He was to *come home!* And take a responsible part in the dynasty! But what was she to do?—the miserable boy didn't answer letters. *Or* cables! And his phone wasn't it turned out listed! So would Mr. Sather have the kindness to go find out what *was* going on? and put a stop to it! And *bring—him—home!!*

Ms. Godfrey murmured, "Goodness," politely.

Well, yes, mothers, Sather'd conceded: a certain cultural lag. Still, he remembered young Newman as very good-looking, last time he'd seen him. Could have done with a bit more Eastern polish, perhaps. But some engaging young woman can always decide to try buffing you up for reasons of her own. So, conceivably, Mrs. Newman had a point—for all he knew, in Iowa that stern-minded archaism 'an unfortunate entanglement' might still be current English. Chad was creeping up on thirty anyway—old enough *not* to have to know better.

"But what has this wayward Mr. Newman been doing then?" Ms. Godfrey asked. "Or do we know."

Sather said what difference what. Been at one point he understood studying architecture. Or some such intellectual pastime. At he thought Urbino. But latterly just, well, it seemed here in Paris. No idea doing what.

"No but I mean," Ms. Godfrey had said, "isn't this all rather—
You don't seem to me to be at all the sort of— Oh dear I guess I
mean isn't this all Mr. Sather rather *personal* I'd have thought? to
call in an agency like ours over!"

Been Mrs. Newman's idea. Though why not—he had no
French to get about with. None since college. And there were all
the unfamiliar foreign logistics in general.

"But why hasn't she simply I mean come herself ?" Ms. Godfrey
asked, as why not.

But what if an 'entanglement' (Sather said) was what Mrs. Newman was upset she might have the outrage of finding if she came?
—and of having to confront! And dear god suppose the delicious
entanglement didn't speak English! Look, he'd said, forbearingly,
even when *he* was an undergraduate some of these musty tropes
were still around. You could even be *expelled* from a college in
those days! There was even such a word as misbehavior!

So she smiled at him over the rim of her glass, sipping.

And said, "But still, how do you, well, *feel*, Mr. Sather, about it."

How'd she mean. Because as one male about another, if Chad
was a marauder or whatever that generation called it, well he supposed who wasn't. Not the point anyhow. And no concern of his if
it were. But as the family's money-man, family firms he had to say
made him uneasy. In principle; but in particular when they were
this sort of autarchy. Because lose the autarch and you never knew
about the financial viabilities. There could even be for instance no
market in the stock! He'd seen such situations, and they were very
unsettling indeed. So it was *very* much in young Newman's own
long-term interest to get back and into the thing himself. Should
have done long ago. And avoided *this* nonsense!

Ms. Godfrey murmured, ". . . couplings," as if lost in dream.

But then here the waiter began serving them. So this they
watched.

Though then she said, "Yes but I meant *is* this all there is to
it, Mr. Sather? Here you are, going after a wayward son practically
as if you were part of the family. I'm not prying, goodness, but
we've found we can be more efficient for our clients if we do know
the ins and outs. Office politics, you know. And other kinds of
emotions. Well, we are expensive, and here *are* we really needed
—so I mean could Mrs. Newman be just giving you a fond and
luxurious vacation as much as getting you a disinterested courier.
So for example does she perhaps want to marry you or something?"

He snorted *god* no!—not even something, looking amused.

"No but is there some reason she mightn't want to? I mean, you can't be all that modest, can you?"

'Presentable,' huh? he said.

"Well aren't you?" she said sweetly.

Ah, well, he said, Mrs. Newman was a, was an unusually able woman, should they leave it at that? If she'd ever been farmington'd into an Eastern deb type, it hadn't taken. In a word this mission was just a mission and no complications, except the damn' awkwardness of it, and he hoped she and her agency would accept it for what it was.

"Alors bon," she said. "Simply then Mr. Newman is a promising young man a wicked woman has got hold of, and you have accepted the mission of separating him from the wicked woman. Oh dear, it sounds practically like a novel we had to wade through in American Lit, Henry James or somebody. Are you quite sure she's bad for him?"

He'd no idea. Might even be good for him. Could have been adding refinement that had been a good deal wanting. There *was* very likely something to be got from lobsters and fancy women, if you had time on your hands.

"So then how do you propose to handle it then?" she said.

Could hardly make plans could he? until he'd seen what was in fact happening. Too many unknown factors—Chad's attitude; what his young woman was like; whether she might be a young man instead; the current state of the attachment. Which for instance might turn out to be on the wane already. So he'd thought he'd reconnoiter perhaps first—at least get a working notion. But *not*, if she didn't mind, this afternoon—always had to catch up on his sleep after these barbarous planes. But he might drop past in good time in the morning. Perhaps she'd have the kindness to pick him up at his hotel afterwards, for lunch? Then they could start to work out what it was he'd found he had to deal with.

So then that, roughly, was how they had left it that first day.

But when next day she picked him up and drove him out through the immense wild vortex of noontime traffic to Versailles ("This is a hotel Mr. Sather I do think you'd be far more comfortable in. I want you to see."), first thing he had to report was a damn' nuisance but there turned out to be a hitch—Chad wasn't in Paris!

Nor immediately expected back, according to a young chap it appeared shared his apartment with him.

He'd asked the hotel concierge was it far, walking he meant, for he'd thought why not; and as she'd know, it of course turned out to be an easy twenty, twenty-five minutes, through the fresh Paris morning. And easy to find—the fellow had whipped out a folding map and spread it, to show: diagonally across those gardens, then this Place, to the Rue St. Dominique, and along it five hundred meters is the Avenue Bosquet intersection, had Monsieur a particular address in mind? because it was simple, street numbers everywhere began always from the Seine.

Ms. Godfrey murmured except when the Seine wasn't there to begin from.

Yes, well, however it was. 41-bis had turned out to be seven or eight stories of massive poured-concrete Modern; seemed to be standard for the neighborhood. Wrought-iron grille of a portal, flush with the pavement; and behind, this broad low-vaulted passage, practically a tunnel, led far in, over cobbles; it could have been a carriage-entry. Through the gloom he'd seen, as if distant, the haze of summer morning in a great cube of a central court, and a fountain, a grotesque stone lizard dribbling water into a flat basin. One of the grilled gates stood ajar. He stepped through, saw what he supposed must be the concierge's lodge to one side, and rang the bell.

There was an aroma of something wonderfully appetizing simmering. From the court he heard, faintly, a piano doing baroque cadenzas: somebody was playing with a window open. He waited.

And was about to ring again when this stringy little woman in a grey smock came scurrying out of the court and down the passage toward him. Jingling a great ring of keys. Gabbling God knew what.

Ms. Godfrey murmured, "Oh *poor* Frenchless ambassador," she should never have left him!

Anyhow he'd finally made out, he said, that it must be the sixth floor at the rear of the court he wanted— Nieumann oui oui oui oui mais oui *là!* or some such, and he had crossed to the entry. High up over somewhere the piano was spilling this glittering allegro down through the sunny air; Haydn, it sounded like, or Mozart; notes like handfuls of facetted jewels; showering down the elevator shaft too as the glass cage rose with him smoothly up and up nearer through the spirals of the surrounding stair, and when he came level with the sixth floor, it turned out that was where it was coming from. And when of the two doors that faced across the landing he rang the one whose card read BINGHAM/NEWMAN, sure enough the piano broke off in the middle of a bar.

So what to expect he'd no idea. He waited.

But at once the door'd been briskly opened, and there was this tall suave young man with a cup of café au lait in one hand and half a croissant in the other. He had nothing but one of those loose towel-robes on. And was chewing something. He gazed amiably at Sather, mumbled "Mouth full; sorry," politely, and went on chewing.

Sather told Ms. Godfrey it had rather taken him aback. So he'd filled the interval: afraid was he disturbing him? forgive him, his name was Sather and he was looking for a Mr. Newman. He was a long-time friend of his family's, and he happened to be in Par—

But "Mr. Sather good god *yes!*" the fellow'd interrupted (having meantime it seemed swallowed), "you're this kindly ambassador we've been threatened with—or is it seen as a Mission? God bless me how d'you do I'm John Bingham. And you meet me at my cleanest. As you can as good as see. Come in, sir, come *in*, Chad I'm sorry's out of town for the moment. But at least this morning," he'd run courteously on, and led him in, to a long sunflooded room where a girl (in nothing but a loose towel-robe either) sat at the keyboard of a grand piano, staring at them—"*this* morning we can offer the local amenities of woman and song. In one delectable package. Miss Barretts is studying at the Conservatoire. And happens to be at *her* cleanest too. As, again, you can see. Or partly see. Or do I mean see in part. Barretts, this is a Mr. Sather, of New York, de passage for our improvement."

The child looked at him with great golden eyes, and said, "Hullo," through a yawn.

"Will you listen to that?" cried Bingham, as if in delight. "Who says women don't reward effort! A mere month ago, when she came floating into the Embassy like Spring in a Botticelli, all she'd have said was Hi. In fact it was the first complete sentence she ever addressed to me. But now by god give me till Bastille Day and we'll have her saying How-d'you-do as if she'd been born to it!"

"He doesn't approve of being from California, is all," Miss Barretts said, to Sather. "He says it disinterests him. Venery, what heaven."

She pushed the piano bench back and came gracefully to her feet, the folds of the robe still more or less around her.

"All *sorts* of things can disinterest him," she went on, to Sather. "You've got to be lucky he let you in at all. You know what he did the other day? the other day a couple of perfectly *sweet* young missionaries came to the door and said, 'We're Mormons,' and you know what he said? he said, 'Why bring your spiritual misgivings to me?' and shut the door in their faces! Well nice met y'by," and trundled off.

At the door, she turned and looked back at Bingham. "Your *friends!*" she giggled. And vanished.

"*That's* how things are," Bingham said amiably. "And as for the foreseeable future if it's not Freud at our case-histories it'll be Bowdler. The content, sir, is the all—take some heavenly creature to see the Sainte-Chapelle and she'll want you to explain the plots in the stained glass to her! God moves in His customary preoccupied way, tossing off universal truths at random intervals. Or quoting Saint Paul—far and away His favorite author. In a thunder of Sinaitic platitudes. But here, sir, dammit, what am I thinking of!—what can I do for you?"

And in short, Sather finished it, with a mild snort, the visit had been preposterous from the word go.

But Ms. Godfrey murmured, "Oh *dear!*" as if stricken.

So naturally Sather looked blank.

But what was she to *do*, she *knew* Jock Bingham! she as good as lamented. She saw him all the *time!*—clients wanted things done for them at the Embassy, and that was Jock. And she saw him at parties! She'd even danced with him, and here Sather was giving her this—this—did she mean unbuttoned or unbosoming? view into the poor man's private life, how *perfectly* awful!

So about all he could say was well God bless.

Well she should think so!

Though how was he or anyone, he protested mildly, to have expected the damn' world to be so small.

But *this* sort of coincidence!

But he said but not really, considering her job and Bingham's?—and Chad an American? Simple matter of course. As had sharing the apartment been, for that matter, according to Bingham. One day a couple of years ago he'd happened to drop past the consulate downstairs on his way out to lunch, and there had been this well-turned-out young guy sitting waiting to see the consul, and damned if he hadn't his own club tie on. So Bingham said he'd stopped in front of him and said wasn't that a Quad tie he was wearing? and the guy'd looked up surprised and said well yes. So he'd said well be damned, what class was he? and he'd said '77, what was *he?* and he'd said '73. And the guy'd said for God's sweet sake fancy meeting him in *this* assembly-line, what was *he* here after? So naturally he'd said he worked here, what could he expedite for him? and it had turned out what he wanted was some advice on apartment hunting. Which was God's personalized service if ever there'd been—Morgan Guaranty were just transferring his current roommate to London. So, Bingham said, he and Chad had had lunch together, very agreeably, and he'd shown him the Avenue Bosquet set-up, and when the roommate moved out Chad had moved in.

Perfect relationship ever since. Minded his own business; also they had a nice selection of random tastes in common. Even found they had some of the same friends. Couple of cocks on a blue-chip midden, yes, but the midden was of course all Western Europe.

But Ms. Godfrey seemed unappeased. Because merely how was she to *face* the abashing man the next time she saw him? she fretted. Because this girl— The things one learned, goodness!

He said, amused, well it was a generation she was a good many years nearer to than alas he was. In his day girls had done their overseas marauding on junior-year-abroad, or on fulbrights. But this Barretts child it seemed was doing spectacularly well on her own. Talented musically but in fact also paying her way with it, composing that bogus-Black stuff for a French nightclub band. Played piano in this band's cellar it appeared some nights herself—'the sort of enterprise our international trade balance could use a lot more of,' Bingham had put it.

—But otherwise, Sather went on, he'd pretty much drawn a blank in the Avenue Bosquet. Chad was 'somewhere in the south of France'; he rang up every now and then to ask about mail or the like; last time, he'd said he'd thought of dropping in on his married sister (who was it seemed staying with a man named Waymarsh, in Grasse); be heading home in a few days. Or probably. Or perhaps. And in short about all he'd got from his visit was that unlisted telephone number.

Ms. Godfrey said '. . . staying with'?

Newman family lawyer. Though what of all people Waymarsh was doing in foreign parts, God knew. Hardly part of his own operation anyhow—he doubted if Waymarsh would be even Mrs. Newman's notion of a fall-back position! And in any case that wouldn't explain what Chad's sister was doing there. What was she looking amused about?

'Overseas marauding' was *his* phrase not hers. But now with the sister too?

He said blandly well no, hardly occur to anybody to think of Waymarsh as dirty-old-man enough. Still, who knew who knew. But to go back to the Avenue Bosquet (how'd they ever got off onto something like Waymarsh good god)—the upshot was, here he now found himself, and in particular might he say *her*, with an unexpected amount of time to kill. From her point of view this might simply— Look, he said, with nothing actually to *do* but wait around until Chad turned up, marking time he meant could well be something her agency didn't—

But this was what they *did!* she cried, what did he suppose?

All the same he felt, well, diffident. So he hoped she would consider— It wasn't as if she'd have to be with him all that constantly, just that he—

But she didn't have to be 'kept amused'! When she liked him?—*and* being with him!

So he mumbled well very kind, *very* kind.

And anyway wasn't he really rather used to it, with women?

He said (and it might have been warily) oh nonsense—simply he'd found women were—how should he put it?—*nicer* to older men. They thought they were sweet or some such adjective. Or at any rate they didn't seem to feel they had to brace themselves to beat off those immediate attacks. The trouble though was it seemed to take a man all those years to find out enough of what a woman was like to treat her the way she baffled him by wanting him to, damn' sad.

Yes she said so stupid. But then if women didn't keep men's morale up somehow in the endless meantime look what they had on their hands, she said. No but to go back, had he found out what Mr. Newman occupied his time with? or was it architecture again. Or still.

Well *this* part, he said, was hardly believable. Certainly to *his* astonishment anyway, but it appeared Chad had been seriously in the stock market from by god college on! During Carter days he'd even done so well with short positions that he'd made a great deal of money. To top it off, on the election he'd not so much bet on national gullibility as plunged—and of course made a killing. A *serious* market-analyst in short! Maybe he ought to offer him a job in his own office—detach him *that* way from whoever-she-was, why not!

But then they were coming into Versailles.

And this hotel, she explained, she particularly wanted him to see, they'd have lunch there and he'd see, because it was not only

Edwardian-elegant but they what used to be called 'cossetted' you. So it would be far more she thought his sort of place than that new rich-American'd one he was in, even if the Empress Eugénie *had* lived there staring sadly out over the Tuileries after she was deposed, she'd died in 1920 anyway, anyway if you were nearly a hundred did you *notice?* But *this* hotel was right at the edge of the Trianon side of the immense palace gardens, at the Porte de la Reine, in fact it was in a sort of woodsy arboretum and rose gardens of its own.

And the thing about the great hotels of the Edwardian era was how much more they were laid out for the comforts of life architecturally. In this one for instance what led to the dining room was a very long room made wide enough for tea-tables and easy chairs and love-seats, it was like an English 'long gallery,' they served tea there in winter, and all along one side of it tall French windows opened out in summer for tea or drinks onto a great terrace toward the trees, and on its inner side there was an absolutely charming white-and-gold-paneled ballroom, of course there were no balls now except at weddings, but on weekends they'd been experimenting with it as a nightclub (after of course sound-proofing the ceiling!) did he like to dance? and off it there was a little bar.

Then at the far end was the dining room and it had its terrasse outside too, toward the rose gardens, for dinner by lamplight or candles in the warm night, in high summer. And today being Sunday they had an immense buffet 'brunch,' usually sixty or seventy first-course dishes, you took a plate and served yourself, and while it was not attitudinized or *haute* cuisine it was always impeccable.

The British upper-executive class seemed to have discovered it but, still, it was a *good* hotel. And it was only ten minutes' walk from her apartment, so if he wanted to see some of France as well as Paris while he waited for Chad to rescue his sister or whatever he was doing, it would save a *lot* of time and energy if he stayed here, he could try the buffet and look at the place and decide.

So he made a first course (which she translated dish by dish as he took some) of escabèche de poissons, fougères à la grecque, jambon persillé, langoustines, salade de riz, salade de concombres aux moules, and an artichaut farci. During which, among other things, she said if they were going to spend time together in this pleasant dallying way till Mr. Newman turned up who knew really when, shouldn't they be sensible about first names.

✦

So next morning she moved him out to Versailles. And saw him settled in.

And then checked off at least seeing Chartres, lunch and the cathedral, where they found themselves caught up in a gaping British charabanc-tour who were being told, window by window, the plots in the stained glass.

Then back in Versailles she said voilà, and now for the evening? should she pick him up about eight for dinner? They could drive into Paris, she'd reserve a table at one of her favorite best places, it was out the Avenue du Maine and one never saw anybody there but impeccable bourgeois doing themselves *extremely* well. Also this man had a rosé d'Arbois which would be new to him, because it didn't travel—and he needn't look skeptical, it wasn't a Midi rosé it was almost a deep ruby. Arbois was in the Jura. Which is off there between Burgundy and Switzerland. It was, did he know? Pasteur's pays. But the *famous* Arbois wine was a yellow, called vin de paille: it was for dessert, like sauternes and those German trockenbeeren wines. She *had* heard they made coq au vin with it locally, but wouldn't he be dubious too?

—It however turned out that with eventually a guinea they had a Beaune; and (eyes smiling at him across the candlelight) she was inquiring gently into his character.

"Are you sort of what I'm beginning to think you are?" she asked, in a voice of almost promises, "—or more anyway Lewis I mean than I thought you were, sort of, at first?"

He said oh he was pretty much standard fare. Made money. Spent it. Made more. Tended to spend that then too.

"No but I meant your—how you *live* generally, do with your time and all I mean."

If she meant his spare time, he had a sloop in the Sound. And played squash winters. But if she meant was he married, no he wasn't. Had been, years ago. Charming girl too. Got tired of each other, of course. Amicably tired, but tired. She'd remarried. Hadn't seen her for years. Amicably tired of his successor too by this time very likely. Restless like anyone.

"But you," she persisted, "you're 'sophisticated' the way Americans are sophisticated when they are. I do like the way you look, Lewis, shall I alarm you by saying? But do you think, possibly, you might be happier if you were sophisticated the way Europeans are? Or think they are—having had their parochial worries longer."

He said, smiling, oh now now. He made do.

"Yes but I mean your character, Lewis, are you perhaps a little, well, melancholy?" she asked, as if in tender amusement. "Should I try to divert you specially somehow?—take you to the Grand Véfour say in my yellow silk? that one of the girls at Chanel (they *all* do, you know) copied for me absolutely stitch for stitch, because how am I to know about you? You make it sound so bleak, 'make do.' "

Well she was sweet, he said; but of course it never struck you as bleak at the time, how could it? One picked up a lovely signal, if that was what she was asking. At a party. Across a milling room. The signals he supposed differed from generation to generation, but suddenly a look would say—and to *you*—'Here I am. . . .' A pretty woman was bored with her husband. Or disillusioned with a lover. Likely of course to be the fellow's own damn' fault. But suppose at the moment one had too much unprincipled indolence to refuse. It could even last the whole season. Then off for the summer, Maine or the Cape or wherever, and by autumn each of you would have gone on, even if a bit apologetically, to something new. A bit of nostalgia and tenderness first time you met again, but that was simply good manners. Did he need to describe it? Been divorced herself hadn't she?

She was silent.

Well but hadn't she?

So she murmured, ". . . differently," smiling a little.

Well, however it was. Simply there was this disenchantment, was the principle. How did women operate either? So it was targets of opportunity. He'd had a wicked old uncle who as good as reduced it to a formula—'Absolute dish of a girl. Married, too, which is always convenient.'

" 'Convenient'!"

Well, he'd admit, yes, it did sound a bit lazy—competition only a husband. Who'd have lost her already presumably—otherwise this lovely thunderbolt wouldn't be poised over your head. No, but his uncle had an entirely humane position even if he didn't put it that way. And even if it looked like a dilemma of egotism! Because what kind of (it might be) desperation *was* it standing there looking her question straight at you? How did you know you weren't being asked for an act of humanity?—being *trusted* for it!

"Oh but *Lewis*," she said, laughing at him, "you can't be saying you think of your sexual behavior as high-minded!"

Plato thought *his* was didn't he? No, be serious—suppose you're her first. She's nerved herself up to something she may even have been brought up to be shocked at. And the *risk* she's running! Is a decent-minded man to back irresponsibly off? And leave a perhaps very sweet woman to some eventual oaf who'll do no better by her than her husband? Hadn't she *seen* what some of her clients were like?

"Are you?" she said lightly, watching the waiter serve their feuilleté aux framboises.

Ah he and they were all pretty much of an age and kind, he said, watching too. Next year his class would have their thirtieth reunion. She know what most of them would turn up thinking?— even saying? 'Well I'm still by god alive anyway!' She conceive of it? Man after man of them! Appalling! Well then what kind of husband was that to stay appetizingly faithful to. Hadn't done what, thirty years before, they'd confidently expected. Or hoped. Hadn't had a respectable number of love affairs. Didn't even seem to be aware they hadn't. Hadn't of course paid enough elementary attention to women to *have* had. Hardly any longer try—poor sods given that up too. Whereas all these goddam young men (they'll complain to you) mind you in our *own college*— All right, he said, giggle, but most of them were a breed that hadn't really *understood* anything much that happens to the race of man since they were told in kindergarten it didn't, and he found it *sad!*

"No but Lewis what I was ask—"

Made all kinds of money, yes, but then what? Just morosely make more? Make enough to parlay it up dear god into Washington? Would she believe that a couple of bankery dull bastards he was at Yale with were now *making* foreign policy, God help us all? . . .

So she teased him. "Are you perhaps just a *little* an intellectual snob? No but Lewis to go back I mean—you can't always just stand there looking humane and available till somebody comes up and says 'Console me' can you, or shouldn't I ask?"

Laugh if she liked, he said amiably, but what could anybody do, considering the reciprocating incompetences? The expectations, the hair-raising myths, one grew up in! . . . For instance the sense in which one was or was not somebody's property was beyond a layman to define. 'Tenancy at will' perhaps a lawyer would call it—but then, at the end of it, were you entitled to emblements or weren't you?

"But Lewis where would men be," she protested, teasing still, "if every now and then a woman didn't make a totally incompetent decision about you?"

Thank God of *course*. But suppose it was God forbid an old friend's wife who'd suddenly looked her immemorial query into your eyes—in that *instant* what black gulfs of revelation had opened! And this, mind you, about a man you'd known perhaps from prep-school on, and assumed was as like you in attitudes as another man could be. And no doubt was. But now?—how many secret hours had she been considering you, wondering about you, weighing you, *comparing* you, and now *this* difference! And if you answered that lovely look, think before the night was out what you would have been pitilessly told, and listened to as comfortless for him as she. He conceded, the consensus was it was comedy. As his old uncle used to say, 'Why not seduce a friend's wife?—far more humane than causing pain to some poor chap you hardly know.' But his uncle had never been anything but a bachelor. So did she see?

"And you don't call *that* bleak?" she cried.

Let him finish, dammit. All this was just the, well, the scenario one seemed to be handed. But the theme, for him, was the actors rather than the action. Or call it style. The beginnings of an affair were of course in themselves a great pleasure. But they were hardly the end a man of experience would have in mind. Who anybody *was* was the final charming secret; and this, the girl in your arms might only decide to let you think you were discovering. Though even for that she had to be convinced you really wanted to know. For all he could tell, the ultimate humanity was *not* finding it out anyhow—the history of Western civilization had been its processes, after all, not our endlessly mistaken 'answers.' Put another way, he said, smiling at her, was there anyone to talk to to your heart's content but someone in your arms?

"But oh *dear!*" she cried. "But Lewis how *wicked* and disarming! Are you really as—"

'Disarming'!—when it was merely how he did see it? good god there'd been times when he felt like Lord Chesterfield, 'the most agreeable things he had ever heard had been from persons in a horizontal position.'

So she looked at him smiling.

But she said, "No but how am I to describe it to anyone who hasn't *been* besieged? your way or not. You all say why *not* fall in love, what good does it do not to?—as if that were the argument! When really there isn't any argument, is there. Because nothing a man says is plausible, it's *he* who is. Or, most of the time, isn't, poor sweet."

He said what kind of heartless stodgy word was this 'besiege' of hers! No man laid siege, in any case, the way she meant it. It was women made these lovely decisions wasn't it? so all a 'siege' was was a man's modest signal that he hoped he might be decided on, and knew he sometimes was.

And so forth and so on.

But as it was still clearly too soon for any of this theory to be put into practice, they had for that evening wordlessly left it at that.

✦

Next morning, though, he had said yes, well, but what was *she* like then generally either? And as this trip he was driving, she could look at him carefully, though what she had the moment before been doing was fill him in on the economics and geography of the Cotentin peninsula.

For though he had said there were some things in Paris he'd like to see, the Jeu de Paume pictures for instance, after New York wasn't Paris in most ways just another great city? and France must have other countrysides rather less bland than those vistas going out to Chartres. Country was in fact what he'd like to see most. And architecture was a hobby of his, if they had time. But also his father had been in the 1944 invasion; in filial piety he ought to go look at Omaha Beach, could they do it in a day?

So they were well on their way to Caen when he asked what she was like then generally either.

"How d'you mean," she said, " 'either'?"

Meant how she happened to be, for one thing, living in France like this.

"But I love France! And the French let you breathe. I had a Tourangelle grandmother, I used to visit her in the summer. Ever since I can remember. France is *home*. So after my divorce I put ads in college alumni magazines, and *very* soon I was so busy I needed a partner. Now after three years and a half there are three of us, and extras on call. And really Lewis it is a lovely life—expense-account lovely anyway. Some clients I told you can be yearning and tiresome, but when they're good-looking and high-powered it's good for one's morale."

Then she mustn't have stayed married long.

"Oh but Lewis I told you—it was stupid. I mean I shouldn't have *married* him, it was perfectly sweet as it was. But then my roommate was having this horsing-around *messy* affair and I guess it was sort of contrast."

'Messy'?

"Yes with this professor of English. Because he had this just devastating campus reputation, among other things he gave a very advanced course in James Joyce and you had to be interviewed to get into it, and then once you were in, *then* he took his pick. Well anyway that was the myth, and girls got besotted about him. On the wall over his bed there was a needlepoint sampler one of his girls had made him as a valentine, all hearts and cowrie shells, and it had a motto from *Finnegans Wake*, 'Hadn't he seven dams to wive him each with her different hue and cry,' and he certainly did!"

He said catnip, huh.

"Well he *was*, I guess. And my roommate was a crazy girl and for a *joke* went to be interviewed. Only she came back looking sort of stunned and out of her mind, and said well she'd *heard* how he affected students 'but oh god Maria that's how he's affected *me!*' Well *hilarious* of course but don't you see also it's rather scary? to see somebody totally lose her head over a man like that? Because *instantly* you think suppose it happens to *me!*"

And sometimes he said it does.

She murmured, ". . . yes," as if humbly.

This Edwardian old uncle of his, he said, used to amuse himself concocting turn-of-the-century epigrams about that sort of thing. They dated, he supposed, epigrams. But he remembered one that wasn't far from the point. 'What the lovely things are up to in bed with us they seldom say. In the opinion of competent observers they seldom know.' The style was, he'd concede, dated.

"But my roommate wasn't!"

Not all that difference! Yale innocently went coed before her roommate's time didn't it? and he gathered the sudden delicious new perquisites had left the faculty exhausted.

"You don't have to snicker!" she cried. "Girls need to practice on *somebody*—and what practice does a boy give? All the *work* still to be done on him, goodness!"

He said amiably they'd let another woman do the buffing-up? Damn' lazy, if you asked him. Not to say running risks! Or had perhaps something of the sort (if she'd permit him to ask, in sympathy need he say not from curiosity)—had something like that been the trouble in her marriage?

"Oh no *that* wasn't the trouble," she said. "He was sweet. I mean I suppose he still is, he's sort of a writer."

He said he saw.

So she stared at him. "I don't see how you can 'see'!" she cried. "What could being a writer have to do with it? Oh well you might as well *know* about me I guess. Simply I fell out of love with him. But he kept on being upset, I mean after the divorce too. So once I did really give it a second try, Lewis. Because he rang up from New York. He was coming to the south of France around Easter, he was going to hole up somewhere near Le Canadel and write a novel, and *please* wouldn't I try again. If nothing else, we could stay at Nîmes or Arles and go to the bullfights, I'd be going south for Easter like everybody else wouldn't I? So I thought oh dear. But it wasn't as if I were in love then with anybody else. And, well, after all I *hadn't* you know made love for practically ages, in love or not. So I said to him well I would *try* meeting him, better perhaps in Arles, I said, we'd be less likely to run into somebody I knew than in Nîmes, which for one thing is three times as big, so all right I'd meet him, the bulls would be fun. And he sounded oh just so helplessly *happy*, all those thousands of miles of lonely ocean away, that I was *touched*, it could have been me, I suppose. So he met my plane in Marseille, and when we got to the hotel in Arles I found he'd been so uncertain, poor sweet, about how he was afraid I might feel, that he'd taken separate rooms for us, and I was touched all over again."

He said dangerous.

"Well *yes!* The most *total* self-trap! But I was so attendrie I almost wondered whether it wouldn't be kind to be a poule de luxe that night for him, the way I used to do for his birthday. And once for Christmas. Only of course *that* would have left him feeling even more bereft when I was gone. Oh dear, what are you looking like that for?—hasn't any girl ever done a Special Occasion for you?"

Hardly though in *these* particular—what should he call them? —these re-marital circumstances.

"But haven't you ever taken up again with somebody?"

He said oh a couple of times, yes.

"Like what."

Usual thing—a bit sad.

"You're ashamed of it?"

Certainly not!

"Then *tell!*"

Why, he said, it was simply for instance like a visiting girl he'd met at a rowdy party of a classmate's and he found haunted him after she'd gone home to her Berkeley husband. So, presently, on a trip to see clients he had in San Francisco, like an infatuated boy he'd rung her number. What opinion of his past behavior he'd have when he was seventy, God knew; but her voice again, answering her phone there in her house across the bay— Was it God's plan to have us unteachably susceptible, or what? The party might have been no more than the night before!

"The rowdy party?"

In one of those formal old brick houses in East 11th, it had been, in the Village. Normal Village party of the era, too—everybody tight in the usual pleasantly pointless way; on into the usual small hours; usual drunken bellows of good night echoing up the stairwell from the dark hall below as at long last it was ending; and suddenly this girl had materialized before him. As if from nowhere. Mind you he hadn't said ten words to her all evening— somebody had introduced them, hours back, and they'd said hello, and so help him not ten words since. But now here this charming thing stood, eyes looking gravely into his. It could have been a dream, it was so strange.

And taken aback he supposed he must have appeared, for she'd reached up, looking amused, and let a wrist fall lightly on each of his shoulders, as if it were a ritual—and what was he to have done. They stood there; they might have been alone in the world. Then she said softly, 'Where do you live? . . .' and that year he happened to be living just round the block, in East 10th.

So, well, in short, when he opened his eyes in the lovely summer-Sunday dawn, she was sitting on the edge of his bed in a yellow Chinese dressing gown of his, with the cuffs turned back from her wrists, gazing down at him with no particular expression. He had gazed back, his mind foggily reconstructing. After a minute or two he'd said, 'Thinking me over? . . .' and after a minute or two of her own she'd murmured, 'Should I?' and then there had been this slightly smiling silence. Until, finally, he'd more or less mumbled, 'I wasn't, you know, standard . . . .' and she'd given this little yelp of amusement, 'Heavens did you think I was?' and toppled giggling down into his arms.

Maria said, "Oh *dear*," looking at him. "Are you always being spoiled like this?"

'Spoiled'!

"Well goodness but don't you think?"

Hardly call it a thing like 'spoiled'—good god the angel had had to go home to her damn' husband before even the week was out!

"Oh *poor* man!" she mocked. "So deserted so forlorn! How could *any* woman!"

Ah, well, he said, amusing wasn't how you saw these things at the time. When you'd been stunned? When there wasn't world enough and time for the feast you were being deprived of? He'd seen her off at Newark as good as wordless with woe. She too: at the end she'd just managed a last choking '. . . Take care of yourself?' and fled down the tunnel to her plane. Without a glance back. And he had turned and come away, death in his soul.

So Maria looked at him solemnly, as respecting this.

Dismal he said in fact all round. And then, would she believe it? in San Francisco she'd, she'd tearfully refused even to see him.

"Oh Lewis how *awful!*"

Been fairly bad, yes. Though likely enough would've been bad seeing her too. Who was to say.

"But why?"

How'd anyone know. Probably been a great mistake to give her time to come to her senses. Or at least decide whether he was worth the, call it the turmoil, the emotional risks. In fact she'd said so— 'Oh sweet do you really want us to have to get over each other a *second* time ? . . .' He found he remembered every accusing syllable. In short she'd been sensible: a damn' shame. Though he supposed how not. Heartbreaking, though, if you liked stately terms. But one had to expect it—women had somehow edited the sensibilities-scenario so it was always they who were nobly wounded. Which he presumed was what conferred on them the right to say Yes or No. It had been she, hadn't it? who'd agreed to meet this ex-husband of hers again! And had the poor devil dared more than take a separate room for her like a gent?

"Oh Lewis don't be tiresome—what was I down there *for*, heavens!"

. . . But he thought hadn't she said she was touched?

"But who wouldn't be? He was sweet. But being touched isn't falling in love, heavens. And how could any man think being unassuming was a way to put me in a swoon about him—well, one despairs! And then oh it was so perfectly *silly*—couldn't I always have said No to him in the same room? But then if I was going to decide to make love with him again, why pay for an extra room! And anyway what on earth did he imagine the patronne thought a man and a girl came to her hotel in the Easter vacation to *do* besides eat and go to bullfights!—so he'd made us look childishly innocent of the world as *well* as perfectly ridiculous. I never did find out who he gave her to understand I was—for all I know he told her I was an old friend or something, and of course what 'une ancienne amie' *means,* poor dear, is 'a former mistress.' When why explain at all! Well naturally the patronne's manners were impeccable, this is after all France, but imagine arriving to find oneself stuck with such a hopeless méprise! And when *anybody* in the hotel could see he was all blissful over me, so the separate bedrooms looked sillier still!"

Hard to bear, Sather said; um.

"And then he didn't know every hotel in Arles is booked *weeks* ahead for the bullfights—so after two days the patronne was terribly sorry for Monsieur's malentendu but we must vacate our rooms! We were appalled; we said but what were we to *do,* go back to Paris at *Easter?*—surely she could find us a room somewhere! She said well she did have a cousin who had an attic apartment that might not be taken, but Madame and Monsieur—well, there were two *beds* in her cousin's grenier, but it was just the one room, if Madame understood . . . ? So I thought very fast and said but had she or perhaps her cousin by any chance a paravent? because something like that, didn't she think, between the beds. . . . So of course instantly she was beaming and d'accord, *much* relieved, mais bien sûr she had a paravent if in effect that would turn the difficulty for Madame, she would send a girl at once to her cousin's to make sure the apartment was still free. I saw I said no difficulties whatever, Monsieur and I were perfectly débrouillards and in any case we had known each other since childhood; and off she went. He said 'What in God's name's a paravent?' I said a folding screen, what did he think. He said, 'She thinks a *screen's* going to preserve your modesty?' I said, 'Heavens d'you think she believes we were childhood friends either? Just this is good manners and *France.*' So, presently, there was this solemn little procession up through the streets to her cousin's attic—us, two maids with our luggage, and a little old man from the cousin's pottering along behind with the paravent. I thought it was *hilarious!*" she finished.

Husband, though, probably didn't?

"No he did too. But then after the bullfights I anyway transplanted us off to Aix—to *one* room, and if he behaved like an undergraduate, what matter."

So for a kilometer or so they were silent.

Presently she said, "But then anyway it turned out I wasn't any wilder about him than before. So it didn't work out."

Ah well, he said, she'd been a sweet to try.

"But now he's written a very dejected novel about it. It isn't published yet, but he sent me a copy of the manuscript. It's sort of what the French called nouveau roman, only of course that's been out-of-date for twenty years, d'you suppose he didn't know? Anyway, *his* is written in what you called stately terms, not French at all."

He said, sounding amused, 'wild about'?—what kind of criterion was that!

"Well isn't it?" she demanded. "You needn't sound sardonic and superior! Haven't you ever lost your head? Or do you just go round being hard to get over!"

Writing a novel about a sad parting with a girl you'd not been able to forget, he said smoothly, hardly struck him as a sensible way to forget her. Though ah, who was sensible. Some heavenly creature took your breath away by walking into your arms—only to change her damn' mind about you and walk out of them with just as little explanation. Enough for any man to hang himself over. Particularly when young. And she, Maria, might he add—well, after these four days of her he didn't wonder at the depths the poor devil's dejection must have plunged him to! Could ruin any novel, what'd she expect! She know that mock-Restoration lyric?—

> Why should a decent-minded God
> Trouble my sleep with you?

—that wasn't a question, God *bless* no, that was a complaint to the Management.

So for a long moment she gazed at him so soberly that she nearly let him miss the turn-off for Dives-Cabourg.

Where, then, before the estuary, they stopped at a charcuterie for pâté de campagne and saucisson sec, at a bakery for a baguette, and at a Suma for a wedge of Brie, three hundred grammes of Breton strawberries, a bottle of Brouilly, and a packet of paper napkins.

Next morning she rang him at breakfast to ask what should she propose they do today? assuming Jock Bingham had still no word from Chad. Perhaps *not* so far as Normandy this time? Would he like to see Rambouillet?—the château and the lovely forest? They could set out late-morning, it wasn't far, and eat somewhere on the way.

At Le Perray there was a charming inn, set in what the French called a parc. Or, a little off the direct route, a *very* good restaurant at Châteaufort. So they could be back for tea, the hotel served beautiful pastry, he could have a tarte aux fraises des bois, and he could phone Mrs. Newman, wasn't six o'clock here midmorning there?

He said fine, fine; if she meant a lazy day, why not; end up perhaps with dinner at the hotel and then go dancing there, she care to? he hadn't brought evening clothes but *she* could dress, to dazzle him.

—And dazzling in fact she was, in half-naked summer black, and they had dinner, late, out on the rose-garden terrasse in the soft June evening, the myriad gleam of candles from table to table so barely luminous a dusk there were aisles as of outer darkness between, each table might have been a little tent of light pitched secret and apart, lit from within, so that women's eyes shone like dark gold in it for you, lustrous and a marvel, or with a glitter as of promise no matter what in their minds lay hidden and unguessed. At a table near, a man Sather's age perhaps and a young woman of Maria's were surely (Maria murmured) in love—it was how they gazed, and twice she said the girl's fingertips had touched his hand. Except but oh *look*, had she brought her *children* to a rendezvous?—for on a dusky balcony two stories above two small girls in summer nightgowns were peering over the railing down, and presently, giggling with love, they'd begun dropping crumbs (from their suppers?) down onto that table, and soon the whole terrasse was sharing in the amusement.

Sather said 'lovers'? nonsense. The fellow was much too old. Must be her father. Or uncle.

" 'Too old'—with *your* history?" she teased. "Hoh!"

What history.

"Well you might admit for once mightn't you? I mean for instance look, you've had affairs with girls *ten* years younger than you haven't you?—well, so then have you with a girl fifteen years younger ever too?"

So naturally he snorted at her. What was this sociological Socratic elenchus leading up to—the difference in ages (alas) between the two of *them*?

She said sweetly, "Well or shouldn't it? No but I mean Lewis for instance that Berkeley girl you seem to've so completely— And if you didn't want me to ask questions about her you shouldn't have boasted! So how much was *she* younger?"

Damned if he'd boasted! He'd merely—

"Fifteen years younger? *Twenty?*"

How was he to know?—hardly the sort of thing you asked! Could have been anything more or less young. What did age have to do with it anyhow.

So she looked at him it seemed astonished.

"But Lewis didn't you even think what she could have been *through* over you?" she demanded. "Because I mean at that age meeting an attractive man who can help thinking 'oh what would it be like to have him?' only then there is the danger too, you *know* how fast you fall in love—so all evening long she could have been in this fever or spellbound or seduced or whatever. *But waiting.* For what if you were working your way toward her through the party uproar. Only what if she turned round and you weren't. Or weren't even near. Or were leaving. . . . And then abruptly there was the party beginning to break up, with *nothing* decided about you, she hadn't even shut her eyes and wished; and she simply— Well what would anybody do! she came up to you in this daze and just helplessly claimed you, do you understand *anything?*" she more or less accused him.

So (if only courteously to the contrary) he was silent.

"Oh well I know not 'claimed,'" she fretted, "but it was a choice wasn't it? I mean, *serious!* Not just a have-bed-will-bundle. Or as if you'd been just anybody. And then next morning a choice all over again, and certainly *then* réfléchi. So I don't see how she could just go back to her life or whatever. Or even why did you let her!" she cried, as if past belief.

—Later, though, as if continuing, and this was hours later, the shadowy white and gold of the ballroom as if softly candle-lit too for the slow wheeling patterns of the dancers—turning and turning in his arms to the music's discourse she murmured, ". . . or did you I guess have your usual New York girl you were being unfaithful to then too?" so gently she might, already, have had a right to indulge him.

So, as such things go, a good deal of what may nevertheless want saying could be considered said.

The rest of the ritual following naturally dans les formes too. "Because what I seem to be trying you know to make up my mind about," she told him, as they turned, "is *are* you more what I wondered whether you mightn't turn out to be than I'd expected I'd think."

He said (amused, having decoded this) why, he hoped an attitude of the most respectful attentiveness—

"Oh Lewis *don't* be bogus-worldly at me!" she begged. "Because but anyway no, what I mean is, somehow we've— It does seem I've— *Have* you taken a fancy to me?"

When she'd dammit explicitly warned him *off?!*

"But sweet that was only—"

And before they'd good god more than sat down at Drouant! In the face of *that* charming No—and at his age!—was he to have presumed on what an absolute darling to be with he'd found her, to insist on telling her how adorable he found her too?

"You're not perhaps just softening my heart Lewis in the usual low male way?"

He said, smiling, dammit he was a modest man! Why was he to think the happy details of how he felt about her weren't exactly what she'd forbidden him to recite?

"But goodness," she said, smiling too, "is it something to sound so sad about? All the average man requires is the services of a small portable woman of some kind. But you aren't *that* average are you? Should I reflect about you I mean d'you think?" she ended, teasing.

So it became merely a question of which of them shouldn't too abruptly suggest wasn't it perhaps time (tomorrow's excursion starting early)—time they called it an evening? and he saw her home? it being, after all, by then, well on into the small hours anyway.

Though she did murmur a gently tactical "Ah do I really fetch you Lewis?—and so soon?" slipping a hand through his arm as they sauntered off through the hotel gates into the summer night of the Avenue de la Reine and along under the lindens in the dark, the gleam of a street lamp only here and there sifting down through the dusty foliage into patterns of leaf-shadow across the cracks and crevices of the pavement. And when at the carrefour they turned into her Avenue du Roi, silent and fathomless it too among its looming shadows, "*Are* you hard to get over?" she asked—but teasing still, so he could answer (as why not?) well he tried his gentlemanly damn' best to be! and in a happy voice she could pretend, "But suppose the lovely roof fell in on us . . . ." until under the lamp at the corner of her cross street they wandered to a stop and kissed, lightly, tastingly, a good dozen times it could have been, before drifting murmuring on.

So at last, at her door in the black starlight, she said almost dreamily, ". . . and when you've never even seen me home before, oh sweet isn't it strange," rummaging in her handbag for her key. "And then *this*," she mumbled, and slotted the key into the lock.

—Hours, then, it may have been, later (dawn, outside, if they'd bothered to look) that she seemed to decide, for whatever reason, to set at least part of the ambiguities drowsily straight.

". . . It was my other partner, you know, not me."

He made some vague dozing sound.

"Who had I mean an affair with Jock Bingham."

Did, huh, he agreed; *well*.

"And still maybe *is* having was why I sounded I guess startled that day."

. . . 'd wondered, yes.

"Because you *aren't* are you sweetie going to be stupid and jealous over me?"

He said no.

They slept late.

—And slept late the second morning too, for that matter.

But then in due course later still ("Le petit déjeuner. De mon amant. Est sur la table. Mon amour get *up*, I am teaching you aren't-you-hungry French") dawdling over breakfast too in the brilliance and happy senses of on toward noon ("'Complacencies of the peignoir' oh sweet 'and late coffee and oranges,' well it's a sortie de bain of course not a peignoir, but 'par complaisance' oh *dear!*") she began the reconstruction of their history, myths and all.

"Tell me something? I mean the *truth?*"

So he looked amused and wary.

"Did you feel I was a *long* time making up my mind about you? Or did you."

"I was to have expected *this?*" he demanded, sounding courteously astonished.

"Oh sweet but sort of weren't you?"

"When the first thing you did was recite your agency's virginal damn' ground-rules at me?"

"As if *you* were in the habit of just letting girls say No to you!" she grieved. "Hoh!"

He said agreeably, "Properly brought up, is all. Did as I thought I was being told. Thought I was supposed to."

"*Hoh!*"

"Look, my angel," he said, as if explaining, "how could any man in his right mind—"

"Well but *was* I? Longer? Than your usual girls!"

There being no such thing as a usual girl, what was a reasonable man to say?

So he declaimed (and in fact reasonably). For quite aside, dammit, from the sheer bad manners of disbelieving her to her face, how could any man in his dazzled senses have had the, the effrontery to assume anything as lovely as *she* was wasn't already—if she'd forgive him the stuffiness of an archaism—already spoken for!

"But Lewis all I told you—"

He said be quiet. Because quite simply— Look, would she have the womanly candor to admit? simply she was a beauty, and against beauty what could a man do? It stunned you, it transfixed you. In a word, for him anyhow (he said rhetorically), it was as daunting as death, and damn' well by now she must know it, he ended, waiting to be smiled at.

So at least she looked at him more reasonably.

And conceded, "I don't really I suppose want to hear about your other girls anyway do I."

He said *god* no.

"No, but about you," she now said, as if in a kind of tender and anxious cherishing, "ah Lewis have you had so *little* pleasure in your life? 'Making do.' *Shall* I take you to the Grand Véfour in full fig and cheer you up, poor sweet? and I mean see?"

Well he said she was a blessing, but what kind of dotty methodology was this?—she been making love with him just to 'cheer him up'?!

"Ah, Lewis," she said, sounding hurt, "can't I worry a little about you besides other things? I never had an affair with a disabused man. Of course I don't mean that was *why*. But you *are* a little melancholy, Lewis. And I started asking myself why you were, I suppose. And was curious about you. And sorry. And I remember one day we were driving—this must have been that second day?—we were anyway driving and suddenly I thought But I'm looking at him differently, heavens does my face show it? and I said to you, 'I'm beginning to think you're not solemn at all.' "

So he mildly snorted.

"And d'you remember what you said? you said, 'Then you might even stop being daughterly to me!'—which you will admit was, well, *was!* because oh dear I realized *that* wasn't how I felt like being to you, and I looked at you in a sort of terror—I mean there you were, experienced and charming and unknowable, how would I ever expect to know how many girls had loved you? And all this so *sudden*, Lewis, like one's doom. So see?" she said happily. "So now I do find myself being a little mad about you, temporarily!"

'Temporarily!'

"Well isn't it?"

This, any more in passing for her than—

"Oh Lewis, do I have to remind you how the dialogue always goes?—this is *comedy*! You say in this romantic voice, sounding just irresistible, 'I don't want to leave ever,' and I absolutely melt inside and say, 'Oh sweet I don't ever want you to,' but does that mean either of us thinks you're going to stay? And sweetie you do rather, well, have a history of living off the country don't you?"

But dammit he said do a man and a woman just any day find themselves in *this* sort of miraculous—

"Oh but that's what I *mean*," she mourned. "Because I don't think I know how to deal with it!—I mean have I lost my head over you like a schoolgirl or do you just so totally please me? Or is *that* losing one's head! And you don't even seem to realize I shouldn't be *asking* such a question, even, this soon!" she reproached him, as if who could not. "Didn't you *see* I was falling in love with you?"

He said but—

"But when so many girls have been in love with you it isn't *possible* you didn't know!"

He said in the first place dammit there hadn't been all that many. And in the second, how was he to have been sure that 'agency policy' of hers was anything but a well-brought-up young woman's way of reminding a man of fifty that fifty, alas, was pretty much the age her father was, champagne to start with or no champagne.

And anyhow, he said, amiably, if he might say so, women's 'falling in love,' as a trope, had often seemed to him to be not so much a passion per se as a way of behaving, a part of the good manners of being a woman. A style; a procedure, even. Of course it was a pastime too—Restoration comedy for instance wasn't even about anything much else, and there were still, God knows— Well, wasn't it a matter of amour propre?—if you weren't in love what was wrong with you!

She said, "You discuss us as if we were some sort of natural phenomenon."

"Ah well," he said, "but aren't you?"

"Oh Lewis of course who now and then doesn't," she admitted. "Because it is silly not to make love now and *then* with somebody nice. One doesn't have to be 'in love' dans les formes—heavens, do men? After my divorce I was dancing once at this party in some-body's studio and he was very nice, and that lovely electricity be-gan flickering. You know? But then I thought oh but this is just what women *do* after a divorce, oh *damn!*—and anyhow I was just back in Paris again and *much* too busy starting my agency. To I mean fall in *love*."

Some Frenchman this was?

"Oh no he wasn't French, I wasn't *that* light-minded, no he was this very nice— Oh well if you'd really like to know it was Jock Bingham," she said, as if abashed. "But I didn't have an affair with him—it was my partner was why I was startled about your Barretts girl. Because Lewis I did have to concentrate on starting my agency. I'd had the idea of it long before the divorce, you know, but commuting, sort of, instead, between New York and France."

That perhaps had something to do with the divorce?

"Oh well that wasn't the real trouble. With our marriage, that is. *That* was, that I fell in love with somebody else. But he did love me, Lewis, I mean my husband. His whole novel's about me, in Arles. About what he calls 'the feast' of me. It made me feel like a Matisse odalisque, goodness! You can read it if you like."

He said oh well, very kind, thank 'ee yes. 'Feast' was a lovely word for her, her husband was a man of talent; why didn't she come round *this* side of the breakfast table?

So when presently she'd fetched the manuscript she did. And perched on his knee so he could read around her in comfort.

Then here I am, without her.

No longer sure who I am, without her. A man lacking routine identity. A man very possibly unrecognizable.

His identity now in an airport bus en route to Marignane; en route to her plane to Rome.

A man, simply, in a daze.

Sather said, "What were you doing in Rome?"

"But visiting my dear mother, pet. She lives in Rome, part of the year. She loves it."

"This thing have a title?"

"He's still deciding on one. He wanted to call it 'Maria as an Art Form,' but I said how silly."

A man, simply, in a daze.

Though no doubt in appearance a normally definable (tall; dazed) pedestrian descending, among other pedestrians descending/ascending, these flights of broad stone stair, these gardens; in a city he would a fortnight ago have spelled (with a non-existent S) Marseilles; proceeding moreover to a definable destination (a Quai des Belges); the data including in particular what the briefest of inquiries would establish, viz., a man perdutamente innamorato, a man violently in love, and now of no more identity than merely that.

Wasn't this all kind of mannered?

"But Lewis I told you! He's being stylistically nouveau roman. Of course in an end-of-the-fifties way. But maybe he's parodying somebody French."

No longer a man who this now vanished fortnight ago had met her plane from Orly; no longer even a man in whose arms only this far-off morning she had woken murmuring, to indulge with sleepy love.

"So Maria was an art form then too?"

She nuzzled him, giggling.

Except then "Oh maybe I shouldn't I suppose have met him again poor sweet at all, or d'you think," she admitted. "Oh dear am I hard to get over too?"

He said god *yes* she'd be!

"I didn't mean for *you*."

No but look dammit, he said, this poor devil—meeting her again was a headlong folly, yes, the odds totally God knew against him, but he *felt* for this ex-husband of hers, helpless or not!— hadn't she *any* idea what a heart-stopping thing she'd be to have lost? So would she mind if they didn't read any more of the thing. The poor guy shouldn't of course have put it on paper if he'd object, but all the same— *Really* she oughtn't to go round reducing men to states like that, over-articulate or not! Himself he hoped included.

But "*You*, my darling," she said forgivingly, "aren't likely to be infatuated with anybody ever. So don't *fuss*," she ended; and in due course they went into Paris for lunch, and afterwards to the Jeu de Paume.

And after that, window-shopping in the Rue du Bac, he bought her a pair of antique gold earrings, apparently Directoire.

✦

So if it had turned out that they were waiting *this* contentedly for young Newman (Sather said next morning at breakfast) mightn't they even have time for some architecture, for instance how far off were the Loire châteaux?—anyway wasn't that where she'd grown up spending summers at her French grandmother's?

But imagine his remembering! yes she was practically du pays, she was even told she had a Touraine accent. Actually her grandmother lived on a tributary, the Indre; at a little place called Veigné. But *yes*, in three days they could have a wonderful trip! And eat *very* well, there was a splendid variety of river-fishes—salmon, pike, perch, and did he like eel? The regional sauces did tend to be mostly crayfish'd, when they weren't beurre blanc, but would he complain? They could spend the first night at Luynes, say, and have a *perfect* regional dinner of mousseline de brochet aux queues d'écrevisses!

But *not*, though, did he mind, visit her grandmother. ("She's much too French—if *we* dropped in, sweetie, she'd think I loved you or something. . . .")

So they decided, and he went back to the hotel to pack.

—Where however the concierge had a message for him: a Mr. Bingham had telephoned, and would Monsieur, at his earliest convenience, have the kindness to ring him back.

And when he did (he told Maria in due course) Bingham reported Chad *was* finally it appeared on his way. The damn' boy'd called in last night, from Annecy, in the Haute Savoie. Which the hotel concierge informed him was 547 kilometers from Paris, 'an easy day's drive.' So that dammit was that; and in the end she just took him to a restaurant in the Rue Le Peletier which did Loire specialties, where they dutifully discussed the prospects.

"Of course you're a sweet to say I've 'made your mission irrelevant,' " Maria said, "but specifically, Lewis, what are you going to do when Mr. Newman's back—argue with him?"

He said god no. Just more or less open-mindedly present the case for the boy's going reasonably home. The financial case. Which was all it was. Then up to him to decide.

"But what about his girl? Or haven't you thought about her. I suppose she's with him. I wonder what she *is* like."

Could be anything. Including couldn't-be-nicer.

"Are you going to see her d'you think too?"

Not really much point, was there?

"But Lewis suppose she's in love with him. In her place I'd be *outraged* at you—coming to piggishly break everything up!

And just for his awful mother!"

But why assume a break-up? God help him would any young man in his right mind, Princetonian or not, want to spend the rest of his days in a couplings-empire in Iowa? Or consider the contrary. Suppose the girl was beginning to be tired of the fellow anyway—what a blessing to her *he*'d be! How nobly and for Chad's own good she could be rid of him! Because they had no idea when this affair mightn't have begun had they? And in any case, what *was* a median duration for enchantment!

"But then what did Mrs. Newman expect you to do?"

So he began to laugh. The discussion with Mrs. Newman, he said, had revolved around the size of the probable expense. . . .

"Oh Lewis *no!*"

He *swore* it!

"But how could any woman think like that!—in *1983?*"

Time-lag would hardly affect a thing like maternal jealousy! Lucky thing perhaps, on the whole, that Chad had made money of his own. Though of course who could tell, it even *might* turn out he'd opt for the factories.

So they decided there was nothing, actually, for them to decide.

And so why not window-shop, she said, through the Sixième Arrondissement, how many friends did he want to buy presents for? Including for secretaries? And they could end up for tea at the Closerie des Lilas, simply enjoying themselves.

At the Closerie however, things being as they are, it turned out she went on with her inquiry into his life and loves.

"Were they all people's wives?"

"Dear God, Maria," he said, "what's natural selection!"

"You mean we all just fall into your arms like me?" she said. "Don't you ever go *after* people?"

"Went after you!"

"You didn't, you just *behaved.*"

"What were you responding to then?" he said amiably.

"Oh sweetie I told you—I just liked you, was all. But you *are* terribly correct, Lewis. And then, the way you are, I didn't see how you could possibly not have a girl in New York. And then anyway you were going to be here only this day or two, weren't you? *Have* you a New York girl?"

"Good God," he complained, "what a question to sound honest replying to!"

"But do you have?"

Dammit he said *no!* California either!

". . . When was the last one."

"But look," he said mildly, "what was all that about I-wasn't-to-be-stupid-and-jealous, a couple of nights ago?"

"I'm not being! Can't I be tenderly anxious about you?"

"That what your generation calls it?"

"Oh sweet don't hedge! When was she?"

Oh, well, he said, last winter.

"Winter ending in March?"

. . . Easter'd been late, this year.

"You mean it isn't really over at all?" she cried.

Oh yes. She'd got a job in Washington. Look, this was the daughter of a client. Three or four years ago—

"It began *four years ago?*"

No no no *no*, the girl was still in college then, simply he'd let her what's called 'intern' during summer vacation, to oblige her father. She was an economics major. Been no question of! Affairs in the office?—at *his* age?

"So then *what?*"

. . . Oh well, the usual thing, call it, what else? An affair. After that summer he hadn't seen her, till one day last autumn she'd rung him up. Might she interview him professionally? Because she was doing a piece, for some learned journal or other, on 'the metapolitics of stock options.' Or some such, and if she took him to lunch could she pick his brains about it a little?

"You hadn't seen her in all that time?"

Or thought of. No occasion to. Been several years. Four, even. But anyway. You did get this sort of request, how not. Clients could ask you to do a talk on the market, for instance, at their club. He'd even done a couple of guest lectures at Yale. So he had lunch with the girl.

"And went on from there!" she accused him.

No no no no, at lunch all they—

"She didn't have somebody already?—in her *twenties?*—in New *York?*"

What if she had? Hardly the sort of question he—

"What was she like?"

. . . What was anybody!

"That's not what I meant!"

But dammit she'd asked him, hadn't she?—and in so many words!—whether he ever 'took off after' people. He was only describ—

"So you did go after her!"

. . . In a light-hearted way, yes, why not?

"You didn't after *me!*"

"What *is* all this?" he cried. "How's a simple man to conduct himself if not on the, what's one to call it? the hypotheses of egotism and experience? There are too many ways the average young man can exasperate a young woman for her not to be looking for a lover she hopes won't. If the fellow's catnip of course there's nothing immediate to be done—she has to be silly and get it over with. She has to discover that all catnip is is catnip. But aside from that—"

"So you mean you just heartlessly dispossessed some helpless young man she had!"

"'Heartlessly'!"

"He could have been some terribly easily hurt mere *boy!*"

"But dammit my angel it was *she* that—"

"Didn't you ever even meet him, to find out?"

"What would I do a cockeyed thing like meet him for!—compare our perquisites and prerogatives?"

"But Lewis you don't just—"

He had, once, *heard* the guy. Sort of, anyway. This'd been late one night; poor guy'd rung her bell. She was up on her arm in an instant, furiously listening. Then he'd rung again, and she'd breathed *Oh damn* and sprung out of bed and off into the little hall, and heard the faint rattle of the door-chain, and then the mumble of their voices, on and on. . . . Though God bless, what can either side say that makes sense in *that* situation! Finally of course she sent him away. But he'd heard the rise and fall of their voices a long while first. Then she came softly back to him in the dark. As if nothing much had happened, come to think of it. So that was that.

". . . Not even a *little* upset?"

"*I* was upset. Look, I felt badly for him! If you lose a girl you lose her, but dear god you might as well go hang yourself as mope and maunder around keeping tabs on whatever unappetizing lout she's replaced you with! Maybe he'd been waiting across somewhere in the shadows, hour after hour, to see whether oh please God *not!*— the impossible off-chance that when she came home at last she'd come home alone. Except there she had come home with me. And I'd gone in with her. And he'd seen the light in her apartment go on. And then (and soon) go out. And there he might have been standing on and on, in the black night of the soul, seeing in his mind how perhaps at that very instant every lovely inch of her—

There's an anguished couplet of Ovid's, my angel, that says it all: 'multa miser timeo—I shake at what he may do with you for I have done it all myself—my own damned example has me on the rack!' How can a man *let* himself be caught like that? And what low Plautine streak in human nature ever decided the locked-out lover was a stock figure for farce? 'Mens abit, et morior'—and you *might* as well be dead! That night, I was appalled. . . ."

"But you went heartlessly right back to making love with her didn't you?" she rebuked him.

"As a matter of fact," he said, "no, I didn't."

"Oh Lewis *truly* didn't?"

"Dammit I was upset!"

So she gazed at him as if decoding this. And finally said, "But I didn't think men felt like that."

Maybe in her generation they didn't.

"No I mean the way you felt. About him."

Why shouldn't he have? Roman comedy or not!

"But how did she feel?"

He said, amused, 'd hardly felt he knew the young lady well enough to ask.

"No be *serious*," she begged him. "Because after my husband— Well, I'd left him, I'd moved to the pied-à-terre my mother has on the East River, sweetie I told you, there was this man I fell in love with, was why. Because the way I'd felt about him, oh Lewis if I'd stayed, my husband's just *being* there would remind me of the, the, of the difference, and change all the other feelings perhaps I'd had about him *ever*! And when I'd felt I thought so fond of him so long, having to face don't you see whether really *had* I! And perhaps only feel sad about him. Because getting used to myself with somebody new— Oh dear why am I *discussing* this with you!"

He said agreeably ah then don't. And in any case, you put everything you'd discovered about love (including a random infidelity only the night before) into each new affair, so why shouldn't each be better than the last?

"Am *I*? Or goodness, am I! Because put *that* way, what does it mean I am?" she protested, and began to laugh at him. "Oh Lewis what a way to look at things! Because then isn't some horrid girl going to replace me for your benefit as easily as I seem to have replaced your last little— *Had* she been with him the night before?"

No no, all he'd meant was—

"Well but are you saying you expect to go effortlessly on and on with these convenient replacements?—and, each time, each of us in this endless series is a, is a what? an improvement? on the one before?"

So naturally he snorted. Was she out of her perverse head? The 'improvement' he'd meant was, obviously, they improved *him*, what on earth else! It was women men learned manners from wasn't it? And always had been. Bedroom and drawing-room both. So why *not* the more the better? And if the way he was (at the peak of his perfection) appealed to her, he said laughing, then what was there for her to fuss at?

"But sweet so uninterruptedly *many!*"

He said but—

"I hate them *all*," she said contentedly; and as this was hardly what they were talking about in any case, they left the theory of the thing, for the rest of that evening at least, unannotated further.

But next day, sure enough, Sather came back to his hotel to change for lunch, and there were these messages the concierge handed him with his key.

The day before, a Mr. Bingham had telephoned Monsieur; the message left was that Mr. Newman had returned to Paris.

The day before, a Mr. Newman had telephoned Monsieur; the message left was that he had returned to Paris and would telephone Monsieur in the morning.

This morning a Mr. Newman had telephoned Monsieur; he had left a number, which would Monsieur have the kindness, at Monsieur's convenience, to call.

This number however, when he rang it, did not answer.

When moreover he then rang Bingham's extension at the Embassy, a voice like a caress breathed Oh was this Mr. Sather? for then Mr. Bingham was not in but had left a message for Monsieur in case Monsieur called, and this was that Mr. Newman was back in Paris, and would call him.

So when Maria picked him up for lunch she said, "Oh damn, now you'll be going home!"

And when she hadn't had even a quarter enough of him!

He said well but God bless, 'home'?—she forgot the job he was here for? These polite embassies took time. You didn't disentangle a young man from the pretty arms round his neck just overnight.

Could take a week. *Could* take a fortnight.

But suppose it didn't.

And even if it did, what was going to happen then? They both *knew* what was going to happen then!

He said but—

And when here they were with a love in their laps!

But dear god—

It was *sad* to think that his dismal 'making do' was all he had to look forward to!

With she supposed the next wandering wife or teenage economist he happened on? . . .

But at lunch in the Rue de Bac (this restaurant had she said been gutted and *completely* refitted and tarted up a couple of years ago, but was now would he believe it as classically what the French called 'loyal' as if it still had its dotty old painted tin ceiling)—at lunch she said simply what he should *do* was open why not a branch in Paris. His clients needed foreign titres too in their portfolios didn't they and he'd get new clients here, and expand. And hadn't he seen, as to amenities, how much simply better one lived here? He'd have the lovely life he ought to have—France was *France!* "And then of course also," she ended it, and laughed, "I could have you and *have* you!"

He said a Paris office? God Bless!—when he hadn't a word of French?

"When you've *me?*" she cried—not to mention all the other fundamental amenities. Which she lovingly listed: nobody bothered you; there were proper domestics still; the bread, once you had found *the* boulangerie in your quarter, was a supreme food; the tax situation had been made advantageous beyond Republican dreams; the wine hadn't had to travel; the trains ran.

And *no* one (she said in tender mockery) would be lurking in the shadows of her street to see how she came home.

So there. And he could réfléchir. . . .

But when she dropped him at his hotel to change for dinner, there was the message. A Mr. Newman had telephoned: could Monsieur be informed that Mr. Newman was driving a friend down into Normandy tomorrow for lunch, and would Monsieur be free to join them. Mr. Newman would be by about ten in the morning. He urgently hoped he would find Monsieur free.

So now it confronted them.

—Though at dinner, and this, again, they had on that terrasse of his hotel, the summer dusk already deepening into night over the fading gardens off into the black leaves of the lindens beyond, so that the massed flaming of a hundred candles, table by damask'd table, made it as if a low pavilion of light without walls had been built out under those vaults of darkness; or again it could have been a lighted proscenium stood out there, set for the staging of a play, and the actors there, and in that soft brilliance, above the crystal and silver of the tables, the eyes of actresses would be like jewels as they looked at you—at dinner then Maria was gently exploring consequences.

"Darling tell me something?"

So he looked need-she-ask.

"About if you come back. *Do* I mean decide. To open this office."

He said hypotheses, huh.

"Tell me anyway?"

He snorted mildly.

"Because I don't want to upset you," she said lightly, "but it's about how I feel."

'Upset' him!

"Yes but it *may!*" she cried. "Anyway *something!* Because I told you—I don't think I know how to deal with this, not any way at all. I'm beginning to be afraid I've got you rather badly. Of course *that* I don't think you'd mind, but I've— Oh Lewis I'm *not* possessive, but I keep thinking about your past with love and terror, how can I help it, so if you do come back will you mind if now and then I'm jealous of your ghosts?"

He said, sounding amused, but what earthly sort of hypothetical anxiety—

"But aren't you even a little jealous of mine?"

Hardly told him God bless enough, had she, to be jealous about! Including about for instance this chap she'd said she'd left her husband for.

"Oh but sweetie simply I lost my head about him, what else, what d'you think, what *does* one do, heavens!" she passed this off with. "Didn't *you* ever feel you suddenly wanted somebody more than you'd ever wanted anything on earth?"

Catnip, huh!

"Don't laugh—it's lovely!" she said; and that was that.

—Later, though, in the contented midnight of their bed ("Mind if you don't seduce me again for a little?" "Only keep us awake anyhow"), half entangled still, lips idly grazing his shoulder, ". . . or anyway lost my head *enough,*" she murmured, conceding.

"Because I guess I half didn't know what was happening to me. You know? The first time I made love with him, and I never had, then, with anybody but my husband, well, the difference of course, but it was the, oh the *discovery*, Lewis! I'd *never* imagined anyone could make you feel like that, and then to have to leave the heaven of those few vanishing hours, so rushing and gone, and go back to— And oh I blew it, I made a scene about *nothing*—and I'd felt so lovely, coming from him, that I thought how easy to feel tender about my husband too, and then I came in and there he was, and I thought but I never *saw* how he was till now—and poor darling I blew up, oh Lewis so *sad!*"

. . . Past consoling, he said. And always had been.

"But you," she said, "you're the same thing, only worse, it's like being stunned. Because one never believes how it turns out it is. And stunned twice over, because the bliss of it, that *anything* can be so overwhelming, and then thinking but what is it, how *can* it be what it is! So you're dazed all over again," she mumbled, through a rosy mouthful of his neck. "Do men ever feel like this too?"

Why, for him at least, yes, he said. Or anyhow, when this happened, somehow one was in it, part of the girl's tumult. Not that it always happened—as things stood between the sexes still, women seemed to be wary of giving in to their senses. For that did, he'd concede, change the whole history of the self for them. Which could upset anybody. So they didn't get what was called 'involved.' For instance, had she with this Bingham?

She whirled up onto her elbow and stared at him speechless.

Well, he said, had she?

". . . How did you know!" she cried at him.

Guessed. How else.

"But Lewis *how?*"

All the denying.

So she drooped, saying, ". . . oh." And she then collapsed humbly onto him again, for some time they lay there in silence.

Till presently she said, "*Does* it upset you?"

. . . Oh, well, he supposed a little. In his generation you rather—

"But sweet I wasn't in *love* with Jock! I was just getting over the, the taste of the other affair. And Jock was attractive and amusing. And *nice.* And it wasn't an affair—it was *nothing* like this with you, nobody's been. Goodness, I only made love with him two or three times, you *can't* be jealous about that!"

He said look, dammit, it was man's simple-mindedness made these things a complexity. To see a girl's body in memory was one thing, and you could endure it, but the dazzling reality of it, tangible and *there*, and past belief temporarily yours, reduced you to idiocy. So why shouldn't the revolting idea that some low lecher of a peasant—

"He wasn't! He was sweet!"

Catnip, huh.

". . . No."

So (he snickered) she'd passed him on to her partner?

". . . Sweetie that *isn't* the nicest way to put it!"

The terminology matter? Ah, well, they were a hair-raising sex. His old uncle used to say, 'Women are women—and it's just as well.' Whatever that meant.

But she said, "And anyway you haven't any right to say anything about it. All those *Sather* girls! They're all alike—and then they come back for more! And that's all you think about us! I should never make love with you again!" she mumbled, kissing him.

But dear god who'd been patiently hearing about her men?— and in quantity!

"But Lewis I was *explaining* myself to you, is all, what d'you think! And I haven't had anything like your disgusting dozens, so there!"

So, in perhaps amusement, they were silent.

Till presently she murmured, ". . . J'ai la gorge comme on les demande?"

. . . What'd that mean.

"Oh what a stupid amant, what have I done to deserve so un-instructed a man in bed with me!" she cried at him. "Un amant qui n'a même pas de bribes de français! Where your *hand* is, my darling! Or are you jealous of my ghosts?"

. . . Ghosts were for an age when they still upset you. Natural enough!—you wanted to be able to think it was only You the lovely thing had ever been like this with, or wanted to be. But any age it was a kind of sadness.

". . . Even not needing to? When was *never* this but you?"

So he muttered something gentlemanly. To which however she paid no attention; for now, as if from some musing midnight of her own, she had begun to tell him, it seemed, how it began.

"Because oh sweet," she said, lips against his throat, "it was the way I found I was thinking about you, and so soon. Thought about you I mean when I was undressing. At night. Or should I tell you, and spoil you more. Because I'd think what it would be like, if you were there, watching. What it would do to you. And what having you watching would do to me. And when oh dear I'd only known you two days! Oh but how wishing you were there, because then— Oh well how was I to know we were going to seduce each other so adorably? Oh anyway, *here!*" she ordered, and rolling up from his shoulder she gave him a long kiss. "There—that's to keep my rope on you! And tomorrow in Normandy you'll *buy off* this 'friend' of your Mr. Newman's—promise?" she ended contentedly, "not just charm her?"

He said *god* no.

—It was deep dawn, that morning, when he left, her little street already silver with it, and the Avenue, full day. At her gate he turned to smile good-bye. She was standing in the half-open doorway, head leaning against the jamb, looking at him almost somberly; but as he smiled, with a sudden fierce gravity she said, "*I love you!*"—and was gone.

Because, said like that, it is a spell.

Ah! par pitié, Madame, daignez calmer le trouble de
mon âme; daignez m'apprendre ce que je dois espérer
ou craindre.

— LACLOS, *Les Liaisons Dangereuses*

. . . avec un coeur de la trempe du sien, un coeur noble
et vertueux, une jeune femme comme celle-là, quand
on lui parle d'amour, n'a point d'autre parti à prendre
que de fuir. Si elle s'amuse à se scandaliser tout bas du
compliment qu'on lui fait, l'air soumis d'un amant la
gagne, son ton pénétré la blesse, et je la garantis perdue
quinze jours après.

— MARIVAUX, *Le Spectateur Français*

Elle ne pouvoit s'empêcher d'être troublée de sa vue
. . . mais, quand elle ne le voyoit plus . . . elle n'eut pas
néanmoins la force: il y avoit trop longtemps qu'elle ne
l'avoit vu, pour se résoudre à ne le voir pas.

— MME. DE LA FAYETTE, *La Princesse de Clèves*

I never thought he would ring up that second time, and ask again.

And *never*, how I would feel.

So how possibly should I have been sur mes gardes. Folly, yes:
c'est normal. But against that *instantaneous* wild mingling of exaltation and dismay? . . .

Or to have set the phone back on its stand again faint with happiness notwithstanding?

Baudouin came out of his dressing-room saying, "Ton américain?" and I heard my voice say, "Mais oui," without the slightest
quaver; and he came across behind me at the dressing-table and I
leaned my head back against him and closed my eyes and said,
"Ah mon Dieu, Chad and I should never have fed the polite man
lunch!" And he said, "Jeu de ravanche, que veux-tu," and bent

and kissed the nape of my neck where I love, and down along into the hollow of my shoulder, and I brushed my cheek against his and said, "So I do mon cher have to let him feed me," thinking *though what shall I find it is I have beyond help said yes to.* "Mais tu sors?" I said, and he said, "Que dans le quartier," and I said, "Tu rentres quand?" and he said, "Mais te chercher!" and kissed the top of my head with love and smiled at me in the dressing-glass, and was gone.

I picked up my brush and began to brush my hair again, and I could not even think what I was doing.

—But what was I to have said.

With not even an instant to think! And with Baudouin là à côté, no farther than his dressing-room.

—Ah, but still!—*why* that half-fainting yes. . . .

And when he had not even been plausible, 'mon américain'! What sort of reason for asking me again was 'before he left France'? And yet I accepted it! As if it had been a reasoned whim of my own! I *accepted* it!

Because ah what could he I suppose have said that would have been 'reasonable' enough—it was reason that would have given me reason to refuse. . . .

—Ah, and anyway!

It was his voice. Asking.

—Alors bon, there *was* no reason I could have accepted and I knew it, voilà, the first syllable he spoke I knew it, I was *done* with reason, it was his voice. I looked at my brushing image in the glass and said to her, aloud, "Et si tu n'es plus à défendre? . . ."

And how can he not know. He has been loved too often not to know. That day at the domaine, even, he knew. And, now, it is five days of knowledge more.

". . . enchantment," he said that day, at the end, the sun on his hair as he bowed over my cold fingers, the sunflooded stone of the manoir towering over us, the dreaming summer of the gardens around us and beyond, but it was I l'ensorcelée, the spellbound. And even then, beyond saving, fascinée. . . .

Though how should he know? Or a mere polite Yes tell him! And when couldn't the man simply feel he owes me a luncheon? —alors qu'il s'en acquitte! Is a polite accession to his American sense of what shall I call it? of social obligations a capitulation dans les formes? Am I in a panic for *that*?

And think how he himself must have felt, coming to 'rescue' Chad but finding *me*! For oh the poor man, the absolute awfulness of his embassy, the sheer malappris of it, and now he knows it. He was I admit impeccable; even that first moment in the hotel court-yard in Versailles, not the flicker of an eyelid. And of course he will not bring it up, across a table from me at the Plaza-Athénée or anywhere else. But it will *be* there, in his mind—an uneasiness, a chagrin, un malencontreux, a wordless hope of appeasing.

—Ah but he *knows*. He knew that day at the domaine. And again in my mind I saw the homage in his eyes as we said good-bye, and that glint too of—was it almost appraisal? as he turned with Chad and they went into the manoir and through it to Chad's car in the courtyard and away. I was lost, and he knew. I looked into my terrified eyes in the glass and that too I said aloud, "Il le *sait* . . . ."

But what if he does know—is *he* a man who would let me see he does, or amuse himself with the knowledge? Ah he could not be so cynical!—il est *bien*, he has been loved often because he has de-served to be loved, or he could not be what he is. Enfin qu'il sache! —am I to be other than myself whether or not he knows? I shall be as safe in the court of the Plaza-Athénée as—

The phone rang.

I think I had been going to add the proviso *à moins de folie*, but oh it was so sudden and imperious, the phone, just when every nerve-end in my body was vibrating with the imminence of him, that who could I think it was if not he?—though why *again*? why possibly? was luncheon off and I was *not* to see him? it rang again, and then again, and even when I did at last pick it up and said allô, all I was thinking was what could I think of to say.

But when it was *Jock*, I was so dizzy with deliverance that I said, "Oh Jock it was *you*?" like a child.

"What's this was-me?" he said cheerfully. "*Is*-me is how I'd hoped my friends thought about me, what's the matter with you! And as it happens I'm at the *very* top of my form. I am breathing down the neck of my time. In fact I've just helped the ambassador cut a couple career throats he's had his eye on for most of the year. 'Why call on God in His great mercy to strike the bastards down,' I said to him, 'when you can do it yourself with a budget?' God's mercies aren't thunderbolts anyway, I told him, just something to be thankful for at intervals. Rather a second-rate sort of thing to base One's reputation on, between you and me—especially if One has tri-personally caused what the mercy's needed for. Yes. Well. Not what I rang up about. I gather Chad's perhaps told you our Mr. Sather has what's called been by, and that Chad is wanted home, d'urgence, for purposes of family empire."

So I must have said yes how sad, for he said, "'Sad'?—but from Chad I gathered you practically said how wonderful for him! Are you heartless? Heartless you are, and what's more, poor chap, you aren't even letting him come round and argue."

"Ah but you *know*," I said, "how Baudouin is, on leaves. And I am devoted to him. And I did you know tell you. At lunch. At Barbizon. I *told* you."

"Ah, well," he said, "let me at least put you in the current picture? Because look, Fabienne my angel, I am doing my disabused best for you *and* for him. I am not Corneille, knocking out couplets on love and duty like so many fungoes, but I *have* been doing the facts of life in short beginner's takes. If some angel tells you she adores you (I say to him) why not believe her? Saves argument. Anyhow girls fall in love with us from time to time don't they?— with an air of selectivity, too! So why *not* conclude they know what they're doing? But in the contrary case therefore *also* (I remind him) the principle obtains: if she is done she is done. As my in-house composer put it, a couple of her ballades ago—

> I do not love thee, sweetie-pie.
> The reason *why*'s the reason why.

God help me, I've even cited the classics for his enlightenment— remember Aphrodite I said in the Homeric hymn? There she was, in the first faint shadows of dawn, eeling stealthily out of bed and tiptoeing into her clothes—never wanted to see the fellow again, what *had* she been doing in bed with a mortal!—and what does this back-country peasant of an Anchises do but wake up and gawk at her! What girl wouldn't fling into a fury, goddess or not! 'Aásthen!' she spits at him. 'To think *I* was infatuated! The whole *thing* skhétlion ouk onomaston—so awful there isn't a word for it! I was out of my *mind*!' And if the oaf ever so much as mentioned— Ah, well, aásthen. Very funny, 'infatuated,' from a goddess whose specialty was infatuation! But not the kind of language you like to hear about a friend."

—But I was hardly I think listening.

Because I can never, really, can I (I was saying to myself) explain what has happened to me. Is happening. How could anyone explain. There is no language to. It is from some ancient chaos before language. Even if I could find words that would explain it exactly as it feels it *is*, it would not be explained.

But Jock was saying, ". . . so I have been *torn* over it! I am on the side of all of you. Comme un benêt. Inconduite and all. But you I adore, and I have put up with my irrelevant reservations. The finality of divine planning is final, I say to myself, but think—*we* are the demonstration? So shall I ring you? I'll ring you."

He hung up, and I picked up my brush again.

—If it stays cool, I thought, I will wear that two-piece summer silk I got chez Goulnár; and I saw it in my mind, the ribbing at the wrists and throat, and where the sleeves are set into the sleek shoulders it is like épaulières in court armor, really *very* elegant, and anyway in that kind of blouson I look inabordable. Baudouin even said on te croirait dans les affaires, and I haven't worn it since.

Tant pis. It is elegant.

And why should I not be.

I will walk there, I thought, brushing. The Avenue Montaigne is barely ten minutes. And in a taxi I should dither. Walking, my heart will beat as if I were only walking, I said to my image in the glass, softly brushing; and after a little, Baudouin came in again, to fetch me, and we went to his mother's, off the Place d'Iéna. My heart beating as if I were only walking.

But in the morning it had turned hot.

So if he should have reserved a courtyard table at the Plaza-Athénée, what to wear.

I tried to remember the court. But when had I had luncheon there, anyway in summer? Or had I ever. Ah mon Dieu I couldn't remember that either! It could be anything. Including *not* a table in the court! Then how was I to know what to dress for! Why of *all* places had he had to settle on a banality like the Plaza-Athénée! How was I expected to decide *what* to wear!

Ah zut I'd wear just something sleeveless then, who cared! And if 'accessible,' tant pis!

And walk anyway. Me détendre. A *slow* ten minutes. Timed to be late un petit quart d'heure.

(Though heavens the way Baudouin had wheedled and courted me *this* leave, how could I not be détendue! . . .)

Désinvolte, anyway, when the time came—so full of the noontide brilliance of the Quai de Passy that I was nearly at the Port Debilly before I thought am I too soon?—and I was, there was the

Pont de l'Alma, ah zut I was going to be almost à l'heure. Or only five minutes late at the most. And one can't *saunter*—should I decently kill time and go up the Avenue Georges V first? and across to the Avenue Montaigne at the level of the, of what *is* that first little— Or should I take the street next beyond and come out in the Avenue Montaigne above the hotel instead? Or what?

Oh or *what*?

But then abruptly oh thank God (I could have crossed myself in deliverance right there on the quai!) I thought but am I une petite nigaude de seize ans, in Heaven's name, and this is my first rendezvous I am headed for, quailing? I was in such a pet at myself I began walking faster still, à grands pas even—very well I'd *be* on time then! Let him think what he liked!—tôt venu tôt en fait even, if he liked, and wonder why! And I would cut the luncheon short too if I thought *he*—if I pleased. At the Place de l'Alma I didn't so much as glance up the Avenue Georges V as I passed it.

But then, turning into the Avenue Montaigne, I did, a little, slow down. In three minutes, in two, I should find him waiting in any case. And discover how he looked. This time I would make sure. I can hardly have glanced at him, at Versailles. I was expecting un fâcheux quelconque, how not. Helping Chad get rid of him, en faisant l'aimable; how he looked mattered no more than he. And it was deep shade under the lindens. I didn't really *see* him at all. Until after we started, and I turned round. . . .

—Anyway now what was left me but a scène à faire he must know by heart! Which *I* had now to play as innocently as if I could never guess how innocently how many women had played it for him a hundred times before. . . .

Then there at the hotel he was, coming tall and courtly to meet me the instant I stepped into the doorway, coming straight at me saying my name as if it were a delight to, a deliverance to—but I was so overcome by my awareness of him, so daunted, that I must have stopped halfway in, mindless, for what was I even to say to this man I knew I should need every defense against, why had I not *thought* what I could say?—only had I even the breath to? but then there he was, before me, saying but *how* kind it was of me to have relented and met him like this but had I *walked* here? said so naturally that without having to think I found myself answering bonjour but heavens how *not* walk, in the lovely noon! and in any case we lived practically à côté, in Passy; and I was breathing again. And he could have noticed nothing, it was so swift and over. And as we went on in toward the courtyard I could even add (and almost lightly, now!), "And I am even on time for you, Mr. Sather!—or do American women go the trouble of spoiling you too. . . ."

But how easy! An omen.

And at the table I found I could even look at him. Also there was champagne ready in a cooler, and he had the sommelier at once there opening it.

Then, it was amusing, translating things on the menu for him—for how could anyone be dangerous, so helpless! And over the rim of the glass I could look at him and be free.

Except how could I any longer, I said to myself, sipping, quite see him even as I had at the last there, up the sun-dappled lawns at the domaine, hardly knowing what I did, in the wild tumult of my dismay, except I knew I must never see him again. And ah, *then*, still thinking I could bear it! Though what mon Dieu was I doing now but tell myself I was bearing it—watching the play of light and expression on his face as he ordered and the captain bent over him, the poise of his head, the glints of grey at his temples, the look of his mouth, the way his tanned fingers held the carte; and I drank off my glass and thought in two short hours at the most I shall rise smiling from this table and thank him for his repas and his amabilités and wish him a smiling bon voyage home, and turn on my stylish heels la mort dans l'âme, and *not* ever see him again.

Et j'en prends déjà le deuil, I said deep in my mind, and if when you telephoned I did not ask why you wished to see me once more, it was because I did not dare to: what could you have said but 'to repay my kindness'? and what was that for me to have *had* to say yes to! and he finished ordering and I fluttered a finger at my glass for the man to fill.

So delicious, I said; and had Chad I hoped been seeing to him properly?

And he said oh very competently. Much improved, he'd found. Hardly barbarian now at all.

So he'd been able to dispense with his—what did she call herself? his 'courier'?

Well, not altogether, he said, no. He couldn't after all expect Chad to drop everything and turn cicerone. So Mrs. Godfrey was still very kindly shepherding him about. A very knowledgeable young woman.

"But didn't you feel a little odd, Mr. Sather," I said, "'hiring' a pretty girl to go about with you day and night? Or isn't she pretty enough to matter."

Oh, being 'pretty,' he said easily, was just part of the job any-where, wasn't it? And then, a thing like beauty, anyway!—it always lay in wait there, in women. Like a beckoning ghost. Of course if you saw her somehow and followed, you were lost. No, but what he'd been in plain fact enchanted by was France itself, the way it seemed we lived here, the whole ambience. The intelligence; the freedom. It had been a—well, simply it had come over him *this* was how he wished he were living himself. Matter of fact, he said, he'd wondered why shouldn't he? At least a part of the time. He had a branch office he visited in San Francisco; why not one in Paris?

But oh dear Heaven he must *not!*—and I said, "But Mr. Sather you don't even understand French!"

He said what of it?—be for his American clients, not French. He'd been thinking for months anyhow they ought to be getting into European investment more. Europe's sheer exasperation with these endless and *total* American foreign-policy ineptitudes, for instance, was going to *end* in the Common Market's taking off on its own, how not? And that meant far more money to be made for his clients in European companies than at home. Not to mention tax advantages! So a Paris office was easy to justify economically. And as to 'spiritually,' he said, smiling, he'd found France didn't need justifying. So he had been making a few inquiries. If only to see.

Then he had said it: "If I should come, Madame, might I hope to be allowed to pay my respects to you, and, well, now and then perhaps see you again?"—and suddenly he was looking straight into my eyes.

As when I'd turned round that morning in the car. . . .

And this time too I suppose I could say I looked a moment too long. Ah, but this time?—*this* time I knew what had happened to me, and dear Heaven was he as near to being sure it had as this?—for him to come back to?—and he was *asking?*

But he was saying, almost humbly, "I realize I could hardly God help me have had a more unfortunate introduction to you. I came on an errand I ought never to have undertaken to start with. I never would have, if I'd known it concerned someone like you. But even without knowing, I should never have."

I must *stop him!* I said, "But my dear Mr. Sather you haven't been désobligeant in the least!"

But wasn't he even listening to me? For on, he went *on* with it!—couldn't he *see* I mustn't care *what* he explained his feelings were? He'd begun (he said) to realize how out of place Americans can be, abroad; what outsiders. Perhaps always had been—he'd been haunted, in Versailles, by a sad adventure of Thomas Jefferson's there, at the court of Louis XVI. This had been before our Revolution—Jefferson'd been America's ambassador. A fashionable English painter was in Versailles at the time, doing miniatures of court beauties, a man named Cosway; he was about Jefferson's age, and he had the usual delicious painter's wife, a talented musician and painter herself—"but also, Madame, Maria Cosway was only in her mid-twenties, and our Mr. Jefferson was alas on his way toward fifty, so you can imagine the man's helpless desperation when he found himself in love with her—Jefferson, who was eighteenth-century Reason in person!"

I watched the blue of his eyes change as his head moved, and I thought Can I believe I am hearing this, the taste of tears in my throat? —ces frivolités d'archiviste, the one time I shall ever have been alone with him?

But he was saying. ". . . letter he wrote to her afterwards, of how he saw her off for England, from the Pavillon de St. Denis. 'I handed you into your carriage,' he says, 'and watched the wheels begin to revolve and slowly bear you away from me. And I turned on my heel, more dead than alive, and walked across the Pavillon to my carriage. And had myself driven back into Paris I cared not where.' It's I suppose a rather plain eighteenth-century style. Byron a quarter century later would have said 'death in my heart' instead. And I know I have no right, Madame, to afflict you with any of this anyway. Even if you have perhaps had the generosity to sense my feelings but forgive them. But when I think of not seeing you ever again, as poor Jefferson never again saw Maria Cosway, I find I am more dead than alive too."

—For an instant I thought I should faint: the court was a spinning dazzle. Ah Dieu du Ciel I was saved, I was *safe*, he was as stricken as I, I could do as I pleased with him, there were not even bienséances, I was *free!* . . . The dizziness vanished, and I could see his face again, and my eyes said I hardly know what except 'I am *not* yours, oh lovely lovely . . .' and that awful trembling was gone as if it had never been; and I thought 'Encore est vive la souris!'

And oh what a surcroît de bonheur, to have given me this too! —to sweetly torment him with, to tenderly pity him for, to live remembering he had said, to be sometimes dazed, remembering. . . .

Oh and no longer to care or have to care what I said or what I did or what he thought! Or what *I* thought—for there were no more bienséances, or if there were it should be *I* who had created them, ah I almost laughed aloud in the pure happiness of my deliverance. . . .

For oh what a lovely game now too! and I said, "But Mr. Sather what am I to say!" (And what could he, poor man!) "Because *this*, Monsieur?—if you understood French I would tell you qu'il revient de l'autre côté de l'inouï!"

Oh but the poor man how stuffy I sounded. And besides not understanding what I said he looked too miserable to answer anyway, so I was cruel too! so as if just amused I said, "But surely this can't be how Americans go about seducing a virtuous wife? On nous fait la cour, oui—even fall in love with us now and then I'm told, to make it more convincing. But *this* quantum leap, Mr. Sather? —to expect me to think you in despair over me after a country luncheon and a quarter-hour of our mere second meeting?"

So at least he tried to smile. "But God help me," he said, "would I put myself in this insufferable position, or subject you of all people, Madame, to the dejecting spectacle of it, if I weren't near the end of desperation? I haven't even Jefferson's eighteenth-century belief in Order, to sustain me. I *am* in despair. I am not even plausible to myself. For all I know the Count is the most charming husband in France."

Of course *some* bienséances must be preserved—one automatically says, "I forbid you to speak of him!" (And anyway!—*that* sort of remark! And so soon!)

But naturally he said, "But for that matter what can there be, Madame, that you can't irreproachably forbid me? I am appalled at myself myself! How am I *not* to appear to you a man his enchantment with you has reduced to the effrontery of hope?"

Oh, he delighted me! " 'Effrontery'?" I said. "On devient donc hardi par ses espérances?—you are even beginning to sound eighteenth-century yourself!" I said laughing. "Even dans les règles, Mr. Sather! You look so ready to sigh that it could serve you in place of sighing. But do think what you are asking me to believe!"

"But what else do you think I have been in despair over, Madame," he cried, "if not the hopelessness of asking you to believe me! My difficulty is the *difficulty*! Can a man ever really think up anything less simple-minded to say to a woman he adores than why *not* fall in love with him, what good does it do not to? God bless, what fatuity!"

"But what would happen to us, Mr. Sather," I said, "if you were all as charming as the way you look makes us think you are? A man doesn't know what he does. And that is désobligeant. And *that* is really what saves us—it's no trouble at all keeping one's head if one's not being tempted to lose it 'very expertly indeed! No but what are you doing really, Mr. Sather," I said. "When you came, you had the, what shall I call it? the malhonnêteté to assume it seems it was *I*, not France, that was keeping Chad from his factories—imagine! And now you're proposing to make the same insulting mistake yourself in reverse? and come to France for *me?*—what *are* you doing!"

He said, "'Doing'? In my indefensible predicament what is there a man can do! Ovid wrote a brilliant treatise once on how to recover, and simply from regard for your feelings God knows I should like to, but what if textbook remedies don't apply? 'Sceleratae facta puellae' is the basic maxim: remember 'the things the damn' girl's done to you.' But you're not some wretched girl, you're an angel—and what you've done to me, Madame, whether you choose to know it or not, is dazzle me, enchant me, en—"

"You must not *say* such things to me!" I said. "Hardi or not, you must not! You *know* you must not! You are making it impossible for me!"—but I heard the caress in my voice as I said it, and I thought aïe I've said it *wrong*, am I so light-headed with relief still that I have let myself *forget* what has happened to me? And the danger? "Are you pretending not to be a textbook case, Mr. Sather," I said, "because a textbook remedy doesn't cure you?—heavens, what a convenient logic!"

But what was I to do with the poor man?—he still it seemed couldn't smile; he was tragic, oh he was lovely! He said, "But that morning in Versailles I wasn't expecting *you*, Madame! Or what happened to me. Or the way it happened—the thunderclap! In my *life* I'd never— Your beauty was like a dagger glittering to its mark. Are you really so heartless as not to care what you do? Or even to bother to notice? There in the courtyard of the hotel you hardly so much as glanced at me!"

"Do you expect women to gaze in your eyes and be lost, Mr. Sather?" I said, laughing at him. "Why on earth should I have more than glanced, with all the day ahead to look at you and be stricken!"

"But all the way down to Normandy," he said—

"But I was down out of the wind, what else!—you *saw* how Chad drives!" I said. "Surely you weren't staring at me?—but then

how mannerless and flattering! But ah Mr. Sather do let's be
sensible. You adore me so convincingly you must be a libertine
born—in another five minutes you will be able to charm me into
anything you please, I shall be lost. But must I really feel you are
lost too? Do let me cajole you into being honest!"

So at least he began to smile. 'Honest'? he said—was anything
as deranged as infatuation to have moral responsibilities supposed
of it? For the matter of that, was he to think it was honesty women
were susceptible to, instead of flattery?

"You say that and flatter anyway?" I said.

But if men didn't flatter us, we'd be certain they were in love
with somebody else, wouldn't we?—so why not, he said—and now
he was almost laughing.

—Oh mon américain que vous me plaisez. . . .

Except . . . am I really to forget that a man as assured and urbane as this man is, ah mon Dieu and as plausible!— For *imagine*
'speaking out' after no more than a mere— And as if so overcome
he was helpless not to! Oh I am faint with admiration at him, at
simply how he made it sound, how *reasonable* he makes me feel I
should be, believing him! oh I could fall in love with the danger of
him all over again, with the tour de force of it, of what it does to
me!

And then, anyway, really *is* it so . . . unheard of? For are you (I
thought) 'desperate' perhaps truly, mon bel américain? and *that* is
why? . . .

I will never ask. To ask says everything. And poses questions
who could let herself believe the mockery of answers to, and of his
answers above all.

For has a man like this man no New York girl to leave behind—
and unexplained to!—if (again and again) he should come to an
office here? leave behind moping or sulking or fuming, or simply
in tears? Leave and come to *me* from? And go back to?

Or even have here perhaps already—am I to think he can't have
enchanted this *very* (Jock said) pretty courier of his? He has been
in Paris a fortnight. Do these American girls resist as long as that?
Has this one resisted?—a man like him? Am I to ask Jock?

As if what matter!

Or bother my *head* whether this is the, the recurring scenario I
know it of course must be! For how straightforward, how classical
even, I thought, looking at him—you could have met me and
voilà, simply decided that I enchant you more than she. Even
much more—I am a dagger glittering to its mark. But what are

weapons? A heart like yours who can think herself the last and deadliest to wound! . . .

—Ah mais tu es *à moi!* (I said to him in my mind), and here in this gay room, this place of flowers and light, place now of my lovely freedom again too, you are mine to tease, mon américain de rechange—for truly perhaps you *are* so desperate that you are being honest, libertine or not. And if you are, think: *really* can you never have guessed what happened to me that morning? when I turned round in Chad's car and saw you for what alas you are, the sun in your blue eyes, the wind fluttering your tie. . . .

—Of course shall I ever be sure.

For how could the sort of man *you* are, mon Sather, have been so bold, or had the effrontery or the mere cynicism to think I would sit and listen, unless you . . . *more* than hoped you knew I would want to?

I shall never be sure. But then, hoh, shall I ever have to let *you* be sure either!

So now? à la fin? à la longue?

A la fin you are mine whenever I want to take the Dionysiac risk of you and your beguiling Paris office-to-be; and I said, "But mon Dieu, Mr. Sather, how can you expect me to advise you? . . ." and let my eyes smile.

A LITTLE DECORUM,
FOR ONCE

To
Harriet Newell

and to
Alice Quinn

and, always, to
Laurice

On a dit, l'an passé, que j'imitais Byron.
Vous qui me connaissez, vous savez bien que non.

1

From the cardiac care he responsibly assured his family and friends could hardly be his deathbed ("At a still marauding sixty-plus? *god* no!") a novelist named Scrope Townshend rang up his many-times-past love Laura Tench-Fenton and said angel look: not to be startled, but how about his doing that glossy high-fashion magazine of hers a civilized couple of thousand words on adultery?—though clearly, in the circumstances, this would take any editor aback.

So, naturally, "But Scrope *sweetie* what is this!" she cried at him, as in tenderest shock and concern. "I mean of *all* possible mad— Oh my dear of course *how* kind to offer it to me I know, but just when we've all been utterly ill worrying weren't you perhaps even dying my old darling?—and *that* topic?" she rebuked him with brisk editorial impatience. "My dear man for *my* readers? heavens!" and in fact this sort of thing it happened they had many times before disingenuously wrangled over, even as often their long once-upon-a-time as bed together.

So he was amused. Woman's happiest birthright and perquisite not for her readers?—dear god who were this sad circulation of hers, faithful wives or something?

"But you're in intensive *care!*" she cried, as if the man were un-hinged.

Any better place to waste time and genius on a thinkpiece in?— tell him what else do, lying there!—regretting his regrettable past with he hoped the required piety, in particular—

" 'Piety' oh *listen* to you!"

—in particular deploring all the passed-up opportunities he'd been too much of a gent, or ah sometimes just too dazzled, to understand this or that lovely apparition was offering him.

"Oh how *can* you be so light-minded in practically Scrope the shadow of death aren't you still?" she denounced him, as if in grief for him already. " 'A civilized couple of thous—' And when it's not a *week* since that ambulance hurtled you writhing and gasping through the night to thank God emergency? so bludgeoned and beaten by that awful thudding pain it took no fewer than *four* injections of morphine, the absolute Sibylla said limit they dared give you, even to begin the— Oh you madden me, sweetie who wouldn't you madden!"

Been a bit, yes, he'd concede, like being beaten to a pulp by jack-hammers. But by now he'd completely—

"And when you groggily asked that duty doctor working on you what kind of heart attack was it you were having, Sibylla told me this man—who *knew!*—this man said, 'The bad kind,' do you deny it? And when at last she went home hopeless and weeping because they didn't even feel they could encourage the sweet darling her father would last the night, she lay there praying and *praying* when practically she doesn't believe in God d'you think in the slightest!"

He said but—

"And even *she* it wasn't till yesterday was allowed to visit you for more than five minutes at a time once an hour! And in *your* condition you ring me up about Heaven knows what wicked sardonic upsetting article you pretend to think I'd for one instant— 'Adultery'! when you've just for all we know been no more than the next heartbeat from *death?*" she upbraided him, in a voice of tears.

So, after a moment, he said, mildly, well God bless. And what a lovely tirade.

Then, for another moment, slightly longer, they were silent. As, perhaps, each admitting.

But then, "No but my elegant creature look," he went back, "the thing's already written, is why, is all. I did it weeks ago. For *Vanity Fair*. Was asked to. Wonderful title, too—'Your Neighbor's Wife, Her Acquisition and Care.' In other words the social decencies of the thing, d'ye see: La Rochefoucauld stuff. Decorum, Laura, dammit! So calm down. Only now this morning here's a letter regretting changing their collective minds about running it! So all I get—"

"The hospital lets you have *mail?*"

"Good god why not!—something the matter with me? So now, d'you see, all I'm getting's a kill-fee for the thing—*me*, Laura! Well, is the stuff just to be scrapped, for God's sweet sake? So I naturally thought all right then, change the slant, nothing easier *or* simpler—change the man-about-town pretexts and fatuities into women's and there you are. Or change into both's, why not—I can for instance see a very handsome layout with a subhead added: 'Your Neighbor's Wife, Her Acquisition and Care (And What She Can Do to Help).' Can you resist it? How can you resist it! And I'll have it in your hands in forty-eight hours."

Mrs. Tench-Fenton demanded, as of a child, was he *totally* unteachable? Or just didn't he listen!

But here was dear god an activity everybody could enjoy! *Did* enjoy! Most of those faithful-wife readers of hers included!

Did he expect her to *purvey* his kind of scoffing irresponsible misbehavior?—indeed *not!*

What was this 'misbehavior'?—when everybody believed in a given way of acting, that way became accepted comportment— was normal *behavior*, not *mis*. What was the matter with her?— been a faithful wife at one misguided period herself hadn't she? so she knew what happens!

"And anyhow dammit," he ran smoothly on, forestalling her, "why not consider running the thing with a matching piece by a woman on the facing page, making sense of the feminine side of the pastime? Or the feminist side even, good god why not—one of those outraged fuming confutations they do so beautifully, demolishing me!"

She said, sounding amused, she supposed what he meant was— Well in particular who had he thought of suggesting to *her* might do this did he mean?

Why should he have thought of anybody. Be up to her, he'd've thought. Only thing was, they wouldn't want some bedroom freudiologist writing it, tone wrong into the bargain! What was called for was blandness. Even in a high-style rebuttal. Why, any-body'd do: couldn't say he'd thought of anybody in particular. Of course if she—

"You haven't *any* alluring little thing you're as usual after in mind, for me to help you with?"

" 'After'!—how d'ye mean, 'after'?"

"What would anybody mean! So then who?"

So he said, in an honest voice, that in point of fact it had oc-curred to him that Sibylla's friend Amy Hallam did somewhat that *sort* of short stories—she might try her hand at it. But *damned* if he was 'after' her or anything like it!—his own daughter's college roommate?

Mrs. Tench-Fenton was silent.

"Anyhow Laura you know the child already, you ran a story of hers a year or so ago. Very gifted young woman. And the thing is, she'd do you a nice sexy *either* feminine or feminist job, whichever. Editorially speaking ideal, in short. What's the matter, you don't think so?"

Still she was silent.

So naturally he laughed at her. "You're not going to maintain the young woman's unqualified to write about adultery because she's not married good god?"

"Well she isn't is she? She just lives with Charles Ebury! Or he with her, heavens do I know which?"

"But they—"

"And when he's so charming!"

"But what's *his*—"

"I don't even like her novels!"

"But the story you ran—"

"Was what my last year's stupid story editor— Scrope *sweetie* how can you be so perverse and unendurable! when why can't you *see* there isn't the slightest pretext I could run your impossible graceless effrontery of an article using! Print *your* idea of behavior for an even remotely— So once for all *oh will you give up* about it!" she commanded, as in an absolute fume.

So (it not mattering much anyhow) he obeyed.

And modulated smoothly into gossip. Charles Ebury had as it happened just this morning—had he told her?—dropped by. Very kind; couldn't have been kinder. Not been allowed to see him of course, but he'd left him an amusing note: "My current in-house othersex sends her fond love too." Very amusing. But then, Charles was a wit. Except ah well, what a way for even a Classics professor to describe a delicious girl, lived-with or not. Did she suppose Amy herself—

But here, "Oh Scrope my dear I do have to ring off, I must go I must go, you *know* this endless magazine of mine, oh isn't one so helpless always!" Mrs. Tench-Fenton wailed, as in ladylike despair. "And when anyway I've only talked *this* long to make sure— for *myself*, poor darling—that you were as well again as oh thank God you obviously are, I mean disputing with me in your usual self-serving bullying chauvinist fashion about things you know to *begin* with are totally out of the question, oh you're distracting!— and when we have all been so *deeply* worried Scrope over you, oh if you loved me you'd promise you'd never argue with me about anything again ever!"

So he snorted—what was this 'if he loved her'! What had he become to her, then, dammit, some sort of merely vestigial him?—a man who'd adored her from the first dazed moment he'd laid eyes on her, as by *god* she knew!

"Allowing you mean for the interludes? *And* intervals, sweetie! *All* those intervals!"

He demanded, with some heat, did she dammit have to affront his feelings about her with these pitiless libels? when there wasn't a heroine in his uncollected works that didn't somehow mirror her!—her dizzying moods, her follies, her flighty sophist of a heart, even that delicious fluttering she used for syntax had got into his novels, where did she think the charm came from?—in for instance scenes like What's-his-name's coming round the corner of Miranda's roommate's house, heart pounding with manly hope—

"Oh Scrope not that memorized passage *again!*"

—to the two girls 'dawdling in garden chairs by a pool, sunning their pretty legs. Miranda was singing some French song or other, clapping her palms together to beat time. She was in summer white, her sleek arms bare; her sun-flooded dark beauty—'

Mrs. Tench-Fenton said oh *really* the purposes he seemed to think women were created for! Also for her taste he had used that 'sun-flooded' of his *much* too much, in fact ever since he had thought it up, why didn't that editor he was always saying was so wonderful (as well as an angel!) call his lazy attention to it? Also anyway it had been her roommate singing too. Also all *right* if he insisted, on occasion she had indulged him, and if that struck him as light-minded what did its even *being* light-minded matter, goodness! And as if she hadn't known it herself!—imagine *any* woman's not knowing she was only doing what she was doing because she was young and giddy even while she was young and giddy doing it! So she had a *right* to worry about him, and if they'd moved him out of intensive care into a private room he still had monitors stuck all over him hadn't he?—so when Sibylla worried why shouldn't anyone who loved him worry too? oh he was detestable!

Yes, well, he said mildly, after a moment, yes the heart unit had, he'd of course concede, been something of a memento mori, how did those splendid duty nurses stand it, hour after hour? For instance in the cubicle across from his there had been this huge dying hulk of (he'd found out) a ship's captain, an enormous man, lost and wandering in delirium on top of everything else, and he kept bellowing for his lawyers.

'Lawyers'?

Well it seemed he thought he was being held captive by sea-going gangsters, in some waterfront dive! So, to escape, he kept pulling out the various tubes they had in him, nurses were lugging blood-soaked bedding out every half-hour or so; amazing! So finally they actually lashed the poor devil's wrists to the bed-rails!—except then by god what did he do but work his way round till he could tear the knots loose with his great teeth, could she imagine such a thing?

"Ah Scrope . . ."

But then, that second night, in the middle of one of those hoarse raging Achillean tantrums, suddenly there had come this, well, it was the *suddenness* of the stillness. And the rush of the nurses. To what was no longer there. . . . Very *moving*, somehow. To have lain there, listening. Though why 'moving'? One's im-personal interest, as at a play? Or is it merely human decency—sympathy for the race of man. Or was it 'moved' (as at a play) in a sort of Aristotelian satisfaction at the well-constructed Sophoclean dénouement, 'Zeus still Zeus' in fact, and the audience homeward bound, purged and edified? . . .

But "Oh sweetie now I *must* sign off," she regretted, "I must I *must*, I am enslaved to this inexorable magazine, and when you haven't even told me how is your heavenly Sibylla of a daughter."

He said need he say couldn't be sweeter?—"Comes to see me in this damn place two and three times a day."

"Yes how does she manage?"

So he said and how was that huge stepson of hers and his latest Guggenheim.

"Do I ever see him, to find out?" she cried. "Though Scrope he does have a splendid I'm told poem in some quarterly, one of those tensely intellectual quarterlies I think, the *Susquehanna* is it? Quite a long poem, too. *Pages*."

He said narrative, huh.

"No I don't think so, just more sort of—oh *you* know, more sort of what he feels about how he feels."

He said um.

"And you don't in the least care anyhow!" she told him, though then, for a wary moment, and this was perhaps mutual good man-ners and forgiveness, they were silent.

But she had to go.

"Because now my sweet old darling I do have to hang up on you, oh how sad always," she lamented. "Except do you never

Scrope wonder a little about the pair of them, those special two of ours, together?"

He snickered bless God what an unseemly question!

"No but I mean about their being married to each *other*. Being who they are."

"What's this being who—Alec you mean yours and she mine?"

"Yes, and, well, being *married*, sweetie. And they d'you truly think happy."

"Happy how? Way we were?"

"Well of course, but happily *married*."

"Why shouldn't they be happy? Sibylla's a lovely thing, what could any man want! And a sweet besides! And, well, Alec's this splendid huge jock of a Discobolos if you like—good god Laura in principle what more'd either of 'em want!"

"But as happy as we've been? Oh Scrope don't you ever wonder whether sometimes— Because can it be the same sort of *match*. My dear she's like you, the sweet, but who Alec's like is his father, who was *splendidly* what you called my bel homme tendency if ever anyone was!"

Her bel homme 'frailty' was the word. Never lifted a finger! Bill Basset was another of 'em. And worse!

"So you see Alec and Sibylla aren't really a sort of thing like you and me at *all*, I mean."

What she mean, 'she meant'?

"But how they feel about each other, heavens!—not like *us* can it be, surely? Because is your lovely Sibylla's temperament any more a cleave-to d'you think than yours?—and Scrope you can't *not* see how like Alec is to his father instead?"

. . . Hadn't turned out to be all that cleaved-*to*, either, she meant? Or was it 'cloven-to.'

"As who knows better than you!"

Ah, well, he said, beaux hommes. They did often turn out to be temptable-from, anyhow. Women being, upon reflection, women. His darling daughter he supposed included, never *had* got used to producing anything so delicious!

Mrs. Tench-Fenton opened her eyes at him instantly. "Do you mean about Charles Ebury?" she demanded.

"Now what's this!" he cried, as in alarm.

"Well but I understood he was helping her with this *very* it seems amusing libretto isn't he? Because *Charles* I should have thought— Well I had a fascinating talk with him at a party, about *Ovid* can you imagine? all I'd somehow thought Ovid'd written

was that collection of nursery-tale myths, but Charles said his
Helen to Paris letter is the basis for the whole genre of psychology-
of-love novels from Mme. de La Fayette on. He promised to do
me an article on it, what an angel, I don't wonder Sibylla's putting
him to work! But surely you'd heard, didn't she tell you? Because
certainly *he* could be a temptation without lifting a finger either."

"Dammit," the father cried, as if humorously, "what kind of in-
terlocking triangles are you trying to upset me with!"

"Well sweetie there *is* after all us! You don't feel anybody's ever
going to think they're proxies for us somehow?"

"Proxies for *our* happy behavior, woman?" he demanded of her,
greatly amused.

"*Now* who's unseemly!" she chanted, sounding amorous; and
they hung up, snickering if only in memory.

2

Those at any rate married children of theirs, whose name was
Urquhart, it happened were discussing them too, late that
evening, before bed.

Or anyhow Sibylla, creaming her fashionable face at her dressing glass, was tenderly fretting about her father.

"Imagine letting a man as near death as Daddy was have a telephone! Have they no sense? How's he to rest properly, Alec? I was
beside myself!"

This however her huge young husband, yawning at his image in
the pier glass beyond, might well have been too sodden with sleep,
by the look of him, to grasp was a concern.

"And you know how Daddy is!" she denounced him. "Now he'll
wear himself out haranguing everybody he knows!"

So the man appeared to search, vacant. Though at last, ". . . nm,"
he came up with, swaying.

"So he's maddening!" the daughter cried lovingly. "For example when I got to the hospital this morning he was just hanging
up from talking who knows how long to of all people your sweet
m'ma, trying to palm off an article on her! And simply because
some other editor had turned it down, well I despaired! Oh and
I forgot to tell you—yesterday when he was still half-stoned and
babbling I found out how the two of them first met, Alec!"

But he, lurched round, was now straggling yawning toward
their bed, and mumbled only a mindless ". . . ng?" in reply.

"Well, parents, yes! But it seems it was the very first piece Daddy ever wrote for her, was how. Way back, darling; she was working for some chichi decorators' thing that isn't published now. You and I weren't even born, can you imagine? One 'theme' of this particular issue it seems was to be Tables— Are you listening to me or aren't you?" she demanded, for he was now toppling, stuporous, onto their great soft-billowing white circle of a bed, into which he now sank, spent.

She watched this, as tolerantly analyzing it.

"But what have you been doing, to be this great tedious tired hulk from, all suddenly?" she now accused him, sounding amused. "Not surely some of your time-wasting little slinks of student groupies again you've put up with!"

He made some vague disavowing sound, stretching happily, as in innocence and contentment, deep in down.

"Goodness shall I be jealous of you or something?" she laughed. "Poor catnip darling, having to fend off sophomores! As I do of course hope you of course do. No, but imagine," she went on, "Daddy said they'd not only never met but he'd never so much as heard of her when out of the blue there she was! Would he consider doing them fifteen hundred of his lovely words on for example strange hosts he had known? Or odd table-conversations. Or eccentric seating-protocols. Or of course any angle he wanted to propose himself instead, because they did so want *him* in this issue, his wit and the way he wrote his brilliant novels—oh well darling you know that coaxing caressing absolutely seducing voice of hers, as if she's Daddy said about to murmur herself into bed with you!"

The son-in-law muttered something derisive-sounding, "nole edger," it seemed.

"Oh ptah, he isn't! Anyway he certainly wasn't old *then!* Anyway if he's unteachable are you with your simpering students all that different? And Amy says Charles either! Well naturally Daddy told your m'ma how flattering, he'd be delighted to, though how about something with perhaps a bit more *his* sort of slant? Of course she breathed at him oh what a heavenly thing to suggest, without bothering to wait and hear what he was suggesting— which of course, it being Pa, was what does happen at tables: he'd do her a man and a girl meeting for lunch at Les Piérides with something in mind. So that's what it seems he did. And sent it round to her without bothering his agent, that voice of hers, goodness! Well but next *day* Alec there on his doorstep was a messenger with an enormous bouquet of bird-of-paradise flowers!—and being Pa he fell in love with her then and there, oh really darling the *seductions* of your mother!"

. . . stepmother.

"So he instantly rang her up and asked her to lunch. And, being Daddy, at Les Piérides."

Said nnnn.

"So I was wildly amused. Only then he got off onto something else. But then coming home I remembered wasn't there a magazine-editor heroine in *A Time Was Had by All?* So I looked it up. And there is; called Miranda. And the second time the hero takes her to lunch it says it's 'the second time they'd ever laid eyes on each other,' which would fit, Alec! And then the way he describes her, because listen to what I found, I marked the place, because it's absolutely—well, listen!

. . . her eyes overflowing with light at him before she'd even sipped her Punt e Mes

—which Alec she *still* drinks now and then, and who else ever does, goodness! Except this second restaurant was way down in what Daddy calls 'the wilds below Canal Street' somewhere, Cacciapuoti's did you ever hear of it? Very elegant, in the book. Except it has an upstairs balcony out over the street but all there is across is warehouses. Would he bother to invent that? So it must actually have happened. Most of the places in his novels of course haven't been there for years by our time; Daddy's geography is sweetly archaic, is all. And then anyway it could really have been almost any random seduced girl, you know how he is."

Her husband grunted something, it could have been disparaging, into his pillow, turned now away.

"Well darling *he* feels like that about *poets!*" she laughed. "What am I to do, between you? Each of you snorting why even consider writing in the other's worn-out form! Oh dear I suppose you're slighting and dismissive about novels to your adoring students too, corrupting them! No, but about your m'ma back then, still young and volage the way who isn't—this affair with Daddy must been don't you suppose long before she was married to your father? Daddy perhaps hadn't met my mother either— darling they *can't* have been lovers with you and me in a crib in the next room, goodness how indecorous, and they were properly brought up, Alec!"

He had however it seemed dozed peacefully off.

"Though what era was it. Do we even know? Also they could have taken their affair up again later couldn't they," this permissive daughter theorized. "I expect it would depend on what they'd broken off over. She could temporarily have met someone else. Or Daddy could've. Or whichever, but still the other one lovingly there, hoping and so on. Or one of them's getting married could have ended it for the time?"

But he it appeared slumbered on, beyond such cares.

"Oh but then Alec how exhausting, in those days! Because think!—being brought up the way they were, to be seriously responsible socially, think of the endless time-taking stealths, to protect each other's spouse's feelings!—the way in Daddy's novels it's not just unkind not to, it's inexcusable! They loved whoever they were married to *too*. Except Amy says but the first time you met a man who was going to be your lover naturally you didn't know he was going to be, so how could they start to be careful and dissembling? Only then hoh, who she met like that was *Charles!*" she mocked, but now suddenly in the glass her eyes were on her husband's slumbering image. " 'Didn't know'?—when who wouldn't *think!*" she murmured, though the sleeper did not stir. ". . . a man like Charles?"

So for a long moment then she seemed to muse, eyes lost in her own eyes in the glass once more.

But soon, "Oh well Amy does fuss about what to have her story characters feel," she went on. "And asks *me* darling! And such simple-minded questions sometimes! If one spouse is having an affair she said doesn't the other spouse sense it? And somehow show it? She said if you didn't wouldn't your husband just perhaps think you didn't care what he did? Well, imagine! Naturally I said why should the wife show she knew, heavens. She said but wouldn't a used-to-you man like a husband notice some difference?—could I for instance just go on making wifely love with you if you were sleeping with somebody so that you'd still not know I knew? I said don't be silly, men are stones. But she said but suppose it was complicated, suppose the affair you, Alec, were having was with somebody I see all the time, like her?"

In their great bed the husband's eyes suddenly opened.

"Naturally I said, 'Oh dear is he having?' and she said, 'Well I adore him don't I?' And she did once have that crush. Of course I said why ask *me!* when why not my dear pa? He's not only an entirely practical writer he's very amusing in particular about other writers' seduction scenes, or men writers' anyway, like Anna

weeping on that hard sofa and Vronski glumly pacing the floor—
he says what in God's name did Tolstoi conceive had gone *on* to
produce this preposterous scene! Did gens du monde of the time,
with seven or eight kilos of Second Empire clothes on, make love
on period sofas in drawing-rooms? Had Tolstoi ever tried it? And
those *tears?* . . . For any instructive particulars, Daddy says the
scene could have been written by Henry James!"

But her husband was staring at the ceiling, as if baffled.
Though even, it could have been, in dismay.

"What Amy really wanted was to know whether I felt she could
'research' Daddy for her new story: how do men his age feel she
said about young women they have to deal with in the ordinary
course of things, for instance this Yale sociology instructress who's
doing part of her dissertation on him. Of course I told her *he* just
seems to be amused; he calls it the 'in-house school of sociology,
who simply move in on you,' and why not. Except Alec when the
girl spends whole weekends at this au pair fieldwork with him?—
'intensively observing' him or whatever it is sociologists do?"

So he mumbled something. Though he had closed his eyes.

"Well the girl *is* very pretty. And she's Danish. But should we
be against her making him sociologically famous if that's what
she's doing? And I certainly can't say, 'Darling Pa should your
dear famblies perhaps worry a little?'—as if *he* would get stuck
with honorable intentions! But is he enough of an expert old marauder to take care of himself?—now that here's his heart? And
darling I am still just a little upset over what I saw that Sunday. It
was past *noon* they were still at breakfast when I dropped by! In
dressing gowns of course, but she was all rosy and tousled, and
under her dressing gown—well, remember that epigram of
Charles's? 'Black chiffon isn't to sleep in, it's to sleep with in,
a different activity altogether,' and oh Alec now he's had this
dreadful setback what could happen, it's every Friday she comes
down from New Haven! 'Lay Patterning in Scrope Townshend,'
oh dear what *is* she writing about him!"

He said um.

But now she had finished.

"There!" she sighed, drifting to her feet. "And at his age, oh
think," she mourned, and slowly crossed to stand beside their bed,
gazing sadly down.

"And now there's been this frightening heart attack. And this
girl. All these weekends *all* weekend at his age, Alec, like that? Au-
pair-ing or not? . . ."

But he, like any son-in-law, merely sighed.

"And you don't even pretend to care! are you going to get over or aren't you?" she crooned at him, laughing. "You're a great torpid Gaelic lout, Daddy's *right* I'm wasted on you!" she cried lovingly. "Move over, or I won't even bother to wake you deliciously up!"

So after a babble of a late evening they made love as usual.

3

The ménage of Amy Hallam and Charles Ebury their friends held to be exemplary and also enduring, it being agreed that, given Charles's wary air of being put upon enough already, students languishing at his effortless good looks were merely unavoidable industrial hazard (though of course job-grade entitlement, depending), and look at Amy's behavior with him anyway: doting.

On occasion helpless, even, with docility.

As for example on this particular Sunday midmorning, Charles seigneurially still abed, "But oh *why* sweetie won't you let me just *ask* dear Scrope?" she was imploring him. "How can you *be* so mean to me!"—when simply this story she had in mind was to be about this younger girl in love with this older (maybe Scrope's age) man but how *much* older, how could Scrope's merely being asked his opinion of their age *differences* upset him, she wailed, dithering about picking up last night's discarded clothes as if distracted —she'd known him ever since Sibylla's and her freshman year at Vassar, she'd even known his last wife, and of *course* that infatuated-with-him classmate of theirs who'd caused that scandal, Scrope was as good as *family*.

So, if only as a responsible bedfellow, he considered her plight with indulgence. "Look, my blessing," he said—

"I am your out-of-my-*mind* blessing!" she cried at him. "Because Charles I could simply remind him he gave me the idea in the first place why couldn't I?—because sweetie he did, I *told* you! We were talking that evening at Sibylla and Alec's and he said he was beginning to think he knew so archaically little about our generation that how was he to write about it? so he wondered wasn't perhaps the practical solution to hire a live-in our-age model, for him to more or less round-the-clock observe, what she did (and even ask why!)—painters hire models, why shouldn't novelists? I told you I TOLD you, why don't you ever *liss*-sunn to me!!"

He said, amused, what was she clutching that armful of dirty clothes for?

She flung them at a chair.

And why didn't she come back like a lovely Sunday-morning girl to bed? In bed he could listen closer.

Anyhow dammit look—if Scrope himself thought he was an archaism, what use did she think his views about young women would be for *her* stories? Why did she suppose a man of Scrope's long and punishing experience would consider, with what *she*'d consider a proper seriousness, the emotions of her baby sister's generation?—Scrope couldn't have been the standard thy-bra-and-bikini-they-comfort-me type even in college, and *now* he'd as good as persuaded himself he treated women as Reciprocal Beings, he even boasted he was one of the few dozen heterosexual American males the census had found who did!

So she brooded at him.

And finally, "Well what I *didn't* tell you," she seemed to decide to confess, "is he said why didn't I leave you for a couple of weeks and move chastely in to instruct him! So, well, *goodness*, but so anyway I told him oh how flattering, was I really all young American womanhood for him? but, well, I had only these two modest talents, I said I write what Charles says my genre is and I make love with him on demand, but a *third* career? heavens!—even temporarily, no matter how clearly glamorous, so *why* do you keep saying it would 'upset' him to ask, he is sort of an old monster but he's sweet, oh Charles *tell* me!" she besought him. "Am I your dearest frantic-over-decisions sweetie or amn't I?"

So (since she was) he replied as a decent sense of stewardship called for: hadn't it occurred to her, given Scrope's noble age, that her questions might strike the man as an inquiry as to his—call it his performance she was having the effrontery to be engaged in?—and how, he said blandly, was she going to dissemble *that*, face to face!

So she stared at him. And presently mumbled, ". . . oh."

And ah, dammit, in any case, he said, laughing, he hardly saw Scrope, of all people, ravening off after some babbling little creature only a feeling of responsibility for the species could make him rest his eyes on twice. How about coming back to bed why not. And unfuss.

She said, ". . . But he writes about them."

What if he did, she coming or wasn't she?

So she dropped onto the bed beside him, if mistrustfully.

He said look, he himself taught for example sophomores, so in line of duty he was metaphorically leered at five days a week. But what possible crosscultural correlations did that imply? *Or* serious undertakings!

"Are you looking sort of your honest-as-daylight look at me again?" she cried, and sat up.

He said, laughing at her, was he not to impart his cultural level to this or that hoping college child? and lovingly pulled her down again.

"Don't *scoff!*" she rebuked him, and resisted. "I get very uncertain about you when you look honest, it's perfectly disgrace— Charles *no!*"

But how could so adorable a bosom become so impervious to his adoring it, when a mere hour ago—

"That was *then!* and when I spoil you you get so spoiled, and anyway," she said, and left him, in fact going back to the chairful of clothes she began sorting them, "we're discussing Scrope. Do you think he *is* in a way fascinating? Except in a way he's also like somebody-you-don't-know-very-well's great-uncle! who may I mean pounce? So he's socially confusing, one feels one ought to see him as just one more old-fashioned— Did they really call them 'libertines'?"

He said 'rakes,' even.

"But then I suppose he *is* isn't he. Only somehow he isn't! Or is it he just seems he isn't but you feel is. Because every now and then there's this sort of glimpse of how he must once have been, I mean I can perfectly *see* girls' thinking of bed about him back then, so therefore now I keep feeling I have to be not just unencouraging but absolutely unfeminine against all my instincts and responses, to save him from misinterpreting and its being sad. Oh dear. Because suppose. For how old is he actually. But then even supposing! Or d'you think. I mean if only because how would one make sure, in advance, whether in bed one mightn't have to— Oh dear, how do you say it! Only now here's this Sibylla says *sexy* Yale researcher weekends, and isn't she some sort of evidence? And don't *snicker!*—she dropped in on her father two or three Sundays ago and they looked practically she said just out of bed! One of which she says *is* double."

Man of sense; just decided on an *all*-categories model; why not! Nothing for Sibylla to worry about.

"But sweetie she's a sociologist! How could that be a *Scrope* model? And it's she observing *him*, not he her! And also she's Danish!"

He said exotic, yes. Unexpected amenities, Yale's! Of course there was that widespread intellectual fatuity at Yale to be compensated for—poor devils, you'd suppose they were refugees from the Cinquième Arrondissement if they didn't keep gabbling as if they'd brought the Arrondissement with them. So perhaps they did need these exotic solaces!

"Well except when Sibylla told me about finding this girl with her father like that, something in the way she— Sweetie it was almost as if she didn't want to tell me! But we tell each other everything! We've never been strange with each other in our lives, but here, it was as if she was being specially confiding, to cover not actually feeling confiding at all! You don't suppose there can have been something we've upset them about, Alec and Sibylla? Or has there been something she feels guilty about toward *us*. Though what? You *have* been helping her with that libretto she's writing for the League, d'you suppose it could be she's feeling apologetic about taking up your time, goodness should I have let you?"

He said, smiling, ecce novum crimen!

She was silent.

Ovid, he explained, amiably. Standard masculine disclaimer. Ergo ego sufficiam reus in nova crimina semper?—'what've I done now!' and so forth.

But she said, "But sweetie when I think about the way *I* felt practically seduced by you even before I began to think about you, why shouldn't I wonder mightn't she be starting to feel that way too? And you needn't look astonished!—don't you really sort of think, to *yourself*, you could probably seduce nearly any girl you wanted to? Oh dear do I have to marry you to keep you virtuous?"

He said dear god why not!

"But I don't think I want to! I don't want anything to keep you faithful to me but *me!*"

What vanity! he said.

"Oh well," she said, and seemed to brood. Though whether in sadness or resentment who could say.

But at last, "Oh well never *mind*," she told him. "But whichever way Scrope feels about this Yale girl, sweetie it is a *relationship* isn't it?—so how can he not have *some* opinions about their age difference. So why can't I research how he sees *himself* in it, older-man-wise, for my story? And don't say I'll tire him and make his heart worse—he can't be all that ill, his *dying*'s not what Sibylla's worried over. Oh Charles can't you *see* I need to be told? I won't upset him, I *won't!*—so don't be so mean!"

And so forth and so on, till eventually she came back to bed to argue.

4

As it happened, when Sibylla had paid that morning's visit to her father he looked so much better that she sat on his bed to kiss him.

He was touched. Even mumbled a 'darling girl' in old-fashioned embarrassment.

In fact picked up her hand and kissed it.

(Which when he let it go she patted him with.)

"Well you are a sweet."

"Well so are you."

They smiled at each other.

"And looking so much better," she told him, and sat on his bedside chair.

"Ah, at any rate," he said cheerfully, "some punctual nurse isn't whisking in with her needle every couple of hours to shoot me in the small-clothes."

"Poor love."

"Not that it isn't you know fascinating stuff. At one point I distinctly remember seeing my sheets had turned into blue-green plastic—anise-flavored, too, can you imagine? So naturally I rose up and by god shed the things—tubes and attachments with them, in one grand crash. Of course the nurses were on me like whippets on a hare, and back I was indulgently put."

"Well and also, pet, when you were babbling you were hilarious. After my five minutes I'd go out into the waiting-room *convulsed*. All the poor hopeless waiting families were affronted by me!"

"Dear god I should think so!—father hovering between life and death, and she's *giggling!*"

"Except darling Daddy it *was* awful."

"Yes. Well. Chest pains. Yes. Still, elements of comedy. Huge dying man across from me ripping his tubes out, nurses just interestedly *watching* the process on their screen! But then rushing in just as he'd got the last one out, cooing 'Oh Mr. Thorgrimmsdatter what are you *doing* to yourself!' with the sweetest womanly indulgence and concern."

"Ah but darling didn't you say he died?"

"So at least God took him you mean seriously? Which reminds

me—this very pretty girl parson dropped by last evening after you'd left. Or was she a deaconess? anyway she was from 'round the corner,' she said, Saint Beekman the Well-Fixed or some such splendid shrine. Extraordinary visitation! I gather the principle is, one may be worried about the relevant theological data—the Afterlife after life, what's the ecology like and so on. So they come helpfully round, and we must feel free to inquire."

"Oh dear."

"What d'ye mean, 'oh dear'! I was a perfect gent—told her thank'ee, yes, but I'd read Dante, anyhow the *Inferno*, which I assumed was what mattered to the generality of the uneasy, but *god* what a delicious minister of hope might I say she was?—was she here to seduce me with doctrine as well as instruct me?"

"Pa *darling!*"

"Well in point of fact I suppose yes, I was a little stoned from the evening needle, still I thanked her politely enough, for either form of ministry—as thoughtful I told her as it was kind; but I said God's behavior toward us here on earth ('donde usciremo a riveder le stelle,' I remember quoting) hardly made a life with Him in Heaven something to look forward to. Did she know that devastating line of Istrati's?—'Tant de besoins, tant de désirs, tant de tumulte, et si peu d'éternité! Seigneur, pourquoi si maladroit avec Ton chef d'œuvre?' But it turned out she didn't understand French. Lovely girl, not a brain in her body."

"Oh *Pa!*" she mourned. "How can you behave that way!—and when you have such lovely manners!"

"Interrupting my writing with her damn' benisons call for anything as civilized as manners?"

But at this, "But darling, *writing?*" she cried, as in alarm. "Goodness, should you be? Tiring yourself?"

She have him just lie there going docilely nuts? What'd got into his women?—her lovely mother-in-law'd even been fussing about his being allowed mail! And in any case he'd been fiddling not writing: subconscious churning out its customary false starts, actually, for the most part. Would she like to hear the cockeyed first thing it had come up with this morning? he snickered, pulling his clipboard from under his pillow—though God knew who it was supposed to sound like, some halfwit recommending himself for cohabitation, or what?

I awake with the lark, genially. At breakfast I am cheerful, affectionate, gynæcotropic, and an informative talker.

Where did this kind of claptrap come from!

I breakfast on kippers and buttered eggs, on kedgeree and Canadian bacon, my fulminating disapprobation of my era at the service of mankind. My glance is mild.

"Well darling he eats rather like you, whoever!"

"Ah well I throw away nine-tenths of the deathless stuff I write anyhow, what's another nineteen-twentieths. Death, by the way (did I tell you?), as a by-product of this run-around of mine with eternity, turns out to be something I'm not alarmed by, *very* surprising! Simply the pain was so appalling that what was death!—and then, once they'd numbed the pain, I was past being frightened by anything as trivial as dying, just lay there sort of courteously interested in all those emergency people working on me with such frantic concentration. I thought, 'Be damned, must be in pretty bad shape, what d'you know!' so then of course I thought about Internal Revenue."

"Yes Daddy you said."

"Well how *do* you protect intangibles like future royalties from estate tax! But then it struck me this wasn't the most fitting topic to devote my last hour on earth to, so I began to think about you and your brother, and that's all I remember until I found my sheets were blue-green plastic."

"Ah darling. It *was* awful."

"Yes. Well. Anyhow. 'Have I woken on the bright morning of my disaster' isn't the thing to say. Or necessarily write about—Priam's roll-call of human catastrophe's taken care of that already. Which reminds me, you haven't said how that comic *Agamemnon* of yours is getting on, what's this about Charles Ebury's helping you?"

" 'About' Charles, darling? how d'you mean?"

"How'd *he* happen to get in on it, what'd anybody mean!"

"But simply he very kindly offered to give advice if I needed it, heavens what else! He lectures on the *Oresteia* in his Greek Religions course as well as in his Greek Tragedy, darling he's a perfect adviser!"

"Well I read Greek too, what of it?—even Æschylus!"

"Oh but Pa you're busy—and anyway you're important! And also it was Amy knowing I was writing it sent Charles. Or practically. Why should I have bothered you, heavens!"

" 'Bother'?—good god, you're my daughter!"

"But darling all the more reason!"

"Well but what's this 'advice' you claim he's giving you dammit," the father complained.

"But heavens all sorts of suggestions! For instance Cassandra sings her first solo aria—woe woe behold her, King Priam's Bennington-educated daughter now a mere slave and concubine, and to this thug-witted provincial warlord, even in bed he talks geopolitics, so funny, and what Charles did was write some absolutely coleporterly extra lyrics for her, some of it he says lifted nearly word for word from Æschylus himself!"

Her father said politely, why, wonderful.

"Then Agamemnon is 'a morose and rumbling basso,' Charles says, and in his opening aria he complains ('in a grumpy and self-pitying roar,' Charles says it should be) about how middle-aged and put-upon he feels, what's he supposed to *do* with this damn' Cassandra!—of course being top trophy she *had* to be allotted to him as commander-in-chief, status is after all status, but why was it his luck to get *this* wincing little finishing-school intellectual! And look at this affair his wife has been having with his cousin in his absence—couldn't the silly bitch have picked somebody outside the royal succession to go to bed with? Why, all he had to do was fall down a stair and break his neck, and everybody'd think she'd murdered him to make the fellow king! The political fatuity he has to put up with! And when all he wants after ten years of war's a little peace and quiet—and a concubine who isn't so everlastingly avant-garde in bed!"

He said this hers or Ebury's?

"Mostly mine."

By god it was wonderful!—could be practically a satyr-play for the original *Oresteia!*

"That's what Charles says too, how did you know? And then we've thought up what's a *really* lovely twist—"

"Look, my sweet child, how do you collaborate or whatever, you and Ebury?"

"How?—but how do you mean, 'how'?"

"What could I mean dammit!—he come to your place, for instance? Or you to his!"

So naturally she opened her eyes at him. "But darling *Pa!*" she cried. "What could 'where' have to do with it! Except it's *my* typewriter I'm used to. But half the time neither of us goes anywhere, we just telephone, goodness. Oh Daddy am I tiring you?"

He mumbled *god* no.

"Then about the twist at the end? Because Orestes, see, comes home from graduate-school in Phocis, and he's just as much a young intellectual as Cassandra, so in act two they fall in love and sing a Liebesduett about the stuffiness of their parents. And in act three they elope back to the Troad—so of course then Agamemnon, in a great bellowing finale, has to muster the Greek host all over again, this time to get *his* girl back, oh it's lovely! Oh but Daddy I *am* tiring you!"

'Tiring' him? she never tired him! Dear god it was she and Botticelli epiphanies like her that kept him interested in staying alive, in this tedious place *and* out of it. No but by god *really* what a witty scenario—she was wonderful! And might he offer a suggestion too? for a possible curtain-effect? couldn't have Ebury making all the contributions, Classics prof or not! So what would she say to this, for the curtain coming down: as Agamemnon plunges off bellowing côté cour, why not have Clytemnestra and Ægisthus saunter off giggling côté jardin, hand in hand?

"Oh Daddy how perfect, Charles'll—"

"Well dammit Clytemnestra was after all Helen of Troy's sister, doesn't she deserve a little self-expression too?—aux jolis minois les baisers!"

"Oh Charles will love it!—he admires you terribly anyway you know. He says he particularly falls in love with your heroines, did I tell you?"

"Well don't let him fall in love with *you!*" he cried.

"*Pa!*" she reproved him, in sheer scandal.

So he mumbled something. Contrite, presumably.

"But darling I thought you liked him!"

. . . Nothing against the fellow. Nothing at all! Simply hadn't perhaps seen all that much of him. For an opinion. Except of course his being a wit. Which he was.

"And in the way *you* are, Daddy, haven't you noticed? Even his subconscious behaves like yours, goodness!—he told me he woke up the other day with it giving him the complete opening sentence for a story he wouldn't even consider writing either!"

What was a father to say.

"And he's just done this hilarious article on modern poetry which is exactly Daddy how you feel about it yourself, I mean he says there's so little tradition of craftsmanship that most of the poor gabbling practitioners don't even know they aren't even far enough along in their apprenticeships to realize tradition exists!"

He said by god *no!*

"And Charles is just as sarcastic about them as you are. Only he says he'll have to publish it under a nom de guerre, because of for instance Alec. Well, and of me. But how arrange it, so I said but I'll simply take it to Laura! Because don't you think? Oh and he has such a brilliant title for it, 'Mr. Molehill's Reasons for Writing,' isn't it lovely?"

. . . Why couldn't the fellow take it to Laura himself!

"But darling *no* reason, heavens! Except why shouldn't I do it for him? knowing her so much better! Being *family!*"

He said well but dear god *Alec* was a modern poet!

"Goodness, I'm being *unfaithful* you mean?" she laughed. "And with my very best friend's live-in—oh *Pa!*"

—But here the nurse swept efficiently in, looking dismissive and put-upon; so for that morning that was that.

5

Mrs. Tench-Fenton rang up her stepson next day at his faculty office, though this she seldom did, "because is this wretched hospital being *guarded* do you think, Alec, about poor Scrope's actual condition, what it truly is? he of course *is* getting I assume better isn't he? and Sibylla they must have told something definite by now surely!" interrupting one of his term-paper consultations ("Non-U and Demotic in Philip Larkin"), and this was a student who, besides an enchanting bosom, had an entrancing lisp. "One gets nothing *nothing* from doctors, he could be even *dying* and you couldn't tell whether they did or didn't know whether they as much as knew!"

He said, well—

"But can't your sweet Sibylla insist a little more? because how am *I* to! You are I mean so lucky to have her, that darling, but mightn't you perhaps suggest to her— Well, the man *is* your own father-in-law, Alec!"

He said but—

"Isn't *she* worried poor sweet he may for instance not even think seriously enough about himself (and you *know* how he can *not!*) to tell us what they may have told *him?* and when I am half frantic!"

He said—

"Alec he never had even a chest pain till this!—and I've known him from *years,* even, before I'd as much as met your infuriating great angel of a father! Or said I'd marry him—*imagine* not telling me you existed, when there you were all the time, off at that hair-raising permissive prep-school, really how do Quakers justify the means of whatever their ends are! No but Alec is he— Oh *how* is he? and can't you do anything but mumble? Or is there some student with you."

He smiled at the girl (who smiled obediently back).

"Because *I* never know whether you're off in one of your inarticulate brooding intervals or not, goodness your lovely speechless father babbled, compared! But Alec *besides* being sick with worry poor darling like all of us about Scrope is Sibylla can you tell me seeing to the housekeeping side of things at his flat meantime?—I mean the poor man's laundry to be picked up from wherever and for instance how much is there rotting in his ice-box. Oh and has she any idea whether he may have let that Yale young woman have a key?"

He appeared to search his memory.

"Because you know how he is! Or hasn't Sibylla are you trying to tell me even asked him whether! Is the silly child— Oh Alec you *can't* mean she knows so little about her father that she thinks he's having something like an affair with the girl, so she's diffident about asking!"

He said he—

"And when she told me the girl seems even considerate about not disturbing him? heavens! Monday mornings she's up dark-of-the-dawn as far as she can make out, and makes herself breakfast and lays out everything for *his*, with a little thank-you note (sometimes in Danish—'playfully,' Scrope supposes), and is off to Grand Central before he'd even consider opening his eyes. And writes up her weekend notes on the train back to New Haven. Of course what *sort* of notes about a man like Scrope this girl can possibly be taking, well *yes* Alec who wouldn't wonder!—it could hardly be just routine time-motion average-minutes between the beset man's breakfast and the day's first word-on-paper mutterings, but who ever knows with these people? even sociologists haven't studied what sociologists study have they? But Alec an *affair* with her? hoh!"

He said um.

"Oh with any normally light-minded flighty young woman well yes Alec naturally of course—'unripeness is all.' But an affair with a creature who for all he knows is carrying out his humane statistics to three sigmas—what *can* Sibylla be thinking of!"

Her stepson sighed, eyes on his student (whose eyes were cast down).

"And in particular since we all Alec know what's certain is, he's taking his wretched wordless mental notes on *her*, oh he can be outrageous! One never knows *when* some innocent offhand remark one's made to him in perfect decency won't turn up in his dialogue in a, well, in a different context altogether, and the shock when you remember the situation *and* sometimes the state you were in when you actually said it, and realize what he's— Because think of all the ones you may *not* be sure it wasn't you who said, and people *reading* them, oh he's detestable!"

He of course, as was civil, was silent.

"And how am I not to worry for him for *sensible* reasons, poor old angel! For one thing, and even if it sounds superstitious, Sibylla says he's taken to being so, well, being *rude* of all things about God, when he's never bothered his head about religion five minutes in his whole life—because Sibylla says *why* suddenly, is he worried about himself seriously? Because there *is* his age. He's been composing sardonic little couplets, she says, for instance

> God (Zeus, Iddio, Bog, Dieu, Gott)
> Does as He pleases. We may not

which he actually seems to *resent*, she says. She'd no idea he even thought enough about God to be down on Him. He said that bloody-minded old Jewish smiter was bad enough, but were Saint Paul's book-length regulations much of an improvement?—so childish really, Alec, imagine! Of course Sibylla says he was amusing too: Creation he admitted was an attractive idea in its way, everything fresh and new, and archangels fluttering in and out with ecological and demographic suggestions of one sort and another. But then he said, that was back *then*; and what we seem to have got is this bureaucracy of angels distributing computerized damnations. So my dear what is one to think?"

And so on, until presently the student mumbled something apologetic and bashful (as to a poet) and left.

6

One midmorning, after a class, Sibylla Urquhart rang up Charles Ebury and said had he a minute? because, first, her father had a beautiful curtain for the libretto she wanted to tell him, and second, to read him something—"because remember you said what you call the 'dream girls' in Daddy's novels are actually symbols?

which help him recall and reconstruct the feelings he felt, not the particular perhaps girls."

"*I* made this meta-critical remark?"

"Yes Charles you did, and so then you said if I was worried about this Yale involvement of his, though you said *you* weren't in the least, why didn't I read up on the traits of the heroines in his novels? and if they didn't match hers, stop worrying; but what it's *done* somehow is make me think I don't perhaps know anything really about him at all! Oh and when here the old darling is, so *ill*, Charles!"

He instantly said should he come round.

"Oh I didn't mean to make you *concerned*, goodness!" she cried, in a happy voice. "When it's oh probably you know nothing but delayed shock don't you suppose?—like remember I told you the time I found out Daddy'd had this devastating-them-both affair with Alec's sweetie of a mother."

He put in '—stepmother.'

"How can one *not* be involved in one's parents' amours!—even didn't I tell you I was a tiny *child* when I heard Mummy laughing with a friend of hers about 'the *tedium* of all those frantic little bitches in heat over my husband,' what age was I?—anyway I remember I had to look 'tedium' up in the dictionary, I thought was it for instance a new dirty word, what could I have been, seven? eight?"

He snorted, amused.

"Oh *well*," she conceded. "No but anyway Charles I've done what you said why not try, researched their dreamy traits, his girls', and I came on this very early one, early I mean if she was real, so it's this passage about her I wanted to read to you and see what you think. Or am I interrupting you in something, what were you doing?"

"Wondering whether to interrupt you."

"Goodness, how kind, and you even sound as if you were, such nice manners, Charles!"

He was silent.

"But what!" she said, surprised.

"Not 'manners,' " he said, lightly. "Never mind. What early girl?"

"In that wartime-London novel of Daddy's, and the hero's uncle had given him a letter of introduction to her m'ma. So he sends it round and then calls—

and there, in the practiced blandishment of her cool young white and gold, was Lady Sophia.

Daddy *loves* that word 'blandishment'!

How tiresome of M'ma to be late and not there! And when how kind of him to have called! His old connoisseur of an uncle had by god told the truth—an elegant dish she was, poised and uninnocent, wanton blue-eyed gaze and all.

Of course the old uncle had had an affair with the mother years before; typical Pa! Well, the girl's married to

a splendid young brute named Hamish FitzEdmund, a rowing-hearty type with the usual brigade-of-guards manner, but he was a subaltern at HQ Cairo, and she was holding her beauty's court in her m'ma's drawing room or levee in her own. Two dozen other young officers were in various stages of fuming rut or suicidal despair over her—

Does she sound like any of Daddy's usual girls to you either? And then listen to this:

She was trained to please, as for centuries only her class has been trained to please. But she had too many generations of libertine ladyships behind her to fancy taking a lover anything but ordinary good breeding: what was one trained *for*?

I mean do you believe in her? Isn't she just sort of novel-character real?—not 'alive,' just with the type-traits you expect from the type."

"You believe in the stylization," he said.

". . . I do?"

"You make the required adjustments and assumptions. The way you assume the non-existent fourth wall in a stage-set. Look, styliz-ing's been here from the beginning, Æschylus and all—if you don't see his Cassandra's a total stylization, think if Stendhal or good god Flaubert had written her! What do you think even our Cassandra is!"

Sibylla was silent.

And for so long that he said, "You still there?"

"Oh *yes*. Just I hoped you were going on."

"About Cassandra?"

"Or anything. I like to hear you talk."

So he was silent. Until presently he said, "Well, but about un-derstanding your father?"

"Oh. Yes, well. Except I suppose this Lady Sophia wasn't all that explaining-him, was it. I just thought I'd read it to you, is all.

And see what you thought. Well I *happened* on it! And you did suggest I 'research.' So I just felt I'd like to read it to you. Is all," she finished.

Then they were both silent.

And for so long it as good as became a stylization.

But at last, "Ah look," he said, "this is God *knows* à l'improviste, but will you have lunch with me?"

". . . 'lunch'?"

"If only to— Since we can't I suppose do anything much more *than* that about whatever-it-is, can we."

". . . Oh Charles."

"Well but can we?"

". . . No I suppose really not."

"But at least at lunch we— Because what you rang me up about wasn't really *what* you rang me up about, was it."

She was silent.

"So come to at least lunch?"

She still said nothing.

"Squarcialuppi's? Les Piérides? Five-Four-Three?"

"Oh Charles I *can't*, I'm seeing *Daddy!*"

"Well then tomorrow?"

"Oh pet you don't understand—I *take* Daddy lunch, the hospital kitchen puts him into rages. So I make him his particular daubes and navarins and heat them in the nurses' pantry. And today it's a coq au vin."

". . . I see."

"And I stay with him while he eats, oh Charles forgive me? Because I'm afraid I am sort of caught! Or at least until Daddy's nearer out and home again."

"But then?"

"Well but those first days home—"

"But good *god*, Sibylla," he cried at her, "am I to assume that if you and I were across a table at Les Piérides instead of at the ends of a damn' telephone cable all we'd do is gaze at each other sadly? —what *is* this!"

But this outburst she of course at once countered with the proprieties. "But what's *what*, goodness! —and so ominous-sounding, Charles!"

" 'Ominous'!"

"Well but what am I to think? When have I ever 'gazed sadly' at you!"

"You abashing me?" he said, and laughed.

"Well *anybody* listening to you!" she rebuked him, smiling.

So he said ah well but to go back then, what was this new finale her ingenious father had suggested for the libretto; so she described it for him, and presently they rang off.

7

That same morning, though after a different class, Alec Urquhart rang up Amy Hallam and said (so dispiritedly she hardly heard him) was she busy? or could he come see her about something, and she said all she was doing was shorten a skirt, would he mind a sewing-machine in a flustered bedroom? she *loved* seeing him, even about something; but when presently he arrived he looked so altogether cast down she was too surprised to kiss him.

"But Alec sweetie this *gloom?*" she protested. "But what possible— Oh sit on the bed where I can *see* you, goodness!" she told him, for he was looming there over her, gazing down it seemed wordless with woe. "No but what *is* this?" she demanded, concerned, as he sat. "Heavens something *that* desponding?—and when Alec you're looking so huge and handsome I could fall swooning into your arms with helpless love!"

He gaped at her, stunned.

She was astonished. "But Alec *sweetie!*" she cried. "What *can* it be!" (For indeed he appeared overwhelmed.) "What I said?— except goodness, said what? I mean heavens-said-what! That I could swoon at you?—oh dear don't tell me you're *upset* I might!"

He mumbled something—hopeless, it sounded.

"But I *wouldn't*, who'd even think I would? even the time Sibylla spotted that lovely crush I had on you she didn't! Oh Alec don't tell me she still thinks I— Oh *not* that it's something *worse*, oh *no!*"

What could he have said but what could he say! He was mute.

". . . but with *me?*" this best friend babbled. "When how possibly! And when simply we *haven't*, Alec! And when is this to have happened, even! And how—am I supposed to have seduced you? and when I don't even dream about you anymore, oh *darling* Alec how appalling!"

Though what could he say.

"Oh poor sweetie can't you do anything but sit there gulping?— so *sad*, and when it was such an innocent crush! Like *everybody's*, and I never do anything about them anyway, oh why have I the fidelity of the raven! And it wasn't an adulterous crush *ever*, just I used to carry your latest published poem around with me in my handbag. For company. And to wordlessly tell it I wordlessly adored you. All the time of course feeling awful at *not* feeling awful about Sibylla. But then I sort of knew I didn't feel genuinely awful because probably I wasn't ever actually going to sleep with you, I hope you don't mind, it wasn't you-as-such I wasn't going to sleep with, goodness every time I saw you I was faint with longing, but just I didn't seem to feel convinced it was likely I'd hand myself over to myself like that. So then I felt better about wordlessly adoring you. And then, well, in bed with Charles I realized I always forgot about you entirely, I hope you won't mind that either, so anyhow being *that* heartless I felt better. Except I still felt like a dopey teenager. Until I got over you. Except I've never I guess got *that* over, maybe I never will, I'll always remember with sweet sadness my crush on you. Because who says nostalgia doesn't change the part of you that's being nostalgic, I think about how I *thought* about going to bed with you, and could I be any more tender than that even if we had? I mean it's how I felt not whether I did what I felt. *Am* I supposed to have seduced you? Or is it you me? Oh dear. Oh *dear*! Do you ever seduce your students?—like Charles, if he does?"

He muttered something unintelligible.

"Or is it they I suppose seduce you. Or I mean try to. *There!*" she said to the machine, lining the seam up again. "Or do you just avoid the situation—so *wicked* and cruel of you Alec, when the poor girl's decided on you! *I* thought I adored you didn't I?— and adored *you*, not your poetry, goodness I don't think I always really *read* the poem of yours I was faithfully carrying around, I just blissfully felt I knew you by heart, you *see* how dopey? Oh well, Charles says since Joyce even freshman girls have epiphanies. Oh Alec how *can* they imagine we are lovers! Charles is my true sweetie, how could he suspect me? Or Sibylla you? What *are* we to do, to be innocent?—how can either of us make love *like* a faithful spouse without the performing's affecting the performance!"

He had no answer—the question having, in any case, merely stated a dilemma.

8

One afternoon, later that week, a delicious child named Amanda Hallam (but called Mimi) and a gangling boy named Richard Scrope Townshend III rolled stickily apart in a bedroom they had borrowed in Blair Hall, and he said "... *whoooh!*" and gaped at the ceiling vacant-eyed, for he in particular of this pair of Princeton freshmen had still, for this sort of thing, some polish to acquire.

So they lay there—she too, for the moment—dozing.

But in time she stretched, arching her slim back in a murmur of luxury, wriggling her toes. She opened her eyes, and, swallowing a yawn, appeared to think.

So presently she lolled her head on the pillow toward the stuporous boy.

Whose jaw hung ajar, slack. He might have been about to snore. She was amused.

And so, finally, rolled up onto an elbow and contemplated him with lazy indulgence, eyes assessing his young-male length detail by detail. She could have been appraising a work in progress. And perhaps signing it, for she put out a ladylike fingertip, and, on his belly, lightly tracked an M.

His flesh winced.

She said, "*My* you sweat!" and wiped her finger in his hair.

His eyes came open, glazed.

"You're practically *trickling!*" she giggled. "And look at me, you great slop—you were trickling onto *me!*"

He stared, still lost.

"Oh and you're trickling *yet!*" she taunted happily—and with practiced ease slid up and knelt astride his moist middle, toes tucked in along his flanks as elegantly as a jockey's.

He yelped *Hey!* and came to.

"So *sad* you're so messy!"

He reared his head and stared down his length to her, sheepish, saying, "... am?"

"*And* so bony!" she told him, shifting in the saddle.

He mumbled, "... aw, Mimi," as in appeasement.

So she smiled down at him, poised there; and for a long moment they were silent again, smiling faintly, both—a girl riding a dolphin they could have been, a marble from Methymna, brought for some Roman fountain lost in time, and, for that later taste, Arion a girl.

"So then anyway you can just stop freaking at me about Amy!" she decreed, and for obedience.

He made an indeterminate swallowing sound.

"Because I certainly *can too* bug her bedroom if I want to, goodness she's my sister! And it isn't as if I'm going to *tell* anybody what I hear!"

He said meekly, "Well but you told me."

"Not what was on the actual tape I didn't! So it's not what she *said*. And naturally it won't be about *her* in my term-paper, stupid —we *generalize* people in Sociology!"

He appeared to reflect on this. But he said, "Yuh but *bug* your own sister's apartment?—that's *real* flakey!"

"Not her apartment, her bed!"

"Well, jesus, her bed—just for some crappy term-paper? *Jesus*, Mimi, where were you brought up!"

"All right then tell me how *else* I can get to actually compare generational affective vocabularies!—you can't *ask*! I have to compare all the subjective-erotic topic-ratios too—so *how* else!"

"Compare with what."

"Well, with our generation. Naturally. But also I thought why not with D. H. Lawrence, I'm tired of Proust. Anyway he was *old-fashioned* gay, so that would screw up my glossary of demotic input too."

"What's 'demotic'?"

"Four letters."

He pondered. "Ah but anyway *look*," he said finally, "it's poor. It's just *poor*!"

"It is *not*! How *do* generations differ? Professor Staling said it will be a fascinating special demonstration!"

"Another durdy old man!"

"Oh, well, professors. But so what. Just they've all read *Lolita* and they think *that's* it. Amy says when she was a freshman she had a professor who couldn't seem to tell her from that sort of White Russian daydream either."

"From *what*?"

"Well he *was* a White Russian. Vladimir something—he wanted her to call him Vovo. He'd say, 'You 'ave never wish to making laaahv with Russian man?'—so wistful, she said. She felt sorry for him, sort of. Only of course not *that* sorry. Oh Richard your mouth *is* so pretty!" she exulted, and traced the line of it with a fingertip. "No but then Amy really baffles me sex-wise. Because Richard on that very first tape I played back, there she was, not *in* bed but in her bedroom, which she's always *neurotic* about men in except Charles, and Richard it was your uncle!"

He said, blank, "Christ what uncle!"

"How many uncles have you got?—Alec, silly!"

"Hey, Alec's not my uncle!"

"Your aunt's husband's not your uncle?"

"Sibylla's not my aunt, she's my father's half-sister. So what's her husband?—he's not anything!"

"He would be in New Guinea, among the Arrhoa! And among the Neshaminy he'd be your wan'h-toc."

"Where'd you get all this—that same crappy course?"

"Listen, do you want to hear about them in Amy's bedroom or don't you?"

"Well he's *not my uncle!*"

"Well and he hasn't *done* anything yet either, but they're certainly going to!"

"Yeah? how can you tell?"

"I can tell—verbally she was all *over* him!"

"Nuts, you can't tell!"

"I can too! I'm not some dumb *boy!* Listen, she was pretending to sew a skirt or something, so she had her sewing-machine between them, unconsciously she goes in for symbols all the time anyway, so it was there as a barrier, to help drive him wild, goodness a sewing-machine in a bedroom? why else! And *then* Richard all she talked about was this swooning crush she'd had on him, but eventually she'd got over it, except she was afraid she hadn't got over it *really*. And oh, nostalgia and stuff, oh Richard it was *lurid*, really she was disgusting, I mean what a fuss that generation turns out to make about it!"

He said unh.

"But when she has *Charles?* oh she's out of her *head* sexually!— she moons over a towering hunk like your uncle when *any* woman would want lovely Charles, I don't care if Alec *is* a very getting-famous poet."

Well he was no clod.

"No but if Amy's going to have this do with him, what about Charles?—maybe *I'll* have to keep him in the family, hoh!"

Her young man was scandalized. "Screw some guy three times your age?—*jesus*, Mimi!"

"Oh taaaah, what about that friend of your mother's on the Cape last summer!—are you so dumb you haven't even worked out yet how you got seduced?"

So he mumbled something.

"Anyway she did a good job on you, what are you grumping about?—d'you think I'd be in bed with a *freshman* if she hadn't? So shut up! You didn't even know what was happening to you. Oh you're all so dumb and helpless! Oh well of course since *then* you've got lovely," she conceded, and squeezed him with her knees. "No but about Charles I don't *feel* I feel cynical, it's just that maybe I owe it to myself to fall in *love,* to see. I mean Charles has this epigram, 'It's disillusion that turns girls into women,' so I keep thinking at what point, sort of, is this going to happen to *me.* What are you looking like that for?"

He said well jesus, keep him tuned!

"Oh come aaaahn!" she said. "Would even Charles be forever either?—what's so awesome! Anyway listen, what time did you tell those two wisps we'd give them their room back? Because how about making you a believer again?"

So, as a child of the technological age, he looked at his wrist-watch.

"Or aren't you up to it!"

But to this he replied as idiomatically as if an English major already, and the intellectual segment of the afternoon concluded.

Except that, in due course dressing again, suddenly she shrieked, "Oh god I forgot to take out my *lenses!* . . ." so they issued forth at last, beneath the spalling majesty of Witherspoon, snickering their heads off.

9

Mrs. Tench-Fenton rang up Charles Ebury from one of her cor-poration's Sabre-Liners and breathed a caressing "Oh Charles . . ." because she *could* call him Charles couldn't she? she'd not thought of him as anything else since that night he'd entranced her about Ovid at Sibylla's party for Miss Hallam's editor's upset-ting divorce, the things young women *did,* and anyhow her darling Sibylla had talked so practically glowingly about him when she brought her his brilliant piece on modern poetry (and which *couldn't* be funnier!) that she almost felt she almost knew him well, *not* just as a party talk-to, it was devastatingly funny, he'd had her laughing since take-off in St. Louis and here they were halfway to Santa Fe (not that opera was one of her weaknesses, it always seemed to be so badly written, but culturally one was helpless, and the *town* was charming) because from the wit of his title *on* it was magisterial, "Mr. Molehill's Reasons for Writing" was goodness so *true!* and then this he'd said about Samuel Beckett, this now where was it, of course Beckett wasn't technically a poet, oh where *was* it? but his sort of drama— Oh here it was!

Beckett has only to intone "Nowhere is now here," and the professors of Comparative Profundity are off—the transit of the letter *w* from the brow of one semantic unit to the sad butt of the other has become a statement of God's plan.

—oh she adored it, and then the way on this next page he *demolished* academic criticism—

in the gesturing and excited hands of insight-mongers and meta-readers and sub-Hegelians and moonlighting sociologists and even a stray shrink, in a pandemonium of happiest self-display

—oh *Charles*, but for alas *her* readership? goodness he didn't imagine readers read did he! quite aside from the delicate circumstance (or was it a quandary!) that her own dear stepson was so splendidly a modern poet himself poor boy, so in practice had Sibylla perhaps not thought before bringing her such a dilemma-making piece, she herself had even for a moment said to herself how Sibylla must admire *him*, had he enchanted her too?— though why hadn't he simply brought her the manuscript himself, was he *shy?* No but in any case, what she thought he'd promised he'd do for her, at the party, was fifteen hundred words about Ovid's poems, the ones about making love, he'd made him sound as if all she or any woman would ever want to do was gratefully lose her heart to the man, ancient Roman or not!

Well, he said, apparently Ovid—

"Because you told me in particular that he was a man who simply, well, who *liked* women not just loved us, remember? or was I just meant to understand," she laughed, "that you were telling me you did too?"

He said well Ovid said—

But "Oh Charles," she teased him, "men who actually do like women you *know* are terribly bad for us, you're so few and far between you're disorienting, I mean are we really to *believe* you think we're people or something?—so we begin to mistrust our very ability to read signals, it's *unsettling!* heavens can we have been wrong all along somehow about men?—because our total relationship *automatically* we've thought what's it been but fending off such endless low marauders! So then how on earth are we to—is the word 'comport' ourselves? I haven't heard it in so long do I even remember how to use it correctly! anyway I mean we think, Look, if he's not attacking me what am I defending myself for, heavens! So in a sort of happy daze we stop defending. And then of course see what happens. But oh Charles you *know* this, you're not like those fumbling Howells-ish characters in Henry James who have to have minor characters explain things to them all the time, you're— Oh *damn!*" she yelped, "my pilot says the ground's saying— Oh Charles it's the call I've had in for San Francisco, it's ready, oh *damn* when we were having this lovely talk but I *must* go, there are four *legal*-pad sheets of details to settle with them before lunch, but you *will* do me your lovely lovemaking Ovid, promise *promise* you will?"

He said he—

"And oh when also I so wanted to ask *you* about how Scrope is really, almost Charles I'm afraid to leave town, not knowing, but I thought—well you and Sibylla are seeing so much of each other if nothing else, over I mean this libretto of hers of course, that doesn't she ever say *what* the doctors think? I know he's in a room now like anybody, not cardiac care, but he's still being monitored, and surely they'd detach the poor darling if they— Oh the ground's *shouting* for me, oh Charles *sweetie* good-bye, *do me your Ovid!*" she wailed, and vanished.

10

When Amy Hallam came to see Scrope in his still sternly monitored room she brought him a gardenia, and went so far as to kiss his cheek in greeting.

So he dutifully grumbled, why, what a sweet she was, every time he saw her he found himself regretting he wasn't a couple of hundred years younger again.

But she said, "But goodness what *was* that I passed going out coming in!"

His ghostly solacer?—the Rev. Ms. somebody. Or was the word 'solacess'? Ah, well, pretty enough girl he supposed. Just been ordained, if that mattered.

"But Scrope sweetie, *wide-eyed* from you?"

Oh, that. Theological petulance, who in God's name knew?—
what'd the blasted girl come bothering him for!—he dying or
something? Anyway all he'd done was ask her was she tempting
him to salvation, looking the way she did, or was the devil tempting him in the other direction by making her so tempting?

"Oh Scrope you *said* that?"

Why not?—normal masculine homage, surely? First duty of
man, *he*'d been brought up believing, was to assure any girl God
had made as delectable as that, that she *was* as delectable as that.
Could even quote himself to that effect: 'Women should be told
regularly, like bells,' to parody Noel Coward. Or didn't homage
from a man his age count as homage. No, but this girl—once she'd
got over whatever sub-Pauline pet it was she was in, she'd look in
her glass wouldn't she? Which might even start a musing doubt
whether God's work *was* what God had in mind when creating
her!

As however none of this had much to do with either of Miss
Hallam's reasons for visiting the man, she at once began a soothing
transition to what were.

Having, besides, found him in *this* sort of mood!

"Oh but Scrope *sweetie*," she cooed, "but when I was so hoping
you'd help me with something?—and here you are all patronizing
and cross!"

'*Patronizing*'!

"Well, to *her*, weren't you? And well you do sometimes like to
sound as if your programs for women were more sensible than our
own, even about making love, as it usually seems to be, though of
course why not, but I have something I hope you'll be a sweetie
and discuss, because I'm stuck in a story I've been thinking about,
about age 'differences.' "

Discuss? Glad to! Whose age differences?

"Well actually anybody's, of different sexes, for instance how do
you see younger women and girls as being?"

. . . As being what?

"As just *being*. Their ambience, sort of. Being the younger *way*
they are. As less maybe how you're used to."

He was amused: dear god, hadn't he, a month ago, told her he
hadn't the ghost of an idea about that generation? Ask his Gael
of a son-in-law, why didn't she. Or Charles—they both taught the
creatures!

"But they wouldn't themselves be at that age difference. And
anyhow this particular story— Oh for instance suppose that girl

minister wasn't a *minister*, and she suddenly adored you and you had an affair, different ages and all, would you feel about her the *way* you would if she were fifteen or twenty years older? Or say twenty-five," she added, in generosity.

What was she doing, interviewing him?

"But Scrope think of the way you write about them, I remember the very phrase the first time I noticed how often you do use it— in this novel your hero's in his pantry getting more ice for a party and this girl's followed him, she's infatuated with him though he doesn't know it yet, and here's how you introduced her, it's lovely—'the door had swung open and swung gently to again, and in had stepped this beautiful child'—*so* skillful, but 'child'? she's in Radcliffe! So is this just technique or *do* you think of them that way?"

. . . well, a certain docileness had to be conveyed, he supposed, yes. Demureness perhaps too? Still, in that sort of relationship, a kind of daughterly deference he'd assume was at work. Of course the corollary was ludicrous—imagine a love affair in which you found yourself muttering, 'Dammit this *can't* be the best thing for the child!' as you clambered into bed!

"But do they feel this older man knows more?—so he's complacent at teaching things as well as at being adored?"

So he snorted—dear god what sort of thing went on in her stories! For all he knew, anyway, girls who fell in love with older men were a special category as much as for instance just working their way through a phase. For dammit look: were they more 'mature'— so that they went for you as being worldlier? Or were they, instead, so much less mature that they went for you as being Daddy! He hoped (might he say?) she wasn't consulting him about some such state of her own! Or was she.

"Oh sweetie when I *love* men? No but *what* ages do you think of as being this girls/young-women category? And *treat* that way, the way the hero in your novel treats what's-her-name, sort of like a valuable pet, I mean he couldn't be more considerate or nicer to her, but doesn't he think she's up to him emotionally or something? Why *doesn't* he make love with her! The woman he's in love with is *just* as silly, only she's forty, oh *do* you see what I'm trying to find out?"

Dammit, he wasn't his characters!

"But you must have some age at which *you* think of us as knowing 'what's good for us' as well as you think *you* do—and consequently stop patronizing us? I mean Scrope men love women but what is the *difference* in how somebody like you sees himself as loving differently at different ages? Or do you just subjectively and arbitrarily decide on sight who's a femme sérieuse for you and who isn't?"

Well, he said, the—

"Am I one?"

He said, smiling at her, had he ever had the misplaced effrontery to try to find out? But 'patronize' implied a value-judgment he never made. Simply he felt women should be thought of as ballerinas; they then responded with every grace. What more they were, *than* that, one discovered as they decided one deserved. Care for an epigram?—she could have that one.

So she looked at him. And seemed to brood.

And finally, "Oh well," she said, and smiled at him. "Anyway I'm *so* glad you're so much better."

At least no worse.

"You're wonderful, to be consulted. And discuss."

Pleasure to!

"Oh but I hope it hasn't tired you?"

He said what nonsense.

She seemed about to go.

But then, "But there is though *one* other thing," she came out with, instead. "Not to consult about, exactly, just it's something you might think of some way to help with if I tell you. Because Scrope partly it's about Sibylla, only it simply isn't something I can think of any way to talk to her about, I mean this is *unbelievable!*"

But good god, he said, in some alarm, she mean something *wrong?*—Sibylla not having a serious spat with Alec or that sort of thing he hoped was she?

She gaped at him, lost.

" 'A spat'!" she marveled. "Oh but Scrope oh *dear* what—"

For God's sake not *leaving* the fellow she didn't mean did she!—even *for* some lout she'd taken a fancy to?

"Oh but *Scrope!*" she wailed, "it's Sibylla thinks *I'm* having an affair! With *Alec!*"

So, parentally or not, the man was taken aback.

"And probably my darling Charles thinks so too!"

He mumbled well God *bless!* As called for.

"But how do you mean?" she begged him. "Because how *can* they think such a thing! Alec and I don't even dream about each other! And the awful part is, what can we merely *do?*—plant ourselves beaming before them saying sweeties we have something wonderful to tell you out of the blue? —we're *un*-having an affair?"

That he certainly saw!

"Especially since one of the reasons we're sure they do think we are is that they've been so unbelievably careful not to give the slightest sign they do!"

He said um.

"And of course your dearest friend's husband *is* your very likeliest lover of anybody, you *see* him so constantly, and his things lying around keep making you think of him undressing. And of in bed with her. And then, well, it happens I—oh dear I wouldn't tell this to anybody but you but I even did have this wild crush on Alec once."

Did, huh; well!

"I adored him for *weeks!* Only Scrope I had I guess *such* a crush I was too terrified of him to think about normally seducing him or anything, can you imagine such a state!"

He said well God bless indeed! But hadn't Sibylla suspected this, uh, this unholy passion at the time?

"Oh no."

Then how'd she happen to now?

"Well *Alec* thinks, from something he thinks she let slip without meaning to— Oh I *can't* tell you!"

So then, for now she seemed not far from helpless tears, for a moment they were silent.

Finally he said well it *was* dreadful for her.

"And I did, once, tell Charles a dream I had about Alec. So, working on Sibylla's libretto together the way they are, Charles could have told her."

So once again there seemed to be little to say.

Though ah, well, he said presently, he supposed one ought to entertain a decent concern for one's offsprings' marriages and the like. Men and women had no pleasure in life like each other; nobody but hysterical crackpots like Saint Paul ever suggested anything else. But had fidelity all that to do with it? Look, if all that our piety-simple writs and prescripts about adultery produced was a divorce rate ten times the civilized average abroad, perhaps we should explore the hypothesis that it was an unsung blessing! *Binas habeatis amicas,* said Ovid—have two loves, and you're a slave to neither. Well, but he himself meant turn Ovid round— with two loves you grow *tired* of neither, and, as things go between men and women, you therefore stay married. And the social structure preserves its stable decencies. So, as a natural bonus—

"Is this your *Vanity Fair* piece?"

He said yes. So as a cultural bonus, the *family* is preserved. What a pity Mrs. Tench-Fenton didn't take the piece—among other nice bits it had an elderly-rake-sounding final paragraph he was particularly pleased with—

"I don't perhaps get the reports from the field I used to," a graying class-mate said to me not long ago, "but by god I see no signs of my kind of woman's becoming an endangered species!"

Ah, well, anyway, he did hope Sibylla wasn't going to be, well, for example upset? Had she back then, when she'd had this ungovernable passion for Alec before?

"Oh no."

Well, it baffled him.

And he wished he could cheer her up; she was a sweet. Would it he wondered amuse her to hear a rejection his agent had just sent him from a French publisher? There'd been a proposal for a translation of his next to last.

On y prend un plaisir réel, à condition de comprendre un argot pratiqué entre l'Hôtel Pierre et Washington Square: du Giraudoux de Manhattan.

Giraudoux?—he *that* much of an archaism abroad too? . . . And what was that 'argot'? *His* dialogue 'argot'? He'd wondered what they'd make of the language his subconscious sometimes came up with!—that very morning, for instance, an opening sentence as cockeyed as it was typical!

My old man was made a living for by a Little Rock call girl named Prairie Anthum, but it was the garbage route put me through Yale.

She edified? Yes. Well. No but then what was book for jealousy in her generation? If for example Sibylla turned out not to be jealous, would that be because she was a liberated young woman and above any such degrading tradition? Dear god, she could just as easily be tired of Alec! . . .

And so on.

Till finally Miss Hallam began to smile, wanly anyway, and he said well at least *somehow* he seemed to have cheered her up! so shortly she kissed him almost fondly, and left.

11

That weekend, and this had been for purposes of research as much as for the hell of it (was there all that plus, sex-wise, in spending the night together too?), Mimi Hallam and Richard Scrope Townshend III were house-sitting the Institute for Advanced Study pied-à-terre of her math instructor, who commuted from Las Vegas. The apartment had disappointed them: in particular, for their specific research, there was no double bed; aside moreover from a bust of Diophantos in travertine the humane amenities were bleakly wanting, the fellow's field being 'assorted sequestrations' in the cyclic-decomposition theorem of modules. They had nevertheless, being responsible children, stayed on. As taught one did.

Also they had made do, trundling the twin beds together and flumping the mattresses side by side across.

So, now, on these, Mimi was sprawling on her elbows, chin in her hands, drowsily listening to her bedfellow (sprawled on his back beside her) explain in exasperated detail how his father *kept* bugging him!—last week snapping if he *had* to have an elementary something for an elective why in God's name not Elementary Russian the way *he* had, what good was this goddam Elementary Mandarin to anybody! and then last night jesus he'd rung him up *again* about going to see his grandfather, poor old guy'd been put back in intensive care and was or *wasn't* he going to see him before he maybe died!—when for god sakes how was he to get away, with two midterms Monday! Anyhow what could you think up to talk about with anybody old?

She murmured, "*Mmm,*" and yawned.

"And then the way my father makes me what he calls clean up my language, visiting Grampa, like for Sunday lunches in summer—it fucking wears me out!"

She said, idly, "So but anyway what happened," almost as if having listened.

"Well, see, he was supposed to be better. Only then there was this girl priest kept visiting him, and my father says Grampa was too polite to tell her to keep the hell out."

Miss Hallam blew a soft *fffffffth* at a white fluff of pillow-feather in the hollow of his shoulder.

"Hey!" he complained.

"Why do you always need dusting!"

"Aw, Mimi," he grumbled.

"So well what *happened* then."

"Well finally he gave up being polite and bellowed at her. So then he had chest pains."

"Goodness," she said lazily, and yawned again.

So he yawned too.

And said, "Yes, well, jesus—people *at* you," and was silent. "Though you can see the poor old guy's point, at that, I guess," he added, generously.

They were silent.

But presently he stretched, as in purest luxury, limb by long young limb, and smiled at her, a question. And as she gazed back at him in what seemed womanly forbearance, why should he not have shifted a near shoulder, and slid a humble hand, palm up, under her sleek belly, in adoration and entreaty?

But she was simply amused.

"No."

"Aw, Mimi."

"Intermission's not over."

"It's *over* over!"

"Then why doesn't it feel like it."

"Feels to *me!*"

"As if you counted!"

"Aw, *Mimi*," he mumbled, as in hopeless love.

"And don't argue!"

So he drew back his hand, in abasement, dashed.

"That's better," she said kindly, and kissed the tip of his nose. "No but about your grandfather, listen you'll never *guess* what the very first tape picked up about his heart attack. Amy told Charles your Aunt Sibylla—"

"She's *not* my aunt!"

"—said she'd figured out what it must have been caused it, oh and this is wild!"

"Well jesus he's just old anyway."

"No *not* just that, no there's for weeks been this girl from Yale, well she's really a professor, she's doing a *book* on your grandfather, you didn't know? anyway she comes down from New Haven every weekend to study him and just moves *in!* Amy says she leaves crumbs all over the kitchen counters. And eggshells in the sink-strainer. And the bedroom smells of she thinks it's *Opium*, anyway it seems she's been sleeping with your grandfather every weekend for *weeks!*—so Sibylla said obviously he, well, *you* know, he overdid."

Her bedfellow was shocked.

"You simple?" he cried. "Look, jesus, old men *can't!*" in tones of scandal.

"Well it obviously doesn't seem they always can't! Anyway what are you so outraged about? Amy said Sibylla said she'd dropped by your grandfather's one Sunday nearly noon and the place was a mess, and this girl (who she said is *very* sexy) looked practically swoony, she was getting their breakfast in a dream, she looked as if they'd—"

"I don't care—old men can't!"

"How do *you* know!"

"Everybody knows!"

"Taaaah, how can they!—anyhow is there a better explanation why he had a heart attack out of the blue? There she's been, weekend after weekend, and she's this sexy Dane. Also your grandfather's *sort* of famous, isn't he?—why shouldn't she decide to collect him! So, making love Fridays Saturdays Sundays *and* the mornings maybe, at his age? Hoh!"

The grandson was decently silent.

She was amused.

"Oh what would you do without me to tell you things?" she teased him. "Oh Richard *think* if I turned you loose."

He shut his eyes. And seemed to turn away, scowling.

"Oh my, are you sulking at me?" she giggled.

He was silent.

"But poor sweetie *listen,*" she told him, humoring him, "I don't think anybody's prettier than you do I? Except of *course* I'll have to turn you loose some time, why won't you see! And suppose my out-of-her-mind sister leaves Charles? Richard I *told* you!"

He opened his eyes, speechless.

"Well don't glare at me, goodness!" she cried.

"But *jesus,* Mimi, your own sister's—"

"But what if the complications are exactly part of what I ought to learn about, how do I know! Including learn how I can be sure I feel how I am—I mean I'd *know,* here, who Charles would be comparing me with. As of course he would—they always tell about their others, so you have a norm. And anyway what *is* it like, at my age, with an experienced man, do you just blissfully lose your head?"

He was silent; he could have been stunned by his doom.

"Well you think about others than me don't you, so what are you glooming like that at me for!" she protested, reasonably. "Like when I first knew you you had an absolute *dog* for that sexy English instructor you have."

He muttered something.

"Well had you or hadn't you? You told me she was what your grandfather calls a 'dish,' it was one of the archaisms I *started* my generation-gap glossary with. Hoh, and you asked me what I thought she did for sex, you *do* have a voyeur-y mind!" she giggled. "And about faculty, *my!*"

He was silent.

"I bet you still think about being in bed with her, too, don't you!" she mocked. "And then you get all upset and stupefying about me and Charles—oh god, *men!*" she denounced him.

He snarled *hell* with Charles!!

"Oh cheer *up!*" she cried. "All I'm saying is if you *want* her why not go *after* her! you can't just spend your *life* letting girls seduce you like your mother's friend!—can't you for once act like a couthie?"

He shut his eyes again. She watched him, yawning.

And presently collapsed lazily prone, head on her arms, gaze on him still, as pondering his case.

But abruptly, "Oh but *listen!*" she yelped, and came up onto her pretty elbows again, laughing happily down at him. "Hey, what if I set her as a project for you!—like remember Mme. de Merteuil did for the Chevalier in *Les Liaisons Dangereuses?* So shall I give you till exams to seduce her? oh or at any rate *get* yourself seduced," she indulged him, "and if you won't give me your word of honor to *seriously* try I'll never sleep with you again? Well don't *glare*, why shouldn't you? I could help with suggestions and instruc—"

But he bellowed, "Mimi-jesus-goddammit-lay-*off!*" and bounded out of their bed and slammed off into the kitchen, where he flung open the refrigerator door with a crash into apparently the counter, and began banging its contents out onto the counter too. "You want a goddam beer?" he yelled.

Mimi rolled over onto her back, and thought. ". . . Not if that white wine's cold," she called, finally.

"Well fucking *okay* then!" he snarled, and rummaged.

But Mimi, lying there, was now lightly pedaling the air with delicious legs, a ghostly bicycling, smiling at their slim beauty as she counted to fifty.

". . . Mme. de Merteuil," she murmured. And started another fifty, giggling, as her scowling charge came hulking in with her wine.

12

Mrs. Tench-Fenton (looking heavenly) had come to visit Scrope so early, the morning he'd been trundled back from intensive care to a monitored room again, that she floated in to perch tenderly on his bed and flutteringly kiss him before the scandalized student nurse had half finished taking his blood-pressure and temperature, in fact the thermometer was still stuck in the helpless man's mouth.

So, for decorum's sake, she soothed the child's shock: "Oh sweetie Mr. Townshend and I have been married off and on for twenty years, goodness!—not of course *all* that often to each other, but I've been taking his vital signs since for any practical purposes he had any, *long* before I expect you were even born (not that vital *signs* are what one goes by with him!), in any case I'm only rushing past with this pot of caviar for the poor man—*will* you, like the lamb you look, just put it in a, oh careful it's heavy, in haven't you a refrigerator on the floor? so there won't be trouble about trays? and tell them he likes to eat it right out of the pot, just *it*, with a dessert-spoon, anyhow he hasn't the slightest fever, has he," she announced in a happy voice, and laid her lips lingeringly against his temple to make sure, "*perfectly* normal, and from his look what's his blood-pressure—his splendid hundred-and-twenty-over-eighty as usual?"

This loving rhetoric however, the nurselet gone, it appeared merely amused him: 'off and on' thank God of course *yes*, but that 'married' of hers?—that 'to each other' disingenuously slipped in as if grammatically connected? . . .

She said smoothly but had he ever seen much point, either, in disillusioning young people before they save you trouble by doing it themselves?—and when anyway she and he might very easily, as he was well aware, have *been* married, it came to the same thing. So how silly. Besides, what made him think he'd ever asked her to marry him all that often!

She didn't call hundreds of times often?

"Oh sweetie what difference whether how often, it always you'll notice seemed to be when I was already married to someone you must perfectly well have known I wasn't at the time *dreaming*, even, of exchanging for you!"

She mean one of those semi-disposable bastards she claimed she adored almost as much?

"Are you insane?" she cried. "I did adore them!—him!"

Which them/him was this—that Siena time?

But "Oh Scrope how can you!" she rebuked him, now in it seemed a voice of tears. "How can you carp and cavil and *upset* me so, just when what have I been able to even think of from the first horrifying instant I heard they'd rushed you here dying, if not night and day worry about you, are you *heartless?* And just *back* from intensive care! and when even Sibylla was hardly allowed to visit you what *could* I do but wonder whether I might actually not ever see you alive again! I was so despairing I finally, oh well doesn't one *need* magics sometimes? I carried all your novels into my bedroom and spread them on my bed, as if somehow they'd—oh Scrope I spent till *dawn* rereading all those haunted places that are really about you and me, in tears over them for you, half the time, you sounded so alive in them and like how I remembered you were when what happens in them happened, that I could almost feel you still *were* alive, till about five o'clock I rang up the hospital, and they were *furious* at me at such an hour but at least they admitted no you hadn't died."

He said, sounding moved too, well she was a sweet.

"Yes but then what I'd *found*," she said in a different tone altogether, "was have you *any* notion how disorienting some of those passages can be for me? for instance that girl in remember the scene upstairs at Fouquet's where the man taking her to dinner is you?—he says was that damn' waiter looking down her dress (remember?) and naturally she laughs (well you sounded so stuffy!) and says, 'Oh pooh, don't you think it's spiritually good for his vanity to catch glimpses of what he can't have? but of course *you* may!' which is *exactly* what I said, I never do know what perfectly private remark I make to you may not turn up in some context I've no control over! yes but then *later* in this novel he takes what you *say* is this same girl to dinner at the Grand Véfour, and she is en grande tenue, she's wearing this apparently heavenly yellow silk evening dress and *long* black kid gloves almost to the shoulder, and when the maître d'hôtel has seated them she looks appraisingly round, table by table, and then serenely settles back, politely smirking, and says, 'How nice, I'm the best-dressed woman in the room, alors bon, qu'est-ce qu'on va manger?' and takes the carte from the hovering waiter pour commander, except sweetie *I* was never at the Grand Véfour with you *ever!*"

He said huh? *wasn't?* nonsense!

"And I hardly ever wear yellow. So you see? there at three in the morning your memory of me was partly heaven-knows-which of your other girls, that flittering little Tory Bingham for all I know, and you don't think *that* was upsetting? And after their delicious dinner of I forget *how* many courses they were going dancing in some Montparnasse cellar you knew about except in the taxi they decided to go back to her apartment and make love instead! can't you *see* what a heartless outrage it is when this man, who *is* you— Well was I to think it was *me* in your arms or whatever girl your lecherous memory had grafted on to me! Or should I just thank Heaven (I suppose you'll say!) you at least aren't the kind of novelist who thinks the way to write love scenes is an exhaustive listing of everything including push-ups he imagines can go on in bed?— oh *dear* what mightn't I turn cold finding this helpless half-me reported as doing!" she ended, laughing.

But good god he knew as well as he did that a character wasn't who this or that enchanting aspect of her came from: the point was always the rightness of the detail *for* the character, not its provenance. Which was irrelevant.

"But it *wasn't* me. So who was it?"

Dammit he said look, in a long and spendthrift life how many expensive girls *mightn't* a man end up having fed at the Grand Véfour? did you keep gentlemanly count? Could've been any girl who felt he should be dressed full-fig for, to dazzle. Tory Bingham included. Except also (he added, reasonably) he could have made the scene up altogether. You often had to, real girls not always meeting specifications.

"Hoh!"

Look, why not sit on the bed instead of that damn' chair she was in?—she have to go *on* acting like the loveliest natural coquette a man had ever crossed himself in awe at finding in his arms?

This invitation was however so clearly irrelevant to any situation not long past and gone that she paid no attention to it beyond a forbearing brief smile, indeed at once she looked almost grave.

"No but Scrope love," she told him in a voice of concern. "I of course above all came to make sure for *myself* you were as much better as they said, but *also* to ask whether— Well by any chance has your lovely Sibylla, or my dear have *you* by any chance thought that just recently, oh dear how shall I put it? but I mean are they d'you think all *right*, Scrope, those married two of ours?"

The father uttered a cry.

"Oh sweetie then something *may* you've noticed be wrong?—or going wrong! Oh *dear*, because all I'd thought (which after all could of *course* have a perfectly innocent explanation) was that

wasn't it a little odd of *her* to be bringing me that article of Charles
Ebury's?—when it wasn't the one *Charles* and I had had such fun
discussing anyway? And then, well, it was this very funny but
Scrope *unkind* job on modern poetry, which is what my poor
stepson her husband writes! And then she rather went on about
how witty the article was. And how wonderful also he was being
about this libretto of hers—which began to sound like a theirs!
in short my dear *all* the happy signs not to say the stigmata! And,
well, goodness, simply *Charles* then! heavens *how* easy to find one
has a béguin for him, five years younger and I might well have
waved myself under his nose myself! Are you listening to me or
aren't you!"

"But what cockeyed scenario's this—*whose* béguin?" he as good
as gobbled at her, as if foundering. "*I* was given to believe, and not
long ago, that *far* from its being what you appear to imagine, my
daughter and your darling Charles, the *actual* trouble is she's got
it in her lovely head Alec's been rolling in the hay with her dearest
Amy good god—and Amy, poor child, came to me frantic!"

This naturally left them staring at each other, blank.

"In particular," he said finally, "she said how does one demonstrate *any* negative, innocence included. A dilemma one shares!"

"But they *are* innocent?"

"I have been seeing life steadily and seeing it whole till I am
black in the face," he said grandly, as if quoting himself, "but how
am *I* to know!"

So she appeared to weigh this.

And presently, "No but sweetie whichever way it *is*," she
pointed out, "it doesn't *preclude* Sibylla's falling in love with
Charles anyway, surely? And she *is* just as easy for a man to have
a béguin for as—"

"Dammit," he cried, wretchedly, "d'you have to tell me!"

"But my absurd old *darling*," she cooed, "you *know* that these
young people—"

"What's that got to do with *my* daughter! I've got nothing
against young people, good god! Except their youth. Nothing
against that either unless they overdo it. But are you suggesting
that I can any day now expect the damn' fellow to come round
dans les formes and ask the hand of my daughter in adultery?"

"Did you ask my fierce black-balling father for mine?"

"But goddammit I *loved* you!"

This so amused her that she came and sat on his bed after all.
"And Charles doesn't adore her?" she teased him.

"Ah but why my sweet Sibylla?" this responsible father snarled. "Why can't the damn' marauder take one of his students to bed with him, what are students for?—instead of *this* kind of disorder!"

"Oh but old darling!" she laughed.

"Something funny goddammit in a parent's wanting a darling daughter in good hands?"

"Wasn't *I*?" she said, and reaching a hand, stroked the inside of his wrist with the tips of remembering fingers.

So, "Ah, well," he conceded, with sentiment, "will my fingertips ever forget a sweet inch of you either? No, but how explain any of us anyway?" he ended, smiling back at her.

"You mean you were always it seemed married to somebody any time I happened not to be?" she said, tenderly.

"That had nothing to do with *us!*"

"Oh had it not!"

"My blessed woman," he besought her, "hasn't it ever occurred to you that one of *the* bonds of long and happy understanding between us mayn't well be that simply we find it natural to be in love with two people at once, provided one of them is the other of *us*? It's what we did!—what's more, if everybody else did too, don't we privately think la condition humaine would be as happy a state as ours has been? Dammit, if I ever decide to rearrange the past with an autobiography, I'll say so! (By the way, I've a splendid title, *Bygones, Begone!*) Ah though, Laura, think!—if we'd married each other would we have stayed as faithful as can't you see we've in fact been, unmarried?"

"I suppose what you're trying to convince me of is would we ever have found anybody as suitable as ourselves to be unfaithful with! And you tout *that* as an example for humanity?—and when you were just now fretting about our children's unhappy behavior? goodness!"

All he'd meant was—

"Which reminds me, Sibylla is in something of a fuss my dear about *you*, I don't know of course whether I'm supposed to tell, but there's this I'm informed rather *sexy* Yale creature you've acquired."

'Acquired'! Good *god!*

"Well everyone is at least *wondering* about the status."

Girl researching him a 'status'? Simply there was this book she was doing! About a couple of poets too. *The Creative Habitat*; not a bad title at all. Or anyway for a university press.

"But sweetie isn't there a certain ambiguity in the—"

At the start by *god* there was!—'d've taken any man in his right mind aback! Hadn't they told her? Because how did he want his sexual aspect stoodied, should she interview his mistress? Or had he groupie-type fans, like poets. Or naturally she could stoody him herself—'I sleep with this other poet while always I stoody him.' So help me, *that* it seemed was how the fellow'd found out he wasn't so gay as he'd led himself to believe ('Ho, so fonny!'). So what methodology did he prefer? For herself, 'A little I like better with girls,' but she was without preconceptions. But mightn't she mix them up—or wasn't she sleeping with the poet now? 'Naw, why. I finish to stoody him.' Dammit she was a study in herself! An *affair* with her?—Sibylla was out of her mind!

". . . So then who did she interview about you?"

There being nobody, *nobody!*

"You hadn't *any* current girl?" she cried, in shock.

So he reached for her, laughing at her: she think he'd have handed her over to the quantifications of sociology if he'd had?

". . . Not even a temporary one?"

No!

"But in prospect, surely?"

No, dammit, nor in prospect!—was he to pry into God's classified intentions? Some years, apparently He was principally interested (as by god why shouldn't He be!) in providing him with an effortless flow of His best syntax and vocabulary. But, other times, He saw to it, instead, that some delicious young woman stunned his mind blank by falling in love with him. Well, he was grateful for both these divine accommodations, how not! but he felt a pious diffidence about conjecturing, in advance, which accommodation he was about to be grateful for.

So, with one topic and another, Mrs. Tench-Fenton so overstayed the permitted visit that she was rebuked with a severe and bureaucratic "But Mrs. *Townshend!*" by the nurse who here came in to end it.

13

Amy Hallam rang up Alec Urquhart, about this time, to fret oh what was she to do?—was her subconscious *obsessed?* All it was letting her think of, as plots, were idiotic real-life adulteries she knew about, and she was frantic!

"—like my by-marriage aunt who dumped my perfectly good

uncle and went off to Antibes with a publisher? He was rich and easily dazed, so she married him and began to write books about genteel French eating, chefs it seems adored her, recipes and all. But then everybody's eating went genteel, so she wrote about being adored by the petit personnel generally, as well as chefs — *you* know, adored like Hemingway? And *told* the way Hemingway told how the Spanish petit personnel adored him, with subordinate clauses explaining how fine and true. And how the Italian adoranti adored him when he was in Italy. Though the Swiss, it seems, not. Of course Charles says, 'Do we have to justify some imputation of Jamesian seriousness to be thought a serious writer? — if the air of unreality fits, put it on.' But in real life she's married five times — does that mean she's very sexy or just not very sexy?"

Urquhart it seemed found no real reason to comment.

"Then did I ever tell you about a Texas classmate who's been sleeping weekends, in Walla, with a lout who heaves groggily out of bed before dawn Mondays and drives two hundred miles home to Crabtree, in Arkansas, where he lives with his regular girl? Well this is, I suppose, sort of extreme Texas behavior, but they do have universities and psychiatrists in case, anyway his name's Lance but she calls him Dick from having said 'For Richard for poorer' once about his ex-wife's alimony, and she's been having this affair for a *year*. But then one Sunday a little while ago he just got into his car and took off after breakfast — like that! Well, she thought what of it, c'est plus moi qui courrai après, like Zazie's mother; but then as the day went on she began to get into a rage, by evening she was pacing round *hitting* things with a quirt he'd given her, and finally about two in the morning she just blew *up!* and leaped into her car and roared off the whole preposterous two hundred miles through the night to his house in Crabtree (by then it was dawn) and began beating his flimsy door in with a tire-iron, shouting everything she thought of him and the slut he was in bed with at the top of her voice, oh *Alec* how sad! So he had to come down and let her in (his girl jumped out a window at the back and fled screeching), and she charged in and the first thing she saw was a beautiful little Sheraton chair she'd given him, so she beat it to flinders with the tire-iron, he hovering round bleating for Christ's sake what *was* this? till she charged through into the kitchen and flung open the cupboard doors and systematically *one by one* smashed every plate dish cup saucer bowl mug and glass into pieces on the floor! Then, as a sort of final *there!* she hurled the tire-iron through the glass of the door onto the patio and marched back into the living-room, where Lance was now sitting helpless on the sofa, and said, 'May I use your phone?' and rang up her analyst back in Mt. Pleasant and talked for the better part of an hour, while Lance made breakfast. Oh Alec *so* sad somehow, and now Charles doesn't want me to visit her!"

This scenario Urquhart appeared to have no comment to make on either.

"Charles says on a *rational* plane it's of course easy to be cynical about women, but think how much easier it is for women to be cynical about men. Except what is the matter with the sweetie? Or is it just Sun Belt tastes in men. Are you listening to me, Alec? you're so quiet!"

He remained so.

"Oh but I *mustn't* keep you! Oh you are so sweet to listen to me going on and on wondering *why* it is whatever it is has so totally— And when it's *both* our woe! And nothing to be done anyway! Oh *sweet* Alec if only we could go to bed and *console* each other for their unfounded suspicions! D'you know, I'm in such a state I lie awake wondering has God perhaps done this to me for writing *nice* stories about unfaithful girls?—and with my darling Charles quietly sleeping right there beside me!"

So, shortly, she rang off.

14

Sibylla having said perhaps Charles *not* (for whatever reason) Les Piérides, it turned out it was the packed and stylish uproar of Five-Four-Three's noontide bar he eventually waited a good half-hour for her to arrive angelically on time in, eyes smiling into his as placatingly as if she were late.

So he kissed her cheek there in greeting but at once took her out of that jeweled din, in to their table, up to which the sommelier immediately trundled a wine-cooler and set to work on the cork, leering courteously.

At which evidence of foresight and sensibility, "But champagne?" she cried, as in bliss. "Oh but Charles how agreeable and fond!"

Had to lure her somehow, he said, and smiled, from this habit she'd got into of feeding her father lunch, how was the poor man today?

"And all iced and ready! Well, oh, but Pa? oh dear he's I'm

afraid so much better he's in a fume at not being let go home—
so difficult. Then it seems when my sweet mother-in-law comes to
see him she upsets the nurses! You by the way," she added, in no
particular tone, "he says she sounds like getting one of her lovely
béguins for!"

He said what nonsense, eye on the sommelier's ballet—simply
she was trying to coax fifteen hundred words on Ovid's *Amores* out
of him. But they weren't letting Scrope go home *yet* surely, were
they?

"Well Charles 'coaxing' is hardly the word that Daddy— No but
what about your Mr. Molehill piece I took her specially?"

Turned down, he said amiably.

"Oh but Charles why!"

Her readers didn't apparently read. Or so she said.

"You went to *see* her?"

Here however the sommelier, beaming, poured their champagne. So this ritual they had to watch, silent.

But then, "To your Pa first anyway?" Charles said, and she said
soberly, "To Pa," and they sipped.

"How's he putting up with lunch though without you?" he
asked. "Nurses dish him up some sad dietician's gruel?"

"But I took him a salade niçoise, what d'you think!"

So they sipped again, smiling.

"I was thinking about him, waiting," he said then. "Or anyway
about that *Town & Country* piece of his last year about a man and
a girl meet by chance one day in town. Same Connecticut suburb
set; same parties; always *look* for each other at parties. But always
of course at parties other people there, and *this* day, into this restaurant he's having lunch alone in, she happens to come, by herself too."

Here however the maggiordomo interrupted with polished
hoodlum mondanità, to demand their every wish. So, with the
usual irrelevances (what was this 'cotriade'?) they composed their
courses.

And as the fellow took himself at last off, here came the
sommelier again, bowing, to pour.

And then to submit the wine card, for the signore's amiable
decisions.

So then in due course:

—in she comes, alone too, and naturally he stands up and waves,
and she threads her way laughing through the crowded tables and
joins him. And after the smiling banalities of coincidence and

amusement, and a sherry's been fetched her, and she's ordered, all at once it strikes the man—her it had struck the moment she saw him—that this must be the first time in all the vanished months they had known each other that the two of them had been—that extraordinary word—*alone*. He blurts it out—

"Oh dear."

"—well, yes, without thinking, but he does, and in the wordless moment of pause that follows (as your father put it) they gaze at each other, and the knowledge of what has happened is so shared, so tangible, it is like a third presence there between them."

". . . Oh Charles," she said.

"Well my lovely thing it *happens!*"

But she only gazed at him, as if helpless, silent.

"And what your father said," he finished, "is, suddenly they're free to say things to each other that are so new they can't even predict what they may turn out to be."

This she of course instantly deplored.

"No but Charles," she cried, "but that's only the way he—I mean oh *poor* Pa don't you think? because such an incorrigible romantic! Oh dear what am I to— Are you like him? Or do I mean goodness-are-you-like-him!" she more or less implored him, trying it seemed to laugh.

All *that* bad?

"Well but think how difficult for his girls—if only what they've had to live up to, heavens! Charles I'm in *awe* at Laura, handling it—and through three or four of their affairs, oh Charles the mere *times* before, the crescendo of it, how possibly could any woman— What are you looking at me like that for?" she faltered, in a voice suddenly near tears.

—Ah how do you coax them out of these equivocations, these immemorial temporizings?—and the sheer skill they do it with! He was bemused.

In fact reduced to mere sound—a baffled "Sibylla, *Sibylla* . . ." though whether reproach or caress had he any idea either? "My sad angel what *is* this!"

She gazed at him as in some wordless misery, gulping.

"*They*'re what we came here to talk about?—Laura and your father? . . ."

". . . I know."

"When all this time it's what's happened to *us?*—in God's name are we going to go *on* not saying it?"

"Oh Charles," she mumbled, as if despairing.

"What else on earth have I been able to think of, all these heart-shaken irrecoverable days you've known it too," he accused her tenderly, and slid a hand, palm up in simple entreaty, across the table to where, by her glass, lay hers,

Which however she had instantly to withdraw to her lap, for that sommelier once more loomed beside them, as in triumph presenting for approval the Montrachet the signore had had the spendthrift good taste to command; and now he slid it deftly into the wine-cooler beside the Moët, draped a spotless serviette across from rim to rim, and, bowing efficiently, whisked himself away.

These displays did however give them time to recover enough from what they had said to be able to deal with it.

At least provisionally.

The proviso being, for the moment, that what had happened had not so to speak all that *much* happened.

At any rate she now said, "Oh Charles . . . ," only a little breathless-sounding. "But then I have to find out about you, oh sweet," she put it off, in happy misgiving.

"Find *out* I adore you?" he cried, as if stunned at her.

"Oh but can't you see?—do I even know what questions to ask! Or anyway I suppose I mean questions you could reply to the way I want you to," she murmured, abashed. "Well, and because nothing like this has ever—oh Charles never like *this,* so am I supposed to *ask* are you what Daddy calls a marauder? Because are you? Only then suppose I mightn't find you so attractive if you a little weren't! And your feeling like this about me—well, so *touching* of you, Charles, as well as all the other lovely things it is, can't you see?"

So, like a man of sensibility (marauding or not), at least one preliminary query he at once answered, and as if in reproach at her thinking she need ask it: "But my *blessing* it isn't as if we were going to jump ship!—either of us."

She said, faintly, ". . . oh."

"But what's this 'oh'?" he teased.

"Well I *said* I had to find out!" she justified it, dolefully. "And now oh *sweet* Charles see what it is we're even this much doing!—meeting about it! and you won't tell Amy we did and I won't tell Alec—oh *already* who we trust is just each other? Oh I don't *want* any!" she fretted at the waiter, who was just spreading a crimson skiving of prosciutto over the cool greens of her melon. "Oh well then *yes* I suppose I do, yes leave it, *leave* it!" she countermanded, as in sheer distraction. "Oh Charles why didn't I order moules, like yours!" she mourned.

He of course said but God bless, take his!—melon'd suit him *just* as—

But she cried, "No but *how* am I to tell you how I'll simply *feel*, if! I mean about myself, feel—I *know* how I'll feel about my darling Alec, I've as good as felt it about him for days haven't I? and how I'll feel about Amy—and feel I suppose won't I on your account as well as my own, oh *how* do these things happen!"

He said, lightly, " 'Happen'?" watching the waiter ladle his mussels from tureen to dish (the fidelity of the raven having no explanation either).

"Well does one get used to it, the feeling? . . . Or isn't it a question to ask? Only oh dear I'm *not* prying, but have you ever loved Amy and somebody else too like this—if you do me really? Or has the other one been just one of your students. And so sort of didn't count? Oh I *shouldn't* ask oh Charles forgive me? all these *low* shameful questions—and so jealous-sounding, when I'm not!"

"But my lovely Sibylla," he implored her, as if mildly scandalized at all this. "*Angel* will you stop!—making me miserable too! What *is* this fuss!—it isn't as if we suddenly love Amy and Alec in the least the less!"

"So you mean we *would* have to be utterly hole-and-corner wouldn't we, oh it sounds so dreadful, said like that! And how can we, Charles—I love Alec, I *do!* so why don't I seem to have the proper scruples I thought I did? All I seem to want to do this instant is *touch* you!" she cried, as in sad exultation. "Do you realize? we never have!"

"You've thought of that too!" he said, as if amazed.

"Oh darling yes!"

"Always some damn' Æschylus present!"

"So *that's* why you went on about Daddy's first-time-alone man and girl! Hoh, and looked so dark and brooding when I came in!— you were thinking up all your low persuasions?"

"Oh god," he said, "I was sitting there thinking of all those wasted months we'd known each other and said nothing—*nothing!*—how many hundreds of times I'd come into a room and you were there, and in my innocence all I'd thought was what a part of the pleasure I have in being alive you were—the instant lilt of delight through my senses no more defined than that! Can you imagine? So there in that shouting bar I sat, astounded at myself. Then in you came, so lovely I was dazed all over again, and I thought—"

"Ah but sweet," she interrupted— But here once more the

sommelier appeared beside them. Where, with ritual gestures, he uncorked and poured the signore's Montrachet.

"Champagne *and* burgundy, goodness how lovely!" Sibylla murmured, watching. "Except Charles how disingenuous and disarming, you *are* planning to seduce me!"

This however being a charge one can neither honorably deny nor concede the truth of (or that calls for answering when moot), he merely snorted.

"Or just shouldn't I put it that *way?*" she teased, as a bus-boy began taking their empty plates. "And anyhow isn't 'alone' what one anonymously is, in restaurants?—ah mais comme c'est *bon* que de pouvoir dire n'importe quoi sans se méfier qu'on n'écoute!" she added, as if French were a foreign language, for their waiter had arrived, chafing-dish and all, and was setting about the serving of their lobster, with its Marguéry counterpoint of contrasted sauces, port and cream.

But what if they do listen!—"Ah, sweet," she said, "how long have you known . . ."

" 'Known'!—when good god I've hardly even let myself believe it was happening?"

"Oh but *how* didn't you! Oh but I suppose how does anyone start, simply I just began thinking about you, was all. After do you remember our next-to-last Æschylus session?—Charles right in the middle of it, how *didn't* you notice! suddenly I just overwhelmingly wanted to touch you. . . . And of course I was so shocked I— because what *was* this!—I looked up at you and, well, I saw it was the lovely way you were looking at me that I must be responding to. But then the shock was, the *way* I had responded!"

"So that was it," he said. "My heart stopped."

"And then Charles the other day. When I phoned you. Because oh dear you knew as well as I did what we were as good as saying."

But here, as the waiter began serving them (*"Très* chaud, madame!"), the maggiordomo loomed up across from the fellow, in liturgical supervision. So they watched.

But finally ("Now may I in God's name have this lady to myself?") they could eat.

And did.

So, in due course, "Ah Charles *so* delicious," she told him. "Will you always adore me with food like this?"

Appeal to her idealism mere matter of principle!

But this she was it seemed too murmurous with Montrachet to answer. Even lost in dream, for instead, "Oh blessing," she breathed, eyes in his, "where would you take me, to make love? Take me I mean 'if' oh sweet. Pa used to say girls seemed always to want to be taken to Venice. But why?—just the Byron in him?" she giggled. "Oh but then Laura always wanted Siena didn't she! d'you suppose it was because Siena was where they began, way back then, and she wasn't even my age? and so Siena was a sweet nostalgia for her? Oh darling where would you take me, to remember?—if I mean we did stop being an if?"

So as who could say which way she was deciding, he said, why, in an ideal irresponsible world, he'd take her to Rome.

"Is that where you took Amy?"

He said, amused, "But Amy wasn't somebody else's wife."

"Oh Charles what a *heartless* thing to say!—and anyway didn't you take her anywhere? Oh how unfair! And when you'd taken her away from that perfectly sweet young—who *have* you gone to Rome with?"

Never with anybody. Look, just he *liked* Rome, was all. And its unlayable Classical ghosts—Ovid's Propertius's, all their sweetly strolling girls' in their summer dresses, tot *milia* formosarum!

But "Oh then but you and I Charles?" she lamented. "Rome or anywhere?—oh how *wouldn't* it be noticed we were both missing at the same time. . . ."

Fatal, yes, he conceded. And saddening.

"Then what *do* lovers do about their wives and husbands—serious lovers! Can it always be as heartbreaking and impossible as this? Or oh dear am I sounding as delinquent already as my darling awful Pa!" she mumbled, in a happy voice. "And Charles even if I were going to be! Oh my love have you thought even where, if?— because *not* some horrid hotel, like your students!"

Ah, well, he said, logistics logistics—anyway other people's rendezvous who knew! No, but for him, he said, and now he reached across their table for the tips of her cool fingers, which he coaxed with his own—but for him, would she forgive him? as a man who —and hadn't she just now said who did they already trust beyond each other!—would she, like the angel she was, forgive his having treated the mere desperate hope she might love him as a working hypothesis for if she did? Because the university ran an exchange, for senior faculty, and if you wanted to sublet your apartment during a sabbatical to a responsible colleague or visiting professor, you put it in their hands.

So, foresight being foresight even if only hope, a month ago he'd begun asking whether— "But *angel* what's wrong!" he cried out (startling that sommelier, who again was about to pour)—for she was staring at him as if in terror, eyes enormous.

"But my darling woman," he protested, "even with the end of term near we've a choice—including a small pied-à-terre in *walking* distance in East 11th!"

". . . Oh Charles."

"Man in semantics's. His live-in poppet's decided to go to Helsinki with him after all. Who *says* fidelity isn't what holds the social fabric together! *Now* what's the matter?" he demanded, amused. "Have I like a low swine taken away your last excuse?"

". . . But suppose I found out I love you more than I love Alec— and then how would you feel either!" she mourned, seeming to despair. "Or do you think I wouldn't even be wondering whether I'd love you more if I weren't terrified I already do? Oh Charles this is unfair I *know*, dithering like a—"

Here however that maggiordomo was again upon them, twin bus-boys trundling the splendors of their laden chariots in his train, for which of his frutte and frivolezze and facezie would it please the signora/signore to expensively desire?

They stared at him, blank, stunned—for what was this, in what world?

But at last, ". . . Oh do we want desserts, oh Charles what are you having? oh give me I suppose a millefeuille thing then," Sibylla told the fellow, distracted, watching the bus-boy spring to life. "What *are* you having," she said mindlessly, for he had already pointed at a glistening tart, greengage it appeared. "—unfair I know, oh my poor sweet are you seething? But it's only that it's been so long I just *admired* you terribly, why didn't I ever think of 'unfaithful' as being such a solemn word!"

"But God in heaven what's my adoration then!" he teased. "Am I a man who loves you or just a mist before your eyes?"

". . . But Charles *is* this how one lives? It's I know how Daddy has, and perhaps you too? because I *haven't* asked—but is my generation like for instance Laura's, goodness! And how can a lover ever have been as simple as they can make it sound! So why do you think I can't decide!"

So again he was amused.

"Ah, dammit, Sibylla," he cajoled, "which side of this dizzy debate with yourself are you planning to end up losing!"

"And you're not even thinking practically about the risks of your wicked garçonnière!—and when not only would this colleague of yours know, but his girl!"

"Dear god," he said, "the poor bastard's a—"

"And have you even thought about my side of us?—do I know whether you seriously adore me at all!" she teased, and now she too was amused. "I'll bet if I asked you whether you love me more than you love Amy you'd say, 'How do *I* know, I've never been in bed with you,' wouldn't you!" she accused him, laughing. "Goodness why do I even consider you for a lover, all you want's an *answer!*"

So this went on.

Through their coffees and brandies, on. On into the long, murmuring, tenderly wrangling afternoon.

Undecided. Her father would have been scandalized.

—But at the end, as he handed her out of their taxi at her doorstep, ". . . But don't you Charles at least *think* I'm trying?" she conceded; and though she only let him kiss her angel cheek, for a moment she made it seem she was in his arms.

15

A day or so after this, Sibylla was allowed to fetch her father watchfully home.

As however he had to be accounted an invalid for a time still, Mrs. Tench-Fenton had said why shouldn't she send her excellent cook over, and one of her maids, to help make do—"because sweetie you know how he can be! so then this way you won't have to lift a finger, just be *there* with him, and of course go out any time too."

Also, for the first night or two (which who knew whether critical), as *she* had after all her handsome husband to see to, she herself would move in—night nurses or not, one never knew, he having been so frighteningly near death so *few* days before. There should be family! Or as good as.

(He remarked vive l'autant-que!)

But then where, he said wouldn't the question be, once he was well enough to recuperate—where would she consent to his talking her into going with him *to* recuperate? and this they were agreeably arguing about in his pantry, dressing-gowned for early bed this third night home, as they finished off the second bottle of their before-dinner Bollinger, with a white peach or so each from a bowl on the serving-table.

She was saying didn't he realize her editors' vacations were scheduled a *year* in advance? and at the moment the only editor she would think of deputizing even for his impossible two weeks, and exchange times with, was Tammie, and Tammie was expecting her stupid baby within the next ten days *besides* having these ghastly dismantling scenes divorcing its father (who said he wasn't). Anyway, anyone in Scrope's still perilous condition, when wasn't he practically tottering actually? how could he consider any such doctorless risk as the back-country isolation-from-everywhere of the Côtes-du-Nord out of season! the nearest even-for-France-modern hospital to Port-Blanc seventy kilometers of dreadful chest pains along that wild coast road to St. Brieuc not even in an ambulance, or for all he knew nothing but somebody's desperate passing Deux Chevaux! And for mere nostalgia?—was he *mad?*

He said but when it was *lovely* nostalgia?—and reached for her, coaxing.

And as they were in any case leaning amiably side by side against the pantry counter, she indulged him.

Anyway for the moment.

So then now at least, his arm lying lightly (transitionally, even) round her shoulders, they could argue in comfort.

So he said, tenderly, did she love him dammit or didn't she. Was he reduced to *reminding* her how once she had, and *at* Port-Blanc? Why else did she think he wanted the two of them to return, even if not specifically to that weathered grey gentilhommière they'd rented then, on its low headland up from the sea, the scrolls and arabesques of lichen green-gold and black on the worn stone of its façade, and over the portico stone beasts and flowers carved, and stone crockets and even finials along the cornices— and the green ferny fronds of the bracken sloping up and away landward, so tall she'd teased him why not make love in them!

"Yes and you fussed about vipers! *Were* there vipers?"

He said god *yes!*—and the terrasse the salon's French windows opened out onto had a rose-granite balustrade, with vased turnings, and balustraded flights of stairs curved down through the thickets of bougainvillea and laurel and white bursts of hortensia everywhere to the blue circle of the sea beyond, and she remember the little oriel balcony the bedroom gave on? rose-granite too, and that first morning she'd woken early, not being alone—so early the first pale cool dawn quiet lay over everything still, and she had stepped out and leaned on the balcony railing and watched the sky turn slowly as deep a blue as the sea, until finally she had come back in and kissed him awake, and said high over the flowering headlands there was a kestrel soaring.

". . . so sweet," she murmured, head against his cheek. "And my dear that *freedom* of being alone."

Even the storms, he agreed, were a privacy: that savage tempête, that second week, she'd curled up by his knees before the fire, hail shattering down the panes, and written her letters.

"As I should've days before, goodness!"

". . . Which damn' béguin was it, Dominic?"

"Bart."

"Bastard off organizing that land-swindle in Damascus!"

"Beirut, sweetie, and he made a *great* deal of money with it. And it wasn't a swindle, I've still enough of his mètres carrés in Bliss Street for a bayt. No but my silly sweet, Port-Blanc?—it was back *then*, our Port-Blanc, you were a mere—"

"Ah Laura *look* dammit!" he complained, and shifted her round to where he could see her properly. "Where could my health, if that's the argument, be in better hands? Brittany's our Bona Dea country, not that moralizing old metic Jehovah's! The Curia hasn't even jurisdiction in Basse Bretagne: Saint Thégonnec and Saint Efflam and Saint Guénolé and Saint Caradec and Saint Tugdual are by god *working* saints there, what's Rome know! *Or* Canterbury."

For that matter (he said happily, for she had drifted closer, in amusement)—for that matter Who did she think had cajoled her into saying that heart-stopping Yes on that cockeyed balcony at Cacciapuoti's at the start of it all?

Or even, Who was it this *moment* having her nuzzle his collar-bone so rememberingly?

So she drew somewhat away, smiling.

Though naturally what a relief (she said) if nothing else, to see him like himself again, even if so tiresomely like. Because how could even a man as lifelong spoiled as he was think reciting these lists of tender memories was all he had to do!—who was it used to quote that marquise of Musset's at her? 'quelques phrases bien faites, un tour de valse et un bouquet, c'est pourtant ça qu'on appelle la cour?' gently taking one of his hands away to put his glass in again. Because *also* things she remembered were the street fair by the cathedral in Tréguier that day, and that enchant-ing little fillette— She couldn't have been more than six, *beauti-fully* dressed (as was her young maman), little white gloves and all, and she'd been gazing so longingly at the booth where they were selling balloons that her mother said *alors bon*, what color had she decided on, "and oh Scrope *remember* how disdainfully she dismissed her plebeian yearnings?—'Mais j'aurais l'air de quoi, dans la rue, avec un ballon!' "

. . . 'd reminded him of Sibylla, little.

"Well sweetie what she reminded *me* of was *me!*" she told him, and simply in it seemed amusement, kissed him.

So he gratefully set his glass back on the counter and would have gathered her in again if "Oh but my old darling," she hadn't murmured, and gently stopped him, "after nearly dying before my *eyes* before I even knew, you expect to go *on* the same as ever? and when even your blessing of a Sibylla has time and *again* said to me, 'The trouble with dearest Pa is, all the women he knows are female.' "

"Look, blast it," he said, reasonably, "whose fault's that?—if a man has the sense to *like* women don't they behave the way he likes?—couldn't be simpler!"

"No my dear what I *meant* was," she said, as if this were so, and smoothing the lapel of his dressing gown, which was not rumpled, "shouldn't we I thought try to deal with the *real* reality of what we've been to each other? Or do I mean 'are.' "

So he snorted. As if she hadn't said this, or something as out-of-character like it, every *other* time it had turned out they ended up concluding they couldn't resist each other that one more time either!

"Yes but sweetie *now* you've just had this dreadful monstrum of a— Oh why have you been such an unteachable marauder!" she grieved. "*Always* a marauder!"

He the marauder of them? he cried, amused—"you lovely flitting apparition are you pretending you don't remember the nonsense that it happens *led* to Port-Blanc? There on my doorstep at two in the morning—"

"It was *not* two in the morning! it wasn't even—"

"—blaming *me* for Bill Basset's stifling-past-endurance mind!"

"Well why had you wickedly *let* me marry him!"

"Good god, woman, was I to *stop* you?—for all I know you *need* one of these damn' bel homme types now and then to remind you how disappointing they are."

"Are you self-satisfied past *reclaiming?*" she cried at him, in a fume. "Or simply don't you *hear* how fatuous and smug about other men's lovemaking you let yourself sound! If *that* was the tone of that outrageous piece thank Heaven at least somebody at

Vanity Fair had the editorial sense, *and* enough concern for your reputation, to reject it! Have you forgot the cloudburst of abuse your arrogant *Esquire* piece brought down on you five years ago?—over what you called 'the scandal a rosy mouth so often astounded and saddened you with,' oh *really* Scrope what a phrase!"

He said ah but dammit—

"Because husbands, you said, were of course no competition, or all those nightlong darlings would never have been there in your arms, telling you!—but were none of their incompetent lovers competition *either?* . . . 'Girl after girl,' you boasted, 'the soft reproaches were stored up in your memory'—your *detestable* memory!—so what could a reasonable man conclude, amazed or not, you said, but that hardly one lover in fifty was an improvement on even husbands, *oh* what simpering self-complacency!" she finished, in a passion.

So for a courteous moment he considered this, as called for.

Though, then, well, yes, if she liked, how it could look, yes he supposed (he agreed, peaceably); but the *fact* perhaps still being he was a modest man? The immemorial trope was, all a woman existed for was to fall in love, and the shocking thing was so many still believed it. But take a calm, a Classical, view for once: what amazed him, didn't she see? was an adorable woman telling him she loved *him*—out of millions, *him?*—and this dammit was not just bred-in modesty but the observed fact that clearly it never crossed the minds of a shattering percentage of the women who bothered to look at him that he was anything to look at twice!

"Well you *are* hardly sweetie a bel homme are you!" she denounced him.

He said but he—

"And don't tell me I *know* you haven't had to be!"

All he'd meant—

"Will you stop *explaining!!* Must you go *on* about your indefensible misdoings like that great stupid prig of a Tolstoi making his fiancé read his diaries?—and spoil every *sweet* memory I have of you mingled in!"

So what was there but be silent.

She had even stopped looking at him.

For she stood there silent now too, gazing down it seemed at the fluted glass her hands clasped as in grave ritual before her, eyelids so veiled he could not see her eyes; she might have been an Attic *kora with kylix*, from the frieze of some ruined temple, of Artemis, or Roman Bona Dea, the long folds of her peplum motionless in time; a khoëphora, perhaps, though the tiny garlands of bubbles the champagne loosed endlessly upward from nowhere a libation to Whom?

And as it seemed things stood, what was he to say?—for was this a mere Laura dudgeon she was in, or was she done with him once for all *and* for ever, as on this or that occasion before.

At last, though (for in fact what else?), warily he stretched out his hands and took her waist in his fingers.

And as she did not move, ". . . all this head-tossing," he murmured, coaxing.

So at least she looked at him again, silent.

". . . Giraudoux de Manhattan not Tolstoi anyway," he said, and smiled.

"As if it isn't bad enough being in love with you!" she cried, "without having you carelessly tear my heart in two by nearly dying!"

But as at least the tone of this nonsense was relevant, he at once turned sober again.

And said, as if earnestly, but good god hadn't they from the first survived things infinitely more upsetting and disrupting than a mere cardiac fright? For two dispossessed years, after the summer they'd met ended, hadn't the whole damn' continent and sometimes the ocean too lain between them? *and* she'd acquired was it Bart? yet the instant—

"It was Dominic!"

Yet from the *instant* they'd once more been within—

"And you know yourself there never *was* a more entirely presentable bel homme—besides, so touching, Scrope, his starting that West Coast edition for me, was I to be mannerless and intractable? heavens! And at least Coasties by and *large*— Well it's *Texans* think they're normal, Coasties know better. So one simply revises a few assumptions, and you know as well as I do, that *first* summer of ours—ah, sweet, who had I ever had or imagined like you yes I *know*, but it wasn't the way it—the way we've—well I was only *light*-mindedly out of my mind over you, was all!"

Well Heaven of course defend him from controversy, he said amiably (and lifting one of her hands gently from her glass he kissed the cool inside of her wrist), but wasn't the way thank God they'd since come to feel about each other foreshadowed, by the time he'd sadly put her on the plane that final day?—like the scribbled note he found she'd tucked into the pocket of his next morning's shirt in the drawer, "Un doux baiser, mon amour, et un bon retour de nos nuits," and taking her glass from her other hand to set out of the way (and this she at least allowed) he gathered her in.

But she laid her fingers against his breast, between, if only as reminder.

And said, "But oh sweetie but Port-*Blanc?*" as in womanly or even in true concern for such folly, "when isn't what you in fact ought to have is somewhere they will look *after* you properly, re-cuperating? instead of just some curtseying gardienne to get you breakfast! Because if you sentimentally insist on Brittany I know this country-de-luxe place with 'de ravissantes dépendances' not fifteen minutes from remember Pont-Aven? that that French-man who was doing me our Étapes series took me to lunch at— well and to engagingly seduce me at he of course hoped too, *so* French to still think one goes to bed with a man because he was brought up thinking one's panting to—I thought in *1984* sweetie you're so hermetically French it has to be explained to you?— because *such* a pity when he really was very attractive—and did behave I admit very well, not only not sulking but hardly even downcast, in fact the only inconvenance qu'il s'est permise was a slight surprise that I could keep my fingers off him, I thought oh *dear* what does that say about French women! because can you imagine making love in that ambience? not only was the lunch very good indeed (and he ordered admirably) but I looked at the rooms of the auberge side of the place and they were *expensively* cosseting. Also, for the way you are about oysters, Belon is literally just round the corner! It's near this no more than village, Moëlan, but it's definitely *not* one of those summer fruits-de-mer establish-ments, *this* one's gorgeous fruits-de-mer salver had for instance oursins, and *no* dismal winkles, oh Sibylla would love it!" she finished, as if helpfully.

Which was as likely to be coquetry as disingenuousness.

So naturally this amused him: what under the sun had Sibylla to do with it!

". . . But sweetie weren't you I thought just a *tiny* bit worried about her?"

So he took her hands again, and mockingly rested a wrist on each of his shoulders. Which, this time, seeming to decide, she cautiously allowed.

"About Sibylla?" he protested. "My devious blessing do you want me to believe you think the way to keep my sweet daughter out of that damn' young professor's bed is to take her off from her husband's too?—and to a place with nothing for her to do in but listen to her dear father by day and merely *think* about making love half the night?—you, of all people? Look, whose rosy mouth d'you think it was that sweetly— Are you going to put your arms round my neck properly or are you practicing being a lovely statue of yourself?"

". . . I don't think this is good for you, is all."

"What in God's name's good-for-me got to do with it!"

"And not for your heart *either*, Scrope, the time it's become— and when you *know* the doctor said bed early! Oh are you going to be silly and overdo and harrow everybody who loves you all *over* again arguing about trifles?"

" '*Trifles*'!"

"But Scrope—"

"Not knowing whether you'll come or not, a *trifle?*"

". . . But suppose I lost my head over you *again!*" she put him off, in a voice it seemed near tears.

"Then come *with* me goddammit!" he implored her (for what's logic?), and slid his fingers lovingly up her slim back, in caress at last.

"But ah why don't you think of *me?*" she murmured, lost.

"When I good god *adore* you?" he laughed, and tilting her head in his fingers he kissed her, for some time.

Till she took her mouth away, sighing, ". . . so irrespon- sible . . . ," smiling into his eyes.

As (after all!) often before.

So, "Alors—à Moëlan?" he asked her, finally.

And at least, ". . . oh darling I'll *see*," she seemed to promise.

But then she reached carefully for her glass again. And shortly after this, early bed it was.

16

That afternoon, it happens, Mimi Hallam and Richard Scrope Townshend III had been celebrating, abed, their first three months of each other abed—this time, again, in 21 Blair, a suite now in fact part of their sense of the pleasures of a stable tradition, Richard having meantime discovered that his Great-Uncle Tom (Class of '31) had in his day not only roomed there but been caught with an improper girl there by the proctors, and resound- ingly expelled.

Mimi had, besides, as an act of amnesty for the occasion, forgiven Richard's blundering into that English instructor of his's husband ("At least you found out what she does for sex!") and had added sentiment by wearing his shirt, unbuttoned, to make love in.

Academically however it had been necessary to bring her notebook ("Mais pour les relâches entre nos ébats, stupid, what d'you think!"), her term-paper being due in only four days more as it was.

So, now, kneeling up beside her dulled boy in their twice-tumbled bed, she was reviewing, for possible revisions of the final draft, her notes for Part II: Parameters.

"—so I don't care, I'm going to *say* there's no statable norm for a spectrum of presbephebic ambience imbalances, weighted for phyletic and era factors or not! Anyway even if your grandfather does seem to set a novel in 1959, *that* could be no more than what Professor Staling calls a 'preening factor.' So when you can't synthesize you *list*, so taaaah. Oh *anyway* the state Staling's in about me, I'll get an A, so what. Oh but listen, *here*'s this quote from your grandfather I told you I was thinking I'd epigraph the whole section with—

This generation baffled him—psychotherapy-simple was what they were! Reliably informed by god they went to Central Park in groups Sunday mornings and solemnly threw stones to work off aggressions, you credit such a thing? And where'd they get the stones—Altman's? In *his* time what you did Sunday mornings was laze in bed with somebody delicious. And have brunch *late*. Though ah dammit how was one to pass *on* one's knowledge of the amenities, one's touch! The very technique was lost. So everything it seemed had to be learned over again, generation after generation to the fumbling incompetent end of time! Or like as not, *not* learned properly at all, and only the sad disillusionments passed on instead.

Well it sounds pathetic, but goodness it's not *us*! And Charles and Amy hardly get up Sundays at all. So who's disillusioned?"

He appeared to reflect.

"Who's this telling whoever-it-is off?" he said presently. "Grampa or some other lecturing old bastard?"

"Oh Richard it's a *character*! In a *novel*! It's this novelist who's being writer-in-residence at Bryn Mawr. And there is this dumb English major who's been sleeping with him, so it's *her* he's talking about the generation gap he has with that I'm quoting in the *text* passage—

. . . like the time he'd said to this demure and naked child (and in sheer awe, mind you!) he'd said *god* what a lovely piece she was!—and so help him, what had she done but go white with outrage, shriek 'So *that's* all you think of me!!' at him, and fling on her clothes and out his astounded door forever! And in fact absolutely refused to sleep with him for a week.

Of course she did have a point—*all* the dictionaries say 'piece' meaning a girl is 'archaic or dialect.' "

So he thought this over.

. . . His *door* astounded?

"Oh Richard it's a *metonymy*! No but then I checked about 'piece' with Charles that night I spent in town, and he said ah, well, Scrope invents his own dialect, stylizing. Also anyway he *has* a lot of old-fashioned prejudices and behaviors, Charles for instance said Scrope claims courtship is every bit as productive an alternative as just saying *You wanna*? Oh it was lovely, Amy wasn't there, so I sat on their bed, and Richard he really *talked* to me! And he *isn't* three times my age, he won't even be thirty-seven till September, and we talked for hours. I asked him how professors feel when some student falls in love with them, what do professors, well, *do*? He said why? was I thinking about seducing one? I said goodness no!—the sort of professors we have at Princeton? my!— no, actually I was just asking what *he* did when a student began to behave as if she wanted him badly, I'd been taking this *course* that'd made me sociologically investigative. Because Richard I wanted to see whether he'd pretend it never happens to him. But of course he just looked mondain and amused, and said '*Do*'? what would any gent do! So I said, 'Oh but Charles not what anybody would, what *you* have,' so he began to laugh and said what was I doing, interviewing him? what kind of course I'd taken *was* this! Because in principle, or anyway *his* principle as an un-marauder, these things depended on your best honest estimate of how any given girl's temperament and experience would bear up under the assaults of your adoration, oh Richard he was a trance!"

Her bedfellow, it seemed sulkily, said nothing.

But she paid no attention. "Because Charles said look," she went on, serenely, "if a girl goes to bed with you to make sure she's as lovely as why *shouldn't* she hope she is—and he said that's always *a* reason, never mind all the silly others—then the only decent way to respond to this gift from Heaven is not just confirm her hope but dispel any last possible doubts she could *ever* have, and for good! So, when the affair's over, she not only has no regrets about herself and folly, she also ends up *fond* of you, and what more can a man want! — and he sounded so charming I didn't even point out how neatly *that* excused a man from responsibility! Though he says the average man never has *any* real idea what he has in his arms. Or how she operates, which is why the poor clod's hardly serious competition, oh Richard he was *telling* me about himself, imagine! But *now* what are you looking all grumpy and sullen for, I didn't *do* anything about him did I?"

". . . Well but *jesus*, Mimi!" he mumbled.

"And anyway, listening to Charles, I thought of something to try for *you* Richard, making love. Oh god you look like that phrase Charles said your grandfather says is the style most novelists write their novels in, 'Henry shook his head thoughtfully' — shall I just give up? No but I was thinking how caressing Charles sounded on my tapes, with Amy, as well as how he *is*, so then I thought how Amy sounded, making love with him, oh Richard *the* most erotic *wildly* blissful little whimpering cries, goodness! and I thought I bet it would excite you too if *I* made them, because wouldn't it? But then I thought but does she do it on purpose, to excite him, or only because she feels so lovely she really can't help it — how *does* one get to know, about other women? What did that sexy friend of your mother's last summer do? Or were you I suppose too dazed by her to notice. No but then I thought but suppose Amy *is* consciously being blissful with Charles, then *oh* what a hypocrite when she's so wild about your uncle she's committing adultery with him! Unless, that is, she's still in total pieces about Charles too? — do you suppose you can actually be *in love* with two men at the same time? I mean goodness maybe there *are* still things to find out!" she crooned at him, exulting.

But her Henry did not even shake his head. Women being beyond us.

17

One morning that week Amy Hallam rang up Alec Urquhart and said could he perhaps did he suppose have been mistaken about Sibylla's suspecting them? — it having been actually mostly inference after all? Sibylla hadn't *said* had she? So what if perhaps she didn't think it either! And so Charles didn't either *either!*

Because, first, the adorable way Charles had recently — well she of course couldn't tell him in detail, but the way he'd been not just making love but oh *everything!* for instance just last night about *adultery* he was adorable, he'd said it was a branch of civilized deportment you had to *acquire* the traditions of, being unfaithful wasn't just something you did by light of nature, as between consenting illiterates, you had to read up on it, and would he joke if he thought?

"Because in particular, Alec, he said the first arms men end up in, as things go, are your wife's delicious best friend's or your own best friend's delicious wife's, so is light of nature going to prepare you for the hair-raising social legerdemain you're then stuck with? So, sweetie, would he have said 'your wife's best friend' when I *am?*" she ended happily.

He said um.

"And then, second, I don't see how otherwise Sibylla would have confided in me (as she just *has,* and for me to use for a story she even said if I liked) this anecdote about her father she has never told *anyone*—never even hinted how amused she felt about him sometimes because of, Alec! This was some year he'd been talked into at least *being* at this literary bash in Berkeley, and he'd said to her why not come by for a couple of days' cultural pub-crawling, he was staying with his editor's cousin, who'd be delighted to put her up too, so one afternoon she'd left Scrope lazing in the sun in the rose-garden behind and gone upstairs, and was standing at her bedroom window for a moment looking out at her father and thinking really how nice he looked for a man his age, when she heard this car turn into the drive and in past the house and it stopped by the gate into the garden right under her window. And Alec out sprang this *very* young wife, Sibylla said she'd it seemed only *graduated* at Berkeley the year before! of the brilliant young professor who was running the conference—and oh Alec Sibylla says she simply *raced* across the garden to Scrope and flung her arms round his wicked old neck, laughing in sort of pure joy, and the easy, *accustomed* way her father—well it was so absolutely in-*bed*-used-to I think Sibylla was even shocked! and then this girl took his hands and practically she said *tugged* him to her car, both of them laughing, and as they went past under her window Sibylla heard her exulting, '. . . and I won't have to go pick him up till after *eleven,* oh angel *think!*' and then they were gone. And Sibylla thought but she's hardly older than I am! and she was scandalized, maybe I would've been too. But then, later, she decided well but what a pleasure for him at what was he? fifty-five? so why not. So *there* is my age-difference story!—but with *two* girls of the same difference, so I'll tell it about one from the standpoint of the other

and it's *perfect!* And then it seems Scrope upset a lot of people with
a public lecture because he said academic criticism was salvos of
stately clucking from the scenery, so I can make my older man
intellectually controversial and sarcastic too. Also, Sibylla once
told me he said Greek tragedy has screwed up literary theory *and*
practice for the last twenty-five hundred years, by making solemnity the basic criterion. And Charles says Scrope is entirely right—
if you don't make your characters suffer he says how are the boys
in the back room to be sure what you're writing is Literature? so
then they can't analyze it. He says William Gerhardi, who he says
wrote the only Chekhov novel in English literature, said critics
feel *uneasy* when a writer isn't solemn. As if comedy weren't serious!—he says for instance Scrope took Housman's

> Could man be drunk for ever
> With liquor, love, or fights

and rewrote it as comedy: 'a pretty girl within grabbing range, a
dazing drink, and somebody to knock down,' and was that any the
less *serious* writing?"

Urquhart said nn.

"Oh though doesn't it feel lovely Alec maybe not being suspected any longer? even if maybe we never all that actually were
anyway! Hoh, and so *free*-feeling!—oh dear if I were still having
that crush on you d'you suppose we'd—because it *would* be the
perfect time, being I mean suddenly all *un*suspected! And when
we've been so agonizingly through it all together already! Or *do*
you think. Oh *dear!* I mean I had this same situation in a story
once, only in the story the girl ran off into the Peace Corps, and
none of my magazines liked it. Oh Alec. I mean I *adore* Charles!
And your students are sort of a groupie thing aren't they. So neither of us ever seriously of course—but then it wasn't a sensible
way to end the story either, or d'you think."

He did not reply.

"And anyway it would be as heartless to make Charles and
Sibylla suffer from our *having* an affair as we thought they were
suffering from thinking we were when we weren't, oh Alec how
can such things ever *happen* to people like us!" she wailed, and
she might have been in remorse already.

But he was silent still. Not being all that ex cathedra articulate
anyhow.

18

Midafternoon by now it may have been, beyond the shuttered windows, even it was late afternoon the drawn curtains helped muffle and close as if evening away, but their bed's tall hangings too Sibylla had loosed from the tester's ties, to swing down around, enfolding, so under that hooded canopy was dusk deep as secrets —even poised on an elbow there, close beside, she hardly made out among those nightfall shadows her lover's eyes.

Which presently it seemed it tenderly amused her were closed, anyhow she now drooped her enchanted head and kissed them, to open them.

So, amused too, he pulled her down. And for a time she lay there, nuzzling him as in sluggard happiness, lips grazing his shoulder, murmuring.

So that presently he murmured, ". . . what," in return.

But in that musing indolence of limbs she seemed too lost in mere contentment, or in dream, to reply.

So they dozed there, wordless.

Except that, at length, she stroked him, laggardly, a mere once, light palm dawdling along his thigh; in torpor; in lullaby.

". . . and so lovely," she whispered. Though of what this was, who knew.

But finally, ". . . even this place, lovely, oh Charles such luck!" she told him, and kissed his throat, for such blessings. "Because how not, you know, wonder. I used to come walk past, along 11th Street, some days two or three times past, before they turned it over to you, I'd look up at our third floor and think 'next *week* it will be ours . . .' and try to decide how I hoped the bedroom would turn out to be, and the bed, oh and us in it, but then sometimes my heart would *sink*, for what if it was in someone's *really* awful taste, because what kind of girls do semantics professors have?"

Needn't've worried, he said. Actually was what her father called a 'dish.'

"But then the heavenly day came and my darling it was *this!*" she exulted. "Oh and from the very first, lovely! . . . And *you* lovely, even the way you simply stood me by the bed and adorably undressed me, ah Charles I felt seduced dans les *formes!*—and to think at our lunch that day I'd been modestly wondering whether to ask, well, 'Are you . . . very physical?'—oh *dear!*"

So he began to laugh.

"*So* practiced and wicked of you!" she teased him. "Poor deprived sweet, have you always had to just dream of having a garçonnière?"

Brought up to have *some* ideals, dear god!—were there no goals to be set before a growing boy, to strive for and attain? No, but what was this 'practiced and wicked' she was disingenuously charging him with—*she* not experienced? Was that delicious delaying him with salvos of fluttering little interrupting kisses the whole time *not* a Special Occasion expertise that Ovid's Corinna herself—

"And you didn't like it?—hoh!"

Good god he'd *never*—!

"And anyway I *felt* like kissing you!—and never stopping ever, and touching you and touching you—and you call that 'interrupting'?"

Well, he said, you could *combine* efficiency with a—

But "Ah, sweet," she murmured, "when my fingers were beginning to learn you too? . . ."—so for some time, then, they said nothing more.

At last, though, she slid up from him, onto an elbow again, gazing soberly down.

And asked, as uncertainly as if it were not altogether a question, ". . . Have we perhaps my love do you think— What have I done to, well, to how you feel about Amy?"

As this could also however mean what *he* had done, to her feelings about Alec, he was warily silent, to see.

"Or shouldn't I ask."

Well, but she had.

So he said, as if lightly, feelings about Amy? when all he could feel was *her*?—what cockeyed time was *this* to ask! with not an atom of his body that wasn't shivering like a tuning-fork with delight in her! Couldn't she realize she'd obliterated every other girl he'd ever as much as glanced at—or that in the future he ever might? Yes, but was *that*, God help him, the way he would presently feel when he was clothed and in his right mind again? and she alas in hers, and in practiced decorum they descended their borrowed stairs, and then sedately down the front steps too, and like the well-brought-up personnes de condition they were set out as if for a Sunday stroll, not even holding hands! . . .

". . . Oh Charles," she mumbled.

"And wouldn't you have to say the same?" he asked her tenderly. "At this undeceived and lovely moment does it seem to you you'll ever again particularly want—"

"I know," she said dolefully.

"Then what?" he coaxed, and slid his fingers up her docile back, to pull her down to comfort and consolation.

But "Ah Charles so much to be endlessly wary about too?" she fretted, resisting. "And then all the feelings that—the edge-of-consciousness— Oh how do I say it? I mean do you sometimes feel, well, *odd* my darling about me, coming to you from you'll never perhaps feel quite sure what with Alec?"

But she didn't feel odd about him, with Amy.

"But you're my *lover*, heavens!"

He was amused: he wasn't Amy's too?

"Only then why doesn't it seem to count!" she lamented. "Or do I just put up with thinking about it because I love you so much?— because that time she had a crush on Alec I stopped even kissing him!—and when poor sweet it wasn't in the least his fault! goodness, all he'd ever said about her was why did I think her bosom made *him* melt, and once we were all at that beach and he said it soothed him to gaze down Amy's curves to the sea. Or no, down her parabolas. So do I just want you more than I did him? Because oh Charles that sounds so *belittling* as well as unfaithful!" she ended, as if despairing, and sank down once again into his arms.

This time then they lay there, it could have been, musing.

But presently, from her private darkness, ". . . Darling tell me something?—even," she asked, "if it's just a nagging little curiosity? which is what it is, not jealousy. But Amy's crush on Alec made me think of it, because at our New Year's party that lovely little menace Mimi was at one point adoring you practically in *public* Charles, so has she ever waved herself as languishingly at you since? Of course you can't possibly I know think about her. Only of course you could, *incest* I mean aside! But, well, one of the nights Amy was off on that publishers' trip, ten days ago, when I rang up Mimi was *there* not in Princeton, and right there beside you because she just handed you the phone."

Ah, well, he said, amused, if she wanted the reprehensible fact, the child was sitting on his bed in nothing but a chastely draped sortie de bain, very engagingly trying to seduce him. Had come in of course about a term-paper—some sociological claptrap on differences, by lustra, between among others her Princeton era and his. A boy in her class for example had made himself ridiculous— ridiculous she meant in their own present peer-context—by tagging hopefully around after his freshman-English instructor till finally her husband threw him out of the house in a rage, and one of *her* professors she'd never given the slightest encouragement to had one day just *grabbed* her!—so would there have been such, well, such incompetent expectations in his time? So naturally he'd said (with perfect solemnity) dear god she was embarrassing him for his alma mater! had they taken to importing professors from Yale or some such place these days? for what sad fumbling!

"But Charles you listened to her?"

Dammit he'd been amused!—anyhow, she'd gone on, she supposed he couldn't tell her personally, because of Amy, but how at his college did students and faculty (or had they said it some other way in his time) make out?

"Oh *dear!*"

Well god *yes!* So, making conversation in self-defense, he'd said, so she hadn't been all that charmed! and she'd said, "When he's twice my age?—hoh!" laughing. So he felt he'd better call a halt! So he'd said *he* was twice her age too, but here she was, sitting on his bed wasn't she? angelically smiling at him, at nearly one in the morning?

"Oh *Charles* how brutal!"

Ah, look, this was a highly charged young intelligence—and they come prepared! For all he knew, she'd read up on for instance 'deceased wife's sister' cases, and had a set piece ready! Or on primitive taboo, or on entail even; or *genetically* sisters fell for the same man's DNA and he for theirs? And this one had come prepared emotionally too—she'd just laughed up at him and said *my*, did he think he had to make her say poor Professor Staling didn't attract her but *he* very much *did?* and simply anyhow was there any reason she couldn't come put in a bid for if and when? . . . , and got up from his bed and sweetly kissed him hardly three seconds more than was sisterly, and was gone.

". . . Giggling?"

No.

"The little horror!"

Ah, now, she'd behaved.

"*Kissing* you, after that 'if and when,' was *behaving?*"

Ah, well, he conceded, no.

"But how possibly think Amy was about to give you up!"

He was silent. It was beyond fathoming. Or hypothesis. They both were silent.

But presently (by whatever contour of logic) "Does it seem to you," she wondered, "that Amy and Alec have been almost avoiding each other, I mean lately? Of course it could just be another of those poets-detest-novelists fumes they have sometimes. Or d'you think?"

He said God bless, for all anybody could tell, they were even having a sad unspoken longing for each other themselves, and were loyally fighting it off.

"Oh Charles you're *cruel*, to laugh!"

But he *sympathized!*—particularly if they were in anything like the lover's despondency *he*'d been in about her! Had she any notion of the— Well, had he ever had so much as a look from her, *or* a word or a gesture, whose lovely ambiguity could have let him hope his adoring her mattered one way or the other? Or assume he could even archaically court her? Good god, her beauty'd reduced him to Prufrock's And-how-should-I-begin! Because suppose, he'd say to himself, just hopelessly suppose—and mind you, *knowing* the supposition was neurotic fatuity!—though yes, but suppose anyway!—he'd say to himself suppose that everything, *every* perilous hope, might in *fact* (never mind any sensible likelihood) depend on the heart-stopping moment in time he'd finally risk telling her he loved her, and on the *one* right opening phrase her father's Bona Dea might smilingly decide to put on his stammering tongue to say—

"Oh *Charles!*" she cried, in complete delight, and rolling up kissed him, laughing. "You didn't *really?*—and so dejected? *Oh* what flattery!" she crooned, kissing him again.

Kind of appalling, yes, he agreed, smiling too.

"Oh my love you even made it *sound* like what remember you said once about Prufrock?—'Why did poor Mr. Eliot just out of Harvard think the mermaids wouldn't sing to him? Or was he wrong, they were just cultivatedly waiting to be asked?' But oh Charles a marauder like you dither about asking?—oh *no!*"

What was she used to—appeals to her idealism?

"Oh darling when I already admired you? No, but it's a little like something that— Well, this was a time Daddy had gone to one of those seminar things on the Coast, and he'd said come be with him a couple of days and let him show me off to his literary friends and enemies, so I did and we were staying in some people he knew's house in Berkeley. But one day after lunch I'd left him sunning in the big garden, behind, and gone up to my room to change, an athletic poet was picking me up for tennis, so when I heard a car come in past the house and stop at the gate into the garden I thought it was my athlete and went to the window to call down. But instead it was this *very* young wife of the professor who'd organized the seminar, and what did she do but Charles *race* across the garden into Daddy's arms, and then almost before I'd realized I was astonished she was tugging him laughing back across to her car, oh she was *dancing* almost! and as they went past under my window I heard her say, '—and this time we've *hours!*' and then they were gone. And I found all I was thinking was oh what a *sweetie* to do that for him!—at his age to have somebody young and pretty and adoring to make love with! and obviously it had been going on but how had they managed? And also I was amused—so *this* was the way women could feel about my pa! of course I knew the way he *writes* can feel seducing, or at least make you curious, but naturally I'd never seen a girl of his I knew'd been making love with him, *alone* with him before. But then I thought—and sort of soberly, my darling—but what heavenly luck for the girl even more, for *any* girl, because how many girls ever do? to fall in love with a man who made you feel like that, made you feel radiant!—which don't you think perhaps," she said, and lightly fluttered his lips with a lingering tongue, "is sort of how"—flick—"I feel about you? . . . ," and slipping her arms under his bemused head she began to kiss him without further analytical nonsense.

So, there being plenty of time in fact still, they went on from there.

19

The craik and wail of gulls over the sea-meadows woke him, so early in the first faint saffron pallor of summer morning no one was he found up and about anywhere, even in this inn's vaulted kitchens, only ranks of breakfast trays lined up set and ready there for this day now begun seemed to prepare for its beginning, the cool dawn stillness everywhere.

No one! He was amused.

But forbearing: so then in Finistère too, where Bretons bretonnent if anywhere, now had there been some Frankish time-motion studies?—and the efficiency of sleep!

So, like a man of forbearance, to wait, he sauntered through and out, into the forecourt's flutter of doves, white fantails tumbling in the now bronze streaks of sunrise, though at once, at the sight of him was it? an instantaneous whirr and slither about him of alighting wings.

Ah, well, he was hungry himself!

—And had nothing to feed them. He set out through the fresh green Breton-daybreak landscape toward the village and breakfast—sur le zinc as in student days, at an early bar.

Across the Place de la Mairie from which, when the librairie opened its shutters, he bought a *France-Ouest,* and a (surprising!) copy of Queneau's *Exercices de Style,* to take back, as amends if needed, to Mrs. Tench-Fenton.

Who in their room's glowing morning he found was contentedly breakfasting in bed.

And in murmuring welcome held out her arms. "But you *left* me? . . ." she reproached him, with love, putting up a smiling mouth to be kissed good morning. "I woke and darling you were *gone,*" eyes smiling too. "*Heartlessly* gone," she regretted happily, patting the bed beside her with a forgiving hand (which he picked up smiling and kissed, and which she then took his wrist with, to gently tug him down). "And sweetie without even thinking what you'd left me to account for?—in of *course* came the little maid with our breakfasts, and where were you, hoh!"

'Account for'?—account for what? (he said, laughing) she think the child wasn't used to this or that offhand 'Monsieur me quitte dès l'aube' for god's sake?

"Well even if you don't you *had* hadn't you?—'d've served you right, and the child's so beautifully trained she'd simply have said, 'Oui, madame,' and not batted a modest eyelash, how *can* you suggest putting the little thing through that! At least I preserved your reputation, I said, 'Monsieur est sorti faire un tour' so would she see that his coffee was kept au chaud? so she said, 'Mais oui, madame' to that instead, darling where did you *go*?"

He said well these northern-summer sunrises he'd forgot how they woke you early. Brittany's latitude was after all Newfoundland's wasn't it? But *ahhh* how lovely she looked! Made-love-to lovely!—if epistemologists could contemplate her at this moment they'd renounce, forever, the doctrine that appearance and reality couldn't be the same! Anyhow, light had woken him. So he'd very quietly dressed and gone to breakfast —except would she credit it? not even a marmiton was up! the kitchen a place of shadows and silence—unheard-of! so by god he'd gone along the voie to the village for breakfast!

"You *walked*?" she cried at him, instantly appalled. "All the way into *Moëlan*? . . ."

He was astonished: this, for a mere two kilometers?

"Oh Scrope how can you *be* so devious, Moëlan's two and a *half* kilometers," she wailed, "which is five kilometers round-trip which is three *miles!*—and when to make sure you were not only properly cared for but cosseted I told them the moment we arrived 'Monsieur n'est toujours pas bien en train'? and now here you wickedly overtire yourself before the day's even begun! And especially when last night *again* you know you—we— Oh sweetie do you think I don't know what heaven it is again? but *so* soon after that dreadful not-yet-one-month-ago crisis, to talk me into letting you run *risks* because I foolishly love you and want you to be happy?—oh *Scrope!*" she rebuked him, and snatched her fingers absolutely away.

"But my lovely *thing!*" he cried, as if stricken—remorseful, even (though God bless, for what!).

"And also you *upset* me, talking French!"

So he was at sea besides. " 'French'?" he stammered. "Last *night?* . . .?" as if scandalized.

"Well you *did!*—and totally *irrelevant* upsetting French too! 'que j'en ai le goût, de ta bouche,' you said, why *shouldn't* it upset me, the way I was feeling how lovely you are!—oh Scrope how was I *not* to think of the last time I indulged you and we made love in French, so did you mean you were remembering it too? And remembering all the other things that particular Paris week?—so of *course* in the middle of everything it distracted me! how was I to abruptly rearrange my feelings to suit you if *that* was what you stupidly wanted! Oh even with only the *edges* of my mind wondering, it distracted me! and then why were you talking about my mouth when you were kissing my throat? And then, well, I adore your mouth too, sometimes I think I'll never have enough of it, but would I say I 'have a taste for' it?—so in the middle of making love was I to be involved in *also* wondering whether the phrase had nuances for you besides what it means literally, for instance who did you learn it from?—oh sweetie I am *not* flighty and jealous and you know it, goodness! but can't you see what such *pointless* random nonsense does to the enchanting concentration you beguile me into? how *could* you!"

Ah, well.

But what endearing claptrap; so he lovingly set her damn' bed-table out of the way and took her by the shoulders. So what actually she'd *meant* was, if he ever again—

"Well you *might* don't you think have woken me and taken me along!" she denounced him.

Inflict his insomnia on her? When she was sleeping like a bliss-ful angel? Looking about fifteen! And not really *all* that upset then anyway . . .

And kissed her. Which at least she permitted.

Because anyway dammit their French hadn't in the least upset her in that little hotel in the Rue de—

"That *grubby* little hotel in the Rue de l'Université!—and *laughing* at what you yourself called 'taking me slumming for once'!"

What slumming?—room'd had a bath!

"It was dingy and on the ground floor on the *street* and unsuit-able and unseemly and even my bed-Italian was better than my bed-French then anyway!"

Peccato!

"And don't snicker! I *remember* our sweet places! And in Paris I always think about you anyway," she said sadly, kissing him. "Didn't I ever tell you about the day I got so suicidally tired of the people I was there for, the Apollinaire centenary wasn't it? anyway I got so nostalgic I decided oh damn *damn*, I'll just *go* off and touch a few bases then!—you know? where there had been something special for me?—follies too?—and, well, the Rue de l'Université darling you know *was* slummy but it was one of our real étapes emotionally, it was where you talked me out of starting a baby and I cried, besides where you said I was 'the caress of a wholly feminine sensuality,' and oh I actually went in and Scrope *asked* had by any chance a Monsieur Townshend been de passage recently, can you imagine? and they were so politely regretful at never having heard of you that I didn't even feel silly. But then I thought but supposing you *were* in Paris where would you prob-ably be? so of course I instantly remembered that Berkeley profes-sor's marauding little centerfold of a wife you'd not only let seduce you but she'd followed you east!"

He said dear god it wasn't just her posturing husband—he'd gathered four or five selected California-beachboy types hadn't held her interest either. But how was it *his* fault they'd fallen so short of her ladylike expectations that she'd turned to such a sad ruin of past gallantry as *he* was!

"Well but you got very fond of her didn't you? And she amused you—you told me she said things like 'When you call me *blessing* I think of church, it's confusing!' "

Damn' priests should reconsider their language.

"And you let her follow you to France too, so I remembered

you said she'd found an apartment in the Boulevard Raspail near
the Rue Stanislas corner, so I took a bus as far as Notre Dame des
Champs. And, well, walked slowly along looking up at house numbers, wondering was it *here?* or was it *this* one, nearer the Rue
Stanislas?—oh what a saddening thing, somehow, walking alone,
just looking my love at *numbers* with longing—except even if I'd
remembered her name *would* I have rung and asked the concierge
whether she was in? oh cities *are* so sad aren't they! But finally I *did*
go round the corner to that crowded little restaurant in the Rue
Stanislas you'd said you and she ate at sometimes, you said it was
good, and it *was*, the patronne made a place for me and I had
lunch there. Afterwards I wanted to ask about you there too. But I
felt too sad to," she said. "And then how was I to put it—'une jeune
femme américaine d'à côté dans le quartier'? when back *then* had
it perhaps even been the same patronne! So *see* what your idle
misbehavior can put me through!" she accused him, happily, and
took his face in her hands to kiss him. "And when I can almost
even forget you for months at a time? And I *do*, almost totally, so
there!—oh sweetie, forget even what you're like, imagine!"

Intermittences du coeur, yes, he conceded, smiling.

"Only then for no reason at all there will be a sort of warm
flooding of my senses from nowhere (lovely!) and I wonder what *is*
this!—and only *then* I suddenly realize my mind has been thinking about you to itself, and has decided I should have my attention
called. So, my intermittences love, we do go on," she said, and
kissed him sentimentally. "Which is why, even lovely-last-night,
Scrope, I risked making you cross."

. . . about Sibylla.

"Yes, and Charles."

"But *wrangling* about it with me?" he teased her. "Lying there
in my *arms* wrangling?"

"As if in any case you wouldn't *far* rather have Charles for your
darling than somebody you'd have to get *used* to not detesting! Not
that either of us thinks for a minute—"

God, no!—thing only too damn' clear!

"So then my old darling why *shouldn't* they live happily ever
after!—once upon a time didn't *we* decide to? And haven't we?
And haven't we always, even so—well you said yourself loving
someone else *too* was part of the secret."

Actually, he said, it was Ovid said it. Even if he said it wrong
way round.

DIALOGUE AT THE END OF A PURSUIT

For Nancy Tuck Gardiner

Scene: an alcove bed (now rumpled). *Time:* a summer dusk. *Personae:* She and He.

She has drifted up from him at last, murmuring. She stretches, arching her slim back in the luxury of it, fluttering her hands to the fingertips. She relaxes. And almost, in contentment, minutely yawns. Finally, she looks at him, over her shoulder, to see.

But he looks as delicious as ever!

Which it seems so delights her that she collapses happily across him, propped on an arm, eyes taking him in again detail by detail, gazing smiling down.

He lifts his free hand, smiling too—to her cheek, down her throat, along the curve of her shoulder, down her side, thumb modeling her breast on the way.

She stoops and, soberly, kisses him.

. . . So see? he teases, and laughs.

But "Ah but sweet," she reproaches him, "why shouldn't I have been especially wary? One doesn't know who one's handing oneself over to till oh dear one's already finding out! And you were adorably after me weren't you? And isn't any marauder? So who'd have thought— Well, one does hear there are men who actually *like* women, but doesn't one wonder?"

He looks amused.

"Oh taaah, you know what I mean! No but don't you see how unsettling? I kept getting all these *other* signals beside the tally-ho! Was I to handle this as if it was just going to be the usual biological onslaught? Life is full of lovely strangers, yes, but why suddenly should you be one I needn't be strange with? You 'liked' me, as well as everything else, but goodness would that translate into a recognizable passion? Oh why did you complicate everything—you *confused* me, liking me!"

She already *reminiscing* about them, for god sakes?—when they'd hardly begun?

"But I have to see you in perspective! Aren't there civilized stages?—for instance I know the *type* of man I like in love with me the first second I meet him, if I have my lenses in. And at that Connecticut wedding we sat in that arbor, talking, for an hour."

He says 'stage'? What stage!—that proconsular lout of hers appeared and she'd let him carry her off!

"*That* stop a lovely marauder?—hoh!"

Had she dammit *no* idea what she'd done to him? He'd stood there and watched her slowly disappear across the darkening gardens and past the marquee away from him—to Bithynia with the fellow forever, for all he knew, death in his heart! A lifetime, and he'd known her barely an hour! And there she was, *gone*, taking her miracles with her. . . .

She kisses him in amusement. "Goodness what endearing Art Deco things you think up to say! But do you really have to fuss?—hardly a month later there I was for you wasn't I, at what's-her-name's decree-nisi party? And stage *three*'s been all this charming feeding me lunch after lunch—Le Perrosien and Fourtie's and La Buonabolgia and *today* that expensive din at A Qui de Droit, darling why *lunches?*"

He snorts. Dear god, what did she take him for!—*commit* a woman he adored?

"Ho, but here I am, happily in bed with you in the afternoon anyway—lunch *not* 'commit' me, oh *dear!* No but what if *my* third stage is only sort of virginally wondering am I d'you suppose *going* to decide? . . . Because I don't *decide* till stage four whether there's all that difference between a man I adore having in love with me, and a man I *might* lavish myself on. Are you to have no interim frustrations I can deliciously make it up to you for afterwards?"

That being stage five?

"Or six. Or seven. Because anyway am I sure that deciding to go to bed with you is *the* decision."

Considering what he'd been given to understand women thought of men as people, what were the heavenly things doing in bed with them at all?

"Oh sweet but where but in bed am I likely to find out how much I've perhaps decided I want to have you discover *all* the things I can be? Or do I ever?—because *darling* how dangerous to put it into words! And what are the chances, ever, really, that a lover will turn out to be as lovely as you thought how could he *not* be, the way he seemed!"

Ah, he says, teasing, but was she putting the poor helpless devil up against the whole catalogue of ladylike misgivings from Eden on?

"But are they any the less misgivings for that? For oh what shall I perhaps find I've told you, finally? Because what if it's only the things I might tell any man! And how can it not frighten me it might be?—because then would you have been no more to me than that? You like me—and oh dear how I've begun to like you back! But what am I being tempted to? And how much of myself may I not even have noticed I've as good as handed over! Oh are you somehow stranger than the usual stranger?—and am I suddenly to think *that* is what love is? Oh why couldn't you have loved me as if the marauder I thought you were is what you are? . . ."

So he says (and what more reasonable) but God bless, couldn't they try that too? There *was* that built-in advantage to afternoons—not only was a perfectly good night still ahead, but a *whole* night.

DECLARATIONS OF INTENT

Why *should* I have felt like talking, driving back to New York that night, after the weekend—I was upset, dear heaven how couldn't I have been! And what was Guy for if not to see I was, what *are* lovers!

Yes, and I'd tilted my bliss of a spectacular new floppy hat down over my nose and leaned my head back against the cool leather of the bucket seat and closed my eyes—*this* much upset I had to think out how *could* it be I was!

Though then what did Guy do but say, and in that bland indulging-me voice, he was analytically alert, as always, to the glittering kaleidoscope of my moods, but was I should-he-call-it brooding?

I thought *hah*.

'Pout' being, he remembered, a word I forbade even my most permitted authors to employ.

So he was making me cross besides?

Well, and *vengeful!* and I thought if you know me no better you superior savage than to think you know what the matter is *ever*, then you can think it's something it isn't!

Oh you oaf *anything* it isn't!!

You and that live-in showgirl, even! so I pulled off my hat and tossed it over back without looking even where and said, "Goodness how I adore hats like that, what heaven, no but what did you make of her finally?" a false scent how couldn't he follow.

He said make of which her was this.

"You have to be stupid too?" I said. "The little thing amusing you right up to the very last, what else!"

Oh, he said, the child.

"*Yes* the child!"

. . . Made of her how? As this unexpected undergraduate? Or as modeling her way through Princeton?

(With a straight face. How can men. How could *this* one, after three months of Me!)

Or was it 'a bit young for him' I meant I felt.

What vanity. "Oh Guy," I said.

So then we were silent. I closed my eyes again. And if he thought I was sulking, what earthly matter.

—Because now, oh anyway!—for what if these three months *were* all there was ever to have been. . . .

But he was saying ah but look (and in his what-*is*-this voice), she was older than average Princeton seniors, how not? Been in shows, *then* decided to go to college, was all.

I thought oh well.

So I opened my eyes and said, "No but merely Guy to begin with, this was a grown-*up* bash of Matthew's, how have you been brightly explaining to yourself she was there at all?"

'Explain' the incidence of pretty girls? God Himself could hardly have been sure about it till Darwin came along! Look, they *decorate* a bash! Jesus, ask Matthew where he'd got her—man was *my* author wasn't he?

Oh Guy. " 'Matthew'!" I said. "You actually didn't notice where she appeared from, both mornings? I mean of *course* whose girl is she!"

He said oh come—moral disapprobation? Were we to deplore our friends' rustic delinquencies? ". . . my love my *love!*"—and his gently reproving hand on my knee.

So at least the false scent was being followed.

And *Robert* not even a suspicion of . . .

—About whom what *am* I to do.

And when how possibly was I to have imagined, from anything Matthew had ever said, that this 'Classicist brother of his at the Institute' would turn out to— That I would— Oh well damn *damn*, does the girl think he's that sort of man either? No wonder she adores him!

. . . And of course, also, the clothes she has—*not* just a part-time model's lagniappe! And that little vintage MG in Robert's garage must be hers. And afford four years of Princeton on modeling in vacations? *Of course* Robert's been putting her through!

And what if it *is* sort of old-fashioned comic and prim-sounding, being 'kept'—Matthew calls her their 'family showgirl' as if she were.

I closed my eyes, and let myself *feel* the silence.

—Oh but it was so perfectly light-minded, in the pantry—simply Robert went with me for more ice, and suddenly—well, he no more than breathed "Eve, Eve—" and as I turned, because *that* tone? "—even your name's an enchantment . . ." and from nowhere this courteous male mouth (tasting of marc?) was expertly on mine, and this questing tongue was asking my lips whether it even needed to ask—oh *dear* how assured, and when at last I drew away, this accomplished—this—this *educated* mouth softly kissed the curve of my throat below my ear. And all this, hardly touching, a mere range-finding hand lightly on my shoulder, oh I was stunned with admiration!

But then what do you do but gaze analytically at each other, revising your realities, while you get both your breaths again. I leaned my head back against the ice-box door and said, "At least your mouth has very nice manners," and laughed, and he picked up my hand and turned it over and kissed the palm, and said, "The rest of me hopes it would deserve your kind approval too."

Ho, but were we to go *on* like this? so I said, "Don't you ever read your novelist brother's disheartening epigrams?—'All catnip is is catnip.' " But he just snorted agreeably; and then with perfect punctilio he held the ice-bucket while I plunked trays of ice into it, the whole thing as stylized and heartless as a ballet, and we sauntered smiling back in to the party again.

Entirely light-minded and party-routine.

—Guy yawned, and took his hand back. "I thought it was a splendid bash," he said. "On the whole didn't you?"

I said oh as house-warmings go.

"Ah, well, no, some of the local classmates that first evening, yes," he said. "Ah but you know how we are. Dewy-eyed with nostalgia, all of us. So a guy comes back and settles in Princeton, like Matthew, and he asks damn' near anybody in his whole Princeton era to come celebrate."

("So at least," Matthew had said, "I'll have seen which of 'em I don't give a damn if I never lay eyes on again.")

"Fabulous woods, though," Guy said. "Imagine *that*, a mere three miles from campus! I mean, God bless, the whole four years I was in *college* there they were! Amazing!"

I said Robert said with Matthew's woods joined to his, now they had nearly two hundred acres altogether. It had been chestnut forest once, but then the blight, and the oaks had taken over. But the lovely aisles of the beechwood where Robert's house stood had been there forever.

"Fabulous," Guy said. And yawned again.

He want me to drive?

"No."

Seriously?

"*Yes* seriously!"

I closed my eyes.

—Because also what am I to do about *you*, I thought.

. . . Will you behave as beautifully as Sean? Well, Celtic tears, no. Ah, but Sean I hurt. I should never have been playful, trying to be tender and console. 'But when I've been your first-ever Wasp?' I remember oh dear as good as cooing, that last morning, kissing his eyes, laughing. 'But sweet, simply think what you've learned!' Ah, that was what the tears were for. We weren't, for him, a cross-cultural divertissement: for him, poor darling, we were Me. And with what I thought were two affectionately disabusing sentences I had disavowed it all. . . .

Easier to leave when it's been longer. Simon was both my last years at Radcliffe. And his Grenoble summer lecturing between. And it was understood graduation was to be good-bye.

And anyway: how many men like Simon are there.

Oh and Guy is my bel homme type anyway! So now and then who doesn't simply need them temporarily why can't they see! Sean was even— Oh Sean was absolutely High Renaissance, he could have posed for Titian! And heavens how good they are for one's vanity, oh they're like sables, aren't they! Only, they are beautiful, so they're spoiled. They've never had to notice things, even—Guy doesn't even realize it's I who am sleeping with him, not he with me!

Imagine.

Ah but then he can be touching. Like that night we'd got in so late we'd *collapsed* into bed, and hardly made love but I was asleep. But then I woke, and there he was, sitting by me, on my side of the bed, gazing silently down at me in the darkness, and in a kind of drowsy wonder I thought but how strange. But before I could even ask but what? he saw I'd woken and I thought he'd smile and explain; but what he *did* was softly recite that early Cocteau—

> Ton rêve est une Egypte, et toi c'est la momie,
> Avec son masque d'or

—well who wouldn't have been touched! and I reached my arms up round his neck and pulled him down, not to make love (though we did) but simply for the sweetness of it, the cherishing in return. . . .

And, now, is he going to think it is my 'mask' he has known, not me?—and be sad again? Oh I do hope not: he has no reason to be! For a bel homme, he's— Well, a *touch* of the pasha, in bed, but no more than a touch. Oh poor darling it's nothing I have against him anyway. . . .

Just I am unfair.

—Because oh Robert.

. . . And you recklessly as good as *said* it, there at the last, in the dark of Matthew's hall. Guy was already out at the car with our bags, but you came so fast out of the living-room, calling after me, that I thought had I forgot something? and I stopped and turned. But then oh Robert the *way* you came up to me in the darkness, it was like terror. Though *why?* the sheer physical there-ness of you? —you didn't touch me, you didn't have to, just *looming* there I was lost! Ah but then it was what you said—"Are we *not* to go on with this?—and at least good god *see?* . . .," sounding so half-desperate I was dizzy with what I found was happening to me. As of course you saw, you put out your hand and I felt your fingertips under mine, coaxing or caressing who knows which, and you said, "Can't I even find out whether you're an angel or a woman?" and now you were smiling, *you knew*, "—and anyhow catnip *is* catnip you lovely thing, so have lunch in town with me tomorrow? or by now is it getting to be thank god today!"

—Oh but my expert marauder *that* was not the way!—so sure so sudden so swift so *soon* after me? triggering, to SET, my innermost alarm? so now the faintest of imagined footfalls will loose that shattering clangor, to preserve me. . . .

I said, "Oh *Robert*," and I'd even got breath enough back to laugh at you. "After as nothing-done a weekend as this? And not just my own arrears of manuscripts but I'm taking over for an editor who's on jury duty! And 'lunch today' anyway!—headlong *besides* all the other preposterous things it is, heavens!"

You said, "I *feel* headlong!" with a kind of happy violence, and your fingers slid up my wrist into my sleeve so urgently my cuff button came undone.

(Symbolically undressing me? oh *dear* how amusing!)

And I might even have said it, only suddenly, at the end of the hall, behind you, I saw *her* appear in the lighted doorway from the living-room, and I had just time to breathe *your poppet* like a conspirator instead, and I turned as innocently I hope as if from a second good-bye, and trooped on out to Guy and the car—though how *did* you explain!

—No but how could she have been as uneasy about you as that, a girl as young and lovely as she is?

Because even Robert if she is too much in love with you *not* to keep that helpless watch, what had there been between us she could possibly have noticed. From the moment I met you, Friday afternoon, *I* knew you are the risk I must keep myself from running, always; and not once, all weekend long, did I let a look or a tone of voice, ever, glide over into uneasy ambiguities.

And for you too, even after that undissembling kiss, I might have been no more than what I had been all along, your brother's editor, just met. Oh you were impeccable—back with our ice, with the others again, I could hardly believe that that blandly conversational tongue had just been making enchanting love to mine, so poised you were—though ah Robert the sheer practicedness of it told me how much greater the danger of you must be for me, and with it my dismay.

—Or was it the very unruffledness of Robert's performance that somehow alerted her. She knows him. She has been his girl Matthew said from before college: she was still in the floor show at Fourtie's when they began. By now every transience of his behavior she can interpret as I cannot.

Ah, and anyhow—love is terror. If you do not find, you imagine, what endlessly you dread.

—I wonder what I feel about her.

I mean actually what. Isn't she as they say 'with' Robert very much for instance the way I was 'with' Simon? She is two or three years older than I was then. And how old is he? thirty-five? thirty-seven? Simon was nearly fifty, but it's the same classical scenario. Except isn't she perhaps more 'in love' with Robert than I was with Simon?—because how else explain being of all things *anxious* about him, heavens! Matthew said she only roomed on campus her freshman year. And didn't even bother about Bicker, just moved out and *lived* with Robert. I suppose when I had Simon I never seriously thought about making love with even a very pretty undergraduate either. But didn't the girl at least wave herself at them, except of course in class? One always has *that* much duty to one's instincts and one's upbringing! But here, all weekend, even my beautiful Guy never really took her attention from Robert.

Still, what a lovely thing she is. All over again, this morning, I thought how lovely, coming along that sun-spattered woodland ride to join us at the folly Robert is building—the sun filtering down through the high crown of the forest like sequined veils of light across her face as she came, teetering elegantly on her high heels through the carpets of fern. She had been to mass; and when she came smiling up to us what nice manners I thought too—holding up a cheek for Robert to kiss as if merely in well-brought-up good morning, and then, just as sweetly, a maidenly cheek for Matthew to kiss too, with only the softest of polite glances sidewise to include Guy as she did.

Matthew was right: 'family' she is.

And if he sounded sardonic about it at breakfast, being sardonic is Matthew's literary style. And this was indulgently sardonic: could I imagine a more presentable young sister-in-law, hand-fasting or not?—*either* side of the wicked blanket in fact. Well-behaved child, too—Robert even aware, through the mists of concupiscence, just *how* well?

"Though can you conceive of treating a stately Queen Anne house as a garçonnière dear god? Beautiful creature like Samantha well *yes* you indulge her, but do you have to outdo Veblen's conspicuous waste doing it?"

Matthew loves women; he *does*. But he can sound as if he found us faintly comic sometimes too, how do his girls put up with it! "Oh Matthew," I said.

"Dammit am I *blaming* her?" he cried. "All you Protestant sweeties have for spiritual backup is some mumbling shrink and do you feel *better* about feeling better about refraining. So thank God for His weekly confessional and statistics ('Combien de fois, ma fille?'), and you're *set* for the next week's mortal sin with us, who wouldn't be grateful! Ah, religion—what a tombola! And any sect can play. Any IQ too, for that matter—and the lower the better!"

So childish of him.

Oh of course he was teasing. And after all why *do* people believe in gods when they think magic is silly? So I only said, "Oh Matthew. Why upset people."

—And now was I to hope a brother would be so different? Ah, Robert, what luck for me you were so headlong! For suppose—No. I will not suppose. I am *dis*enthralled.

I opened my eyes and looked at Guy's profile silhouetted against the river of headlights in the opposite lanes, and I thought oh poor sweetie, are the real consequences for you more than me?

'I must come for the whole weekend,' Matthew had said—'not just the damn' bash. He *never* saw enough of me! So come for the weekend? Oh, and Sean of course, bring Sean *too*, he said—*naturally* Sean!' So I said I supposed he meant Guy?

As good as anonymity.

But never to have thought of good-bye that way before?—how couldn't I have, oh how couldn't I! . . .

Ah well.

—The kindest way is probably the way our flitting grandm'mas did it. Mary McCarthy's ladylike 'note on the pin-cushion' for Edmund Wilson for instance was surely the— Oh but wouldn't she have taken her pin-cushion with her? oh dear was it *his*? Of course my good-bye I'll magnet to the ice-box door but the principle's the same: the *kind* way is make it possible for them to be alone when they're told—perhaps especially *we* not witnesses to the insult of our being done with them forever.

So then how am I to put it.

Perhaps what I told Robert?—for I *shall* be taking on a few of Sandra's authors till she's through her stupefying jury duty. And instead of 'a few' I can say 'most'! And I *shall* I expect be overworked.

I could say *Guy sweetie I didn't*— But oh poor darling he deserves better than that! A man I've made love with at least a hundred times? heavens even statistically he deserves better! So for instance *My lovely Guy*, which he *is*, what else have I been living with him for, *My lovely Guy I couldn't bear to tell you and spoil our weekend, but* and then about Sandra and so exhausting would I even be any sleep-with good to him, much less—

Oh but how *awful*, pretending it's just an interlude, if I'm being unfair I can at least be fair about the way I'm being it can't I?—and turn him loose for whoever's next: all those little office groupies I rescued him from are still there aren't they?

—At which point, and I was still gazing at his profile, thinking I'll phone Mummy after breakfast and have her send Bessa to help me pack, goodness by noon I can be gone!—at which point Guy said, "You think Samantha's her real name?—christ she's a Daisy Miller type! Or Fitzgerald's Daisy Buchanan. Or even Edmund Wilson's thought-of Daisy. She comes from *Nebraska!*"

—Oh poor sweet. All that time a false scent? When what was *happening* was, he was losing me? I put my hand on his knee, and let it rest there, till nearly the Tunnel.

✧

But morning as decided on.

And I rang up Gillian too of course and said for a *bit* I was going to be at my number at my mother's in East 11th, so would she deal, herself, with all my calls she possibly could, and those she couldn't, tell I'd call back; and the *smaller* pile of work on the left-hand windowsill with the mockup of the new cover for *Mega-Boy* either on top or near the top would she send down by messenger, with of course anything important that had come in over the weekend, and Sandra should have left two manuscripts for me to take over, so those too.

Gillian said, "Oh dear. Like that?"

I said yes, so would she be helpfully vague also about whether I was back from the weekend.

—Mummy had said *oh dear* too. And not just a maternal reflex: Guy she had thought seriously well of from the first ("—simpatico, darling child, *besides!*").

I was half packed when Bessa arrived, so while she finished I wrote Guy my pin-cushion note. Finally I just said I loved him, but if I stayed on much longer— Only what was *love you* to a man I was walking out on, so I put in *and I adore the way you make love* after it and started over—if I stayed on I was afraid I could become more attached to him than either of us (didn't he think?) would end up wanting, being independent and highly charged as both of us were? and these months with him had been so *especially*— Oh, well, and so on, and instead of the ice-box door I put it on the seat of a chair facing the door in his little hall.

Mummy was gone when we arrived in East 11th. On the phone she'd lamented oh but sweetheart just when she was *helplessly* being lunched uptown? so it was one of her men. But Bessa gave me lunch properly in the garden atrium anyway, a shrimp salad and one of her heavenly mirabelle tarts, and she finished making up my rooms while I fed.

Also, a muscadet I found in the ice-box I opened. So I began to unwind.

I love our tall old-New York house, always it's been home; and now the whole third floor is mine all my things live there even when I'm living away, furniture rugs books everything. Of course Mummy borrows it, when I'm away, for old-friend guests or ex-family like P'pa down from Maine. So I finished unwinding in my own blissful bed again before unpacking and settling in.

But I'd barely begun before she came floating up my stair, great blue eyes and looking-*my*-age as ever.

And so pleasantly delighted with me always— "Oh blessing *here* again how wonderful!—for of course *me* I mean wonderful, but it *can't* love surely have been *all* that shattering happened? a man as beautifully well-brought-up as Guy? oh I won't believe it."

I said well if she wanted a report on *roughly* why—

"Oh but my angel not if it's not *entirely* to your credit and of course it *is*—no but it is so sad, always, isn't it, the sort of thing one has to say, telling them, instead of what really is! Because *exactly* that a mere hour ago I had to face with—though oh dear, Ralph Bispham haven't you I expect *not* met? he's been couldn't-be-love-lier about me for almost two months only now it seems he's all along wanted me to *marry* him, heavens! and could I tell him how, well, 'disillusioning' I suppose isn't the word, it sounds so rude, but it's the *thing*, and here I'd been so *entirely* pleased with him, unsuspecting! And he is a sweet, fifty-four, and a little greying but he's played squash since prepschool, he could hardly *be* more presentable, and now that he's 'of counsel' he doesn't even go downtown unless a case comes in they think will interest him, *ideal* to depend on day in day out. Of course in Italy we were seeing other people too, he has a *very* nice sister in Venice, and I looked up all your father's old friends in Florence, and then we had *fun* showing each other our different Romes. But today—and today he'd said let's try this new La Boum place, if only to find out whether it was the cuisine they meant by it or the décor—why today *again* did he still think my not having started to feel tender about anyone else means I can be talked into *marrying* him?—if nothing else can't they remember how the preliminaries, with them, tended to overlap with whoever it still was? and so the *inevitable* risks if they got to be en titre themselves—and which they *hate*! And when he's been married twice himself it's *scandalous* one can't simply *say* hasn't he learned about captivity?—any more than you I expect said whatever it finally was you couldn't say to Guy, oh *darling* girl it's such a blessing to have you back to talk to again, why don't you just leave your things for Bessa to put away properly, and come down, it's early for drinks but we'll have tea?"

So we did. And presently I told her the roughly-why was I'd met a man I was terrified I might fall badly in love with, he was my novelist Matthew Talley's brother and I was so upset I'd almost decided I'd hand Matthew over to Sandra to edit as soon as she was back from jury duty.

His name was Robert Talley.

He was this brilliant Classics Fellow at the Institute for Advanced Study, in Princeton.

He was just finishing a book on how Athenian foreign policy in the time of Peisistratos led to our having the *Iliad* and the *Odyssey* instead of why not this or that other equally good he said parts of the epic cycle.

Only of course that wasn't what he was like at all.

And, well, what else. Well, I thought he was perhaps thirty-seven. And not a bel homme—oh dear it was bad enough without that! The girl living with him was—

Mummy said oh.

No, *not* 'oh,' Samantha wasn't the trouble, it was he was *after* me, was why I was upset! And the *way* he was after me! He was the sort of— Oh, simply you felt, the way he was, always he'd had us in love with him without lifting a finger, how couldn't he have! so your heart sank. She knew the signs—that disorienting subculture of male that see love as the Daimon women do, so there are no preliminary skirmishes left us: they *know*, and when we meet them, either we take to our heels or Marivaux will be right, nous serons perdues, and not anything like so long as quinze jours après! Risk seeing him again *ever?*—hoh!

Of course she was scandalized. " 'Risk'!" she cried. "My blessed *child* what's happened to your morale!—'not ever again' oh *dear* what a— Never again see a very attractive man *because* very attractive is what he is?"

I was amused. I said but she knew as well as I did what folly it was not to be 'in command' in an affair!

"But sweetheart do you have to be *told* at twenty-what-are-you? you're twenty-*eight?*—have to be *told* a man can be what you shock me by calling 'after' you, without *getting* you, heavens! Wasn't that *I* thought rather dangerous Noel after you? Wasn't Curzio? Were any of them anything but child's play for you? Oh Eve you put me out of *all* patience!"

So how was I to explain.

"Oh darling," I said, "but this wasn't the usual sort of change of lovers, that you see coming and have time to prepare your emotions for—after all, one has been discarding one acquisition for another from the first grubby little second-grader on. And it *is* sad; but then there is always this new enticement—and, well, the first lovely breathlessness at what suddenly you know is going to happen, and the shivery sense that he knows it too, oh dear almost the feel of how it will be to touch him! But this wasn't just another charming marauder, or your senses temporarily—"

"But 'changing' lovers?" she cried at me. "But darling child you're *not* changing! You haven't anyone else! You *can't* just— Oh we have to *discuss* this!"

I said but what happened *happened*—and so suddenly! One minute I was having an entirely beguiling affair, and the next *instant* it was as over and done with as if I were merely remembering this man named Trowbridge from somewhere in my past! and the *shock* of realizing—

Oh but my *blessing* (she wailed) *just* when it was my first night home was she having to abandon me and go dress? with all *this* unsettled and undecided?—and when for all anyone knew making it 'easier' for myself very possibly the *harder* way? but she did have to be à quatre épingles, Henry made such a thing of the ballet, so she— What did I mean 'Who was Henry?' how many men with a name like Henry was one likely to know? "Henry *Laird*, darling, you saw him at our New Year's party, he's six-feet-five and almost as imposing as Mr. Galbraith. Even if not almost as witty—oh dear I'm afraid not *nearly* not-almost-as."

So I spent the evening putting my rooms in order. Peacefully: Guy didn't call. So I was glad for him. Whichever way he was taking it, glad—self-esteem or some instant girl.

I even went to bed having got back the feeling of being selfishly free again.

But it was a long night, and all of it Robert.

Mummy likes good breakfasts if only as foresight, and that morning it was broiled bluefish and bacon, because dear John Rodney was squiring her to Sotheby's and who knew when the bonheur du jour she hoped nobody else wanted would come up, to put between the French windows in the back drawing-room overlooking the garden, instead of that Baltimore card-table—four-leg or five-leg they were never anything but a table, just something to put things *on*, even a light sidechair looked pointless stood by it, so nobody ever sat there, but a bonheur du jour *was* a desk, anyway was seen as, even if not for you to write any very serious-minded letter at, and she would put that little Louis XVI caned chair from her sitting-room at it, she might very well *use* it as a desk, the card-table belonged to my angel of a father anyway, simply he had lct her keep it, borrowed, because he was a sweet—why not go visit *him* if I really meant to stay away from the office for a bit? he adored me, and *no* one had to know where I was. "Except oh sweetheart I can't understand your what am I to call it? your *depriving* yourself?—what are attractive men *there* for! and this brother of Mr. Talley's it sounds especially! darling child I lay awake till *all* hours worrying about you!"

I was amused, I said, "Oh sweetie are you inciting me to delinquency?"

But *love* what a thing to say! All she'd meant was—

I said, "Oh dear how do you put up with such an unwayward daughter," and got up, laughing, and kissed the top of her head, and took myself upstairs to Gillian's bundles.

And worked straight through till tea.

Except that, midmorning, a gentlemanly armful of white roses was delivered, with just his engraved MR. GUY HEREWARD TROWBRIDGE (no message—which was the message), and about four my phone rang and it was Gillian, *accusing.*

"Why didn't you *tell* me what to expect!—*and* what to tell him, heavens!"

I thought but then why on earth the roses? and I said, "'Tell' Guy?" baffled.

She shrieked "'Guy'!" sounding outraged. "Sweetie are you being disingenuous and *ladylike* with me?—Matthew Talley's *brother* is who I'm talking about, what *did* you do to him last weekend!—yesterday morning he rang up *twice* asking when you'd be in, the afternoon? and then again about a quarter to four; and then this morning there he was again at nine-thirty and I nearly rang you to ask what you wanted me to say when he phoned before lunch again, except just before lunch he *appeared!* I was just rushing for an elevator when I heard this man asking that new receptionist was Miss Fremantle in, 'Mr. Talley, tell her,' and I *fled* into the down car!"

I said oh *damn.*

"But do you think *that* was all? heavens, he came back *after* lunch!—which how was I to have expected! what do you *do* to men? I mean you don't seem to do anything at all, you don't make even minimum concessions, you just blithely stand there, *being!* anyway I was just back from lunch when reception rang and would I see a Mr. Talley? and what could I do to protect you but go out and speak to him? Well he isn't your bel homme type but goodness would he ever have to be! but anyway he said he hoped he wasn't being exigent but could I tell him when I expected he might find you in? he of course realized I might feel I had to say I had no idea, but if you were out of town could I give him a general idea of when you might be back? So I said but often editors simply holed up somewhere when they had extra work, and I said about Sandra, but *where* you might have holed up I had no idea, once I remembered you'd taken a huge stack of manuscripts up to your father's in Maine, well what *was* I to say, and *naturally* he looked politely skeptical!"

I said, "At least you didn't I hope tell him tomorrow is staff-meeting day!"

"Heavens, why should I have? Sweetie you *do* sound a-dither— what on earth's happened to you!"

"Oh Gillie," I said, "don't *you* ever now and then feel like a little celibacy too?"

Silence.

But then, "Oh dear, am I perhaps do you mean oversexed?" she giggled. "Oh very well then! but all the same, sweetie, if you're *not* going to use him let me know?"

(Ho, as if she'd asked would I mind, when Matthew gave up on me and took off after her! Oh well, she's so pretty I suppose her affairs confuse her. And she doesn't believe in *living* with a man: so constricting—'the *fuss* there can be about infidelity!')

—Mummy didn't bring her Mr. Rodney back with her. She hadn't got her bonheur du jour: the wretched thing had turned out to be *signed*—and went for eighty-seven thousand, people *totally* out of their minds! I said how high had she been prepared to go? She said oh darling how was *she* to know, anyway she hadn't known it was signed. Would I mind dinner with just her? for this one night? and with why not a bottle of the *good* champagne— she'd called Ralph off, she was beginning to think she was seeing too much of him anyway.

So it turned out we had rather a confiding-things dinner, at one point I think she even came near telling me she sometimes sleeps with P'pa on his visits down from Maine. And I have wondered. Because he *is* charming, and is there some reason one can't with perfect propriety, after a decent interval, have one's divorced husband as a lover now and then? For suppose I ran into Simon somewhere. Though which of them decided to seduce the other? But she did clear it up about that Santa Fe painter *this* year— "Oh sweetheart when I think I even considered marrying the man, next after your adorable father, I can't imagine what I could have been *thinking* of!"

So we had brandies too, and felt very fond of ourselves, in fact when I kissed her goodnight at her bedroom door she was tenderly on the edge of tears about me. "Because this *so* isn't like you, darling girl!—nobody to even take you about? when at a moment's notice you *know* all one needs is a sensible heartlessness if one has to! And didn't Gillian say 'What did you do to the man?' so he's obviously upset too. So he's helpless. And even if he's not, Eve a *little* shouldn't you think what you leave it open to him to suppose about you, with *this* behavior?—he'll simply *guess!*"

I said oh taaah, one sits out a dance now and then.

"But my *love!*" she mourned, "am I really to think this brother of Mr. Talley's has somehow— For how *can* he have so— Well whatever it is he *is* wouldn't it be sensibler to face and oh darling *dispose* of? If only because *not* having one's convenient man, how not risk some perhaps—"

I said as if I'd ever, goodness! But there *there*, I'd sleep on it; and I kissed her good night, patting her, and went on up to bed.

Though once again not to sleep.

For perhaps wasn't she right.

For what had been that teasing *Was I an angel or a woman* of Robert's, there in the darkness of the hall, but as good as blandly telling me he knew what had happened—oh, *coaxing* me, almost, with his sureness of it!—as one practiced marauder to another, even, coaxing! So what possible unbypassed preliminaries was I to pretend there still were, to be ritually gone through?

And anyway the absurdity of what I was doing!—an implausible No about nothing more than a lunch, oh *dear!* Mummy was quite right: what had happened to my morale! Follies we all have—is one to deprive oneself of everything? But *fright?* hoh! And for that matter, Curzio had been as 'dangerous' as Noel, but had that addio been effortless either? Ho, and he had laid siege to my office too.

The easiest place to say an effortless No in this time too. If I decide to.

So at my usual before-nine-ish I trooped out our handsome brass-knockered front door and down our steps so carefree I was nearly at the pavement before I saw that a man leaning in easy elegance against the fender of a double-parked red Porsche, hands in his pockets, morning sun glinting on his fair hair, was—though how could it be?—Robert!

. . . *Here* after me?

And as sure of me as *this?* . . .

For a dizzying moment it was my dismay all over again—and *shock* at myself! Three days, almost, since I'd fled from that dark hall, safe (though, ah, knowing how barely safe!) and was the danger of him as instant still as *this?*

Though what did I mean by 'this'?—and dangerous to what in me? And there he came, *at* me, between the curb-parked cars, tall and straight, smiling, the sun in his blue eyes, on his beautifully trimmed hair, and I thought is it starting *again*, that overrunning of my senses, flooding me with his nearness?

And he was saying, as blandly as if it made sense, Well but we'd been interrupted, hadn't we? so now when *would* I let him feed me lunch?

So thank heaven for a split-second subconscious! (And it *was* preposterous, his being there at all, on this pavement in front of Mummy's!) "Oh *Robert!*" I said, and I could even laugh at him, "what hideous country hour can you have got up! And just to come say *that?* What *is* the matter with you!"

He merely looked amused. And said (as indulgently as if he owned me!—had he *no* idea how he sounded?) 'matter'? my dithering office was the matter—one very pretty young woman had been so frantic, putting him off about me, that so help him she'd tried to convince him I was in Maine!

"But when Robert I *told* you!" I said. "I am busy! And anyway you *know* better!—catnip if you like, even quite lovely catnip, but surely you're not turning whatever it was into a *pursuit!*"

He said, laughing, ah but dammit, what else *was* that whatever-it-was!

I said, "But why should I have lunch with you at all!"

What was he asking me to have lunch with him *for* but to (he hoped) find out? But ah look, was there anything against arguing about it (if I *had* to) in comfort in his car? while he drove me up-town? instead of on this pointless Village sidewalk? And held out a cajoling hand for my briefcase.

Oh well why fuss. I said, "From Maine or not?" and let him take it; and we went around his car and he handed me in, and off we went into the shimmer of city morning.

—I leaned my head back against the seat and looked at his profile, wondering how long would I remember it like this, my every haunted sense remembering. Profile it had been, coming back from the pantry. Yes, and at the folly, watching him watch

Samantha picking her way through the ferns of his forest ride, waving to him, laughing, as she came. Though then it had been his left profile, not this. But the sun flecking his long lashes then too.

Ah, and when to think perhaps I have only to turn and *say*—for my enchanted fingers to rove and discover and memorize and *have* this male body that is so elegantly understating what it knows it is, oh the *luxury* of you, Robert, why am I commanding myself not to, why *not* think 'perhaps just this one time. . . .'

We stopped for Fifth Avenue.

So till the light changed, I said, "But how long were you going to absurdly wait there, in front of my m'ma's?"

'Absurd'?—here I was, wasn't I?

I said, "Well but *how* long?" Which of course was just teasing.

And of course he just snorted; and the light changed, and we turned downtown and to the light at 10th.

He said amiably, "You might decently have expected me! *I* knew what was happening to me five minutes after we met, Friday—and how long was it before your angel antennae had picked it up? You pretending you don't remember how suddenly *careful* with me, how méfiante, you became? Dear god I was light-headed at your lovely carefulness!"

"Oh dear," I said, "you sound like Matthew."

'*Matthew*'!

"But why should I think you so different?" I said, laughing at him. "Are you behaving as if you took women seriously either? He really just likes our décor—you know?—and whichever of us happens to come with it? anyhow, the way he thinks she is, with!" (The light changed, and we turned into East 10th.) "We're this adorable ballet for him. But does one have to be a ballerina on demand? And why should I want to be 'adored,' heavens!"

But what tirade was this? he said, sounding amused. When all he'd done was ask me to have lunch with him? . . .

"Oh but then Robert you *know* then another lunch," I said. "And then lunch again. And then again, and so on as long as it turned out to take?—till I was dessert? Oh Robert of *course* how flattering, who wouldn't be touched! And by such constancy of purpose! But, well, 'constancy'?—my dear man there *is* Samantha!"

We stopped for the light at University Place, and he looked at me. "I shouldn't have thought Samantha was the difficulty at all," he said coolly.

"Oh Robert what does it matter what either of us thinks?" I said. "You aren't going to throw the child out are you! So what am I to think you have in mind?—a 'selective infidelity' shall I call it? Sweetly ad hoc? Just for *me?*"

So the light changed, and we turned uptown. Silent. Until almost 14th Street, silent.

Then he said, soberly, "You are all temptations, once one learns how sweet you are. But *you?*— My lovely thing, are people like you and me to conduct this cockeyed argument as if either of us thought a word like 'practical' had anything to do with what's happened? Samantha you know damn' well I've no intention— I may not have a respectably stuffy sense of responsibility, but I do go through the motions like a gent. Men and women are étapes for each other, and I'm still one of Samantha's. And on your side of the random decencies, Trowbridge is at any rate 'there,' isn't he, one way or another?"

"Oh Robert," I said, and laughed, "do you think *listing* my reasonable objections before I've had a chance to, *disposes* of them? hoh!"

"But *Samantha* one of them?" he said.

I thought But do you expect me to say she isn't?

"Because ah, anyway, dammit," he cried, "what *is* this? Lady-like disingenuousnesses one's been long taught one puts up with. And coquetry's part of the enchantment. But *this?*—you're not even taking an honest pursuit under advisement! Good god, as things go between a woman and a man, you're not even being civil!"

(. . . and of course it was true.)

"So then what way *is* it you're behaving!" he demanded.

—I looked at his profile and thought But mightn't you have guessed?—since you're so serenely sure you know 'what's happened' anyway? How am I to say it but how it is. I am Me! I never want not to be! *Nothing* have I ever wanted more than being me! But suppose I began to find I wanted you more. And do I have to tell a marauder like you how easy that could be?—the special danger of you is that you know how easy! So am I to risk everything I am? Is that so hard for of all men *you* to understand?

—Oh but I thought But make a *manifesto* of it?—he'd simply laugh at me: *Was I saying he was so God help him attractive to me that he frightened me* off? *What fabulous feminine encoding was this?*

And anyhow leading to what? A dozen blocks more and he will pull in at my building, and turn to me, and what do I do? Because *not* have decided—about a *lunch?*

—But to go to pieces about it? Am I to mumble a wretched 'I ought never to have kissed you, oh Robert forgive me?' scrambling out clutching my briefcase like a schoolgirl? For simply he could say, 'Frights one gets over—but what if neither of us gets over the rest of it?' And what would I do?—flee, choking, into the soaring cathedral of our building's lobby, tasting my tears?

Oh *dear* what a Henry James thought-up of a scenario! How Simon would have teased me. . . .

—Yes, well, but sensibly, then?

'Practically,' even, what. Since Robert knows.

Oh well since both of us know!—are we experienced marauders or aren't we?

Because about Samantha he must know even better. I mean *I* said good-bye to Simon after two years. As doesn't one expect to? Even if it's special and will always be. Just it's . . . become affection? And Simon knew: it was I felt him knowing made me see I did too. And Samantha—well, graduation is a rite de passage too. Not that faithful or unfaithful has anything to do with it. *That* wasn't why I left Guy!

For are you *truly*, Robert, 'dangerous,' or just 'against my better judgment'?

Which isn't the same category of thing at all. And has an escape-clause. Of a sort.

Or could have.

But how would that leave him any the less dismayingly attractive?—or me *not* in this lovely tumult still, this disarray, flooded with the mere nearness of him. And what if one may not always have Mummy's 'sensible heartlessness' at one's fingertips! Oh Robert no wonder you don't believe I mean it!—do I believe it either?

Or heavens should I let you *have* your lunch, to *show* you I mean it!

—We were at 53rd Street. Four more blocks to argue in, but the argument is in feelings, not words. Even if even marauders never quite outgrow thinking it is blandishments cajole us.

"Oh Robert," I said, almost laughing, "how badly do I have to treat you to make you give up!"

AS I SAUNTERED OUT, ONE MIDCENTURY MORNING . . .

Un homme naît duc, millionnaire, pair de France;
ce n'est pas à lui à examiner si sa position est
conforme ou non à la vertu, au bonheur général
et autres belles choses.
—STENDHAL, *Lucien Leuwen*

I both loved and admired my Uncle John Coates, and if the family deprecated the way he lived, and frequently said so, it was for Old Philadelphia reasons I never thought anything but absurd: what if he did 'live abroad,' and 'unproductively'? Cousin Edmund Kennet's adjective for him, 'unprincipled,' was even sillier: all it meant was, Uncle John spent money in ways, and in sums, that old clubmen like Cousin Edmund find outrageous ("Other men's wives, for instance!—cost you *any* figure!"). And what was left of Uncle's money why leave to *me*, namesake or not—distaff-side nephews too, weren't there? Family money was *family* money!

It is true, Uncle John was only my father's half-brother. And he did, I admit, see to my bringing-up, after my parents' deaths, sometimes from a considerable distance. But Rome or the south of France, he did a good affectionate job of it: I always felt he was *there*. Holidays, he always was; and in the long happy summers he'd have me with him here at 'Byberry,' with his horses to exercise, and our endless woods to explore and shoot at squirrels in, and, later, the instructive babble of parties and house parties I was allowed to appear at. Above all, perhaps, in all those years I don't remember a single stuffy or officious lecture; indeed the only time he took more of a hand in my life than I felt was fair, was his blandly decreeing I was to go to the French Riviera with him, the summer after I finished at Penn Charter.

That had *not* been my plan for the summer! A beguiled girl of mine was to have her m'ma invite me to their summer place in Maine in July, and another, hers to theirs, in Rhode Island, in August. A couple of weeks each, and I was looking forward to the tranquillity of one at a time, after the impromptus and improvisations of Main Line logistics. But my uncle said, firmly, yes, well, but a flattering supply of East Coast prepschool girls was only *one* of the amenities of Western Civilization. There were others, for the most part less single-minded, and one or two of them I could do with more exposure to than I'd so far had. He could hardly, come September, abandon me on a sociological midden like Princeton these days, in a state to cause comment on his guardianship! My manners were adequate; they were even, he felt, a sound start; but they could still benefit (I mind his saying?) from a couple of civilizing months among his friends and summer neighbors on Cap Nègre. I was a bit cocky for eighteen anyway; I could do with a little random civilizing. Also it would straighten up my French.

Do me no harm, either, come to think of it, if I picked up a little polite Italian too. There were always agreeable estatanti at the Cap, idle bel mondo creatures who'd be amused indulging a presentable boy's ungrammar. Usually played good tennis these days too. And their husbands only came up, from Rome or Milan, weekends. For all I know he may even have had Carla Montaperti in mind.

There anyway in the rich villa beyond ours she was, and from the moment my uncle took me there and presented me I was lost to every amenity of his Western Civilization but her. I remember that morning in happy detail still—the long driveway curving in through a taillis of mimosa and cedar and bougainvillea, the sun-blaze on the cobbled forecourt and the white villa among its soaring pines, the maggiordomo's respectful familiarities to my uncle in the porte-cochère ("Monsieur s'en souviendra—Madame ne se lève toujours pas de bon matin!"), the cool formal rooms he led us to the garden terrasse through, and then at last—oh god even the way she moved stopped my breathing!—this unbelievable Botticelli loveliness springing up from her breakfast table with little jewelled cries of welcome, to come laughing toward us through the soft summer morning, slender and tall, hands outstretched to my smiling uncle.

(But to me *too?* . . . I might have been my uncle's contemporary, so like the way she greeted him did it seem to me she greeted me. Somehow she didn't notice I was only a boy, six-foot-two or not? And her wide eyes, for that long moment straight into mine— could I have put it to myself, in my innocence then, that a, well, that a Grown Woman had in my *life* never looked at me that way before? . . .)

She clapped her hands for fresh coffee; and as the maggior-domo served us I listened, dazzled, tranced, to the lilting bel canto of her Cap news for my uncle—who had come since he left, who hadn't yet, and ho, the scandal of who wouldn't be coming at all ("—*bolted* wiz him, caro! To Algiers—imagine! Ahi, madonna, if she *had* to have an affetto, where were *you*—vergogna!"), my uncle snorting, amused.

But most of what they said I find I have little memory of. I was in such a state of awe at how beautiful she was that I may not even have heard it. I felt—how describe an epiphany!—I felt I had never, till now, even *imagined* what woman's loveliness could be—and not just could be, but holy god there before my eyes *was!* By what dizzying benevolence of Mediterranean divinities was *I* in this Presence?—and I was going to be, all summer! And she was saying to my uncle, in a voice like a caress, but this very afternoon we must come, she was having a tennis, what a pleasure to have him back!—e questo Apollino di nipote, why had he never told her he had nephews even handsomer than he? . . .

She played good tennis; everybody did. But her elegance in white tennis-shorts turned my blissful awe into a kind of happy despair—for how can you ever put into words, even to yourself, the adoration it undoes you with! By the time Uncle and I left, I felt I was hers for life.

And that night I lay awake into the summer dawn, thinking of how her dark eyes had looked at me (because *how?*), of the tone of her voice saying ciao—could it be she was even deciding she *liked* me? Or had she only picked me for a doubles partner for my uncle's sake?—because all of them, not just she, had been kind, including me in their swift French gossip at the courtside. She was nearly thirty, Uncle had said: God help me, why should she espe-cially notice me at all?

Still, when we left, she had said I must come *every* day if I liked—she'd known my incantatore of an uncle for years! I must use her pool, too, did I take anglosaxon early dips? or even not-so-early?—simply come through the pinewood between our villas, sans façon. . . . Before at last I daydreamed myself to sleep I vowed I *would* go for early dips, if only to prove how I adored her! That I adored her with a mixture of wonder and exaltation that amounted to innocence, never crossed my mind.

So things took a certain time. I went to tea as well as to tennis; and with my uncle, to lunch. She sunbathed an afternoon hour by the pool with me; it became almost natural to talk to her. She was sweetly amused at my Beginning Italian; as part of it I graduated to calling her Carla. My uncle gave a supper-dance for weekending husbands, and I danced with her five times, so confused by how unbelievably her ballerina body handed itself over to mine that I almost overcame my agonized dread of boring her. I memorized the second person singular of fifty Italian verbs, for daydream dialogue.

So, all told, it took a good fortnight.

Then, one afternoon, a sudden shower scratched the tennis. Ma poi? I could stay for tea, it was even a weather for my lamentable Italian—senti, I could read aloud to her, and she correct me, vorrei? So presently there we were, on the long couch in the salotto, I obediently stammering Pirandello dialogue for her at one end, she lolling among the cushions at the other, the soft murmur of summer rain beyond the open French windows like a counterpoint to the soft Tuscan vowels of her voice correcting me. What I was reading, who cared!—it was her voice saying it, sounding amused, that my mind was on. Ah, and with her attention on *me*, if only for a quarter of an hour, who was Pirandello!

But after a bit I began to think she was correcting me less often: was I doing better? or was she just indulging me? But it struck me I hadn't noticed her correcting me for *some time* now—oh god was this boring her after all? and I looked up from the Pirandello, *stricken*.

But she was gazing at me with no particular expression, in silence. So was I to go on with the stuff? Or was it basta? . . . But the silence went on so long that perhaps was I to *ask* which? and so, finally, I mumbled what I thought was a blameless ". . . Cosa?"—and (thunderstruck!) found myself *told*.

"*You* ask 'what'?" she said gently. "Do you not think it is I who might? Ho, am I to see you are in love wiz me and *not* wonder why you are afraid I should be cross wiz you, that you do not say it?"

. . . She knew?

The sacred, the *unsayable*, taboo of my adoring her put into *words*? I gaped at her, stiff with horror.

"Do you think it is not charming, a man who pleases you, in love wiz you?" she asked, as if tenderly reproaching me. "And if also he is handsome, one is unmoved?"

(But was I supposed— God help me, were you expected to *know* what to say?)

"But wiz your little American girls you have made love, no?" she asked, softly. "Ebbene, wiz your first one how did you begin? Did you think *she* would be 'cross' wiz you?"

('Begin'?—did *I* know? Somehow a girl sort of— I mean exactly *how* a girl— Look, it was an *atmosphere!*)

But she had uncoiled from her cusions; she was ending it. "Madonna, what was the poor girl to make of you, your little first one?—vergogna!" she gently mocked me, and stood up to go. But when I scrambled to my feet, wordless with anguish, "Bello as *you* you think saying 'I love you' can ever be a disobligeance?" she said, eyes straight into mine—and took the Pirandello from my incompetent hands, turned on her heel, and was gone.

I was dazed. Was I supposed to leave? or helplessly stay! Was she *rebuking* me?—because good god if I was supposed to ask her to forgive me, what was I to ask her to forgive me *for*? What could I do?—but in sheer misery tag after her, across the hall into her piccolo salotto.

Where she turned to confront me so abruptly I almost ran into her. "Ho, *now* you come after me, capriccioso mio!" she said. "Ma di grazia, what am I to do wiz you?"—and with one step she was against me (this was *happening?*—to ME?) and her hands slid under my arms and up, and closed over my shoulders as if forever, and there was her mouth coming up for mine. The last thing I remember thinking was a wild *She* MEANS *it?*—and then I was gone, into the maelstrom.

—I came to, being grazingly kissed more or less all over, in the softest bed I'd ever lain in. *This* was Reality? . . . Between stunned disbelief, helpless gratitude (though to Whom?), the simpleminded pagan delight throbbing along my arteries, and a total astonishment at what the logistics must have been, I was beyond speech. It was a thunderbolt: *this*, then, here in my dazzled initiate's arms, *this* was what a woman could be? . . . I must, I suppose—if only because what could a mere adolescent say!—I must have groaned aloud, for the kissing stopped, and there was her face above me, gazing down with a sort of teasing indulgence: madonna, did I require explanations *too?* But then, simply, "Dunque!" she said, soberly, and kissed my eyes; and so it began.

Yet what I *was*, was bewildered. Was I to take it that I had (God knows how!) 'seduced' this adorable Woman? . . . Sociologically speaking, somehow *I* was the lover of a femme du monde? . . . Girls slept I knew with older men—but the other way round too? . . . . No, but *Carla* 'older'?—this angelic body had felt and tasted and murmured and (so help me!) *behaved* the way my Main Line loves' had, hadn't it? It was past belief lovelier and more knowing, god *yes*, but what it had *done* was, well, recognizably the same sort of thing. And what had 'age' to do with this sunburst of the senses!

All of which must have shown in my face, for suddenly she was amused at me: "Ahi, the time I have had wiz you! So slow, so innocent?—when there I was for you? And what was I there for you *for*, timido mio!" Had I put my little Americans to the trouble I'd put her to? Or were the little stupids helpless themselves! Had they taught me nothing at all? Madonna, che nazione d'incapaci! . . .

—So mean it she did?

And with a sweet violence it had never occurred to me making love could be? I took a long breath and, half fearful still, worshipingly pulled her down. For hours.

—Of course at last I was indulgently kissed and sent home. "Ma si, idiot of a cuore mio! ma come vuoi che resti?—out of the blue am I to tell my people I am dining alone wiz a bellino like you?—and gazing across the table at me like at me now? hah!" *No*, and what made me suppose I might come back after dinner either, had I no sense of le buone creanze? No!

I said, humbly, all I meant was, once the servants—

Soprattutto not then!

But just to say good night? I *swore* I'd only—

Macchè 'good night'! Was she to decide I was a bore as well as a golosino?—va via va *via!*

('Greedy'!—after such a feast? And who was it had fed me every mouthful!)

But now at least I knew where her bedroom was, and which were its windows and which her dressing-room's—so *macchè* to that macchè of hers! was I *not* to say good night (I almost said aloud as I wandered blissfully home along the evening voie)—not even a chaste good night to a Being who had changed the world for me, good god?

For what if I— For *suppose* around (say) midnight— For would she *really* not expect me?

So suppose there *was* a light in one of her windows. And I stood outside and tapped on the pane. After *this afternoon* wouldn't she at least— But holy god *anyway* what would she think of me if I didn't even try!

. . . But wait *till* midnight? Uncle had dinner at nine; unless we had invités we'd finish by ten-fifteen. And with no invités he might take off for the Casino. No but if Carla had dinner at nine, her servants wouldn't have cleared up and gone to bed before ours. And what if Uncle suggested backgammon? . . .

But if I waited too long I might find she'd oh god gone to bed hours ago! . . .

So in short when at last I slipped out the French windows of my room into the soft summer night, in a total fume between dithering hope and helpless forebodings, the moon was long set, and the path through the dark pinewood I stumbled along was such a tunnel of shadows that twice I thought I'd lost my way. But now, when I came out at the forecourt, the dusky radiance of starlight lay over everything—I could be goddammit *spotted* crossing! So round back of the villa? servants' wing or not? I cut along the edge of the pinewood, and down across the lower garden, and then, holding my breath, back up, under the towering pines on the villa's far side, the starlight only here and there a dark brilliance sifting down. Only then did I realize I had never been this side of the villa at all.

But I knew *roughly* how far in from the front Carla's rooms ought to be, didn't I? And if there *was* a light, at this hour, it could only be hers. I rounded the bay of the biblioteca, almost willing to hope.

And oh benedizione d'Iddio, a light there was!—a glow, at least, behind the drawn curtains of the French window nearest me. I was *not* too late!

But what if it was only a night-light? Her bedroom, I remembered, had three windows; had the dressing-room only one? But *all* the windows toward the front were dark; if the light was a night-light, I *was* too late.

But those next three I saw were open a slot, on the espagnolette. Did Europeans sleep with their windows like that, or shut? (God *blast* the things I didn't know!) But then, nearer, I saw the long curtains were still looped at the sides, *not* drawn—God bless!—in fact gods of the lovely Mediterranean bless!—she hadn't gone to bed yet after all? I drew a long, shivery breath (Dei del Mezzogiorno siatemi di buona voglia!) and tapped on the nearest dark pane.

And waited.

. . . Hadn't I tapped hard enough? What *was* a proper mean between a (hardly unjustified) expectation and a (oh god unthinkable!) presumption? I tapped again, a bit more daringly.

What happened next I suppose I was in too wild a turmoil for a clear account now. The light went out in the dressing-room. But that may not have been right away, and I'm not sure how soon afterwards I heard the clank of an espagnolette-bolt at the dark French window next beyond me. I do know, though, that I got there just as she threw both tall casements open, and stepped across the sill and confronted me, silent. She had something filmy and white on; she must have been brushing her hair, for it was tumbling loose over her bare shoulders; perhaps she was barefoot? for I remember she seemed somehow less tall than I had expected. But what her expression was, what mood I was finding her in, her eyes were too deep in a midnight of shadows to tell. Ah, and anyway!—beauty like hers, in starlight? I wasn't just struck dumb, I was transfixed!

And God help me, when finally she spoke, it was in *Italian!* It must have been something like Non serve a niente dirti, no? but all I might have understood was that cascade of negatives if my despairing ear hadn't caught the lilt of (Could it *be?* . . . Those ancient Divinità had *no kidding* intervened? . . .) the lilt of a sweet amusement in the mocking "Ma che foga!" that followed. But was she mocking me? Or just teasing? (But how did you ever *know!*) No telling *what* simple-minded thing I mightn't have done, if suddenly—holy god was she *unbuttoning my shirt?* And laughing at me: "What if I hadn't given you till midnight, vergognoso mio?" and all I could do was helplessly mumble her name as she ripped the last button and jerked my shirt up and out and back over my shoulders and down my arms and *off*—and from then on I find I don't remember the logistics this time either.

—So we both soon took to sleeping late, mornings.

Four times, too, before the end of summer, my uncle went for a night or two to Rome, and the villa, with his blessing, was *mine!* I could have Carla to dinner, and to stay on; we could *really* sleep together; wake together, and make sleepy love before I saw her home—carried her, once!—through the pinewood in the first grey light, watching till she'd slipped in at her French window, safe, and blown me her a rivederci kiss. Love even took over Beginning Italian: was she to put up wiz a lover who pronounced it no better than he pronounced French? so there tra zuffe I'd be, on a footstool by her bed, stammering out the amorous vowels and consonants of a Moravia seduction scene, while she followed the page over my shoulder, gurgling at my mistakes, her breath warm on my cheek, the loveliest breasts in Western Civilization against my naked back. Or there would be a little explosion of amusement: Dio what was I doing wiz my lips to make such barbarian sounds! —and I would be commanded to turn my head and watch *her* say it the way a Tuscan Iddio intended it to be said!—and there would be her mocking lips and curling tongue-tip, not ten inches from mine.

But I learned, too, and early, the outrage a husband is. Baldassare's first weekend up from Rome, it's true, making love with Carla was still so new and a miracle that I was humble (di molto!) to think of anything but envying him. For what rights had I?—and he was a charming and witty man! By his second weekend (*many* more proofs of her béguin for me later) my confidence was back to normal, yes, but now I was embarrassed by—so to speak—the discourtesy of what I was doing to a perfectly decent man, and a friend of my uncle's besides. Carla's being older than I was even made it more man-of-the-worldly regrettable of me somehow— had I really good god grown up? . . . Well, I found I *had*, by the third weekend: not only was Baldassare an intruder, but his damned air of ownership enraged me—once, that weekend, she very nearly sent me home, and for three days, afterwards, she refused even to let me touch her hand. The fear of God is the beginning of manners.

All the more inevitably, then, at the end of summer, parting from her was a corollary that left me half-stunned with grief. Indeed, that final night before my uncle put me aboard the Train Bleu for Paris and Princeton, the alternating agonies of adoration and despair that Carla tenderly saw me through were pure Romantisme: Constant to Musset (dear god, I might've been *inventing* the course!) and the abandon she consoled me with, the fiery sweetness, Stendhal himself could hardly have found short of the transports sensibility required. Day was breaking before at last I could make myself go: the first cool shadows of dawn lay already across the lawns as Carla saw me off from the porte-cochère—poised there in the greying light, one slender hand resting against a pillar, the other clutching the slipping silks of her vestaglia to her breast, till at the curve of the drive I should turn (as how often, before!) for a last blown kiss and wave of the hand. Ah, but turn, *this* time (I said to myself, wretchedly) for perhaps the last time ever? I even muttered it, for more doleful effect still, in the language she had taught me love in—l'ultima volta? che mai della vita mia la vedrò? . . . But turn of course I did; I was helpless not to; she blew me her kiss—with both hands, laughing as the vestaglia slithered open—and what could I do but turn, to my doom, away, to stumble out, choking, through the grilled lodge-gates, and along the voie in the first lovely stillness of summer morning, dazed, to my uncle's slumbering villa, and bed.

Onto which I tumbled, haggard with self-pity, and fell instantly asleep.

—In an hour, of course, Uncle was gently shaking me awake: had I forgot we had all our good-bye calls to make before Toulon and the train?

I gaped at him; even bleary with sleep, I was appalled! Go through that anguish all *over* again?—put *Carla* through it?—tarnish such a memory with drawing-room pastiche? . . . Yes but—instead?—blurt it out to my uncle that we'd already *said* good-bye? affronting his good manners by making him take notice of what, all these weeks, he had been so blandly and affectionately blind to? . . . Letting anyone suppose *any* woman was your mistress was God help me bad enough, but expose *Carla* to such a charade? before a man who'd held her in civilized esteem for years? Yes, and why wouldn't she assume *I had told* Uncle?—I, who'd have died first! I was *doomed* by the mere dilemma of my consequences!

And this was *Europe*, and I was my uncle's guest as well as his nephew: in Europe, for all I knew, seducing your host's neighbor's wife was held to be the last, the unthinkable, discourtesy!

But my uncle—I was thunderstruck!—seemed to take it all for said! Come, come, what was the matter with me? Did I think a woman who was pleased with you didn't make it easy? *Of course* I was to come prendre congé with him, dans les formes! The most tenderly private addio in the world didn't excuse not calling as manners require: in usage there are *no* substitutions! All I need do was behave myself. Dammit I'd had six weeks of as elegant an attention as Iddio was likely to indulge a man with in a life-time—and I was *sorry* for myself? *No!*—we would go make our adieux to Signora Montaperti exactly as to all the other donne who had been kind to us. "And why the devil shouldn't you behave convenevolmente?—*she* will!"

As she of course did. And at least I managed to only gaze at her, numb, and listen, more dead than alive, to the effortless bel canto of her good-byes to my uncle. Also, at the end, I bowed over her hand and kissed the air an inch above her cool fingers as taught to, and followed my uncle, wordless, out through those rooms of my memory and away, off to our other calls—off forever, without a look behind.

—So I suppose it can be said that, in the immemorial tribal way, Uncle John left me the essential traditions of tribal comportment, and the tribal opinions and perquisites that established them to start with, as well as more money to maintain them—as

Cousin Edmund might put it, 'what it is expected of thee thee will expect.'

One of course chooses, among these formidable structures. I don't, for example, live abroad. Nor, again, am I unproductive: I am a political journalist, and known. But most of my uncle's traditions I have dutifully or gratefully taken to heart. In particular, this Bucks County place, which we've had from almost Penn-grant times, I have as deep an affection for as he had. And why should I not have taken his view—certainly it has been my own experience—that women are perhaps at their happiest when they're being volage: every new falling in love, with its sudden blinding bliss of *freedom*, renews their happiest illusions too. (Nor, as Uncle amiably put it, need any very great social disaster follow—"God bless, if the angel's scruples stop working, can't yours take over?")

But that freshman autumn his example wasn't of much good to me. He had sympathetically overseen my being taught an advanced lesson in what a woman in love can be, and (up to a point) how to behave to her; but how to get over her he had left to the grandeurs et misères of Darwinian chance. And no doubt on purpose, for how otherwise couldn't he have foreseen that the standard Ovidian remedy, a new girl, might *not* work? Princeton weekends offered me new girls immediately—but sua quemque moratur cura, says Propertius, 'each keeps his own distraction still,' and Carla had plundered my senses once for all.

I doubt whether even Uncle, though, had imagined what a disconcerting dilemma, in consequence, I now found my Penn Charter loves. Both were now in college themselves, and naturally I had to have each in turn for a football weekend; but how avoid what might damn well happen then? God help me, my category wasn't prepschool boyfriend *now!*—I was an experienced *lover*, the experience moreover a full-scale Mezzogiorno passion, and how could their memories of how I had been not shock them with my difference?—and each, helplessly, not interpret it as a difference about *her*, and be wounded and outraged? Up from Goucher or down from Vassar, I would meet them at the Junction; there would be the happy rush into my arms, the shining eyes—but then what?

It turned out to be even more harrowing than feeling badly about them: I was made to feel *guilty!* Because why was I so strange? "You don't even kiss the way you used to! You don't do *any* of our things the same! Oh Johnnie you used to be so sweet, and now I don't know *what* you want! And I was so— I thought we'd—" and humiliated tears. But Goucher *fury:* "Why did you

ask me at all! I don't know and I don't care, but I *believed* it was just
your stupid uncle kept you from visiting me! And all summer long
I thought about seeing you again, hah!"—and dressed again in a
fume, and packed her bag then and there, and had a *taxi* drive her
to the train. . . .

Man's fate: doing what was expected of me I was a low swine,
and denounced!

Yet what could I have done! I had 'felt badly,' whatever that
meant; I had perhaps been (that neat Quaker term) 'unkind'; had I
also been that fashionable literary uncastigation, 'corrupt'? (How
high-minded, how apodeictic, how weighty and status-conferring,
how Jamesian a chiding the term has become since then—it
almost calls for a rotunda for its echoes to resound in!) Yet all I'd
done was learn to be *better* with them! I'd disillusioned them, yes;
and I'd learned it elsewhere; but for the long run what was more
necessary for a girl, or more useful? Disillusionment was part of
maturity! What were they fussing about?

So by the Christmas deb dances I was a little disillusioned
myself, and my heart wasn't even cynically in it. I was desolate: I
was *in mourning* for Carla. There were of course girls, in quantity,
with no nostalgia whatever for my lost innocence, and who even
seemed charmed with me as I was, but were mortals to console
me for a lost goddess? I think all that saved me from a full-dress
Romantisme melancholy was my uncle's taking a hard look at me
at Christmas, and coming up with a serious distraction, if not a
cure—why didn't I consider moving to the old 'dower house' here
at Byberry, had I forgot it was barely a half-hour's drive now from
Princeton? *Sell* Chestnut Hill, he meant, and move here for good;
I already had my father's half-ownership hadn't I? so why not enjoy
it? He'd send me an admirable local woman, a Mrs. Grammace,
to cook-housekeep for me. God bless, I'd always loved the place,
hadn't I? Look, I could even move in in the midwinter break. Be
settled by Easter! How about it?

So I did. Byberry had meant 'home' to me, after all, from my
childhood summers on; and now it soon began to mean this stone
house in from our 'river-road' entrance, low-ceiling'd and ancient
enough to have been the original messuage (though first houses
must have been timber)—a handsome old house, barely modernized at all; nor has the barn been, except for loose boxes instead
of stalls; beautiful eastern Pennsylvania pointed stonework it too.
Landsdown the estate-manager and his sister had lived there when
I was little; in fact my mother had driven me over with her on

some errand to them the first time I think I ever saw my uncle: he'd come looking for her, just back from a long stay abroad; I couldn't've been more than four. So, partly perhaps the simple-minded comfort of returning to a childhood landscape, partly the pleasure of entering physically upon my inheritance—even the mere being busy, moving in—whatever it was that lightened my heart, my uncle's concern for me had found it. 'The dower house' may have been the family name for it, but a flitting Bryn Mawr girl helped me rechristen it 'the garçonnière' that Easter vac, and in due course a good quarter of my undergraduate weekends I spent there. If it turned out some angel still needed courting, I had Uncle's permission to put her up (with his housekeeper for property chaperone) in the 1790-ish brick elegance of his 'new' house, a mile or so through the woods, in from the lodge entrance on the Newtown side.

It, properly speaking, was 'Byberry.' It had brick-walled formal gardens off one wing, and a box maze and a water-stair off the other, the stables and paddock and carriage-house fanning out toward the green labyrinth of the woods behind. (Why it was called 'Byberry' no one knew. We were nowhere near Byberry Meeting. Had some marauding ancestor married a Byberry Meeting girl, and in infatuation let her name it?) Technically it had been my father's and my uncle's, but it had always been treated as a 'family' house, for the use of any of us. My stately Great-Aunts Emmeline and Amanda, for instance, had for most of a lifetime made its tall cool rooms their annual refuge from the heat of Philadelphia summers; no doubt it would have been they who said to my mother, that year I was four, 'Why doesn't thee just bring that little boy of thine *here* with thee, away from it.' And certainly my father and my uncle, in their own Princeton days, would have used it as a private maison de passe themselves—even a very recalcitrant girl would have been helplessly impressed. Though in those days you got there by Washington's Crossing.

Still, by the end of my freshman year, I had also settled into the normal amenities of a Princeton undergraduate, conceding girls their ladylike Yes or No, and then, as my roommate Hank Talbot put it, 'expanding the perimeters of permission.' Summer was back to normal too—house parties in July in Edgartown and Harwich Port and on one of those little four-acre granite islands off Maine you have to rowboat water to; and part of August as crew on the Talbots' big ketch, cruising up port by port around Grand Manan and back, living on lobster picnics and the last sweet strawberries,

with the temporary adoration of Hank's kid sister as spiritual en-
richment. A *good* summer; but back at Princeton for sophomore
autumn, I decided Byberry was more my sort of thing.

Not that a Byberry weekend was always easy to find Princeton
time for. For one thing, I'd gone out for the *Prince*, and the competition was talented and hardworking. I did end up think-piece
editor, senior year, but a satisfying Byberry Friday-through-Sunday
by then was rare. Besides, the senior-thesis topic I'd picked for its
being about Bucks County—the farm-foreclosure revolts there, in
the Depression—turned out to be fascinating in itself: what our
Bucks County politicians had imagined was happening, and the
wild swings of what they thought of as their plans for dealing with
what they imagined, I decided were in fact a parody, in miniature,
of American foreign policy from the days of my fellow-alumnus
Dulles '08. My conclusion, accordingly, was a sardonic fundamental that Aristotle had (naturally) overlooked: political blundering is a constant, because an electorate of simpletons cannot elect
politicians smart enough to deal with the behavior of the simpletons who elect them. My department pleasantly surprised me with
a 1+ and a magna; but it had taken a *lot* of time from Byberry and
girls.

But also, by senior year, I had begun to find myself thinking,
Byberry weekends, of Carla—*baffling*, for surely, by then, oughtn't
I to have become as contented with American college girls as if I'd
never known anything else? I had recognized myself, a little, in
Diderot's self-portrait I'd happened on in French 306:

. . . j'ai un coeur et des yeux, et j'aime à voir une jolie femme, j'aime à
sentir sous ma main la fermeté et la rondeur de sa gorge, à presser ses
lèvres des miennes, à puiser la volupté dans ses regards, et à en expirer
entre ses bras

—and, well, I had eyes and a heart myself, hadn't I? But by senior
year my Byberry girls tended to be three years older too, they were
so to speak turning into women, lovemaking no longer the romp
and scamper of their rite de passage; they had even begun to wonder whether perhaps what they were after was—if not quite the
primitive grandeurs of Love itself—at least some semblance of,
well, of *love*. There was a sweetness about them now; a simple tender phrase could bring their arms round my neck. It was touching.
And I do have eyes and a heart; it would have been very easy to be
overcome.

Yet what it seemed to do was bring back an ache of longing for Carla I'd have sworn I'd lived my way through long since. Sometimes a girl murmuring her contentment in my arms could almost seem to mock me with her difference from my senses' memories— the difference perhaps no more than Diderot's 'feel of her round breast in my hand.' Or I'd find myself forgetting the girl altogether, my mind so bemused that I *was* at the Cap that long-vanished summer again, reliving it, scene by scene, from the unknown goddess coming smiling to greet my uncle in the blaze of Mediterranean morning, to the last laughing kiss a nightlong mistress had blown me, that dawn-shadowed ultima volta of my despair. What kind of cockeyed heartlessness *was* this, to girls who'd at the very least had the good manners to behave as if they wanted me as much as I'd said I wanted them! But there I lay, seeing in my mind the white villa among its towering pines, the sun on the cobbled forecourt I'd crossed so often, the porte-cochère; I could guess at Fabrice's well-tipped welcome ("Monsieur me permettra-t-il de lui dire qu'il nous a beaucoup manqué?"); I would be led in and through, to the terrasse; and there, at last, and after four years' deprivation how *not* four years lovelier— But what lingering adolescent vanity let me suppose she'd even be amused by 'how I'd turned out'? God bless, what did my idiot subconscious think it was telling me to pack my bag *for?*—above all since, now, I could quote immortal sound sense from a course in the Latin poets: 'the vows a woman breathes to the lover nightlong in her arms the winds and the waters carry away.'

—I put it to my uncle, finally, the morning of my graduation. He was standing me and my roommates a full-fig buffet-lunch, families, girls, and all, in our rooms in Campbell; and well along in the champagne din I asked him, simply, how would he feel ("and being I mean *frank*, Uncle!") about having me at Cap Nègre for a couple of weeks this summer—assuming, I of course meant, that he was going to be there anyhow himself?

So he gazed at me for a long moment, with no particular expression except his usual judiciously tempered affection. Then he said, and in no particular tone either, he didn't suppose he had to ask me why?

I said, well, no.

. . . But to fall in love with her all *over* again? And in due course say good-bye all over again too?

I thought oh god *damn* it, Uncle! but I just said, "You going to expect me to argue both sides of it?"

"Well," he said amiably, "can't you?"

(What else had I been doing!) I said, "No, but Uncle look—just I don't seem to have— I mean Uncle I *don't know* about this sort of thing!"

So naturally he snorted: what *was* this!—the cultural differences of women are impenetrable to us and beyond count anyhow, but was I pretending my guesses about this particular blessing weren't likely to be—how should he put it?—'rather better informed,' say?—than his could decently be! Also, I'd adored her *without* being boring about it, hadn't I?—an amenity a nice woman responds to. And then, there had been a (I mind if he called it?) a sweetness about me that *any* nice woman—

But here, from nowhere, the sleekest of my roommates' m'mas appeared, drawling, "Who's a sweetness?—both of you?" in an amorous Greenwich contralto; and as she then slid a caressing arm through mine, and drooped her pretty lashes at my uncle, I decided that was that, and I was on my own.

—So in due course the rite de passage came to an end. I was lingeringly kissed good-bye by all three mothers, shook hands with six or seven fathers and stepfathers, patted my uncle on the shoulder and told him I loved him *anyway*, and issued grandly forth onto the green summer lawns of intellectual freedom at last, my destiny now in God's presumed hands rather than my uncle's or the dean's, and in a champagne haze anyhow.

. . . So all right, Hume's theory of probability is *Either it happens or it don't.* I would toss a coin!

I would proceed with fitting formality to the farthest edge of this lovely girl-strewn campus (where never again would Melancholy mark me for her own) and spin my ritual quarter up and out into the symbolic wide world of University Place—I would by god *find out* whether l'univers était no kidding égal à mon vaste appétit! With fitting formality I paraded, swaying, across, and through the arch between Blair and Joline, till I stood on the ultimate inch of alma mater earth, and ecco! catapulted my coin ("Heads I'll *go!*") high into the air. It glinted in the sun, spinning as it fell, bounced musically on the Borough pavement, caromed wildly off over the stone curb, clinked on the grating of a storm drain, and vanished into the hollow earth.

. . . So much for David Hume?

. . . And for that matter, God!—eye on His sparrow instead? I turned, snickering away, up University Place, and in a brisk half hour at American Express had a plane reservation to Paris for Thursday, an Airfrance connection to Nice, a room at the Négresco, and a car for Friday morning at nine.

—The Alpes-Maritimes I drove off through, that brilliant morning, was not the Var I knew, but the sun-flooded landscape was the landscape of my memory still, the dusty green and gold of Mediterranean summer seeping into my senses again as if I had never been away, the sky the deep ancient blue of enamel, and after St. Raphaël the turquoise sea to my left a dazzle to the round horizon. It was as if it was all *there* for me again, set before my dreaming eyes just as it had been, the days and nights of Carla there so believable I almost had the fantasy that the Mediterranean gods were pointing my way: how else, from the A.8, had I found the coast road so easily—Les Issambres, Ste. Maxime, Port-Grimaud, Cavalaire, Le Canadel. And as I drove, my memory began to see the private landscape of my enchantment as if superimposed the two villas and the sun-flecked voie between, now at long last almost before my eyes. I would leave my car at Uncle's, with the gardien (was his name Emile?) and *walk* to Carla's. As I always had. And how else but walk now either, superstition or not, if she was to be 'there' for me again now too? . . .

So, heart high, lips I suppose half-smiling already with the phrases of greeting to come, every happy nerve tingling, I walked up the curving drive at last, and rounded the taillis.

And jarred to a halt, stunned.

A glistening Bugatti and a huge vintage Daimler were drawn up at the porte-cochère in the blaze of Mediterranean noon—there were PEOPLE there? . . .

And *not* people I'd know?—both cars had *Rome* plates, and the only Roman friends I remembered were Uncle's!

—Then the *difference* hit me, and I stood there, numb. For what 'strangers' could there have been, what possible malaise either, four years ago? I *knew* Carla's friends; I shared them; *all* her life I felt I knew; it was mine, as she was! But here, in a mere four years—well, *look* at it!—she had a whole life apart from me? a life *of her own* I'd God help me never thought of?—in fact if I went round to the terrasse as I used to, for all I knew *I* could be the intruder!

. . . Well but then what do I do?—do you *send in your card* to a woman you've caressed every sweet inch of? I choked.

—All right all *right* I should have telephoned first! I turned and stalked back down the drive, and back to my uncle's, in a fume. Emile'd give me lunch. I'd phone when they'd *gone*.

... And *all right* I was behaving like a goddam child!—how *shouldn't* her life have gone on without me!

And even if I'd phoned, would she have asked me to lunch?— and had to 'explain' me! And risk my calling her 'tu'—oh god risked I suppose *any* of my behavior! I lugged my bags into my old room in such sudden misery I even wondered whether there was going to be much point in unpacking at all.

For say I phoned, and was let come to tea—how would she greet me? After four years, what fantasies could make me expect a laughing *Dunque! Let me look at you—ahi, madonna, no wonder I had an indiscrezione wiz you!* or what vanity let me hope we'd impossibly go on from there!

For why should it be anything (I saw) but cold displeasure. I had *come* here? and wiz no warning? Di grazia, what follies did I expect of her! To leave her charming and honorable husband?— her every friend?—her *life?* Was I so ingenuo, so untaught still, that I thought a summer caprice was a grand passion?—*she* to have lost her head over a *boy?* . . .

. . . But as heartless as that? I opened the French windows, and stood staring out, in disbelief, at the sun on the pinewood I'd carried her through that time, in the first cool pallor of summer dawn —nuzzling my neck, murmuring, as I carried her: caprice or not, was that a memory she'd have let 'the winds and the waters carry away'? And dammit was I *not* to go find out?

—But on what possible pretext, go? Even supposing you had the effrontery to pay a *social* call on a woman you'd spent half a summer in bed with, what bland explanation had you for all the non-summers since?—until, suddenly, now! Good god could I persuade *myself* I'd be here at all except for Hume and his damn' coin!

In fact, put in stately terms, had *I* had a grand passion that summer either, or just a hair-raising initiation? And would a man of sense expect to be initiated twice?

. . . I should never have come.

—Well, but I had. So was I going to take off for home again, like (possibly) a man of sense, without seeing her? Or ring up, midafternoon, and be (perhaps) asked to tea?

Or simply God bless take off for Paris!—and the early-summer ebb-and-flow of American college girls through the front rooms at Morgans till I spotted one I knew, the Ovidian prescription itself; and we would fall deeply in love till her fiancé got in next weekend.

It was noon. I had four hours to make up my mind.

—And perhaps for god sakes even *reflect* a little!—after four at least theoretically enlightening years was I behaving like a *kid* still? . . .

Had I for instance so much as thought about Carla's side of it? Even generally: what *was* it, to be a woman, apart from being the woman a woman is in your arms? How much of any Yes or No could I tell myself I'd perhaps not misunderstood? . . .

What *had* Carla felt about me?—whether or not she did now. I remembered what once, long afterwards, my uncle had said: "Never strike you just *how* scandalous about you she was? *Damn* I was uneasy! What if she'd decided she didn't intend to give you up? Thank God she behaved like a gent! You realize she didn't *risk* touching you good-bye? . . ."

So he'd felt it had been a folly? even a toquade? Because then what mightn't I be doing, calling now, but make a woman I adored remember what she might totally want to forget?

I should *never* have come!

. . . Yes; but couldn't Uncle's judgment have been biased? By, say, his guardian's concern for me?

For dammit how could a woman as di gran mondo as Carla be thought to have allowed herself anything more than a, well, than an indiscrezione? She had in fact *not* "touched me good-bye" but why need she have wanted to! She in fact *had* behaved (Uncle's word) convenevolmente! Why then expect her to be any less serenely mondana if a sometime lover presented himself in her salotto and bowed over her cool fingers now too?

So by god why shouldn't I!

And leave whatever happened then up to *her*: if a femme du monde couldn't impose the tone she wanted on a conversation, who could?

So in fact *basta!* I'd ring up after lunch, and *go!* And if some goddam new maggiordomo answers instead of Fabrice, I'm simply this ancien ami américain qui tient à présenter ses respects à Madame—hoping to God *that* polite context makes "ancien ami" mean "an old friend" not "a former lover." . . .

But it turned out to be Fabrice still. And as respectfully welcoming ("Quel plaisir que de revoir Monsieur! Nous avions failli en faire notre deuil!") as if I had been my uncle. Madame was in the terraced garden; she was profiting by the expectation of Monsieur to cut fresh bouquets for the salotto; the iris this year were early in flower; and through those haunted rooms (each one a stab) once

again I was led to the terrasse of my memory, knowing no more
what I should find there than I had known that first time, now four
years almost to the day gone by.

She was in the lower garden; she was bending over a cutting
bed, a trug on the turf beside her heaped with the long stems of
the iris, a tousle of white petals to one end, of blue to the other.
Fabrice called out my name, and she turned, waving and laughing, and came (oh god that lovely tilting walk—four years but
all *over* again was it taking my breath away?) —came up the slope
to meet me, chanting a smiling "Djonnie, Djonnie, *you?* . . ."
secateur in one gauntled hand, flower-laden trug swinging from
the other (so slender, so lithe, and I'd known it all, every heartbreaking inch—and now not even a hand free for me?)—sweetly
reproaching me as she came near: ma vergogna! not to have *told*
her I was arriving? And what was this inumanità Fabrice had reported! I was only di *passaggio?* (holding up a polite cheek to be
kissed) "—to come only to *go,* crudele?" (the other cheek, drooping her lashes). And to arrive just when she had *people!* ahi, and
what people! (dumping trug and secateur on a bench) —*not*
amici, a pig of a playboy of a cognato of Baldassare's (stripping off
her gauntlets) and his chiacchieroni of hosts in Cannes! "But what
is this unkind 'in passing,' caro?—you are not to *stay?*"

That, at least I had an answer ready for, senses in a riot at her
nearness again or not: Uncle John wasn't opening the villa for a
week or so yet, and as I'd never seen much of France—

"Turismo?—and beginning wiz me! Mi commuovo!"

('Touched'!—she was laughing at me? . . .)

"Ah but come sit down, let me *inspect* you after four years!"
she went on, sweetly. "Till Fabrice brings tea. Are you as bello as
ever? Shall I embarrass you and say 'Madonna *si!*' Ah, but not,
perhaps, so schivo about it, so bashful, now? No, but let us be
serious—what have you done, these four years? Worked hard, at
your university? And done well? And are now baccelliere—bravo!
And wiz distinctions?"

I said a magna. In History.

"Ah *bravo!* And now? What does one do wiz history?"

I explained about journalism; the *Prince,* the Press Club; and
now, in the fall, Columbia Journalism.

"And then the wide world," she said, smiling.

I said secondo come la gira.

"I think we should speak English," she said smoothly. "It has
been some time, since in Italian, no? four years? And meantime

your accent— Shall I be cruel, and ask you— Ahi, the things I could ask you! Your little first ones, after the summer, did you not feel a little—do you say 'abashed'? A little, even inconstant?"

(And I'd thought I might 'upset' her, by coming? *hah!*)

"How many girls—did you keep count?—have lost their pretty heads over you? And when this one has decided she has been foolish, always has there been another? Ah, Djonnie, it is *bad* for a young man to be so handsome he need only rely on our folly! It is not grazioso, caro, to let us seduce ourselves!"

(As if it made a difference!)

"No but in four years, Djonnie," she went on, lightly, "not to have got over even a serious affetto? Because one learns that one *does*—viene a capo, and why should *not* the end of it be the end of a time, the last day of a villegiatura, the end of summer, caro, and one lover goes one way, the other another way. Is it a betrayal that one recovers?—e riceve al tè!" she finished, laughing, as Fabrice set the tea-tray on the table before her.

So (ah, well) we had tea.

With farfallette and that Milan cake; it could hardly have been more convenevole. Even as (*this* time) l'ultima volta che mai della vita mia la vedrei, it had its conventional side—hands-on-my-shoulder presently good-bye, not sleek arms round my neck. And if she saw me off from the porte-cochère, at least it was from the porte-cochère.

Of course, as I walked away down the curving drive, I did wonder whether, if I turned to look back, at the taillis, *might* she, just possibly, still be standing there, light hand against a pillar, watching me go? . . .

But the question lacked dignity. At the taillis I did not even bother to turn my head to see.

2

. Arms to assuage you are always there, and that fall I teamed up in a two-bedroom Heights basement with a *Prince* classmate who'd decided on a year of Columbia Journalism too, a very nice guy named Ike Trimmingham, and we spent an ideal partying first-year-out, an occasional slight borrowing from each other's strings of blessings taken as a given.

But what made the year for me was politics: the fatuities of the 1952 presidential campaign turned out to be what launched me as a journalist. I was lazing over the *Times* one Sunday morning when it struck me that the total disparity between political realities and our politicians' descriptions of them was exactly the high non-sense my senior thesis had analyzed in Bucks County, and I set briskly to work on a sardonic (and I still think funny) couple of thousand words on campaign rodomontade as a national treasure. (Of course, Ad Stevenson '22 had been managing editor of the *Prince* before us, but his elegance and his wit made a hilarious counterpoint.) I got Ike to edit the thing down to twelve hundred words, gave it a selling title ("Claptrap from Riffraff"), and tried it on *Esquire*. So help me, they bought it! I was amazed—god sweet sakes, if it was no harder than this, shouldn't I consider myself a pro already? I damn near got myself an agent!

But it was my fourth or fifth try that was my real entrée to serious attention from editors, a think-piece the amenities of our Heights basement had inspired: fifteen hundred words on the intellectual disjunction I pretended to find between the cosseting arms nightlong round my neck, and the beratings, at breakfast, of my crass male-chauvinist ignorance of everybody from Lady Mary Wortley Montagu and Mary Wollstonecraft to (what world *was* I living in!) Ms. Greer. I called it "Love Makes You Go *Whee*"; the instant feminist outcry was as good as a contract.

I, naturally, hadn't a drop of anti-Lib blood in my body. God knows, from kindergarten on I've *liked* girls, as well as the rest of it; I'd even got used to girls with careers in mind. The flightiness of young women being what it is, they and I were simply targets of opportunity for each other, and why not? Even romantic or idealis-tic girls' experience of me and my like would leave them sweetly skeptical: why suppose a love affair was for more than (say) the first few months of 'the rest of time'? And as no ideal guy ever turned up, girls found a presentable fill-in (me, on occasion) for mean-time. In consequence (and women being the affectionate creature they are), you grew used to assuming that any new girl you met was in love already, and that there would *be* this carry-over to deal with for a start; but as you also had to expect to become a carry-over presently yourself, as some low supplanter began to take her fancy, this was acceptable. (Even normal: one was sometimes tempo-rarily encumbered oneself.) An impromptu of Ike's, on an affair of his, I felt summed it up:

Swirling your sweet skirts at me, yes;
But migrants, all of you—having or not having
A where next, and (always) no doubt aflutter
At the culturally disconcerting
Recurrence of the amenities of landfall.
　　　Must you go?—as I was brought up one should say,
And as you were brought up to (fuming!) expect me to.

If the arms round my neck were not Carla's, at least the girls I cajoled weren't concerned with irrelevances like devotion.

After Columbia, though, Byberry my base again, the creature comforts and Arcadian pleasances of the dower house made the Heights basement seem threadbare; it also, naturally, led to a change of style in the comedy of manners. As my uncle put it, that Columbia spring, if I had (no business of his, but *if* I had) a serious young woman, might he say he'd found that if they *lived* with you they tended to take *trouble* about you? very gratifying. Not that he meant anything like 'settle down'—Dieu l'en garde! No, but it was the pleasure it gave them. Which of course they then sweetly rewarded you for.

And it happened that an elegant Radcliffe enchantment of mine named Andrea Boulton was just then in a flounce about our summer. She had been indulging my delight in her since Thanksgiving; in June she would graduate; and yes, seven months *was* brief for how we felt we felt; but also (hoh!) fancy trying to finish her novel in a family summer on the Cape! So I said wasn't perhaps the cook-housekeeper'd peace and quiet of Byberry, and the dreaming woods, an agreeable answer? She was amused ("Oh dear, are you asking my hand in cohabitation?") but when we drove down and I showed her round, stables and all, she was charmed—what a *stylish* archaism of a place! and with a cook you addressed as 'Mrs.'? Even a grand piano to work off fumes at me on?—*yes* she'd come live with me! Anyway till she finished her novel. I did, though, realize, didn't I?—Thanksgiving *would* be a whole *year*. . . .

As it turned out, she didn't finish till the following Easter. And almost decided to marry me, to celebrate. But then she decided to *rewrite* to celebrate, so— Ah, well, it had been a ménage not a mere fantaisie; and when the book appeared it was dedicated to me even if by then its author wasn't. Anyway, as my uncle remarked, years later, the girls I cajoled had careers in mind, not anything as irrelevant as devotion. The bind was, only smart girls enchanted me.

Or, perhaps, single-minded ones. Ike's young Vassar cousin Paula had always been going to study voice in Florence, *no* matter what. Julia Langham's eye was on Washington even before she began to think about bar exams. True, she made it up to me, for leaving, by handing me on to her roommate Adriana Eustis; but that was Adriana's next-to-next-to-last year at Hahnemann, and then she took off too. Megan Stead was constantly coming and going for the United Nations, and was always having to look in on her London husband anyway—and anyway why couldn't I take it the way her Russian colleagues did: proshchaí meant 'forgive me' as well as 'good-bye.' Each of them, I admit, seemed to dote on me in her turn, without thinking of it as a 'turn' at all, and to be as tenderly upset at going as I found it heartbreaking to see her go. And certainly my uncle approved of them ("You *do* do yourself well!"), wear and tear or not: volage, yes, but been properly brought up. He'd have us to dinner, and to parties, when he was in this country; we'd take him with us to plays and concerts in Princeton. He'd ride over a couple of times a week, if only to exercise his hunters. The girls adored him.

Now and then, naturally, one of them would surprise him. I remember one early-October morning I was working in the woods, and he heard my saw and rode up. We've always 'forested' our woods, as they do in Europe (and now, for tax purposes besides), and I do a lot of the work myself—for pleasure as much as for anything: simply I suppose I feel *happy* in the woods. And I think out my next article as I work. They are splendid woods: a century ago it was half chestnut forest, and there are still a few huge weathered silver-grey stumps scattered through it; but red oak took over after the blight and the logging, with some hickory and white ash, and the usual oak-forest understorey of dogwood, and in spring there is wild azalea everywhere.

It was a dazzling morning. I remember thinking had I ever seen a more gorgeous fall, such *brilliance* of color—the dogwood carmine and vermilion, the egg-yellow tulip, the crimson and bronze and puce of the ash, and the last two or three days the great spreading groves of beech turning copper and tobacco-brown; even the oaks were beginning to show their rubies—the first full splendors of autumn launched at last, and the air glittering like crystal. I like to look at all that; and I was stopping work now and then, just to gaze, when here came my uncle, cantering out of the cathedral aisles of the beeches on a Morgan mare he was fond of. He pulled up by my Jeep; God bless, how was I; *what* a magnificent morning; and tossed his off leg over and dropped smartly to the ground.

He'd rung up to see would Meg and I be free for dinner Tuesday? but whoever it was answered said I'd already— Look, it was no business of his, *god* no, but he'd have sworn wasn't it *Julia's* lovely voice again?

I thought ah dammit what do I keep Mrs. Grammace for! but I had to say, well, yes, Julia did visit from time to time. She got into fumes about this or that in Washington; who didn't. So she'd flounce up for a weekend. Like this time. Spiritual refreshment, was all.

He said, mildly, but 'from time to time'? Wasn't that rather a hit-or-miss sort of logistics?

I said Meg was in Geneva.

But sometimes hadn't Meg arrived rather— Ah, well, always perhaps been too many been too sweet *not* to now and then get in each other's way; what could a man do.

Ah, now, Uncle, I said, nostalgia had its agréments.

Yes. Well. No doubt. Yes. Still, *this* particular young woman? Even admitting it of course spoke well for me, coming back for 'visits' like this. Except then why have left! Not that it was at all clear, he'd admit, how women had ever taken to pretending to anything as un-Darwinian as fidelity in the first place! And when you considered the *fuss* they can decide to make about being properly adored!—the emotional expense they've put you to!—the *rant* you've had to fall back on! . . . Ah, well, young women. No, but give her his love, would I kindly? Unless possibly it would embarrass her?—or did such things, nowadays!

(Though Julia was perhaps a bit more complicated a girl than my uncle's reliance on 'proper upbringing' led him to suppose. On trips to Washington, for instance, I now and then took Julia to dinner and a show, or dancing, and now and then she would ask me in for a nightcap when I delivered her home to Georgetown. And then, well, what *were* the signals? (a) Straightforward? for moving to Washington didn't necessarily, after all, mean her *feeling* for me had changed. Anyhow (b) surely I was as free of old-fashioned scruples as she was—and why should Adriana know anyway. Or was it (c) she was amusing herself seeing whether I *had* old-fashioned scruples? Or, God help me, (d) girls being what they are, had she and Adriana a *bet* on about me? Or, to the contrary, (e) she was seeing whether she could score on her dearest friend? And (f)—though I refused to consider it—were there kinks? . . . Naturally, any hypothesis except the first, any gent would dismiss as unthinkable the moment he thought it; and she *was* a beautiful thing wasn't she? so I would let the ballet proceed as how often before, picking up my cues as she lightly tossed them to me, and we would have as lovely a night as Adriana and I had had in Philadelphia the night before. And next day I'd return to Philadelphia and Adriana's amused and clinical "Sleep with you nicely?" and be as baffled as ever.)

It was my uncle, however, who got me started—without in the least meaning to—toward a more settled kind of life. He rang up one morning: did I expect to be by myself that weekend by any chance?—dinner he meant Saturday? Because he'd be grateful if I'd give him a hand with the social life of a young cousin who was just turning up at the grad college. No relation of mine—*his* mother's sister's granddaughter, but he thought I might be kind enough to introduce the child to a few of my younger Princeton hostesses, if I thought proper. Name was Francesca Drewes; Bennington girl; going to do architecture, he understood; *beautiful* young creature—her unforgettable mother all over again! So was I free for dinner? Not to dress—he was having a few of his *his*-side Philadelphia cousins for her too. He'd fetch the child, but I could run her back to college afterwards if I liked.

Uncle was right; she *was* a beauty! But family forgatherings being what they are, I hardly had a word with her all evening. By the time the minutiae of their family history had got round to a debate whether Caln Meeting's double meetinghouse dated from the Hicksite schism of the 1820s, or from Fallowfield Quarter's differences, later, over helping runaway slaves, I was desperately willing Francesca to in God's polite name rise to her feet and murmur alas she must go.

But driving back afterwards she made up for it. "Oh what genealogical archives we inflicted on you! And you were so nice about it all!"

I said, yes, well, Philadelphia conversation, yes. *Not* an articulate culture, Philadelphia. We had splendid painters, Cassatt and Eakins, and we'd been kindly to the gibbering mad from Ben Franklin on, but where were our writers?

"Oh but I didn't mean about Cousin *John!*" she cried. "*He* is absolutely the— Well, Mummy even warned me about him! she told me the first time she met him she was thirteen, it was at a family wedding in Harwich Port, and she never dreamed about *anybody* else till practically freshman year in college! And even after that she had crushes on older men for years. What does he do? besides be hard to get over!"

I said oh he had the standard law degree. Qualified to practice in Rome, even. But Philadelphia rentiers weren't expected to 'do' much of anything. Except, naturally, behave well in a well-fixed way. If they saw fit to. But Uncle John, I felt, wasn't just provincial about it.

"You mean he's a model for you?"

Look, I wasn't a full-time rentier—I moonlighted at it, was all. Still, if Uncle was of such dream-about quality, by god what better model!

"Ho, and be hard to get over too?"

I thought what *was* this! Feminist confrontation? Méfiance? Skittishness? Or just ranging shots, at a younger level than I was used to! I said well but it was men found girls hard to get over, not girls men.

"Oh poor darlings!" she mocked. "So pathetic so *mistreated*-sounding!"

But we were brought up, I said mildly, to be suitably stricken, weren't we, when one of you took it into her disenchanted head to take off?

"Are we to give up what we *want to do*?" she cried. "And merely because we've taken a meantime fancy to one of you? And we *love* you while we do, don't we? before we what you call 'take off'? And we look after you too, *my!*"

So all the way back to the grad college it was Careers.

—But a girl saying good night to you in starlight is a lovely illusion; and *this* one— Abruptly it struck me that (God bless!) wasn't I perhaps being seriously tempted to pursuit myself? . . .

So, next day being a Sunday, I took her to Trinity and a (resulting) hospitable after-church brunch on Edgehill Street; on Tuesday to a cocktail bash on Battle Road; got us invited to lunch Thursday at the faculty club; and so, finally, Uncle's behest attended to, I took her to Byberry, Saturday, for myself. If only to see whether, if it *had* been méfiance, mightn't it, by now, be decently gone.

I let the archaisms of the dower house's architecture begin the beguiling—the 1700s heating advantages of six-foot-eight ceilings (six-three, upstairs); the four-flue chimneys and the efficiency of their paired inner-corner fireplaces, the second storey's exactly over the first's; the waxed chestnut wainscoting, though in the dining-room still painted colonial blue; the queen-post framing of the garrets. The barn was simpler; but she was enchanted by the stonework's being as finished and elegant as the house's, and by the great chestnut beams.

I'd borrowed Uncle's Morgan for her, and we picnicked by a spring in the 'up-river' beechwoods, and afterwards gave the horses their heads for a good run; and finally we rode home through the Newtown-side oakwoods, the brilliance of autumn leaves showering down about us. And as we unsaddled and rubbed the horses down, she was so *damn'* pretty, cheeks flushed with the exercise, eyes shining, that I thought You know this could turn *serious?*—except of course how could anything as enchanting as *this* one not already have been spoken for. . . .

We had tea, and she pounced on my record collection, with little cries of delight at my 'antiques'—did I know how to ballroom dance *too?*—so we rolled back the rugs and danced.

Danced, in fact, till Mrs. Grammace announced dinner.

Where, finally, we got round to what my uncle once called, in a vaguely Vergilian phrase, 'the amenities of things.'

"I only love people one at a time," she said. "Do you?"

I said well, in practice, I supposed *yes*.

" 'In practice'! What's *that* mean!"

Ah, look, I said, what did 'one at a time' mean.

"It means you're *sincere!*" she cried. "It means you break *up* with whoever!"

She expected a decent guy to forget his *feelings*, I said, about a girl who'd had the sweetness to have been making love with him for maybe years?—merely because she'd now said good-bye, and it was another girl?

"You mean you *in detail* remember about her?" she demanded, sounding scandalized. "Like *in bed?* You *compare* girls?"

I said *god* no!—a girl in your arms, for one thing, wasn't just the ultimate blessing, she was a total event in *herself!* She was the only thing *of* her kind—which was what 'unforgettable' meant!

So she brooded at me. Finally she said, "But you don't mean you *don't* have a girl do you?"

I was amused: had her generation of girls gone undissembling on us? Ah, now, now, I said, if I did have a girl she'd hardly put up with my claiming she was anything as ownership-sounding as 'mine' would she?

"No but I meant this girl you said you *didn't* compare the girl you remembered about with—this girl you said was there *now*."

Dammit I said *what* girls?—I was *generalizing!* About *theoretical* girls! And were even real girls a dependable datum for generalities anyway? Anyway shouldn't we go have coffee?—and if Mrs. Grammace hadn't put the rugs back we could dance again, would she like a brandy? because I also had some *good* marc de Bourgogne.

—But now, as we danced, she was silent, close against me, cheek in the hollow of my shoulder; and when presently she did speak, it was as if, from where we'd left off, her mind had gone on in a dialogue I was being gently invited to join.

Not that it was clear at what point, in whatever we were to discuss, I was being invited—for what she said was, ". . . But are you?" as if she had already asked a question (and I perhaps ambiguously replied); and only then, "About girls I mean are you? You almost sounded, well, *faithful*-sounding!"

'Faithful'!

"Yes! Remembering, like that!"

Then she was silent again. I thought God bless, can this be going in the happy direction it begins to sound as if it might be?— basic skittishness or not?

(Though what did *I* know about this generation's signals!)

The record ran out. We put on a new one. She said, "I guess I didn't think you were like that at all, at first," as we danced again.

I said like what.

"The way I've decided you *are*. I mean I thought you were like Cousin John. Who I told you, Mummy warned me about."

I thought ah dammit angel *enough* of this! and I said, "Fancy thinking *I* was like him!" and gently stopped us dancing, and bent my head and kissed her. A *long* kiss, while I was at it; and when at last she drew back and gazed gravely up at me, all she said was, ". . . oh," so I kissed her again, a serious kiss this time too. Several serious kisses, till finally she murmured, ". . . but we're supposed to be dancing," so we danced till the record came to an end.

But then I started it again without letting her go, and we danced on. Wordlessly on: everything that needed saying had I thought been said; once, even, I stopped us dancing again, and kissed her, to make sure. But when the record ended, she drew away, murmuring oh dear, and I was terribly sweet, and what a lovely ending to a lovely day, but she *had*—and I *knew* she had—to go.

(And if I naturally thought *damn* I also thought but why argue —if this time wasn't the time, didn't next time look as good as certain to be? and I protested merely as a gentlemanly matter of course.)

But we were barely halfway to the Scudder Falls bridge when she said in an uncertain voice, "Can I ask you a question I don't seem to know how to put?"

I thought now what.

"I mean you're more than three whole college *generations* older than me, aren't you? I know that sounds— But you *are*! Anyway, what it *is* is, have you been— *Are* you what I suppose you probably call 'falling in love' with me?"

Ah, well.

"You lovely thing," I said, "mightn't you have thought of asking that *before* the record stopped?"

She was silent.

"What do you mean, do I *call* it 'falling in love'!" I said. "Good god, from the first heart-stopping moment I walked into Uncle's drawing-room and there you *were*, I've— What do you think I've been doing! Four days out of the last six doesn't qualify as pursuit? And why shouldn't I?—have you shown any signs of being in whatever *you* call the state I'm in, about any other guy at all?"

She was still silent. I thought God *blast* the difference of generations!—*no* girl, in mine, would have kissed me like that if she had another guy seriously in mind!

Or anyhow no girl ever had.

Or anyhow I didn't think had.

Or just were my generation's ground rules such an archaism it was no longer even general knowledge such niceties had ever been held to exist?

—Ah, but what it turned out the angel was deciding, no simple-hearted man (of *any* generation) would have had the impossible assurance to predict! For now, as if the silence had been a solemn prelude to a ritual she was about to perform, she said softly, ". . . Let's go back," and tilted her knee against mine; and so it began.

I suppose I had forgot what sweetness they can be, young; but what idiot boys had Francesca been wasting her loveliness on, to be so little confident of its sorcery, its absolute dominion!—so uncertain, that first morning, so (for God's sake!) *shy*, that I decided I understood her generation even *less* than I'd assumed!

For instance: —the preposterous conversation we had as I drove her to Princeton, midmorning, for a change of clothes. It began, again, halfway to the bridge: she put her hand on my knee, and her fingers gently explored it, and presently she murmured, ". . . You're nice to touch," so I picked the hand up and kissed the fingers as called for, and returned them to my knee; and for a mile or so we were silent. Then she said (and so help me, sounding surprised!), "You know? last night, the way we— I've never— You seemed so sort of, oh well so *delighted* with me, Johnnie!" (Good god '*seemed*'?) "Because I guess you delight me too," so I pulled her over against my shoulder; and then we were silent again.

But a mile or two along, she sat up, and said, "From how your Mrs. Grammace said good morning to me she's *very* used to girls at breakfast with you."

I was amused. I said, " 'Good morning, Miss'?—overnight guests, what else would the woman say!"

"No but Johnnie it was the bland *accustomed* way she said it! I don't mean it was impertinent, in the least, but how *couldn't* it make me feel she— I mean I know of *course* by your age every-body has had all kinds of affairs, and anyway I suppose you're sort of the latest in *my* series too, aren't you, even if I haven't *had* very many! But Mrs. Grammace sounding so used to your probably *years* of girls made me remember what you said at din-ner about remembering them, every detail—so how *amn't* I to wonder whether all last night perhaps weren't you! with *me!* all night *long* remembering! Oh and when you were so lovely!" she mourned.

I said but God bless, I'd do a *survey?*—with every sweetness a man could ever hope a girl would be, right there in my arms?

"Oh I don't mean *then* I felt I was being compared! And I'm not jealous! Just I—"

I said *god* no!—jealousy was 'sans trêve, sans variété, sans résultat,' *and* Proustian! But was she going méfiante on me again?—after last *night?* God in heaven couldn't she tell the dif-ference between a man in love with her and a marauder?

So for a while she was silent. But then she said, "Did they live with you?"

Sometimes, I said. Some of them. When they could.

"But I never even spent the *night* with anybody!" she cried. "And here, the very first time I do, oh sort of *everybody* knows!"

I said but good god—

"Well she's going to *make the bed* isn't she?"

—Ah, well, one's responsible, and we were nearly at the turn-off to the Princeton Pike, so I pulled up off the throughway and petted her back to sweetness and sense; and in fact the only con-tinuation of the silly topic was that she said, "What does 'trêve' mean?" and I said, " 'Let-up,' " as we were passing the battlefield coming into Princeton.

I even had no trouble, back at Byberry again, persuading her to cut a Monday lecture, and not leave till Tuesday morning.

—Talking her into coming to live with me, though, took a good month. I was *sweet* to want her to have both the bedrooms across the upstairs hall from mine all to herself, they were lovely, and, yes, one she could make into a study, and set up her drafting-table in it—and she of course *could* sleep alone there (she murmured, nuzzling me) any time she was having a spat with me—but *move* from the grad college? move *in?* . . .

Because why on earth did I want her to?—goodness, it would be practically like *marriage!* And how would she explain the new phone exchange to her family!

And even if I did buy her a car she'd be *commuting* to classes wouldn't she?

And was *I* to be her only social life?—and way off here in the woods *besides?* And how would I explain, to *my* friends, her being my hostess!

And *Cousin John* would know!!

So I had to be patient. But by our fourth Saturday, the weekends had demonstrated, if nothing more, at least the routine housekeeping as well as the lovemaking conveniences a ménage can be. There might even, she conceded, be a special *domestic* amenity in kissing me good-bye as she set off to class in the morning, knowing I would be there to kiss that night when she returned. So that Saturday we spent the afternoon and evening moving her in—making a celebration of it, with a magnum of champagne and smoked salmon and thin cucumber sandwiches as a peripatetic picnic to sustain us, as I lugged suitcases and boxes up the stairs, and she unpacked and distributed and stowed away and fretted over proper places for.

But I was so delighted with her that it never crossed my mind that this was also her first exposure to my devotion to champagne in quantity; so when in due course I came upstairs at last from putting the cars in the barn, seeing to the horses, and locking up for the night all round, God help me there she was in a lovely heap by the slipper chair—*out*, a last tumbled armful of blouses strewn on the floor around her.

I was stricken. Ah dammit if I *loved* the child mightn't I have watched over her properly? Marriage or not, I'd acquired her hadn't I!—I was *responsible* for her! Good god, for that matter, I was hardly five years shy of being old enough to be her *father* and responsible! And I'd let *this* happen to her?—the very night she'd had the sweetness to come live with me I'd let *this* happen? I could have hanged myself in sheer champagne remorse!

Ah, well. I slid my arms under her knees and her shoulders and gathered her up—so limp, so light—and carried her to her new bed, as moved as if I were carrying a bride over a threshold. She murmured something sad-sounding as I lowered her onto the coverlet, but she didn't open her eyes. Nor did she change from the position I'd laid her down in. Was she going to be all right? Or wasn't she.

I sat down on the bed beside her, and tried to look at her clinically. She was at least all *right*, I decided: 'a burning forehead and a parching tongue' is Keats's ghastly sparkling Burgundy, not vintage Bollinger! I picked up her unresisting hand: how angelically, in this mere month, these fingers had learned to caress! Should I spread a quilt over her and let her sleep? Or undress her properly and put her to bed. But dammit, undressing a girl to make love with her was one thing, undressing her to put her to bed was a different activity altogether—for all I knew, it was a male-chauvinist invasion of privacy! And to be *resented*!

—Ah, and anyhow. Sitting there, gazing sentimentally at this in-vino-Campestri but nevertheless adorable acquisition of mine, I found I had begun to meditate. Whether from man's built-in naïveté or our Darwinian helplessness, the beauty of woman we are always in a kind of awe before; but here, with Francesca, what was this sense of cherishing her that I seemed to be feeling besides, this surprising concern? I remembered an offhand remark of my uncle's, that the sort of men women liked most were the sort that was worst for them; and I'd thought ah, well, epigrams, but it wasn't the sort he *or* I were self-conceited enough to be. But now, I thought, what if, a little, I *was*? A lot of girls *had* liked me; but had I ever particularly worried about the outcome? Prepschool and college love affairs are of course de rencontre and suivant l'occasion (and perhaps the first-three-years crop of your classmates' disenchanted wives are too), but my *serious* loves? my live-ins? It was all very well to say (and also it was true) that it was their careers, not some fundamental heartlessness of mine, that made them leave me. But now?

—Ah, well, but here and now, I could hardly leave a girl I was falling in love with (if that was it) to wake, alone, lost, in a strange bed in an unfamiliar room! But carry her across the hall to 'ours' and *not* undress her?—so I simply turned off all the lights but a small lamp on the dressing-table, and sank into the hearth-chair, to finish off the champagne before I went to sleep.

So, at least, come morning, she was no worse than abashed: oh dear, at twenty-*one* not to be used to champagne? And contrite: oh not to have *christened* the bed with me! And when I'd sat up all *night* in case she'd need me? oh *dear!* But she spent the day contentedly re-arranging everything she'd arranged the night before, so I felt the omens were favorable: perhaps I was going to lead something of a regular life at Byberry at last, with domestic routines as well as editors' deadlines, and this endearing child growing up to be part of it for good. At any rate, I seemed to be feeling domesticable enough to wonder whether a live-in girl to waste emotional time on wasn't an amenity I hadn't this *seriously* tried: if I 'doted' a bit on this one, what of it? — did that make it folly?

And certainly, as domesticity, Francesca seemed to be very happily settling in, and even taking over. Shouldn't we (didn't I *really* think?) have a housemaid? This *wasn't* a small house to look after properly with the kitchen too. Because also think if we got Mrs. Grammace a *Larousse Gastronomique* and some Elizabeth Davids, and set her free to *cook*. With the girl to chop parsley and stuff and beat sauces, besides serving in the dining-room?

And didn't I ever *give* parties? — not just pay back all my Princeton hostesses (as I *had* to, now I wasn't just an available bachelor). Because we had to know each other's friends; and mix them. Also, if she showed me off to some of her yearning gradschool people maybe they'd give *up* — ho, and all those hostesses' lecherous husbands too!

And she had moved her bank account (she told me, kissing me) from her bank to mine.

Even her first shyness about my uncle she felt lady-of-the-house enough to deal with, when he came back on a visit in the spring — and this, though I was in Berkeley, on a student-riot story, and not there as moral buffer. "He came in and oh darling there I *was!*" she reported when I returned. "I was making up a shopping-list in the kitchen with Mrs. Grammace, it couldn't have *been* plainer! — what was I to *say*, even, when the last time he'd seen me I'd no more than met you! so what could I do but ask him to lunch, I said Mrs. Grammace had made one of her delectable pâtés parisiennes, wouldn't he stay? so he did. And of course he's so charming I got over my dither, I even took him upstairs and showed him that set of elevations I've been doing, and where I — well, I showed him *all* upstairs, I didn't think you'd mind. Oh Johnnie he *is* a lot like you, now I love you it's practically *confusing* he's so like!"

I was amused: she'd forgot her m'ma's cautionary tale? I wondered what my dear uncle's version of the visit would be; I rode over to find out. He greeted me with a bland "You surprise me!"

I was taken aback: 'surprise' him!—going after as lovely a thing as Francesca was *surprising?*

Ah, well, he said, perhaps he might say Francesca surprised him too. Last time he'd seen her she was a serious-minded young New England female relation entering graduate school. He'd returned a mere seven months later to find— Well, might he put it, what an enchanting thing they can turn out to be when they've been let *feel* the full luster of their beauty! He'd always (as I knew) had a high opinion of me, he said, smiling, but to have presided over *this* sort of transfiguration?—by *god* how gratifying!

I said ah now, Uncle, they *evolved.* I hardly thought feminists—

Allow him the affection of irony, would I? No, but the 'surprise': was he to gather that some new attitude of my own was evolving? I'd never moved a girl *in* quite like this, had I?—child'd endeared herself into as good as half the house! Then, she'd shown him that beautiful little mare I'd bought her. And hadn't it struck me Mrs. Grammace was showing signs of long-suffering hopes rewarded at last? Called the child 'Miss Francesca' God bless like family!

I suppose I'd by and large begun to risk thinking of her as 'family' myself. Certainly we had 'married' rows: three or four times in those years she'd fume off across the hall to 'her' bed, and sometimes it would be half an hour before I'd cross after her or she'd be in my doorway again ("All right I *accept* your infuriating apology, aren't you hungry?"), and we'd go down to the kitchen for a quarter-to-three reconciliation on (say) leftover blueberry tart and the rest of a Barsac. She would report, with the sweet mockery of contentment, her various professors' and fellow students' hopeful invitations to delinquency—Christmas in the Virgin Islands? Easter vac? Venice Cintra *Ireland?* ("—and he's *almost* every bit as nice as you are!") She found a drawerful of old photographs and made up an album of pictures of me from the cradle on. In general, I felt that pretty much every spiritual agrément a young woman can flatter you with, Francesca was happily lavishing on me. I hoped I was never to see an end to it. I saw no reason I should: for me she was no more an architect than I was a political journalist to her. I was delighted her department thought her highly talented, and had had her apply for half a dozen of the most opulent fellowships; but to me she was a blessing who would come riding through the woods with a picnic lunch when I was working there, who saw to it we had people to dinners and parties half the evenings we weren't at dinners or parties of theirs, who'd wake for sleepy love if I was starting the day early, who in a word spoiled me with such simple sweetness that it hardly occurred to me I was being spoiled.

Then, midmorning one day, I was at my typewriter in the library when I heard a car screech to a stop in the forecourt, and a car door slam, and I looked out just in time to see her (but hadn't she a class?) scudding headlong, *bolting*, for the house, and she was in, and at the library doorway, wild, almost before I was on my feet to greet her, her face so woebegone I was struck dumb; and she raced to me crying, "Oh Johnnie forgive me I *got* the two-year Urbino! . . ." and flung herself into my arms, choking, and began to shake.

I was stunned. Of all possible fellowships, *that* one? . . .

She clung to me, face smothered in my shoulder, and told me, in little shuddering gasps. It wouldn't be announced till next month. But Professor Lemoile had told her. The direttore or the preposto or whoever it was had phoned him, and he was so delighted he'd told her, oh he was sort of *cawing* he was so delighted, "and oh my love I was so overcome and upset I let him *kiss* me!" she finished, wretchedly, and now she was in tears.

So I was losing this one too?

Had I then God help me reached the age of fatalities? At which young women are deadly?

And when perhaps all I simple-mindedly wanted was to sit quietly in a room, looking at this one?

I have fed your Lar with poppies, said Ezra—and now only for what?—for *this* desolation? I could almost hear my uncle: Inform an agreeable young woman of the state of your heart, and listen happily to her antiphonal misinformation about the state of hers—but ah the helpless *innocence* of this one's apostasy!

And the corollary for my own life now? What if even parties now, without her, left me abruptly misanthropized?—a past participle perhaps I'd find the language had long been in want of.

Ah, well. I stroked her hair; what else was there to do? There *there*, what was the matter with her! She'd got the absolutely top prize in her field—and she was weeping about it? When with *this* in her résumé, jobs would be hers for the choosing? Even the where was ideal!—was there a more humane people on earth, to live among, than Italians? Or, by and large, a handsomer?

But then I thought but good god what kind of pointless assuasion was this!—had I never had a weeping girl in my arms before? Don't argue, modulate! so I picked her up and carried her upstairs, heartbreak and all; and little by little we went on from there, as the topic changed.

(It wasn't till afterwards that it struck me what a saddening parody I could see it as, of that first long-ago night she'd come to live with me, when I'd found her sweetly champagned out, in a scattering of unpacked blouses on the floor, and I'd scooped her up and put her to bed, dressed, and sat on the bed beside her in simple champagne sentiment, falling in love.)

And now, afterwards, warm and close against me, murmuring, it was the *helplessness* of unhappiness, she said, that her tears had been for. All the way driving home she had seen it in her mind— "Oh my love how was I to *tell* you, even, it was so awful, what was happening, and would go *on* happening, without our even knowing how it would feel! Because you *will* meet somebody nice, but how can I think about how I'll probably feel when you do, when I can't know *when* it will happen, I mean how will *I* be feeling when it does? Will you give her my rooms? And will I *care* if all she feels about me is just what I feel about your ex-girls, that I'm only a 'before her'? And oh Johnnie it doesn't seem to help to tell myself I'll meet somebody too—how can you think about somebody you haven't the slightest idea even *if* you'll meet! And who I love is you anyhow, oh *making love* is just you, and how am I to think how it would be in bed with anybody else, ever!"

And suppose my whoever wasn't good with horses!—should she take her lovely Pouliche with her to Italy? Were there parks you could ride in? Or would I ship her after her, if?

—So the end began.

And next morning I said to her, angel look: shouldn't we try to cut the unhappiness short? so let her simply take off. She could do with a couple of months getting used to the language, before Urbino. My uncle would give her letters, to friends in Rome. Who'd introduce her to people, and be delighted to help her convert her Bennington Dante into Beginning Italian. . . .

On the whole we went through the motions 'responsibly.' Only the last night was too much for her: for hours all I could do for her was murmur on and on the helpless rhetoric of parting—now now now, if her professors said go to Urbino and let her lovely talent flower, what they meant was *go* to Urbino, and *let* it flower, and was that something for a woman I loved to weep about? She said she was *not* weeping. And she was not weeping about leaving me anyway, she was just *weeping*. About things. About me. The way she'd wept that night of our second anniversary. About *love*.

—But in the morning, she might have been no more than taking off for a weekend—hugged and kissed Mrs. Grammace almost
as gaily as she'd kissed Pouliche's nose, and kissed my uncle as
lightly as if they were seeing each other in Rome next week. Me, of
course, she'd spent the night in good-byes to; one last shaky kiss,
her lips a voiceless *I love you*, and she was in her car and away, with
a wave of a hand, for Boston. And beyond.

—So I said to Uncle, kind of him to have come over; stay for
lunch? I'd give him a sherry and a couple of my last pieces to read
meantime, he care to? and settled him in the front living-room
while I went to the kitchen to let Mrs. Grammace sob on my
shoulder, and in due course hand her over to Dillie for the finishing touches; and so down to the cellar for a wine. Back in the living-room I found my uncle not only cheered up but even amused:
dear god, an editor had had the brass to *print* this thing?—how
could you say, even of the kind of people we elect, that the difference between his ass and first base had never been adequately
explained to him! I said well but think what kind of people we
must be to *elect* that kind of people, and in due course we went in
to lunch.

But saddling up, afterwards (Mrs. Grammace had done the sweetbreads périgourdine admirably. Uncle said God bless, where'd she
learn *this?* I said 'Miss Francesca.' He said nm.) —saddling up to
go, he got round to it. What a darling of a girl—and so lovely to
look at too! And when they were pleased with one of us what a
sweetness they could be! J'étais *fort* à plaindre! He meant, dammit,
hadn't she lived with me going on three years? You think a girl's
more or *less* yours, and then suddenly you find yourself reciting
Wiat's

They flee from me, that some tyme did me seke.

But at least I could tell myself *I* wasn't just one of those first happy
fancies they shudder at later. Been perhaps a certain dreamy in-
competence about some of Francesca's decisions, but God bless
shouldn't even endearing young women aspire to be mature or
something?—become George Eliots?—Georges Sands? ". . . and
you've doted, dammit, as well as the expected verbs," he finished
briskly, and swung himself up into the saddle. "Thank 'ee kindly
for lunch. Tell Mrs. Grammace again what beautiful food. Look,
all I'm saying is, I suppose, it's the endearing ones throw your
judgment off. And I'm *fond* of you!" he cried, and was away.

But at the edge of the woods he pulled up and turned round in the saddle. "D'you think she's ever likely to forget you though either?" he called, and waved an arm, and was gone.

I was touched. But when I went up to change for the afternoon's work on the folly I was building in the 'near' beechgrove, a Palladian tempietto, I found the bed neatly made up, with fresh sheets. As if it were the day for it. And, of course, with fresh pillow-cases too.

3

So, generally, I suppose I was vulnerable to the amenities of almost any enticing disorder.

For example, an end-of-term faculty party I'd been dispirited enough to go to: there, across the room, gazing at me, was exactly the kind of blue-eyed Celt I knew nothing about whatever. So I crossed the room.

And sure enough, her name was Mairead, and her eyes had begun to ask me their unanswerable questions before we'd so much as exchanged our preliminary biographies. She was new faculty; a medievalist; her husband was new faculty too; in philosophy; but he was (could I imagine it?) philosophically *supercilious* about Aquinas! We took our drinks and sat on the stairs, out of the din; she didn't know my articles; was I as Wasp as I made them sound? her husband was a Wasp too; why were we so difficult; sometimes she could hardly bring herself to speak to him; and *not* because of just Aquinas! There was a grape arbor in the garden, behind; presently we were strolling there, to and fro, our drinks held ritually before us, the warm starlight filtering through the dusky trellised tracery of the vines too faint to see a face by; being attracted to someone was just being attracted, what did I *mean*, a 'classic posture' of women! ho, was I stuffy as well as a Wasp? a willingness to take me or *any* man 'under advisement' was merely how one was brought up! But if I *understood* that, yes I might see her home, this happened to be (again!) an evening she wasn't speaking to her husband—and in the darkness of her portico she'd have handed herself over to me till he found us there, but by then I knew I was being used for trouble, and I kissed her merely as called for, and left.

Still, it was luck that '52's Fifteenth Reunion happened to be the very next week.

We had a marquee and a dance-floor, that year, out in the warm June night; and somewhere along toward the small hours Friday I spotted a very pretty girl sitting it out with the stuffiest of my old roommates—a waste of humane resources that I instantly, as a man with eyes and a heart, felt to be intolerable. So I hailed him, and was jovially introduced ("—lovely bride of old Studdy Sheward, whaddaya know!"). . . . 'Sheward'? ah, well, the Class abounds in people I never saw in my life, campus or anywhere, but clearly old Studdy was a man of taste: his Mrs. S. was far more than just pretty—close to, she was by god an absolute dish! So we disposed of the preliminaries: her name was Suzanne (or wasn't I formal); she was from Wilmington; Studdy was with Du Pont there —he was plants-manager for one of their dynamites; where he'd careened off to, at the moment, she had no idea, wives weren't at Reunions to be companions were they? I said ah but at Reunion we were all of us wandering apparitions; *terrible* people to marry, Princeton men; but wasn't she dancing? and she said but when not! and she was as lovely to have in your arms as she was to look at. We did dutifully go back, after three or four encores, to see to my ponderous roommate; but God had seen to him, he'd vanished, so she and I smiled an unspoken *Think of that!* at each other, and tripped decorously back to the floor.

But now, the way she felt in my arms—suddenly I found myself thinking but holy god am I *imagining* this? so *soon*, this lovely signal? . . . That soft flutter of breathlessness against my cheek, was it hers, or in my mind, and mine? Though ah, what is it that happens, and one knows?—*both* know! Or what is it that women do, so that for a dizzying moment it is as if, somehow, one had heard the first murmur of a promise, in a secret room? . . .

So (as a man of taste myself) I explored: did she ever come to Philadelphia?

Oh, sometimes. Shopping. Caldwells and places.

I said I meant for lunch? I meant with me.

So she leaned back in my arms and gazed at me.

For instance I said next week some time?

The gaze turned faintly mocking.

I said no, but *seriously*. Meet her the pavement outside Caldwells, even, why not. Come out jangling her summer bangles and there I'd be?

She murmured oh dear.

Heart on my '52 blazer sleeve!

Oh but so *headlong?* And so *soon!* (But she was smiling.) Because what if she— She meant she— Oh *dear!* because what if she very carefully didn't eat lunch!

I said but girls who didn't eat lunch could still be *asked* to lunch good god couldn't they?

She said sweetly, that was what she meant!

I thought well be damned if that'd been the signal! So I protested: was I some kind of marauder? What cockeyed category was she consigning me to!

But now she was back in my arms, close and warm against me again. And murmuring: Oh but such a fuss? and when didn't she at least *very* much like the way we danced together? . . . So I gave it a miss for that evening, and just enjoyed the slender arms round my neck, the elegant chignon against my cheek, the ballerina body—till, finally, her damn' husband came lurching blearily in, and reeled off to bed with her. Stumbling drunk as that there's nothing to be done with them, and I'd talked her as far as she'd go into anything that evening anyhow.

But Saturday night, dancing again, we found we had come a long way. Now, we talked so little, as we danced (and were cut in on; and I cut back, and we danced again), that it was almost as if we knew so well what we would say, if we spoke, that part of the secret pleasure was to leave it unspoken. Or, perhaps, it was as if everything that needed saying at this stage had been said; everything decided, even; as if we knew, already, that the private language we might (and soon!) find ourselves speaking was so full of discoveries, so new, that the vocabulary of our separate pasts was obsolete, inadequate to what we would want to say. So why bother with words at all, till it was time!

But about midnight this enchanted nonsense was interrupted. I saw the Club steward signaling to me from the edge of the dance-floor; and when we danced over, 'Scuse him but was this Miz Sheward? count of he was afraid Mistuh Sheward, he— Well looked like Miz Sheward ma'am she better *come!* And ah, well, there was Studdy, slumped forward over a coffee-table in the billiard-room, head on his arms, and by god so passed out he wasn't even mumbling.

I was nobly *outraged!* The offense of it to the Club and civilization in general was supportable, not to say what they were long used to, but the affront offered the adorable girl I was in the process of disseizing him of was *unspeakable!* And look at the sodden son-of-a-bitch!—haul *that* seventeen-stone-minimum up two

flights of stairs to his bed? *hoh!* I said to the steward, here Henry
lend a hand, and we dragged the body over to a couch and shov-
eled it up onto it. Let him sleep it off; it's a warm night; the hell
with him.

I thanked Henry, and sent him off. Then, finally, I turned
round to— Well, she was still the lout's wife wasn't she? so what
would I find. Rage? Derision? Shame? Fuming exasperation?
Tears? . . . Or would it likelier be (since it began to look as if
this could have been going on) some variety of conjugal stoicism.
Ladylike inurement? Womanly desolation?

Well, none of them! Simple *fury,* and I was delighted with her
—and by god *for* her, the properly-brought-up angel! And mightn't
I have had enough ordinary common sense to tell her I adored her
by *saying* so?

Instead, "Poor guy," I heard myself mumble. "A damn *shame!*"

She said in a voice of ice, "I don't think you are necessarily the
one to know!" and spun on her heel and was out of the room without a look behind.

. . . Not even a good night?

No, but the logic of it? Is a man to be deprived of a girl because
the competition *isn't* competitive?

—Ah, but the poor sweet. What dignified justification can a
woman offer herself for having married a jock?—and with a pro-
spective lover who knows there isn't any (me) right there looking
on! And for all she knows, *pitying* her!

Dear God, I thought, what if it turns out she'll never want to see
me in her life again?

—Ah well. I crossed Studdiford's manly hands on his chest like
a fallen crusader's, and went upstairs and out to the marquee, to
find her. She wasn't *there?* I charged back through the Club and
out into the echoing night. There was a solitary drunk shambling
along toward me from Washington Road, and a folkmoot of cel-
ebrants cruising off in the other direction, beyond Olden Street,
but no girl either way. Could she have gone to bed, and the hell
with me? Or just gone to the loo. Did she give a damn about me
at all! I ran back into the Club, and through the public rooms.
She wasn't in any of them. Nor in the marquee. I began to feel an
immense disquiet. But what do you do? I gave her a gentlemanly
quarter of an hour. And then another. And then goddammit
another! until finally I got my car and took off for home, cursing
the men young women in their folly marry.

And went to bed snarling: was I falling in love with the damn' girl, for god sakes, or just was I frustrated? And suppose in the morning I found I was both!

And what if I also found, when I got back to Reunion, that she'd simply—and heartlessly!—*gone.* . . .

—Well, gone, yes, I found she was, and early—they'd it seems loaded Studdy into the car for her at practically dawn, and she'd taken off, with a mere coffee for breakfast. But can a matter-of-fact man *ever* quite imagine what an angel they can decide to be?—the minute I walked into the Club, there God bless was Henry with the note she'd left for him to hand me:

Oh dear oh dear. But if you are on the pavement outside Caldwells Wednesday noon you will see me come out.

I was stunned—this was TRUE? . . . I floated in among the sleep-sodden hangovers of my breakfasting classmates in such a haze of blissful solipsism that I might have been alone in the dewy morning of the world.

But it was a Philadelphia noon in the past-belief here and now that I had to see to the logistics of, and I took care of what contingencies a man of sensibility could. Be in town, I told Mrs. Grammace, till *late* Wednesday night; leave me a midnight supper, would she kindly? and then take the day off? Dillie too. I drove into Philadelphia, Tuesday, for a couple of timing runs round the Caldwells block: if the angel said noon, with luck noon it would be. I made sure (with, I admit, a pang) that the bed in Francesca's room was made up—décor or decorum, as might be called for. I rode Pouliche over to my uncle's. And walked back through the green early-summer woods in such an astonished confusion at what seemed to be happening to me that I suppose only long habit kept me from losing my way.

So, Wednesday, I pulled in to Caldwells' curb at a very competent 11:57, heart beating high with simple-minded hope; and sure enough, at 12:01 there she came, serene and town-shopping elegant in skirt and summer cardigan, faintly smiling at me as she crossed the pavement to the car, sun on her hair in the lovely day, shoulder-bag swinging. Which I took, smiling too, and we went through the charade of public greeting as taught to, cheek kissed and all; friends, you'd have thought, seeing us, from the blameless kindergartens of our childhood; and by 12:04, so help me, we were *off!*

(And if, even this, it was still a bit breathtaking to believe, could I have so much as conceived of it, of *any* of it, a mere five days before either?—yet now, no more than a thirty miles of I-95 until honest to *god* this adorable stranger I had still not even kissed would be stepping out of my car into my arms?)

—But it was hours on, many hours, the long murmur of afternoon fading into evening, before we bothered with accounting for either this headlong accommodation to chance or the wordless assent that had got us here. I remember her, at last, kneeling back beside me in the now shadowy bed, her body the pallor of silver in the summer dusk, gazing down at me as if in grave appraisal, evening by now so lost in the soft edges of night that I hardly made out her eyes.

Though it turned out what she was was gently amused. "*Fancy* this!" she said. "And without a word spoken!"

Well, but she'd as good as. I said, "There *was* that about how we danced."

"We needed to say that either?—hoh! And when anyway I was making it I thought oh *dear* how much too plain I was pleased with you!"

"I was to think *this* pleased?"

Which amused her again. "The things you seem to have been taught to expect!" she mocked. "And when I am *not* volage? Because my sweet you know as well as I do, this shouldn't have happened as fast as this at *all!*"

As if 'volage' (or not) had anything to do with it! I put a deprecating hand to her cheek, to her temple, fingers in the warm tangle of her hair, and she tilted smiling across me. ". . . and almost I *didn't* leave that ladylike note for you?" she murmured. "Oh sweet *think* how awful!" and gently collapsed, uncoiling, legs slipping down and in along mine; and so to sleep.

I lay there, watching the day fade beyond the windows, the soft flutter of her breath in the hollow of my shoulder, an elegant knee between mine; volage or not—*husband* or not!—how was I ever to let this one go? Yet what man of sense would expect— Ah, even that soft ". . . what a *pleasure* pleasure can be," lips against my throat, an hour ago, how suppose it was more than just that hour ago's entrancement? A girl who could say it, good god what man of sense would ever let go!—but what vanity, or what simpleton besotment, could let me tell myself that this or any angel had never murmured it to a lover before? or the winds and the waters not carried it away each time then too!

But now she was waking. The arm round me stirred; its fingers drifted, exploring. Down the back of my neck; off along the curve of my shoulder; lightly back again, up into my hair. She stretched her length against me, murmuring; her knees hugged mine. Awake and—what?

And competent. She rolled up onto a shoulder, and smiled at me; I wasn't even beginning to feel hungry? —"but what flattery!" She kissed me briskly, and sat up. "And anyway *I*, my sweet," she finished, "am having a *bathe!*" and was gone.

Ah, well, I got into a dressing gown and went down to the kitchen to ice champagne and see what Mrs. Grammace had left as supper. Coq au vin, it turned out, and a casserole of rice, cooked. I set them to heat, and put dinner-plates and serving-dishes in the warming-oven. The ice-box also had a bowl of hulled strawberries and half yesterday's charlotte au chocolat; I set the table for whichever. Perhaps give the salad a miss? The dining-room's sconce-lights, I decided, rather than risk the candelabra— the beauty of women in candlelight has been a blessing from the beginnings of time, but what if this cool stranger I so badly wanted to acquire felt candlelight was for adolescents (say) or, still worse, *romantics!* I was untwisting the wire from the champagne cork when I heard the light tripping of high heels in the pantry, and I turned, and there she was—and if the déshabillé was a good deal too frivolously elegant to be romantic, dear god did it matter?—all over again I could hardly believe it, even now I'd begun to think (almost) that I knew better.

And almost she behaved as if I did—a kiss as light as a greeting, and as amused (and why not!—a *pledge* needed, by now?); and when I had poured our champagnes, how approving she seemed, drifting about, sipping, inspecting things, while I finished my cas-seroles. "What a spotless kitchen," she said. "*And* pantry. You must have a very good woman come in. Or have you a man."

I said woman; a Mrs. Grammace; been looking after me fresh-man year Princeton on. Old Retainer by now! But getting on— these last years I'd added a maid.

"You have a housemaid? you mean *too?*"

Good-sized house; why not?

"But isn't a housemaid-too rather grand for a bachelor?"

Ah, well, I said, Mrs. Grammace—somebody who'd been with you that long?—and not so spry now as she was?

"Oh dear," she said, "a *real* old family servitor—that you *look* after? So she does then perhaps a bit run you I suppose?"

. . . Ran the house.

"She doesn't I mean cast a cold eye now and then?"

I said nonsense (was I to for god sakes *say* Mrs. Grammace was long used to the decorum of a tumbled bed in the guest-room too when status required, if that was what she meant?), anyhow *look*, dinner was ready, would she take the plates out of the warming-oven and put them on a hot-pad on the sideboard while I served up? and the champagne bucket too? so the critique of my staffing practices gave place to higher things.

And the night held no more questions than had the afternoon.

Still, in the morning, as I took her on a wandering tour of the house, and the barn, and the springhouse, and the edge of the beechgrove where I was building the little tempietto of a folly over another spring, she came back to my 'staff.'

Because it had been she said so unexpected!

"Because naturally a woman would see the house *is* a bit big for even a young and energetic à tout faire, all those gleaming fire-place brasses if nothing else, goodness! but it's not the sort of thing a man thinks of. And that kitchen *Larousse* and Elizabeth Davids? I mean is it a topic of conversation but sweet I do have a husband, so perhaps haven't you a girl? Or maybe don't, but did, and she added the maid? I don't mean I haven't been— I mean the lovely way we— Oh dear I don't seem to be putting it the way I want to, because I am *not* how it sounds, but *do* you have a girl? Not that I see how it could be you couldn't have, the way *I*'ve been behaving about you! But hasn't a girl been living with you?—even perhaps till just now?"

I said, mildly, ah now, nobody lives alone.

"But is perhaps whoever it was coming back?"

"Look, dammit," I said, "from that first heart-stopping half-hour at Reunions have I behaved like a man with *any* part of his mind on any woman on earth but you? 'Coming back,' *god* no!"

"But you've kept her maid for her, haven't you?"

"Kept for Mrs. Grammace, not *her*! She's gone to Italy—for a couple of years! On a scholarship at Urbino!"

"She was still *college-age?*"

"Ah angel," I said, "what *is* this! She's *gone*. For *good!* And any-way she was in *grad*-school! And Bennington before that—she's pushing twenty-*three!*"

". . . What was her name."

I said Francesca Drewes; a Boston girl; very *proper* Boston girl. But then she got this one-of-a-kind fellowship in architecture. For which her professors said she had extraordinary talent. So she took off. In tears—having after all been properly brought up. As said.

Was I to have stood in her way?

"You sound as if your mind was a little on her still."

I said dammit the girl'd *lived* with me! Two *years!*

"Except now suddenly you're deeply in love with *me?* Oh dear," she said, sounding amused, "are you perhaps a *bit* volage?"

(*This?*—from a wedded wife who—*oh-dear-oh-dear* or not—had made me a ladylike assignation a bare thirty-six hours after we'd *met?* . . .)

But what's casuistry. "You lovely thing," I said, "had you any idea, either, this short week ago, that you'd be strolling in a Bucks County beechwood, this or *any* midmorning, amusing yourself mocking the helpless adoration of a man you wouldn't know existed till the next day? Was I to expect to feel the way God help me I find I do? As if the *timing* of a thunderbolt mattered!"—but of course by now she was laughing at me.

—And first times I suppose yes anyway: the random irrelevances! A first time, in principle, is a guided tour (in this case, of me and the habitat that came with me) that you offer a nice woman as a statement of the devotion she has only to say, to have as hers forever. (It is also of course an affectionate warning of whatever it is you hope she's about to let herself consider being talked into.) But here, *now,* for the first time in my life, a girl I wanted to be as pleased with herself about me as she seemed to be with me, had this blasted *husband,* and how badly *was* it likely to spoil things?

—With Carla, between my awe and my innocence, it had hardly occurred to me to wonder how she accounted to herself for me; nor had I bothered about Megan's husband—with the guy way off in London, *was* it adultery?—New Jersey, after all, hadn't been a British jurisdiction for two hundred years! But Suzanne I suddenly found I— Why had she walked into *anybody's* arms? To begin with, she was too serenely beautiful to need reassurance. Or 'damage control.' How *did* she feel about her damn' husband?—should I, in decency, take into account the feelings she must have had for the guy back before she gave up on him?—if only because wouldn't it have a bearing on the practical logistics of where we should meet, and how?

I admit, I had always more or less taken my uncle's relaxed view of husbands. They should be thought of, he once said, as a (preferably offstage) character in the unchanging comedy of manners that marriage has been from Classical antiquity on. Ovid's worldly *Paris to Helen* letter can translate into purest Congreve: *Sure, madam, our manners are not so ill as to use his lordship's absence from your bed with the incivility of disinclination.* For if the style is Restoration, the scenario is immemorial.

Yes; but in this particular *Epistle*, Ovid has his Menelaus conveniently off on a royal visit to Crete, whereas Studdy it appeared was hardly ever away, touring his damn' plants, longer than overnight, and even that, God help us, only every other week. Even the logistics of keeping in touch might be a nightmare! In fact all we'd as much as settled, when I put her on her train in Trenton, midafternoon, was that I clearly shouldn't risk calling her; *she* would call *me*; so I spent the weekend in a fume of frustration as good as adolescent.

And the fatuities of doubt. For though the Saturday mail brought a Friday special delivery—

> my thoughts this morning are
> as tangled as my hair
> —Lady Horikawa

—did it mean she was as happily haunted as I was, or that she was upset, and this charming couplet was Japanese second thoughts? Suddenly I found I was *appalled* at what I could see happening to me. . . .

But the difference from Francesca? (Which perhaps was *not* that there might never have been a way to annul, to outgrow, the difference of ages: I was in my next-to-last year at Penn Charter, dammit, when she was born!)

For instance (and bluntly), hadn't she—well, at first hadn't she amused me? Then of course *also* delighted me; and I'd acquired her. Naturally I'd then (by and large) taught her to make love—a flattering pupil I'd in consequence pampered; and indulged. So hadn't I then pretty much created her? Created dangerously endearing, I admit, but *yes*, created! As a delight. For myself. And then in due course I'd found I was—probably the simple-minded word was 'deprived'—of my creation; et voilà. Simply that? . . .

Whereas now, *this* girl—if we were dealing with reality in exotic couplets, God help me,

> this girl will bring
> annihilation upon me

if she heartlessly didn't ring me Monday morning early. . . .

But she did: a tinkling shower of small change into a coinbox, and then a bland "It's *you?*—imagine!" and would I feed her lunch? Because she was driving to her sweetie of a godmother's in

Bernardsville; she *often* did; she *loved* her; and now think of my having that river-road entrance on the very *way!* And it had been there I'd said since 1702?—what foresight! So see me in an hour? and was gone.

'Godmother'? . . .

—But phoning from where, 'an hour'? What was a likely socio-economic geography for upper New Castle County?—for example, did Du Pont middle executives who lived in Wilmington live *in* Wilmington?

Though what matter—she'd have been phoning from somewhere on the way: Claymont, Marcus Hook, Eddystone. So 'an hour' meant 'an hour at the outside': God bless, she could *be* here in forty minutes! I spent twenty of them discussing a light summer lunch with Mrs. Grammace (ice a champagnized Saumur too, would she?), and took off for the river road, the rest of my life suddenly an undelivered doom.

—But what is there, ever, to think of, waiting, except the irreducibles?—what, given the nature of woman, will have to be accommodated; what (discreetly) changed; what you can be seen as offering, beyond the vanity of your adoration. . . .

—Anyway what if it turned out 202 was her usual route to Bernardsville instead? She'd hit the river up at New Hope! And take *longer* than forty minutes!

Except she'd said '*on* the way.' Which would be I-95.

. . . Still, what *is* there to think about, waiting. I began a two-way traffic-count, if only to think about something else.

So among other things she was the twenty-second up-river car (just after the thirty-fourth down), a big Volvo, coming so fast its left-turn signal burst out blinking a bare fifty yards away—still braking violently as she shot skidding in past me and sprawled to a stop in a wild scattering of gravel beyond, and as I raced to the car she tumbled out laughing and gasping ("—I nearly drove *past* you!") and fell into my arms.

So it was some time before we bothered to speak.

Or were competent to. I seem to remember mumbling something about ". . . four DAYS without you . . ." but for all I know I may only have felt it, hardly even thought it into a phrase. Once, too, somewhere along, she leaned back in my arms and murmured an equally simple-minded "It *is* how I remembered, imagine! . . ."—good god, you'd have thought it hadn't even begun to occur to either of us how far this helpless delight in each other was the discovery of a pledge!

But she put it in words before I did. She pushed back in my arms, wrists lightly on my shoulders, and gazed at me, sober at last. ". . . See?" she said, gently. "It *is* as bad as I was afraid it was—oh my love what can we do but try to *face* 'What shall we do'?"

—Well but good god *that* topic could turn out as ambiguous as her tangled hair! I changed subjects instantly: what was all this about a godmother?

Didn't Quakers have *any* of the civilized amenities? "Marraine's my *marraine!*" she cried. "Who I tell *everything* that matters! So how not about you? She *loves* me—so if I'm even a little to go on misbehaving with you, she has to understand why."

'*Misbehaving*'!

"But oh sweet what would *any* loving godmother say! 'This Mr. Coates, darling child, seems to have made you feel what in my day I'm afraid we called "wanton"—heaven of *course*, sweetheart, but is that a reason for telling me you "love" him?' She is *old-régime* New Jersey, Johnnie!"

I said but God blast what if the woman—

But "Oh sweet as if I'd tell her if I thought she'd all *that* disapprove . . .," she said, and came back into my arms.

But at lunch she said no but what Marraine probably *would* be was— Well, she must have had lovers herself once, she'd been (you could *see!*) very beautiful, so she'd be *concerned* for her. Because love was upsetting, and what if it were *seriously* upsetting? "And Johnnie you *are* disorienting— I tossed for *hours* Thursday night trying to remember what we merely *talked* about, driving from Caldwells, Wednesday! I couldn't think of a single topic— can you imagine being so bemused? All that way, and I couldn't even remember whether we'd talked about something we must've talked about, like Reunions. . . . I lay awake there, on and on and on, and all I remembered was things like leaning my head back against the seat and looking at your profile as you drove. You know? And speculating about what it would be like, goodness was *going* to be like, touching you! And whether I was going to be pleased with myself about you. (Though I thought but how possibly couldn't I be!) And you know, we must have been *saying* things all the time! . . ."

—All very well; but I was still worried when I saw her off, after lunch, at the river road. I said, "You telling her *how* bad I am for you?"

"She *loves* me; am I to tell her you're not? . . ."

"But 'concerned' for you?—holy god what kind of old-régime New Jersey lovers' incompetences has she had to put up with!"

"Hush," she said, and kissed me. "And anyway I'll phone tomorrow morning, and tell you. Tell you *everything* she said. So don't *fuss!*" and was gone.

I walked slowly back in (to a house I now *knew* was how empty!) in a kind of grim disquiet. For *when*, even, I might see her again was as much in the goddam air as ever! And had we even got round to discussing a way to keep in touch with each other!—and for all I knew, the reason we hadn't was that God help us what if there *wasn't* a way! . . .

But midmorning next day would I accept a collect call for anyone from a Mrs. Sheward in Hockessin, Delaware? and then a caressing "*Me*, reporting."

"Are you *all right?*"

"Sshhh, I'm *reporting*. Marraine says *eventually* perhaps I should have her inspect you, if only to decide whether I'm deplorable or just rather—"

" '*Deplorable*'!"

"Well sweet I told her about us from the *very* first, I mean looking up and seeing you coming through the marquee straight *at* me, and then the way we—oh Johnnie *all* of it! So she said, 'As wickedly attractive as *that*, sweetheart, but not married, fifteen years out of college?'—hadn't I wondered whether you mightn't be a bit heartless?—or been always 'in love,' which comes to the same thing! Hadn't I wondered whether an interval now and then, even if only for properly-brought-up appearances, would show more character? . . . So you see?"

I saw.

"So what was I to say. But then she said 'Coates?'—she'd *known* a Princeton boy named Coates, back when she was going to proms and weekends. She didn't remember his given name, but it seems one June night he very charmingly tried to seduce her in a canoe on your Lake. So *think* how amusing, she said, if it turned out you looked like him!"

(. . . My *father?* . . .)

"Because if it happens you do, do you think she'll need to meet you to find *out* you do?—old-régime New Jersey is still a *very* efficient social network, even if it's not the Establishment now. Oh Johnnie they all *know* each other! Two or three phone calls and she'll have her Princeton boy's given name *and* anything else she wants to know about him. And if it turns out you're not his son or whatever, *who* you are! And at least two or three of your Princeton hostesses will be Old New Jersey, so their m'mas and aunties will have *decades* of authentic gossip, about you and your various ménages. And what your taste in girls has *really* been—oh *dear!*" she finished, laughing at me.

—But in God's name what was all this about? A woman's judgment of a man's taste in women depends on whether he's to *her* taste (she bother, if he isn't?)—so was this somehow about Francesca? . . .

Or was I just to take this elaborate Old New Jersey social-registering to mean a provisional nihil obstat?—when what in *fact* obstabat was this heartbreaking off-limits geography (including wherever the hell Hockessin was!) that we'd not even begun to deal with? . . .

But then she took my breath away. "No but sweet *the* thing I'm calling about," she went on, in a different voice entirely, "is so lovely I saved it till last—out of the *blue* at breakfast Studdy announced he's taking his boss deep-sea fishing in his new boat *Friday*, and they won't—"

"*You angel!*"

"Yes oh *think!*—and till *Monday?* . . . Johnnie I feel as if some— I feel *shivery!* Oh sweet *imagine* only three days till *three days!*" So she had decided shouldn't she perhaps go visit her old roommate, in New York; but since the Washington–New York trains that stop in Wilmington sometimes very affectionately stop in Trenton too, what if she got off a 10:53 one, Friday morning? In good time for lunch. I was not to draw conclusions: just she freelance *loved* me, see? And still expected to at 10:53 Fri—oh what a *pity* I was a Quaker and couldn't thank God properly! And rang off, laughing.

—Yes, but God bless, *lunch* first? after a week of agonizing deprivation? with every bedroom in Uncle's great empty house at our disposal? *huh!* I rang the lodge, told the manager's daughter I was putting an overnight guest in the acacia room Friday night, 'd be eating at my place, breakfast too, thank her I'd see to the room's being ready but be kind of her to do the straightening up afterwards; and took off, to see to it.

—Had it been Great-Aunt Amanda who'd decided to have the lovely room repaneled in acacia? I slung the tall curtains back and threw open the windows to the warm amenities of noon; I found sheets and pillow-cases and made up the elegant four-poster. (With a light summer blanket? Or not. I decided *with*, but a bedspread, no.) I laid out towels and a couple of sorties de bain in the bathroom; the hot water I'd turn on Friday, on my way to the train.

(How many undisillusioned years had it been since I'd met a—could I still call it 'a beguiled girl'?—on a station platform. . . .)

At the door I turned: it looked I decided *damn'* charming, my stage-set! The blond paneling mellowed the noon from beyond the windows to a soft radiance, everywhere, inside; even under the bed's stately baldaquin the luster of summer was floating in. By god how *couldn't* a properly-brought-up young woman find the scenario as charming as the set—godmother'd or not!

("... Though my improvising love mightn't you have *told* me?" she murmured, nuzzling me, Friday afternoon. "All the way on the train I wondered. I mean how would we simply *manage!* Because I thought 10:53 is eleven, and then the drive, but then lunch at *one?* So shouldn't I have taken an afternoon train instead, for better timing? Yes except no matter *what* schedule, was I simply to arrive and disappear upstairs with you? like *that?* in your *not*-all-that-big a house! We can hardly behave as if as mothering a for-years servant as Mrs. Grammace just wasn't *there!* Well but your barn either?—with your little maid nervously clearing her throat below the hay-mow to announce that lunch was served? *hoh!* So I thought oh well, the woods, then, I suppose, oh dear why hadn't I worn something that wouldn't get totally— I never *thought* of your lovely uncle's, imagine!")

So we passed up tea as well as lunch. "No but spiritually so smart of you too," she said, still amused, as at last we drove round to the dower house. "Now I'll be able to go for minutes at a time without having to reach out and touch you. . . ."

—But it was 'the rest of time' or a reasonable equivalent that *I* badly wanted this weekend to arrive at a Sense of the Meeting about—and what if all she had in mind was an affair, a passade, a *nice* folly, the unregretted kind a woman is due now and then? So I had to play the weekend dialogue by ear.

Was it for instance a good omen, or a bad, or not even an omen, that she began to explain herself to me. Saturday afternoon I took her to Uncle's ("There's *more* to see than Great-Aunt Amanda's bedroom?") and as we walked through the green summer woods I'd been describing my father's and uncle's likely escapades there in their college days—what scenes the old ladies' spinster ghosts must have been affronted by (imagine wandering in, unwarned, from Elysium, to find *this* was how the human race conducted itself!), and she had described how, when *she* wanted to know things, she'd asked her m'ma's Venetian maid, who if she wasn't always accurate was hair-raisingly explicit; and then, with the only transition a softer voice, would I mind? but she thought we should clear things up about Studdy. . . .

Because she'd seen the look on my face when he'd come reeling in Friday night. Because among other things I'd obviously not thought I'd ever seen him in my life!—"when Johnnie he'd *rowed* at Princeton! all four *years*, rowed! And as far as you were concerned he'd never existed? What kind of intellectual snob were you! And when I *knew* I was falling in love with you? . . ."

I said *nonsense*, all I'd—

"And he's *not* a drunk! Just it was Reunions. And seeing his old friends beginning not to look all that young anymore, or the way they looked when none of you had any responsibilities. Studdy's a *very sweet man*. And always has been. He was also the most beautiful jock *any* of us had ever had after us, and he was crazy about me, so why *shouldn't* I fall in love with him! And sleep with him, and marry him. Johnnie that's how I *was* then! Then, Saturday night, in the billiard room—"

"I was an *oaf!*" I said.

"Yes my darling you *were!* And I was stricken—for then I mean how did you feel about *me?* Because by that time I'd begun to realize *how* badly I'd fallen in love with you. So it was a *disaster.* I went up and took a long shower, to try to deal with it. Then later, one of the wives and I were brushing our teeth and she said, 'Sweetie where *were* you? Not *hiding* from that nice Coates man—he was frantic, that last hour, looking for you!' So I felt grateful to you, for being upset. Even though I only thought I knew *why* you were upset. So then I thought about how we'd danced together—and so of course *didn't* get to sleep! At last I crept downstairs in the dark club, to the writing-room, and wrote you my letter."

—So what was I being told.

With impenetrable complications moreover in how she felt about *me*. "Because I just seem to feel so pleased with myself," she told me, late that night, "—and when on the train, yesterday, I thought but what am I doing? I mean I'm in a perfect folly about you, I *know* that, but how am I to *behave*, knowing it? Because don't you see how frightening? What if I find myself behaving in ways I know perfectly well women *can't* behave! In half an hour there you'd be, on the Trenton platform, and in another half-hour— When what if I oughtn't even to *consider* making love with you till I'm a little sobered up about you!"

I naturally snorted.

"But my sweet I'd hardly known you a decent two weeks!—and

there I was, *lawless* about you! Anyway breaking every *feminine* law there is! And what if, Monday morning, I wasn't going to be able to make myself leave? I am not *made* for such disorder!"

But was a Sense of the Meeting about me to be left undetermined this time too?—the 'meeting' simply prorogued? So, Sunday morning, half by chance, I took the risk.

We were in the barn, seeing to the horses. I was at the feed-bin, scooping oats into a bucket; she had been inspecting the Great-Aunts' elegant surrey. I was topping off the bucket, when she came up behind me and leaned sweetly against my back, arms round me, lips lightly nibbling the shoulder-seam of my shirt, murmuring ". . . mmmmmm?" I was amused; I thought God bless, this was *Suzanne* being flirtatious? what next what next; but I said mmmmmm *what?* But when she answered, ". . . feeling like this *without* champagne isn't 'mmmmmm'?" and came round into my arms (upsetting the bucket back into the bin) I decided God help me am I ever likely to find her more simple-mindedly persuadable than this? and chanced it.

"Champagne or no champagne," I said, "will you behave like the angel I think you are and at least *begin* to consider marrying me? *I love you.* If I can't somehow— Suzanne my life *stops* when you leave!"

"Ah Johnnie," she said.

So at any rate I'd sobered her. "This time *too*," I said, "are you going to take off without facing up to the ordinary civilities of what's happened to us? What good's fluttering your flighty lashes at me when you live fifty totally nullifying miles—"

She put her fingers over my lips, and gazed at me dolefully. "Do you think I haven't been out of my mind too?" she said. "At not being day and night where I could put out my hand and touch you? No but sweet suppose— I mean do we have to be *married?* Would it make you unhappy and uncertain about me if we weren't? Because most of us got married because marry was what you *did* then, after college. And now a lot of us find ourselves wondering oh dear why did we! And of course there really aren't all that many high-minded excuses, so you give up and have a baby."

I said but *she—*

"So when I find I love you like *this* what can I do but worry whether just coming to live with you— Have you thought how you'd handle *us* for your Princeton friends? Because with your girls it's been simple: people have got used to *girls'* living with a

man, it's an extra rite de passage everybody *knows* is what happens.
So Francesca you just introduced to your friends as the replacement of whoever had been the replacement of whoever it had
been before that, and why not? But my love *I* am a Married
Woman, and have people quite decided what to *decide* about that
particular status in this particular situation? Because in for instance Marraine's day, if your darling goddaughter turned up as
a new wife (there was of course *no* acceptable divorce, but you
could be new thanks to, say, death) you told your friends there the
lovely child *was*, in Bucks County or wherever, and everybody
called. Or left cards, there being maids then, to answer the door.
But that was then. And even today—I don't think Studdy would
divorce me for adultery, he's *much* too nice (even if *you*'ve only
seen him at Reunions), but isn't there a good bit of Old New Jersey
about Princeton still? And in any case Princeton's so full of *money!*
Mightn't I be exposing you to—oh *you* know the sort of stuffy remark people can make, 'Late thirties, isn't he?—you'd think he'd
be thinking of settling *down!* Huge place like that and all that
money just go to some distant cousin or other? . . .' "

Ah, well. A *little* irony was called for. I said, good god, and suppose Studdy decided to sue me for changing his tax bracket—
wasn't she worried I couldn't afford her?

"I'm *serious!*" she cried.

But I was encouraged by her light-hearted—even teasing—an-
nouncements of the changes she would make in my establishment
if she came to live with me. She would bring her silver (though
some of mine wouldn't have to be stored). And she had a *great* deal
of china. Her great-grandfather's secretary could go against the far
wall of the back drawing-room if she took the finials off; the Pem-
broke table I had there now, she'd have upstairs—for of course *all*
Francesca's rooms would have to be stored, where else would we
put *her* sitting-room and dressing-room furniture? "Oh dear the
number of Francescas you've faithlessly recovered from since college!—think what any woman would risk, taking you on! Not that
any of *them* married you either, did they! But if career girls are
what you go for, how am I to explain your being after *me?*"

(Oh and *anyway*—how possibly did I think she could decide
reasonably about me when she was *with* me?)

Or again, Monday, as I drove her to her train, she said how
would I feel (*if* she came to live with me)—how would I feel if
she took her maiden name back? Taking it back would be a symbol for her Wilmington friends. And new people wouldn't know

she'd ever been called anything else. The deed-poll formalities could wait; it might complicate the divorce. But she could send her friends a faire-part. Or didn't I think.

So I began to be seriously hopeful. Ah, and anyway—this would be a Wednesday Studdy'd be off at his factories, and at least she'd be with me again.

But it was more. Tuesday midmorning, the phone: would I accept a collect call from a— I said god *yes*; and past belief, she'd *decided*: "I'm to take you to Marraine's tomorrow, for luncheon, poor sweet d'you mind so soon? Because I rang her up a little while ago and said, 'Darling I think I may be being acquired, so shouldn't you perhaps see why?' so she said ah, well, bring him to lunch, at least she'd— But what's the matter with you?" she ended, laughing.

'*Matter* with me'!!—the rest of my life suddenly this miracle? and I was *not* to explode at the fifty insupportable miles between us? . . .

And twenty-four hours to wait *besides?* And hours still, even *then* —to Bernardsville, *and* lunch, *and* back, God help me, *first?* . . .

—I had to *talk* about it to somebody!

And at any rate Mrs. Grammace had to know. I found her by herself in the kitchen. I said I knew how she felt about Miss Francesca. It had been heartbreaking, for both of us: there was a sweetness about Miss Francesca one didn't meet in a lifetime. But all this last year we'd known she would get her degree, and go. Perhaps she, Mrs. Grammace, had managed to accustom her feelings, as I had mine, to the inevitable good-bye.

But now I had had the great good fortune to meet Mrs. Sheward, whose marriage had played itself out; she was getting a divorce, and I had persuaded her to come live with me meantime; then I hoped she'd marry me.

She was bringing her silver, and her china, and a few pieces of her family furniture. Some of our things we'd store. Or my uncle take for Byberry.

But I very much hoped, needed I say, that these various changes would not affect her, Mrs. Grammace's, feelings about me, after these twenty years she'd looked after me with such wonderful kindness, and that she'd welcome Mrs. Sheward, who was *the* sort of young woman I'd just about given up hope of ever meeting—and perhaps Mrs. Grammace herself given up hope of my bothering to look for! And as "Well, sir," she said blandly, "we did wonder, me and the girl. But a very nice young lady she does seem, I will say,"

I felt free to spend the rest of the day dismantling (though with a pang) Francesca's rooms.

I got through the next morning rewriting the lead of a piece on our government's genius for picking *the* faction, in whatever country we were dealing with, that was certain to screw up whatever we were dealing with the country about. Could I for instance say the flaps and fiascoes had also occurred before corporation lawyers were standard at State? And when had that black-comedy slogan *Princeton in the Nation's Service* been thought up? Hibben's time? Dodds's? God knew, any day now some mute inglorious classmate of my own might loyally raise *his* voice too. But my mind wasn't really on it.

For goddamit, if nothing *else*, Bernardsville was twelve miles beyond Somerville, which was twenty-seven miles of 202 beyond New Hope, which was eight miles up-river from *here*; and *here* it was now past *eleven*—and did or didn't an Old New Jersey twelve-thirty-for-one mean what it said?

I went *out* to wait, fuming.

But that did it: there suddenly her Volvo came, charging round the stand of ash at the final curve of the drive—headlong *at* me, in fact she skidded and slithered the thing to a stop just short of lovingly running me down. And then she was out and into my arms and who *gave* a damn what o'clock it was. . . .

Though "Oh dear, instead of *all that*," she reproached me happily, when at last we'd taken off for Bernardsville, "I was going to give you just a chaste kiss of betrothal! Or don't Quakers know about that ceremony either? . . ." I said look, a lovely mauling's a lovely mauling; stop fussing and *drive*. So we made it by twelve-twenty.

And ah, well, Marraine. She was even more elegant an Establishment chatelaine than I'd expected, tall and straight, and still beautiful enough to take homage for granted: that first time, when she held out her hand in greeting I only just stopped myself from bowing over it and lifting her fingers to my lips. But she was not daunting: she addressed me as 'Mr. Coates' only the first half-hour or so's bland interrogatory, before (provisionally) I was admitted to the transitional informality of a simple 'you.' If her sweet godchild *must* insist on having a folly, I did, it seemed, appear to be an acceptable sort of young man to have it with—reasonably presentable, apparently well brought up, *more* than able to afford her (no matter what), of an age to show a few signs of character, and if a journalist at least a political journalist, and with a byline. Experienced enough, also, presumably, not to be *trying* about Suzanne's disinclination to marry again. ("Conformity is for people who don't have the position to make the rules, not for *us*.") And by the look of things the child had bewitched me to the point of a serious attachment. Which was as it should be, even if it was all one could expect. It was moreover clearly in my favor that I had appreciated the *generous* amount of saffron in the paella. In sum, when we made our adieux I was told I might kiss her cheek.

"Feel all better now?" I said, as we drove off.

"Don't be superior—family inspections are a *necessary* part of betrothals! How else can I be sure I'm not doing something unspeakably silly? And anyway, since I am not going to marry you, poor darling what other anniversary will you have, except our betrothal, to give me I hope very expensive bangles on? Ho, and such an easy date to remember—or didn't you know it's Midsummer Eve?"

(I was amused: neither of us had a druidy gene in our Sassenach makeups, but didn't she at least know Midsummer Eve is the shortest night of the year? . . .)

"And anyhow," she went on, "it *is* from this day forward, my darling, that I, Suzanne, take thee, John—and *that* 'thee' is honest Episcopal english, not Quaker dialect!—take thee, John, to my unwedded lover, to have and to hold, to love and to cherish, and most of the rest of it; and thereto I give thee my troth. What a pity all *you* can do with your troth is plight it, oh poor man, how sad!" she mocked, happily.

But then suddenly, "*You* drive," she said, and pulled up off the road.

I thought now what. "You all right?" I said.

"Of course I'm all right! Why shouldn't I be?—I've just handed myself over to you to be all right *with*! But do I have to put up with even a man I love's gazing gratefully at my profile for the next thirty-something miles?"

I said it was forty-seven, but we changed places.

Presently she said, as sweetly as if nothing had happened, "My love I didn't tell you, you didn't leave me breath to! but the car trunk is solid with luggage. I've brought at least half my clothes, d'you mind? winter things too. Because I—well, it's only practical, but I thought if I get Dillie to help me unpack and put away and find places for, it will make everything plain about *us*. And save time explaining. Anyway I will *not* go on indulging your Victorian attitude about servants' sensibilities with that absurd charade of tumbling the bed across the hall—as if Mrs. Grammace and Dillie believed it!"

Ah well, I was brought up, from time to time, by selected nannies. Who naturally believed what it was their duty *to* believe. But that wasn't the topic I was interested in. I said, "No affair of mine, but what *was* all that about, there leaving your godmother's?"

"Was all what about."

"Your profile going shy on me, for god sakes!"

"Oh taaah," she said, and leaned across and kissed me. "Don't you think even an insensitive Quaker might have guessed? It was just—and don't laugh!—suddenly I just found myself feeling very—oh, well, *newly betrothed* about you, why shouldn't I have, now Marraine's approved of you too, scandal or not! And in *that* fatuous condition was I to sit there feeling your eyes on me for even *one* of your forty-seven miles? *hoh!*"

4

It wasn't till the next June that my uncle met Suzanne. He had decided (sentimentally) to come back for Reunions; and when he got in, and rang up, I happened to be out—"and so," as he put it later, "here was *another* of these entrancing unknown voices you specialize in, introducing herself as blandly as if but-who-else? and sweetly asking me to dinner." And with womanly *concern*: had he jet lag? should we eat early? seven? But Johnnie'd want a *lot* of champagne first, so come say six-ish, even? *oh* but how pleasant, she was to *meet* him at last! . . . and from the moment she greeted him in the drawing-room doorway, smiling mouth held up for his kiss, he wanted her in the family.

As he as good as said, when I rode over a couple of mornings later. "Ah Johnnie," he said, straight off, "this *is* a lovely one!"— and the disposition of an angel besides! Was there a— No business of his, but was she might-he-affectionately-ask perhaps serious about me, did I think? Getting for instance a divorce?

I was amused. I said what made him think she had to be somebody's wife?

Beauty like *that* at—what'd she be? twenty-eight? thirty? and God bless not at least *between* undeserving husbands?

Up to *her* to go into her reasons; so I merely said, "Ah now, Uncle, remember that couplet of Donne's of yours—

> What! should we rise because 'tis light?
> Did we lie down because 'twas night?

With anything as lovely as Suzanne, is married or not-married the point either?"

But he was serious. "No but dammit Johnnie," he said, "a married woman can you know go *back* to her blasted husband! And for nothing more sensible than to have the fellow's baby—you conceive of such light-mindedness? *Heart*-breaking! *And* leaves you wondering, for the rest of time, whether you were anything by god to her but a nice folly yourself!"

(But what was this!—it'd happened to *him?* . . . The only 'married woman' of his I knew of was the beautiful Mrs. Hervey, and she'd been living with him from damn' near my first year out of Columbia. . . .)

But I said, "Oh, now, Uncle, aren't they *due* a nice folly now and then?—totally wasted on most of us the way they soon find they are, good god!"

So he looked at me. And finally said, "Ah, well, yes, I suppose how not. But been a grave mistake, giving women this strange right to Yes and No—how can a male god in his right mind have got conned *into* such a thing! Thank of course *Who*ever for their immemorial addiction to folly—what an enchanting characteristic to have thought up for them! Not that the sort of man they find to their taste isn't in as short supply now as it ever was. . . ."

(I finally said to Sue shouldn't she perhaps clear things up for him? He adored her; he'd accept whatever she told him. But remember, his undivorced sweet of an Anne Hervey had been living in Rome with him, *very* happily for both of them, ever since she'd bolted with him years ago; only *there*, there had been random forces majeures, including the pope—her English Catholic husband was a vengeful son-of-a-bitch who wouldn't've set her free even if the Church had allowed it. So analogies had to be avoided.)

Uncle John of course wanted Sue for me for keeps. When she told him she (forgive her?) didn't want to marry me or anybody, he was as courteously taken aback, and bemused, as if she had been a present he'd picked for me himself. "Dammit look," he said to me presently, as he was getting over it, "not marrying Francesca's one thing—and understandable: she was lovely, and did either of us ever meet a girl, of *any* age, we thought sweeter? but mightn't marrying her have caused comment? You're after all a *bit* young for a dirty old man!" Whereas one of the built-in amenities of a married woman was that she'd got over her virginal follies by marrying one. So now she'd offer a man a reasonably folly-free wife.

I said, "No, but Uncle, why not a folly-free live-in instead, if she wants it that way?"

"But what's this dejecting disinclination to marrying you," he cried, "if she means to stay! And by the look of it doesn't she? So then in God's name why not make it straightforward *socially*? There must still be *some* proper, old-fashioned drawing-rooms in Princeton, aren't there? Good god, in *my* day, there were even a couple of properly-brought-up millionaires! . . ."

And come to think of it, she had money of her own: hadn't it occurred to her the *taxes* you'd both save, married, good god?

("Oh dear," she said, when I reported this, "has he never heard of tax-free municipals? Yes but *marry* you, my love," she went on, kissing me. "What if I did and then felt I wanted to own you, as well as the rest of it? And what if that took *over* the rest of it? And think how bad for you owning me would be! And why is he being so out-of-*character* old-fashioned? This *isn't* his 1923—even Mar-aine's friends have behaved like old sweeties, and why not!")

So on the whole he accepted it; in fact the last time I ever saw him the subject didn't even come up. It was an autumn morning I was cleaning out a spring that had abruptly welled up in the forest floor halfway to Byberry (if there was going to be a serious flow it had to be dealt with)—and there he was, on a chestnut filly he'd recently bought, pulling up by my Jeep: dear god what a *mess*, why hadn't I got one of the men to give me a hand with it, how *was* I? 'd been on his way to make his adieux to my sweet of a young woman, and spotted me. Find her at home, 'd I think?

I said she'd be fetching us a picnic lunch in a quarter-hour or so, why didn't he join us? Cold-water set-around, but there was a jug of California plonk in the Jeep—every amenity!

She'd be the amenity! But no; lunch, alas no. He had to go to Boston before he took off for Rome. Memorial service. Friends beginning to die on him right and left. Made you *feel* your mor-tality! Not that, at *his* age, merely staying alive didn't sometimes strike him as a relatively trivial thing to stay alive *for*. No, but Suzanne coming he'd wait.

I said, dutifully, but who'd this been? an old friend?

"Ah, poor charming old bastard, yes," he said. "Roomed in Blair tower with him junior and senior years. And now he's gone. At *my* age. But imagine getting yourself shot dead in that squalid way before you could even scramble up out of the wretched girl's bed, whoever she was! You conceive of such disheartening maladresse? Of course on any reasonable theory of probability something of the sort should've happened years ago. Fornicating across cultural lines is a *fool* mistake!"

"Now, now, Uncle," I said, "*we* aren't peasants?"

"All right, across parochial traditions then, is it a matter of vocabulary?" he demanded. "Are there no maisons de passe in this goddam country but motor-courts? Ah, though, what a shocking thing to have happened to a perfectly decent church-going Presbyterian! Or was the poor guy an Episcopalian. Though wouldn't you think pretty much *anybody* literate, by this stage of civilization, would be more or less discouraged about our current Creator? Your grandfather'd plain given *up* on Him, they ever tell you?—felt He'd 'turned out badly.' Hardly bothered to wash the blood off His hands from one religious war to the next. . . . Ah, well, people like us are dying out too. But will you tell me what in God's kindly name I can say to the poor guy's widow?"

But he wouldn't stay to lunch with us. Boston was Boston, and he had to be there decently early; fly to Rome *from* there; so, come to think of it, this was a rivederci till spring. Could it be going-on-*four* years now that Suzanne had had the sweetness to give some direction to my life at last? He and I patted each other's shoulders, Sue gave him her tenderest kiss, and he swung himself into the saddle and was gone, with a last backward wave of an affectionate hand. Naturally it didn't occur to us that we shouldn't see him again. Why should it have?—man in *perfect* health, and no more than—what'd he be? sixty-nine? seventy?

So it was sudden. I was getting out of the shower early one morning, that next May, when the phone rang in the bedroom and I heard Sue answering, and then her shocked voice calling— "It's Anne; in Rome; it's your *uncle*; my darling he's *dead!*" and I knotted the towel round my waist, and ran in, incredulous still, to take the dressing-room phone, dripping.

The elegant Anglo-Irish voice was as poised, as beautifully controlled, as a formal call. The servietta had found him, when she'd brought the morning tea. I was *not* to grieve; he loved me; the last thing he would have understood was grief. Nor was I to worry about *her*. The doctor thought it almost certain he'd died in his sleep; and peacefully, from the look of his face. 'Une belle mort.' She'd thought she'd heard him snoring, in the night; he often did; no doubt that had been the—been his—it had been then he had been dying. ("And oh suddenly the loneliness in her voice!" Sue said, later.) How soon could I arrive? Not to bother with a letter of credit—she had plenty of cash. And I should of course stay with *her*. And Suzanne would she hoped be coming too—Jack had adored her, even more for herself than for me. We could decide on a service when I arrived; but did I remember? he wanted to be cremated, but she of course had no authority for it, so until I arrived she was having the customary things done; they were required it appeared before a cremation in any case. His will, and a certified Italian translation, were in his safe; the Embassy said my passport would be enough to certify me as executor. . . .

(But as I listened to the bleak, the irreducible recital, what I thought was Ah, Uncle, perhaps I find myself 'alone' now too. Not like Anne; but can I any longer feel what I've felt from childhood, that you were 'always *there*'? Suddenly it is as if it is my final liberty I have lost, the last carefree tag-end of who I was, young— no longer is your elder generation between me and the bounden duties you have sheltered me from with such affection, such long indulgence. Now a dozen unthought-of livelihoods depend on *me*; the destinies of some thirty horses have become *my* decision; *only* I can defend from despoilment these twenty-two hundred wooded acres still almost as Penn granted them a quarter of a millennium ago; and if it is no longer reasonable to toast one's irreplaceable house, as our ancestors could, with a stately

> May Taste respect thee, and may Fashion spare,
> Till Time preserve thee to the twentieth heir

—at least I am Byberry's eighth or ninth, and as far back as I can remember I have loved it: *my* help it is, Time has to depend on.)

But now Anne was talking to Sue on the bedroom phone: ". . . though one thing my dear you can help me decide. Jack has left me the villa on Cap Nègre along with everything else here, but I *don't* want it, without him. But rather than coldly sell it I think you should see it. Jack told me Johnnie adored it in his college summers. And if you find you like it too, may I simply give it to the two of you, with Jack's blessing? Furnishings of course and all, except I do want to keep that Paul Matthews portrait of Jack, in the piccolo salotto. Now, when shall you arrive? tomorrow?"

We took a night flight; but she had already seen to everything except the few legal chores she could not. She met us at the airport, dry-eyed and smiling, and told us how things stood, as she drove us back into town. Half Rome was consecrated basilicas, every conceivable religion including none; but none having been Jack's, none there should *be!* For herself, of course—well, we *knew* him, he'd affectionately forgiven her prayers for him while he was alive, why shouldn't he now too? As to a memorial service, secular or not, his ombra would deplore it, as pretentious, so she'd had the newspaper obituaries say his ashes were being returned to the States for burial, and that would perhaps take care of that. The inevitable onslaught of Mediterranean condolences she would of course sit through, hundreds of friends or not; but we knew none of them; once, then, I'd cleared what I had to, at our Embassy, we were dears, why shouldn't we take Jack's car and simply escape to Cap Nègre?—and if it turned out we liked it, there we'd be, we could find out how you transfer real estate in France, she'd give us a note to Jack's lawyer, au Lavandou—et voilà, by the time we left for the States the villa could be ours.

I naturally had two serious caveats, though I was waiting to see whether Suzanne mightn't decide against accepting such a place anyhow. First, what was I to *do* there? I had no book in mind, to settle down to. Nor did I see myself turning part-time (and amateur!) foreign correspondent, summer after summer, as American politics went on, unrebuked, without me: even spectacular événements, as in '68, I could hardly cover from the Riviera. And second, there, a due passi, would be Carla, almost certainly as beautiful at forty-seven as ever, and the risk of an unconscious— But good god, '*risk*'?—it was the one *certainty!* There always *is* an unguarded word, a tone of voice, a glance, the gesture of a remembering hand: the betrayal is irreparable and complete, and was I to 'risk' Suzanne's being saddened by such a confrontation? How I'd proceed, if it turned out she adored the villa, I had no idea. But a reasonable lie, in a reasonably good cause, I had found can with luck be persuasive.)

A plane to Nice or Cannes would of course have been the efficient route to Cap Nègre; but Suzanne had never seen any of Italy, so we took Uncle's car, and spent the night at Nice. And sure enough, as we set off in the morning, on the easy two hours' run to the Cap, she began to amuse herself with questions.

"What did you do at the villa, all those college summers?"

"It was just one summer. After Penn Charter."

"But what did you do?"

"What'd anybody? Played tennis. Learned some French."

"Do for *love*, darling—what *would* I mean!"

"With everybody Uncle's age, good god? *You* never had to spend that kind of summer?"

"Your uncle didn't think of inviting your girl too?"

"She had to be with her family. In Maine."

"You had only one girl? At *eighteen*?"

". . . The other had to be with her family too. In Rhode Island."

"Oh my poor *pet* how sad!—two beguiled Main Line angels to be unfaithful to and nobody to be unfaithful to either of them *with*, how thwarting!"

"What *is* this!" I protested, amused. "*You* hadn't a circus of dazed and helpless teenage louts to practice your lovely disingenuousnesses on, at eighteen?"

"I wasn't *sleeping* with them, like a revolting *boy*! No but my ingenious love how did you manage your simultaneous Penn Charter two? Mary even days Martha odd? And did you really suppose they didn't *know*? . . ."

(It *mattered*?—that summer of 1948 she was still in pigtails! Yes, but as we passed Fréjus, and one by one the names of villages murmured like echoes in my memory—Les Issambres, Ste. Maxime, Port-Grimaud, Cavalaire, Le Canadel—I found I was glad we'd bypassed my itinéraire sentimental of '52.)

—It turned out I needn't have worried about the villa either. Our second morning there—she was standing in the open French window of my old room, gazing out at the sun on the pinewood and the blue dazzle of the sea beyond—oh she adored it *all*, she said, the lovely tall rooms, the style, the sense of space, the paysage of Provence like an endless garden, the villa's splendid site here above the sea; the richness of it unspoiled by grandeur; what a happy introduction to Europe it must have been for me—and at eighteen! "Except it *is* rather a *place*, Johnnie, isn't it."

I said I supposed so; yes.

"And among other things you don't actually know any of your uncle's friends or neighbors now, do you. Even if you did, a few, twenty years ago."

Nineteen, I said.

"I mean they may not even be the same people, by now."

Ah, well, things then still hadn't—good god, the *war*'d barely been over three years, then! There was still a black market in coffee—and they'd only just dedicated the memorial to the '44 local landing of the Free French—'dont les corps jalonnent la route de la libération du territoire.' The British hadn't begun to come back;

some of the rich French had been ruined. There must have been a *lot* of property changing hands, since then.

". . . The only reason for a big place *is* to entertain."

Like Byberry.

"Which you already have. Oh sweet, would you d'you think *terribly* mind? It's so touching of Anne, and the *kindness* of putting it as if it were your uncle giving it to us!—but do you *really* want another place either? . . ."

And so therefore.

But we could at least, Sue said, go through the house, for Anne, to make sure nothing was left in armoires or commodes or secrétaires or placards or bibliothèques; also, she would inventory the linen and china and vaisselle, and I could do the wine-cellar and go through the desks and see whether any books were worth keeping; and so, midmorning, methodically clearing out the provincial Louis XVI secretary in my uncle's study, in filial innocence I pulled out a drawer crammed to the top, spilling *over*, with photographs of—but holy god she'd been *this* beautiful?—my young *mother!!*

But my *uncle's* keepsakes? . . .

Studio portraits, 35-mm enlargements; color and black-and-white; dressed for tennis, for town, for horse shows, for full-fig balls, for nightclubs. Her expression indulgent mocking bland tender faintly-bored; one or two holding a solemn baby (me!)—Main Line deb, Main Line young wife, Main Line young mother, the whole well-fixed untroubled Philadelphia showcase of her it was my *uncle* had hoarded, and what was I to make of it, now?—and make, perhaps in particular, of the series of her *here*, in this villa, in this *room*, one of them writing in fact at this very desk, when the photographer must have spoken to her and she'd turned; or, again, on the terrasse beyond these open French windows, this color shot had her breakfasting, the sun hot already on the pins marins, the turquoise sea flashing behind, the blaze of Mediterranean morning everywhere; she is in a white sortie de bain, her hair piled high in a topknot from the bath, and she is stretching out a beguiling hand, laughing, to—and mustn't my uncle have been the photographer then too? And ah, well, enough bra-and-bikini Botticellis of her to break a man's heart. . . .

But hardly one of them *my* memory of my mother?—in *any* way! I had been only four when she died, yes—but could I have forgot such loveliness? Whereas clearly my uncle—good god *any* man with eyes and a heart— I was stunned.

. . . But why hadn't my damned uncle at least mounted his trea-sures in albums, like a man of sense?—didn't he ever even *look* at them? . . .

And this little packet of letters, what was I to do with *it*? Her letters, I assumed. But whoever they were, was I to open and *read* them good god?

Letters are the property of the recipient; but what they *say*, the property of the writer; and either can prohibit their 'publication.' So the packet (and for that matter the string round it) was Anne's, inherited from my uncle, and among other things, she could refuse me access to it; but the letters' content was mine, as my mother's heir—and without her permission, was I to let *anyone* read them? much less her 'successor'!

But didn't this 'anyone' include me? Quite apart from never opening other people's mail, do we think what a woman says to *her* lover any less privileged by decency than what she says to her hus-band?

Nor was settling possible doubts about my paternity a plausible excuse: in those days people behaved as they *should:* if my mother had thought I was my uncle's child she'd have left my father and *gone* to him—'scandal' wasn't what *mattered*.

—After which Cartesian review, I decided but she was dammit *my* mother; if she hadn't written these letters for *me* to read, their few and irrelevant words were all she *had* left me, for me to know her by; to justify her folly by, even, why not; so was I to deny all family feeling, and *not* read what chance had handed me? I snapped the string of the packet, and began.

The letters weren't dated, but clearly all but one had been writ-ten before I was born. At some time after my mother's marriage to my father, she and my uncle had found themselves in the imme-morial plight:

. . . lead us not into frustration, but how have the combined sensibilities of you and me, my darling love, led us into *this*? Was there no danger in it until we put it into words? Or was it when the autumn separation loomed, that first time, and we *knew*. . . .

At one point, they seem to have tried simple-mindedly staying apart. Or call it high-mindedly; either way it didn't work: one short letter ended almost in a cry—

. . . I know everything we said and decided, everything everything every-thing everything, but are you *never* coming home?

So presumably at some point they gave up. Perhaps, as the villa pictures suggest, she had somehow managed to join him in France without my father. But the last sentence makes it likely that, by then, they were already lovers:

. . . That tearful phrase you found in Constant, nous nous affligérions ensemble, wasn't so *at all*—there were no afflictions *there*, in each other's company. Just we adored each other! Ah que c'était bon que de me retrouver dans tes bras!

But then what? Did they dear god call it *off*? Or only get it under proper control? Or was I misreading the 'carefree' sound of what must have been the latest letter of all?—

. . . When are you coming home from stupid old Europe and *see* my enchanting baby?

Me; but when had she written this?—how old was I? Had my conception so outraged my uncle that he'd refused to lay eyes on me? It was of course his own damn' fault—*imagine* letting her risk going back to my father at all! *Her* going I can understand: in those days a woman needed *time* to decide such things! She just took too much, and had the bad luck to start me; and do you dance blissfully off to your lover carrying your *husband's* child? Quite apart from considerations of scandal, good taste, ordinary decency, and (possibly!) a charge of kidnapping, who'd ever believe the unhappy child was legitimate!

But did my uncle *stay* 'outraged'? For, whatever the letter's date, for me it loosened a rubble of memories, and abruptly I was back in one of those set-piece scenes from one's childhood that one not so much remembers as has been so often reminded of that it has become memory; and this was a scene from a story ("The First Time He Ever Saw Me") that my uncle had indulged me by telling and retelling when I was little. I was in the dower-house kitchen. It was the summer I was four years old. The Landsdowns lived in the dower house then. My mother had driven over in the dogcart on an errand to them, and had taken me along. It was late afternoon, nearly my supper time; but it wasn't a long visit, and my mother was just saying good-bye, and I'd slid down off the hearth-bench where I'd been sitting, and turned round—and there in the doorway from the hall was this looming *Stranger!* ("Because I didn't know it was *you!*" Yes, because *he*'d lived way off in Rome.)

So, because I was a properly brought *up* little boy, I looked at my mother to see what to do: was I to come forward and bow and ask how he did? But this man was smiling at my mother, not at me. And he went straight *to* my mother and, before my astonished eyes, he picked up her hand and *kissed* it! Ha! and did I remember what had happened *then?*—which of course was my cue to laugh in triumph and shout, "*Yes!* I rushed across and took her hand *away* from you!"

Rudely *yanked* away (he'd correct me, smiling); and then he'd said to her, "So *this* is who you belong to now!" and everybody had laughed. Then we'd left and driven back to Byberry, he riding his hunter Selim along beside my mother and me in the dogcart. And the next day ("I remember?") we had all driven in his car over to a horse-farm near Downingtown, and he'd bought me Mister, my first pony, and we'd brought him back in a horse-trailer.

Ah, well.

But what can one make of an episode one's handed *not* as a draft shooting-script, for sarcastic comment and exasperated revision, but as what has, irremediably, already happened? And from a temps perdu as good as legendary! Nemo tum illicere et illici *saeculum* vocabat, says Tacitus: 'nobody, in those days, called beguiling and being beguiled *the fashion of the period,*' no matter how they themselves happened to be behaving; but why, now, were so many questions so unanswerable? Was I for instance here on earth only because my mother chose what she thought the least unhappy way to end an affair, or because it was expedient and easy—and need *not* end it at all! Again, in all that time (I was *four*), had he only *then* returned from Europe?—for a man who hoarded that drawerful of photographs, it was past belief! (Good god, would *I* have?) And how at ease with each other they'd been, when he'd come with her, at my bedtime to tuck me in, and she'd sit on the bed beside me to kiss me good night. What *had* happened then?—and why shouldn't it have, with my father in Philadelphia, that summer, except for weekends, and the great-aunts withdrawing early to their rooms? The lovers would have been alone with the beating of their hearts. (Was my uncle so different from me?)

And least answerable by *me* perhaps of all: on top of everything else was I god help me plain *jealous* of my uncle! . . .

I scooped up a half-dozen pictures, and went to find Sue.

She was standing in the pantry; she had a clipboard, and was working on the china inventory. I fanned my pictures out on the counter in front of her; but I was still upset, so when I said, "There's a whole damn' *drawerful* of these in Uncle's desk—you conceive of such a thing?" the resentment or bafflement or whatever it was in my tone made her look at me, surprised. So I tried to smooth it over: "Be a gallery of his fine taste in young women, except it's all the same girl!"

"Goodness," she said. She began taking the pictures up one after another. "But Johnnie the *clothes!*" she said presently. "If she was a girl of your uncle's it must have been in the *Twenties*— we weren't even born! Who could she have been?"

"From the sheer quantification," I said, "the love of his life!"

"Do you wonder? She's *lovely!*"

"And turned *out* to be a heartbreaker!"

" 'Turned out to be'! You *know* about her?"

Ah, well. "I knew *her,*" I said.

" '*Knew* her'!!"

"Dear god you do too!" I said. "You see her every day! You didn't *recognize* that elegant portrait over the fireplace in the back drawing-room?"

". . . These are *your mother?* And your *uncle* was in love with her?"

"*Yes!*" I said, "and God bless, she with him!"

"Oh Johnnie *no!*"

"Love of *her* life, very likely, too! There's half a dozen letters of hers to him in that same desk drawer that God knows sound as if he was!"

". . . Ah Johnnie!"

"Except then, by bad luck, she started *me.* And that perhaps ended it. *Virtuously,* if you want to be sardonic about it. *And* if it did in fact end it!"

"Ah my poor love," she said, "it *has* upset you!" and came and put her arms round me. "But Johnnie it was *their* life. You feel betrayed, but 'betraying you' wasn't what they were *doing!*"

(Perfectly true: wasn't I perhaps merely in shock from discovering that an innocent childhood memory hadn't been of innocence at all?)

But why not tell her? imaginary dialogue would have to be dubbed, but was I an experienced political journalist or wasn't I? I'd 'quoted' what politicians ought to have said, or tried to say, a thousand times; if I couldn't report what my mother and her lover must by and large *have* said on a dramatic occasion, I should turn in my typewriter!

So I said to Suzanne look, this was something that had happened the summer I was four. My mother had driven over to the dower house on an errand one afternoon, and taken me with her.

I suppose the errand was to the estate-manager, Landsdown, who lived there then with his horsey spinster of a sister. It was late afternoon; the sunset must have been pouring through the western windows of the kitchen in long shafts of dusty gold across the waxed oak of the floor. As it does now. The tone of my mother's voice must have told me she was ready to leave, but anyhow I'd slid down off the hearth-bench where I'd been sitting, and was just turning round, when in the doorway from the hall there appeared this total Stranger! I suppose I looked at my mother, for guidance: did we know this man? and how was I to behave. But I was immediately confused, by *how* she looked: *this* look I'd never seen on her face in my life! Naturally I translated this into the disquiet of the unknown, and I looked instantly back at the intruder to see what the menace was. But he was *smiling!* And not just a social smile, but a family-affection smile I was perfectly familiar with, because everybody smiled that way at me. But the man didn't seem to notice I was there; he came straight to my mother!—and to my total astonishment picked up her hand and *kissed* it!

And I suppose she could have said something like ". . . oh Jack," in a kind of sigh (I told Sue). But how am I to translate that, forty years on? Had she conceivably *not* seen him again until now? and reconstructed her life around me and my father? Or *had* the affair gone on, after my birth, hole-and-corner or not? and by suddenly appearing like this, to have his presence noted by *people*, he had broken their strictest rule?—so her sigh was a reproach. And I suppose he was blandly saying, "Oh how d'ye do, Miss Landsdown—afternoon, Landsdown, *wonderful* see you again!" with hardly a glance at them.

But by then *I* was pattering furiously across, to jerk my mother's outraged hand from his. And he said, "So *this* is who you belong to now!" and everybody laughed.

And no doubt he may have gone on, "Perfectly clear to *him* anyway! You bringing him up to be no more generous with his possessions than this?" And my mother could have answered, "But what did you expect?" in a voice I'd never heard before.

Or, again, she could have said nothing at all. . . .

But, whichever way, they'd hardly have stood there much longer, smiling unguardedly into each other's eyes (and no doubt I was brattishly demanding who-is-he-who-*is*-he?); we must have left at once. But I imagine my mother could have said, as we crossed the courtyard to the dogcart and my uncle's tethered hunter, "Miss Landsdown may be watching from behind the curtain," even before she lifted me into the dogcart or began explaining to me what an 'uncle' was.

That much, I said to Sue, is a reasonable reconstruction. Of an episode. But then? It is guesswork!

So she looked at me. And presently said, "Or do you just mean you don't want to guess."

"Guess as a decent-minded observer of my uncle's behavior? Or as perhaps his fellow-marauder!"

She said gently, "As a romantic, my love," and kissed me.

But ah dammit, I said, what man in his right mind would see this drawerful as anything God bless but a beautiful girl why *shouldn't* my uncle have taken off after!

"But if you're not blaming!"

"What d'you think's *upsetting* me so!" I demanded. "If I'd been there, am I to tell myself I'm so different from the uncle who brought me up that I wouldn't have behaved as he did? Because obviously *if* I'd been there, then the lovely thing wouldn't have been my mother—what d'you *think*'s been upsetting me! I mean the whole affair's totally understandable and *normal*, Sue! So what if they *were* my mother and an uncle I've loved and admired all my life!—does that make it any the less ludicrous to find myself solemnly asking whether I'm not perhaps, of *all* cockeyed emotions, *jealous* good god!"

But by this time she was sweetly laughing at me.

I scooped the damn' pictures together and shuffled them straight. On top was a 3 x 5 black-and-white close-up. She was wearing a dark turtleneck sweater that I remembered; a breeze was ruffling her hair; she was smiling into her photographer's eyes; with love. But if I remembered that sweater, the picture must have been taken that summer I was four: my uncle must have taken it, after that day he'd come back from France and ridden over to the dower house to find her. So, suddenly, I saw the picture for what it was, and with a sense of helpless pity so strong I forgot my other emotions—for it had been an *early*-fall Princeton game that she and my father were racing home to a dinner-dance from, when he took a curve near Langhorne too fast, and killed them both—poor angel, there in the picture she is, smiling at her lover, without a thought in her careless head that, for love or for anything, there could possibly be no time left for her at all. . . .

Ah, well. At least there was a structure to society in those days, and none of this psychologically fashionable Guilt. Or if there had been, had she been brought up to feel it? *We* were the establishment: rules were for people who weren't in the position to make them. Ah, and anyway—as my uncle would have said, women are an establishment of themselves.

—But Sue was saying, "If I'm going to have a beautiful rival, may I at least see the rest of the creature's pictures too?"—so, back in my uncle's study, we spread out his hoard. I set up an extra card-table, and there was still an overflow.

Sue was a long time looking at them, one by one. "Oh dear," she said at last, "she *was* beautiful, wasn't she. Are you going to ask Anne for them?"

"And have her say, '*What* pictures'?"

". . . Oh."

"And what would I do with them?—keep them as mementos of, well, of what? But throw *away* all I have left of her? . . ."

We began to gather them up. Presently she said, "Shall I keep them for you? Till you decide?" and I said, "You're an *angel!*" and we left it at that.

—And she is keeping them for me still. But I have always thought, how can my uncle have wanted me to see them? They are *his* hoard; it is *his* eyes she is smiling into, picture after picture. In *any* picture, only he could remember the ambience, what they had been doing, what they had done next. Above all, would he have left me her letters? None of any of it fitted his long and happy relationship with me. I had taken it for granted that he loved me because I assumed that was simply how a reasonably affectionate uncle did behave—kept an eye on me, made infrequent mild suggestions as to my conduct (and manners), had my long-term good in mind even if I hadn't, and kept officious demurring to himself; a proper Wasp upbringing, in short.

But now that I knew far more about him than I'd ever expected to, decently or not, was any of all that to be seriously altered by a slight irregularity added to the nomenclature of our relationship? I am still what he brought me up to be; am I to see him, now, as other than his long affection has taught me to? Not only he, but his *concern* for me, was always 'there'—he approved of Sue for me, I suppose, to 'settle me down' very much as he'd approved of Carla as an antidote to settling down too soon.

And if he didn't perhaps form my views, he did help shape my language. For one thing, there were his epigrams—both the classical kind (*The saving grace of woman is her Darwinian folly*) and a kind of surrealist wit of *his* sort (*What if the blood on your unbowed head is not your own?*). Or again, some of his intellectual tirades, as my confidence in my political column grew, I found I could simply steal whole paragraphs of, and adapt for uses of my own. Multa senem circumveniunt insulsa (I happen to remember Horace said), and as Uncle John grew older the spectacle of human ineptitude sometimes had him at the sardonic limits of his tolerance.

How had the country been allowed to *get* into this dejecting condition? I remember his demanding, on one of his last trips home. The American electorate didn't perhaps actually believe the earth is flat, but it thought God could have made it round if He'd wanted to. Ah, well, 'American'—the sheer disorder that adjective had come to connote left him feeling he was a mere survivor of something, hardly knew of what!—perhaps of nothing more than some tallage-cursing thirteenth-century forebear, and how far was *that* from the upheavals and dispossessions after 1066? How'd we *come* to this state of things?—Puritan bigots on Plymouth Rock, wild younger sons and transported felons in Virginia, Quaker *Tories*, God help us, in Philadelphia!—*whichever* among the lot of us had let it happen, la position en était-elle moins foutue? . . .

"Mind you," I remember his saying once, "all our kindly accustomed own-sort-of people couldn't *be* easier to put up with, you know, or better brought up, wouldn't *think* of wondering why we're not Episcopalians like everybody—but what, actually, do we have in common, beyond an occasional pretty wife?"

I said ah well, the picture was black, yes. But weren't we reliably informed it was Created to be?—even on purpose?

"What kind of certainty's that?" he demanded. "Stained-glass windows and endowed pews are well enough for our fellowmen, theologically adither as they are, poor devils, with all that fear-and-trembling called for. Not that I don't entertain the most tender sympathy for man's longing to outlast the anonymity of time, but what decent Quaker would think of his soul as a Concern? Would a birthright Quaker of *either* Meeting expect a special status in Eternity for his name up in brass? Your name's for your headstone—it's Property! What's thee looking at me like that for?—at my age we're allowed to pontificate!"

And, I suppose, God bless, why not.

But how I remember my uncle, generally, could be that last autumn morning I ever saw him, riding over to "make his adieux to my sweet of a young woman," as he put it, before taking off, once more, for Rome; and as we were talking, there she came, bringing my lunch. She was on the sorrel he'd given her, trooping out of the high woods into a glade of ash between us, now warm and ablaze with noon, the sorrel coming along at his rapid walk, glossy head nodding in time, picking his way smartly among the trees. The ash sheds its leaves early; and now, between us, they were showering down through the satiny air in myriads, crimson and bronze, flashing in the sun as they sailed and spun and fell, as if a veil sewn thick with sequins was endlessly descending across the brilliant autumn day, horse and rider half lost in the glint and wink of it. Suzanne saw us, and waved, and put the sorrel into a trot, and he came up to us scuffling nimbly through the drifts of leaves, nickering politely to the filly, ears cocked. "Ah *god*," I heard my uncle mutter, "what a pretty thing a pretty girl *is!*" and he went to meet her, holding out his arms.

And, well, young women were fond of my uncle: she dismounted into them, to be kissed.

Afterword

> Virtuosity and style were for him the chief merits of
> literature.
>> —Osbert Sitwell on Ronald Firbank

Many novelists get off to a late start, or wait years before receiving proper critical attention, but few can match W. M. Spackman in this regard. His first novel wasn't published until he was nearly fifty, his second not until he was over seventy. But that second novel, *An Armful of Warm Girl*, won widespread critical acclaim, and for the next half-dozen years Spackman published a novel nearly every other year, a burst of creative activity unusual at any age, but all the more so for a gentleman in his seventies. And what novels they were: stylish comedies of manners, audacious arguments for adultery, by turns cheeky and charming, haughty and haunting, and impeccably executed. A few years later he was dead, and those delicious novels out of print. But the man deserves to be remembered and (more importantly) the work preserved, hence this omnibus edition of all his fiction.

William Mode Spackman was born 20 May 1905 in Coatesville, Pennsylvania. His Quaker ancestors had lived in Pennsylvania since the beginning of the eighteenth century, and Spackman himself prepped at the 200-year-old Friends School in Wilmington, Delaware. (His family moved to Wilmington the year after he was born; his parents owned a large hardware store with a substantial steel operation.) Quaker traditions and practices run through his novels, even their use of *thee* and *thou*. More important than his Quaker background, however, is his Princeton background, which is so pervasive in these novels that this book should be bound in orange and black, the school colors. Under the influence of F. Scott Fitzgerald's *This Side of Paradise*, Spackman was matriculated in the Class of 1927, the same as that of the protagonists of his first novel, *Heyday*; in fact nearly all the male characters in his novels are Princetonians. His writing career began when he was an undergraduate: a brand-new magazine called the *New Yorker* published several of his poems during its first year. In his sophomore year Spackman was chairman of the *Nassau Lit*, and caused something of a scandal by publishing his "Sketches from a Madhouse" there, a piece he later described as "straight Aldous Huxley" (but which, as juvenilia, is not included in the present collection). Spackman graduated from Princeton with honors in French and Italian literatures, and as a Rhodes Scholar (1927-30) took a second Bachelor's degree at Balliol College, Oxford, where he read "Greats" (Greek philosophy and ancient Greek and Ro-man history—though his best final exam paper was on classical Greek prose). Just before his last year at Oxford Spackman married Mary Ann Matthews (to whom *Heyday* is dedicated), from a family even older than his (her first ancestor in America was one of Cromwell's lieutenants).

Returning to the States at the beginning of the Depression—he lost a small fortune in the stock market crash of 1929—he taught Classics for a year at New York University, then returned to Princeton in 1933 to do graduate work. He spent the rest of the Thirties working as a copy-writer and account executive for vari-ous public relations agencies in New York City (he was a Rocke-feller Fellow in opinion research 1940-41); often this required work in radio, and Spackman won three national awards for edu-cational radio programs in the OSU annual judgings. During much of World War II he was director of the Office of Public Information at the University of Colorado in Boulder, where he had gone largely for his wife's health. Towards the end of the war he studied Russian at the Navy Language School there and be-came an agent for the U.S. Navy. In 1945 he became assistant professor of Classics at the University of Colorado, and it was during a sabbatical in France in the fall of 1949 that he wrote his first novel; after *Heyday* was published in 1953, he resigned and returned to Princeton to devote himself full-time to writing (and part-time to architecture; over the years Spackman designed and built two Queen Anne houses for himself and his family, even the rough carpentry and panelling, and later remodeled a modern-style house as well as a large seaside villa in France). Quitting teaching seems to have been an easy decision given his immense frustration and exasperation with how literature was being taught at the time.[1]

Spackman's next two books wouldn't appear until 1967. The first, *Twenty-five Years of It*, is a slim book of poetry, a limited edition—six hardbacks, 250 paperbacks—privately published in France. (He was spending six months a year living in Perros-Guirec at the time, which is given as the place of publication.) It's a gathering of verse dating back to his undergraduate days—some first appeared in the *Nassau Lit* and Oxford's *Cherwell*, and had been anthologized in *Princeton Verse between Two Wars* and in Blackwell's Oxford Poetry series—mostly of a traditional sort, some with Latin titles (and apparently based on Latin models). The poems more closely resemble those of Ovid or Catullus than any twentieth-century poets, except for a Marianne Moore-like poem about a tortoise. The longest poem in the book is a take-off on Byron's *Don Juan*, written in the same ottava rima form and good-naturedly addressing what Spackman believes are the shortcomings of Byron's comic epic. Entitled "Proem to an Unwritten Epic," it doubles as a proem to his fiction of the next two decades, the central thrust of which could be described as a modernization of the Don Juan theme:

> . . . a century plus has passed since Byron
> Dispatched that earlier Juan to the press.
> Our literary needs have changed—require an
> Array of symbols, far less fancy dress,
> A modern bitch instead of gothick siren,
> A hero with a haircut . . .

> . . . .

> However. Here's the issue as I find it:—
> Byron would make you think the mischief's done
> By lovers half tongue-tied and seven-eighths blinded;
> Neither of them, you'd swear, is having fun;
> The lady, if not downright absent-minded,
> Never seems conscious quite what's going on
> (In fact the situation's so abused
> I'm never sure she knows she's being seduced).

---

[1]See his blistering indictments "The Menace to Curriculum Reform," *Classical Journal* 44.5 (February 1949): 293-97, "Topic Sentences" and "The Learned No" in his *On the Decay of Humanism*, and "Literature as Literature, and Why," *Cultural Affairs* 3 (1968): 5-9, published under the pseudonym Alexander Neave (see n. 9 below).

And since such rapturous stuff'll hardly go down
    With anyone who's ever lived the part,
What I propose is the plain modern low-down
    On what does happen in her pretty heart
When passions rev up and refusals slow down.
    Half way through Canto One (a flying start
And you'll be through before it's time for dinner)
My little saint turns every inch a sinner.

Spackman here could be describing *An Armful of Warm Girl*, which he had completed some years earlier. If nothing else, his poetry pays tribute to the writers with whom Spackman had the greatest affinity: the classical love poets—Catullus, Propertius, but above all Ovid (especially the *Amores* and *Ars amatoria*), Renaissance and Cavalier poets like Wyatt (or Wiat, as he preferred to spell it), Donne, and Herrick, and finally (despite his misgivings) the author of *Don Juan*. (Byron's poem is also parodied in part 3 of *A Presence with Secrets* [290].)

The other book Spackman published in 1967, *On the Decay of Humanism* (Rutgers University Press), is a dazzling collection of essays treating more recent literature (though two are on the Classics) and the inadequate way such literature is taught. Like Harold Bloom more recently, Spackman castigates those who exploit literature for its psycho-socio-political content at the expense of its artistry, its technique. In the first essay, "Topic Sentences," he writes: "In our time, from various accidents of fashion and personality, the basic disagreement—for everyone but the narrowest of philosophers—is whether literature is something a writer writes or the synthesis of signs the establishment tends to deal in instead." Rather than explore the former, academics prefer the latter, which he likens to "a roll in the catnip of semantics." In words as applicable to today's literary theoreticians as to those of the sixties, Spackman warns: "the more articulate your professor, the likelier he is to deal with a work of art less in its own terms than as a mere starting point for whatever he has thought up to say instead." This point is reiterated in his long essay on Henry James, whose defects as a writer, he feels, have gone unnoticed by critics because "a professor of literature is not so much trained to *look* at what he is reading as to find things to say about it."

Focusing himself on what a writer actually writes, Spackman offers numerous iconoclastic readings of canonized writers, displaying an Olympian self-confidence (which some reviewers found hubristic) and an enviably encyclopedic range of background reading, everything from Homer (in Greek, of course) to Raymond Queneau's *Zazie dans le métro*. Those whom he weighs in the balances and finds wanting include Socrates, Aristotle ("a marine biologist," he reminds us), Wordsworth, James, and Ford Madox Ford. In contrast, he finds much to admire in less-celebrated writers like Benjamin Constant, Ivy Compton-Burnett, Henry Green (a recurring touchstone for disciplined, artful prose), and Edmund Wilson's fiction. This isn't an indulgence in studied iconoclasm; in passing Spackman expresses great admiration for such canonized authors as Ovid, Stendhal, Proust, Joyce, Pound (especially as a translator), Auden, Faulkner, and Beckett. It is a brilliant, provocative book and deserves to be reprinted someday, perhaps augmented by the essays and book reviews Spackman continued to write (especially for *Parnassus*) in the seventies and early eighties.

At an early point in the book Spackman notes "the typical first novel . . . tends to be naturally gloomy and emotionally out of balance / *Sto sospirando o lagrimando vado* / and so forth," but "second novels are noticeably different *if* the writer is artist enough to see that every new book calls for a new form, and perhaps style, as much as for a new topic." Spackman probably had himself in mind, for this accurately describes the difference between *Heyday* and *An Armful of Warm Girl*, which he had "just finished" according to the jacket of *On the Decay of Humanism*. (Incidentally, in the latter Spackman tries out the title of his second novel: "We read Vergil for other things entirely, putting up with his aesthete's character-drawing by the same convention that lets us accept, say, a travertine Galatea as representing an armful of warm girl.") Actually, he had finished a first draft of the novel in 1955; the book made the rounds without any luck, then was submitted to Stanley Kauffmann at Knopf in 1959, who liked the book and suggested revisions, which Spackman made, only to have the book rejected again. It was shopped around elsewhere during the sixties—Spackman later said it was rejected by fifteen publishers—but with no takers. It was resubmitted to Knopf in the early seventies, but he was told that the advent of the feminist movement made his novel unpublishable at that time. It wouldn't see print until the summer of 1977, when the editors of *Canto*, a new literary magazine, decided to publish the novel as the complete contents of their second issue. It was spotted by Gordon Lish, then fiction editor at *Esquire*, and recommended to Knopf once more; this time they accepted it and offset the *Canto* text for book publication in the spring of 1978. (In the process, a line on the bottom of its page 79 was accidentally dropped, which has been restored here.) The novel enjoyed enough critical acclaim that Knopf became his regular publisher: *A Presence with Secrets*, which Spackman had written in 1971-73 but which likewise failed to find a publisher at the time, followed in October 1980, *A Difference of Design* in June 1983, and *A Little Decorum, for Once* in October 1985. The novels were favorably reviewed for the most part, but like most innovative fiction, they didn't sell particularly well.

A heart attack in 1975 caused Spackman to abandon his plan to settle permanently in France. The failing health and eventual death of his first wife in 1978, the year *An Armful of Warm Girl* was published, was another tragedy that altered his life. He later moved in with his second wife, the Laurice to whom the later novels are dedicated, and continued to spend most of his time writing.

The remaining works in this omnibus date from the last five years of Spackman's life. The brief "Dialogue at the End of a Pursuit" was first published under the title "After Glow: A Dialogue" in *Town & Country*, October 1985. To make it suitable for publication there, Spackman had to rewrite a few lines and change the opening stage directions to the following: "SCENE: The appointed place. TIME: Now and then. PERSONAE: Corinna and Ovid." The version published here, including its original title and dedication, is taken from Spackman's typescript.

"Declarations of Intent" was first published in the autumn 1987 issue of *Southwest Review*. The same journal also published a short story entitled "As I Sauntered Out, One Mid-Century Morning . . ." in its spring 1989 issue, adapted from chapter 2 of the short novel of the same name published here in full for the first time. The novel was sent to Spackman's editor at Knopf, Alice Quinn, for book publication; she visited him once in Princeton to work on it, but his illness in his final years, along with Quinn's move from Knopf to the *New Yorker*, left the work unpublished. The manuscript has numerous corrections in Spackman's hand, as well as an errata page, so it seems to be in finished form. (There is an awkward leap at the beginning of chapter 2 from the early 1950s to the mid 1960s that still needed to be finessed.) A few superior readings from the *Southwest Review* chapter have been adopted (under the assumption Spackman would have made these changes for the book version as well), and what looks like an unintentionally duplicated passage dropped; otherwise, aside from routine copy-editing, the novel appears here just as he left it.

Just as some of his novels were dropping out of print in this country, they started to attract attention abroad. A German translation of *An Armful of Warm Girl* had appeared in 1981 (as *Die Unschuld der Fünfziger*, claassen Verlag), and a French translation of *A Presence with Secrets* was published by Quai Voltaire under the title *L'Ombre d'une présence* in the autumn of 1987. In 1988 the French magazine *Le Promeneur* published a translation of the unexpurgated version of "Dialogue at the End of a Pursuit," and the following year Quai Voltaire published a translation of *An Armful of Warm Girl* under the title *L'Embrassée*. (This novel came out after *A Presence* because Spackman was unhappy with the initial translation and felt it needed work. Even the title proved troublesome; Spackman told a correspondent at the time that the title *Une Brassée de fille épanouie* "has been suggested, but it's up to the publishers. I myself find that *épanouie* lovely, but the ambiguities of the French word for 'girl' aren't something a foreigner should deal with.") Both French novels were translated by Bernard Turle and were well received by the French press.

W. M. Spackman died 3 August 1990, in his beloved Princeton, of complications of prostate cancer.[2]

2

Spackman's first novel, *Heyday*, was published in 1953 by Ballantine Books as an early experiment in a "split" edition, whereby a book is published simultaneously in hardcover and mass-market paperback formats. In a lengthy author's note at the end of the book, Spackman described the novel as follows:

---

[2]My sources for this brief biography are (1) the author's note in the first edition of *Heyday*, (2) the entry on Spackman in *Contemporary Authors*, vols. 84-88 (based on information supplied by Spackman himself), (3) correspondence with Harriet Spackman Newell, the author's daughter, (4) brief interviews with Spackman that accompanied a few of the reviews of his books, and (5) Maurice B. Cloud's "A Conversation with W. M. Spackman," *High Plains Literary Review* 4.1 (Spring 1989): 51-63. This informative interview is followed by Cloud's appreciative essay "How Watchful of His Muse . . . : In Praise of W. M. Spackman" (64-69). The only other critical essays published on Spackman to date are Sallie Bingham's "Maenads and Satyrs: Some Thoughts on W. M. Spackman's Novels," *American Voice* 2 (Spring 1986): 30-37, and John Whitehead's "An American Arcadia: The Novels of W. M. Spackman," *Contemporary Review* 265 (October 1994): 206-11.

Heyday is among other things an elegy upon the immemorial loneliness of man; a statement too about its causes (varied) and customary cure (someone charming to hold one's hand); though these things are of course said about a particular group at a particular time, viz. the young American upper class in that era of its disaster, the 1930's. *Heyday* is thus also the spiritual biography of a generation hardly anyone has written up, the generation a decade after Scott Fitzgerald's (his story *Babylon Revisited*, for instance, is about the Class of 1917 very much as *Heyday* is about the Class of 1927). *Heyday* is incidentally too, then, a statement about American values, for the Class of 1927 was perhaps the last generation brought up in those traditions of moral competence and severe pride in the individual which progressive education and the welfare state have nearly stamped out by now forever.

To those who know only the later novels, this statement strikes an uncharacteristically somber note, and indeed *Heyday* is the most "serious" novel Spackman ever wrote. (It could hardly be otherwise, dealing as it does with the coruscating effect of the Depression on his generation.) One reviewer described that statement as "Pretty large claims for this nostalgic and singleminded chronicle of Greenwich Village sex-capades, featuring nubile ivy-leaguers whose hearts belonged to Eighth Street even during sidetrips to Paris, France, and Coatesville, Pa. Regrettably, therefore, one must judge *Heyday* by how close it comes to the author's elaborate intentions, which is not very." The reviewer (James Kelly in the *Saturday Review*) went on to remark: "If Max Bodenheim, Scott Fitzgerald, and Ezra Pound had at one time pooled their forces (shocking thought) to write a definitive Depression Novel, the chances are it would have turned out something like this parodiable amalgam of classical allusions, large social observations, and explicit sexual vignettes. As a one-man tour de force, *Heyday* is remarkable." Other reviewers had similar mixed feelings, and though the novel was published in England by Frederick Muller in 1954 (with many of the racier sexual vignettes censored out), the novel soon went out of print and was never reprinted in Spackman's lifetime.

The text of *Heyday* printed here is the revised version that Spackman was working on at the time of his death. The original version consisted of three parts: parts 1 and 3, largely about narrator Webb Fletcher, were set in the novel's present (1942) and provided a frame around the longer part 2, largely about his distant cousin Malachi (Mike) Fletcher, and set in the early 1930s. The frame was intended to give formal elegance to Webb Fletcher's narration, "enclosing within my fate your fate; the action of your tragedy exhibited within the symbolic border of its contrasting counterpart" (206). Part 1 indicated that Webb, like Spackman himself, was born in 1905 and was a member of Princeton's Class of '27, and that the novel was intended as a kind of book-length obituary for the *Princeton Alumni Weekly*, which Webb thinks might be called "Obituary with Female Figures." Not satisfied with the original, Spackman dropped the first and third parts, made numerous cuts in part 2, switched the order of a few chapters, and made an occasional word substitution or added a transitional phrase. In the surviving manuscript (a photocopy of part 2 of the Ballantine edition, worked over in pencil), he also indicated eight places where new material was to be inserted. These inserts either were never written or became separated from the manuscript and lost. Consequently, those places are indicated in the present text with bracketed ellipses. Although the rest of the manuscript shows considerable evidence of work, it is impossible to tell whether it represents his final wishes (save for the missing inserts). However, the Spackman Estate and I agreed that, even in its not-quite finished form, this version is the one that should represent his first novel in this collected edition.

In its revised form, the novel shifts the focus away from what Spackman called (in the original author's note) the causes of "the immemorial loneliness of man" to their "customary cure," exchanging the mask of tragedy for that of comedy, or at least tragicomedy. Love in all its phases, from flirting to adultery, is the central theme here, as it would be in all of Spackman's fiction. Webb Fletcher remains the narrator, but in a greatly reduced role, though the novel is still, in essence, Webb's monologue to Stephanie Lowndesden, the woman he loves and loses. The debilitating effect of the Depression remains, especially in the near-hysteria that keeps the female characters on edge throughout, but the tone is a bit lighter than the earlier version. Although Mike's trip with Kitty to a Quaker graveyard remains, the novel's tone is softened from funereal to valedictory. The feelings of jealousy and betrayal felt by some characters are retained in full animal force, feelings that will be all but absent in the arcadian affairs that follow. While he cut many of the philosophical meditations of the original edition, Spackman retained the precious, fluttering adjectives (*angelic, blissful,* etc.) that he would continue to use to describe women, and his fine ear for the variations in female voices—displayed here in Kitty's offbeat emphases, Stephanie's lan-guor-ous drawl, Jill's childlike prattle—would only get better. The revised version is more compatible with the later novels than the original is, but finally *Heyday* belongs to a different world, aesthetically and historically, and it will probably always strike most readers as a prelude to (rather than a part of) his true oeuvre.

From the vantage point of the 1990s, the 1950s may likewise seem a different world, but there is a world of difference between the tone of Spackman's first novel and that of his second, set in June 1959. The first paragraph of *Heyday* sounds like something Fitzgerald or O'Hara could have written, but I can't think of any other writer who could have written the outrageous opening of *An Armful of Warm Girl*. (The closest thing to it is the first paragraph of *The Catcher in the Rye*, which in fact Spackman may be parodying.) At first the haughty arrogance is like a slap in the face, but soon enough the reader understands why Nicholas Romney is so damned irked and thus why the narrative tone is appropriate. The reader is addressed as though he were a Princeton crony of similar age and temperament, a disarming tactic deployed to win the reader's tolerance, even affection, for this bellowing rake. As quickly as the second page, though, a second mode is introduced—the pastoral—as Nicholas broods on his now-forsaken Pennsylvania property. Presiding over this novel is Thalia, muse of comedy and bucolic poetry (but in a Coco Chanel dress rather than her usual shepherdess garb). This mode will find its purest expression in the four choral interludes featuring Nicholas's daughter Melissa and her friend that occur at regular intervals, enchanting dialogues that read like Theocritus as translated by Ronald Firbank ("Hours long, a soft gabble, musing, as in Arcadia, choral turn and turn"). There is even a dash of Restoration comedy here—Spackman greatly admired Congreve's *The Way of the World*—both in the novel's deliberately artificial diction ("Yes; who in love with; oh hideous!") and in its bedroom-farce plotting.

It's easy enough to sit back and enjoy the novel as though it were a Fred Astaire musical—indeed, that approach is more advisable than a politically correct one of how people should be represented in fiction, otherwise Spackman will seem the very Antichrist of sexism and elitism—but closer attention reveals some rather unexpected elements. For a novel in which everyone is committing (or contemplating) adultery with everybody else, it is surprising to note how often the concept of responsibility is raised. In fact the word appears over fifty times (in one form or another) within the short novel, and is applied to virtually every character. In love begins responsibility as far as Spackman is concerned: responsibility to the loved one, to oneself, to family. In Spackman's view, adultery is a *civilized* activity, and like any civilized activity presupposes manners, thoughtfulness, education, certain standards of behavior, and so on. In a word, responsibility.

Even more surprising are the darker elements of the novel. Spackman's world may seem like a kind of Arcadia, but *et in Arcadio ego*. Death stalks these pages, with classmates of Nicholas's dropping dead right and left. Though Nicholas is still hale and hearty at fifty, these deaths add a certain poignancy to the novel, and encourage the *carpe diem* motivation that drives him and the other characters to live life to the fullest. But most troubling are the hints of incest; the possibility is often raised that Morgan, the young actress who is pursuing Nicholas with such passion, may be his illegitimate daughter, but he also has an almost unhealthy regard for his legitimate daughter Melissa. (In addition, there is a suggestion on page 166 that Nicholas's son may be pursuing a woman that his father once had an affair with.) The suspicion of incest is never verified, but it is flirted with often enough to give the novel an unsettling tone, less like Fred Astaire's *Top Hat* than de Sade's *La Philosophie dans le boudoir*.

But these are passing clouds in the novel's otherwise blue sky. The style especially is a delight: a heady mixture of Edwardian elegance, colloquial breeziness, and Mayfair slang ("Sweetie, champaginny and all, well how *coo*"). Latin quotations dance cheek-to-cheek with risqué nightclub lyrics, traditional syntax is unbuttoned, and several species of rather outlandish female dialogue are heard, ranging from Melissa's gushiness to Morgan's theatricality to Mrs. Barclay's "femalizing." It could all be criticized as cloying if that isn't exactly what Spackman is after: at one point Nicholas insists that he "wanted a sweet dessert to be really and *elaborately* sweet, no nonsense about de-cloying it" (160), which explains the excesses of Spackman's style. *An Armful of Warm Girl* is Spackman's most entertaining novel, if not his best; that distinction would go to his next one, *A Presence with Secrets*.

Nicholas Romney confesses to "a lifetime's delight in the mere look, the mere tournure, of women, in the posed and lovely portraits they always somehow made him half-think they were" (160) —and in fact at one point refers to his namesake George Romney, the British portrait painter. Spackman pursues this conceit even further in *A Presence with Secrets*, whose protagonist is an award-winning painter named Hugh Tatnall, and whose story involves a veritable portrait gallery of delectable women. (Tatnall was based to some extent on a Princeton classmate named Alfred Young Fisher, a poet who taught at Smith, one of whose undergraduate poems is quoted at the end of *On the Decay of Humanism*. *An Armful of Warm Girl* is dedicated to him.) Like several of Spackman's novels, *A Presence with Secrets* has a three-part structure: in keeping with the protagonist's vocation, the novel is intended to be a triptych, three portraits of Tatnall from three different perspectives. Part 1 takes place in Florence, Italy, in the spring, when Hugh is thirty-six, and is narrated from his point of view (though in third-person); part 2 takes place in Brittany in the summer, perhaps a few years later, and is narrated in first-person by a nameless cousin of Hugh's. Part 3 takes place a month after Hugh's death, a decade or so after parts 1 and 2, and is narrated by a friend of his named Simon Shipley, who reviews their mutual careers as "marauders" at Hugh's funeral service.[3] Together, the three views create a rounded but deliberately incomplete portrait of a typical Spackman libertine, but in a tone that leans more toward tragedy than farce, closer to Mozart's *Don Giovanni* than Byron's *Don Juan*.

The portrait is incomplete because Hugh Tatnall—like any human being—is at most a presence with secrets, never capable of being completely understood by another person. Each part of the novel dramatizes this is in a different way: in part 1, Hugh wonders what to make of the young woman delivered to his bed by (he fancies) a benevolent Bona Dea, at the same time brooding on his year-long adulterous liaison with Alexandra Fonteviot. Solicitous of each woman, he realizes he knows neither in any real sense. In part 2 Tatnall's cousin has one assumption after another overturned, surprised at Hugh (whom she has known since age nine), at her host's behavior, at the Gaullist assassins (whom she

---

[3]As Spackman explained to interviewer Keith Fleming, the book had a complicated composition history: "I wrote the last part first, as a separate novel; then rewrote it so often I began to detest it *and* its style; so I threw out everything I could no longer stand looking at—and there was the present novella. Then I used my painter character as protagonist for two other novella ideas I had, adapting him as I went along—*et voila*, I'd cobbled a novel together. I did the first story next, starting out stylistically as if I were doing a pastiche of Henry Green; then the middle story last" (*Chicago Literary Review*, 13 March 1981, 7). Further revisions were made for the Dutton Obelisk edition (1982).

took for Breton separatists), and even at herself. And in part 3, while playing Leporello by cataloguing Tatnall's many conquests, Shipley recounts coming across a drawerful of Tatnall's mementos that upsets everything *he* thought he knew about his lifelong friend. Shipley also emphasizes how misleading biography can be when trying to make sense of an artist's work; wondering "whether the painter and the libertine were two aspects or components of a creative unity" (281), he provides a good deal of data to support such an argument, but finally retreats from any final judgment. For that reason, he burns the contents of the drawer, apparently deciding that Tatnall's work will have to be judged on its own merits, and that the man behind the work should remain a secret.

The prose is especially lush. Appropriately, there are frequent "painterly" descriptions — of rooms, landscapes — that demonstrate an artist's eye for color and light. The novel shares *Heyday*'s valedictory tone, but is less ponderous, bittersweet rather than gloomy. A few of the recounted affairs are somewhat comic, but most are sweetly sad or — in the story of Hildegarde on pages 316-23 — utterly heartbreaking. The novel is technically interesting for its experiments in non-linear narration: both parts 1 and 3 advance by retreating, with the narrative present continually interrupted by flashbacks that nevertheless carry the narrative forward. The rich prose, the aesthetically satisfying structure, and the parade of Spackman dreamgirls make *A Presence with Secrets* his finest achievement.

The idea of redoing *The Ambassadors* occurred to Spackman in 1973, but his dissatisfaction with Henry James's novel was longstanding. In a highly critical essay in *On the Decay of Humanism* entitled "James, James," Spackman agreed with F. R. Leavis that in *The Ambassadors*

I cannot find anything to admire at all. Women perhaps find it more readable than men do. One trouble, technically, is that male characters, which are never what James did best, take up so much of the total wordage. In particular, the Jamesian-male shilly-shally of Strether is excessive, and the endless bleating of Bilham is really not to be borne at all. Again, the love affair which James's plan puts at the center of his action is both a sensory and a narrative blank: there is not even enough physical presence bestowed on Mme. de Vionnet to suggest that she had ever been in anybody's bedroom. The choral commentary of Bilham (with hemichoria by Maria Gostrey) is as crude as it is wearisome, mere third-person narration disguised as dialogue: nowhere is Mr. [Edmund] Wilson's cruel phrase "the fumes of Jamesian gas" more just or more apropos. One is even exasperated by opportunities programmatically thrown away—Miss Gostrey starts off beautifully only to fade into a mere annotation upon the action, yet how could anyone overlook the sheer comedy of making her the American parallel of Mme. de Vionnet and seduce Strether? And so on. The ladies can have it.

Many years later, reviewing a public-television film version of *The Ambassadors*, Spackman said rather cattily, "If the new BBC production is more of a success than [the original], then the sometimes headlong condensation of James's 165,000 words into a 90-minute script is certainly in part why."[4] Spackman's 90-page novel *A Difference of Design* is not so much a condensation of *The Ambassadors* as a makeover. Set in 1983, Spackman's novel uses James's cast of characters, with slightly different names—James's Lewis Lambert Strether is called Lewis Lambert Sather, Maria Gostrey is Maria Godfrey, Chad Newsome is Chad Newman (probably taken from James's 1877 novel about another American in Paris)—and differs from *The Ambassadors* largely, as the title announces, in design. Instead of a linear narrative consistently rendered from the point of view of the male protagonist (which Spackman considered wrong-headed), *A Difference of Design* is broken up into three achronological sections that focus on the women: the first and third are narrated in the first-person by Fabienne, the Comtesse de Borde-Cessac (playing Madame du Vionnet's role) and record her coup de foudre with regard to Sather, while the second section, like *The Ambassadors*, is in third-person but from Sather's point of view and deals with his affair with Maria. "How could anyone overlook the sheer comedy of making her the American parallel of Mme. de Vionnet and seduce Strether?" Spackman had asked in his James essay, and that is what he set out to do here, though it's an open question who seduces whom in Spackman's version. James used a linear form to track Strether's growing awareness of the limitations of New England life in light of cosmopolitan Paris, affording him a "glimpse of a possible 'civilization' in which the manners belonging to a ripe social intercourse shall be the index of a moral refinement." Spackman's Sather already belongs to that "civilization" and merely comes to a realization that a more comfortable life can be lived in Paris than what he is used to in America, especially with the added attraction of two lovely women head over heels about him.

---

[4]"H.J., O.M. (TV)," *New England Review* 4.1 (Autumn 1981): 95.

Another difference in design is signaled by the numerous references to French writers: Spackman's is a *roman libertin* rather than an American bildungsroman, closer to a Marivaux comedy than to a James novel. Spackman was deeply read in French literature, and *A Difference of Design* is studded with references to this reading: obscure writers like Marivaux, Pellier, and Fontenelle are quoted (usually in French), as are better-known writers like Corneille, Giraudoux, Constant, Musset, Rostand, Choderlos de Laclos, and the Comtesse de La Fayette. There's even a parody of the *nouveau roman* at one point (397-98), part Marguerite Duras, part Alain Robbe-Grillet. Throughout there is an emphasis on *les bienséances*, which is a French principle of literary decorum as well as manners, but which still allows a traditionally French form of farce to develop as the characters juggle lovers. In this regard, *A Difference of Design* is as much an homage to French literature as a makeover of *The Ambassadors*.

Reviewing Laurie Colwin's novel *Happy All the Time* in 1978, Spackman described the structure as "simple and amusing, a mock-formal three-part composition of six couples in a kaleidoscope of the patterns and stylistics of the urban love-affair, the two principal sets of lovers serving as story-line, the other four pairs (all with splendidly various eccentricities) rushing in and out as chorus, running commentary, and the ironies of antithesis in general." He goes on to say, "Good manners, as it happens, are also the novel's ambience—the title in fact might better have been *A Little Propriety For Once*."[5] Spackman's fifth novel, *A Little Decorum, for Once*, has a cast list similar to Colwin's—one principal couple, three other pairs—and could likewise be described as "a kaleidoscope of the patterns and stylistics of the urban love-affair." But it is not only a far greater achievement than Colwin's relatively lightweight one, it is also his most self-conscious novel, his most metafictional. Every major character is a writer of some sort, and literary discussions pop up on nearly every page. The principal male protagonist, Scrope Townshend, is clearly a stand-in for Spackman himself (though a decade younger than Spackman was at the time) and the novel functions as both a demonstration and defense of Spackman's style of writing.

[5]"Undeath of the Novel," *Canto* 2.4 (Winter 1978-79): 152, 153. This is a useful essay because it has more to do with Spackman's aesthetics than with Colwin's novel.

Reminiscent of *An Armful of Warm Girl* in some ways, the novel is Spackman's most audacious justification of adultery yet: introduced in the very first paragraph, adultery is defined by Scrope as "Woman's happiest birthright and perquisite" (425) and is defended by him (with help from Ovid) as a means of preserving family values:

Look, if all that our piety-simple writs and prescripts about adultery produced was a divorce rate ten times the civilized average abroad, perhaps we should explore the hypothesis that it was an unsung blessing! Binas habeatis amicas, said Ovid—have two loves, and you're a slave to neither. Well, but he himself meant turn Ovid round—with two loves you grow *tired* of neither, and, as things go between men and women, you therefore stay married. And the social structure preserves its stable decencies. So, as a natural bonus . . . as a cultural bonus, the *family* is preserved. (463-64)

Later, another character is reported to have argued adultery "was a branch of civilized deportment you had to *acquire* the traditions of, being unfaithful wasn't just something you did by light of nature, as between consenting illiterates, you had to read up on it, and would he joke if he thought?" (495). As much as these arguments are calculated to outrage, Spackman in fact offers a delightful novel (an entire oeuvre, actually) where one can indeed "read up on it." Scrope is upset at first to learn that his daughter Sibylla may be having an affair, but by the end of the novel realizes this is all for the best, just as his various adulteries with Laura Tench-Fenton over the years have deepened their love for each other.[6] By treating this theme comically, Spackman is of course going against the grain of traditional treatments of adultery in literature; in American fiction in particular, from Nathaniel Hawthorne's *Scarlet Letter* to Alexander Theroux's *An Adultery*, adultery is a grim and corrosive business, withering the souls of all involved. Spackman takes a continental approach, exemplified by Ovid and by his beloved French writers, to argue that adultery is a blessing, not a curse, of civilization. Again like Firbank (whose works seem

---

[6]Mrs. Tench-Fenton is based somewhat on Spackman's image of Nancy Tuck Gardiner, the editor at *Town & Country* with whom he worked (though he never met her), and who (Mrs. Newell tells me) "flattered him outrageously by sending him flowers, and notes such as this one in which she wrote: 'My dear Mr. Spackman— What a joy to hear your voice! As ever, mischievous and merry. . . . With apologies to your friend, Mr. James, it's not 'summer afternoon' which I find the two most beautiful words in the English language, . . . but a secretarial shout, 'William Spackman' is on the phone.'"

frivolous but contain devastating critiques of Edwardian mores), the airy inconsequentiality of the medium makes the message all the more shocking.

When not defending his case for adultery, Scrope defends his manner of writing, which violates conventional style just as adultery does conventional morality. Spackman's novels were favorably reviewed, by and large, but there were of course those who objected to his precious vocabulary, unapologetic elitism, and the rendition of his "dream girls," as his son-in-adultery Charles Ebury calls them. It's all meant to be stylization, he points out, not mimesis (450). For example, when Scrope writes a sentence like "the door had swung open and swung gently to again, and in had stepped this beautiful child" (461—echoing Morgan's entrance in *An Armful of Warm Girl* [127]), Amy asks, "but 'child'? she's in Radcliffe! So is this just technique or *do* you think of them that way?" Scrope, like a gentleman, overlooks her "just technique" and argues "a certain docileness had to be conveyed, he supposed, yes. Demureness perhaps too? Still, in that sort of relationship, a kind of daughterly deference he'd assume was at work"—that is, the use of *child* isn't sexist or patronizing but a compact designation that carefully conveys the exact nature of their relationship. That is, "child" is aesthetically correct, if not literally or politically correct. (I can just imagine what Spackman would have thought of *that* provincial intellectual blight.) As the quotation here indicates, Spackman's defenses of his style are casually confident; either one has the taste and education to appreciate these things, or one hasn't. No point in arguing.

Death is even more of a sobering presence here than it is in *An Armful of Warm Girl*. Gerontic love is rarely portrayed in literature, which gives *A Little Decorum* a special place in romantic fiction, but Scrope's romp with the Danish sociologist and his more considered affair with Mrs. Tench-Fenton take on special poignancy when it is implied that the former caused the heart attack that put him in the hospital at the beginning of the novel and the latter may cause another, fatal attack at the end. But the novel is anything but solemn; like most of Spackman's works, the novel is set in summer, the season of romance (in Northrop Frye's paradigm), with three generations of lovers celebrating life and literature. It is Spackman's most ebullient novel.

The remaining works in this omnibus provide delightful variations on Spackman's characteristic themes and concerns. The two short stories can be read as companion pieces, dealing as they do with a romantic "pursuit" ("Declarations of Intent") and a "Dialogue at the End of a Pursuit." The sexual act itself was of no literary interest to Spackman; it was the social dance that led up to it, and the tender relations between lovers immediately following, that engaged his attention. The female speaker in the "Dialogue" itemizes the stages in a pursuit *dans les formes* (a French phrase that appears in several of Spackman's novels), and Eve Fremantle of "Declarations" knows that her pursuer knows the forms as well as she, which causes her no little distress. Eve is the editor of a writer like Spackman named Matthew Talley and is being pursued by his brother Robert, a classicist at Princeton's Institute for Advanced Study currently involved with a Princeton undergraduate who models on the side.[7] At one point she expresses her impatience with her predetermined role by accusing Robert of being like his novelist brother:

"But why should I think you so different," I said, laughing at him. "Are you behaving as if you took women seriously either? He really just likes our décor—you know?—and whichever of us happens to come with it? anyhow, the way he thinks she is, with! . . . We're this adorable ballet for him. But does one have to be a ballerina on demand? And why should I want to be 'adored,' heavens!" (531)

The passage is interesting for several reasons (not the least as an example of the kind of adventure in syntax Spackman can lead the reader on). If Robert is a typical Spackman marauder, he likes both woman *and* their décor—it's not an either/or choice—but there's no denying that Spackman's characters, male and female, are like dancers, and his novels like ballets. Stylization, artificiality, and self-conscious display of technique are common to both the ballet and Spackman's novels—indeed, to many works of literature. In *An Armful of Warm Girl*, Nicholas compares even the *Iliad* to "a ballet, matched heroes dancing forward at each other in opposing pairs to fling their antiphonal taunts and spears, then dancing back, and then after a choral movement of the ordinary infantry another pair coming on, another pas de deux; and this he said was how it often seemed to be with love" (201). Spackman's novels could be called "adorable ballets," and Eve's declaration

---

[7] Though the undergraduate Samantha is described as a showgirl, one can't help but think of actress Brooke Shields, who was attending Princeton at the time Spackman wrote this story.

has the unsettling effect of a ballerina stopping in mid-performance to complain of sore feet, breaking the illusion. Eve speaks of an "escape-clause" near the end, from the same legal vocabulary that the story takes its title, and provides a rare instance in Spackman's work when *dans les formes* threatens to become merely going through the motions. Eve is one of Spackman's most complex female characters, but, despite her reservations, the circular form of the story (which begins and ends with Eve in a car admiring a man's profile) suggests that Eve will put on her toe shoes for yet another performance.

Spackman's final novel, *As I Sauntered Out, One Midcentury Morning . . .*, is a more relaxed work than the ones that preceded it—a saunter rather than a gallop, as the title indicates—without quite the whirl and wit of *A Little Decorum* or the tour-de-force ambitions of *A Difference of Design*. In fact, it recalls *Heyday* in some respects: the Princeton/Quaker background is once again emphasized, and like the first novel it covers a longer span of time than the other novels: despite its brevity, *As I Sauntered Out* is Spackman's most spacious novel, ranging from the summer of 1948 to the late sixties or early seventies.[8] It is also his most domestic novel, the only one in which the protagonist shows any concern for "settling down." Johnnie Coates, the narrator, is a self-confessed "marauder," but he's a domesticated marauder, not a campaigner like his Uncle John Coates or Spackman's other rakes. He even proposes marriage to a woman, one of the few men in Spackman's fiction to do so.

Broadly based on the career of Spackman's son Peter (1930-1995), Johnnie Coates graduates from Princeton in 1952, does graduate work at Columbia, and later becomes a political journalist. (Peter Spackman edited a political journal called *Cultural Affairs* in the late sixties; his father contributed an essay entitled "Literature as Literature, and Why" in 1968 under the pseudonym

---

[8]The internal chronology for the novel is shaky; as I said earlier, there is an awkward leap at the beginning of chapter 2 from 1952 to the mid-sixties, and although the novel is intended to conclude in 1967 (the narrator states on p. 602 that he went to France in the summer of 1948 and that it is now nineteen years later), several years intervene between the Class of '52's fifteenth Reunion in chap. 2—i.e, 1967—and the conclusion of the novel. Such discrepancies undoubtedly would have cleared up had the book been edited in his lifetime, but I felt it would be intrusive to try to correct his chronology for him. There are a few anachronisms as well, but these too have been allowed to stand, with one exception: the substitution of "plane" for Spackman's "Concorde" at the bottom of p. 552.

Alexander Neave.[9]) The novel recounts Johnnie's sentimental education, with special attention to his relationship to his Uncle John—who recalls to some extent Hugh Tatnall's rakish uncle in *A Presence with Secrets*, with his palazzo in Italy and a drawerful of amorous mementos. Uncle John proves to be another "presence with secrets," with one secret in particular that shakes but doesn't destroy his nephew's love and respect for him. Like Spackman's other novels, *As I Sauntered Out* is concerned with adultery—the theme is spelled out on pages 583-84—but with few of the shock tactics of the earlier novels; adultery here is merely an alternative domestic arrangement, and a sensible one at that. And like the other novels, it is chiefly a "comedy of manners" (559), but less hectic, less mannered. It doesn't represent a falling-off of Spackman's powers, but an attempt at a different mode; though several scenes are characteristically set in summer, the novel's conclusion and overall tone are autumnal. Those who find his other novels too self-consciously brilliant may actually prefer this quieter demonstration of his skills. I find it charmingly appropriate that the last word in his last work is *kissed*.

3

Up through his final work, style, not content, remained Spackman's chief interest and, as he argued in his critical writings, the principal (if not the only) criterion by which a writer should be judged. From the earliest essays in *On the Decay of Humanism* through his last published essay, "An *Ex Parte* for Comedy," Spackman railed against the professoriat's (and book-review media's) reduction of a work of art to "its 'content'—the thing's theme, its 'ideas,' its everlasting Meaning."[10] "Content is not really what any decently gifted novelist is chiefly concerned with," he wrote elsewhere, and he quoted with approval Nabokov's state-

---

[9]Alexander and Neave are old family names, Mrs. Newell informs me: "Apparently Elizabeth Neave was his great-grandmother; she married Thomas Peirce, and their daughter, Priscilla, in turn married WMS's grandfather, William Mode, who owned, with his brother Alexander, paper mills at a small town called Modena, just down the Brandywine River from Coatesville, PA." Cf. *Heyday*, pp. 13-15.

[10]"An *Ex Parte* for Comedy," *American Voice* 1.3 (Summer 1986): 50. This essay is essential reading for Spackman students, for it is the most succinct statement of his aesthetic principles and a defense of his work against unsympathetic critics.

ment that "Style and structure are the essence of a book; great ideas are a lot of hogwash."[11]

Style, at its simplest, is a matter of vocabulary and syntactical organization. Spackman's signature style is a unique combination of decorum and playfulness, Edwardian vocabulary and contorted syntax. A scrap of dialogue like "Webb sweet, you are plying me with drink, surely a girl shouldn't just let ply?" (from *Heyday*) is both formal and informal, taking an antiquated phrase like "plying me with drink" and giving it a Wodehousian twist that violates traditional grammar but makes perfect sense, amuses the reader, and adds to the characterization of the speaker. There are few antecedents for such a style: Wodehouse, Firbank, the Stevie Smith of *Novel on Yellow Paper*; among contemporary writers, such a sentence might be found in James McCourt's novels, David Markson's under-appreciated *Springer's Progress*, or in one of Karen Elizabeth Gordon's delightful books, but not very many other places. Where Spackman shines, however, is in paragraphs like this one (from *An Armful of Warm Girl*):

Mrs. Barclay being as it turned out late and Nicholas early, or as early anyway as a man in his right mind waiting for a pretty woman, he'd sat damn' near twenty minutes in Veale's unrecognizable bar, bolt-upright and presently glaring, before with a ripple of high heels in fluttered his angel in this breathless rush at last, blissfully gasping "Oh Nicholas oh simply now imagine!" as he lunged up from the banquette with a happy bellow to grab her—though this act she parried, after one radiant flash of blue eyes, by seizing and tenderly pressing his hands while uttering little winded cries of salutation and reminiscence; and having let him merely peck at one heavenly cheek eeled out of his arms to the seat, onto which she at once sank, blown.

One first admires the velocity of the passage, a single sentence that strains the rules of syntax and the proper use of dependent clauses to render the "breathless rush" of the action. It opens with a phrase that could have been written by Jane Austen but quickly races through a number of other registers before coming to rest onomatopoeically with two monosyllabic words. The tone is conversational rather than expository, as though Nicholas were retelling the event to a friend, but consists of carefully chosen vocabulary— Nicholas lunges, bellows, and grabs (mostly in earthy trochees),

---

[11]"Undeath of the Novel," 149; "A Time Was Had by All" (a review of Nabokov's *Lectures on Literature*), *Canto* 3.4 (January 1981): 164.

while Mrs. Barclay flutters, parries, tenderly presses, eels (in lacy sibilants: "this breathless rush at last, blissfully")—his bluntness contrasted to her wariness, which sets the tone for their relationship throughout the novel. It gives one example of Mrs. Barclay's "little winded cries of salutation" to stand for the rest and efficiently conveys other descriptive matters like her footwear, the color of her eyes, and her sleek ("eeled") figure. The aptness of the diction and economy of the passage are amazing; most writers would have taken a page to convey what Spackman does here in a brief paragraph. The care and precision of the composition will be self-apparent to anyone who has tried to write. And that, Spackman always felt, rather than the characters' morals or sociopolitical outlook, is the only thing that should matter in a work of literature.

It is tempting to quote and analyze other passages—especially those showing Spackman's brilliant use of what grammarians call "free indirect discourse," where conversation and exposition are blended without clear demaracation (a method William Gaddis has likewise developed to great advantage)—but I'll leave such pleasures to the reader. It is Spackman's instantly recognizable style that elevates him above the ranks of other novelists of manners and places him among the most accomplished writers of our time. The content of his novels, and his characterization of women especially, will always create problems for some readers, but not for those who agree that style is what a writer is to be judged by. In his review of a new translation of the *Aeneid*, Spackman wrote that it is, finally, not the content or philsophy but "the noises, the language, that make Vergil Vergil."[12] Similarly, it is the charming noises and Olympian language that make Spackman Spackman.

STEVEN MOORE

---

[12]"Pascua, Rura, Duces," *Parnassus* 1.2 (Spring/Summer 1973): 101.

DALKEY ARCHIVE PAPERBACKS

FICTION: AMERICAN

BARNES, DJUNA. *Ladies Almanack*	9.95
BARNES, DJUNA. *Ryder*	11.95
BARTH, JOHN. *LETTERS*	14.95
BARTH, JOHN. *Sabbatical*	12.95
BOYLAN, ROGER. *Killoyle*	13.95
CHARYN, JEROME. *The Tar Baby*	10.95
COLEMAN, EMILY. *The Shutter of Snow*	12.95
COOVER, ROBERT. *A Night at the Movies*	11.95
CRAWFORD, STANLEY. *Some Instructions to my Wife*	11.95
DAITCH, SUSAN. *Storytown*	12.95
DOWELL, COLEMAN. *Island People*	12.95
DOWELL, COLEMAN. *Too Much Flesh and Jabez*	9.95
DUCORNET, RIKKI. *The Fountains of Neptune*	12.95
DUCORNET, RIKKI. *The Jade Cabinet*	9.95
DUCORNET, RIKKI. *Phosphor in Dreamland*	12.95
DUCORNET, RIKKI. *The Stain*	11.95
EASTLAKE, WILLIAM. *Lyric of the Circle Heart*	14.95
FAIRBANKS, LAUREN. *Sister Carrie*	10.95
GASS, WILLIAM H. *Willie Masters' Lonesome Wife*	9.95
GORDON, KAREN ELIZABETH. *The Red Shoes*	12.95
KURYLUK, EWA. *Century 21*	12.95
MARKSON, DAVID. *Reader's Block*	12.95
MARKSON, DAVID. *Springer's Progress*	9.95
MARKSON, DAVID. *Wittgenstein's Mistress*	11.95
MASO, CAROLE. *AVA*	12.95
MCELROY, JOSEPH. *Women and Men*	15.95
MERRILL, JAMES. *The (Diblos) Notebook*	9.95
NOLLEDO, WILFRIDO D. *But for the Lovers*	12.95
SEESE, JUNE AKERS. *Is This What Other Women Feel Too?*	9.95
SEESE, JUNE AKERS. *What Waiting Really Means*	7.95
SORRENTINO, GILBERT. *Aberration of Starlight*	9.95
SORRENTINO, GILBERT. *Imaginative Qualities of Actual Things*	11.95
SORRENTINO, GILBERT. *Mulligan Stew*	13.95
SORRENTINO, GILBERT. *Pack of Lies*	14.95
SORRENTINO, GILBERT. *Splendide-Hôtel*	5.95
SORRENTINO, GILBERT. *Steelwork*	9.95
SORRENTINO, GILBERT. *Under the Shadow*	9.95
SPACKMAN, W. M. *The Complete Fiction*	16.95
STEIN, GERTRUDE. *The Making of Americans*	16.95
STEIN, GERTRUDE. *A Novel of Thank You*	9.95

DALKEY ARCHIVE PAPERBACKS

STEPHENS, MICHAEL. *Season at Coole*	7.95
WOOLF, DOUGLAS. *Wall to Wall*	7.95
YOUNG, MARGUERITE. *Miss MacIntosh, My Darling*	2-vol. set, 30.00
ZUKOFSKY, LOUIS. *Collected Fiction*	13.50
ZWIREN, SCOTT. *God Head*	10.95

FICTION: BRITISH

BROOKE-ROSE, CHRISTINE. *Amalgamemnon*	9.95
CHARTERIS, HUGO. *The Tide Is Right*	9.95
FIRBANK, RONALD. *Complete Short Stories*	9.95
GALLOWAY, JANICE. *Foreign Parts*	12.95
GALLOWAY, JANICE. *The Trick Is to Keep Breathing*	11.95
HUXLEY, ALDOUS. *Antic Hay*	12.50
HUXLEY, ALDOUS. *Point Counter Point*	13.95
MOORE, OLIVE. *Spleen*	10.95
MOSLEY, NICHOLAS. *Accident*	9.95
MOSLEY, NICHOLAS. *Assassins*	12.95
MOSLEY, NICHOLAS. *Children of Darkness and Light*	13.95
MOSLEY, NICHOLAS. *Impossible Object*	9.95
MOSLEY, NICHOLAS. *Judith*	10.95
MOSLEY, NICHOLAS. *Natalie Natalia*	12.95

FICTION: FRENCH

BUTOR, MICHEL. *Portrait of the Artist as a Young Ape*	10.95
CÉLINE, LOUIS-FERDINAND. *Castle to Castle*	13.95
CÉLINE, LOUIS-FERDINAND. *North*	13.95
CREVEL, RENÉ. *Putting My Foot in It*	9.95
ERNAUX, ANNIE. *Cleaned Out*	10.95
GRAINVILLE, PATRICK. *The Cave of Heaven*	10.95
NAVARRE, YVES. *Our Share of Time*	9.95
QUENEAU, RAYMOND. *The Last Days*	11.95
QUENEAU, RAYMOND. *Pierrot Mon Ami*	9.95
ROUBAUD, JACQUES. *The Great Fire of London*	12.95
ROUBAUD, JACQUES. *The Princess Hoppy*	9.95
SIMON, CLAUDE. *The Invitation*	9.95

FICTION: GERMAN

SCHMIDT, ARNO. *Collected Stories*	13.50
SCHMIDT, ARNO. *Nobodaddy's Children*	13.95

DALKEY ARCHIVE PAPERBACKS

FICTION: IRISH

CUSACK, RALPH. *Cadenza*	7.95
MAC LOCHLAINN, ALF. *The Corpus in the Library*	11.95
MACLOCHLAINN, ALF. *Out of Focus*	7.95
O'BRIEN, FLANN. *The Dalkey Archive*	9.95
O'BRIEN, FLANN. *The Hard Life*	11.95
O'BRIEN, FLANN. *The Poor Mouth*	10.95

FICTION: LATIN AMERICAN AND SPANISH

CAMPOS, JULIETA. *The Fear of Losing Eurydice*	8.95
LINS, OSMAN. *The Queen of the Prisons of Greece*	12.95
PASO, FERNANDO DEL. *Palinuro of Mexico*	14.95
RÍOS, JULIÁN. *Poundemonium*	13.50
SARDUY, SEVERO. *Cobra* and *Maitreya*	13.95
TUSQUETS, ESTHER. *Stranded*	9.95
VALENZUELA, LUISA. *He Who Searches*	8.00

POETRY

ALFAU, FELIPE. *Sentimental Songs*	9.95
ANSEN, ALAN. *Contact Highs: Selected Poems 1957-1987*	11.95
BURNS, GERALD. *Shorter Poems*	9.95
FAIRBANKS, LAUREN. *Muzzle Thyself*	9.95
GISCOMBE, C. S. *Here*	9.95
MARKSON, DAVID. *Collected Poems*	9.95
ROUBAUD, JACQUES. *The Plurality of Worlds of Lewis*	9.95
THEROUX, ALEXANDER. *The Lollipop Trollops*	10.95

NONFICTION

FORD, FORD MADOX. *The March of Literature*	16.95
GREEN, GEOFFREY, ET AL. *The Vineland Papers*	14.95
MATHEWS, HARRY. *20 Lines a Day*	8.95
MOORE, STEVEN. *Ronald Firbank: An Annotated Bibliography*	30.00
ROUDIEZ, LEON S. *French Fiction Revisited*	14.95
SHKLOVSKY, VIKTOR. *Theory of Prose*	14.95
WEST, PAUL. *Words for a Deaf Daughter* and *Gala*	12.95
WYLIE, PHILIP. *Generation of Vipers*	13.95
YOUNG, MARGUERITE. *Angel in the Forest*	13.95

Dalkey Archive Press, ISU Box 4241, Normal, IL 61790-4241
fax (309) 438-7422
Visit our website at http://www.cas.ilstu.edu/english/dalkey/dalkey.html